# IN THE SHADOW OF A GIANT

DAVID FITZ-GERALD

outskirts press

In the Shadow of a Giant

v2.0

Edited by Lindsay Fitzgerald



Outskirts Press, Inc.
http://www.outskirtspress.com

ISBN: 978-1-4327-7075-4

Library of Congress Control Number: 2017915039

Cover Image by Patricia Fitz-Gerald

PRINTED IN THE UNITED STATES OF AMERICA

## Foreword

A couple years ago, I started researching my family's history and had the good fortune to run across a website that had historical newspapers from New York State, all the way back into the 1800s. I was particularly interested in the story of my family's business, Paleface Ski Center and Dude Ranch, established in the early 1960s by my paternal grandparents, Aaron Boylan Fitz-Gerald and his wife Jean Allen Fitz-Gerald. I dutifully clipped every citation I could find, and cataloged them by year. As I was doing that, I began to feel compelled to bring the family business back to life by writing a book.

It occurred to me to write up the facts, figures, dates and chronology and essentially write a "history book." What I really wanted to do was re-create Paleface so that people could experience it the way it was experienced by my family, the people that worked there, the people that vacationed there, and the local community where Paleface was located, which is to say just on the town line between Wilmington and Jay, New York, just a short distance from Lake Placid. If I was "filthy stinking rich" I would buy the property and turn it back into what it once was, however I would need a time machine, which mankind has not yet invented.

I thought a lot about the best way to capture Paleface on the page. I could write a book as a memoir, that is, Paleface from my perspective, as I recall and imagine it was. From my perspective, to do so would make the book about me, and my intent is to make the book primarily about Paleface. Also, I was very young at the time. I wish I had a better memory to recall more details. Fortunately, I have been able to talk to many people who were older at the time, and who have better memories than I do.

Another option would be to write an historical novel. At *The Harley School*, in Rochester, New York, where I graduated from High School in 1980, I took an elective class, taught by a professor named Alan Sparrow. I think it was called *History as a Novel*. We read James

Michener's *The Source,* and as we were reading the novel, we researched the history within the book. To this day, I love the way a good historical novel can put me right in the setting with the characters I'm reading about. This is the option that I was drawn to.

Over the last couple of years, I have been keenly aware that the characters in this book are real people and happily, quite a few are still living. Those who have passed away have descendants who would not appreciate having me fictionalize their loved ones for dramatic effect. In a novel, part of the fun for a reader is experiencing conflict, and identifying with the inner feelings of characters in a book. I remain steadfastly dedicated to presenting the real characters in this book in a manner that they and their loved ones would be proud to read about, and willingly sacrifice the potential for the character portrayal to be deeper and richer. To make up for it, there are fictional characters in the book. I had lots of fun creating them, and some of them I fell in love with myself.

Before you begin, so you won't be disturbed when I suddenly arrive in the first person, hundreds of pages into the novel, I wasn't born when the Paleface story began. I will exercise my option as author and narrator of this combination of historical facts and made up fiction, and drop in and deliver perspective from any of the characters in the book along the way. I will speak of my relatives by their given names or nicknames except in those sections where I am writing in the first person.

If I achieved what I set out to do, then you, the reader, will be transported into the heart of the Adirondacks, during the 1960s and early 1970s. This is primarily a story about a place. A family business. The entrepreneur's family. The towns of Wilmington and Jay, New York, and to an extent also the neighboring towns as well. It is also a collection of brief stories about local heroes, and everyday people.

## Acknowledgements

From a personal standpoint, working on this project was a tremendous delight. There was a certain amount of irony involved in researching and writing about my grandfather, and I was often struck by the thought that he was exactly the same age then as I am right now. Also, given this project has taken me several years, it's amazing to think that Paleface sprung to life so quickly, in less than a year, whereas bringing it back to (fictional) life has taken more than five times as long. As I've been working on this project, several noteworthy events were commemorated such as the 50th anniversary of the Montreal Expo, the bicentennial of the Battle of Plattsburgh and the 50th anniversary of the debut of *How the Grinch Stole Christmas,* just to name a few examples. It was fun comparing the original coverage in the newspaper to the coverage of these events 50 years later.

I have also enjoyed meeting and corresponding with people about this project. In particular, meeting Jane and Dana Peck and hearing about Paleface from their perspective was such an honor. As the chief financial officer of Carris Reels, an employee-owned company which cares deeply about the well-being of employee-owners, and as the volunteer chair of The ESOP Association (Employee-Stock Ownership Plan) with so many member companies who are also dedicated to the well-being of their employee-owners, I was hoping to find out that my grandparents, Doc and Jean, were great people to work for. Jane and Dana didn't have to say so, but I was so pleased and proud to hear that from them. I felt honored to meet with them, and given the choice to meet them or the president, the pope or the queen of England, I would have easily chosen to meet with Jane and Dana Peck!

I am grateful to Jane, Dana and their sons Greg, Doug, and Dana David Peck for sharing their recollections so I could weave them into this book. I'm also thankful for the memories shared with me by Heidi Jost, Susan Pulitzer, Dennis Keegan, Maureen “Mickey” Miller, Royal “Red” Nadeau, and others. Thank you.

My happiest memories of Paleface are unquestionably connected to my beloved Aunt Patti. As a small boy’s hero, there was no one in the world more fun to be around. As a middle-aged man, my Aunt Patti continues to inspire me. I think all of the personal hardships Aunt Patti has endured, and I am inspired by the ways in which she still demonstrates positivity, a love of life, and creates beautiful happy moments even in the bad times. I can’t help being moved to aspire to the same attributes.

I want to acknowledge the graceful patience and loving guidance provided by my cousin Lindsay Fitzgerald, who took on the enormous task of helping a debits and credits guy dip a couple of toes into a creative realm. Hopefully, you the reader will benefit tremendously from the fact that I have been well trained through the years to take good advice to heart. During our collaboration on this project, one of the compliments Lindsay offered me really touched my heart, and I was so glad she mentioned it because it hadn’t occurred to me as I was writing the manuscript:

> *You look at the joys and griefs of the characters with equal sensitivity and respect; the storytelling indicates that the life of an entrepreneur and the life of a chambermaid are deserving of equal consideration, investment, and empathy. This is a wonderful (and rare) quality in writing and in life. So much of the time in this world, we pay tribute to the people whose selves or lives are most conspicuously impressive; we do not often enough honor the people whose humble lives and daily efforts are also important.*

Thank you for all your help, Lindsay.

## Dedication

I dedicate this book to my wonderfully nurturing, patient, and super supportive wife LaRena and our awesome son Kolton who didn't complain about me living in the past for the last several years. Perhaps Kolton did suggest I was spending too much time on my "boring research!" Hopefully someday he'll be glad I did.

I further dedicate this book to my mother, Carolyn, and fondly recall the special bond we shared.

This book is also dedicated to my very special aunt, Patti Fitz-Gerald, on the occasion of her 70th birthday.

# '54 Overlook

Patti slid as silently as she could from the top of the bulky, antique, four poster bed, in which she had been expected to nap. Her tiny feet landed silently on the small, rag rug beside the bed. On all fours, Patti crawled a few feet from the rug, across the hard-wood floor to the bedroom door, which had been left open a crack.

Patti thought about how to get through the door without making a sound, and wondered if she should open it quickly, and hope it didn't squeak. She decided instead to use the slow and steady approach, which resulted in a protracted groan from the ancient hinges. When the door was open, Patti remained crouched and frozen, waiting to see if anyone else had heard. Her heart was beating fast, and blood was rushing through her body. Six year old Patti knew that she was being naughty, yet she couldn't stop herself.

After a couple minutes, it was clear that nobody had been called to the sound of the door. It was quiet in the old house, except for the sound of Patti's parents talking in a distant room. Patti worked up the courage for her next move.

Once out in the hallway, just beyond the bedroom door, Patti crept quietly around the balcony rails which protected people from falling through the big square hole in the second floor of the large, old gambrel house. Patti thought for a moment, maybe it was a hole in the first-floor ceiling! What a grand house, Patti thought. She had been accustomed to more modest accommodations. All the rooms emptied into the hallway, which completely surrounded, on all four sides, the balcony which over-looked the most beautiful, comfortable living room Patti had ever seen. Still, the voices of Patti's parents remained distant.

Finally, Patti's crawl brought her to a long, dark, narrow room. Fortunately, the door was open. Quiet as a mouse trying to sneak past a sleeping cat, Patti crawled into the room. There were no less than five small beds, running along the exterior wall, three of which were beneath dormer windows. Triangular pennants were tacked to the wood paneled walls, and there was a small wooden chest and a small wooden chair at the foot of each bed. Aside from the bed, there was not enough room for two adults to walk side by side down the length of the room which came to be called *the dormitory*.

Just a couple of feet into the room was a large, iron grate, two feet long by two feet wide, which allowed the heat to rise from the rooms beneath. It was also the perfect channel for secret eaves-dropping. The distant voices of Patti's parents were no longer distant; Patti could hear everything they were saying, as plain as could be. Quietly, Patti lay down beside the grate, using a bent arm to pillow her head, not even realizing the discomfort of lying on a hardwood floor. A thought crossed Patti's mind, as she recalled her grandfather who frequently reminded Patti that "children should be seen, not heard." She almost giggled and revealed her presence. Instead, she would be neither seen, nor heard.

It had been a very long day for Patti and her parents. Not long before her mandatory nap, Patti told her parents that it was the best day of her life. They shared smiles, and Patti's parents agreed that it was a very special day. The Fitz-Gerald family had been vacationing in the Adirondack mountains of New York state for many years. That day they became owners of a home of their own in the town of Jay. Jay sat one town away from Wilmington, the home of Whiteface Mountain where the family stayed many times as guests at Wolfe's Bonnie View, during many happy vacations. Jay was two towns from Lake Placid, the famous resort town and host of the 1932 Winter Olympic Games.

Patti was initially comforted to hear the contentment in her parents' voices. Their conversation was unhurried, and the tone of their voices was pleasant, warm and comforting to a small child. As Patti listened on, she couldn't believe the things she was hearing. How could her parents talk so calmly about such things? Patti wanted to spring to her feet, jump up and down and scream. Though it crossed Patti's mind that she wasn't sure whether she liked what she was hearing or not!

Patti's father, Doc Fitz-Gerald, properly named Aaron Boylan Fitz-Gerald, Junior was a Methodist minister in New Jersey, like his father. Doc's pastorate and residence was in South Orange. It never occurred to Patti that the family might move away from their home, and it never occurred to Patti that her father might be anything other than a minister. As Patti listened, she heard her father reassure her mother that he still had a great love for God, and helping people. The unsettling part for Patti was to hear that Doc was thinking of taking an important job as a magazine editor in Manhattan. Patti wondered, "Isn't that New York City?"

Jean, Patti's mother, wasn't very surprised. She had certainly noticed that Doc's interest in his hobbies had long since eclipsed his passion for his chosen profession. Jean loved Doc's paintings, and she loved traveling with Doc and their family to the remote natural locations where Doc liked to hunt, fish, ski, and paint. Jean was always ready with a fully-loaded picnic basket, blankets, and tablecloth. Perhaps the only thing she loved more than a picnic was being a minister's wife. Tending a flock was a lot of work, and a minister's wife was as important to the happiness of the community as her husband. Jean was the only child of a prominent businessman who also served a couple years as the mayor of Ottawa, however Jean wished for a life of service rather than a life of privilege. Doc and Jean were perfect partners in public service. Now in their early forties, both were comfortable acknowledging that the changes in their lives had brought them to the point where Doc would resign his post as pastor and accept the job of editor of *The Artist* magazine in New York City. Doc did most of the talking, eloquently painting with words the picture of their new life together.

Jean mostly listened, asked a couple of questions, and from time to time, her thoughts wandered away from their current conversation about the future. Jean thought back to the 1941 commencement ceremony when Doc was awarded his Ph D in philosophy. Though she hadn't fully realized it at the time, she knew even then that one career wouldn't be enough for Doc. It was hard to believe that thirteen years had passed since that special afternoon, and over twenty years had passed since they began their service in the church. Jean was thinking about the day she married Doc, twenty-one years earlier, but sensing that Doc was coming to the end of his pitch, Jean's thoughts returned to 1954. Jean verbalized consent for the plan, and with a slight shrug acknowledged to herself that she could serve God and her fellow man wherever she happened to be and whatever she happened to be doing.

Patti was amazed that her mom and dad talked about such important things so calmly and made such big decisions with so little fanfare. Patti felt her stomach tighten and turn. They hadn't even slept one night in their new home in the Adirondacks, and now they were going to move to Manhattan! Patti couldn't imagine living in such a big city. Earlier in the day, Jean had explained that the home in the Adirondacks was only meant for summers, but Patti wasn't listening to her mother, and had missed that important detail.

As Patti listened, Doc and Jean talked about Doc's aging parents who lived in Mountain Lakes, New Jersey. They were getting up in their years. It didn't take a long discussion to conclude that Doc, Jean, and Patti would move to Mountain Lakes. Either they would move in with Doc's parents or they would rent a small home nearby. Now that Doc and Jean's older sons were grown, they wouldn't need as much space. Doc would take a small room in a boarding house in the city and be gone for a few days in the middle of the week. Patti felt a tinge of sadness to hear that her dad would be away each week, although Patti was used to Doc being gone several days at a time. Patti thought about her Granny in Mountain Lakes, and how much fun it would be to live with her. On the other hand, Patti was a little fearful of the thought of living with her grandfather, who didn't have much tolerance for the fancies of a rambunctious youngster who didn't like being quiet and lady-like. Patti thought it sounded like a better idea than living in an apartment in the city.

Doc and Jean went on to talk about how pleasant it would be to have his parents accompany them to the Adirondacks for the summer. Doc had hoped that much of his work as editor could be done from far away, and then he could work long days in the city to meet the monthly deadlines.

Having charted an entirely new future, Doc and Jean went on to discuss their boys, Allen and Chuck, then 20 and 18 years old. Having failed to fall asleep earlier in the comfort of her new bed, Patti fell asleep on the floor by the grate as her parents discussed the academic prospects of her older brothers.

Half an hour later, Patti woke up. Her mother's shoes were inches in front of her face. It took a couple moments for Patti to realize that her mother was standing in those shoes. Way above, her mother's head shook slowly from side to side in a mild state of feigned disapproval, further affirmed by her crossed arms. Patti smiled sheepishly at her mother, and Patti's smile widened as she heard her mother ask, "What are we going to do with you!"

Minutes later, Patti had her gun belt strapped across her hips, a toy revolver on each side and a dolly tucked into the waistband between the guns. A long, coiled spring slammed the screen door shut just behind Patti as she ventured out into the beautiful yard, fully ready to defend the baby doll from whatever maliciousness could be found. Doc was right behind her, and they spent the next couple hours exploring the woods and clearings on the large ten-acre lot of their new property.

Jean loaded the picnic basket with fried chicken, warm biscuits, baked beans and more food than three people would need for a week. Doc spread the large blanket over the dry, sparse grass on the gentle hill just behind the new house. It was a late dinner, and the sun was setting earlier each day, it seemed. It was still warm, almost like summer, and the leaves were beginning to share their brighter shades. Perhaps the best feature of their new house was the view to the west of enormous, mysterious, rugged Whiteface Mountain, and there was no better place to enjoy that view than from the picnic blanket at the top of their little hill.

As the sun set over the mountain, Jean said, "I think we're going to be very happy here," adding emphasis, "in the shadow of a giant." Jean explained to Patti that the property was called "Overlook" and

Patti was impressed that the house had such a grand name. Patti had never heard of houses having names before. The next day, the Fitz-Geralds returned to New Jersey, and immediately Doc and Jean began to set their new plans in motion.

## '58 Substitute Minister

In addition to editing *The Artist* magazine and contributing a large portion of its content, Doc had plenty of time to devote to his painting, his family, his outdoor interests and have some time left over to inspire souls. One week a month, Doc would work eighteen to twenty hour days in Manhattan, in advance of each month's publishing deadline. The remaining weeks, editing the magazine was more of a part time job. Doc would arrive in Manhattan on Tuesday mornings and leave Thursday afternoons. It didn't take Doc long to appreciate the rhythm and freedom that his new life afforded him.

The more time that Doc and his family spent at Overlook in Jay, the more in love they became with their mountain home, the Adirondack mountains, and the people in their new, adopted home town. From time to time, Doc was called upon to lead Sunday services, both in New Jersey and in the Adirondacks. While the Fitz-Geralds were in residence at Overlook in the summer of 1958, the Methodist church in Jay asked Doc to fill in while the Reverend and Mrs. Carter vacationed.

When Sunday came, Jean and Patti were dressed in their finest, and Doc's parents, Florence Mary Ferrier Young Fitz-Gerald and Aaron Boylan Fitz-Gerald, Senior were at their side. Jean could recall many such times in the past, standing at church, waiting for Doc to arrive. Jean was always prompt, and on Sunday, arriving at church on time was her top priority. Doc often tried to get a lot of other things done before church. Patti, then 10 years old, was beginning to think her grandfather would have to deliver the sermon instead of her father. Patti thought that it was too beautiful a day to think about the fiery depths of hell and damnation.

It was almost five minutes past time for services to begin. Jean checked her watch and looked up in the sky. Observers might have thought she was checking the placement of the sun to verify the time on her watch, or maybe it was to pray to God for Doc's timeliness or forgiveness for Doc's tardiness. Jean shifted from one foot to the other, and turned her body to look up the road toward Upper Jay, then down the road toward AuSable Forks and finally around the corner toward Wilmington. Where could Doc be?

Even the habitually late arriving members of the congregation arrived at church before the doors opened. Instead of making the shameful walk to their seats in the front row, they joined their more punctual friends and neighbors on the walkway and the steps in front of the church. Jean shared brief apologies with each family, and was answering an interrogation from her neighbor, Pat Smith, who lived down the hill from Overlook, when all conversation came to a halt. The loud, thunderous sound of a motorcycle had been approaching from a distance for a while, and had come so close as to halt conversations among the waiting worshipers. Jean had a cross look on her face as she turned from her conversation with Pat Smith, toward the oncoming motorcyclist, and then her jaw dropped in shock before her brain could process what she was seeing.

It was her husband, properly dressed to lead the congregation, sitting on top of a two-toned, cherry red and bright white Indian Chief motorcycle, decked out with western style accessories, including a buckskin colored seat cushion, and dangling fringe like you would expect to see on the blouse of an Indian's tunic. The front fender had a black leather skirt with decorative tacks like a Spanish parade saddle, and the back fender had a smaller matching skirt. No longer fidgety, Jean stood frozen in amazement as Doc quickly parked the flashy bike on the curb in front of the church, and greeted the waiting crowd as if there were nothing extraordinary about seeing a 49 year old minister jump from the seat of a shiny, loud motorcycle in front of church, more than a few minutes late on a Sunday morning.

Once settled inside, Doc delivered an inspiring sermon on the importance of feeding your soul and dreaming big dreams. Patti was greatly relieved to hear happy uplifting messages instead of dark and dreary, threatening warnings. Jean had heard variations of this sermon many times before, and thought that it sounded even more inspiring than it used to. Momentarily, Jean fantasized a full-time, permanent parsonage for Doc at the Church in Jay.

Within the sermon, Doc shared with the congregation that he had delivered a series of six large paintings to a customer in Lake Placid who was furnishing their new home on the lake, and that his customer had offered to pay him with a motorcycle instead of cash. Though it looked brand-new, the Indian was a couple years old. As Doc described the joy of riding the Indian on a fine summer morning, with the wind blowing through his curly white hair, Jean imagined all kinds of potentially horrible endings to that ride, and finally resolved to think about how to make her case against motorcycles later in the day.

The sermon was very popular with much of the crowd. Pat Smith whispered charitably behind the back of her hand to Margaret Madden, "That was a very *interesting* sermon."

Doc's father whispered to Doc's mother, "Do you think Doc is spending too much time with all those artists in New York City?"

Doc and Jean exchanged glances from across the church. Doc knew the look and got the message, and could almost hear the words, "What are we going to do with you?" These were the same words Jean often said to Patti. Doc shrugged ever so slightly. Jean smiled slightly, and they followed the rest of the churchgoers who were being liberated from the confines of the church to the beauty of a cloudless summer afternoon in the Adirondacks.

After church, back at Overlook, Florence and a couple friends were chatting and working on an enormous United States flag, a sewing project which had occupied their efforts much of the summer. Boylan, Senior was seated nearby, reading some letters from friends in New Jersey. Jean was making sure Florence and her friends had everything they needed, when Doc walked into the living room. "Well, that went well!" Doc joked.

Looking over the top of his round, wire-rimmed glasses, Boylan remarked partly with pride and partly with a tone of chastisement,

"They won't soon forget that sermon, son," and then added, "it wasn't that long ago a good sermon was paid for with a couple fat hens," perhaps forgetting that Doc's Indian motorcycle was a payment for six paintings rather than for the sermon. As Boylan, Senior dozed off for a nap, he thought about the letter Doc had sent him years ago, asking for permission to follow in his footsteps and become a minister rather than study law. A little eccentric at times, but yes, that boy had made him proud, and it was hard to believe he would soon turn 50 years old.

## '60 Whiteface Mountain

It was the dawn of a new decade, and less than a year since the passing of his father. Doc thought back a few years to when he and Jean had purchased the house in Jay, and when he had traded the pulpit for the paintbrush. Riding up the chairlift on Whiteface Mountain, on a late spring morning, Doc smiled and thought of how he had loved both professions, and loved them still. And yet, it seemed Doc might have to answer another calling. Once again, a big change was on the way.

Doc and his oldest son, Allen, were enjoying a few days in the Adirondacks. Allen was on a break from his studies and it seemed like a perfect opportunity to enjoy some early spring skiing. There was plenty of snow, and yet it was not as cold as in the dead of winter.

In the evenings, Doc enjoyed the company at Carl Steinhoff's Sportsman's Inn. Steinhoff's was a skier's paradise. It was also a fisherman's dream—located near the foot of Whiteface mountain, the AuSable River had some of the best fly fishing in North America. Steinhoff's featured a restaurant and bar, with rustic décor. Spending time at Steinhoff's felt like being with old friends at hunting camp.

By the time Doc left Steinhoff's at the end of the week, a freshly painted scene hung on the walls at the Inn, a gift to Carl, not that a gift was necessary to cement the relationship that was fast becoming a lifelong friendship.

Even when Doc was studying theology, he had also entertained notions of going into business to become an entrepreneur. As the years unfolded, Doc found a yearning to build and run a ski center. What had been far flung, undeveloped thoughts began to dance in the front of his mind as the means to realize those dreams became tangible. Doc had not wanted to become a skiing "mogul" in order to strike it rich and create a business empire. His first dream of a ski center involved a rope tow and a hot dog shack.

Doc was an extreme extrovert who always enjoyed being around people. Doc's dream, however, was to create a unique place, inspire future generations to have a love and appreciation for the Adirondack mountains, and to help families experience wonderful vacations together.

After one week at Whiteface in March, left alone on the chairlift by his son who was skiing with people his own age, Doc had a detailed business plan laid out in his mind. In obsessive fashion, he had reviewed every detail of what he hoped Paleface could become. All day, every day that week, it was all Doc could think of as he skied the slopes of Whiteface instinctually and painted Carl Steinhoff's picture as if he were painting it while sleepwalking. The front of Doc's mind was occupied with the urgency of a plan that must be realized. Fortunately, it did not take long to find just the right setting for the dream.

## '60 Basset Mountain

It was a rainy Tuesday evening. Dinner was finished, Jane Peck had washed the dishes and Dana, her husband, had dried them and put them away. It was an unusually quiet moment in a house where three young boys lived. Gregory, aged 10, was reading a library book about children from around the world. Douggie, aged 4, was playing with some small wooden toys on the floor and Dana David Peck, aged 2, had just fallen asleep on a blanket on the floor.

Dana was sitting at the kitchen table filling out an order form from the Henry Fields seed catalog. Spring was just around the corner and soon it would be time for planting.

Jane was sitting across the table bringing order to a stack of papers that had become shuffled. She wanted to be prepared for morning, and another busy day working on the 1960 census. Jane's census territory was enormous and included the towns of Wilmington, Bloomingdale, St. Armand, Jay, and Keene, New York.

Jane was the sort of person that took on every challenge with an enormous smile, a big heart, an open mind, and a positive, can-do spirit. If you had asked her how she would get the job done, she might not have been able to tell you. Nonetheless, at the end of the day, there was a job well done.

It had been so quiet that Dana and Jane jumped when there was a loud knock on the front door. The heavy rain had masked the arrival of a car in the driveway. Doc Fitz-Gerald introduced himself to Dana and was invited in. A real estate broker followed Doc into Dana and Jane's home.

Jane moved the census papers off the kitchen table, offered the unexpected guests some cookies and coffee then excused herself to put the boys to bed. When Jane returned to the kitchen about 9:10pm, the men hadn't moved much.

The cookies were gone and a third pot of coffee was bubbling in the stove top percolator. The real estate agent had hardly said two words since arriving. On the other hand, Dana and Doc had quickly found themselves to be kindred spirits, sharing stories from building lives centered around faith and family.

Jane picked up her knitting basket and her favorite set of needles and sat down to continue working on next winter's mittens for her growing boys. Mittens were a necessity from October through April in the North Country, as the region was generally known.

As Jane was getting settled, Dana said to Doc, "If you don't mind me asking, Reverend, would you repeat what you told me about your plan and your proposition? I would like Jane to hear it as well." Jane set her basket down and listened attentively at first and then with a slight look of shock as it became clear what Doc was suggesting.

Doc had come to visit Mr. and Mrs. Peck with the intention of offering to buy their property. Doc described his vision in long form for Jane, and Dana got to hear it a second time. Once or twice as Doc was repeating the plan, Doc glanced at Dana, who seemed outwardly enthusiastic, whereas the first time Doc told him, Dana appeared skeptical, with worried eyebrows and a clenched jaw. Jane also glanced at Dana a couple times, and reassured by his expression, she devoted her attention to fully comprehending Doc's proposal and the advantages and disadvantages that came along with it.

Doc showed Mr. and Mrs. Peck a postcard. On the front of the postcard was a picture of snowcapped mountains in the background, four A-Frame buildings at the bottom, and in the foreground, an upside-down skier, caught by the photographer in the middle of a flip. On the back of the post card was the description: "Stein Eriksen, former Olympic and World's Champion Skier, now head of Aspen Highlands Ski School, performing in late spring his regular Sunday somersault on skis at Aspen Highlands, Aspen, Colorado."

"I want to build a lodge like the one shown on the front of this postcard," Doc explained. Incredible as it might seem, the dream was so compelling and credible that Jane and Dana became engulfed in it and before the evening was over, an agreement was reached.

Doc had heard about Dana's experience at the old Marble Mountain Ski Center, the Whiteface Mountain Ski Center, and the Haselton Lumber Company. Doc also learned about Dana's time at the aviation mechanics training school at Plattsburgh, and the Glen Martin airplane factory in Baltimore, Maryland.

Also, Dana had told Doc about Jane's experience working as a secretary for the army in 1944, during the war, when the army had set up offices inside the Lake Placid Club. Dana also mentioned Jane's work on the census.

Mostly Dana and Doc had talked about the extensive volunteer work Dana and Jane had done in service to their beloved Nazarene Church in Wilmington. Dana and Jane had recently returned from a couple of years in Wolcott, Vermont where Dana served as pastor, and Dana periodically served as guest pastor in Vermontville, New York which is about ten miles north of Saranac Lake, New York.

Dana and Jane were both extremely active in every aspect of the local church, and were greatly committed to the church's international programs. Doc could identify. What's more, Doc recalled meeting Jane's father Keith Hardy on the golf course adjacent to Wolfe's Bonnie View. Doc clearly remembered the high praise Mr. Hardy had for his daughter and her husband, as he spoke of them on numerous occasions. Mr. Hardy just couldn't say enough good things about the Peck family.

It was getting late, long since time to say good night to a young family on a school night. There was already a handshake in place, so all that was left was for the lawyers and the bankers to catch up. It was well past 10pm and still Doc showed no sign of making an exit.

One of the best business decisions Doc made was the decision he made on the spot that night in April. It was made without planning, deliberation, consulting with experts, or thoughtful prayer for guidance. Sometimes a decision is just so right it naturally evolves in the moment. Before leaving, Doc had offered both Dana and Jane jobs in addition to offering to buy their property. A deposit check was left on the kitchen table. Doc wished Dana and Jane a good evening and the real estate agent followed Doc back out to the car.

A week later, Dana and Jane's mountain property was transferred and the first news began to hit the newspapers of Doc Fitz-Gerald's plans to transform the lovely Basset Mountain, elevation 1,893 feet, into a family oriented ski center resort. Doc and Jean, and Dana and Jane were on their way to creating Paleface.

## '60 Survey

Although their home had been sold to Boylan Fitz-Gerald in April, Dana and Jane's family remained in the home until September. By the end of April, Doc had also convinced the owners of undeveloped land adjacent to Dana and Jane's home. The last of these deeds was filed in the County offices in Elizabethtown on the 26th of May. Meanwhile, work on the trails began three weeks earlier.

One thing that might have slowed down progress was the need to survey all the new properties. The local surveyor was a very hardworking man named Norman Briggs, who was always able to get the job done, and meet virtually anyone's deadline.

It was a particularly exciting time in Norm's life. At 44 years of age, Norm had found the perfect woman, the lovely Miss Luella McComber who had been busy managing the front desk at The Feek family's Holiday Motor Lodge at the foot of Whiteface Mountain. It was the first property on the right-hand side, just after turning onto the highway that went all the way to the top of Whiteface Mountain.

Fortunately, Norm got all the surveying completed in good time, and caused no delays, either in the building of Paleface or in his June 12th wedding. From that day on, if anyone asked Doc about a surveyor, Norm Briggs was the only man referred.

There was lots of work to do. Time was of the essence. The mountain was heavily forested. Like a giant sculpture, trails had to be carved out of the mountain.

## '60 Voice of the South Wind Bird

On the 7th of June, Doc lost his mother.

Patti had lost her beloved Granny, who had been such a kind, sweet spirit. Since their move two years earlier, Patti had grown even closer to her grandmother. Granny told Patti such fascinating stories of living amongst the Indians on distant prairies in the wilds of Canada and sang so beautifully that Patti hung on every word and every note. Sometimes Granny spoke of things that happened so long ago it was hard for Patti to remember Granny was talking about things that had actually happened, let alone things that had actually happened to her. Many of the stories Granny told were stories her father, the Reverend Egerton Ryerson Young had written and published. In those stories, Granny was just a young girl, no older than Patti, younger even. Sometimes when Granny told stories and sang songs, it seemed to Patti like a dream. Since Granny had all but lost her eyesight, Patti had been a great help, guiding her around the house and describing things in detail so her Granny could picture them. Similarly, since Granny's eyesight faded, her stories became even richer, full of lots of brilliant, beautiful detail.

Jean also had a great love and admiration for her mother-in-law. And every time Jean heard Florence telling Patti stories, Jean resolved to take the time to read the books Granny's father had written. More urgent, pressing matters always seemed to intervene. As the family grieved the loss of such a close family member, Jean was reminded of the sorrow of losing her own parents, far too soon, so many years earlier.

With work beginning on Paleface, Doc was in the Adirondacks when his mother passed away. Jean made many of the funeral arrangements, and worked to prepare the household for the family's next transition. Jean loved the community of Mountain Lakes, and her friends there. Jean had also been very comfortable and happy living with Doc's parents and caring for them. Without Florence, it didn't seem like home. When Patti wasn't at school, she moped haplessly around the house, and Jean felt like she was exhibiting that same behavior herself. Jean couldn't wait to move to Overlook for good, not just for the summer.

The task of writing and delivering his mother's eulogy fell to Doc. Moments after Doc hung up the phone, he was in the car on the way to Paleface. Doc parked the station wagon and climbed the mountain, taking a notebook and a pen from the glovebox and wrote:

*85 years in a Methodist parsonage could well be the sub-title of the life of Mrs. A. Boylan Fitz-Gerald.*

*Born May 9, 1875, of a pioneer Canadian Methodist missionary, 500 miles away from the nearest white people other than her parents, Florence Young received the Indian name of Sou-wan-ak-wa-na-peek, meaning "voice of the south wind bird."*

*Much of her early training was with Church choirs, later with concert teachers. For several years, she was the contralto soloist of the Mendelssohn Choir of Toronto, Canada. In 1907, she left the parsonage of her father, the Rev. Egerton Ryerson Young, to become the bride of the Rev. A. Boylan Fitz-Gerald, and for more than 50 years she shared his life as a member of the Newark Conference.*

*Of outstanding significance was her happy disposition and sunny nature. This was especially noteworthy when we reflect that this sensitive vocal artist was hard of hearing for more than 50 years. More recently her blindness was even more of a handicap. Yet, with it all, she maintained great sweetness of character. She was essentially a wife and mother. Her home was her castle. She loved people and was always concerned about the well-being of others. Hers was a long and useful life, and a spirit full of sunshine.*

Doc finished the task, then it registered in his heart and soul that his mother was gone. Doc permitted himself some time alone for grieving, then forced himself to hurry along, back down the mountain. He had several construction details to tend before making the long drive to New Jersey. Doc was keenly aware and feeling guilty about Jean's having to prepare for his mother's funeral and their move, on her own. It helped to be busy with so many urgent tasks, plus Doc had a long car trip to make. It crossed Doc's mind that now both of his parents had passed, he should contemplate his own mortality. Doc dismissed the thought, postponing such contemplation until later.

## '60 The Big Move

It had been weeks since Granny's passing and Jean was concerned that Patti didn't show any sign of reclaiming her normal demeanor. From time to time, Jean tried to console Patti. Jean understood that children understand and experience grief differently, and often asked Patti if she had any questions or wanted to talk. For the most part, Jean moved quickly and efficiently, preparing the household for the big move.

Finally, moving day came. Patti looked around at the empty house that her grandparents had lived in. Patti felt bad that she didn't seem sad to be leaving. It wasn't the same there without Granny. At that exact second, Jean said to Patti, "Granny will be with you, in your heart, everywhere you go." She smiled slightly, and took Patti's hand in her own. Patti wondered how her mother had known exactly what she was thinking. They walked out the door together, and didn't look back.

Jean had prepared a bag full of activities designed to distract Patti during the long ride. Patti rifled aimlessly through the bag, and just stared out the window until she fell asleep. Hours later, Patti woke up, looked around and realized that she couldn't wait to get to Overlook. With each passing mile, her mood improved. Jean could tell the fog had lifted. Patti was herself again. Jean felt a warm, happy feeling within her heart as well.

When they pulled into the long driveway, Patti thought, "We've been away too long. It's good to be home!" Patti pulled a small paper calendar from her activity bag, circled the date, and drew three hearts in the box.

Doc was sitting in a lawn chair, waiting at the end of the long, shady driveway. Doc opened the door for his wife, and Patti burst out of her door, barely waiting for the car to stop. Jean hugged Doc, and Patti impatiently joined the hug. Tears streamed down Patti's face. She hadn't realized how much she had missed her dad. Inside, Doc had the table set, and dinner ready, and barely ate himself as he updated Jean and Patti on all the progress at Paleface.

## '60 Demolition and Excavation

For the demolition and excavation projects, a great, hard-working core of guys was hired. Word had spread throughout the area so there was no shortage of men for Dana and Doc to employ. Most men brought their own chainsaws. There was plenty of work for men and boys without chainsaws also. The trees were cut and trimmed, and then cut in large sections. All summer long, several large fires were fed tree limbs and brush, almost continuously. There was plenty of wood for everyone's woodstoves and fireplaces for the next couple of winters.

Dana was kept very busy supervising his large crew all summer, just outside his front door. Dana's sons couldn't get enough of the constant activity. Greg, Doug and Dana-D had front row seats for the most exciting show in town. The sights, sounds and smells of demolition captivated the boys all summer. And their Dad was the boss!

Each night at dinner, the boys retold the days' events, summarizing the progress on the mountain, as if Dana and Jane hadn't witnessed those events as well.

When the well was being drilled, Doug told about how the house shook, and imagined that an earthquake must feel just exactly like that. The boys tried to compete to count the number of trees they saw drop to the ground each day. One day Doug got to ride in the tiny John Deere, 2-cylinder bulldozer, and all day long impersonated its "PUH-ta-PUH-ta" engine sounds. To five year old Doug, the dozer seemed enormous. Another night, at dinner Doug breathlessly talked about laying under a truck with his dad, for cover, and hearing the explosive handler shout, "Fire in the hole!" Doug watched as the man pressed down the handle, and took cover himself. They knew the sound was coming, yet jumped as if surprised when it came, and Doug watched in amazement as dirt, gravel, pebbles and rock showered to the ground. The sights, sounds, and smells of tractors, chainsaws and explosives on the mountain was pretty heady stuff for such a small boy to witness.

Though Greg was much older, and celebrated his eleventh

birthday during the summer of demolition, the work on the mountain was no less astonishing for him to observe. Greg loved to see the enormous fires burning, and Greg liked to watch the men work, knew the equipment by heart, and could describe the machinery down to the last detail.

Being older, Greg had the good fortune of being able to ride with his Dad in the vehicles, almost every day. Greg rode in the passenger seat of the bright yellow, snub-nosed Jeep, as Dana made his rounds supervising activity on the mountain. Dana surely knew their real names, but Greg wondered sometimes whether Kruchev, Gooseneck, and the others had real names, or were given those strange names by their parents. Greg loved sitting as far forward as he could in the Jeep, which had almost no dashboard. He could almost see the ground immediately in front of the Jeep, which looked kind of like a cross between a Jeep, a van and a pick-up truck.

One night, Greg made the whole family laugh as he described seeing Doc at work on the mountain, laying out the design for the trails. Greg said that he looked like he leaned so far forward as he walked up the hills that his nose would drag on the ground.

Another night, while Dana was working late, Greg told his mother about a conversation he had overheard. Dana and Doc had observed that they could tell who the goof-offs on the crew were because their saw engines would always be idling until they spotted the boss approaching. Jane took the opportunity to mention the importance of doing the right thing, even when nobody was looking, and the importance of working hard when you are paid to do a job.

At last the day came in September when the family had to move. Summer was over. Plans had been completed, materials had begun arriving, and the old house had to come down to make way for the grand lodge that was to replace it on the site.

Another house would soon become home for Dana, Jane, and the boys. Dana and Jane promised the boys that they would buy a color television set, and the boys were looking forward to watching the World Series in color for the first time that fall.

Doc watched the Pecks' car pull away from their family home for the last time, and his eyes met Greg's. It didn't seem fair to have to ask the young family to move. Doc felt he could read Greg's mind, and a terrible wave of guilt blew through Doc's soul, making him shiver.

The next day, the house was literally on its side. Men were pulling the house apart board by board and feeding it to the fires that had been burning all summer long. Watching Dana's house burn, Doc thought about the fact that a happy, loving family had breakfast together in that home just one morning prior, and now it was gone completely. For the next couple months, the sounds of construction added to the chorus of more than a dozen chainsaws that continued buzzing on the mountain all throughout the fall.

Dana Peck never did get his vegetables planted that summer.

## '60 Pine Knot Restaurant

It was well before dawn on a crisp, foggy September morning, the day before the close of fishing season. Doc parked in front of the Pine Knot Restaurant, a place so small you wouldn't know it was a business unless you knew it was a business. Doc entered briskly, which he tended to do even when he wasn't in a hurry, and made himself right at home on a sawed-off stump that served the purpose of a chair.

"Good morning, dear," Fanny said sweetly as she placed a piping hot homemade donut on a small dish in front of him. "What's got you up so early this morning?" she asked, as she always did, knowing full well what the answer would be, of course.

With her customer's nose in a newspaper, armed with coffee and a donut, Fanny went back to frying bacon in a cast iron skillet, humming "Wings of a Dove," along with Ferlin Husky on the radio. The Pine Knot didn't have much in the way of furnishings, but it did have an old radio that kept Fanny happy all day. Fanny had seen her husband three times since they got married 47 years earlier. The last time he brought the radio, and then headed off again in search of fortunes elsewhere.

Doc looked up from his paper and said to Fanny, "Hey, you should sing in the church choir!"

"Aw, I'm not that kind of girl," sighed Fanny, "and besides... who would make you boys coffee and donuts if I sang in the church choir?"

Fanny went back to half-humming and half-singing, poking at the bacon with a fork and flipping the slices that looked done enough. Out of the corner of her eye she watched as a fly got stuck on a strip of spiral sticky paper hanging from the ceiling in the corner.

When the bacon was done, Fanny picked up the coffee pot. "Anything in the paper today that is worth sticking on my wall?" Fanny interrupted as she topped off Doc's cup of coffee.

"No, I think they could have made the paper much easier to read if they just printed 'today nothing happened' and left the rest blank, Fanny," Doc shrugged.

Moments later, the door opened causing a bell to ring. The second customer of the morning walked in and set on the stump next to the first. Fanny placed another perfectly shaped, uniformly brown fried donut in front of Arthur.

"How's life treating you this fine morning?" Doc said to Arthur, folding up the paper and putting it on the 2 X 6 plank bar in front of them. They shook hands and introduced themselves, exchanging small talk about the weather and complimenting the food before them. Of course, it would never have occurred to either man that one day they would be related by the marriage of Doc's oldest son to one of Arthur's granddaughters.

With a twinkle in Arthur's eye and enough of a smile to reveal the good-natured intent of the words to follow, Arthur said, "So you're the fellow that's building that big fancy new ski resort down in Wilmington. You must be filthy stinking rich to up and build a place like that." After many years of looking after camps, cottages and lake houses in the Adirondacks, Arthur knew a good number of rich people, or nearly rich people.

Arthur raised a large family, and he never was fully able to provide for the needs of his brood until he stumbled on to the caretaking business. Arthur's clientele would generally come to camp between one week and two months a year, sometimes making a second trip during hunting season as well. Arthur's job was to make sure everything at camp was in the exact same condition as the day they left after their previous visits, only clean, fully stocked, and ready to go. Making rounds checking camps was a darn sight easier than making rounds and checking traps.

"No," replied Doc with a smile and a wink, "but my uncle was!" Doc's uncle was the famous Bishop James Fitz-Gerald who travelled the world, all expenses paid. All of the moderate income the Bishop was paid through the years was invested in a portfolio of stocks and bonds. Doc's father, Aaron Boylan Fitz-Gerald, Sr. travelled the world with the Bishop in 1907 as the Bishop's private secretary. In fact, by the time the investment portfolio was inherited by Doc, it was worth over a million dollars.

Every square inch of the walls at the Pine Knot was covered with old newspaper clippings. Some were fresh. Most had yellowed over with time. Even the ceilings were covered with clippings. Arthur pointed to a clipping by the door and said, "Take a look at that story over there, Reverend."

Doc went over to look more closely. The headline read, "Arthur Ling Kills a Tough Customer." The story was dated May 18, 1917. Doc read aloud, "Arthur Ling killed a nine-foot black bear near the foot of Whiteface Mountain on the Franklin Falls side on Friday. The bear was found chasing sheep and Mr. Ling took his rifle and started out. He tracked the bear up the slope of the mountain to the vicinity of Terrio's lumber camp, where he was able to come up with bruin and fired a shot that finished him. The bear probably weighed 450 pounds. The beast was an ugly looking old customer. When Mr. Ling took the head before the town clerk to get his bounty, he was told that he had earned a double bounty by ridding the district of the animal. The hide was purchased by Paul Smith."

When Doc was done reading, Arthur smiled proudly and said, "They called me 'Mr. Ling', can you imagine that!" Then Arthur pointed to another old clipping. The headline read "Bloomingdale Couple Feted on 50th Year."

Arthur watched as Doc read the very long, detailed story, and was impressed by how quickly Doc read it. Arthur could see Doc's eye's moving at a fast pace. What's more, Arthur couldn't help but notice wave after wave of changes in Doc's expressions as he read along. Arthur observed that Doc had a very expressive face.

As Doc read, he was struck by how a small-town country newspaper painted such a vivid picture of a couple's life and the enormous change in the world during their 50 years together. Doc felt like he could experience the love, joys and hardships, of Arthur's parents, Baron and Flora.

Arthur's father, Baron Ling, chopped wood, swinging his axe all day cutting two cords of wood each day for the going rate which ranged from 40 cents to 65 cents per cord. In addition to working from dawn to dusk, Baron walked seven miles to get from home to the job and back at night.

Doc read about the time that Baron Ling surprised Flora with a brand new $70 sewing machine. Doc paused to think that represented some fifty days wages, and Doc felt tears start to well up in his eyes. Of course, it wasn't just a matter of saving fifty days wages. All the family's other financial needs had to be met before wages could be saved. In days where clothes were made at home, and mended when they became worn out, a sewing machine was one of the most valuable furnishings in a home. It would never have occurred to Doc that in another fifty years people would just throw clothes away when a hole appeared, however it did occur to Doc to think about how much work it was for Flora to keep her large family clothed and what a loving gift and sacrifice that sewing machine truly was. Doc finished reading, and a warm smile appeared on his face as he looked up from the article on the wall and thanked Arthur for sharing his parents' story with him.

Before Doc and Arthur returned to their coffee, a couple other local clippings caught Doc's eye, featuring his new friends, the Pecks. One was dated March 27, 1954 and it said, "Mr. and Mrs.

Dana Peck have had a phone installed in their home." Another, dated April 17, 1953 noted the fact that Mrs. Dana (Jane) Peck of Jay, tied for first honors in an oratorical contest. A third, from April 28, 1955 said, "Dana Peck and son Gregory both had their tonsils removed last week at Placid Memorial Hospital." Doc considered what it must have been like having both father and son in the hospital at the same time. These three simple little stories made Doc feel like he had known the Pecks for years. Then Doc thought for a fraction of a second about his fishing plans, shrugged, and returned his attention to Arthur Ling.

Arthur smiled, and pointed to a feature dated July 27, 1944 with a headline "New Speeding Excuse from Ardent Angler" and the article went on, "A new wrinkle in excuses for speeding was presented by Michael Schultz of Wilmington arrested near here for exceeding the speed limit. Stating he was an ardent fisherman on his way to indulge in his hobby, Mr. Schultz explained that a look at his bait pail disclosed the unhappy fact that his live minnows were dying. Thus, he continued, he stepped harder on the gas to get his bait into the water. The judge, while agreeing that it was refreshing to listen to something new and original in alibis, nevertheless imposed the $10 fine." Doc and Arthur shared a smile and a thought that only a fisherman could fully understand how compelling Mr. Schultz's defense truly was.

"Good morning Fran," Fanny said to Francis Betters as he came through the door. "What can I get for you, son?" Fran Betters was another notorious North Country fisherman enjoying the season.

With a new order to fill, Fanny went to work at the stove, quietly singing "Am I Losing You" along with Jim Reeves, to herself, or so she thought, not aware she was singing loud enough that the customers could hear her.

Doc and Arthur returned from reading the walls to sit on their stumps. While they were away, their coffee cups had been magically refilled.

In most conversations, Doc liked to find out everything he could about the man he was talking to. On this day, these two gentlemen shared whole life stories and hours passed as they talked. Arthur was as curious about Doc's story as Doc was about Arthur's. Both men may have thought they were going to hit the river fishing at dawn, and both had long forgotten that they ever planned to go fishing that late, September day.

Arthur told Doc about his wife Augusta and all their kids. Revealing the depth of the wrinkles on his forehead, Arthur quietly recalled a time, thirty years earlier, when he did not have the means to feed his family and shot a deer out of season. The authorities apprehended Arthur as his family was finishing the first substantial meal they had enjoyed in several days. Arthur couldn't pay the $12 and 50 cent fine, and fortunately a kind stranger in the courthouse that day lent him the money to pay the fine. With no transition, Arthur's voice became much louder and years of worry seemed to evaporate from his face as Arthur next recounted the story of the time he was paid a $35 bounty for shooting a coyote twenty years later.

Arthur talked a bit more about his daughter's large family, trying to make ends meet out on the Bonnie View Road. Ada and her second husband Ernie Schultz, son of the speeding fisherman, lived mostly on the modest income from raising pigs and chickens. The ham and eggs served at the Pine Knot came from the Schultz place, and the money that came from them helped raise a large family.

As Arthur was talking about trying to feed his family while working in the Adirondacks, Doc thought back to his sermons over the last couple of decades on the importance of conservation. From his vantage point, the Adirondacks had been raped and plundered by greedy industrialists living extravagantly, never imagining how important the work was from the standpoint of people making their homes and barns from the wood that floated down the river or the hardworking people in the Adirondacks feeding their families while swinging their axes, tending camps for the well-to-do, making donuts and flipping bacon, or slopping pigs and gathering eggs.

Arthur asked Doc, "So I'm confused. You talk about being a preacher, so why are you called 'Doc'?"

Doc raised one eyebrow. "Well let's see, I am a doctor of philosophy. I don't heal the sick, but I have spent many years trying to heal people's souls. After serving the better part of thirty years as a Reverend in Methodist churches in New Jersey I left that work to become a painter. Now I'm going to try my hand at being a businessman."

For the next couple hours, Doc entertained Arthur with his family stories and bits and pieces of Doc's best sermons through the years.

Many customers had come and gone, and it was closing in on noon when finally, Doc said, "Fanny, can you fix me some sandwiches to go?"

"Sure honey," Fanny replied. "You can have whatever you like as long as it's a ham sandwich!" The Pine Knot was not known for having an extensive menu or lots of ingredients.

Doc wrapped his thumb and index finger around his chin and wrinkled his eyebrows as if deep in thought. Now that Doc had received an enormous inheritance, he wondered whether a filthy-stinking rich man should buy his new friend a filling lunch, and certainly it would be appropriate to buy him coffee and donuts as well. After a dramatic pause, Doc concluded, "I'll take four ham sandwiches." Fanny had a supply of ham sandwiches on buttered bread wrapped in wax paper and tied with twine all ready to go.

"Well you sure have worked up an appetite sitting around all morning drinking coffee and eating donuts," Fanny said to Doc with a smile. "Stop in again soon, dear."

Doc left $15 dollars on the counter, more than enough to cover the cost of breakfast and lunch for both men and still be quadruple the tip that Fanny would ordinarily receive. Doc winked at Fanny and said, good day to the other customers. Outside the Pine Knot, Doc tossed two ham sandwiches through the open window of the old pickup truck parked next to his station wagon. Doc chuckled to himself, at the thought that Arthur might accidentally sit on the sandwiches, since of course Arthur wouldn't expect sandwiches to magically appear on the seat of his old truck.

Instead of spending the morning fishing, Doc spent the afternoon painting. He had his eye on a beat up old barn that looked like it needed to be preserved on canvass. As Doc worked, he thought of the toilsome effort expended by a family, friends and neighbors to build that barn, and how that barn had certainly helped generations of that family survive the long Adirondack winters.

Fishing would have to wait. Doc smiled to himself, knowing there was another day left before the close of fishing season.

## '60 Yodeling

It was high noon, and plans had called for a prompt departure. That trip didn't involve the usual planning and preparation. The hunting gear, fishing poles, camping gear, skis and sleds were staying home. It was a short trip considering the distances the Fitz-Gerald family often travelled. Finally, at 12:15pm Jean came out of the house carrying a bag of apples and a hot tin of apple muffins, fresh from the oven. Patti was in the car, waiting and ready for adventure and happy to be missing school.

A short while later the station wagon was in the driveway at the new home of the Jost family to pick up Karl, Putzi and Heidi. The Josts had moved in just two weeks earlier. Everyone was excited to make the trip to Old Forge to attend the New York State Winter Sports Council at the Four Seasons. Doc's grand, infectious dream had completely enveloped the Jost family, just as it had the Fitz-Gerald and Peck families. With that trip, the first of many such conferences, association meetings, and industry gatherings it finally felt to Doc like the dream was being realized.

It was a warm day for mid-October in the Adirondacks, 63 degrees and climbing. It was fairly cloudy, and threatening to rain. What would have been an extraordinarily scenic drive instead had limited views which might have been enjoyed by the riders in the back. The men in the front seat were blinded by purpose and locked in conversation before the wagon even left the Josts' driveway.

Doc had met Karl and his wife Putzi a few years earlier while on a skiing vacation at Gray Rocks in the Laurentian Mountains, in Quebec, Canada. Karl was born in Austria, trained in Canada, raced internationally, and prior to teaching at Gray Rocks Karl taught at Mt. Snow in Vermont where he met Frances Shuster, better known to everyone as Putzi, also a ski instructor at Mt. Snow.

Karl was the first to hear Doc's dream of building a ski center in the Adirondacks, years before it was a fully formed concept, and long before Doc mentioned such a thought to Jean. Doc was painting on the deck at Gray Rocks and Karl was passing by. Karl stopped to check out what Doc was doing. Doc was just completing his signature at the bottom right of the painting and gave it to Karl on the spot. Afterwards, Doc and Karl remained in touch.

Doc had settled in for a long drive. As he often did during road trips, Doc sat forward, with his left forearm across the top of the steering wheel. Instead of a relaxed position, Doc almost appeared to be sitting on the edge of his seat, not wanting to miss a thing. Karl started the conversation by asking Doc to explain how he came up with the name Paleface.

Doc answered that it gave recognition to the proud heritage of the Indians who populated North America and it paid tribute to Doc and Jean's ancestors in the Methodist missions who worked to convert the Indians to Christianity. Doc felt that the name Paleface turned the white man into the outsiders, in the opposite manner to how the word redskins turned Indians into the outsiders.

Doc went on to tell Karl about a special night when Doc and Jean went to the movies, shortly after Patti was born. Doc had to admit he didn't know anything about the movie before they went. Western comedies were rare, and though he should have, he didn't know it was a comedy, or even who was in it until they got to the theater. The funny parts hit Doc and Jean by surprise. The slapstick comedy was so ridiculous; they just laughed and laughed.

For instance, not too far into the movie, a whole train of wagons was moving out of camp one morning. First one driver, then another gave their teams the old "giddy-up." When it came to the wagon with Bob Hope and Jane Russell, the Bob Hope character cracked the whip, jostled the reins and the horses took off. The wagon did not. Someone had forgotten to hitch the horses to the wagon. Bob Hope's character was dragged away with the horses, reins in hand and Jane Russell's character was left sitting in the wagon. Slowly, exasperated, Jane said, "My husband." Later in the movie, it happened again. Jane said, "Our hero" in much the same manner. Miraculously, the same gag got Doc and Jean a third time at the end of the movie. The happy couple was about to ride off into the sunset. That time Jane Russell's character was driving the team and got dragged away by the horses. The audience in the theater roared with laughter, and Doc and Jean also thought it was hilarious.

After the movie, they stopped for coffee and desert, and relived their favorite parts of the movie, and some of the lines from the movie, kind of cementing those lines in their minds. Of course, Jean's personality and Jane Russell's character in the movie couldn't have been further apart, and it was really silly, but they kind of adopted some of the lines between Jane Russell and Bob Hope as if they applied to themselves and each other as a couple; like a running joke.

They felt like a couple of care-free teen-agers, who had only just started dating. The movie was called The Paleface.

Finally, Doc concluded with the observation that cowboys and Indians were very popular with kids, and that westerns were always playing at the movies and on television. Doc opined that our country was destined to always harken back to frontier times. The *Old West* was within our fabric, part of our culture, and would never go out of style. Doc told Karl it seemed like a great theme to build on.

Karl listened intently as Doc shared his story about Doc and Jean's night at the movies, and was struck by how easily and comfortably Doc talked about personal matters. Karl began to imagine how it would materialize. "So, we name the ski trails Papoose, Wampum, and Tomahawk? Kind of like that? I hope you don't expect the ski instructors to dress up like cowboys and Indians!"

"Exactly," said Doc, getting more animated. "Of course, the ski instructors will need to dress for the cold weather and we will want a very professional image for the ski school. We can't very well have you guys skiing in breechcloths! But remember the dude ranch aspect I told you about for the summer? That will tie into the western theme too. The horses will look like Indian war ponies, and be named after the different tribes or warriors. Inside the lodge, we can decorate in the manner of the *wild west*, and we can have western square dancing on Saturday nights."

"Maybe we could get a big bell," Karl suggested, "and use it as the muster point where the skiers meet their instructors and it could be called the *Rendezvous*. Like each year when the trappers and the Indians would get together to trade their pelts and other treasures."

Doc smiled and nodded. "Perfect!" And with that, Karl was in on the theming of the ski center. "And if an old veteran preacher can't turn up a big old bell I guess he can't be very well connected!" concluded Doc.

Karl inquired, "How did you get Jean interested in this resort plan, Doc?"

Hmmm, thought Doc, "Of course you know it had been in the back of my mind for years, but not fully developed. Then much of the plan crystallized during a week of skiing at Whiteface in early March. I enjoyed skiing during the day. And then it was great to come back to Steinhoff's in the evenings. You could say I returned home with the entire blueprint and business plan figured up in my mind."

Jean had cheerfully followed Doc from one career to the next, but that time she had several questions! Two or three questions into her interrogation, Jean realized the snowball was well on its way down the mountain, growing in size and gaining speed and would crush anything it its way. This mission had already become unstoppable. Still, Jean was not a risk taker.

It was undeniable that Doc had the fire in his belly, and Jean had a menagerie of butterflies in the pit of her stomach. With a sigh of consent, Jean turned away, shook her head begrudgingly, and using her inner Jane Russell voice, said, "My husband." Doc was off and running. Though she didn't say it out loud, Doc seemed to hear her begrudging consent, but consent nonetheless.

"So, you only had all this figured out a couple of months ago?" Karl was incredulous.

"That's right, Karl," said Doc, "and the first thing I did after talking with Jean was to call you. I knew right away I wanted you and Putzi to join us."

"I guess Sacajawea, Geronimo, Crazy Horse and Sitting Bull weren't interested," Karl joked. "It seemed a little crazy to tell you *yes*. We both had good jobs at a winter vacation hot spot, as you know and to leave that to come to a place where there isn't even a ski lift yet, maybe we should have our heads examined! But the fun of course, working with you and Jean and being part of building something from scratch and then running the ski school instead of being just one of the instructors, well, here we are!"

"And mighty glad to have you on board, Karl," said Doc. "And I want to tell you I can get wound up in all the things I'm doing from time to time. I want you to understand you can come to me at any time and say, let's talk. I've never built or run a ski resort before, and I must have people on my team who will let me know what's on their minds. So, promise me you will let me know how things can be better, and don't just keep your ideas to yourself. I may not always agree with what you suggest, but I'm sure most times I will."

"Well," Karl replied, "one thing I will tell you is you can't go from no ski center in September to a finished, fully functioning resort in December. C'est impossible!"

Doc admitted it was an aggressive plan but voiced confidence in the team that had been assembled. Though Doc still spoke of completion by the first of December, Doc quietly admitted to Karl, as if the builders were listening, that he really was shooting for the end of December.

The decking was finished and the A-Frame timbers were in place. The Van Cott family at the Unadilla Silo Company did great work on short order. The beautiful, massive beams were 7 inches thick, 26 inches wide by 40 feet long, and each beam weighed 1,800 pounds. Each of the beams had thirty-five laminations. The beams were a critical part of the foundation of the building, fundamental to the external structure, the external beauty of the architecture, and the internal ambiance being created at Paleface. Fortunately, an 80-foot crane working over at the Flume Bridge in Wilmington just happened to be in the area, when it was needed to help install the gigantic girders.

Karl said, "You must be magic, Doc. I admit when you first called me in April I had serious doubts. Remember you didn't even own any land then. You sure found a beautiful spot. And I'll never forget, walking that mountain with you and Dana Peck on that chilly early April morning." By the end of that day, they had a rough map of the ski trails penciled out.

Doc chuckled, "I guess I've always been that way! When it's time to go, I go full speed ahead. I appreciate you spending that day with me on that mountain. You know exactly how the trails should look on the land."

The day after Dana and Jane Peck shook hands with Doc and agreed to a deal, Doc headed to see attorney Dan Manning, Esquire of AuSable Forks. Doc wasted no time securing the services of Mr. William Prescott, Sr. of Keeseville, representing the architectural firm of Howell Lewis Shay from Philadelphia. Whenever Doc spoke of the architects, and in an attempt to justify using a big city, prestigious firm, Doc explained, "It isn't like my paintings, once it is built there I can't just paint over a part I don't like!" News spread through town, like wildfire of a new ski center being built between Jay and Wilmington.

"Good thing my bosses don't read the newspapers in the Adirondacks," joked Karl. "I had not quit my old job yet!"

"Ah," sighed Doc ominously: "non-believer! You must have faith in the ability of great men such as ourselves to achieve great things" taking his right hand off the wheel to add a royal flourish with his right arm.

After a boisterous shared laugh, the two men returned to reviewing details.

Doc brought Karl up to date on the research he and Dana had done on chairlifts. One would be placed as the north lift and the other would be the east lift. The north lift would pull a T-Bar for a length of 3,000 feet and the east lift would carry double-seat chairs for 2,500 feet.

Karl asked about the work done on the trails. Doc told Karl about the enormous undertaking. "We've got a big crew of local men and boys, including George Sprague, Jackie Nutbrown, and Luther Taylor of Jay. They got started right away in May with the assistance and under the supervision of Dana Peck of course, preparing ski trails, cutting down trees and burning brush."

"I can see the men are well underway," said Karl, who had stopped by to take some pictures the day before. Karl was putting together a scrapbook showing the progress at the site as it progressed. "It's hard to believe people were living in a house there on the site less than a month ago!"

"Yes," said Doc, "they've moved up to Wilmington now. I will forever be grateful Dana and Jane signed on to the dream of Paleface. If they had not sold their property none of this would have been possible. I can't tell you how sad I felt watching them pull out of their driveway with their boys and their possessions." There were a couple moments of silence as Doc reflected on how touched he was by Dana and Jane's faith, sense of adventure, and willingness to trust a man who knocked on their door one rainy spring night. Some things are just meant to be, he thought.

Doc and Karl talked at length about the construction work. Following a competitive bid process, the contract was awarded to Torrance and Trumbull, more particularly David Torrance and Howard Trumbull from AuSable Forks. Torrance and Trumbull had previously been contracted to place a much smaller A-Frame near the top of Basset Mountain. Doc named that structure Smoke Rise Lookout, and the views of the AuSable Valley and of Whiteface were heavenly. You really could imagine sending smoke signals from Paleface to Whiteface. Torrance and Trumbull's work on the Smoke Rise Lookout helped them win the bid. In the years that followed, many chilly skiers and snowmobilers would enjoy warming themselves up by the woodstove at the Smoke Rise in the winter, and in the summer many delightful picnics would be enjoyed there as well.

Doc confessed, "I think I have been making too much of a pest of myself." Karl knew what Doc said was true, because he had heard it himself from the men on site. Doc continued, "The men can't get their work done if I'm in the way asking questions all day long. Just image how much they'll get done while we're at this conference!" Doc and Karl shared another hearty laugh.

They went on to discuss the subcontractors, including Maurice Southmayd of Jay, A. Mason and Son of Peru, the Ward Lumber Company of Jay, and Anson Washburn of Wilmington. Anson's job was to oversee the blasting for the lift lines. Next the men discussed the atmosphere Doc wanted to create inside Paleface. Doc wanted a place where people would enjoy relaxing in the lounge. Doc described his vision for a nice warm, cozy place to gather après-ski. They talked about the furnishings for the hotel rooms, the seating for 100 people in the dining room, what the lodge and lounge should look like and even discussed stocking the bar and kitchen areas.

Karl talked about some of the areas of interest to the director of the ski school, such as lockers and the first aide station. They talked about Walter Prager and his wife Eleanor who would set up a ski shop inside the lodge. Next the idea of establishing programs for skiing with the local schools was identified as an immediate priority. As instructors, Karl and Putzi were naturally in search of protégés. From a public-relations stand point, Doc thought the future would look bright if great skiers in the future could say they got their start at Paleface. Finally, Karl and Doc talked about the ski patrol.

By that time, the station wagon had reached Lake Placid. After a leisurely rest stop, everyone got back in the car with refreshments. Putzi had picked up the newspaper and entertained everyone in the car by sharing the news of the day. As if that weren't enough, Putzi also reported the weather, sports and summarized the advertisements and the sale prices for select items at the Grand Union supermarket.

Putzi read, "Dwight D. Eisenhower is a record-breaking 70 today, the first man ever to serve to that age as President of the United States." Putzi updated the car on the antics of Fidel Castro of Cuba and Chiang Kai-shek of China. Putzi continued, "In the third debate between John F. Kennedy and Richard Nixon, they debated from across the country with Mr. Kennedy in New York and Mr. Nixon in Los Angeles... This keeping the candidates a continent apart seemed to work out all right, especially for Nixon. Since Nixon is, as he puts it 'a heavy sweater,' the broadcasting studio was kept at 58 degrees. Furthermore, it develops that Nixon likes to jab his opponent without having to look him in the eye. On the air: Kennedy smiled and appeared fully at ease. His demeanor and voice were calm as the proverbial cucumber." Just like a commercial, Putzi announced and read the movie listings at the Palace theater, most notably, "Alfred Hitchcock's exciting drama, strictly adult entertainment, Psycho, starring Tony Perkins and Janet Leigh."

By the time Putzi had completed reading the highlights from the Adirondack Daily Enterprise, for Friday, October 14, 1960, Heidi was fast asleep on Jean's lap and the station wagon had traveled through Saranac Lake and most of the way to Tupper Lake.

In deference to a sleeping child, there was complete silence in both the front and back seat as they passed through Tupper Lake, Long Lake and into Blue Mountain Lake. When the wagon came to a stop in the middle of the town of Blue Mountain Lake, Heidi woke up, looked around briefly and apparently not at all surprised to wake up in a car, Heidi said, "Daddy, can you yodel something for me?"

Karl was an excellent yodeler, and he entertained the captive audience as it rolled past Raquette Lake and into Old Forge. Doc pulled up in front of the Four Seasons in the middle of the afternoon. The bellhop arranged for the luggage, the valet took over the station wagon and the two families picked up their room keys at the front desk. Plans were made for an early dinner.

The next morning, Karl, Putzi, Jean, and Doc were at the registration desk picking up the final program for the 1960 Winter Sports Council meeting. A light breakfast was being served as Tom Cantwell, President of the council welcomed everyone, raved about the attendance for the meeting, and slowly reviewed the schedule of activities for the next two days.

The group split up to attend various sessions. Jean spent the morning at a session moderated by Mrs. Kay Eldred, the former Miss Kay Cameron of AuSable Forks who married Bill Eldred, editor of Ski Magazine. Karl and Putzi spent the morning at a session titled "Competitive Skiing for High School Athletes." Doc went to a session called "What Other States Do to Help Skiing."

At lunch, Doc, Jean, Karl, and Putzi were joined by Art and Lili Draper. Art Draper and Doc had become fast friends at a summer meeting of the Lake Placid Chamber of Commerce, both being skiing enthusiasts first and foremost, and both having fallen hopelessly in love with the Adirondacks.

For Art Draper, it happened when he was a reporter for The New York Times assigned to cover the 100th anniversary of the first ascent of Mount Marcy. The top of Mount Marcy was the highest point in the State of New York, with great views of the Adirondacks in every direction. That love at first sight caused Art to give up his promising journalism career.

After a few years as a forest ranger, and after serving in the Army, Art became manager of Belleayre ski center in the Catskills for about seven years before taking over command at Whiteface in 1957. The way Art and Doc talked about trails, and general management of ski centers you would never know they were set to become competitors, but rather you would think they were working together to accomplish a shared dream.

And ironically, one warning from Art to Doc simply stated was this: "When you are the operator of a ski center, the buck stops with you and you are responsible for everything, and you take it so seriously even you begin to think it's your fault when it doesn't snow or when it's too cold or too warm." Listening to Art, Doc raised an eyebrow, tilted his head slightly, and briefly a flicker of doubt flashed through his brain. Art continued, "You have to learn how to relax, and take it easy, and when I figure out just how that's done, why, I'll let you know!"

Lili Draper laughed along with Doc and Art and confirmed Mr. Draper's vacation record.

"What would I do on a vacation?" questioned Art, though it sounded more like a statement.

"We'd probably spend it all skiing somewhere," laughed Lili.

Jean joined in, with a rare and slightly out of character joke. "Well, now that Mr. Fitz-Gerald is going to be a big deal ski mogul, perhaps we will have to give up our vacations!" Through the years, taking significant time away from work for vacations was always a priority. Doc scratched his chin, and looked away from the group. Doc wondered how much he would have to sacrifice to make his newest dream a reality.

As desert was being served President Cantwell returned to the podium and made a lengthy introduction on behalf of a special luncheon speaker, Mr. Harold Wilm, the New York State Conservation Commissioner.

Commissioner Wilm addressed the audience about the increasing popularity of winter sports, and the load on present facilities. The importance of those winter activities was recognized, for its impact on the economy of the State. Commissioner Wilm claimed the State encouraged private enterprise wherever possible, and then reminded the audience, or perhaps informed some who may have learned of such details for the first time, of the provisions of the New York State Constitution regarding the Adirondack State Park.

And so, Howard Wilm concluded his remarks after about forty-five minutes by formally asking the Winter Sports Council to endorse a bond issue amendment. After Commissioner Wilm's remarks concluded, confident that the case had been sufficiently made, he and the Deputy Commissioner and their entourage left the meeting, and left Old Forge.

Later, Doc was introduced to the room to say a few things about his new endeavor. As a public speaker, Doc was never shy about performing live in front of a crowd and entertained the audience with a short story and several clever remarks, making sure to also let everyone know they were invited to attend a Grand Opening at Paleface on January 21st, 1961.

At the conclusion of the business end of the Winter Sports Council's meeting, President Cantwell asked whether there was any new business for the council to consider. A motion was made to formally endorse the bond issue Commissioner Wilm had presented during lunch. President Cantwell did not get the opportunity to ask whether anyone wished to second the motion.

Mr. Perry Williams rose from the audience, walked to the front of the room, faced the crowd and made the following remarks:

*For those of you who don't know me, my name is Perry Williams. I am the owner and operator of the Snow Ridge Ski Resort on the West Road in Turin, New York. We are on the western, or perhaps even southwestern side of the park. You could say we're about half way between Watertown and Utica.*

*Anyway, you don't need a geography lesson, and you don't need me to lecture about how difficult it is to turn a profit running a ski center! It's all well and good to be the pillars of an industry, as you all are, and to get together and enjoy fancy meals.*

*This is the only place where I can come and talk to other people who know exactly what it's like to wait for that phone to ring so we can book a reservation, people who know what it's like to wait day after day for the snow to fall from the sky, people who know what it's like to watch the payroll gobble the cash out of the checkbook week after week without having good money coming in.*

*How many of you have had years where you increased your*

*business, and yet the bank account closed the year smaller than it started? And hey, it would be great to expand our operations, put in a new lift, get a new grooming machine add some amenities, why not. I can't just go to the taxpayers and say, hey let's float a bond.*

*I have to have a sensible, well thought out business plan to sell the stingy banker. Don't get me wrong, Mr. Banker must do a careful job. My point is the government should not be in the business of doing any kind of business. That's not the role of government at all.*

*The most beautiful part of the country, and certainly the most beautiful part of the state of New York, and what does the government do? The whole damned thing they practically had condemned and then all the folks in the big cities who never set foot outside the cities vote a constitutional amendment that says only the state can develop such land.*

*Fast forward years later, and the State of New York is in the business of running Ski Centers at Whiteface, in the Catskills, and as you heard here today plans for expansion, and lip service about bringing customers to their competitors. Men, how are we to compete?*

*With congratulations to the two new guys, I think the count is now fifty-nine ski centers in the State of New York. In a good year, I've got an operating season of ninety days to make a profit, and I have to convince people from Buffalo to Albany they'd rather come to Turin than go to Whiteface. But what do they see? Advertising from the state that only features Whiteface Mountain, and then you gentlemen sit here with me and listen to how they support private endeavors. To add insult to injury our tax dollars help fund the advertising that convinces our customers to go to the*

> *State-owned facilities at Whiteface and Belleayre—and nothing mentioned about our family run businesses. I should say our tax dollars do this, but the way we're going we won't have any tax dollars because we won't be making any damn money. You may all want to give a rubber stamp endorsement of a blessing and it doesn't matter anyway. The downstate voters will just blindly vote for the bond like they do everything else. For my part, I'll be damned if I am going to sit still and be quiet and get taken advantage of and then be asked to be part of unanimously supporting that which is taking advantage of me. Come, men—surely I can't be the only one who feels this way!*

Mr. Williams made a mock gesture as if to wipe the sweat off his forehead and turned toward the stage, thanked President Cantwell and returned to his chair in the audience, at which point about a dozen men tried to speak at once, and many in the audience whispered to their table neighbors.

President Cantwell rose, and in a loud voice addressed the room. "Thank you for your remarks, Mr. Williams. I hear the points you are making and I understand you are very passionate about this issue. I also can see that many men in the room feel as you do. I want to give everybody a chance to speak on this issue. With that, President Cantwell tabled the motion, and promised to take it up again the next morning. The Council members headed for their rooms to dress for cocktails at six and dinner at seven.

There was certainly plenty to talk about over cocktails and dinner, and after a couple of drinks most of the men were as animated as Mr. Williams by the time they were seated for dinner. Certainly, some were more passionate about the issue than others. And yet, some made the point that the Council's endorsement wouldn't matter one way or the other. Downstate voters aren't really concerned about whether the Winter Sports Council endorses a bond proposal. Like it or not, there really isn't anything the Winter Sports Council can do to change the situation Perry Williams spoke about so passionately.

As sizzling steaks arrived on the table, Art Draper excused himself.

Out in the lobby, Art went to the pay phone and called the Deputy Commissioner at home to let him know what had transpired during the afternoon. Of course, the Deputy Commissioner was surprised and disappointed. Art Draper understood from the increasingly elevated voice on the other end of the line that the Deputy Commissioner was not looking forward to having to tell the Commissioner that the Council was not going to endorse the bond.

Mr. Williams may not have thought the voters cared about the Council's endorsement. Evidently the Commissioner and the Deputy Commissioner cared very deeply. Given the popularity of Art Draper, the Commissioner and the Deputy Commissioner had thought the Council would quickly endorse the bond. Art Draper further informed the Deputy Commissioner that discussions would continue in the morning, and perhaps a compromise resolution would effectively endorse the bond proposal, and then excused himself from the call. The Deputy Commissioner had the last word, and his last sentence as you could imagine included several words not suitable to be repeated.

When Mr. Draper returned to the table his steak was no longer sizzling on its plate. Mrs. Draper asked if the call went okay, she knew of course *okay* was about as good as could be expected. Art told Lili, "Well, he was not happy!"

Fortunately, Mr. Draper's table was the first table served, and most people were still enjoying their dinners. Lili had finished half her steak and all her vegetables and was now picking at what was left, not very hungry but trying to decide whether to eat any more or hold out for desert. After a few bites of dinner, Art rose again. "Are you okay?" Lili asked.

"I don't know. I just feel like I could use some fresh air. I'll be back shortly. Go ahead and enjoy dessert, dear," Art said and added, "excuse me, folks" for the rest of the table. If he had to admit it, he felt worse than he'd let on. It was not a feeling he'd had much before, nor one he could well describe, but surely some fresh air was all that was needed.

Art walked out of the dining room, and down a set of stairs. Fortunately, a man was coming up the stairs. As they met, Art collapsed at the landing. The other man caught him, got Art Draper down the stairs and quickly hollered for someone to find a physician. Tragically, it was too late. Art Draper, General Manager of Whiteface Mountain Ski Center had died of a heart attack at 51 years of age.

Most of the Council members finished their deserts and left for their rooms, oblivious to the death of Art Draper in the stairwell. The passions of a contentious afternoon meeting had been cured by airing their thoughts over cocktails. Emotions were further satiated by a fine steak dinner.

In the morning, President Cantwell addressed the Council attendees and informed them of the passing of Art Draper. He told the council that all thoughts and prayers were with Lili and Art's family and Art's colleagues at Whiteface and at Belleayre. President Cantwell held up remarkably well through a difficult speech. Those at the front table could see a tear roll down his cheek. Then President Cantwell concluded the 1960 meeting of the Winter Sports Council. Breakfasts were abandoned half eaten. Whatever folks thought of the State and its competitive advantages, Art Draper was loved and respected. The meeting had turned into a wake.

It was a quiet, sad trip home for Doc, Jean, Karl, Putzi, Patti, and Heidi. No happy stops in Lake Placid, no dramatic reading of the newspaper and certainly no yodeling. At least it was a brilliantly clear day. The forests, lakes, and mountains looked exquisite. Frosted sparkle glistened on top of the last of the fall foliage that was still clinging to the trees. The spectacular beauty refilled hearts and souls that needed rejuvenation.

On the way home, Doc wrote a letter to the editor in his head. Five days later it was typed and mailed to Stephen W. Harnett, of AuSable Forks, New York and was published on November 10th. You would think Doc had known Art his whole life. Perhaps Doc never wrote more beautiful words, combining his thoughts, as he often did, with the words of famous poets. This is how Doc concluded his letter to the editor:

*Our admiration, love and sympathy go out to the family and close associates of one of the grandest leaders of the North Country. Henceforth, to look at Whiteface, will be to remember Art. No man ever had a better monument. And no mountain ever knew the handiwork of a better man. Through the likes of Art Draper, we are the beneficiaries of a testament of beauty, of majesty, and of joy. May his tribe increase and may the good Lord continue to give us men to match the mountains.*

## '60 Preparations

There were so many details to attend to. Of course, the building had to be completed. The heating system had to be installed. It had to be wired. Plumbing had to be installed. Each hotel room had to be furnished. The kitchen equipment had to be in place. There would need to be office equipment. There needed to be dining room equipment. The lounges also needed to be furnished. And the walls needed to be decorated. The fireplaces needed to be built. The giant glass windows needed to be installed. There would need to be people ready to work at Paleface. So much left to be done, and it was already late in October.

For the most part, getting everything finished was beyond Doc's control. The builders had been hired, and understood their deadline. The subcontractors were also working overtime to meet deadlines, which meant most of the men were missing hunting season that fall. All the furniture had been ordered, and was due to be delivered the second week of December. The dishes, silverware, and stemware were scheduled for delivery. So, every morning Doc woke up, ready to go, powered by adrenaline, and yet all the details were in the hands of others.

Halloween was a few days away when Jean had a coffee party at her home in Jay for the women from the Methodist Church in Jay. Not one for dramatic speeches, Jean did have an announcement that Sunday afternoon.

"As you are all aware, the progress at Paleface is coming along and we hope it will be completed soon. We are preparing to have a Grand Opening. We will need lots of people to work at Paleface, so if you or somebody you know might be interested please let me know. And this afternoon I'm going to be working on planning menus. I need all the ideas I can get so if you think it might be fun I'd love to have your help with this, but by all means, don't feel obligated to stay. I didn't ask you all here to put everyone to work for goodness sake! Doc and I have been through a lot of churches, and I think the ladies from the North Country are the best cooks anywhere. And we are very thankful and appreciative to have made such great friends here in our new hometown. So, thanks for coming and I'll let you all get back to visiting."

One by one the Methodist ladies left until there was just Mary Wallace, Bea Lincoln, Bobbie Southmayd, and Agnes Ward. Jean had a notebook full of empty pages. Mary started with a question. "So, dear,"—Mary called everyone dear—"lots of restaurants have a particular theme, you know. For instance, Tirolerland specializes in German food, Steinhoff's has lots of wild game and local fish dishes. What do you have in mind for the Paleface restaurant, Jean?"

Jean answered, "We think that people will come for half weeks, or full weeks and many of them will stay with us for all their meals. We want all their meals to be great, wholesome home cooking. Most people maybe don't want venison or German food every night. And we need to have food that kids will like, since they'll be on vacation too. I think the menu lineup should have tried and true well-loved standards, and maybe there could be a nightly special, but also some things people wouldn't make for themselves at home, some things that are a little daring maybe. And I think we should have a tradition of great baking and deserts."

"Music to my ears," laughed Mary, who was known for being a great cook and party planner. Mary's decorated cakes appeared at almost every event in town.

For the rest of the afternoon the ladies talked about their favorite "go to" family-pleasing recipes. Jean wrote everyone's ideas in her notebook: pork chops and applesauce; ham steak with curried fruit sauce; chicken cacciatori; home fried chicken smothered with onions; charcoal broiled chicken; coq au vin; lobster newburgh en casserole, rich and delicious; frogs legs provencale, sautéed in garlic butter; broiled Danish lobster tails, the favorite of The House; French fried shrimp, with tartar or cocktail sauce; and fish du jour.

For side orders, the ladies called out: vegetable, potato or rice, relish and salad. The list of appetizers included: fruit cup supreme, chilled juices, chopped chicken liver, marinated herring, shrimp cocktail, and celery and olives. Soup tureens included: French onion au gratin; sea food bisque; consommé; and a soup du jour.

It was decided that top billing would go to the steaks. Jean labeled this section "red meat (unless you insist on grey!) followed by options: charcoal broiled t-bone steak with wine and mushroom sauce; charcoal broiled filet mignon with mushrooms; charcoal broiled Delmonico steak; broiled open steak sandwich special, with onion rings and French fried potatoes; and chopped sirloin steak with onion rings. Paleface should become known for premium quality steak cooked to perfection.

In addition to dinners, the ladies talked about lunches and breakfasts. After about four hours, Jean had the basics for the menu for breakfast, lunch and dinner. Of course, it was 1960, so chocolate pudding and multi-colored Jell-O squares found a home as lunch-time desserts!

More importantly, Mary Wallace and Bea Lincoln were interested in working at Paleface, and Mary suggested a couple other ladies who were known as great cooks in the North Country.

---

As the month of November drew to a close, Doc Fitz-Gerald studied a list of disbursements that totaled $300,691.63. It was an enormous sum of money, and Doc felt a pang of doubt unsettle his gut to see the grand total.

As if the list of bills paid so far wasn't daunting enough, there was still a long list of checks to write. The list of debts added up to $203,210.

The project was only slightly over budget, and Doc had heard the half a million dollar estimate. With more than a half a million dollars spent, the enormity of the risk struck Doc. He was not accustomed to the sensation of self-doubt. He turned his head sideways, like a puppy trying to understand his master's commands, then was disturbed by a question from Mr. Torrance, who had suddenly appeared at Doc's side.

The glass was installed at Paleface during the second week of December. Nobody knew how it worked, exactly and it seemed a miracle beyond technological comprehension. The glass seemed to have magical qualities. At night, a warm bright, amber light shone through the glass. During the day time, each giant pane appeared a different color. Some of the colors complimented the lightly colored powder blue exterior and other colors contrasted. The overall effect was dramatic, striking and memorable.

With the Grand Opening deadline fast approaching, it was nice to have the windows in place so that everything on order could be delivered and installed. For the next couple of weeks, it seemed one delivery man was followed immediately by another in rapid succession.

The first storm of the season had held off. The building was finished. Everything that was critically necessary for a Grand Opening had been delivered. Grand Opening plans were finalized. Everything was ready to go, with two important exceptions. There was no snow, and the chairlifts weren't operational.

## '61 Double Chairlift

Five days before Christmas, Walter Warner from Wentworth, Pennsylvania arrived at Paleface with a pair of assistants who were half his age. It was up to that crew to get the chairlift and the T-Bar running properly. Their reputation preceded them. At the meeting in Old Forge, Doc had been told, "Don't hire anybody else, and don't invite them into your home!"

Everything had been prepared as recommended by the experts. The towers were installed up the mountain during the summer and fall. Sheds had been built around the motor and terminal or station at the base of the lift.

The tricky part seemed to be getting the cable properly installed. The cable was like a big bicycle chain around a gear on the front and back wheels of a bike. The terminal at the top and the bottom of the lift were like the bicycle wheels. For everything to work, the cable had to be exactly the right length. With the weight of the cable, the chairs, and the skiers, plus the burden placed on the system by winter conditions, everything had to be installed with great precision.

Calculating the length of cable needed was one thing. The tricky thing was joining the start and the end of the cable. Somehow that detail hadn't been fully anticipated when Paleface plans were put together. Cable for chairlifts was highly specialized. The cable was made of six strands. Each strand was made of between nineteen and twenty-six thin wires. The six strands were twisted around a fiber core. To join one end of the cable to the other in a continuous loop utilized a highly specialized process called splicing. The small strands were braided together in such a way as to keep the total cable thickness within four millimeters of the overall diameter of the cable. This braiding process was called epissure, and required an expert hand. And the expert hands belonged to Walter Warner.

It didn't matter to Walter whether it was the customer's wife, somebody's grandmother, or a whole room full of women from church. Walter used the worst cuss words as nouns, verbs, adjectives, and even punctuation. The first day at Paleface he whistled at Jean Fitz-Gerald, pinched Mary Wallace's behind, and told Patti a dirty joke. From then on, Doc was placed in charge of delivering meals to the men from Wentworth. And Patti was kept a great distance from the work on the lifts.

True to their reputation, the cable was joined on the double chairlift and it was up and running by Friday, December 23rd.

As the men were packing up to return to Pennsylvania, Doc asked

Walter how soon he would be returning to get the T-Bar running. Somehow no one ever told Walter about the T-Bar. Fortunately, Doc got Walter's boss on the phone and arranged for Walter and his crew to return on January 2nd. Doc thought it was too bad Walter couldn't just stay and get the job done without having to come back a second time. But Christmas was two days away. It amused Doc to think someone's Christmas might be ruined by the absence of Wicked Walter. Certainly, there were lots of wonderful human beings in Wentworth, Pennsylvania but Mr. Warner had to come from somewhere.

## '61 Waiting on the T-Bar

"It's an ill wind that doesn't blow some good," or so they say. After holding off throughout December, Mother Nature dropped a two-foot whopper of a storm on the North Country on New Year's Day.

It was great news for Whiteface. Paleface would of course benefit too. However, the snowstorm delayed the cable splicer from Pennsylvania another five days. And the big worry was whether there would be enough time to get the T-Bar running before the Grand Opening on Saturday, January 21st. It would be even nicer if it were running before the Open House on Sunday, January 15th.

If the construction crew from Torrance and Trumbull thought Doc was hovering over them as they were building Paleface, well, that was nothing compared to Doc's impatience with Walter the splicer.

To make matters worse, Walter seemed to enjoy telling Doc about all the things that could go wrong. For instance, "After several days of trying to join the strands in the bitter cold, it might not be perfect and the lift might not pass inspection." Then he might have to start over.

Almost every hour, or so it seemed, Doc went to check on the men. Almost every time, Walter tried to hang a new fear on Doc. On and on this went, and probably Walter could have gotten the job done a day sooner without Doc's supervision. Yet Walter couldn't ever remember being so well cared for at one of his jobs, nor could he remember having had so much fun with it either. Then finally, just a couple days before the Open House, Walter told Doc the job was done.

Dana Peck was on hand to see if it would work. The moment of truth had arrived. Much to Doc's relief, and to Dana's as well, their fears had failed to be realized. The T-Bar was up and running. It still needed an official inspection, but Walter guaranteed it would pass. From then on, the T-Bar and the Double Chairlift were left in the good hands of Dana Peck.

## '61 Open House Weekend

There were a few little things that hadn't arrived in time. However, none of those omissions were noticed by guests or remembered for long even by the staff and owners of Paleface. Everything that was critical for a successful Open House or preview inspection was installed and was looking great.

Visitors from all the local towns stopped by that day. Since the first news of Paleface hit the newspapers, curiosity had been building. Every day it seemed that more and more cars were passing by. Often cars would drive up, pull into the parking lot and people would get out, look things over and then get back in their cars and return in the direction from which they had come.

Finally, the doors were unlocked and tour guides were waiting.

It seemed that every resident of the towns of Jay, Upper Jay, and Wilmington passed through Paleface that morning. What's more, it also seemed like maybe half the residents of AuSable Forks and Keene stopped in as well. It even seemed that a quarter of Lake Placid dropped in for coffee and a donut. Doc and Jean couldn't have been happier with the turnout.

It was a real thrill to show everyone in town what was going on at Paleface. Doc and Jean had made it a point to build and staff Paleface with as many local people as possible, only going outside the area when specific technical skills weren't available locally. Doc and Jean were completely committed to the business becoming a valued part of the local community.

Just after Doc concluded his brief remarks to the folks in attendance at the Open House, Dana Peck and Karl Jost carried an enormous "package" through the front door. Jane Peck was right behind them carrying a card, which she gave to Doc. Doc opened the envelope, and read aloud:

*Dear Doc and Jean, best wishes on your new endeavor. We took up a collection and all your friends and acquaintances in Mountain Lakes, New Jersey pitched in. We figured Paleface would need a mascot of sorts, and this 'little guy' seemed to do the trick. Though we don't see you often enough anymore, please know you are missed and that you are loved.*

*Congratulations, Bob.*

As Doc finished reading, his tongue stumbled over a lump in his throat.

Jean's eyes welled up with tears.

Patti couldn't wait to see what was under all those blankets. Doc sent Patti over to check it out. Even with Dana's pocket knife it took several minutes to get the twine off and unroll the blankets.

Inside was a very soft, bright white teddy bear. It had been custom made for the occasion, and the face of the bear was made of painted wood. It had an exuberant expression and the cheeks were so rosy it looked like the bear had spent three hours in 30 degree below zero weather.

The bear was easily the largest stuffed animal anyone there had ever seen. It was wider than two grown men standing side by side, and just about as tall.

"I love it," Patti gushed.

"I've never seen anything like it in all the world," Jean announced.

"What in tarnation are we going to do with this!" Doc exclaimed with a chuckle. The chuckle distracted Doc from his emotions. Before the chuckle, Doc had been so touched he thought he might weep openly.

## '61 Fuzzy Wuzzy

When the general public had gone from sight, a long thick rope was dropped over the head and arms of the giant stuffed bear. Then a ladder was brought into the lodge.

As luck would have it, it turned out there was a place for the mascot that couldn't have been more perfect if Paleface had been built around the gigantic teddy bear in the first place. It was in the dining room, just above the lowest section of giant picture windows, and right where the roofline from the entry way intersected the dining room. It would be almost impossible to enjoy any meal, snack, or coffee break without admiring the cheerful bruin.

Every time Jean saw it, she hummed the childhood rhyme, "Fuzzy Wuzzy was a bear, Fuzzy Wuzzy had no hair, Fuzzy Wuzzy wasn't fuzzy, was he?" And so, he was. Though everyone put effort into a more perfect name, days turned into weeks and then weeks into months and years, and at last Fuzzy Wuzzy always remained Fuzzy Wuzzy.

## '61 Grand Opening

For weeks, suspense had been building. Doc had told everyone that a super famous mystery guest would appear at the Grand Opening. Not even Jean could get him to elaborate. You might have thought Doc was referring to snow!

The snow from the big storm on New Year's Day kept the mountain covered with snow for half a month. Those who skied during the Open House weekend had good skiing on Saturday. By Sunday skiing conditions had deteriorated to fair.

Every morning Doc awoke, adrenaline shooting through his body; there was so much to tend to, to worry about. Not normally a list maker, Doc had made a list and checked everything on the list several times a day. On the top of the list was a four-letter word... SNOW. Someone could do something about everything else on that to-do list.

In the many years since 1961, very sophisticated weather prediction services have become available, and though we tend to joke about its unreliability, we might have to concede that it is remarkable how well we can count on weather predictions five days to a week in advance, most of the time.

In 1961, they did have a weather satellite. TIROS-1 was followed by TIROS-2 and in July TIROS-3 was launched into space. In September, TIROS-3 had identified hurricane Esther, and was able to warn the mid-Atlantic and New England in advance of its arrival.

The Television Infrared Observation Satellite (TIROS) failed to predict the two feet of snow that descended from Canada into the Adirondacks on New Year's Day. The big storm came with no warning. Weather forecasting at the time was more of an exercise of reporting on current events than it was predicting the future.

Yes, Doc worried about snow, and of course Doc also worried about the super famous mystery guest, because super famous mystery guests are inherently unpredictable.

Two days before the Grand Opening, an enormous nor'easter hit Washington DC, where plans were being made for John Fitzgerald Kennedy's inauguration on Saturday.

On Saturday, as President Kennedy was delivering his inaugural address in Washington, the first ever televised live and in color, the powerful nor'easter brought snow to New York and New England. Great news for ski centers!

Doc and Jean took a few minutes out of their day on Saturday to watch President Kennedy deliver his memorable speech. Some of the phrases that caught their attention were: "a beachhead of cooperation in a jungle of suspicion"; "not a pledge but a request that both sides begin anew the quest for peace"; and "civility is not a sign of weakness, and sincerity is always subject to proof." It wasn't always possible to tell when President Kennedy was talking about foreign adversaries or whether he was talking about political opponents.

Doc loved the phrase imploring mankind to "invoke the wonders of science instead of its terrors." The line which captured Doc and Jean's attention was the memorable phrase, "the torch has passed to a new generation of Americans."

The inauguration of Paleface the next day included enough of the white stuff to make a very respectable showing. They didn't get the bountiful ten foot drifts found elsewhere in the northeast. The Adirondacks had been on the outer fringes of the nor'easter but the snow was plentiful enough for the Fitz-Gerald family to count their blessings.

When Doc woke up on the morning of January 21st, Paleface looked just as he pictured it would, wrapped in a fresh white blanket of snow. The low overnight temperature had dropped to 20 degrees below zero, which was not unusual at all during January in the North Country. The festivities at Paleface were scheduled for 2:00pm by which time the mercury in the thermometer had climbed to 3 degrees above zero.

Friday night the lodge was sold out, filled mostly with friends and family of the Fitz-Geralds plus some of the dignitaries who were in attendance for the Grand Opening. The dining room was busy with breakfast guests from 7:30 all the way until 10:00. The trails on Paleface were busy with happy skiers enjoying a little bit of fresh snow.

A crew from television station WCAX, Channel 3 from Burlington, Vermont arrived a few minutes after ten. The television crew broadcast live from Paleface several times during the day. At 1pm, a low flying plane passed over Paleface, commemorating the occasion with an aerial photograph. Car loads of people had been arriving all day.

The board members of the AuSable and Lake Placid Chambers of Commerce were in attendance and of course all of the board members of the Whiteface Chamber of Commerce were at Paleface. Officials representing the Whiteface Mountain Ski Center were there to offer their support publicly, including Mike Muiry the new director and Lili Draper, the widow of the late director, Art Draper.

Santa's Workshop was represented by Peter Reiss and John Zachay. The legendary theme park along the highway to the summit of Whiteface Mountain, Santa's Workshop, established in 1949 was among the earliest theme parks in the world. Could the super famous mystery guest be Santa himself?

A special podium had been built for the Grand Opening presentation. Paleface had invested in an amplifier and microphone. The elevated podium was decked out in patriotic bunting.

At about ten minutes before 2pm, there was one more sound check. It seemed there had been dozens of sound-checks throughout the morning. The final sound check passed.

Promptly at 2:00pm, Daniel T. Manning, Esquire, who served as the Essex County district attorney in Elizabethtown and who had a legal practice in AuSable Forks, stepped up to the podium and took to the microphone. Attorney Manning welcomed the crowd, lending formality and significance to the occasion. "It is my honor and pleasure to welcome you to the Grand Opening for Paleface Ski Center. Paleface is the newest attraction in the North Country. What started as Boylan Fitz-Gerald's dream has developed into this wonderful vacation spot. For the Fitz-Gerald's this is a family business. For us in the community it is a phenomenal economic development opportunity. We wish all the best for Doc, Jean, and the Fitz-Gerald family, and congratulations on building such a beautiful business." Dan Manning passed the microphone to Doc.

"Good afternoon, everyone. I know it is very cold today. I will only take a couple minutes of your time this afternoon. On behalf of Jean and my family, thank you so much for coming out today to support us by attending this Grand Opening."

One by one, Doc invited those responsible for building Paleface to be recognized before the crowd, starting with the Torrance and Trumbull Construction Company who served as the general contractor. "Just look at the beautiful building they created," Doc said proudly. David Torrance, Howard Trumbull and their families and staff were invited forward to wave to the audience of over 1,000 people. Next, Maurice Southmayd and his family were recognized, and Doc emphasized the enormous task of work completed by the plumbing contractors. Doc continued, "I also want to recognize Anson Washburn from Wilmington. Mr. Washburn had a blast working on this mountain!" Collectively the audience groaned. "Well, he did!" Doc paused dramatically. "For those of you who don't know Anson was responsible for blowing up whatever needed blowing up, and putting holes in the rocks to set the lift towers." Finally, Doc warmly thanked Ward Lumber Company and the Ward family from Jay, which supplied lots of the lumber and building supplies.

Doc continued, "We haven't been a part of the community for generations like many of you have, but in a few short years, you have all made us feel so welcome. We appreciate the hard work of everyone who had a part in building Paleface. We had a tight deadline, and everyone delivered championship work in splendid fashion. After today, please don't forget we are here." Doc added a welcoming smile and a brief pause. If you don't know how to ski, our great staff will teach you. The lodge features a wonderful restaurant, and we happily serve the public. If you have out of town guests, consider putting them up in our great new motel rooms. If you have a business affair, wedding or anniversary celebration we have plenty of great space for that as well."

Doc's tone changed from earnest to playful after a slight pause. "And now, you may have heard a little something about a super famous mystery guest." Magically, right on cue a round man in a bright red suit came zooming down the Paleface Chair Lift Trail right behind the podium. "That's right, everybody," Doc said. "It looks like Santa has a little free time on his hands now that winter is here!" Not far behind Santa, another skier was coming down the hill. "Ladies and Gentlemen, notice the big pile of snow a little way up the mountain." Moments later, the approaching skier hit the top of the snow pile and flew into the air, spread his legs then did some fancy footwork in the air, and landed back on the trail. "May I present Art Devlin, our world-famous ski jumper from Lake Placid!"

Art arrived at the podium moments later, removed his ski hat and goggles, and put his arm around Doc's shoulders. "How about a big round of applause for Art Devlin, the voice of ski jumping on television and our National Champion and World Champion ski jumper. Art will be signing autographs inside the lodge this afternoon. How about a big round of applause for Art Devlin everybody!" When the applause subsided, Doc continued, "And now I'd like to direct your attention back up the trail." The audience watched as Dana Peck removed the giant jump with the tractor. "For Art Devlin, that was just a little mogul. For the rest of us, that jump would be considered a safety hazard!"

Doc turned slightly to his right for his next introduction. "Finally, everybody, I would like to present Mrs. Kay Eldred to christen the chairlift. For those of you who don't know Mrs. Eldred, she is the wife of Mr. Bill Eldred, the editor of Ski Magazine. Mrs. Eldred herself is a local girl. Mrs. Eldred's family founded the J. J. Rogers Company in AuSable, and as if that isn't enough, Mrs. Eldred also helped the Land of Makebelieve get its start in Upper Jay!" Next to Mrs. Eldred was Arto Monaco, the creative genius, and owner-innovator of the Land of Makebelieve. Arto Monaco was holding a bottle of champagne.

"And now," Doc announced, like a circus announcer directing the crowd's attention from one ring to the next, "Ladies and Gentlemen, let me direct your attention to chair number one." A sign with the number one was visible to all on the back of the chair facing the audience. The lift was stopped. Mrs. Eldred and Arto Monaco made a big show of approaching the chair and holding out their arms as if modeling the fashionable chair on a runway.

Arto Monaco passed Mrs. Eldred the bottle. Mrs. Eldred held the neck of the bottle in both hands, lifted it up over her head. At the microphone, Doc counted down "10, 9, 8, 7, 6, 5, four and one half, four and one quarter, four and one eighth." The audience groaned. Doc wanted to savor the moment, however briefly. Doc chuckled and finished the countdown "3, 2, 1."

Mrs. Eldred unflinchingly smashed the bottle to bits over the chair. Foamy bubbles gushed into the snow beneath the chair. The crowd applauded while Mrs. Eldred took several bows and then Arto Monaco escorted her away. Paleface's Grand Opening was now a smashing success. After a quick clean-up of the broken glass, the lift was turned on.

Doc and Patti boarded chair number one and set off up the mountain. With the Grand Opening behind them, Paleface was officially in business. For Doc and Patti, that brief ride was a quiet, precious, island of a moment, like a father-daughter dance at a wedding.

## '61 No Snow

The inaugural snow storm, such as it was, didn't last very long. Two back-to-back warm days in late January just about wiped the last of it away.

Fran Betters, who was working in Bergenfield, New Jersey drove by Paleface, and pulled into the parking lot. Fran was a native of Wilmington, and was home to visit family. Curiosity got the better of Fran, and he stopped in for coffee even though he was just a couple miles from home.

Fran was sitting at a table, enjoying a cup of coffee and staring at the big bear in the rafters. Doc Fitz-Gerald stopped at Fran's table. "Do you mind if I join you for a few minutes?" Doc asked. The two men had met briefly at the Pine Knot Restaurant at the end of fishing season back in September.

Fran said, "No sir, please do." Doc asked about Fran's trip from New Jersey. Fran told Doc he couldn't believe what he saw the closer he got home. All along the way, snow everywhere, but in the Adirondacks almost no snow.

They talked a little longer, mostly about fishing. Also about Fran's dreams of permanently moving back home to the Adirondacks from New Jersey. Sometimes a man had to travel far from home to find the means to support his family. Doc offered encouragement, and asked Fran if there was a way to make a living doing the things he loved. Fran finished his coffee, told Doc it was nice to see him again, and then Fran headed home to see his beloved daughter and the rest of his family.

## '61 Spring Skiing

Toward the end of March, business slowed down. Many people enjoyed spring skiing conditions, on the other hand, by late March many people were thinking about warmer weather and are ready for the change in seasons.

Between the breakfast and lunch service on one slow Tuesday morning, Jean was sitting down for a break with the ladies from the kitchen and the dining room. Bea Lincoln had something to share with everyone. She had waited for that break and she could contain herself no longer.

Bea's son was in the Navy and was based in Spain. In a letter he sent to his mother, he had included a dozen pictures from Barcelona. Bea passed the pictures around to the ladies from Paleface. The architecture and statuary were very impressive, certainly very different from what the ladies were familiar with in the United States. The one picture that Bea was most drawn to was a picture of a small donkey drawing a cart of flowers.

Bea was proud of her sons. That letter from her son touched her heart. She was beaming with pride and beside herself with excitement to be able to share it with her friends. For the rest of the season, that letter shared space in the pocket where Bea carried the little "GUEST CHECK" order book, with its unused green and white pages and its completed carbon copies rolled around the top. Several times a day, Bea would take out the letter and read it again.

During the final days of ski season, Putzi Jost took a rare fall and broke her thumb. Often spring skiing came with icy conditions and limited snow cover which could make skiing treacherous even for experts. Not to be sidelined by such a minor adversity, Putzi continued her work instructing skiers. With her hand in a cast and her thumb entombed in plaster, it looked like she was hitchhiking up the mountain.

## '61 TV Stars

Even after the Paleface launch, the Paleface story remained popular. During January, Doc had the occasion to appear on the local program "Ski Trails" with Al Cahill a couple of times, Doc made for a good television guest, and appeared on the program frequently thereafter.

Part of the Paleface plan was to appeal to the ladies and bring in the families. In February, Doc and Jean's son Chuck Fitz-Gerald had the chance to appear on the program "For You Madame." Mary Wallace, who initially managed the cafeteria at Paleface, also appeared on the program. Mrs. Wallace mentioned her work at Paleface, however she was primarily there to talk about her unique "doll cakes." Chuck Fitz-Gerald talked about the beginner and intermediate ski trails, family friendly resort environment and free baby-sitting services offered at Paleface.

Chuck and Mary rode to Plattsburgh together to appear on the program, and on the way home it started to snow. Paleface received a couple of inches of snow that night.

The next stop on the calendar was a Ski Fashion show sponsored by the Whiteface Chamber of Commerce. The Ski Shop at Paleface was owned and operated by Walter Prager, a two-time world champion alpine skier from Switzerland. The fashions demonstrated were of course available from the Prager Ski Shop at Paleface. In addition to Mr. and Mrs. Prager, there were several men and women in the community who modeled the fashions, and even Patti Fitz-Gerald and Heidi Jost got to model the fashionable skiing outfits of 1961. The evening concluded with singing by Charles Walker from Lake Placid, and dancing to music by Ernie Vaughn at the organ after that.

The next Friday evening, Jane and Dana enjoyed dinner together at Paleface. The boys were left in good hands with their favorite Aunt Natalie. You would think after spending all week working at Paleface they would want to go somewhere else for Jane's birthday dinner. Jane and Dana were proud of Paleface, and it was wonderful to enjoy a leisurely birthday dinner with their friends, Mr. and Mrs. George Haselton.

A couple weeks later, a full color movie called *Tale of Two Skis* was shown at Paleface. The loft at Paleface was perfect for showing 8 millimeter movies. When the lights were turned off, it was dark in the loft. Hundreds of people showed up, and Doc had to scramble to come up with enough chairs for everyone.

By the end of the month, the snow had run thin. When the newspaper called for the ski report, Doc described the skiing conditions as "white frosting on chocolate cake," with tongue in cheek of course. Doc learned never to report the ski conditions on an empty stomach. Doc thought the cake report was better than saying "half an inch of snow over six inches of mud." Or just simply to report that ski conditions were "poor."

Tirolerland, another favorite local restaurant and hotel, reported a 90 percent cancellation rate. In late February, it was too warm and there was not enough snow at all. The warm late February temperatures led to ice jams in the AuSable River that caused great concerns about potential flooding problems. It got so warm in late February and early March that Paleface had to shut down the ski lifts, only operating the restaurant and motel.

Finally, another big snowstorm dropped from the sky on Wednesday, March 15th and Paleface was back to putting skiers on the mountain. The lift operators, ski instructors, and ski patrol were back from being laid off. Extra staff was put on in the restaurant and the bar. Jane Peck had spent much of the previous week with her youngest son Dana-D who had the mumps. Fortunately, David was feeling much better, since even the office was busy after the big storm.

## '61 Jukebox Delivery

All week long, Patti had been looking forward to the delivery of a jukebox. The piped in music at Paleface was pleasant enough, mostly instrumentals like the number one song from all of 1960, "Theme From a Summer Place," by Percy Faith and his Orchestra. It seemed to play on the service every hour. The service also included popular music from the 1950's with the vocals removed, plus Brat Pack and big band standards from the 1940's. Patti wanted to hear the modern kind of songs they were playing on the radio. Those songs which would be later referred to as bubble gum music. Patti also liked the folk, country, rock, and rockabilly songs.

Stan and Tom from the vending company finally arrived on Friday. Patti had been mulling around the lounge with her best friend, Cookie, whose real name was Linda Cooke. Patti always had an infectious positivity, a robust sense of humor and unending reserves of energy, and Cookie even more so. The girls had handfuls of quarters, and once that jukebox got set up they intended to dance all afternoon.

The men from the vending company had delivered many jukeboxes of course, and were used to having an eager audience. Tom was very friendly and answered all the girls' questions with a look of mild amusement. One on his left, the other on the right. He'd no sooner finished answering one girl's question before the second girl would pile on with another question. Stan, on the other hand, wasn't the sort of guy to stop to listen to questions from kids.

The girls were very disappointed to hear the jukebox had been filled with records at the warehouse. They had stayed up very late the night before making lists of the songs they should ask him to put in the box. Tom said, "If you give me your lists, I'll take them back with me and next time I'm here, I can't make any promises, but I'll see what I can do!"

When Stan and Tom left the girls just stared at it for a while. Patti and Cookie agreed it was the most beautiful thing they had ever seen. Cookie said it looked like it was constructed from solid silver. It was so shiny you could see your own reflection in it.

"It has its own lights inside it," said Patti. Though it was nearly noon, the girls wanted to see what it would look like in the dead of night.

The girls went running through the dining room, past the office, and around the bend to the chambermaid's closet to get a couple blankets. Mary, Bea, and Jean hardly noticed them zoom by. Nothing gets by a Mom, though! On the way back through, Jean stopped the girls and asked, "Where are you going with those blankets in the middle of the day in the middle of summer?"

The ladies had a good laugh. Imagine, putting a tent over a jukebox! Considering how it just arrived, and it wouldn't do any harm, Jean said go ahead, but fifteen minutes is it. "This is a business and the jukebox is here for everyone, not a private plaything." Fortunately, all the customers were headed for lunch, not the lounge.

Mary Wallace had dropped in for a visit between the breakfast service and the lunch service. While the jukebox was installed Mary, Jean, and Bea visited over coffee and donuts. Mary had been away from work for several days, at her daughter's side and just had to sneak away for a couple of hours to tell everyone about her new granddaughter, born just two days earlier.

Bea was already a grandmother three times over, although she was only 44 years old. Mary and Bea had raised their kids together, and on that morning, they enjoyed sharing some of their favorite memories. They took turns teaching Sunday school, together with three other women, and spent most of the 1950s together.

One Friday, late in June, six years prior, Bea took her Sunday school class for a hot dog roast down at the river. Her husband, Abe came down to set up the grill, prepare the coals and grill the hot dogs, and Bea set up an enormous bowl of potato salad, hefty slices of watermelon and gallons of Hi-C Punch. Bea made a good show of enforcing the rule of no swimming for twenty minutes after eating. She had a way of standing, with a firm commanding stance and a stern strict look on her face, and then with a slight turn at the corner of her mouth and an almost imperceptible lift of her brow and a tiny shrug of her right shoulder her soft side was revealed. Most of the kids knew what to look for and knew it when they saw it. That day Mary Wallace's oldest daughter got the look, and she was off. Everyone else followed without confirmation. Bea shook her head from side to side as if to say to herself, "kids will be kids."

Abe took the station wagon and left Bea, the cooling grill, and the kids at the river. As he was leaving Mary arrived at the river. Out of the back of her wagon came an enormous wooden board covered in aluminum foil. There must have been about three dozen plump cupcakes each decorated in a different color and pattern yet each one a work of art.

First Mary successfully negotiated her way down the steep dirt path from the side of the road, and then Mary managed to hop-scotch across the boulders at the side of the river. With sixteen kids cheering her on, and with a smile on her face as wide as Lake Champlain, Mary hollered, "Who wants some desert?" Mary kicked off her shoes and stepped into the water. The kids moved toward Mary, and Mary moved toward the kids. The third step in was one step too much!

Down went Mary, up went the cupcakes and moments later when Mary surfaced her wide smile only grew wider. All the kids' eyes were wide with shock, and several rushed to help Mary up out of the water, but Mary stood on her own, put her hands above her knees, bent at the waste and laughed harder than she could ever remember having laughed before. Mary wondered what in the world Bernard was going to say. Mary laughed even harder at the thought.

The kids were relieved of course, and perhaps Mary's daughters were a little embarrassed. The kids couldn't help themselves, and neither could Mary and Bea. Everyone just had to see if the cupcakes would make it down the river and over the rapids. In the Town of Jay, the rapids in the river were the main attraction and on a nice warm summer day there were dozens of people sliding down the rapids. That day, the kids were mostly unaware that soggy frosted cupcake crumbs were shooting the rapids with them.

As Mary headed back to her car she turned to Bea and said the moral of this story is when it's someone else's turn to tend to the kids, stay to home! Bea could hear Mary laughing her larger than life laugh all the way up the path to the car.

Mary and Bea never grew tired of telling and re-telling that story to one another. Jean on the other hand had lived in New Jersey at the time, but enjoyed reminiscing with her friends. If Jean had a jealous bone in her body, she might have had to confess to being a little envious of her friends and their grandchildren. Perhaps one day she would join the club.

It was way past time for Mary Wallace to get back to her daughter and granddaughter at the hospital. As they parted, Bea said, "Next time we'll have to tell Jean about the time Mary hosted a skating party in the town green." Bea took out her waitress order tablet, and Jean went to check on the girls at the Jukebox.

They were at the jukebox of course, and as Jean rounded the corner the girls were Twisting away, Chubby Checker's classic dance song was coming out of the shiny new machine and the sight of the two young teens Twisting away in the lobby struck her funny, and at the same moment she thought of her friend falling in the river with the cupcakes and Jean herself got a rare case of the giggles. She wasn't known to be much of a giggler, so this got the girls' attention. "Uh, uh, are you laughing at us?" asked Patti, who had stopped dancing, and strangely had crossed arms and legs, as one might do if they were caught unexpectedly coming out of the shower.

Jean said, "Well, honesty is the best policy. For some reason watching people do that dance looks so ridiculous to me! Anyway, you girls have fun and I'll come back for you after lunch and we'll go picking raspberries. I want to make some pies and put up some jam." Jean scooped up the two blankets that had been dumped on the floor and headed back to the dining room to help make sure all the guests were enjoying lunch.

## '61 Raspberry Picking

Shortly before 2pm, Jean checked on the girls. They had finished dancing and were quietly sitting and talking. Conversation ceased when Jean came in. "Let's have a glass of lemonade and then let's go pick some berries," Jean said.

It was nice to get out of the lodge for a little while. With a quick stop at home to pick up some pails they were back in the car again and headed up in the Glen to Frank Blakely's farm. Jean had heard that the raspberries were particularly good that year. Jean was looking forward to spending some time outdoors, getting some fresh air and perhaps enjoying a little solitude away from all the customers at the lodge. But it wasn't to be! Frank had advertised extensively, and word had spread that the berries tasted even better than usual. Even without the peace and quiet, Jean enjoyed dropping the fat red berries in her bucket.

The girls had long since grown tired of picking berries and were sitting in the car, again locked in conversation. Still, between them, they had picked ten quarts that afternoon, which set Jean back $2.50. Frank had been charging a quarter a quart for years. Jean couldn't help but think he should raise his prices, then it crossed Jean's mind to wonder whether Paleface was charging enough for rooms and meals.

## '61 French Cut by Alma

Cookie lived up in the Glen near the Blakely farm, and she hadn't been home much over the past couple days. Jean and Patti dropped Cookie off at her house along with two quarts of raspberries. Jean thought it was nice to have her daughter Patti to herself for a few minutes. Before heading back to Paleface, they made a quick side trip to AuSable Forks. Jean needed to pick up some groceries. Just the right amount of time to talk to Patti about a few things.

"Your dad and I were talking about letting you get your haircut before you go off to school in September. I know you and Cookie have been talking about 'the French Cut' and it is a lot of money to spend for a haircut. But if you're still interested, we will pay the $6.95 to get your hair done. I called Alma at the Ark Beauty Salon and she can fit us in at noon on Tuesday. What do you say?"

Patti was amazed. All the girls she knew were getting new-fangled haircuts in all the latest styles, and Cookie was crazy to get 'the French Cut.' Patti preferred to keep her ponytail just like it was, maybe not as anxious to want to grow up as fast as the other girls, but peer pressure seemed to get the better of her. When Jean told Patti that it would make her look more lady like, Jean almost lost the argument. But when Jean said that Doc thought it would be a good idea, the deal was sealed.

The rest of the trip to the store, Patti and Jean talked about Patti's studies. Jean tried to make the experience sound like an excellent adventure and a chance to meet new friends and learn exciting new things. Inside, Jean tried to hide the sadness of being away from her baby girl. Patti wasn't too keen on going either but everyone had agreed that attending St. Johnsbury Academy would give Patti the best options possible for a bright future.

As it would turn out, Alma's French Cut looked great on Patti, but didn't help her at all in French class.

## '61 Whiteface Mountain Museum

Doc told Patti to get ready quickly. "We're heading out on an adventure today, just you and me!" Jean smiled knowingly and Patti went from lazily poking at the last of her breakfast to a state of excited intrigue.

"Should I grab my bathing suit?" asked Patti. Doc shook his head. Nope.

"Should I pack a lunch for you two?" asked Jean.

"That would be nice," said Doc. "How quick can we get ready?"

"Do I need to grab the fishing poles or our backpacks?" asked Patti. Doc shook his head again. Nope.

"I think all we need is the car keys and we're ready to go. Maybe while Mother is making lunch you can run to the bathroom, just in case. It could be a long trip. Or it could be five minutes down the road. How mysterious!" Doc stretched the last word out to make it sound kind of spooky.

A few minutes later they were in the car, headed toward Wilmington and then Lake Placid beyond it. As it turned out, it was not a long car ride after all. Even so, Patti incessantly pestered with questions about where they were headed. Doc brought the car to a stop in the parking lot at the Whiteface Mountain Museum, taking the second to last place.

Doc turned the car off and turned to Patti. "There's somebody I'd like you to meet. You see, once upon a time there was a famous Adirondack Hermit that lived alone in the woods for thirty-three years. About a year before you were born, they convinced him to come out of the woods and took him on tours of sportsmen's shows from Buffalo to Boston. I got to hear him talk in New York City when he was at a sportsmen's show there. Today he is here at the museum and I can tell you he is quite a character. I think you'll enjoy meeting him!"

"Okay, let's go," said Patti, which pretty much described Patti's personality in three words. It was five minutes to ten, and there was a long line at the door. Outside the museum was a man-made pond fully stocked with trout. Next to a small dock beside the pond there was a small gumball sized machine filled with tiny fish food pellets. Doc gave Patti a couple pennies and she ran to the pond to feed the fish. The lively trout jumped out of the pond, greedily gobbling up pellets, as Patti tossed the food. It didn't take long before she was looking for more pennies.

The museum had lots of interesting exhibits. Doc walked through the museum at a slow pace. The exhibits from the 1932 Winter Olympics were interesting enough, but it was hard for a kid to stand in front of a single exhibit for too long.

They looked at pictures and memorabilia in a covered display case featuring hometown hero John Amos "Jack" Shea who won two gold medals in speed skating, first the 1,500 meter and then the 500 meter. In all the U.S. team took six gold, four silver and two bronze medals for a total of twelve. Norway came in second with ten medals and Canada placed third with seven.

Certainly, the star exhibit and main attraction was Noah John Rondeau—Adirondack Hermit. There were display cases full of pictures of Noah John at his camp at Cold River Flow, and memorabilia from Noah John's many sportsmen's shows. It was interesting how one person's story could consume a community, a nation even.

Truly Noah John lived a life outside of the ordinary and survived a self-imposed exile, even thrived in it. As a hermit, Noah John lived off the land and found beauty all around him. Considering the extreme climate of the Adirondack back woods winter, Noah John's survival story was impressive indeed. Perhaps most surprising was that Noah John emerged from his hermitage and revealed himself to be an outgoing, interesting man strangely capable of speaking in front of crowds that numbered in the thousands at some events, and in the millions, all added together. All the while, Noah John maintained a self-effacing humility, thus breaking many of the stereotypes of what a hermit was like even as he accentuated other assumed hermit characteristics.

Around noon, Patti and Doc returned to the parking lot to get their sacked lunches and sat by the pond. Noah John was due to appear in person inside the museum at 1pm. In between the bites and the crunches, Doc told Patti about meeting Noah John in New York City when Patti was just a baby. Back in the museum, Patti and Doc took seats in the front row.

## '61 Adirondack Hermit

"Ladies and Gentlemen, boys and girls," started Noah John, "It is a pleasure to be here with you today and thank you for coming. I guess you are here to hear stories about my life as a Hermit and how I became the Mayor of Cold River City, New York, population one. But I might be mistaken. If you would rather hear me talk about geology or philosophy for an hour, everybody please raise your hand and I'll do that instead!" Noah John made a show of scanning the audience, left to right and then front to back. Very well then," Noah John continued with a smile, "we will do the hermit speech then."

Noah John petted his long gray beard pensively, as if he were planning to settle in for a long afternoon of telling tales. "Every good story starts with once upon a time. Perhaps instead I could begin my story with, 'In a hole in the ground there lived a hobbit.' You would be surprised how many people call me a hobbit instead of a hermit. Maybe it's because I'm only five foot six, which is a bit short for a man, I guess. Yet I am definitely too tall to be a dwarf."

Noah John went on to tell the audience about having been born in 1883 in nearby AuSable Forks. His Dad worked in the pulp mill and Noah John tried out several different professions including working in a barber shop. "I guess AuSable Forks was way too big for me. Eventually I made my way to Tupper Lake and tried to make a living as a guide. I guess I wasn't very good at the business end of running a guide service. On one of my tours I had no customers so I just went into the woods and stayed, longer and longer each time until I hardly ever came out of the woods any more at all. I was about forty years old when I founded Cold River City. That was in 1923. When I was working at the sportsmen's shows one of the newspapermen said I 'couldn't have picked a more isolated place to live with an Ouija board'. All around me were towering mountains—Panther, Santanoni, Henderson, Seymour, Seward and the Sawtooths." Noah John went on for several more minutes about the unrivaled beauty of the scenery.

"Cold River City really was more than just a home. In fact, I often had a whole series of buildings. Each kind of had its own purpose and worst come to worst if something happened to the first I could fall back on the others! Sometimes, maybe once or twice a year I'd get company. It's always nice to have a guest cottage to put your visitors up in. Every year during the summer and fall I built about a dozen teepees. Probably wigwams would be a better way of describing them. Maybe if you saw them you would think they looked like beavers' dams. Anyway, each one had a very small area in the middle, just big enough to stretch out and sleep in, and just enough room besides to set up my small handmade wood stove. Piled all around was a giant stack of long poles, each with a notch every three feet. When the fire died down and I needed more wood all I had to do is strike it once with my axe and the wood split to a perfect size for my fire. When one of my wigwams was almost burned up I'd move into the next. It took a couple of years to perfect this system, and it worked great for me. I've heard others describe it like this: 'he lives in a hole in a wood pile' and I guess I can't argue with that!"

Noah John went on to explain how he felt living alone and providing for himself as he grew older. "I seem to spend most all my nights in the town hall, which also wasn't much bigger than my wigwams. The newspaperman also referred to my town hall as a 'hovel' and called my décor 'gaudy'. It had plenty of room for me, my bear skins, my bed and my stove, and beautiful white, yellow and red candlewax drippings decorated all my shelves and tabletops. I think you would agree with me, I was living in the lap of luxury!"

He described the various implements and tools of convenience that he had constructed over the years and showed the audience pictures of his wigwams, his furnishings, his camp, his town hall and his hall of records. "Now I'm not just famous, but it would seem I've become a veritable relic. After all, you came to see me today in a museum, and you can find my 'hall of records' building at the Adirondack Museum at Blue Mountain Lake. So, my village and my wigwams may have left a lot to be desired, I'll give you that. And sure, it could get cold, way below zero even and at that for weeks if not months at a time in the dead of winter. Even in the dead of winter it was a place of beauty. The way the sparkling frost and snow look on the trees and around the cabin, and the sight of the smoke twirling and curling into the sky from my makeshift chimney warms your soul just to see it. If you can take the everyday beauty around you and see it in just the right way, you'll find great contentment." At this point, Noah John paused, and appeared to be so content, Patti thought he might just drift off into a nap.

Noah John was just getting ready for another poetic description. "And to hear the call of a bear on the mountain, the wind harping through leafless trees or a babbling brook, ah, these are more beautiful sounds than a classical symphony. The smell of the trees when you get just high enough on the mountain are just as pungent as a cedar filled pillow. You can fill your lungs with the best of the pure air. Rather than a village full of friends, you receive daily visits from hummingbirds, deer bounding over the bushes and trout so pretty they might have been varnished. Sometimes I think that God must have made this place just for me. At other times, I think that He made the world and started it rolling downhill from Cold River. To live such a charmed life requires a lot of work though. Don't think you can run off into the woods and just lie around and relax all the time. I can recall when I maintained over thirty miles of trap-line and hiked it all winter on snowshoes. And then once a year, around Christmas time I would hike to town and stock up on supplies. This snowshoe trek would start well before dawn, last all day long, and finish several hours into the evening."

He read from a clipping of the newspaperman's account, quoting himself, "He called the winter sunset over the mountains, the snow and sparkling frost around his cabin and the smoke curling out of his stovepipe the good, necessary parts of living."

He put down the clipping and continued, "Lots of people ask me 'what do you eat out there in the woods?' Perhaps your Mother told you breakfast is the most important meal of the day. Well sometimes, when you're a hermit it's your only meal of the day" laughed Noah John. "One day I was enjoying a perfect breakfast when a whole herd of old maids comes waltzing up the trail. You can laugh," Noah John said to his audience, "but they looked mighty good to me. I was in the middle of flapping some jacks in a crackling pan of bear grease. I begged the ladies' forgiveness, as I didn't want to burn my breakfast. I took the finished flapjack out of the pan, rolled it up like a cigar as I always do, ate half the flapjack in one bite and washed it down with a giant swig from a plastic ketchup bottle full of my personal stock of my home brewed maple syrup. Then I ate the other half. Then I cleaned up proper by wiping off my sticky whiskery face on my shoulder and sleeve. With breakfast finished, my manners returned and I offered my new friends some homemade flapjacks. One of them made a critical remark about dried ketchup on the seams of my syrup bottle. Not one of those ladies was hungry for bear grease flapjacks with ketchup flavored maple syrup. Evidently, they all had enjoyed a hearty breakfast already. Even so, the ladies stayed and talked for hours before returning the way they came, and they were wonderful company. I half wondered whether they might return with clean ketchup bottles and other such niceties on another visit."

Noah John went on to talk about many of the interesting people, colorful characters and travel weary hikers that stopped and visited in Noah John's City through the years. And then as always, time went by quickly and then the hour was just about up.

"I guess the moral of my story," concluded Noah John, "is get outside more. Enjoy nature. If you're going to run away from home, you best be very, very sure of what you're doing. I suggest you wait until you're 40 years old, like I was!"

Then Noah John asked the crowd for questions. Patti's hand shot up into the air, excited to have the opportunity to ask a question before her brain even had a chance to form one. "Yes, young lady," said Noah John. "What is your name, and what is your question?"

"I am Patti Fitz-Gerald from Jay, and this is my Dad, Doc Fitz-Gerald," she said and then she added, "of all the things in the universe that one could do, is there anything you've never done that you'd still like to do?"

"Great question, Patti," said Noah John slowly, making a show of scratching his chin as if deep in thought and perhaps leaving a longer pause than necessary to be truly convincing. "You know, a couple of months ago President Kennedy delivered a speech. Perhaps you saw it on the evening news, where he said, 'this nation should commit itself to achieving the goal, before the decade is out, of landing a man on the moon and returning him safely to the earth.'" Noah John looked at the ceiling as if he were looking at a clear, night sky. "In your question, you asked of all the things in the universe, so I'm thinking I might like to make that trip. Why they wouldn't even need to bring me back. I could just stay there and get the place ready for all the colonists that would follow on the next rocket ship."

At that point he began twisting his mustache, "I guess these whiskers are a little too long for the modern space age, but not long enough for a primitive Moses. So, I would have to either shave them all off or grow them out a bit longer before I leave. Why if I could be the first man on the moon. I would be the most famous man in the Adirondacks," concluded Noah John, ironically as he took out a pen and wrote on a photograph of himself setting in his camp holding a pipe 'to Patti and her Dad Doc, signed Noah John Rondeau, Mayor of Cold River City, New York (population one) August 9, 1961.' Thanks for your question, Patti. If anyone else would like one of these priceless artifacts I'll be here for another hour, quantities are limited, he chuckled pointing to an enormous pile of the photos on a desk, so prices are high naturally. You're lucky today though, I'm running a sale... only 50 cents each. Thank you everyone for coming out to see me today." And Noah John took a deep bow as the audience clapped.

After most of the audience had met with the Adirondack Hermit, Doc made his way to visit with Noah John. Doc shook his hand, thanked him for taking Patti's question and giving her the photo, and asked if Noah John would like to come to Paleface, give talks and sell pictures, without the full exhibit of course. Noah John seldom missed out on such opportunities, and they agreed late afternoons would work well. Doc would pick Noah John up in front of his place in Wilmington on Saturday.

## '61 High Falls Gorge

Route 86 connected Lake Placid and Wilmington, New York and was known more fondly by the name "Wilmington Notch." It was a particularly windy road, not safe for fast travel and always tricky during severe weather. There were high elevations and deep forestation at the side of the road all along that stretch of highway. The morning sun hit the highway late in the morning, and the days ended early as well. Mankind must have really needed to join those two places to put a road there.

On the way back through the Notch, Doc pulled into the High Falls Gorge's parking lot. Doc had been there a couple of weeks earlier for their Grand Opening weekend. Now Doc wanted Patti to see the enchanting beauty of the place, and Doc also was curious to make a more leisurely visit.

The property was owned and operated by a group of several men, mostly from Keeseville, New York and some of whom had a business connection to AuSable Chasm, another absolutely stunning privately owned nature park in the Adirondacks. At High Falls Gorge, Doc and Patti walked on groomed trails and on bridges, steps and catwalks right over the mighty West Branch of the AuSable River in a heavily wooded area at the foot of Whiteface Mountain. Patti was excited by the heights. Doc couldn't help but think Jean would have worried, although it seemed there weren't any chances children could fall. Doc admonished himself for the thought; Patti really wasn't a child anymore.

Doc and Patti enjoyed a leisurely walk through the trails, all together about a mile and a half. Not strenuous exercise, but beautiful and majestic, at the same time somewhat dark and foreboding.

Though their visit was complete, Doc didn't feel quite ready to leave. He wasn't tired, but an empty bench beckoned, seemingly imploring Doc to sit. As Doc sat he said to Patti, "Just a couple minutes more, then we'll head for home."

Patti smiled and sat by his side.

Seconds gave way to minutes. Doc lost himself in a world of thoughts about how to capture the scene. Drawing rectangles in his mind as he panned the scenery before him, quietly surveying the options and concluding that there were lots of great choices. A decision for another day. Doc made mental notes of the prominent color combinations, the way small rays of light filtered through the tall trees of the forest, and which half of the tree trunks before him were darkest with shadow. Doc had forgotten Patti was with him.

Patti had enjoyed the setting for a minute or two, then thoughts about being sent away to boarding school returned to the front of her mind. Her mom and dad had patiently, gently, and lovingly explained why they thought it would be the best opportunity for Patti to learn great things and become inspired to realize the future she was meant for. Doc and Jean had agreed that the challenging curriculum would better prepare Patti for college than the local school in AuSable. Patti knew her parents had made this decision, but she didn't want to go. She knew she didn't belong in St. Johnsbury, Vermont. She belonged in the Adirondacks. Who cares about school, or college, or the future anyway, thought Patti. I just want to ski, and ride horses, and have fun with my friends. Patti thought about how unfair it was that parents could just decide such a thing, and good, well behaved kids just had to do what they were told. Questions were permitted, arguments were not. The more she thought about it, the more angry she became. It was rare for Patti to be cross with her dad, but the longer she sat there the more furious she became. Every day was one day closer to having to go off to school. Her anger began to manifest itself as tears running down her sweetly freckled cheeks. Patti didn't try to hide her emotions, and she didn't try to bring attention to them either. She just sat there stewing. Streams of salty tears ran down her face before Doc completed his thoughts about how to capture the mood of High Falls Gorge in two dimensions.

When Doc saw Patti's face, he thought, could she really be moved to tears over the spiritual and physical beauty of the landscape? "What's wrong, Patti?" Doc asked, putting his arm around her.

They spent the next half hour talking about Patti's education. Some of Patti's questions were traps, and tested the limits of Doc's empathy and compassion as he tried to relate to a young girl in her early teens. "Why do you want to send me away? Don't you love me anymore? What have I done that is so bad I can't stay at home and go to school like my friends do? Is it because of Paleface?"

Doc's reply to the last question came a little too slowly. Both Doc and Jean had felt guilty about the fact that their business required their attention from dawn to after midnight during the high season. At those times, they worried that they didn't spend enough time with Patti. Doc gathered his thoughts for a reasoned, intellectual response to the question. Patti only heard the pause. Patti loved Paleface with all her heart, and yet at that moment, Patti felt the stinging bite of jealousy.

Doc reassured Patti that she hadn't done anything wrong. Doc repeated the reasons why going away to school would be best for Patti, and that she was beloved nonetheless by her family. Doc thought to share with Patti that she was his favorite child, but thought better of saying that out loud. There was nothing new to add to the conversation. It was time to go.

On the way home, Doc told Patti that Torrance and Trumbull had worked on the High Falls Gorge project after building Paleface. Doc declared, more to himself than to Patti, "Next time I come to High Falls Gorge, I'm bringing my easel, paints, and canvass!"

## '61 Room Number One

Most days at three o'clock in the afternoon, Doc and Jean would retire in seclusion for an hour, unless of course more important things came up, like picking raspberries for pies and jam or visiting hermits at the museum. They retired to room number one, one of two "suites" in the hotel. They each had a favorite recliner. Doc's was red, and Jean's was green. In between there was a coffee table, a small magazine rack and one of those floor lamps that had three different lights at different heights that could be adjusted in one direction or another, and had a little metal knob that as you twisted it the three lights would light or not light in various combinations.

Most days, Doc and Jean would sit and talk, read the paper or a magazine, relax and maybe take a five or ten-minute nap. It was mid-August. Summer was beginning to come to an end. The hottest days of the year were beginning to loosen their intensity, and some evenings there was beginning to be a hint that autumn was just around the corner.

They talked a long time about Patti going away to boarding school. Fact was, it made them both sad, but they believed it would provide greater opportunities for. They talked about Doc's sermon for Sunday's service at the Jay Methodist Church. Although "retired" from the ministry, it was handy having Doc in town to fill in when the regular pastor was on vacation or when the church was in between pastors. They took turns reading the paper, or at least parts of it. They discussed the news of the day and the state of their business affairs. They discussed plans for future expansion, and they discussed all the things they planned to do during the "off seasons." With their busy lives and many interests, it was nice to have this small slice of time kind of set aside each day just for one another.

Jean and Doc were looking forward to attending a wedding. Their good friends, Bertha and Carl Steinhoff's daughter Carol was getting married. The groom was Arthur Draper's son Charles Draper. Doc and Jean's son Charles Fitz-Gerald was in the wedding party, and the wedding itself was shaping up to be a major local event. All the rooms at Paleface were booked for that weekend with out of town guests, as were most of the rooms in Wilmington and certainly all the rooms at Steinhoff's Sportsmen's Inn were taken.

Drifting haphazardly to the next topic, Jean told Doc, "I ran into Nellie Weeks at the Grand Union the day before yesterday. She has finished writing a book and has been setting up in area businesses, selling and autographing it. She mentioned that she had a good time at Feek's Pharmacy selling the books and asked if she could set up in the lodge for a couple hours each afternoon for a week. I told her we'd be glad to have her and she plans to be here starting the day after tomorrow, from two to five each day. Some of our guests might get a kick out of meeting Nellie and they might enjoy going home with her book as a souvenir."

Doc chuckled, and told Jean, "I don't know Nellie very well, but she seems nice and also seems to be quite a character but the reason I'm so amused is that yesterday at the museum I told our world-famous Adirondack hermit Noah John Rondeau that we would love to have him come and tell stories in the afternoon to anyone who might be interested in meeting a world famous hermit. Noah John can be expected each afternoon from four to six. Between Nellie and Noah John, the guests and crew here are in for quite a treat!"

Doc told Jean all about the exhibits at the museum, and about the beauty and majesty of High Falls Gorge. They agreed it was wonderful to have another great attraction in the area. It was amazing to read that the museum was drawing in 500 people a day and High Falls Gorge was attracting 1,000 people a week. Doc and Jean agreed that after Labor Day when business slowed down they should go spend an afternoon together at High Falls Gorge.

Back in the paper, Jean noticed a brief story that claimed, "A big Wilmington project is now in the dream or talking stage. Just as a thought to how Whiteface Mountain should operate winter and summer was talked about until it became a fact, we now have a dream project of a lake below the Paleface development. It seems that a dam at Mulvey's would back up water and create a beautiful lake which Wilmington needs for swimming, boating, and ice skating. It could be a fine recreational center in summer and winter."

Doc and Jean thought it would do wonders for Paleface's business. A big lake just down the hill could provide a source of water for snow making even. Doc thought maybe spreading talk of such a development would be a great idea. Ultimately Doc and Jean agreed that it was probably not a good idea to hold their breath waiting for that dream to come true.

Doc noticed in the paper where it mentioned that Mrs. Roger McLean was now employed at Paleface Lodge. "How is Dorothy doing, Jean?" asked Doc. Jean reported that Dorothy was doing great and of course fitting in well with the rest of the crew.

There wasn't much that escaped the notice of the local papers. Jean read aloud, "Miss Nancy Kane of Dannemora is caring for her horses rented by Paleface for the summer. Miss Kane is a famous horse woman and owns many horses. She is staying at the home of Mr. and Mrs. Boylan Fitz-Gerald."

"It's really been nice having Nancy stay with us," said Jean. And the horses were beautiful to see in the pasture in front of Paleface with the backdrop view of Whiteface Mountain behind. As she said it, Jean thought to herself, "Uh oh."

And just as she feared, Doc sat up and started talking quickly about his plans to buy a string of horses and run the riding operation directly rather than hiring it in. Jean loved horses too, but there was a lot of work involved with year-round upkeep and they were busy enough with the rest of the business. Jean sighed a deep sigh, let her glasses drop on her chest, held there by the chain that went around behind her head. "I'll shut my eyes for a few minutes, Doc, and I will try to imagine it."

Doc picked up a magazine, tried to read an article about IBM's new electric typewriter, called the Selectric, which the company had just introduced to the market. After a couple of minutes, he realized he wasn't reading the article, but rather thinking up plans for fixing up a barn, buying horses, cutting riding trails, hiring cowboys, and putting up fencing. Doc put the paper down, took off his glasses, shut his eyes and moments later he was dreaming about Pinto ponies.

## '61 Lucky Star

Nellie arrived on Saturday August 12th at ten minutes to two. Promptness was a hallmark of Nellie's long working career. When Nellie took a job, she committed to it completely. Nellie's book *Lucky Star* was mostly about the years while she was growing up in the town of Lewis, near Elizabethtown, the Essex County "seat."

She was a stickler for details, and she wanted to convey exactly what those days were like to the people who would buy her book. Nellie was dressed up in the manner of a country woman on her wedding day. Inside the book, just after the title page is a picture of Nellie on the day of her marriage. She had kept that dress all those years and to Nellie's credit it still fit and she looked very pretty in both the picture and in person, even at 74 years of age.

It didn't take Nellie long to set up a card table, with a slightly faded white, fancy table cloth draped over it. Underneath the table, Nellie set a box full of books. On the top, she fanned out seven or eight books and a handful of blue ink pens. As she was setting up the table she recalled her days running the Holt Variety Store on the Main Street in Lake Placid during the 1930s and 1940s. Nellie's husband Will, had a sister who married a man named Frank Holt and their son Ernest owned the Variety Store. Nellie worked for him after Nellie and Will's store went out of business in 1935, a casualty of the Great Depression. Nellie stepped back from the card table, hands on her hips, trying to put herself in her customer's shoes. "That will have to do," she told herself. And Nellie felt just like she had finished decorating the window display and was standing on the busy Lake Placid sidewalk looking in the store window to see if everything was placed in such a way as to force customers through the door.

In the summer, it wasn't nearly as busy in the Paleface lobby as it would be in the winter. There were fairly long periods when nobody passed Nellie's table. Even so, Nellie remained standing and greeted everyone that came nearby in a very friendly and accessible manner. Almost everyone was willing to give Nellie three dollars for a copy of the book and almost everyone enjoyed the chance to talk to the author about her book. Since she had finished the book, Nellie had recalled a few other charming stories that she had neglected to remember when she was writing the book in the first place.

By 4pm, Nellie had sold two dozen books, grossing $72 dollars. Nellie had been very careful with money her whole life, and always was very enterprising even as a child. Most of her life she worked for others, but was always planning a business of her own, even if such thoughts were pure fantasy. When her husband died in 1942, she left the Variety store and moved from Lake Placid to Upper Jay and realized her life-long dream of owning her own business and being completely independent, raising poultry and writing a book. Nellie was glad to have a very profitable chicken ranch, to be sure. As for *Lucky Star*, Nellie never expected to make much as an author. She was just happy to put all those years to paper and leave them behind so that someone might find them later. In fact, Nellie started the book with the following:

*The past always looks good to those who gaze back upon it. Impossible as it seems, I have no doubt that the 1950s themselves will be recalled as Good Old Days by people writing or speaking of them in future decades. At any rate this is the story of my life—and of my parents and the rest of the children. And it deals largely with the olden days before the world was as modern and hurried as it is now.*

Jean brought Nellie a tall glass of cold iced tea. In the glass was a long metal straw with a maple leaf shape at the bottom. As Nellie was thanking Jean, Doc was showing Noah John, who had just recently arrived at Paleface, the way to his spot in the lobby.

## '61 Noah John Rondeau

Doc brought Noah John over a nice comfortable chair with lots of padding and good back support. After all those years of roughing it, sitting on stumps and sleeping in a wood pile, Doc figured that Noah John would appreciate a nice, cushioned chair. Noah John smiled and said, "I can just sit on the floor. Don't want to be a bother, Doc!"

"How are our customers going to see eye to eye with the world's most notorious hermit when he's sitting on the floor, my fine Sir?" replied Doc. That matter being settled, Doc and Noah John walked over to greet Jean and Nellie. Doc introduced Noah John to the ladies. "I'd like you to meet my wife Jean, and Nellie Weeks from Upper Jay who is here to share her book with the public at large, such as it is."

"It is a pleasure to make your acquaintance," said Nellie Weeks, offering an old-fashioned mini curtsy.

"We're happy to have you here with us, Mr. Rondeau," said Jean. "Doc has told me all about your exhibit at the museum. I can't wait to come see it myself. I'd like to stay and visit, but I must get back to the kitchen. People will be looking for dinner soon! I will make sure you get a nice cold glass of tea."

"The pleasure is all mine, ladies," said Noah John and he reached for his head to lift his hat, forgetting that he neglected to put one on that warm summer's day. Everyone chuckled at Noah John's attempt to tip a hat that wasn't there, then Noah John added, "And I reckon I could stand to whet my whistle after a long day at the museum."

Jean returned to the kitchen to oversee preparation for the dinner service. Based on the eye contact between Nellie and Noah John, Doc offered his leave, stating, "I'll leave the two of you to become better acquainted. Don't hesitate to let us know if you need anything at all!" To be honest, Doc was a little disappointed that he would be out of earshot as these two interesting old-timers forged an acquaintance.

Right off the bat, Nellie sold a copy of her book to Noah John, and signed it, "To the former Mayor of Cold River, with kindest regards, Nellie Weeks. Thank you." Nellie placed her autograph right under her wedding picture.

Noah John complimented Nellie, remarking on how photogenic she was, and added that Nellie still looked just as pretty as she did when she was a newlywed. On the page opposite, Noah John read aloud the following phrase, which appeared all in capital letters: "ALL NAMES IN THIS BOOK ARE FICTITIOUS ANY NAME PERTAINING TO ANY ONE DEAD OR ALIVE IS PURELY COINCIDENTAL." He scratched his chin. "Interesting."

Nellie quickly laughed. "The publisher and their lawyers made me write that! In fact, it is true, the names are fictitious. But the people and the stories were very real. For instance, my name in the book is Eillen, which is obviously fictitious, and short of proper spelling. The fact that if you spell it backwards you get my real name, Nellie... well that is PURELY COINCIDENTAL, of course," Nellie laughed some more. "I changed our family's last name, and the name of all the kids and the neighbors. I don't think I ever used Mother's name, and the fact that Father's name in the book and in real life is David is PURELY COINCIDENTAL as well. I just didn't have it in me to change his name. Anyway, all the stories are mostly real. I might have made a couple of the stories just a touch more interesting but I shall never admit that."

"I know exactly what you mean," said Noah John, "I do that all the time myself. In the fourteen years since I came out of the woods I have found my recollections get a touch more colorful each time I recall them." Their eyes met, and they smiled warmly at one another, a recognition of their shared passion for telling interesting stories. Noah John concluded, "Adding a little sparkle to your story keeps the audience on the edge of their seat and flipping pages."

Noah John randomly flipped Nellie's book to Chapter 4, page 34 titled, Red Blanket Hens. "Would you read me a chapter of your book, ma'am? I've been on my feet and talking most of the day, and besides I can't remember where I put my glasses."

"Why, they're perched on top of your head, which is maybe why you thought you had your hat on!" Nellie exclaimed, "but I would be happy to read to you. Make yourself comfortable!"

Nellie told the story about how her pet hen Tamie and her sister's pet hen Singer had lost most of their feathers due to molting and so Nellie, renamed Eillen, was worried that they would be cold at night. Nellie's sister, who had been renamed Clara, aspired to be a dress maker and turned an old red flannel undershirt into dresses for the pet chickens, complete with ribbons and fancy silk tape. Unfortunately, the pets did not appreciate their lovely dresses, went crazy and ran off into the woods, which made Nellie cry. Clara couldn't help laughing. Mother remarked later that the pets would have tolerated the dresses if they had been anything but red.

Noah John interrupted Nellie's story only once to ask whether the lawyers and publishers had required Nellie to change the names of the pet chickens. "You can't get anything past them," declared Nellie, "but somehow they missed that detail!"

Nellie went back to her story. She read:

*My fondest wish had always been to own and care for chickens. As soon as I was old enough to plan anything, I resolved to keep poultry all the days of my life, but cruel fate decreed otherwise. Whenever I mentioned chickens to Clara, she would say sneeringly, "You can have them, I don't want the dirty stinkin' things!*

*I tried to explain the sparkling personalities, the many pleasant and attractive traits found among chicken-kind, but she insisted that the only time they looked pleasant or attractive to her was when she saw them roasted, fried or stewed and on the dining room table, and I desisted from my argument, realizing that she voiced a majority viewpoint.*

When Nellie finished reading, Noah John said, "That's right-fine writing and a very compelling story. Usually I only read books about astronomy, philosophy and geology. Hearing your stories and talking with you makes me feel like a kid again, and just looking at you makes me feel like I fell into a time machine!" Noah John went on to tell Nellie about all his years watching birds from his hermitage, considering she had such an interest in poultry.

On and on they talked, and soon it was five o'clock, time for Nellie to head home. The lobby was now starting to get busier as the last horseback riding customers were returning from their trail rides. Business at the bar was picking up, and the early diners were beginning to arrive. The smell of steak dinners was filling the lodge. The more people arrived the busier Noah John became, and he never seemed to tire of telling about his years as a hermit. One small boy asked, "Are you still a hermit now even if you don't live in the woods anymore?"

Noah John scratched his chin. "A new question. I haven't had this question before." After a brief pause, Noah John continued, "Well son, once a hermit, always a hermit. It isn't a classification for the census takers, but rather describes something deep within." Noah John had well-rehearsed answers to the rest of the questions that were asked that afternoon.

By seven o'clock, Noah John had overstayed his planned visit by an hour, and Nellie had overstayed by two hours, not that either one had cared in the slightest. Nellie had sold more books since Noah John arrived than she had earlier, and her box was almost empty. Being as how they were on vacation, most of Paleface's customers had cameras, film and flash cubes and they left with pictures of two of the Adirondacks' great storytellers. Chuck Fitz-Gerald, who was working at the bar across the lounge, was called over time and again to press the button on the cameras. As luck would have it, photography was a hobby of Chuck's, if not his true calling. Most customers would have great souvenirs in a few weeks when their film returned from processing via U.S. mail.

On the way out, Noah John saw the poster in the hallway near the front doors advertising the Starlight Ski Ball on Wednesday, August 16, 1961. He turned to Nellie and asked, "Would you do me the honor of attending the ball with me, Nellie Weeks?"

"It would be my pleasure," said Nellie.

The new friends said goodnight to each other. Nellie drove home to Upper Jay, all the way thinking about the dance, her new friend, and feeling glad she never had to sleep in a wood pile.

## '61 Starlight Ski Ball

Cookie had begged her parents for weeks and finally they had given in. Jean and Doc had also given Patti permission to be at the Starlight Ski Ball until 11pm. Of course, Jean and Doc would be at the dance. Cookie's parents might not have let on to Cookie that such was the case, but they were looking forward to going to the ball as well.

The day before, Jean took Patti and Cookie to Alma's for their brand-new hairdos. Alma operated a beauty parlor at the Ark Motel, a handsome well-tended property of about fifteen motel rooms, beside the AuSable River along Route 9N, midway between Keene and Upper Jay. Miss Alma had one of those well diversified businesses.

Jean thought, one day in pigtails and ponytails, the next day in highly fashionable modern hairstyles. It occurred to Jean that it would take some getting used to, looking at those girls. Try as they might, the girls couldn't talk Jean into a new fashion for herself, though she did get her hair done that afternoon as well.

For the better part of the past three days, the girls had spent countless hours in the lodge listening to the jukebox, talking and making decorations. Doc had generously volunteered Patti and Cookie's time to make two thousand fancy snowflakes, and just as in the natural world, no two snowflakes were to be the same. Cookie got carried away and volunteered to make paper tissue snow flowers as well, which added significantly to the chore, but broke up the boredom of non-stop snowflake making.

The girls had fancy paper to work with in various shades of white, blue, silver and pale yellow. Each afternoon the floor would be covered with chunks of discarded paper. Anyone who has made snowflakes in school by folding paper in half, then in half again, and sometimes in half a third time then cutting out chunks before unfolding the resulting paper snowflake knows what an enormous pile of waste is created by snowflake making.

To add to the mess, many of the paper snowflakes got the glitter treatment. Patti, who had lived in New Jersey until the year before, told Cookie about how glitter was invented by a man in New Jersey. At first it was fun making each glittered snowflake into a masterpiece, albeit extraordinarily time consuming. As the final afternoon of mass-producing snowflakes passed, standards were abandoned and the girls focused on cranking out as many snowflakes as possible as fast as possible.

Around noon, Doc let the girls off the hook. "I had no idea that 1,500 snowflakes would add up to such an enormous pile! I think we have enough to make Paleface look like a winter wonderland. After lunch, you can help me hang them all over the place."

That afternoon, they strung up all the snowflakes, joined end-to-end. All the while, Cookie was popping dimes in the jukebox, and listening over and over to the same song, The Shirelles' "Will You Still Love Me Tomorrow." It was far and away her favorite of the moment. Some of the lyrics made Doc cringe a little bit. It was a beautiful song, but not a great song for thirteen-year-old girls, especially when one of the girls was the daughter of a minister, albeit retired. Fortunately, Cookie only sang along with the first two lines and the chorus.

There was no time that afternoon for Jean and Doc to relax in their armchairs. It was a beautiful summer's day and people were coming in and out, buying tickets to ride the chairlift to the Smoke Rise Lookout, only 50 cents for adults and 25 cents for children. It was also a busy day for Nancy Kane's horses across the street, however everyone had to stop in the lodge to buy tickets to ride the horses, and many were tempted to buy film, flash cubes and bug spray as well. Many also had lunch while they were there.

Nobody had the day off. The entire staff of Paleface was dedicated to preparing for what they expected to be the busiest day of the summer. The kitchen was fully provisioned, all the vendors had delivered doubled the normal orders. The special was spaghetti and meatballs, and sure they sold a good number of the special, but more than anything, the Paleface chefs would be sending out steak after steak with mashed potatoes, green beans, and corn.

Most of the evening, all twenty-five tables were filled with happy well-fed customers. Some people had to wait a little while at the bar or in the lounge nearby. The glittery snowflakes overhead swayed slightly, and twinkled in the candlelight. The jukebox was jumping non-stop, and playing a much wider variety of songs than earlier in the day.

By six o'clock, the girls were in room number one, getting ready for the evening. They took showers, fixed their hair, put on their new sweaters, skirts, bobby socks and dancing shoes. Then Patti and Cookie had dinner with Cookie's parents. Neither girl was very hungry, or much interested in having dinner. They just wanted to get to the dance!

It wasn't just the teenage girls. Men and women, young adults and teenagers of all ages were looking forward to the ball and getting dressed up in their finest party clothes.

Finally, it was nine o'clock. A steady stream of well-dressed tourists and locals came through the door and checked in with the hostess, Mrs. Nancy Robare. In the lounge, the Bob Luppy Trio was tuning up their instruments. After finally being released from the dinner table, the girls were standing in front of the musicians, watching them finish their preparations.

The last of the tables, chairs and rugs were being removed from the lounge, making lots of room for a spacious dance floor. Chuck Fitz-Gerald, who was working at the bar, pulled the plug on the jukebox. And with a "one-two-three" Mr. Luppy and his orchestra kicked off the evening with a trio of old Elvis songs: "Heartbreak Hotel," "Hound Dog," and "All Shook Up." Certainly that made for a strong start, and everyone was dancing right away.

Behind the band, the double doors were open to the Starlight Terrace, and the light breeze through the doorway was appreciated by the band and the dancers, and the garlands of handmade snowflakes overhead swayed with the breeze if not to the beat of the music.

By the time the third Elvis song was over, there were at least 200 partiers at the ball. The next song on the set list was the Twist. The girls were well rehearsed, and didn't miss a beat. Doc, a mighty fine dancer in his own right, was right in there on the dance floor himself. Jean was watching from a corner with her friend Mary Wallace, amused as always to see grown adults doing the Twist right along with Patti and Cookie. Mary's youngest daughter was there too.

When Jean saw Nellie Weeks and Noah John Rondeau all dressed up and twisting right along with everyone else, Jean laughed even harder than she did when Lucille Ball tried to say "vitameatavegamin." They were Twisting on the dance floor. There was a terrace full of Twisters out on the patio. The two cocktail waitresses had set their trays down at the bar and were Twisting in front of the jukebox. It seemed everyone was Twisting except Jean and Mary. And the song which normally was over in two and a half minutes had been extended to four times that long. In the last couple of minutes, Mary talked Jean into giving it a try. Surely nobody was watching them, and wouldn't think anything of it if they had. Jean laughed even harder watching her friend Mary do the Twist. The more Jean laughed the harder Mary laughed. By the time the song was over they had tears running down their faces.

Next the horns in Bob Luppy's orchestra came out and they played a pair of songs by Fats Domino. First up was "Ain't That a

Shame" and next came "Blueberry Hill." Doc had been practicing the guitar so he could join the band from time to time. Doc joined the band for the Fats Domino songs. He was a better dancer than player, but he enjoyed trying new things, and the Paleface audience enjoyed seeing Doc play with the band.

Noah John, Nellie Weeks, and a few of the other older guests had taken a seat in the dining room at one of the tables and were sipping lemonade. Nellie was telling everyone a story about how ten years prior she had heard that if you put spectacles on hens they wouldn't peck each other's feathers off. Nellie herself had tried it on a few of her hens, and it seemed to be working. So, she promptly placed an order for the whole flock and found that it did the trick.

Nellie also told the story from her childhood about her pet hens in their red dresses, and then went on to tell everyone she had a carpenter build her a special pen where she made up each nesting box to look like a room in a doll's house complete with little windows. Unfortunately, the hens didn't like the rooms until Nellie made curtains for the windows, because most of her hens preferred a little more privacy when setting on their nests. Nellie could talk about chickens all evening.

Like most entrepreneurs, Nellie thought about her business constantly. When Nellie talked about raising chickens, her stories portrayed a very frugal and thrifty business. It might have surprised Nellie's family to learn that she turned a very handsome profit from her chicken ranch. She didn't seem to have more eggs than she could sell, and she sold many, many eggs. Where Nellie really excelled was in raising chickens for meat. Sister Clara would be so proud!

All the tables in the dining room were filled with people sipping iced tea, lemonade, or coffee. Many of the older party goers needed to rest up between dances. A significant number of guests came to support the cause and out of duty to one of the organizations who had committed to supporting the cause. There was a large group of people from churches that didn't permit dancing, and they seemed more than happy to visit with friends. Many enjoyed playing Checkers, Dominoes, or cards.

For most of the evening, Jean found herself more comfortable with that crowd then with the party crowd at the bar, in the lounge, on the terrace, or on the dance floor. The crowd in the dining room seemed to enjoy themselves every bit as much as the rest of the crowd.

In particular, Jean spent a fair amount of time with Leon Doremus and his wife who had scheduled themselves a nice long vacation at Paleface. On the way home, they planned to drop their daughter off at Green Mountain College in Poultney, Vermont. She was entering her senior year. She enjoyed ski racing in the winter, and hiking and riding in the summer, so the frequent vacations were enjoyed by the whole Doremus family.

Every time Leon Doremus vacationed at Paleface, which was about three or four times per year, he purchased one of Doc Fitz-Gerald's paintings. That trip he picked up a painting of a barn and a barnyard populated with poultry. Of course, Leon also picked up a copy of Nellie's book and one of Noah John's autographed posters.

The Elizabethtown County Clerk, Harry McDougal also attended the Starlight Ski Ball. Harry liked to entertain crowds with his backwoods, lumberjack, border-style brand of barely understandable English-French mix, and Harry tried to dress the part as well. His costume was very convincing and his performance was very authentic. People who only met Harry's alter ego would have been hard pressed to believe he was a bona fide attorney and long serving County Clerk.

About 10:30pm, Bob Luppy announced it was time for the couples to line up and "Stroll." As the men lined up in one line, the ladies lined up in another, facing them. Patti ran to get Nellie Weeks and Noah John Rondeau, who were resting at one of the tables.

Cookie lined up on the men's side with Patti opposite her. As Bob Luppy and his orchestra played Chuck Willis' 1958 song "Betty and Dupree," each couple took turns strolling down the path between the line of men and ladies. Of course, everyone had to "stroll" to the music.

To properly perform the stroll, you had to cross your leg behind each step, walking down the path in kind of a zig zag fashion. Some couples would make a point of looking like they were having a great time doing this, and other couples would display cool as cucumber strolling techniques.

To get everyone down the path, the Bob Luppy Trio had to repeat several verses multiple times. As the last strollers came down the walkway, the song ended and everyone cheered. All the other stollers were decades younger than Nellie and Noah John, and seemed to be enormously impressed with the fact that Nellie and Noah John were willing to stroll. Nellie and Noah John took their bows and then returned to the dining room. The band took a break and the jukebox was plugged back in to play a few songs.

As the eleven o'clock hour approached, Jean took Patti and Cookie back home to Jay. It had been a long day. Jean subscribed to the notion of "early to bed, early to rise" and was happy to get to bed before midnight.

Nellie Weeks also left at 11pm, knowing that she would be awake at 4:30 regardless of how late she stayed up. On the way out to her car, Nellie stopped to take in a deep breath of air and make a mental snapshot of how it felt to be out late at a dance on a beautiful August evening.

All at once, she felt completely surrounded by mountains so close that she felt as if she would bump into them. Yet at the same time, she felt a cosmic sense of comfort, the kind of comfort that transcends time, like a warm hug from outer space. Nellie's eyes followed the landscape's silhouette, looking at the outline of Whiteface Mountain in the dim light of a newish moon.

The popularity of "dancing on the terrace" on Wednesday evenings at Paleface had been building all summer, and was fast becoming a local tradition. After the Starlight Ski Ball, with hundreds of people coming out, that tradition would be further established, attracting local residents from as far away as Lake Placid to Keeseville to Elizabethtown, even as far as Plattsburgh, and of course all the more so among the closer towns of Wilmington, Jay, Upper Jay and

AuSable Forks. For those who felt there wasn't enough weekend in the week, dancing on Wednesday nights at Paleface divided the week up nicely.

By the time the evening was over, The Starlight Ski Ball had raised a couple hundred dollars. The Wilmington Chamber of Commerce was raising the funds to donate to the Whiteface Ski Council. The Council planned to use the funds to support the 1st Annual Draper Cup ski race scheduled for March, 1962. Everyone thought it was a great way to honor Arthur Draper and his family. The Draper Cup was the first of the Ski Council's events to be sanctioned by the United States Eastern Amateur Ski Association and was sure to bring much greater interest in ski racing to Whiteface and many more tourists to the area along with it.

For Doc and Jean and the folks at Paleface, events like the Starlight Ski Ball and the fantastic reception to Wednesday and Saturday dances on the Terrace meant that August would be one of only four months where Paleface's checking account would have a bigger balance at the end of the month than it did at the beginning of the month.

Out on the terrace, the stars shone brightly. The crescent moon offered just a decorative sliver of luminosity against the dark, late-summer's night sky. The evening ended with a couple slow dances and waltzes served up by the jukebox. "Love Me Tender" by Elvis Presley gave way to Patti Page's version of "The Tennessee Waltz" and then in turn to "At Last" by Etta James.

Just at the edge of where the lighting from the lodge surrendered to the darkness, young lovers could be found stealing kisses.

I was born about nine months later.

## '61 Three Billy Goats Gruff

That fall Doc noticed several large patches of poison ivy on the trails. In particular at the front of the Smoke Rise Lookout. Doc borrowed 3 goats from his friend Arto Monaco at the Land of Makebelieve. Doc chuckled at the thought of the fabled story of the *Three Billy Goats Gruff,* as he drove the bleating, blatting bunch back from Upper Jay one day in early September. Arto probably had suitable names for those goats, but Doc thought up temporary replacement names for them on the way back to Paleface. The oldest one Doc named Grandma Moses, in honor of that famed artist who took up her craft at the ripe old age of 78 years old and had just recently turned 100 years old. The most vocal goat Doc named Ella Fitzgerald whose jazz records Doc had been enjoying on his record player in the evenings in his study. The least vocal goat Doc named Robert Louis Stevenson, representing one of his favorite poets, and a poet that was once connected to the region. The trio worked hard and cleared up Paleface's poison ivy problem prior to Halloween, then Doc took the goats back to the Land of Makebelieve, where they belonged.

## '62 Staff Meeting

Doc started a meeting of the staff one Friday in early February. Unfortunately, Paleface was on a staff reduction due to lack of snow. Paleface was running with a little bit more than a skeleton crew but not much.

"Somehow, we got through a snowless January," started Doc, "and managed to do all right. Of course, after all our efforts to advertise the *après-noel* week in Canada we were fortunate to bring lots of people down from the Provinces. We continue to get lots of inquiries due to the great press we received. Thanks to Anne Heggtveit, Canada's Olympic Gold Medalist and two-time World Champion skier and her husband Ross Hamilton spreading the good word about Paleface, we have managed to fill the rooms nicely. It's true our guests haven't been able to ski at Paleface, but thankfully Whiteface has invested in snow making machinery."

Next on the agenda, Doc updated the staff on a trip to Gray Rocks in the Laurentians the prior week. It was a great opportunity for the Fitz-Geralds and the Josts to talk about skiing in the Adirondacks with people there. Doc shared that he hoped to implement some improvements at Paleface in the coming months and years, inspired by what he had seen at Gray Rocks. More immediately, Doc officially announced that major renovations would begin between the seasons, just as soon as the Easter Ball was over, adding ten new motel units bringing the total number of rooms to twenty-four. The plan was to build out a new wing, forming an L shape, extending past room number one toward the Jay side of Paleface. Torrance and Trumbull were selected to be the builders again.

Doc went on to say, "You may have seen my letter to the editor, published in yesterday's newspaper, but I'll read it to you just the same.

*LETTERS TO THE EDITOR*

*Dear Sir:*

*In last week's issue of the Adirondack Record-Elizabethtown Post you carried a letter of criticism concerning the expenditures of money at Whiteface Mt. Ski Center for the snow making machine. As the owner and operator of Paleface Ski Center, I should like to present the opposite point of view, namely one of congratulations to the Whiteface Ski Center and appreciation for what the installation of the new snow machine has done to better our economy. I will say, very frankly, that a considerable number of our house guests at Paleface Lodge have been kept in the area only because they found snow at Whiteface. Since the rains of a week ago, when we lost our snow here at Paleface, our learn-to-ski week guests have been able to stay with us and our own teachers have been allowed to instruct them on the Whiteface slopes. As nearly as I can estimate, the installation of the snow machinery at Whiteface has been responsible for at least $3,000 gross business for us here at Paleface during this first month of operation.*

*Again, let me express through your columns my appreciation to the Adirondack Mountain Authority for what I believe is a real boost to the winter economy of the eastern Adirondacks. Also, let me reiterate the gratitude of Paleface Ski Center and of the Karl Jost Canadian Ski School for the courtesy afforded them in the matter of ski school teaching privileges at Whiteface.*

*With the firm belief that both state enterprise and private enterprise can, and will co-exist to the mutual satisfaction and profit of both, I remain,*

*Cordially yours,*
*Boylan Fitz-Gerald, President*

Doc went on to tell the staff about his latest appearance on Al Cahill's *Ski Trails* program on Thursday, January 18th. Then, before closing the staff meeting, Doc asked if anyone wanted to make any announcements.

Bea Lincoln mentioned how much she and Abe, Senior were looking forward to news of a new grandchild, which they expected to receive any day.

Chuck told everyone about registering to participate in a gymkhana for cars in the summer, and that he and Karl Jost had signed up as had Charles Draper.

Jean reminded everyone to make the new and part time employees feel welcome and reminded everyone that Linda Ward and Billy Ward would be working on the weekends.

Carl updated everyone on the 18 year old man whose car flew twenty-eight feet through the air, skidded 600 feet across the Paleface parking lot, hit a lamp post and then flew another 130 feet again through the air finally brought to a stop by another light post. "Miraculously, the young man was only slightly injured, suffering only a cut on the forehead. He was charged by state police with driving while intoxicated, but you would think he should consider himself lucky to be alive after a ride like that."

"Okay," concluded Doc, "So keep up the great work, keep your spirits up and pray for snow! We will also pray for a healthy grandbaby for Bea and Abe and we will pray for that young man in the flying car."

Doc had been saving big news for his final announcement. "We have another famous, special guest coming to Paleface. On Friday, February 24th Robert F. Wagner, Junior, the Mayor of New York City, will be attending a fundraising dinner here at Paleface. Of course, we will want to put our best foot forward that night. If you want to have the chance to see a big city mayor, let me know and we will put you to work that night. I know it will make a long day for those of you who work breakfast and lunch. Needless to say, it will be an honor to roll out the red-carpet treatment for Mayor Wagner and his wife.

## '62 Stocking Trout

As if it weren't enough to roll out the red carpet for New York City's mayor and his wife, Paleface had also scheduled the Wilmington Fish and Game Club meeting at six o'clock that evening. The club tended to important business, such as setting dues at $2 for individuals and $5 for business people. The club discussed a newsletter, an advertising brochure, prizes for fishing contests, a member's only accidental death insurance policy, and a summer camp scholarship fund.

Of course, most of the club time was spent talking about fish. The New York State Conservation Department had a supply of trout they were making available, and the club members debated the best places to release the stock. The club also talked about the feasibility of making a big purchase of stock from private hatcheries for release the following year.

And as is the case in all such organizations, a good deal of time was spent discussing membership recruitment.

## '62 Pat Smith, Lobbyist

Before dinner, Adeline "Pat" Smith introduced herself and her husband, Philip to the Mayor. "I have a small gift for you, sir," Pat continued. In her hand, Pat had a copy of her new book entitled *I Will Look Unto the Hills*. "I took the liberty of assuming you would accept a copy of my book, and I made an inscription inside the cover. It is an honor to meet you and to have you here with us. And I hope my book can give you a little insight into what life is like outside of the big city!"

Mayor Wagner neither had time to accept or reject Pat Smith's gift, as Pat continued without pause. "I have to tell you we don't take too kindly to the idea of passing laws requiring that pasteurization dates be marked on milk. We were glad to see that the legislature passed a law preventing New York City from requiring such nonsense. Putting dates on milk creates a psychological impression that milk isn't safe. Not only that, Mr. Mayor, now that we have pasteurization and now that we have refrigeration in people's homes, it is obvious that there is no need for putting a date on milk."

Mayor Wagner, finally finding an opportunity, gently explained to Pat that he was aware of many complaints from citizens in New York City about sour milk. As a public safety concern, it was the duty of politicians to address the issue.

Undaunted, Pat replied, "Well, I should think, Mr. Mayor, that common sense would dictate that if it smells sour, or tastes sour then it has gone bad. You don't need the bottle to tell you it has gone bad. Perhaps if the good people of New York City drank the proper amount of milk, it wouldn't sit around and go sour all the time! Oh, pardon me for making such a nuisance of myself Mr. Mayor. It's just that it is hard enough trying to make a living on a dairy farm, we would hate to see the government scare people away from drinking a proper amount of milk."

Then Pat Smith tried to explain the difficulties of doctors serving patients in the North Country. She didn't get very far when she was interrupted by the arrival of dinner. Mayor Wagner shook hands with Phil and Pat Smith, and said, "It was wonderful meeting you tonight. Thank you for the gift, I will treasure it and congratulations on becoming the author of a new book."

For the next hour, Mayor Wagner enjoyed Paleface's finest

cooking and the company of the county's top Democratic donors. As there weren't enough Democratic donors in the county to fill a room that size, an invitation was extended to community leaders as well.

## '62 Mayor Robert Wagner

At the request of the Mayor's staff, at 8:30pm exactly, Doc promptly rose from his seat to address the crowded room. "Ladies and gentlemen," began Doc, "as some of you might know, not too long ago I worked for a couple of years in New York City. You see, I was part of a club of artists. Some of these creative geniuses were internationally famous artists. One evening at one of our banquets, we were honored to have as a guest speaker, Mayor Robert Wagner."

Doc went on to tell the audience about Mayor Wagner's professional career, college history, and significant achievements, reading from a piece of paper prepared by the Mayor's staff. Then, inspired by news and opinion from the local papers, Doc continued, "Now Mayor Wagner is in his third term and perhaps when he speaks to us he will give us some indication of whether all the rumors are true. Will Mayor Wagner run for Governor of New York State, or does Mayor Wagner have other intentions for the future?"

At this point, the Mayor rose from his seat, and stood next to Doc facing the audience, and Doc concluded, "Please join me in giving his excellence, Mayor Robert Wagner and his lovely wife, a warm hearty Adirondack welcome." Doc began to clap, all the dinner guests rose to their feet and clapped as well. And Mayor Wagner took the microphone from Doc.

"Thank you everyone!" began Mayor Wagner, who for some reason was holding Pat Smith's red book in his left hand. "It's wonderful to be here with you this evening. I can't tell you how lucky you are to be living in such beautiful country. I am sure most folks from the City have no idea such a wonderful natural paradise exists here at the other end of the state. I appreciate the warm welcome,

Doc. As you were talking I can recall speaking in front of your audience. As a politician, you get used to speaking in front of people on a regular basis. I long ago stopped being nervous in public speaking situations. However, with Salvador Dali, and Picasso in the audience, even a seasoned politician would be a little apprehensive, let alone a new Mayor."

Mayor Wagner left a pause, which inspired the crowd to react, and many in the audience rewarded the mayor with a chuckle. Robert F. Wagner, Jr. continued, "So, thank you all for coming tonight, and attending this fundraiser. I can assure you your donations will be put to good use. From talking with many of you before dinner, I guess you get plenty of news about City politics in your local newspapers and certainly you get lots of statewide news in the paper. I do confess I am giving some thought to running for Governor, since everywhere I go people ask me to do it. Clearly, if I run, the voters would get the opportunity to consider a very different direction from the direction Governor Nelson Rockefeller is headed. And if we were to win, perhaps that would give Governor Rockefeller more free time to think about running for President!"

Mayor Wagner shifted Pat Smith's book from his left hand to his right hand, and looked at the cover, then looked into the audience and continued, "Earlier this evening, I was talking with Pat Smith about her husband and his brother who are local farmers. I hope Mrs. Smith won't mind if I also share that she told me that all of her friends at church think that Democrats only speak to issues of concern to people who live in cities and not to issues of concern for people who live in the country. I can't understand how people come to these conclusions! I know for a fact there are numerous Democrats right here in the North Country, and I know our party is working hard to get even more elected in the future."

During dinner, it occurred to the Mayor to make an example from the popular television show, *The Honeymooners,* as if the characters were actual constituents. Mayor Wagner smiled, extended both arms out from his sides, as if to pull the audience into a warm hug, and continued his speech, "And I understand some of you might not think it is necessary or even desirable to stamp pasteurization dates on milk. Just imagine if you will, Alice Kramden has three glass bottles of milk in the refrigerator. Imagine that two bottles of milk are used and the milkman brings three more. Instead of putting the new bottles in the back the way Alice would do it, let's say her husband Ralph puts the new milk in the front. Now let's advance our story forward. That oldest bottle has now worked its way to the front again. Can you just picture Ralph coming home from work taking the bottle from the fridge, and of course he should pour it in a glass, but let's just say he drinks it directly from the bottle and chugs down many gulps before realizing that the milk he is drinking has gone sour. You can just imagine the grief that poor Mrs. Kramden will go through when her husband threatens once again to send her to the moon! And perhaps you are aware of a proposed law to require that beef be at least thirty percent lean. We think such a requirement will make our citizens much healthier. You can imagine that our friend Mr. Kramden would be better off with a little less fat in his dinner."

The mayor spoke for a few more minutes covering several additional topics of interest, and then asked his audience if there were questions anyone would like to ask. Before anyone else had a chance to think of a question, Pat Smith's hand shot up. "Mr. Mayor, I have read that unscrupulous politicians have themselves conspired to sour milk with vinegar to advance their cause. Have you heard or read about such matters, sir?"

Mayor Wagner took Mrs. Smith's question in good spirits, and joked that politics is a rough sport, but didn't think anyone would go to such lengths to win a political debate. She was probably reading an editorial from a conspiracy minded newspaperman.

Pat Smith thought it wise not to mention that she had read that Governor Rockefeller himself had suggested that a hypodermic needle had been used to inject vinegar into milk.

Mayor Wagner concluded, "I have taken up enough of your time here this evening, and I know our hosts are eager to serve coffee and dessert. I understand we're going to have apple crisp with vanilla ice cream, so I won't keep you from it any longer. Thank you so much for having me and Mrs. Wagner here with you this evening. It is a real pleasure to be here, deep in the heart of the Adirondacks this crisp February evening. Thank you for your support. God bless you all."

With that, Mayor Wagner returned to the table to await coffee and dessert.

## '62 Mayor Snow Storm

The next day, Paleface was blessed to receive a substantial snowstorm. No doubt, the snow interfered with Mayor Wagner's ability to make a prompt return to New York City. The following weekend Paleface had no vacancies, and experienced its busiest weekend to date.

Just after Mayor Wagner returned to New York City, the Mayor's proposal to limit the fat in chopped meat to thirty percent was enacted.

## '62 Ken Tucky

Jean didn't feel quite herself, and had been putting it off. It was time to go to see the doctor. It took a lot of energy to make it seem like nothing was wrong. Maybe a couple more weeks, thought Jean. If only I can put it off until the snow is gone and we are closed for the season.

The breakfast service was just about over. Jean sighed a distant sigh, put down the rag she had been using to wipe the stainless-steel surfaces clean and got a cup of coffee.

Just as Jean was sitting down for a break after being on her feet since 6am, a man came running through the door.

"An emergency!"

"A horse is hit!"

"By a truck! A milk truck!"

"Lying on the side of the road!

The man was in a panic. Jean jumped back to her feet. "Just one minute. I'll get Doc!" and off Jean went. She found Doc in the office and told him about the man in the dining room.

Doc raced out to see the man, and seconds later Doc followed him out the door. Jean watched out the window as the two men raced down the walkway to the parking lot, cross the parking lot to the road, and then around the corner toward Wilmington.

Jean returned to her coffee. A tear rolled down her cheek. Jean said a prayer for the horse, whatever horse had been hit. A feeling of dread overwhelmed Jean. She didn't have a good feeling about the situation.

A couple minutes later, Doc came running back through the front door. Doc and Jean locked eyes and Doc shook his head slightly from side to side, confirming Jean's intuition. Then he ran into the office to get his rifle and hurried back out the door.

Unfortunately, the fence had failed and the horses had found their way through in search of greener grass. There's no telling what possessed the beloved family horse named Ken Tucky to cross the road, and just at the point where a tight corner reduced visibility for on-coming traffic. A truck was coming around the corner a little too fast at just the wrong moment.

Poor Ken was in in bad shape. Doc's brain outpaced his heart. He knew at first sight what needed to be done. Before Doc let his heart in on the deal he had sunk a bullet in the brain of his beloved horse. Then grief got the better of him.

Doc had purchased the horse four years earlier. Ol' Ken Tucky was the first horse Doc had ever owned. Ken was dear to Doc's heart, and had taught Doc how to be a horseman. Of course, Doc discovered he loved riding and that riding made him feel connected to history. Doc imagined himself in the boots of Buffalo Bill Cody. And when Doc participated in gymkhana events Doc imagined he could understand how Buffalo Bill felt touring with his "Wild, Wild, West" show.

Doc thought of his mother, Florence, and how much she had enjoyed visiting the horse in her later years. Honestly, Doc hadn't fully grieved when his mother passed away two years earlier. Doc laughed and cried at the same time to think it took the death of his prize horse to allow him to finally confront his grief over the loss of his mother.

Doc remained slumped over the body of the dead horse for some time. The milk man turned his back, and wandered a distance up the road to give Doc space.

When Doc had sufficiently regained his composure, he rose to his feet, approached the man and said, “I'll send someone to take care of this horse. Thank you for coming to get me! Please forgive me, though it isn't appropriate for a man my age, sometimes I can get emotional. Would you like to come in to the lodge for a cup of coffee, some breakfast, or to make a phone call?”

The driver of the truck politely declined and offered Doc his deepest sympathies and then continued down the road with a newly dented bumper, a heavy load of guilt and sadness and more than a couple bottles of spilled milk in the back of the truck.

## '62 Dear Diary

At church a few years earlier, the Reverend R. Emerson Dunkel had encouraged Jean to keep a journal. At first Jean felt self-conscious and self-indulgent about keeping a diary. The Reverend thought it would be a good outlet for a woman who carried the weight of the world's problems on her shoulders. Though he would never know it, Jean wouldn't be any more likely to unload her burdens in writing than she would with a close confidant.

Instead Jean used the large book to record her thoughts about the beauty she encountered in the world. She might write a few paragraphs about something she read in the *Reader's Digest*. If Jean heard an inspiring story from a friend or someone at Paleface, she would write about how the story made her feel. Mostly Jean wrote about sunsets, flowers, and birds. Just as Doc could paint a picture with brushes on canvass, Jean could set a scene by choosing humble words to reflect the beauty she saw around her.

When confronted with hard times, Jean might write a very short sentence, such as, "Doc's beloved horse Kentucky was killed by a truck today." Or she would ignore the bad in a situation and focus on the one little nugget of beauty in the situation. For instance, while noting an absence of snow, Jean might write about how the deer are more easily able to find forage.

## '62 Putzi's Certification

Jean had finally gone to see the doctor, who recommended she see a specialist in Hanover, New Hampshire right away. Putzi Jost had to make a trip to New Hampshire the following week. Jean confided in Putzi and it was agreed Jean would keep Putzi company on the trip.

Putzi already held the "Maple Leaf" indicating full certification from the Canadian Ski Instructors Alliance. Putzi planned to add to her credentials by becoming similarly qualified by the United States Eastern Amateur Ski Association (USEASA) as well. Putzi was looking forward to proving equal to the challenging examination. She had been fully prepared by her husband Karl who carried both the Canadian and Eastern U.S. certifications. And she had diligently practiced every required element many dozens of times!

Jean and Putzi left early and arrived in Hanover, New Hampshire about 11am. Putzi waited while the Doctor examined Jean, had X-rays taken and confirmed the referring Doctor's suspicions. The Doctor wanted to get Jean into surgery as soon as possible. Jean asked if the surgery could be done in Plattsburgh, New York rather than Hanover, New Hampshire. The Doctor assured Jean that they could do a great job for her in Plattsburgh.

In Jean's diary, there was a note about how kind the x-ray technician was, and how smart and understanding the doctor was. Not a word or worry recorded about Jean's thoughts or feelings regarding having to have a major surgery. And nothing against Putzi, but if Jean could have avoided telling Putzi about the news from the doctor, she surely would have. As of yet, she hadn't even told her husband, or any of her other friends or family members either.

Putzi and Jean spent the next two days at Cranmore Mountain in North Conway, New Hampshire. Mostly Putzi was very busy. Jean had plenty of quiet time to relax, take it easy and read a couple of books. In her overnight bag, Jean had the books *By Canoe and Dog-Train* and *Three Boys in the Wild North Land*, both by the Reverend Egerton R. Young. Reverend Young was Doc Fitz-Gerald's grand-father. Jean had been meaning to read those books for years, and just never seemed to find the time.

At the end of the course, Putzi was awarded the certification in a short ceremony. Only three women were certified that week. Putzi became the first woman certified by both the Canadian and the Eastern U.S. credentialing authorities. Jean told Putzi how proud she was. "What a tremendous accomplishment!"

Putzi beamed. It was nice to have her talents and abilities recognized. And although Putzi was an extremely valued member of the Paleface ski instruction staff, this certification would add even more to her credibility and Putzi was enormously pleased to have earned the additional credentials.

## '62 Earthquake

The breakfast service was very slow. The lifts at Paleface were closed. The lodge and restaurant remained open, but barely. Doc was awake. It was early for Doc, and Doc was sitting at a table with a plate of bacon, eggs, and toast in front of him. Jean sat down with him. They talked about upcoming plans for the Easter Ball on Saturday evening, at Paleface. Then they talked about Easter Sunday dinner at home the following week.

Then Jean told Doc about seeing the Doctor, and explained about the surgery that she had scheduled in late May. Doc observed that Jean seemed to be addressing the butter dish. From prior experience, Doc understood that Jean didn't like to be the center of attention, particularly preferring to keep medical concerns private, and didn't ask more questions than necessary.

Doc was still thinking about what Jean had told him. From the first word, he was worried. He was trying not to miss the details she had shared. He knew she would not want to repeat them. As quickly as possible, Jean transitioned to another subject. Doc wasn't really listening, as Jean talked happily about a combination flower show and art exhibit she was looking forward to attending at the Adirondack Gardens Greenhouses in Lake Placid. Jean told Doc about her plans to take her friends Mary Wallace and Bea Lincoln with her to the show.

Just about then, the ground started to shake. Not enough to knock anything off the walls or shelves, but enough to notice. An earthquake. Earthquakes were rare in the North Country. It was big enough that all the customers and staff at Paleface wanted to congregate and share amazement at having felt the earth move beneath them.

It wasn't long before the earthquake and its aftermath were over. Everyone returned to what they were doing. Jean retired to her easy chair in room number one and picked up a newspaper to read for a few minutes before talking a brief nap. Jean reflected on her conversation with Doc, and was glad it was over, relieved to have told him, and hopeful that she wouldn't need to discuss it further until after the surgery. A little observation in the newspaper she was reading referred to the winter of 1962 as a "sick winter." Jean let out an almost imperceptible snort, put the paper down on the side table, removed her glasses, and fell asleep.

---

On Friday, Jean and her friends Mary and Bea made that trip to Lake Placid. Jean enjoyed the slow, peaceful ride with her friends. It was nice to get away for a few hours. Jean drove as her friends talked.

Mary talked about her daughters and Bea talked about her sons. Most of the way there they talked about their grandbabies.

Bea had pictures of her new grandson. Mary had lots of stories to tell about her granddaughter, born the previous August.

Maybe it was the way Jean sighed when Mary mentioned her granddaughter's new Easter outfit. Mary inquired, "Are you okay, dear?"

Jean admitted she couldn't help wishing for grandchildren herself. Then after a brief pause, Jean went on to mention her worries about having surgery the next month.

Mary reassured Jean that everything would be okay, and went so far as to predict she would be back to herself by the end of the summer. "What's more," she said, "I'll bet you are a new grandmother before you know it!" Mary had no basis for her prediction, just a hunch.

Bea and Mary bowed their heads and closed their eyes as Bea offered a prayer for their friend. Bea and Mary had been praying together for many years. Jean kept her eyes open and on the road before her. When Bea was finished, Jean expressed her gratitude.

Once in Lake Placid, the ladies stopped to pick up Bea's mother, Nellie Connors. The ladies enjoyed the greenhouses, flower show, and art exhibit. Then Jean treated everyone to lunch at the Howard Johnson's Restaurant. It was Bea's favorite place in the world. Bea and her mother loved the clam roll and the ice cream at Howard Johnson's. Bea's mission was to try every flavor, and had her running list with her that day. Bea's Mom always made a big show of trying to decide which flavor to try. And then every time Bea's Mom ended up ordering the butter pecan.

When they returned from Lake Placid, Jean sat down to make some notes in her journal. Jean spoke of the warm, healing power of good friends in a difficult situation, and then went on for several pages about the beauty and the intoxicating smell of twenty-five Easter Lilies closed into a station wagon.

## '62 Easter Ball

The next day was the 3rd Annual Easter Ball at Paleface, sponsored by the AuSable Valley Chamber of Commerce. The Ball was scheduled for 9pm and included a banquet at 7pm. The kitchen staff was very busy preparing for a full dinner service.

The Ball was deemed a huge success. The music was provided by the Ernie Vaughn Trio, who performed quite regularly at Paleface. After the obligatory speeches, much of the fun revolved around the contests and prizes.

The Waltz Contest was won by Mr. and Mrs. Thomas Keegan of Wilmington. Mr. Keegan's prize was a set of highball glasses. Mrs. Keegan won an Easter Lilly. The Twist Contest was won by Mr. and Mrs. Larry Capdeville of Keene. Mr. Capdeville won a bottle of whiskey from Fitzsimmons' Liquor Store of AuSable Forks and Mrs. Capdeville won a gold pearl bracelet from Dennett's Jewelry Store, also of AuSable Forks. The Grand Prize drawing winner was Mrs. Reginald Thwaits of Jay, who won a Kodak flash camera donated by Harvey Branch's store in Keene.

Everyone had a great time at the dance, but Jean was tired and left for home in Jay just after the banquet portion of the program.

## '62 Easter Dinner

With Paleface closed for the season, Doc and Jean had plans for a small, quiet Easter dinner at home in Jay with their family. Their oldest son, Allen arrived late Friday night, while everyone in the house was fast asleep. Jean was quite surprised to be introduced to a new daughter-in-law first thing Saturday morning. The fact that the newest Mrs. Fitz-Gerald was expecting a child, perhaps imminently, was impossible not to notice. Especially with Jean's impending surgery, if she had been prone to fainting she could have hit the floor. It was a lot for Jean to take in all at once. Ironically, Mary Wallace's prediction had come true, and more quickly than even Mrs. Wallace could have imagined.

To say it was an awkward weekend was an understatement. Of course, Jean wanted to be a grandmother. But first she would have liked to have attended a wedding. Jean hardly knew this girl, Carolyn Ann.

And Jean was tired, really tired. Meanwhile, there was work to be done in the kitchen to prepare for Easter dinner.

The next day, during Easter dinner, Doc and Jean's second son and his girlfriend announced their engagement. Their plans called for a wedding in November.

After dinner was over, the leftovers piled in the fridge and the dishes washed, dried and put away Jean excused herself to lie down. In the bedroom, Jean put her feet up, picked up a newspaper and noticed an advertisement that said, "OUTSIDE OF A NEW HAT... NOTHING PERKS UP A GIRL LIKE A NEW CAR!"

As Jean fell asleep, she was thinking a new hat would be much nicer than having surgery. Normally a new grandbaby and two new daughters-in-laws would have been very cheerful news. Jean wished she was feeling better, and she wished she had exuded more enthusiasm.

After Jean had retired for the evening, the rest of the family sat in the overstuffed easy chairs by a crackling fire in the stone fire place that dominated the large living room. Carolyn observed quietly, "I don't think Mrs. Fitz-Gerald likes me very much." Doc took advantage of the opportunity to explain to the family the circumstances of Jean's medical situation, adding as well that she would not appreciate him sharing this with them. Jean preferred to keep such problems to herself, not wanting to burden others.

Doc's immediate reaction was joy at the thought of a new baby in the family. It crossed Doc's mind that as a former minister, and pillar in the community, he should experience some emotion about the fact this baby was conceived before marriage vows were exchanged. Doc had remembered Carolyn from several of the dances at Paleface, and had enjoyed talking with her on more than one occasion. Doc enjoyed Carolyn's company. Doc knew that Jean would find a warm, soft place in her heart for Carolyn in the months and years to come.

Everyone else had turned in for the evening. Doc retired to his study, got out his watercolors and painted a fish jumping from the water in pursuit of a fly. Happy thoughts filled Doc's mind, and were reflected in the bright, sunny spring day that appeared on his canvass. Thoughts of Jean's coming surgery and thoughts of the costs of summer construction were blocked from Doc's mind as he painted until after three in the morning.

## '62 Whiteface Ski Council

At the annual meeting of the Whiteface Ski Council, Lili Draper was elected president, John King was elected vice president, Mrs. Hans Sowka was elected treasurer and Mrs. Donald Eckley was elected secretary. The rest of the Board of Directors included Serge Lussi, Lili Draper's son in law, as well as Doc Fitz-Gerald, Mr. Richard Brennan of Elizabethtown, Mr. John Manning of AuSable Forks, Mr. Walter Prager, Mr. Arnold Roberts, and Mr. Paul Twichell all of Wilmington, NY.

When Doc told Jean about the honor of being named to the Board of Directors of the Whiteface Ski Council, she just smiled warmly and shook her head slightly from side to side as if to say, haven't you got enough to do? "My husband," thought Jean.

## '62 New Motel Units

As in the past, Doc hired Torrance and Trumbull to serve as general contractors, Maurice Southmayd of Upper Jay for the plumbing contract, and Robert Gill of Jay to do the electrical work for the spring construction. The new motel units were projected to be ready by July 1st. During the past winter season, the motel business had doubled when compared to the prior winter season and there were seldom any vacancies, at least when the lifts were running. The new units would be a very welcome addition.

Doc had always been pleased with the work of David Torrance and Howard Trumbull, and couldn't wait for the new units to be completed. That time, the contractors would not have to worry about Doc looking over their shoulders. Doc and his family had plenty of other things on their minds.

## '62 Gone Fishing

One of the things on Doc's mind was fishing. Doc would claim that it was important to keep up to date on all the great fishing in the area, so he could help advise guests at Paleface. Doc found fishing relaxing, and thought it allowed his mind to stretch differently, and more creatively than during his other favorite activities.

One morning, Doc ran into Fran Betters at the river, and a little further down the river, Doc ran into Francis Lawrence. Both men reported catching trout more than twenty inches long. Doc had heard complaints that the rivers had been fished out. After talking with Fran and Francis, Doc concluded that the rumors were completely inaccurate.

Spring was cold, windy, wet, and late. It was well into May, and still, so far it seemed there were none of the horrible black flies that make being outdoors in the Adirondacks so difficult in the spring. The fish were ready for the flies, and the fishermen who had the right flies caught some nice specimen.

Another day, Doc had run into Carl Buehler, the president of the Wilmington Fish and Game Club just after he had caught a nice fifteen-inch trout. Doc was less lucky, catching enough to make it worth his while, but none of the really big fish that were so exciting to reel in. Nonetheless, Doc always enjoyed spending time fishing the West Branch of the AuSable River.

## '62 Mother's Day

On Mother's Day, Doc took Jean to the Royal Savage Inn, which had just re-opened for its 31st season under the direction of Marion and Newton Keith. The Royal Savage was one of Doc and Jean's favorite restaurants. They loved the food, the charm, and the views of Lake Champlain. Jean particularly enjoyed having a nice meal where someone else took care of all the details, from ordering it, pricing it, planning it, making sure there was staff to cook it and serve it, and making sure the guests were happy and satisfied. It was a welcome break from all the work and all the worry. Doc knew

Jean needed just such an evening, and they lingered for hours enjoying the candlelight buffet.

## '62 Club Grandma

It was early Thursday morning on the 17th of May. Doc and Jean were home in Jay, at the property named Overlook. It was a warm, sunny, spring morning. Doc was sleeping in late, as he often did, and Jean had been out for a lazy stroll.

Jean had collected a couple dozen daffodils in a basket. Each flower was to end up in a small vase on the tables at Paleface. Jean had enjoyed watching Robins busily pecking around in the grass. She stopped to listen to the Phoebe's song. Then Jean heard the phone ring through the open windows and hurried inside to answer the phone.

"Just a quick call, to share the news," reported a friend of Jean's son and daughter-in-law. Jean hurried to wake up Doc to share the news. They had become grandparents. Moments later, Jean was back out the door, in the station wagon, and headed to Mary Wallace's house where she ended up spending the whole morning.

Mary was busy making a huge cake for a big weekend wedding, but was fully able to do that while talking with Jean and making coffee. After a couple of hours that morning, Jean felt like she had joined a secret society, Club Grandma.

After considering the choices of how she would like to be addressed by her grandson, and future grandchildren that could well follow, Jean decided on Nana, pronounced like banana without the first syllable.

Jean was back home a couple hours later, still reveling in the thought that she was now a grandmother, but very tired, and ready for a nap. She wished she could get right in the wagon and drive to Connecticut. But there was a busy weekend to contend with at Paleface. Then Jean had to have that surgery. She had forgotten about that for a couple of hours.

## '62 Citizen of the Year

Two days later, the summer season opened with a full-capacity crowd at Paleface. The Annual Banquet for the Whiteface Chamber of Commerce had been extensively marketed. As usual, the menu featured a gourmet steak dinner with all the fixings, for a price of $3.50 per person, including gratuity.

The members of the Chamber and their guests, and those members of the general public who had purchased a ticket in time, plus the evening's speakers, enjoyed a leisurely two-hour dinner. When most guests had completed their deserts, Mr. George Haselton, the town supervisor for the Town of Wilmington took the microphone and began the evening's program. First Mr. Haselton introduced the featured guest speaker named Dr. Richard Lea who managed the forest lands of the Diamond National Corp.

Diamond was the principal employer for the city of Ogdensburg, New York, at the confluence of the Oswegatchie River and the Saint Lawrence River. The border between the United States and Canada runs through the middle of the St. Lawrence River. The population of Ogdensburg was approximately 14,000. It was a thriving community.

Ogdensburg relied very heavily on Diamond, its largest employer. In turn, Diamond relied very heavily on one significant product. In those day's butchers wrapped meat products in a special kind of paper. Diamond manufactured that paper.

In New York City, lawmakers decreed that meat be packaged so it was visible to consumers. New York City was a significant market for meat products, and therefore also for meat packaging. Before long, Diamond was faced with laying off a significant percentage of its workforce.

In the years that followed, more and more butchers and grocery stores followed the lead of New York City. Eventually, the renewable paper used to package meat was replaced by a combination of Styrofoam and plastic film. By the late 1970's, the market for Diamond's product was gone and the plant was closed in May 1978.

Ironically, lawmakers in New York City have since banned the use of Styrofoam for packaging beginning in 2015.

Of course, all of that came later. In May of 1962, Diamond National was a healthy, prosperous organization. Dr. Lea was a young professional with an important job and was a sought out public speaker. People were very interested in the work that happened in the woods.

Dr. Lea graduated from the College of Forestry in Syracuse with a PhD in 1953. After a few years on the staff at the College he spent a couple of years as a forester for the Singer Mfg. Co in Quebec before joining the Diamond National Corp in 1957. Dr. Lea was a popular speaker, enjoyed by audiences ranging from classrooms and Scout troops to civic organizations and experts in the forestry industry. Dr. Lea's speech at Paleface covered several interesting topics.

First Dr. Lea talked about how maps of the wild woodlands are created and the types of tools that are used to get the job done. Next, the presentation went on to talk about multi-use forests. This was of interest to people at Paleface, because of course this meant skiing, hunting, fishing, hiking, and living within a thriving forest that was also capable of working to supply materials needed by humankind.

Then Dr. Lea talked about the process of manufacturing paper at the Diamond National plant in Ogdensburg and Dr. Lea passed around pictures of the impressive plant and equipment while he talked.

Dr. Lea seamlessly transitioned into talking about all the volunteer activities the management, office, and supervisory staff of the company participate in to help enrich the community at large.

Finally, Richard Lea concluded by pointing out the impact of a healthy employer within a community. "Of course, employers provide workers with pay and benefits, and payroll taxes go to support the activities of government. The employee and their families use all the goods and services provided locally in the community, meaning jobs for people at banks, post offices, schools, supermarkets, laundromats, and so forth. In a robust local economy, everything is interdependent." That message of course was a good conclusion for a keynote address to members of a local Chamber of Commerce. Dr. Richard Lea was rewarded with a long round of hearty applause.

Supervisor Haselton returned to the microphone briefly. Mr. Haselton proposed a grand toast to the evenings guest of honor, the Citizen of the Year, 93 year old Mr. Abram Kilburn. Then, Mr. Haselton introduced Mrs. Marjorie Porter, who was the official Essex County historian. Marjorie told everyone in attendance the story of Abe Kilburn's life and service to his home town. Then Mr. Haselton presented Abe with a handsome plaque, and asked if he would like to say a few words.

Abe took the microphone and talked about the miraculous transition from hauling freight with horse and oxen to now being able to use trucks and trains. Another miraculous thing Abe mentioned was being able to drive up Whiteface Mountain to enjoy the view in less than a half an hour, compared to having a day long hike to enjoy the view when he was a young man.

When George Haselton got the microphone back, he invited everyone to enjoy the dance. "The band is paid until 1am," George concluded. "And ladies and gentlemen, it is now fully official, Abe Kilburn is our Citizen of the Year." The entire crowd jumped to their feet, giving Justice Kilburn a long and hearty standing ovation.

## '62 Surgery

Jean really did prefer to keep all medical matters personal, and when she didn't feel well, she preferred to be left alone to get better on her own. However, in 1962, communities were much more insistent about recognizing when people were in the hospital by sending flowers, gifts, cards, and casseroles.

Jean entered the Physicians Hospital in Plattsburgh on May 21st, and made a special request that if anything happened to her that her body be donated to science. Perhaps in some small way she could help cure people in the future.

The next day, Jean had a complete hysterectomy. The doctors also removed a 9-pound tumor from her abdomen. It was a couple of weeks before tests were able to confirm and doctors were available to explain to Doc and Jean that the tumor had been benign.

Great news! Jean's spirits soared. There was still a long way to go to recover from the surgery. She resolved that no one would hear her complain. Doc and Jean bowed their heads in thankful prayer.

Jean returned to Overlook twelve days later to continue her recovery at home. Mary Wallace took care of managing the kitchen and dining room at Paleface for her friend, straight through to the 4th of July.

## '62 Gymkhana

Paleface was continuing to establish itself as a great summer attraction in addition to the winter activities. In addition to the motel and restaurant, Paleface again had horseback riding operated by professional experts.

What was the best way to appeal to skiers in the summer time? For those who enjoyed ski racing, maybe something fast and a little dangerous?

Several members of the Paleface Ski School joined Chuck Fitz-Gerald in a Gymkhana sponsored by the AuSable Valley Sports Car Club. The second annual event was staged on Sunday, August 19th with Whiteface Mountain in the background. Jimmer Ransehausen organized the event and a professional timer, Mr. Lionel Alberts, was brought in from Montreal.

A well-known professional driver drove the course as an exhibition event, and did log the fastest time. The race course featured a whole host of obstacles. For example, at one station you had to drop a ping-pong ball into a one-quart oil can from a lofty perch at the top of a ramp.

There were about a dozen contestants who participated in the race, from across the North Country and as far away as Montreal. Third place went to the Draper Team, featuring Charles Draper and his wife Carol Steinhoff Draper. Second place went to Karl Jost, Director of Paleface Ski School and his colleague, ski instructor Vic

Pelkey. The first place prize went to Doc and Jean's son Chuck Fitz-Gerald and his friend Tim Devins.

The races drew a large crowd of locals, including Mr. Leo Cooper from Wilmington who showed up anywhere there was something happening that had anything to do with cars. And wherever Leo Cooper went, his friend Gus Elliott came along as well. Leo and Gus showed up for the event in Leo's antique, 1921 Model T Ford Roadster. Mr. Cooper was teased a bit, and Mr. Pelkey offered to pay Mr. Cooper's entry fee. It would have been fun to see Mr. Cooper put the Roadster through the course. Leo politely yet insistently declined, preferring instead to remain a spectator.

## '62 Jean Carol Marries Chuck

A couple of weeks later, Doc and Jean attended Chuck and Jean Carol's wedding and celebrated their marriage. Jean Fitz-Gerald thought Jean Carol looked stunning. Jean Carol's parents, of course had to agree with that! In fact, Jean thought that all the young ladies looked very pretty. The wedding reception was held at Steinhoff's Sportsman's Inn in Wilmington.

The newspaper the following week seemed to be short of details when they reported, "On Saturday noon the comparative normal quietness of the off-season in Wilmington was suddenly shattered as the wedding cortege of Mr. and Mrs. Charles Fitz-Gerald wended its rapid way to Steinhoff's where the wedding reception was held. Mrs. Fitz-Gerald is the former Jean Carol Devins, of Jay."

Following the wedding, Chuck and Jean Carol went on a road trip honeymoon to Alexandria Bay and Niagara Falls. Meanwhile, Jean, Doc, and Carolyn threw Patti a surprise fifteenth birthday party. While Patti was celebrating with her friends and family in the loft, the staff of Paleface was busy downstairs preparing for a meeting of the Adirondack Shrine Club. All Shriners were invited to attend the event, which included a social hour at 4:40pm, a business meeting at 5:30pm, and dinner at 7pm.

It was a busy weekend for the Fitz-Gerald family!

## '62 Moose Hunting

With the wedding finished, Doc left Paleface in the good hands of its excellent staff while he joined his friends on a Moose hunting expedition in Newfoundland. Carl Steinhoff, Dr. Goff, Judge McNamee, Doc, and William Grossman, each were lucky enough to get a moose.

Carl reported that the moose were so plentiful where they were hunting that they were causing damage to the forest. A guide was required in order to get a license to hunt moose, and there were very few guides available. Therefore, many hunters were unable to hunt, hence the dense population of moose.

The men enjoyed hunting from a very remote and desolate camp. Their cars had to be left forty miles to the south. To get to camp, they had to take a sea plane. Getting five men and their gear to camp was one thing. Unfortunately, the sea plane had to make five trips to get the moose out.

## '62 Dog Team

While Doc was hunting Moose with his friends in Newfoundland, Jean spent a day or two at Paleface, a day or two at home and spent a couple of days on a road trip with her friends to Vermont.

Mary Wallace's daughter was enrolled at Champlain College in Burlington, Vermont. Bernard Wallace thought it would be nice if Mary attended parent's weekend with her friends instead of her husband. Mary packed her sister Agnes Ward, and her friends Della Straight and Jean Fitz-Gerald into her car.

The ladies left for parents' weekend on Friday, in the middle of the morning, and took an indirect route. Someone had told the ladies about the Dog Team Tavern in Middlebury, and given the rave reviews, they thought they would give the place a try.

They arrived shortly after noon, a little later than intended. It was a little bit off the beaten path and they had some difficulty finding it until they stopped to ask someone in town for directions. Two hours later, after a fun lunch the Dog Team Tavern became Jean's favorite restaurant.

The Dog Team was known for a couple of things. First, and foremost, the sticky buns. Light, fluffy, buttery, warm, and coated in soft sticky icing. The sticky buns were almost a meal in themselves.

The second thing the Dog Team was known for was the giant Ferris wheel of relishes. One was brought to each table. A little hand operated crank made the little square buckets of condiments move around so the ladies could reach the contents of their choice. The choices included pickled and fermented fruits and vegetables, including cucumbers, beets, cauliflower, onions, as well as different mustards, flavored mayonnaise, and different varieties of olives. No two ladies decorated their sandwiches the same!

Mary, Agnes, Della, and Jean spent a lovely couple of days on the road, and Mary was very happy to visit with her daughter at college in Burlington.

## '62 Republican Women

One of the busiest nights at Paleface that year was the rally of the region's Republican women a couple of weeks before Election Day. Ladies came from all the local towns. All together, 150 women enjoyed a banquet, singing, and speeches.

The highlight of the evening was when each woman delivered her husband's stump speech. The candidates were allowed to attend briefly at the end of the evening but were not allowed to speak to the audience. There was a distinct advantage to the one or two ladies who themselves were candidates that fall.

Another highlight of the evening was a film presentation on the "Rockefeller Record" which was narrated by the husband of Mrs. Morehouse, who briefly introduced the film.

Of course, the conclusion and rallying cry from the evening was "Vote Row A – All the Way."

Paleface closed for the season after the Republican Women's rally.

## '62 Week of Prayer and Self-Denial

The Week of Prayer and Self-Denial had been a tradition among Methodist women since 1887. The purpose was to provide a special time for study, a time for prayer and a time for giving. For Jean, this tradition was a very special and meaningful part of her membership in the Methodist Church.

Unfortunately, the town of Jay was between pastors in the fall of 1962. Jean had asked Doc to step in and deliver a sermon, the one he often delivered during the Week of Prayer and Self-Denial. Jean herself offered to lead the prayer at the kick-off on Friday evening, October 25th.

Friday evening would begin with a dinner. Each lady would bring a dish. Pat Smith served as food chairman and organized the gathering of the casserole dishes. After a nice dinner, Pat played the organ and the ladies sang several hymns. Then Jean led a meditation, after which she reminded everyone of the meaning of the Week.

"In the words of Mrs. J.W. Payne, The Week of Prayer and Self-Denial invites you to go on a magnificent adventure to spiritual realms as you observe the Quiet Day and study the projects that need your help. We are so earthbound we rarely allow our spirits to soar. Let us try to forget the fast schedule on which we have been running our lives, and let our souls catch up with us." Jean looked up from her notes into the audience which included many of her friends and fellow members of the Women's Society of Christian Service (WSCS) and concluded, "Good night, friends."

## '62 Bahamas

A couple weeks later, Patti, Jean, and Doc flew from Plattsburgh to New York City, then on to Nassau in the Bahamas. Jean savored every warm relaxing minute spent on the beach. When she got warm, she walked into the ocean for a few minutes. When she had cooled off, she returned to her chair. Jean thought the week of self-denial only added to the enjoyment of the ten days of rest and relaxation. One of her favorite sayings regarding the key to happiness was how important it was to have something to love, something to do, and something to look forward to. Jean had looked forward to the trip to the Bahamas for a very long time.

One evening, they attended a beach party at the resort. Just like at the social functions at Paleface, there was a dance contest. Doc and Patti entered the Twist contest, and both made it to the finals. The grand prize winner of the Twist contest that evening was Patti Fitz-Gerald. All that practice at Paleface had paid off, and Patti was crowned Queen of the Twist.

Several days while they were in the Bahamas, Doc and Patti went on deep sea fishing trips. Jean preferred to relax on the beach and catch up on her reading. Doc wasn't very good at relaxing on the beach. The warmth was nice. The views were beautiful. But whenever Doc closed his eyes he pictured himself skiing and running through the required elements for the ski instructor's certification examination. And how to make Paleface an even more attractive destination for tourists and North Country residents. Doc preferred to find exciting things to do and experimented with surfing, snorkeling, even horseback riding, and wandering around the island exploring. Sometimes Patti went with Doc, and sometimes Patti remained with Jean.

On the last evening before the end of their vacation, the Fitz-Gerald family enjoyed a lobster dinner—a non-traditional Thanksgiving dinner to be sure, however Patti, Jean, and Doc could not have felt more blessed after ten wonderful days in a tropical paradise. Jean found herself thinking that they should return to a traditional turkey dinner with all the fixings the following year.

## '62 From the Beach to the Slopes

A couple weeks later, two carloads of ski instructors from Paleface made their way to Chateau Lac Beauport, about a hundred miles north of Quebec City. Karl and Putzi Jost, Maureen Parrow, Laura Trumbull, Robert Waldorf, and Jim Gregory made the trip with Doc. Although Jim Gregory was moving to Beartown for the next winter season, Doc warmly welcomed Jim to accompany the gang from Paleface even so.

The instructors who weren't already Maple Leaf certified took the examination. Doc went last, and was by far the oldest seeking certification. When Doc completed the examination and all its required elements, everyone cheered. The results would come in the mail in a couple weeks, but it looked to everyone in attendance that Doc had completed the required elements perfectly.

While Doc was at Chateau Lac Beauport, he never once thought wistfully about relaxing on the beach in the Bahamas, though he did enjoy painting dramatic pictures of waves crashing into rocks. So the ocean did hold some appeal, lazing around on the beach did not.

## '62 Announcing the 1963 Ski Season

Just before Christmas, the newspaper carried a long feature introducing Paleface's third skiing season. It was reported that even with the new units, Paleface was booked solid for the Christmas to New Year's holiday period, as well as the week of Washington's Birthday in February.

The story went on to herald the improvements to the ski trails, and the experimental trails cut into the upper mountain. It was hoped those would be further developed the following year, and that another T-Bar would be installed as well.

Another new feature for the winter of 1963 was a special program called "Ladies Learn to Ski Special." The promotion would run from January 7th to January 11th and feature 5 two-hour lessons between 10am and noon each day. On Friday afternoon, there would be a competition, and prizes would be presented on Friday afternoon at the cocktail lounge. A special promotional price of $17.50 was announced for that week.

The piece in the paper went on to name the staff for the coming season. In addition to the returning instructors, Karl and Putzi Jost, Vic Pelkey, Laura Trumbull, Theresa Devlin, Howard Snow, and Ralph

Ruffell, as well as Doc himself, there were a few new names on the list. Jacques Thibault and Dave Mallette from Montreal would also be on staff. New Ski Safety Patrol members included John Foley, Director and John Dreissigacker, assistant.

In the lodge, the cocktail lounge was re-branded "The Happy Hunting Ground" and Walter Prager's Ski Shop was relocated to the A-Frame balcony over the main lounge. The restaurant featured a new hostess, Mrs. Joan Dreissigacker and a new waitress, Mrs. Thelma Sorrell. Mrs. Pearl Pearce joined Paleface as a new cook at the end of December, 1962.

## '62 Island Princess

While Doc was away in Quebec, Patti practiced the trumpet tirelessly.

Patti's music teacher at school suggested that Patti play a trumpet solo at the Midnight Mass at St. James' Episcopal Church in AuSable Forks (though the Fitz-Geralds were members of the Methodist Church in Jay). The invitation was for Saturday evening, December 29th.

The music selected for Patti was "Trumpet Tune in D." The musical piece was taken from a mini-opera and was composed by Clarke and Daniel Purcell. The mini-opera was titled "Island Princess." Having just been named Queen of the Twist in the Bahamas, Island Princess sounded like a bit of a demotion, but Patti agreed to tackle the piece nonetheless.

The whole piece was about a minute and thirty-five seconds long. It was fairly easy to play, and pretty easy to learn. It got a little complicated at a point just about a minute in, and then again, the very end was a bit difficult.

During the month of December, Jean must have heard Patti play the Trumpet Tune ten times a day. After the first couple of days, Patti played it quite well. Still, Jean had grown quite tired of hearing it, and was sure that Pat and Phil Smith down the hill were growing tired of hearing it also.

Finally, the night came for Patti to play. Jean had insisted on a long nap in the afternoon. A 15 year old shouldn't have to take a nap, protested Patti. It was pointless to argue. Whether it was the nap or the month of practicing, Patti played perfectly, performing in spite of a sick, nervous feeling in her belly.

Jean and Doc were very proud of Patti's trumpet solo. Jean thought that it sounded much, much better in church than it did at home.

## '63 Fifty Mile Hiking Fad – February, 1963

It was early in the morning on the 13th of February and the guys at the post office in Lake Placid had been talking about the latest craze, the fifty mile fitness march that seemed to have taken the nation by storm. It was typical each morning for the guys to poke fun at one another before making their hikes, and Denny Miller, not known to be much of a morning person, always seemed to end up on the wrong side of the morning banter. Denny should have known better, but before his brain stopped him, he said, "Shoot, I'd do it for $100," and walked out the door to make his rounds.

That was all the guys needed to hear, and within the space of five minutes, they had a plan cooked up. One of the guys made a quick call to news director Fred Ellers at WIRD, the local radio station. Mr. Ellers took the bait and ran down the hall to talk to the morning DJ. All morning between songs, the DJ talked up the challenge, and the urgent need to raise $100 to close the deal.

One of the listeners that morning was Bill Ruocco, who was instantly struck with a brilliant idea. Mr. Ruocco called the radio station and suggested that Denny could deliver a letter to the postmaster in Plattsburgh, inviting him to join the organizing committee for Lake Placid's bid to host the 1968 Winter Olympic Games. Mr. Ellers called the post office and spoke with the Lake Placid postmaster who checked in with his boss in New York City. Before Denny had completed his rounds, $100 had been committed by four businessmen. What's more, Denny had completely forgotten his off-handed boast two minutes after saying that he'd do it for $100.

When Denny got back from delivering the mail up, down, and all around "Humdinger Hill" one of his buddies told him the boss wanted to see him. Denny couldn't imagine what he could have done to be called into the boss's office. In fact, Denny worked very hard to never have a reason to be called into the boss's office. The boss was very excitedly telling Denny about all the arrangements, and Denny was several sentences behind the boss in listening to what he was saying.

Finally, it dawned on him. The morning chatter about the fifty mile challenge returned to his mind. His heart sunk realizing his buddies had not just done it to him again; this time they had taken it to a whole new level. "Well," Denny, shrugging and drawing inspiration from John Wayne's famous words, "A man's got to do what a man's got to do." As he thought about it, Denny wasn't really that upset about having to walk fifty miles. It was having everyone make a fuss over him that seemed daunting.

In high school, Denny had competed in baseball, basketball, swimming, and hockey. He was a good enough swimmer to have come in second and third in a couple races. It was hockey where Denny really excelled, and Denny was good enough to make the all-star team hosted by Clarkson College in Potsdam, New York. Only the best high school hockey stars participated in the invitational tournament, and Denny had even beaten out his brother. "I guess," Denny thought, "I got through that, I can get through this, and then life can get back to normal." The next thought that went through Denny's mind was, "What in the world is Mickey going to think about all of this?"

To Denny's surprise, Maureen (who had always been called Mickey) was waiting for him at the door when he got home. The phone had been ringing off the hook all afternoon, and Mickey felt like a Hollywood movie star. Denny had worried that Mickey wouldn't appreciate this sudden intrusion in their lives. "Nothing to worry about here," thought Denny happily. On his way to get changed out of his work clothes, Denny started to hum "Walk Like a Man" by Frankie Vallie and the Four Seasons.

## '63 Valentine's Day

The next day was Valentine's Day. Denny picked Mickey up at home, just after work, shortly after three in the afternoon. Denny changed from his uniform, and they were ready to drive the route Denny would hike. The starting mileage on the odometer was measured precisely.

From the post office at the corner of Main Street and Parkside Drive, they followed Main Street to the east. Fairly quickly, the town gave way to countryside. Along the way, they passed the entrance to Whiteface Mountain Ski Center, The Blue Bowl Restaurant, the Flume, Steinhoff's, and then entered Wilmington. They followed Route 86, which meant making a right turn at the intersection where going left would have brought them up the highway to the summit of Whiteface Mountain, and where going straight would have taken them up the Bonnie View Road. They continued along Route 86, passing Paleface Ski Center on the right hand side and a couple miles later came to the end of Route 86 in the Town of Jay. They turned left on to Route 9N, with still a great distance to go before hitting the fifty mile mark. They passed through the towns of AuSable Forks, Keeseville, and Peru, and still they weren't at the fifty mile mark. Finally, the odometer crossed the fifty mile mark at the Plattsburgh city limits just south of the city near the Plattsburgh Air Force Base. "Well," Mickey joked, "I'll bet that was a lot easier in the car than it will be on foot, and yet it still took us an hour and a half!" Denny turned the car around and returned the way they came.

On the return trip, Denny pulled the car into the parking lot at Paleface. The baby needed a diaper change, and Mickey had been curious to see the inside of the place. "Let's go in, and seeing as how it is St. Valentine's Day, maybe I can buy you dinner," said Denny.

It was early as far as dinner was concerned, but it was starting to pick up. Even before the baby was born, they didn't get out to eat very often. So it was certainly a nice treat. Denny had steak and potatoes with peas and carrots and Mickey had fried chicken. They both had German chocolate cake for desert. Baby Denise was especially well-behaved. Everyone who passed by had been sure to stop and fuss over her.

At the next table, there was a rowdy bunch, which included Karl Jost, Putzi Jost, Doc Fitz-Gerald, Vic Pelkey, and Jacques Thibault. Paleface's best ski instructors and members from the ski patrol had spent most of the day at Whiteface. Each Thursday there were ski races for the pros from all the ski centers in the region and these events were billed as sort of grudge races pitting skiers from ski schools against ski patrols. Certainly, if you were to ask a bunch of pros which was the better skier, you would hear a hearty debate as there was a long standing rivalry and this was one of the unsolved mysteries of the ages. Truth be told, from the perspective of the Paleface pros, these Thursday races were much more a rivalry between the Paleface and Whiteface ski centers. It was a definite matter of pride that the Paleface pros often beat the pros from Whiteface. On that day, first place went to Paul Jenick from Mt. Whitney's patrol with a winning time of 51.3 seconds. So, bragging rights went to ski patrol, and ski instructors had to bow their heads in shame. Vic Pelkey of Paleface came in second with a time of 52.5 seconds beating Bernie O'Grady who represented Whiteface.

So, as a result of one second's difference, the five of them were brought together in celebration. They retold the day's events over and over while drinking beers, hooting, hollering, and laughing merrily over the victory of the day and schemed for how to attack the race course the following week. And though all of them had seemed to forget it was Valentine's Day, they never forgot that there were families all around them. In fact, Jacques spent most of his time making faces, imitating monkeys, and playing peek-a-boo with baby Denise at the next table.

Jean Fitz-Gerald stopped by the Miller's table to ask how everything was, if they were enjoying their dinner, and what had brought them to Paleface. Mickey told Jean all about the hike that Denny was preparing to undertake on Monday with pride and excitement. It was almost as if Mickey herself was on the verge of making the trek.

Mickey went on to tell Jean that at first, she thought it was a wonderful challenge, but then as she thought about it for a few hours, she became frightened about the hike, and that she had insisted Denny see Dr. Bergamini before taking the risk. Dr. Bergamini advised against it. Mickey looked at Denny, as if checking to see if maybe repeating the doctor's opinion might have changed his mind.

Denny shrugged, and confirmed what he told the doctor. Denny had given his word and couldn't back out.

Mickey added that Dr. Bergamini emphasized the importance of hydration, and noted that Denny was only 31 years old. The doctor had concluded that delivering the mail on foot every day was good physical training.

Jean remarked that Dr. Bergamini was very sensible, however fifty miles seemed like a very long walk indeed.

Knowing Denny had made up his mind to keep his word and follow through on the dare, Mickey concluded, as she often did, "It's all in God's hands. We're just going along for the ride." Once again, the matter was settled.

Mickey went on to tell Jean, "It's fun being around vacationing people, sharing in their enjoyment of your facility." Mickey had been born in New York City, and followed her older sister from Manhattan to the North Country when she was 17 years old. Mickey told Jean about the joy of swimming in Mirror Lake in the summers, how happy she was to get her first pair of skis, and how magical it felt to ride around Mirror Lake in a horse drawn sleigh.

Jean liked talking with Mickey. Jean felt her own heart warm as she listened to Mickey's optimistic enthusiasm, and Jean nodded heartily when Mickey said, "I love Lake Placid and I feel like I live in paradise." Jean looked at Denny. They shared a warm, friendly smile.

After a few minutes, Jean wished them a happy St. Valentine's Day and wished Denny the best of luck on his hike, and told them to be sure and stop in again real soon.

Having finished her rounds in the dining room, Jean passed through the lounges and went upstairs to the meeting room to check on the members of the AuSable Forks Chamber of Commerce, holding their monthly meeting in the loft at Paleface. As Jean approached, the Board was appointing officers for the coming year. Mrs. Glenna Bombard had been named Secretary of the Board. Jean stood by and waited as the Chamber took up its next topic on the agenda, which was a new brochure featuring all the local attractions and tourist related businesses, a project which Mrs. Bombard was leading. The Board authorized the printing of 25,000 brochures, a significant increase over the prior year's 15,000. After that unanimous conclusion, Jean politely interrupted and inquired whether anybody needed anything. Of course, the group had been well attended to and had everything they needed. As Jean walked away, the board entered into executive session and talked about the proposed AuSable Acres project that appeared to be clearing the hurdles for approval and possibly construction of new homes would begin within a year, which would be a big shot in the arm to local construction companies and all the various subcontractors.

As Jean returned down the stairs, through the lounge and back into the dining room, the celebrants were saying goodbye to each other and to the Millers. Other guests were just getting seated after freshening up in their rooms after a great day on the slopes, or after enjoying cocktails in the lounge. Business was good that fine winter's day in the Adirondacks.

It had snowed much of the morning, with occasional mild flurries through the afternoon and evening. It wasn't as cold as it often was in February, comfortably in the twenties rather than being below zero, as it often was. The Millers headed home, put the baby to bed and went to bed as well. A postman gets up early in the morning, and seldom stays up late at night.

## '63 Radio WIRD Crazy

The story exploded on Friday. The radio station had something to say about Denny Miller and his walk to Plattsburgh on the top of every hour after the news and the weather reports. The newspaper featured the story front and center on page one. Denny read the story and chuckled at the quote, "Well, for something that started out as a joke, I guess we'll have to go through with it." Denny asked his boss, "Did I say that?" Fact was, Denny was looking forward to getting out on the streets and getting away from all this talk of walking to Plattsburgh. On his way out, Denny paused for a moment to listen to the radio. They were talking about whether Denny Miller would finish his hike before midnight, whether a postal worker could do what a U.S. Marine did and whether there was any chance Denny could break the record set by a Marine at Camp Lejeune the previous week in North Carolina. Eleven hours and forty-four minutes was the time to beat! "Well," thought Denny, "they can talk about this all day, I've got work to do," and out he went.

Friday morning after a very busy breakfast service, the gals at Paleface were enjoying a break and chatting. Every day after all the guests had been served breakfast, Jean liked to sit down with "the gals" for a half an hour and have a slice of toast, generously buttered, and a cup of tea. That morning, the ladies included Pearl Pierce, Dorothy McLean, and Carrie McDonald from the kitchen, Bea Lincoln who served the guests, and Jane Peck from the office.

Jean hadn't mentioned it earlier, as Mary was scheduled to have the day off anyhow, but Jean told the ladies that Mary Wallace was feeling poorly, not sure what was wrong but that she wouldn't be coming in until further notice. Jean told the ladies that Mary's daughter was home from Champlain College for the weekend and was taking good care of her mother and her dad.

The ladies made plans to get through the busy President's Day holiday but encouraged Jean to hire another woman, at least part time. Jean did most of her hiring from among the ladies of the Methodist Church in Jay, a smart move because church was a great place to discover who the best cooks in town were.

The half hour daily "meeting" went by quickly as Bea told all the ladies about her son and his girlfriend's wedding on Saturday in AuSable. Of course, Bea always liked to talk about her boys and she had a right to be proud. Bea's boys were turning out to be great citizens and were starting young families of their own.

Pearl talked about how her husband Frank seemed to be coming down with something, and might have to close the garage for a few days. Bea told Pearl that she saw the ad in the paper that said, "Frank Pierce Garage, Jay, NY—In Business 34 Years at the Same Old Stand. We Sell Fine Grade Mobil Gas and Oils—Lubrication." The ladies agreed that it was a very fine ad and that Frank and Pearl should be very proud of the garage.

Jane had to run to the phone every time it rang. Between calls, Jean wished Jane a very happy birthday, which in fact wasn't until Sunday.

Though it was almost a week later, the ladies were still talking about the annual smorgasbord benefit put on by the Women's Committee of the Whiteface Chamber of Commerce. Paleface was filled almost to capacity with 250 people each paying $1.50. The Chamber raised a hefty sum. The dishes were prepared by the best cooks in the area. The theme was international dishes, and the ladies were still exchanging their favorite exotic recipes from faraway lands.

Finally, Jean told the ladies about having met Denny and Mickey Miller the evening before. Jane's jaw dropped to the table in awe. She had been listening attentively to the radio in the office all morning, and had gotten completely pulled into the story. Jane told the ladies that the route would bring Denny right through Wilmington, past Paleface, and on into Jay. Then and there the ladies decided they would turn the whole building inside out to greet Denny as he walked past on Monday morning. Each lady talked about what they were going to make for Denny, as he would surely be hungry after walking there from Lake Placid. Jean chided, "How is he supposed to march to Plattsburgh carrying your chocolate cake, Dorothy!"

Jane told the ladies that she heard on the radio that he would be carrying his own concoction of grape, pineapple, and lemon juice mixed with honey. She also heard that Denny was a big fan of that new soda pop called Mountain Dew. The ladies agreed at the very least, they could give Denny some cookies and Mountain Dew.

Jane suggested that they take up a collection so they could also hand Denny an envelope on his way by. Jane converted a coffee can into a piggy bank, and made an appealing sign to paste on the side. It was already a few minutes past eleven, and the ladies needed to get back to work to get ready for lunch. It wouldn't be long before hungry skiers were looking for Paleface's famous hamburgers, cheeseburgers, chocolate pudding, and Jell-O, in one of three bright and jiggly colors.

All weekend long, the Maxwell House piggy bank received donations ranging from small change to an occasional bill, as the story on the radio continued to draw the interest of Paleface staff and guests who would stop by the registration desk every once in a while for updates. Of course, the updates over the weekend were mostly rehashed facts from Friday and whatever the DJs chose to make up and add to the legend of Denny Miller.

## '63 Departure

At long last, 6am Monday morning rolled around and Denny stood there with his pack on his back and a small crowd gathered around him to cheer him on as he prepared to start his epic journey. Everyone from the post office was there, as well as the mayor, the folks from the radio station, a couple of newspaper reporters, his wife Mickey, his Father Gus, and his Brother Jerry.

Denny hugged his wife and kissed his baby girl, shook his Dad's hand, gave his brother a high five and waved to the crowd. "What's on your mind this morning, Denny?" shouted the man from the newspaper.

"Well," Denny said without a thought, "heck of a way to spend my day off. Thanks for coming out this morning everybody. I guess I have an important letter to deliver today."

The Mayor approached Denny, and in a booming voice counted down from ten to one. With that, Denny went to work.

If Denny was to have a chance to beat the record, he would really have to move. His strategy was to walk almost as fast as he could, as steadily-paced as possible for as long as he could without taking any breaks. On the other hand, he knew nobody expected him to break a record, he really just needed to complete the task and deliver the letter. With all that was going on, Denny had almost forgotten the $100. Almost!

Bill Ruocco invited Mickey to ride in his car with him, and they followed Denny at a safe distance. Bill told Mickey about his plan to get a snippet of the story onto the Huntley Brinkley evening news on NBC in order to publicize Lake Placid's bid for the Olympics. If that didn't work, Mr. Ruocco felt certain that the New York Daily News would cover the story. The third time Bill mentioned the plan, Mickey suggested that the matter be left in God's hands.

Mr. Ruocco didn't have much to say for a mile or two. Then he warned Mickey, "Should I have a heart attack, my nitro pills are in the glove compartment."

Mickey didn't drive in those days, and wondered how she would manage to safely set baby Denise down, take over driving the car, park it, and then safely administer nitro pills to Mr. Ruocco. For a while, Mickey forgot to worry about Denny's long, fast hike, and quietly prayed for Mr. Ruocco's good health.

Along the side of the road through the Notch, there was always a bit of snow. Always the optimist, Denny told himself that the slushy road made for soft walking. The Notch was heavily wooded and the road made lots of twists and turns. The Wilmington Notch was known to be a pretty treacherous stretch of road, and through the years, lots of dreadful car accidents happened along that road, even in the summer. But it was a beautiful road if you had the chance to walk it, under the cover of trees, the roaring river along the side of the road at many points. Almost two hours in, Denny passed the entrance to the Whiteface Mountain Ski Center. At the Blue Bowl Restaurant, which a couple years later became The Hungry Trout

Restaurant, three ladies and a little boy were waving at him and shouted, "Go, Denny, go!"

Then Denny went over a bridge and saw the Flume, a roaring waterfall that he hadn't noticed as they drove the route a few days earlier. After passing the Flume, Denny started to realize that a small brown hound dog had fallen in with him. There were an increasing number of hotels, houses, and restaurants and there were people in front of each one, waving and shouting, taking time out of their day to cheer him on. Denny couldn't figure out how everyone knew he was coming along.

Clara Hazelton, the Wilmington correspondent for the newspaper, stood outside her shop in the middle of Wilmington and had a great view of Denny Miller's arrival in town. Though he was walking well off to the side of the road, traffic had built up solidly behind him. Cars had pulled off along the side of the road so that the drivers could jump out and cheer him on. Then other cars couldn't get by. Clara couldn't recall ever having seen so many cars parked in the middle of town, especially at 8:40 on a gray Monday morning.

Clara saw Ernie and Ada Schultz parked at the foot of Bonnie View Road, holding up traffic behind them. Ernie was honking and waving, and it looked like Ada was giving him the business. "Get out of the way, dunderhead. What do you think you're doing? We're blocking everyone's way." Ernie and Ada were on their way to make a delivery of ten dozen fresh eggs to the Pine Knot Restaurant.

Clara saw one of the school board trustees, who also served unofficially as truant officer chasing after Professor Balch who was coming down the road with a station wagon bulging with kids. When he stopped the wagon, she stopped her car and jumped out. Clara didn't hear her say, "Where do you think you're going?"

Professor Balch exclaimed, "I don't know, I'm being taken!" As the kids jumped out of the wagon, Clara looked back to see Mr. Miller the marching mailman, and noticed there was a small dog following him. "How juicy," thought Clara, already thinking of how to put this in her weekly news column. "Man's Best Friend Often Mailman's Worst Nightmare, I don't know, something along these lines, maybe?" Clara looked back at the school children and their teacher who must have finished explaining their absence from school. The whole gang, including the trustee from the school board, was cheering loudly, and hopping up and down as Denny Miller got closer and closer.

The WIRD station car pulled in next to Clara. Fred Ellers jumped out, and tried to talk to everybody he could. He recorded some short enthusiastic exclamations, but mostly people wanted to hoot and holler, not talk with the man from the radio station. Fortunately, Mr. Ellers found Miss Hazelton. As Denny hotfooted it past them, Mr. Ellers recorded a very lengthy interview for the station.

As Denny passed Mr. Balch's group, Denny thought, "Can't let the kids down!" Denny was naturally very friendly, and was happy to wave at everyone and freely shared a warm smile with everyone he came into contact with. As a mailman, Denny was used to saying, "Howdy ma'am" with a tip of the hat, and a smile many, many times a day. "Maybe being the center of attention isn't so bad after all," thought Denny.

Those who saw Denny walk that day remarked on the constancy of his pace. Some people joked that he had a metronome in his pocket, in fact many years later he still hadn't overcome the nickname "the human metronome." One reporter went so far as to state that "Denny was described as pure ped-o-metric poetry every step of the way." Yet another reporter referred to Denny's legs as "precision machines."

Another three miles down the road, just past Hardy's corners, Denny walked around a bend in the road and Paleface came into view. Denny thought briefly about Valentine's dinner a few nights earlier, and it occurred to him that he was getting hungry for lunch, but it was only about 9:30am Then Denny realized that there was an enormous mass of people outside of Paleface along the side of the road, and he remembered the hike he was on. He picked up his pace so the audience wouldn't be disappointed.

As he drew closer, an older gentleman approached him. "I'll walk with you for a while, if you could use the company, son," Doc said.

"Sure, I'll be glad to have the company, but I have to move quickly, you understand," said Denny.

"No problem," said Doc, "go as fast as you like, I'll try to keep up as best I can. It looks like your little dog is having a great adventure!"

"Well," said Denny, "he sort of adopted me in Wilmington, but it is kind of fun having him along. I worry about him getting home and I hope he doesn't get hit by a car on account of me. But he seems to be very street smart."

To Denny's surprise, Doc had no difficulty whatsoever keeping up with Denny.

Doc told Denny, "The ladies in the kitchen at Paleface are worried about you and want to make sure you have enough to eat, to keep you going. They loaded me down here with some of Bea Lincoln's famous oatmeal cookies, a couple of sandwiches and a giant soda pop. One of our ladies heard on the radio that you like that brand new yellow soda, Mountain Dew."

Denny slowed down a little bit. The meal Doc just described sounded like a luxury, seven course meal. "Thank you, sir, I am most obliged. And I was just thinking about the fact I was getting a bit hungry." Denny had a few bites of a roast beef sandwich, two cookies and gave back the rest of the food. "Please tell the ladies it hit the spot. I am very grateful." Then Doc passed Denny the soda. "Sometimes what you hear on the news is true," Denny said to Doc with a grin. "I don't know what it is about this stuff, but it just tastes like the Adirondacks to me!"

Doc said, "Oh, I have a surprise for you, son," and passed Denny an envelope. "We took up a collection for you. The Paleface staff and the guests this weekend made contributions and here's $24 to add to your funds. I also wrote you out a letter good for a free weekend in our best room at Paleface. I want you and your family to join us as our guests, and I'll take care of your meals, skis, and lift tickets plus we have complimentary babysitting. I've got you down for two nights, arriving February the 22nd!"

Denny was shocked, and hardly knew what to say. "Golly, sir. Gee, this is so generous. Please tell everybody 'thank you.' I just don't know what to say." Denny put the envelope in his pocket. "I have to tell you sir, you are a very fast walker. Maybe you should do a fifty mile hike yourself," Denny said, smiling.

"Please, no need to call me sir, just Doc will do. I'll leave the hiking to you, Denny but what you're doing is very important. You know, you have become quite a hero for people today. I've got to get back to business, but we'll see you next week. Godspeed, Dennis Miller!" said Doc, then he turned and walked back toward Paleface, stopping to leave the rest of the food he was supposed to have given to Denny with Mickey and Mr. Ruocco.

Denny walked on, just about a mile and a half more to the center of the town of Jay. At that point, Denny was very conversational with that small brown hound that was still tagging along. Denny had taken to calling him "Jay" since he saw the sign a while back, welcoming him to the Town of Jay. Route 86 came to its abrupt end, and Denny turned left headed up Route 9N toward AuSable Forks. The little dog made a stop at the firehouse, and never caught back up. Denny was back on his own again.

It was just about 11am when Denny arrived at the Lyma Club in AuSable Forks. Denny stopped for a couple minutes, had a little bit of his grape, pineapple, lemon, and honey concoction, changed his socks and shoes, and had a drink of water. One big sigh, and Denny continued on his way.

The next town was Keeseville, which was about two and a half hours from the rest stop in AuSable. As Denny passed one house, a woman flew out the front door, ran down the walkway handed him an envelope and planted a smooch on his left cheek. The note said, "Good luck, Denny," and the envelope had $2 in it.

A long walk meant a lot of time to think, and sometimes Denny thought he could think for hours without realizing what he was thinking. Denny kept his mind entertained with stories, songs, and recollections to pass the time during that long leg of his journey.

In Peru, Denny took another break. He felt he just had to stop and give his legs a couple of minutes, but on the other hand he worried if he stopped too long he wouldn't get back up and finish.

In any case, the crowd was so loud and so supportive, he just knew he had to continue. After a twenty-minute break, Denny was back on the road and back on pace for the last leg of his hike.

Denny really appreciated having company for that last 8.5 miles. Plattsburgh DJ "Tiny" Hare from radio station WIRY walked with Denny, and asked him lots of questions. Denny gave short answers, and concentrated on completing his task. It helped to have someone who had the energy to set the necessary pace.

A quarter mile from the finish line, Tiny said, "We're almost there, Denny!"

Before he could think about what he was doing, and pushed on by a rush of adrenaline, Denny jogged the last quarter mile, waved at everyone, gave his wife a hug and then got in Mr. Ruocco's car for the rest of the ride to the center of Plattsburgh.

And so it was that Dennis Miller entered the city limits of Plattsburgh, fifty miles from his starting point in Lake Placid having walked for ten hours and fifty-seven minutes, plus thirty-nine minutes over the course of two breaks for a grand total overall time of eleven hours and thirty-six minutes, beating that Marine from North Carolina by eight minutes!

There was a large crowd of well-wishers at the Court House Square, and many of them appeared to be very important people given the fancy suits they were wearing. The first man to approach Denny was Postmaster MacKenzie from Plattsburgh. He asked Denny if he had a letter to deliver.

Denny replied, "Oh yes, I almost forgot why I was here!" He handed the letter to Postmaster MacKenzie, which his boss had placed in his custody earlier that day. Denny couldn't believe it was the same day he had put the envelope in his pocket.

Everyone from the Plattsburgh post office was there, and many postal carriers from other towns were there as well to see one of their own celebrated. The Regional Director shook Denny's hand and told him how proud he had made mail carriers everywhere.

After that, the boss's boss from New York City, introduced himself to Denny and applauded Denny's patriotism for doing his part to set an example of physical fitness and following through on a challenge he had committed himself to. The Mayor of Lake Placid, the Honorable Robert J. Peacock, was also there, and announced to the crowd that Denny was invited to the bobsled races and the ice show the following weekend. He would be presented with a special plaque.

Mr. Ruocco expressed great appreciation to Lake Placid village officials, the people at the radio station, and the sponsors that contributed to the $100 prize. In Mr. Ruocco's speech, he listed two dozen people to thank, and he became most excited talking about how glorious it would be to have Lake Placid host the 1968 Winter Olympics, how glad he was to have Mr. MacKenzie join the organizing committee. "Thanks especially to Mr. Miller here. You just never know. Publicity is a funny thing. This hike to Plattsburgh might just be the thing that puts the Olympic bid over the top. One thing is always connected to another. If Lake Placid *ever* gets to host the Winter Olympics again, Denny—" he paused for dramatic effect. "You can claim *THAT* credit for that yourself!" The crowd roared with applause.

Denny's wife gave him a big hug and planted a kiss on his lips as the crowd continued to yell, clap, and cheer.

The next man to shake Denny's hand was the Mayor of Plattsburgh, the Honorable Robert Tyrell.

One of the reporters in the crowd shouted out, "How do you feel, Denny?"

Denny replied, "Tired, sore, $100 richer, and AWFULLY glad it's over," which became the headline in the newspaper. Then Denny said, "I want to thank all those who helped me on my adventure. Everybody has been just great. It really helped me keep going having everybody out there cheering me on. If I had ever thought about giving up, I couldn't do it with everyone counting on me."

A kid shouted from the crowd, "What will you do with your hard earned $100?"

"My wife will take it over!" Denny shouted back with a grin.

With the TV cameras rolling, someone asked Denny, "When did you first begin feeling tired?"

Off the top of his head, Denny said, "Right after I got out of bed." Everyone in the crowd laughed, but then Denny added, "I did pretty well until I got to AuSable Forks. I hadn't planned on stopping and resting anywhere specific, but rather only where I needed to stop. Problem is once you stop and rest it is very hard to get started back up again. A fresh pair of socks and shoes helped a lot, but then I had to stop and rest again in Peru. Anyway, the mail got delivered. That's the important part." Everyone saw that interview on the late news on TV. The story was featured on both WPTZ in Plattsburgh, and WCAX TV across the lake in Burlington, Vermont.

Then, Denny and Mickey were put in a fancy vehicle with the mayors and the postmasters and taken quickly away for a fancy formal dinner. It happened so fast, Denny didn't have time to dread it. Mickey thought to herself, "It doesn't get any better than this!" At the Hotel Witherill they were more than happy to waive their regular dinner attire rules to accommodate a sweaty postman, his proud wife, and their baby girl.

At the end of the day, Doc Fitz-Gerald wrote a letter to the editor about the importance of physical fitness. Doc tied Denny Miller and President Kennedy's fitness challenge to the local ski program sponsored by the Rotary Club.

## '63 I Can't Walk Very Well

Denny had fully planned to go to work on Tuesday but his leg muscles were just too sore. When asked, Denny responded, "I feel pretty good except I can't walk very well!" Denny's buddies at the post office thought it would help to work out the kinks if he would do his regular job that day. After all, it was just a short five mile walk. Denny told everyone that his wife Mickey still made him do his chores at home, sore legs or not.

## '63 Snowflake Race

Paleface was able to boast on their own Pete Pelkey, who won the final Snowflake Race of the season. Pete edged out Bernie O'Grady of Whiteface by one second. The third place finisher, Jacques Thibault, was also from Paleface. Imagine the humiliation for the folks at Whiteface, being beaten by the little tribe of skiers from Paleface!

## '63 A Hero's Reward

February 23rd, 1963 was one of the busiest days Paleface ever had.

There was a lot of snow on the mountain as a result of a major blizzard several weeks earlier, plus several minor snowfalls since. The warmest days hadn't been warm enough to melt snow. The perfect conditions coincided with a holiday weekend.

Denny and Mickey Miller enjoyed the skiing. They had taken an early morning lesson with Pete Pelkey and were ready to strike out on their own. Mickey was doing okay with the skiing, but had a fear of heights and was afraid of getting on the moving chairs.

That morning, immediately ahead of the Millers were two young boys: Doug and Dana-D Peck, Jane and Dana's young sons. Doug was about eight and Dana-D Peck was about five, and overdue for a growth spurt. As the chair before them took off with an older couple, Doug and Dana-D hustled to get in position so they could meet the on-coming chair.

As always, the boys landed in their seats perfectly.

On that morning, young Dana-D had failed to raise his ski tips, and the dangling tips of his skis clipped a snowbank just as the chair was getting ready to take off. Dana-D was flung from the chair and landed face-first in the snowbank.

Billy Ward, who worked at Paleface as a lift attendant during the weekends, hit the kill switch and the chairs stopped their continuous laps around the base station. Billy helped Dana-D out of the snowbank, brushed him off and easily lifted him up into the chair next to his brother.

Dana-D was fine, perhaps a bit chagrined. His brother told

him he looked so funny, flying into the snowbank. Dana-D got the giggles trying to picture himself flying into the snow bank. Together Doug and Dana-D lowered the safety bar into place and waited for the chairs to start moving again. Dana-D learned his lesson that day, to never fail to raise your tips when you get on the lift.

The whole scene wasn't lost on Mickey Miller, who had been dreading trying to get on the lift without instructor Pelkey's assistance. That time around Mickey got lucky. Mickey and Denny got into the chair while it was still stopped, and lowered the safety bar before Billy Ward turned the chairlift back on.

The first time up the mountain, Mickey had clutched the safety bar with both hands and closed her eyes the whole way, telling Denny to let her know when the chair was almost to the top. The second time was a little better. The Millers could hear the boys in the chair ahead of them, singing at the top of their voices, in unison at a very fast pace.

Mickey could hear the words: "The ants go marching one by one, hurrah, hurrah," through verse upon verse in their quest to get out of the rain. As Mickey listened to the verses, she forgot about the heights and smiled, thinking of the boys in the chair ahead of her, and thinking about her own youngster who was enjoying the free babysitting service inside the nice warm lodge.

By the time the boys got off the lift up at the top, they had completed thirty-two verses, beating the previous record by two verses.

The song was replaying over and over in Mickey Miller's mind all afternoon. A little later, Mickey and Denny were slowly making their way down the mountain. They stopped to watch Dana-D Peck navigating the T-Bar.

It looked like Dana-D was having a tough time of it. He wasn't tall enough or heavy enough for his skis to maintain good contact with the snow. There was a little dip, just before the last hill, prior to reaching the mid-station, which was always the spot that seemed most problematic. That trip, that day, Dana-D held on. He had both arms wrapped tightly around the mid-pole, and with one leg stretched as far as he could stretch it, and the end of the ski pointed down, he was just barely able to stay on. It looked like quite a fete, and the Millers smiled at each other to see the triumph of Dana-D's accomplishment.

Near the end of the afternoon, Mickey and Denny saw the boys again. The Millers were resting in a glade with two other couples, enjoying a brief break. First Doug zoomed past, going as fast as he could, hit a little jump, landed back on the ground and zoomed off down the trail.

Moments later, Dana-D came down the trail. Skiers that age rarely went slowly, and rarely made those back and forth motions that slowed them down. Preferring rather to bend the knees, tuck the poles into their armpits and bomb down the trail as fast as they could. Dana-D hadn't hit the jump on the trail since the previous weekend, and it had changed since then. Perhaps there was a bit more snow.

Dana-D hit the jump, which had a little lip on it. Dana-D flew into the air, higher than expected. And the path of motion resulted in three quarters of a back flip, which meant that Dana-D landed on his back instead of on his skies. Moments earlier, Dana-D had it in his mind to impress the bunch of lazy skiers resting on the side of the trail.

After the resting skiers checked on Dana-D, who was fine of course, and after Dana-D politely thanked them for checking, Dana-D reflected on "that old truth that pride goes before a fall." The bruised ego of a young child heals quickly. And Dana-D beamed with pride later in the afternoon when Mrs. Miller told Jane Peck that Dana-D was a great skier and an extraordinary young man. Mickey said, "You should be very proud."

Dana-D said, "Thank you, ma'am."

Jane added, "That's very nice of you to say."

The Millers checked on the baby, who was happily occupied and tended by the babysitter. Then Denny and Mickey headed for the lounge.

## '63 Glühwein

By the fireplace, Doc was passing out glasses of Glühwein, his own secret recipe, carefully crafted and perfected over the course of many years to the point of ritual. Only Doc and Jean were permitted to make the mulled wine; not even their own children were entrusted with the secret recipe.

First a glass of water was heated, with a quarter of a cup of honey. Three cinnamon sticks broken into one inch pieces were added with a heaping spoonful each of nutmeg, coriander and allspice. An orange was cut into quarters and cloves were pressed into the orange which was then added to the mixture. Next, a bottle of wine was added. Then came the non-traditional secret ingredients, just a small, subtle amount of each so as to protect the secret. Five blue berries, half of a plum, and a single ring of pineapple were added to the pot.

Just as the pot looked like it was about to begin boiling, the heat was turned off. The pot was covered and allowed to sit for about two hours. The contents of the pot were strained twice, then brought back nearly to the boiling point and served hot. After a cold, vigorous day on the slopes, a hot spicy wine helped everyone relax and warm their hands and bellies at the same time.

## '63 Introducing Red Nadeau

The Millers thanked Doc for their glasses of Glühwein. Once everyone had a glass in their hands, Doc proposed a toast: "To a great day of skiing!" Everyone raised a glass, and added their own version of "here, here." Then a clean-cut young man brought out a stool and placed it a short distance from the fireplace in the lounge.

His name was Royal, but everyone called him Red. Red grew up in Chateauguay, New York, not far from the Canadian border. Red Nadeau was a very serious young man, graduated at the top of his small high school class then went to college on a scholarship. The priesthood almost became Red's calling, but in the end, Red's passions for folk music and science won out. Red was a regular at

Paleface during weekends and school breaks. During the school weeks, Red taught science classes to high school students in the southern Adirondacks.

Red opened his guitar case and placed it at his feet, put a dollar bill and a pocketful of change inside the case with a handwritten sign that said, "Thank you for supporting the arts." Red climbed up on his tall stool and dreamily, lovingly began singing and strumming his favorite songs.

Mostly Red sang obscure hymns and local folk songs. Occasionally he would play a recognizable song that would get people humming or even singling along, such as Ray Charles' "I Can't Stop Loving You," Nat King Cole's "Ramblin' Rose," and The Drifters' "Up On The Roof." More often than not, he quietly sang songs most people weren't familiar with.

There were two lounges, and Red set his stool between them. Both lounges were organized in rectangular fashion, with dark brown leather sofas facing each other on the long side, and two chairs facing each other on the short sides. The seat and back cushions of the chairs were a bright, cheerful orange colored Naugahyde.

In between was a coffee table with dice, decks of cards, picture books, magazines, a backgammon set, chess, and checkers on shelves beneath the table. On top there were many coasters and ashtrays.

Denny Miller and his wife Mickey were seated on one sofa. On older gentleman named Leon Doremus was sitting in one of the chairs. A young man named Jim Bailey sat next to Mr. Doremus. Jim had grown up in nearby Elizabethtown and went on to teach high school mathematics in Beekmantown, north of Plattsburgh. Jim was spending the weekend at Paleface with a couple of buddies he knew from having been camp counselors at Camp Poke-O-Moonshine in Willsboro a few years earlier. A young, fashionably dressed couple sat on the other sofa. Ribbons of cigarette smoke curled their way toward the rafters in the tall A-Frame ceilings above.

In between songs, Red would briefly join conversations in the lounge, and often his next song choice fit the subject matter. Red's singing and playing was soft enough that nearby conversations were possible, yet loud enough to set an upbeat mood.

Five days after Denny's epic journey, Mickey was still excited to tell anyone she could about her husband's hike. Denny, though happy to be around people would rather have talked about almost anything else. Mr. Doremus was fascinated with the story and asked lots of questions, and everyone around the table contributed a question or two. Mickey told everyone about the potion that Denny carried, and how his father Gus, who had a passion for good nutrition, had concocted the potion to help Denny keep his energy level up. Denny thought that it tasted something like the Glühwein, only not nearly as good. As Mickey concluded telling Denny's story, Red was finishing a song about a hardworking harmonica playing lumberjack from Saranac Lake.

Doc then began to talk about the fifty mile hike fad. Almost instantly, Doc went into his "preacher's voice." Red set down his guitar. Doc had a way of telling stories that pulled everyone in.

"Let me tell you about another local hiking hero! Back in 1837 there was a man named Ebenezer Emmons. It is said that he is responsible for naming the Adirondacks by twisting around a Mohawk Indian phrase *ratirontaks*. Of course, we can't call this place RAT IRON TACKS, Adirondacks just sounds much better. Actually, the Mohawk Indians really did mean the phrase to be an insult, aimed at their rivals, the Algonquin Indians. The phrase ratirontaks meant 'they eat trees' generally, and perhaps 'they eat bark' specifically, and 'they' most certainly referred to the Algonquin Indians. Neither tribe really made their homes in the Adirondacks, but both hunted and regularly passed through the area, and sometimes they had very uncomfortable encounters. But back to old Ebenezer Emmons. Emmons was a famous geologist who climbed most of the tall peaks in the Adirondacks while mapping and cataloging the rocks and rock formations. In 1837 Ebenezer Emmons and his hiking party made the first recorded climb up Mount Marcy. Also on that journey, Emmons finally completed his quest to track down the headwaters, or starting point of the East Fork of the Hudson River. There is a very small pond very near the Summit of Mount Marcy, which I understand is a tiny jewel of a pond. They named the little pond 'Lake Tear of the Clouds.' I can just imagine how beautiful that little lake must be."

Jim Bailey raised his hand suddenly, as an eager student in school would do. "Yes sir," said Jim, "I can attest to the beauty of Lake Tear of the Clouds. You see, I am an Adirondack 46-er which means I have climbed all forty-six Adirondack mountains that are taller than 4000 feet above sea level. Some of them I have climbed several times. So far there have been only a couple hundred people who have done this. I started with Giant Mountain in '56 and I finished on Emmons Mountain, just last summer, after I got back from a six-week voyage to Alaska in my VW bus with my college roommate. Of course, Emmons Mountain was named after and probably named by Ebenezer Emmons." All at once, Jim Bailey realized he had been blurting his story as if he had to finish it within a certain amount of time. "Oh, but I only meant to tell you about Lake Tear of the Clouds," Jim finished with a proud smile.

"Well, goodness sake, man," exclaimed Doc, "it would seem we have another local hiking legend in our midst. I would like to raise a toast to our Adirondack hiking heroes, Denny Miller, Jim Bailey, and Ebenezer Emmons. I would also add President Theodore Roosevelt and my late friend Mr. Art Draper. Here, here!"

For those that hadn't heard about Art Draper, Doc went on to explain that Mr. Draper had been so inspired by the sight of Mount Marcy that he devoted his life to making the Adirondacks more well known and more accessible, particularly to skiers, as the General Manager of Whiteface Mountain. Mr. Draper had been a reporter and was assigned to cover the 100th anniversary of Ebenezer Emmons' climb. On that day in August, 1937, Art Draper fell madly in love—love at first sight, you might say. He later became a Mount Marcy climber himself.

Doc continued, "Now, you may notice I added President Roosevelt to my toast! Of course, you know President Roosevelt was our Vice President under President William McKinley. Teddy of course was also a former New York Governor. Once upon a time, Teddy Roosevelt had a hunting camp which he named Tahawus. In the Mohawk, Indian language Tahawus meant 'cloud splitter.' On the 14th of September, 1901, Teddy had just completed a hike up Mount Marcy. He was relaxing back at camp when a messenger brought him word that President McKinley who had been shot the week before had seemed to be declining rapidly. It was clear that Teddy Roosevelt must immediately return to Washington. Teddy and his party hiked ten miles down the southwest face of the mountain to Long Lake. At Long Lake, a stage coach was hired. The stage coach took the party to North Creek, and today that route is known as the Roosevelt-Marcy Trail. And as you know, President McKinley didn't survive so that epic hike ended with an oath on a Bible in Washington, D.C. as Teddy Roosevelt was appointed to the high position of President of the United States of America!"

Jim Bailey interjected, "Well, someday I'd like to become President of the Adirondack Mountain Club."

"Well I say, make it happen, Mr. Bailey," said Doc.

Jim replied, "Oh, just call me Beetle."

"Okay, Beetle," Doc paused and thought for a moment. "I kind of like that nickname, but there has to be a limit to your future success if you take on a moniker such as that."

Doc had studied up on the fifty mile hiking challenge since meeting Denny Miller, and shared the results of his research. "One day last year, President Kennedy's U.S. Marine commandant came across an old executive order issued by President Teddy Roosevelt that challenged every U.S. Marine to complete a fifty mile march within a twenty hour period to indicate sufficient physical fitness for adequate military preparedness. As you know, our modern Presidents have begun to take an interest in physical fitness. Eight years ago, President Eisenhower established The President's Council on Physical Fitness and Sports. President Kennedy wanted to take these initiatives even further. As President-Elect, President Kennedy published an article titled *The Soft American* in the December 1960 issue of *Sports Illustrated*. President Kennedy noted that changes in the world and in the work place meant that people were getting less exercise. In an automated world, machines are doing everything for us. Kids take the bus to school instead of walking. It is wonderful that our women don't have to take buckets of clothes to the rivers and beat them against rocks to get them clean, but that was more exercise than putting clothes in a washing machine." Doc enjoyed adding points of his own to President Kennedy's message.

Doc continued, "President Kennedy asked one of his Generals to report on the strength and stamina of the modern Marine as compared to Teddy Roosevelt's Marines. Further, President Kennedy asked his Press Secretary, Pierre Salinger to investigate the fitness of his staff in the White House. From all accounts, it was clear to Mr. Salinger that President Kennedy meant for 'HE' himself to make the hike, which became something of a running joke in the press. Mr. Salinger didn't look like the sort of man who would be making a fifty mile hike any time soon. Finally, just six days before Denny made his journey Mr. Salinger made a humorous but firm public statement that left no doubt that he would be declining the honor of making the walk, and that it would no longer be necessary for himself to prove the fitness of the President's staff since Bobby Kennedy had already proven that the President's staff was physically fit. Of course, Bobby Kennedy is President Kennedy's own baby brother, who serves our country as Attorney General. Recently he completed the fifty mile hiking challenge on an impulse wearing leather oxford shoes through snow and slush. If you think young Denny here made his hike on a whim, you would certainly be placing him in distinguished company. What's more, I am made to understand that everyone who completes the challenge in less than twelve hours will be entitled to a Bronze Medal to be presented by the Amos Alonzo Stagg Foundation. So, I guess Mr. Miller, you will be entitled to one of those medals!"

Doc concluded by telling his audience that he must move along. "Don't miss our dinner special tonight; our man Chef Bowen makes a great steak dinner and our Paleface gals make the best deserts in the North Country. At eight we're showing a movie in the loft called

*Winter Wonderland,* filmed at Whiteface and Paleface. And at nine there is dancing with the Bob Luppy trio. In the meantime, please enjoy Red's wonderful folk music here."

## '63 James Bailey

Jim had been thinking about Denny Miller's amazing walk, and had mentioned it to the students in his math class at Beekmantown High School, just outside of Plattsburgh, New York. Jim's retelling of Denny's hike succeeded in inspiring three of his students to recruit Jim to serve as their coach.

Jim and his students would not set out to best Denny's time merely to prove that they could complete the walk for their own personal satisfaction. Mr. Bailey preferred to walk more slowly and enjoy the trip, and wasn't really interested in exploiting the journey for the sake of publicity.

Jim planned out a route of backroads that led from Beekmantown to John Brown's grave, preferring a path less travelled. However, that trip measured out to be a distance of fifty-six miles rather than fifty miles. So, Mr. Bailey set out from the famous abolitionist's grave to find the proper starting point, and had a flat tire before he could complete the task.

And then, as frequently is the case in late winter, the weather forecast on the appointed day was a huge disappointment. The walk was postponed indefinitely, and then the momentum was lost. The guys never did make that copycat walk.

## '63 Outstanding Sportsmanship Award

In March, Denny was honored with the Schaeffer Brewing Company's award for outstanding sportsmanship and a special plaque from the community of Lake Placid was also presented at the North American Invitational Indoor Speed Skating Championships.

## '63 Miss White at the Volunteer Firemen's Convention

Doc and Jean's friends stopped by for a visit in the middle of June. Tom and Ruth were the proprietors of Keegan's White Brook Motel in Wilmington. They had left the business in the hands of their son for the afternoon. It was a beautiful, sunny day, and unseasonably mild. A shuffleboard course had just been installed at Paleface, and the two couples enjoyed a couple of games of shuffleboard, which was so popular in the Adirondacks at that time that there were organized leagues and the standings were published in the sports section of the newspapers.

The Keegan's team beat the Fitz-Gerald's team at shuffleboard that afternoon. Then the two couples relaxed on the patio near the front door of Paleface. Just as they were getting comfortable, Doc and Jean's grandson was placed in their charge while his parents went on a trail ride.

Jean entertained her grandson, who was quickly outgrowing his mechanical swing. At the same time, Jean enjoyed conversing with Ruth Keegan.

Jean complimented Ruth on her pretty, cream-colored sweater, adorned with a series of circles on the front, which she combined with bright yellow pants. The sweater was a gift from Ruth's son Dennis, who was a second lieutenant in the Air Force and at that time was stationed in England.

Tom and Doc enjoyed a glass of beer, and got to talking about business. "I've got a good story for you!" Tom told Doc. "You may have been aware that we hosted the Northern New York Volunteer Fireman's Convention in Wilmington, and all our units were filled, which is pretty good for the month of June! As you know the downside with conventions is sometimes they can get out of control. You know volunteer fireman are hardworking, dedicated heroes. They are, however, a fun-loving crowd when they get together." Tom moved his chair closer to Doc's. Meanwhile, Jean took her grandson from the swing, and started to rock him in her arms, thinking he might fall asleep.

"So, let me set the stage," Tom said, returning to his story. "You know George Broeck in Wilmington. His pretty white cow was standing in her pasture munching on lush green grass, minding her own business. Along comes one of my guests, who decides to assist in Miss White's escape from her enclosure, most likely not in the full light of day. Imagine Miss White being led for a mile along Route 86, going from bush, to shrub, to shed to avoid the troopers." Tom shifted his torso from side to side, forward and back, as if he was demonstrating hopping from one hiding spot to the next.

"Somewhere along the way, poor Miss White got artistically decorated with a can of green spray paint. What happened next, so it was told, was Miss White was led up the stairs to one of my upper motel units. I can't imagine how that feat was accomplished. Along the way, Miss White was introduced to conventioneers as 'my new girlfriend' by my esteemed guest." Tom took a drink of his beer while Doc encouraged Tom's retelling of the tale of Miss White with a hearty chuckle.

"And then," Tom continued, "It's not polite to say, but it was reported that Miss White was 'put to bed' in my guest's room. Miss White must be an early riser, because when the sun came up the next morning, Trooper Cavellero and Trooper Anasky found Miss White tied to the Whiteface Mountain Memorial Highway sign." The sign at the junction of route 86 and route 431 was not far from the White Brook Motel, but it was a good distance to lead a cow.

"You can imagine the surprised look on Mrs. Broeck's face to see two state troopers standing at her front door leading a green and white cow. Trooper Cavellero told us that Mrs. Broeck bemoaned the fact that she didn't have a camera on hand to take a picture of Miss White, who might perhaps need to be renamed Miss Green." Tom spread his arms wide and expressed his opinion that the incident was worthy of national news coverage.

"Anyway," Tom continued, "Mr. Broeck wasn't quite as amused as his wife was. George and his sons gave Miss White a thorough bubble bath and scrubbed as best they could, but unfortunately, they were unable to get their cow back the way she was. On account of Mr. and Mrs. Broeck's concern about contamination of the milk, I have found myself responsible for paying for the equivalent of five quarts of milk a day until Miss White's milk is again considered to be safe." Tom put his head down between open palms, as if expressing the sort of extreme financial hardship that might bankrupt someone.

Returning to form, and suspending his feigned distress, Tom concluded, "Interestingly, that morning, Miss White's room was the cleanest room. As for the rest of our rooms, it would seem like our guests had loads and loads of fun. We had a lot of work to do to clean them up!" Tom tilted his head in mock sympathy toward his friend, and competitor, whom he had seemingly bested, and said, "So, don't feel too bad about losing that convention bid to us!" Tom concluded. The four friends shared a hearty laugh, just restrained enough not to wake the sleeping baby.

The two couples went on to talk about their kids, what they expected the summer season to be like, and plans for travel after the end of the summer season.

## '63 Lady in the Lake

After Labor Day, the Adirondacks could be desolate. For those in the business of tending to tourists, there were so few customers that there was hardly any point in remaining open for business until the foliage began to turn. In the fall of 1963, Paleface remained open. A couple of motel rooms were occupied. A few lunches and dinners were served, mostly to local townspeople. Jean made a trip to visit friends in Mountain Lakes, New Jersey and Doc set out on a fishing trip with friends to Labrador, Canada.

Chuck tended to business at Paleface while Dana and a crew of men worked on clearing the new trails Doc hoped to debut over the coming winter. A new T-Bar lift—or bum-tow as Doc preferred to call it—was being added, and this time the plan was set around the cable splicer's schedule. The new trails, named Teepee, Bow, Peace Pipe, and the Lower Big Horn were typical novice and intermediate type trails like most of the existing trails at Paleface. Another new trail was being cleared for expert skiers and racing. This trail was named the Snow Eagle and was modeled after a famous run of the same name at the Grey Rocks Inn in the Laurentian Mountains of Quebec.

The checkbook would reflect the cost of being open, as workers outnumbered customers by a frightful margin.

Captain Frank F. Pabst and his crew of club members walked through the door of Paleface late in the afternoon one Sunday in mid-September. If anyone had been there to notice, their entrance was full of the sort of swagger you might expect to see from men who had been through an exhilarating ordeal and lived to tell about it.

The Wreck Raiders had spent the day in Lake Placid, on what was supposed to be a leisurely final dive of the season. Instead it turned out to be a day of mystery and adventure. The guys were thirsty and hungry, and they had a need to tell their story. Never mind there was only an audience of one, or an audience of four if you counted the heads mounted over the bar. Monday morning would be coming fast and the guys would be going their separate ways for the week and for the season.

Chuck had been sitting in the lodge lounge when the guys came in. In front of Chuck was a pile of paperwork, catalogs, contracts, and files. After working with his parents at Paleface since it opened, Chuck was ready for a new venture and was planning to make his living as a photographer. He had the plan all worked out in his head, but he knew he needed to put something sensible on paper to get the funds he needed to furnish a studio.

During the summer, the bar area had been remodeled, and now Chuck could get to the other side of the bar from the lounge without going all the way around through the kitchen. It didn't take Chuck long to set each of the guys up with a mug of beer. Frank raised a mug and offered a toast: "Here's to the Wreck Raiders, the Witch (referring to their boat) and the Lady in the Lake." The Wreck Raider's first favorite hobby was diving, and their second favorite hobby was drinking beer. Each man finished their first mug of beer in one continuous chug, even the fellows that were still in high school.

Chuck served each man a second beer and drew a draught for himself as well. With the toast out of the way and a new audience, the day's events were retold.

Frank Pabst introduced The Wreck Raiders diving club members. Then Frank talked about having gotten up very early to get together all the gear they would need for their last dive of the season. They wanted to make it a memorable trip, and go somewhere a little out of the ordinary. Instead of Lake Champlain the divers were headed for Lake Placid, and more specifically selected the area of Pulpit Rock, about three quarters of a mile up the east shore. It was thought that the waters there were deep and clear and perhaps there was a possibility of finding underwater caves.

Of course, once all the gear was gathered, there was a road trip. It would take almost an hour and a half to get from Plattsburgh to Lake Placid. The town of Lake Placid is situated on Mirror Lake, with the body of water named Lake Placid just a little bit to the north. The guys put into the lake approximately 11:30am. The divers planned to take turns, diving in pairs and exploring the depths of the lake. The very first pair to enter the water was a sargent from Plattsburgh Airforce Base and a high school student from Rousses Point.

The sargent and the student dived to a depth of about ninety-eight feet. The water was clear and cold. The temperature at that depth remained at about 38 degrees year round. Something caught their eye. There was a bit of a shelf. Something was on the shelf. As they drew closer, it looked like an Egyptian mummy. They drew closer still. It looked like a department store mannequin. They couldn't believe what they were seeing. It was a body—a human body. And there was a rope around the neck, attached to something, buried in the three feet of silt at the bottom of the lake. With blood pumping, they swam for the surface. Back at the top of the lake, both the sargent and the student talked at once, telling the other guys about the body on the shelf near the bottom of the lake.

One of the boats was sent back to get the authorities. Another pair of divers went down to check out the find. They had taken a burlap blanket with them. As they were getting the body ready to be brought to the surface, they found a ladies' shoe near the body. They had originally thought they were dealing with a man's body, as if only men were victims of crimes or accidental drownings. The ladies shoe made some of the guys think of their girlfriends, wives, or mothers, and that filled them with an extra sense of urgency.

As they were trying to get the body on to the blanket, it quickly began to break into pieces. By the time they surfaced, all they had left was the top part of a skull. And by the time the authorities arrived, the silt at the bottom of the lake had been stirred up to the point of not being able to investigate the scene any further.

Over the next couple of hours, the guys told their story over and over until it seemed that every law enforcement official in the county knew about it. Investigators were busy at the library going through old newspapers trying to find information about anyone missing that could be the lady in the lake. Ultimately, the mystery would take some time to unravel.

As the guys would often report, it was not the first time any of the men had seen a dead body, nor the first time any of the men had brought a body from the bottom of a river or lake. They were torn between feeling empathy for the woman, while at the same time feeling proud of having discovered a marvel of science—a "scientific first." Whoever had inhabited the body had been dead a very long time. Due to the great and constant coldness at the bottom of the lake, a process called "adipocere" had occurred, which is a gradual substitution of mineral salts and other chemical substances for body tissue. Over time the body had been replaced by a cast of the person who had existed before.

Chuck listened with amazement and awe as the divers told and re-told the story, full of the sort of detail that experienced divers might like to include. Not every man got the chance to dive that day, but they all felt like they were a part of the discovery.

The guys further celebrated over sizzling steak dinners with all the usual fixings, Paleface's house specialty. Captain Pabst further entertained the crew with his Swedish accent, not his natural speaking voice, but it always seemed to accompany a couple of beers.

Captain Pabst also enjoyed telling Chuck the story about how the movie star Buster Crabbe, who famously portrayed Tarzan in the movies became an honorary member of the Wreck Raiders. He wasn't just the kind of honorary member who showed up once for an award. Buster Crabbe, who owned a boy's camp near the town of Gabriels, actually attended several meetings, and accompanied the Wreck Raiders on some of their expeditions.

After dinner, Chuck took pictures of the Wreck Raiders outside of Paleface. And with Chuck's permission, consent he didn't have the authority to give, Frank indulged another one of his hobbies–deadheading marigolds with a borrowed golf club in Chuck's mother's garden. Chuck captured some great pictures with his camera and he couldn't wait to get them developed.

## '63 Special Delivery

The next morning, Frank Pabst was back at Paleface as usual. Frank's day job was delivering orders for the Bouyea Bakery. After a very slow weekend, and with a very slow week ahead, there wasn't much to deliver, but it took about an hour for Frank to tell everyone at Paleface the story of the lady in the lake.

## '63 Another Dive

By Wednesday, the authorities were anxious to get more clues to the mystery. Frank took the day off from Bouyea's and got a couple guys together to make another trip to Lake Placid. The silt had settled, and the divers were able to find an arm and a jawbone, complete with teeth and gold fillings. The divers were also able to find the outline of the anchor that was attached to the rope that had been around the neck of the body. It was a fifty pound iron block. The divers tried to lift the block, but the rope broke, falling back to the bottom of the lake, which a local reporter described as being "like dropping lead into talcum powder." Before the divers could make another attempt to rescue the block and whatever was still attached to it, one of the divers began to bleed from his mouth and nose. They had to return to the surface. The rest of the body and the iron anchor were lost forever and never to be found again.

## '63 Doc and Jean Return

The following Tuesday, Doc returned home from his fishing trip.

Chuck was anxious to pitch his plans of starting a photography studio to Doc, though it would mean a lot less involvement in Paleface on a day to day basis. First, Chuck broke the ice by telling Doc all about Captain Pabst and the Wreck Raiders and the lady in the lake and the pictures he had taken of the guys enjoying steak dinners and golfing in the garden at Paleface. That gave Chuck a pretty good set up and he found his father surprisingly agreeable with respect to his planned new profession and business venture. What's more, Doc was willing to provide the start-up capital.

The next day, Doc inspected all the work on the new trails on the mountain and he spent the following day in the office. Jane was ready with all the bills that needed to be paid and the latest subtotal in the bank account. Fortunately, reservations were looking good for the Christmas to New Year's period and that lifted Doc's spirits. Jean returned from New Jersey after having gotten a very early start that morning. Doc and Jean retired to suite number one. There was so much news to catch up on.

Doc updated Jean on his fishing trip with Dr. Goff, Judge McNamee of Hudson, Jim Cooney of Albany, and Carl Steinhoff. The men always enjoyed their hunting and fishing trips together. Doc told Jean about their car trip to Maine, the seaplanes they took to Labrador, and how they had been unable to find the camp that first night. With the rough weather, it was tough to see exactly which of the 10,000 lakes they needed to land on. After an hour and a half, the pilot spotted a power line that led them to Wabush City. The following day they got to camp. Every day brought snow, though it was early September. In addition to catching a lot of fish and seeing a lot of wild geese, Doc landed a good-sized caribou. Doc had a perfect spot behind the bar and was looking forward to getting the caribou head back from the taxidermist. Jean had long since reconciled herself to living among mounted heads, both at home and at the lodge.

Doc told Jean about the progress on the mountain, and about Chuck's new venture. Doc and Jean agreed that would be a great opportunity for Chuck to make a living doing something he loved.

Jean told Doc about visiting with all their old friends and neighbors in Mountain Lakes, New Jersey. She went into great detail, and hadn't been particularly looking in Doc's direction. Jean paused for a moment about half an hour into her update. It became obvious that Doc was snoring, and probably had been asleep for quite some time. Jean smiled, and considered the fact that she had gotten an early start that morning. She put her glasses on the side table, and closed her eyes as well.

Jean woke from her nap a couple minutes before five, and went out to check on the restaurant. There were two groups of four in the dining room. They seemed to be very well tended, and Jean returned to the suite. There was a big stack of newspapers that had piled up while she was away. She put them in order by date, and spent the next couple of hours working her way through the pile.

Though Doc had told Jean about the Wreck Raiders, she found herself surprisingly intrigued by the story as it developed from one daily paper to the next. At first there was great controversy about who the body belonged to.

From the beginning, the authorities had zeroed in on the likelihood that the body belonged to Mrs. Mabel Smith Douglass of Philadelphia, Pennsylvania. Mrs. Douglass was a widow who had been staying in Lake Placid and had disappeared at the age of 56 years while rowing on Lake Placid on September 21, 1933, some thirty years earlier. And Mrs. Douglass was no ordinary tourist. In fact, Mabel Smith Douglass was the first Dean of Douglass College in New Brunswick, New Jersey, a unit of Rutgers which had been named in her honor.

With the retrieval of the jawbone, it had been hoped that there would be enough clues to confirm that the body belonged to Mrs. Douglass. However, a lot of years had passed. Amazingly, the newspapers reported that Dr. Harold Bergamini Senior, aged 71 of Saranac Lake, had somehow managed to recall tending Mrs. Douglass' son about fifty years earlier and further managed to recall having been referred by a New York City dentist and the name of the dentist's junior apprentice.

Ultimately it turned out that the forearm provided the authorities more information than the jawbone. It seemed that Mrs. Douglass had suffered severe anxiety and exhaustion, a consequence of what her colleagues called overwork and the Four Winds Sanitarium at Cross River in Westchester, where she stayed had record of a broken arm that perfectly matched the fracture in the calcified cast of Mrs. Douglass' forearm.

The newspapers went on to note that Mrs. Douglass' son William Douglass Jr. had passed away at the age of 16 years in 1923 and her daughter had passed away at the age of 42 in 1948. It made Jean sad to think of the Douglass family's misfortunes.

The next day, Jean met Frank Pabst when he pulled up in the Bouyea delivery truck. Jean was curious to hear Frank's opinion about the newspaper's conclusion that the cause of Mrs. Douglass death was accidental drowning. It was clear to Jean that Frank didn't agree with the newspaper's conclusion, and what's more Frank had convinced Jean as well. Jean was quick to forgive Frank for the mess in her garden. Frost would soon kill the marigolds anyhow.

During October, the new ski trails were completed before the weather turned cold. The new J-Bar installation went smoothly. The cable splicer arrived as scheduled and completed his work in three days. The new lift passed inspection and was ready to go. With the foliage season past Paleface closed for the season. Doc and Jean moved back to Jay to relax and pray for a snowy winter.

## '63 Assassination

Meanwhile, Chuck spent the fall fitting up his new photo studio behind Jack's Diner in Jay. It was a happy time, filled with anticipation, and Chuck could see himself capturing family portraits and making keepsakes that families would treasure for generations. Jean Carol was expecting their first child the following May. On the 17th of November, Chuck was surprised by a birthday party celebration and Chuck received many fine gifts, including a pet raccoon named Anthony.

Chuck was in his living room on November 22nd working on advertisements and flyers to promote his new business, enjoying making plans and imagining the future. The TV was on in the background, tuned to CBS's early afternoon program "As The World Turns," and Chuck wasn't really paying attention to the television when Walter Cronkite's voice interrupted with an astonishing announcement. "Here's a bulletin from CBS news. In Dallas, Texas, three shots were fired at President Kennedy's motorcade in downtown Dallas. The first reports say that President Kennedy has been seriously wounded by this shooting."

Chuck and Jean Carol sat in their living rooms, completely stunned. Chuck reached for the phone without looking at it. The soap opera returned to the screen. Chuck called his father. Doc hadn't heard the news, and was just as shocked to hear it as Chuck was. It was comforting to hear Doc's voice, though words couldn't make sense of the situation. Within an hour, Walter Cronkite reported that President Kennedy had died. It seemed the TV ran nonstop from that moment all the way through Thanksgiving. Chuck and Jean Carol, and Karl, Putzi, and Heidi joined Doc, Jean, and Patti at Overlook, not feeling particularly thankful as Doc found the words to express their grief and help the families cope with that which they could not understand. They prayed for President Kennedy's family, President Johnson, the United States of America and they prayed for continued blessings in their lives. Then they prayed for a snowy winter.

## '63 Christmas Shopping

Jean wasn't particularly in the mood to go Christmas shopping that year. Normally, Jean would have thoughtfully selected a unique gift for each person on her Christmas shopping list. Instead, Jean picked up the newly introduced Kodak Instamatic 100 cameras for almost everyone on her list. It was a beautiful, rectangular camera with a big square flash cube on top. The flash cube allowed the camera to take pictures inside, however each of the four sides of the flash cube could be used only once. Thankfully, the cube spun automatically after each picture was taken.

## '64 Landscapes

Two days before Christmas, Mother Nature smiled on North Country skiers and the tourist industry. Ten inches of snow fell and then temperatures remained below freezing. On Christmas Eve, the storm tapered to snow showers and further diminished to snow flurries. That powerful storm had previously dropped fourteen inches of snow on Memphis Tennessee and then barreled North. In its wake, an arctic blast numbed most of nation.

The bountiful snowfall blasted Paleface into its most successful early season opener ever. The ski report on Thursday January 2nd boasted good to excellent conditions and six to eight inches of fresh powder on a packed base. Doc and Jean couldn't be happier.

Every motel room had been sold out since December 20th. The kitchen and wait staff served a record number of meals. Skiers were delighted with new trails as Paleface entered its third winter season with a new third lift. Paleface boasted twenty-three trails. Three new expert trails and two advanced trails provided more challenging terrain, allowing the whole family to ski together at Paleface. No longer would the family always have to split up for a fun day of skiing.

At the front desk, a newspaper clipping was made into a sign for all to see. The handwritten message, "This Just In" preceded the newsprint, "Paleface Has Climbed Into the Top 10 Among the

State's 81 Ski Centers." This was an accomplishment that everyone at Paleface was very proud of—to have made such an impression within the industry in less than three years of operations.

The steepest, most challenging new trail was the Snow Eagle trail. This was the trail where Doc planned to stage future racing events. On the trail map, the Snow Eagle trail was number eleven. The new Big Horn lift rose from an elevation of 1,250 feet to 1,750 feet at the top of the mountain. Alternatively, skiers could take the Upper Big Horn trail to the Lower Big Horn trail all the way from the top of the mountain to the lodge, enjoying an enormously long run of intermediate glade skiing, enjoying views of Whiteface almost all the way.

What's more, Paleface also featured night skiing on Saturdays along the Chairlift on the Paleface and Brave trails. Paleface advertised that there was only 200 feet from bedroom to chair lift. On Saturday nights, you could enjoy a gourmet meal, go skiing, and go dancing without having to get in your car.

## '64 Oil Painting Demonstration

A couple weeks into January, Paleface was again waiting for fresh snow. Ski conditions had deteriorated to "fair," not the sort of conditions that excite the ski enthusiast, yet the sort of ski conditions that at least keep the doors open. To put thousands of skiers per hour on the mountain required at least good to excellent ski reports as well as snow in all the back yards from New Jersey to Boston to Montreal to Buffalo.

From Paleface's very first days, skiing programs with the local schools were a major part of the Paleface business strategy. Convincing young people to take up the sport made sense on several levels. The newspapers loved to report stories about kids winning races, which made for great publicity. If one member of the family fell in love with skiing, maybe it would rub off on others in the family.

An exciting addition to the 1964 Paleface season was Monday

night oil painting demonstrations. It had been talked about at area schools for months, and advertised in the newspaper since before Christmas. Doc's first class had close to 150 people from throughout the community. Every chair in the dining room had been filled, and extra chairs had to be pulled in from the lounge, the loft, and the bar, and still a few people were left standing.

Promptly at 8:30pm, Miss Elaine Reilly from Wilmington stood up to introduce Doc. Miss Reilly was a teacher at the AuSable High School and chaperoned a good number of students that evening. "Ladies and Gentlemen, boys and girls," began Miss Reilly. "It is my pleasure to introduce a very special, talented artist who will perform an oil painting demonstration. Before our very eyes he will create a splendid work of art. Of course, you know him best as the owner of Paleface. For many years, he was a Methodist minister, author, lecturer, and educator. Before moving to Jay and buying a mountain, he was a nationally renowned artist. Of course, he is well known locally for his beautiful landscapes, and you can see his paintings almost anywhere you go, from Whiteface Ski Center, to the Castle at the top of Whiteface Mountain, to Steinhoff's, to Tirolerland, to Stonehelm, why you can even find one of his paintings on the wall down at the bank." She tilted her head slightly and smiled sweetly.

"There's a few things perhaps you don't know about Doc Fitz-Gerald. You may not know that he has exhibited widely throughout the metropolitan area of New York and New Jersey. Or that for six years Doc was editor of *The Artist* magazine, a magazine created for artists across the country. Or you may not know that Doc is a former national president of the American Artists Professional League, a former president of the National Arts Club and a former member of the board of directors of the Salmagundi Club. In addition to donating his time to serving other artists, Doc has won many prizes, including the prestigious first prize in the 1953 Water Color Exhibition at the Salmagundi Club. Doc has personally met such famed artists as Pablo Picasso and Salvador Dali. It takes a great public speaker to entertain personalities such as Picasso and Dali, to be sure!" She paused to give the audience a moment to catch up and appreciate the fact that Doc was acquainted with such renowned artists.

"Oh, and on a personal note, I have heard that Jean Fitz-Gerald is now home from the Mary Fletcher Hospital in Burlington, Vermont, where she had surgery on her toe. We have been assured that Jean will be fine and is well tended at her home, so that we can have Doc here with us tonight. Without further ado, it is my honor and my pleasure to introduce Dr. Boylan Fitz-Gerald."

Doc stepped up before the gathered crowd and thanked Miss Reilly for the introduction. Doc's demonstration was performed with his back to his audience, so the audience could watch the painting as it appeared on the canvass. Doc performed without a microphone, in a voice loud enough to carry to the corners of the dining room, a skill honed over decades of delivering sermons.

Doc began his lecture by comparing painting to romance. "As with all romance, that of painting is personal. It is an inner experience which cannot be imitated by anyone anywhere. The artist is stimulated by the people and places, the shapes, colors, and lines of outward experience. And he rightly 'returns to nature' for both information and inspiration. But he sees all of this with his own eyes, passes it through the alembic of his own mind, fashions his materials with his own hands, and produces a highly individual creation whose precise formula remains unknown even to himself. Indeed, the true artist is inimitable. One of a kind. Herein is one of the greatest sources of satisfaction to an artist. The creator is alive. Only he can accomplish this, for only he has this vision. Only he has done this, for only he has even attempted it."

Doc turned to scan the audience. Convinced he had their attention, he turned back to his canvass and continued. Doc spoke of each new painting as an adventure. A journey into the unknown. Choices made, potential alternative choices abandoned as the artist realizes his vision, and mourns the losses of what might have been had he made different decisions. Doc set down his brushes and wandered very briefly among the crowd, stopping to make eye contact with people he hadn't met before, while progressing from discussing the artist's inner turmoil to discussing the artist's relationship with his audience.

Back at the easel, Doc began painting again, without a pause in his lecture. Continuing the romance theme, Doc progressed from the fellowship between artist and enthusiast to the relationship between the artist and other artists. Doc used the word *torture* to describe discussing a mentor's work, and Doc used the word *scolding* to describe the mentor's criticisms of a student's work, but then also the occasional praise as well. Doc opined, "The fellowship of artists is one of the most sweetening influences in society. What a thrill to share something that we have found good!" He turned to the audience again, raised both eyebrows, exposing four rows of wrinkles on his forehead. He stretched his arms wide, as if to engulf the audience. "And who has not grown the most himself at that very moment when he was helping some youngster take his early steps?"

Doc returned to his easel again. "Are you afraid your pupil may outshine you? Then I invite you to share the real romance, guerdon of immortality, which Socrates knew when his pupil Plato took up the lighted torch of a wiser and better humanity. Believe me, the fellowship of pupils is a part of the life creative." Doc turned back to face the crowd. "A transmitted treasure compounds its own interest. And a communicated joy is an everlasting gladness." Doc turned and faced the other side of the room and repeated those two sentences for emphasis.

Then Doc returned to talking about the relationship of the artist with his audience. "What artist has not felt a keen satisfaction in finding someone who has really understood his message? We do not live in a vacuum. We do not paint for the public. We paint for an inner audience, a critical jury whose most austere member is the artist himself. And yet, when the work is done, the whole point of it is communication. This is not the aimless doodling of idle minds. Nor was it meant to hang in an attic. It was intended to wear a frame and to be seen. As with the theatre, whatever else happens, the show must go on."

The pace of Doc's painting sped up, his brushes moving quickly about the canvass. As he painted quicker, his speech grew louder and quicker. "The very genius of our profession is that we are showmen. The true artist knows that he has something to say. The romance of painting is a two-way street. And the creative act is not complete until it takes place in the mind and affections of the viewer. To understand the inner thought process of our public and to paint for someone other than ourselves: this is at the very center of the romance of our work. We *are* trying to register, to transmit an idea, an impression, a message. When we succeed in this, when someone else has seen our vision, dreamed our dream, even feared our fears, then is youth renewed and ours are the wings of eagles." Doc paused and stepped to the side, keeping his back to the crowd, so the audience could see the progress on his canvass, just for a moment before he continued.

"So it is that we acknowledge with pride that we do not walk alone as humans and as artists. And the day may come when others will be glad to say the same of us. For we have chosen the creative life and are among the builders of civilization. Our vocation in the city of everyman is constructive. In this fashion, the romance of painting becomes high romance. It is not a cheap thing, no mere meal ticket, no self-gratifying hobby. We are not just putting in time. We are putting in eternity! The dream must become the deed. The spirit must become flesh. The creative imagination is imperative. Hence, for me, painting becomes high romance." Doc turned, smiled and winked at the audience, in the general direction of the back of the crowd, then turned back to his work.

"For the romance of painting is its very hopefulness. The creative life can be found. We have confidence that man has the capacity and the right to dare to create and re-create. This places him in rapport with the Divine and is the truest guarantee of his manhood. Whether sun or rain or snow, whether land or city or sea, whether an epic or multum in parvo, it is yours to love into existence, for someone else to know and to love too. Of course, there will be a tomorrow, for you, and for that someone else! Do you know any life more truly romantic, more adventuresome, more satisfying, more responsible, more free, more alive? And it 'teases as doth eternity.' The fullness of its very joy is often compounded of 'blood, sweat, and tears.' But the tears are life-lighted with the glory of another dawn!"

Doc turned to face his audience and put the back end of his paint brush in the corner of his mouth, as if it were a long cigarette holder. Doc remained silent for some time so the students could appreciate what had appeared on the canvass so far. Doc took the brush from his mouth and flicked it slightly as if to dispense with a bit of ash, and then continued.

"So you can see my canvass tonight is fifteen inches tall, by thirty inches wide. I prepared the canvass with a base of different colors in different sections of the canvass to get us started. And I sketched in with pencil an outline of the plan. In the background at the upper left is a mountain, off in the distance. On the right is a steep ski trail. A gentle sloping trail comes in from the bottom left side of the painting. Several skiers will be on the steep trail, and one skier will be on the gentle sloping trail. In addition, you will see a couple buildings just to the left of the center. Perhaps these buildings are the ski lodge. There will be one big tree here at the bottom left. And there will be lots of trees here to the left of the steep trail. And a little bit of brush at the bottom right of the canvass. So that's the basic plan for the picture."

Then Doc returned to his painting and lecturing. "In many ways, the supreme creative satisfaction of painting is found in composition. There is nothing more thrilling than this adventure. It starts with the most abstract idea, in this case the idea is Converging Trails, and it continues to the last dynamic accent and the final quality nuance. From first to last, painting is composition, the composing of ideas, lines, masses, and colors. The first requirement for composition is the idea. Ambiguity of idea will inevitably destroy any ultimate unity of composition. Remember, this is not many but one picture. Make it one and keep it that way. The chief goal of composition is unity. There is nothing democratic about a good painting.

From beginning to end the whole process is selective and aristocratic. To paint a lobsterman is to make him king of that picture. As the good composer of music has his 'leitmotiv', and the philosopher has his 'Weltanschauung' so the artist must have his single purpose. The end is in the beginning. Singleness of purpose means simplicity and unity. These mark the greatest creative works. The simple is classic; the classic is simple. When every part of the painting talks with equal volume you have anarchy and chaos. What the composer wants is order. He wants a civilized place, not a jungle. Therefore, you will exercise the greatest control and restraint in the interest of your main idea, your Queen. There can be no real composition without her. If you haven't a Queen idea, admit it. You have nothing to say. Remember Demetrius? 'To embellish the ridiculous is like trying to beautify an ape.' If you *have* a Queen idea, you must enthrone her. All things else must adore her. All other elements of the painting are only page-boys whose chief function is her coronation and enthronement."

Doc went on to discuss many technical aspects relating to good compositions. Doc talked about how to decide where to place different elements within the corners of a painting. Doc explained the various lines along which a story is told. Doc spoke of the laws of climax, and about how to keep the spectator's eyes moving around a painting.

Doc had been talking for quite some time when he turned suddenly to the audience, almost surprised to see the crowd, and caught them quite off guard. Doc's lesson may have been too technical for a crowd of novices. Doc thought, the crowd will be smaller next week. He smiled and continued. "A good plan for the beginner is to mark the exact center of his canvass and avoid it like the plague. That spot is static. Then roughly sketch your center of interest, the area of the enthronement of your idea and the major movement of your idea. Place nothing important in the corners. Remember the frame. It is part of your picture. Your center of interest should not be too isolated from the frame but rather en rapport with it. This relationship is established best, not at the corners, not at the centers of the sides, but somewhere in between. Plan to have some element of your composition 'break through' from the frame at all four sides. This helps us to avoid that obvious parallelism near the frame which so marks the amateur. While you will need the 'stoppers'—framing devices within the frame—you also will need to establish this rapport. In general, when you place human figures, animals, boats, vehicles near the frame, have them entering, not leaving, your picture. Some, used as foils, may point outward, but the total effect should be a dynamic, forever inward-turning movement. All elements outside the center of interest are like faithful page-boys. They serve only to lead the visitor to his audience with the Queen. They are secondary and should be signs pointing away from themselves toward her. Consider the matter of dynamics. A dynamic painting moves. The spectator should never be allowed to stay in one place. There is something about our human nature which makes us delight in a journey. The eye wants to take a walk. It will not choose to stay in one spot unless you compel it to do so. If the spectator stares you are lost. The eye prefers to caress, to move rhythmically from part to part. Your job as an artist is to make sure that you place no barriers between the final goal you have in mind and the adventurer-spectator. That final goal should include movement to and from and back to it again. Sometimes by direct signs, sometimes by indirect or mysterious means, your mastery of dynamics must lead the pilgrim into the very heart of your undiscovered country. The spectator should be compelled to look at least *twice*."

Doc turned and faced the audience. Somehow an almost complete painting had appeared from what had just a short time earlier been a bunch of colorful smudges. Doc gestured toward the canvass. "The Queen idea in this painting is converging trails; that point where one trail meets another." Miss Reilly pointed at her watch. Doc delivered the conclusion of his soliloquy using his paintbrush like a conductor uses a baton. "Always be sure to allow the spectator the creative joy of making many of his own discoveries. Let his journey be one of romance and a thrilling adventure, too. Help him, guide him, but do not tell the whole story. And do not side-track him in a cul-de-sac, howsoever delightful you must find the painting of it. If it is that good, save it for another painting where it can have the whole stage! A Dynamic composition moves because of a certain inevitable or integral logic of its own. Select your material with care and reject with equal discrimination. So-called spontaneous paintings are deceptive. What seems spontaneous has generally had years of experience behind it, months of seminal thought, and many hours of gestation. Planned spontaneity may sound contradictory, but then the fullest romance of life consists precisely of this duality, this paradoxical nature of our deepest experience. Though your Queen idea may have come to you in a flash, but did she really? The whole establishment of her court and empire is surely worthy of time. As Rome was not built in a day, so a good painting is not 'knocked off' in twenty minutes. If your painting is so executed, you run the risk of usurping the throne of your own Queen, you clever charlatan! So we speak of dynamic composition as a serious and often complicated matter. Simplicity is reached by the road labeled complexity. Many factors can be brought into play to make your painting 'move.' Dynamic line, perspective, mass, color, brushwork, all these and more. Even the selection of an appropriate frame makes a difference, too ornate and the spectator admires the frame too much! Dynamic composition includes many living, moving elements which determine much of the romantic journey which your spectator is to take. And you cannot expect him to take a journey unless you have taken it first. Dream! Plan! Think! Revise! If your painting is to be dynamic, alive, *you* must live. There are hundreds of little things all of which contribute in their minor ways toward the major movement of your painting. Sometimes it will be a dark accent within a shadow, a bit of flotsam, a random gull, a wind-kissed branch, a mysterious reflected high light, or a passage of color intensity."

Doc went on for some time in a detailed discussion about an artist's use of colors, and then began to compare painting to writing and poetry as Miss Reilly began to squirm in her seat. It was time for the audience to have a break. Oblivious to Miss Reilly's concern Doc continued, "In the last analysis, to speak of dynamic composition is to speak of the spirit. Along these lines will be found the life creative. May you know it, thrill to it, and live it. And may you communicate some of its glory, truth and beauty to a world which stands in need of the creative and re-creative labors of its artists. Above all, work at it. The spirit *must* become flesh. With Elizabeth Barrett Browning we must be certain that 'the ghosts of our unborn children' do not haunt us forever. To be truly creative is to find our fullest humanity. To be freely creative is to realize our individuality. To be responsibly creative is to accomplish our social immortality. Wherefore, dream and plan and think. Study and experiment and grow. Work and compose and live. When fancy becomes fact and theory ripens into practice, when the dream becomes the deed, then we have that romance of truth which is higher than fiction. By so much the real world becomes ideal for by this much the ideal has been realized."

Doc set down his brush, turned, and tilted his head slightly upward, fixing his gaze on the large stuffed mascot sitting in the beams above the crowd and concluded his thoughts. "The romance of painting is the incarnation of the beautiful, the good and the true in such fashion that the world knows the victory and the glory. And to you all is given the high honor of the Creator whose chief concern is that the spirit shall become flesh and live for others to appreciate."

Poor Miss Reilly had been trying to capture Doc's attention for several minutes. Doc had entered a strange world where he alone could concentrate on the work at his easel and the lecture being delivered simultaneously. At times, Doc seemed to have forgotten that he was speaking to non-artists, high school amateurs, dreamers, and doodlers. Doc put down his brush and lit a Viceroy cigarette. Most of the audience headed for the bar to buy a draft beer or a cold soda pop.

## '64 Beatlemania

During the break, a group of Miss Reilly's students were talking about the music phenomenon that was sweeping the nation. The students were so excited as they talked about the British quartet that Doc couldn't help but overhear them. "What are your students talking about?" Doc asked Miss Reilly.

"I don't know much about this myself," admitted Miss Reilly, "but I have been hearing about it for the past several weeks now. It seems all the high school children are talking about these Beatles. I read an article in the paper that said something like 'parents of teen age girls are mystified as to why their daughters have gone "ga-ga" over the Beatles. Four boys with "way out" haircuts and an even farther out way of making music.' I have heard a couple songs on the radio. They have an insistent beat, which I am sure will make the music very popular at the dances and the prom. And I have seen some pictures. They aren't very impressive looking, but they're very popular in Europe and from what the kids say they are planning on coming to New York next month. You know how it is, Doc. This year the kids can't talk about anything but the Beatles. Next year, probably nobody will think too much about them!"

After a ten minute break, everyone returned to their chairs. Doc made some remarks about the wonderful qualities of working with snow within a painting and about the luminosity of snow. He noted that a whole bunch of subtle colors can be brought to snow, and that working with masses of the white stuff in a painting must be very carefully thought out.

The night was nearing an end, and the painting was pretty well completed. Doc turned to the audience and exclaimed, "Now our painting needs skiers! Would anyone like to appear in the painting? Or would you like me to put someone you know in the painting? Someone famous or infamous perhaps?"

Someone from the back of the room hollered out, "Jackie Kennedy."

"Very well," said Doc. A minute later a tiny figure near the front of the painting appeared on the canvass. The figure wore black stretch ski pants and a white Siberian Arctic wolf fur hat. The former First Lady skied away from the viewers of the painting and toward the lodge.

"And how about some skiers coming down this path toward Mrs. Kennedy?" Doc asked his audience.

One of Miss Reilly's students who was sitting near the front raised her hand. Doc called on her, and she suggested, "How about the Beatles, sir—John, Paul, George, and Ringo!"

"Why not," answered Doc. "So that's what these fellows are named!" One by one, four skiers appeared on the canvass, big enough to tell they were skiers but way too small to make out their faces or hairstyles.

"I don't know whether you realize this or not," Doc continued. "You will recall when I was talking about composition? The Queen idea was the converging of these two trails. In your minds, I have painted the former First Lady of the United States and a band of mop-headed ragamuffins from Great Britain. Of course, they are not the stars of the picture but they do bring mystery and add a sense of drama. You might wonder, are these guys from the steep trail going too fast? Will they crash into this woman on the converging trail? You might identify with the skiers headed toward the lodge. Maybe they're looking forward to a hot cup of coffee or some lunch. You get to make up that part of the story."

The next morning, the painting was hanging on a nail at Paleface, and available for purchase as a souvenir. Through the years, a battle raged within the checkbook at Paleface. Deposits versus disbursements. For the most part, the epic battle was won by disbursements. When guests purchased paintings, deposits sometimes beat disbursements! The Monday night demonstrations continued throughout the winter, and into the following year.

## '64 Winter Olympics at Innsbruck, Austria

The 9th winter Olympic Games held at Innsbruck, Austria were the talk of the town in early February, 1964. After a busy day skiing on very minimal snow coverage, guests gathered as usual in the lodge. Replacing the usual casual conversation, a television set had been placed in the corner of the lounge. Instead of gathering around the fireplace or the bar, guests were gathered on sofas and chairs around the television.

Everyone was captivated by the men's slalom. In the first qualifying run, a pair of French skiers had finished first and third, and a German skier had finished second. American skiers Jimmy Huega and Buddy Werner had finished fourth and fifth. Austrian skier Pepi Stiegler tied a Swiss skier for sixth. Another American skier, Billy Kidd, finished eleventh. Jean-Claude Killy, who had finished twenty-ninth in the first qualifier, came in first in the second qualifier.

Jim McKay provided the official, play by play commentary. During the commercial breaks, friends Karl Jost, Walter Prager and Doc Fitz-Gerald provided additional, more colorful commentary.

As the first skier prepared to make his run, the spectators at Paleface placed their final bets. Everyone put a dollar in a large bowl. Each spectator chose a country. Everyone wrote their name and the country on a line of paper in a notebook, their prediction for the gold medal winning country.

Doc sweetened the pot. "I'm all for the Americans, but no American man has ever won an Olympic medal in skiing. It's not going to happen! If it does, why, I'll double the pot!"

Most of the spectators who hadn't chosen the team from USA wished they had!

As the hours went by, and it came down to the end, most of the spectators' countries had been eliminated. One or two had bet on Japan. Two or three had bet on Sweden, Norway and Finland. Nobody predicted the Soviet Union would win. Most of the crowd had settled on Italy, Germany, Austria and the USA. By far the largest contingent predicted the French would win. From the beginning, the supporters of the French skiers had been the loudest and most boisterous.

One by one, countries fell out of contention, as the top time got harder and harder to beat. The American skier, Jimmy Huega, number twenty-four finished with a blazing fast time of 1:01.36. His two-run total of 2:11.52 knocked the top French skier out of contention. More importantly, the crowd of spectators supporting France turned into a horde of moaning, mourners. Those supporting Norway, Sweden, Finland, Italy, and Germany had already suffered the same fate, and those supporting Switzerland had their hopes dashed as their skier wasn't able to post a fast enough time to hit gold.

Near the end of the program, Billy Kidd from Stowe, Vermont, wearing the number ten made a speedy run of 1:00.31, besting his team mate Jimmy Huega by a fraction of a second in the combined total.

There was still a chance that the Austrian skier Pepi Stiegler could take the gold medal.

During the commercial break, there was plenty of banter between the spectators. Then Walter Prager said, "It looks like you are going to have to sweeten the pot, Doc!"

Doc said, "Not so fast! Pepi could win!" Doc had put his dollar on the Austrian team, as had Karl Jost, and a good many others in the crowd.

Karl turned on his comrade, "Doc you said you would sweeten the pot if an American won a medal. You didn't say it had to be the gold medal!"

Some were cheering, hooting and hollering, taunting friends, neighbors, acquaintances and strangers. Everyone was making some kind of noise, and then the commercials ended. Jim McKay came back on the air. There was total silence in the Paleface lodge, a rare occurrence.

Pepi Stiegler stepped up to the gate. One minute, 2.1 seconds later the Paleface crowd roared, some with glee, some with disdain and others with laughter. Mostly, the patriotic crowd was disappointed to see Billy the Kidd from Stowe, Vermont miss the gold medal by fourteen hundredths of a second.

Doc was simultaneously winner and loser. Having to double the pot cost him forty dollars. As one of the winners having predicted

Austria for gold, Doc got sixteen dollars back. All in all, not a bad night considering the bar at Paleface did a brisk business that evening.

## '64 Ski School

Doc woke up earlier than usual the next morning and grabbed a cup of coffee on his way out the door. As he often did, Doc began the day with coffee and a cigarette. Doc sat, perched on the large rock next to the ski lesson muster bell.

Doc watched as Pete Pelkey worked with half a dozen beginning skiers, teaching them to side-step up a slight incline. Doc smiled to see their guest, Rosemary Robinson, the wife a Newark, New Jersey bank president who—despite annual trips to Paleface for the past three years—had failed to excel beyond the beginner's level. Each year Rosemary insisted on being placed in Pete's class, a strong endorsement for the charm of Victor Cecil Peter Pelkey, but perhaps not an indication of his great teaching ability. Fortunately, most of Pete's beginners did graduate to the intermediate level.

Then Doc watched a bit further up the slopes, as Putzi Jost worked with a group of students on slow, meandering snowplow turns. Doc thought that group looked like it was doing as well as it could, with the thin layer of snow that had fallen overnight, on top of the thin coverage that only just barely covered the short-cropped grass on the hillside.

Walter Prager was taking a rare Sunday off from his shop in Wilmington to help Karl Jost mentor the prize pupils, Wayne Wright and Chucky Morgan. Karl and Chucky hopped one chair up the lift, followed by Walter and Wayne in another chair. There wasn't a better time to work on slalom lessons with a couple young American boys, who had also seen the Americans' triumph in the men's slalom the night before. Karl imagined Chucky and Wayne winning the silver and bronze medals in the 1972 winter Olympics. Maybe it would even be in Lake Placid! Maybe one of them would win gold.

Doc joined Karl, Walter, Wayne, and Chuck for lunch.

The boys were hungry after vigorous work-outs on the mountain.

As good manners dictate, the boys didn't have to be asked to remove their hats before sitting down to lunch. Wayne's mother, Jean Wright, was working in the kitchen at Paleface that afternoon, and couldn't resist taking a minute off to come out and say hi. Without noticing that she was doing so, Jean patted down Wayne's cowlicks, also doing the same for Chucky and making a quick getaway before either boy protested too heartily.

The men were talking about how the morning's training went, barely conscious of the fact the two boys were sitting with them, most likely hearing everything they were saying. Most of it was quite complimentary. The boys had finished their hamburgers, and were working on their chocolate pudding when Walter Prager told the boys he had gift for each of them.

A couple minutes later, Walter returned from his car with a bag containing two brand new goggles from his shop in Wilmington. The goggles were the top of the line, featuring the newest technology, guaranteed not to fog up and amber colored for enhanced clarity, making it easier to see, regardless of whether it was sunny or snowing.

Wayne and Chuck were appropriately appreciative of the new gift, with an "aw shucks, gee whiz and a by golly." Walter felt good about giving his gifts.

Bea Lincoln brought each of the men a cup of coffee. Karl asked Walter to tell the boys about his World Champion ski racing career. Walter Prager was the very first men's World Cup champion skier winning at Murren in his native Switzerland in 1931, and then again at Innsbruck in Austria in 1933.

"I can personally attest to the importance of goggles during a ski race," Walter told the boys. "You see, during that race in 1931, it was snowing something fierce. The flakes were as big as old-time silver dollars. Nobody could see anything. Now, as a boy I lived in those mountains. I had to ski to get to school, or anywhere else for that matter. I was used to those big old snowflakes. The trick to keeping those goggles from fogging up was to rub soap on them. I was the only one who could see the quickest path to the finish line that afternoon!" Walter Prager paused briefly, and swirled his coffee around in his cup.

"Unfortunately, a broken leg kept me off skis in 1932," Walter said sadly as he looked up, "and don't you know I broke that same leg again in 1934. You would not believe the kind of equipment we had to ski on back then!"

After a moment of reflection, he continued, "The proper mental attitude for downhill racing is an extremely significant factor. Absence of fear is essential. Fear, of course, is an instinct, but fearlessness can be cultivated to some degree. Tumbling, diving, or summersaulting from a springboard are good ways of gaining self-confidence and daring, which in turn eliminates fear considerably. These exercises are especially advantageous in improving coordination and quick reaction, too.

With a couple more questions from Doc and Karl to guide him, Walter Prager recounted for the boys his service during World War II. In 1941, Walter Prager was drafted into the U.S. Army. As part of the 10th Mountain Division, Walter served in the Italian Alps where he saw combat. Chuck Morgan and Wayne Wright were sitting on the edges of their seats listening to Walter Prager talk about fighting a war on skis.

"Let's see," Walter began, "we trained for years and became an elite, highly trained, highly specialized fighting force. Before being sent to Europe we spent twenty-one months in the Colorado Rockies. I told you about the ski equipment we had in the 1930s. I can tell you it wasn't any better during the war. The skis were more commonly known as 2 X 4's and the bindings were referred to as bear-traps. By 1944 we were experts at surviving in rugged, harsh mountainous regions, and physically conditioned to carry ninety pound packs with us up and down the mountainsides. It was around Christmas in 1944 when we landed in Naples, Italy. From there we moved north up the Appenine Mountain chain. During the next eight months we lost 992 men, almost a thousand, really. But sitting around was the worst part. Most of the moving and marching happened at night. During the day we camped, but that's when we took incoming fire. That's when men were injured or killed. Anyway, the worst part was trying to dislodge the Germans from the top of a Mountain near Mt. Belvedere in the Italian Alps. We were supposed to be able to complete that mission before sundown and it ended up taking us all night."

Walter seemed all at once to have gotten tired of talking about World War II, and concluded by sharing how happy he was to return home in August of 1945. Walter joked, "You would think all those years of being a ski-vivalist would make me want to pursue some other line of work. But I guess skiing is what I was meant to do."

Walter told the boys about coaching skiing at Dartmouth College in Hanover, New Hampshire, before and then again after the war, and about his time coaching the 1948 Winter Olympic ski team that traveled first to Walter's home town of Davos, Switzerland for training, and then on to St. Moritz to compete. None of the US team members finished better than seventh in 1948, unfortunately.

Karl told the boys, "One thing Walter didn't tell you is that Walter is widely recognized as the best all-around skier that there ever was, competing in cross-country skiing, ski jumping, downhill, and slalom."

"Well, I don't know about that," Walter chuckled. He said humbly, "I never could beat those Swedes at cross country skiing."

Doc, who had been listening as intently as the boys, finally remarked, "Bet you boys didn't know how famous Walter Prager is, did you! We didn't name a ski trail after him just because he's a nice guy. Thank you for all you did during the war to keep the world safe and free, Walter. Oh, and boys did you know our very own Walter Prager has been awarded a Purple Heart and two Bronze Star Medals?"

"Well, enough of this ancient history," Karl said, bringing everyone back to 1964, after an unexpectedly long, two-hour lunch, "you boys better get back to training if you want to be the next Billy the Kidd."

Later that afternoon there were many fewer patrons enjoying

après-ski in the Paleface lounge. Many guests returned to their homes in New Jersey, Pennsylvania, New York City, Connecticut, Long Island, and Boston. Most of the local crowd was home as well. It was a school night.

The television was spending its last evening in the lounge. The last winter Olympic events included the gold medal hockey game and the ski jump championships.

Doc was washing some glasses in the sink behind the bar as Jim McKay was summarizing the 1964 Winter Olympics at Innsbruck, and reminding viewers yet again how, of all years, this was the year that Austria got "little to no snow. The Austrian Army had to bring it in and place it on the mountain so that the competitions could be held."

Doc laughed because he knew what that felt like. He wished he could call in the Army to bring in some snow when the chips were down.

A couple of nearby guests had looked up as Doc laughed, briefly distracted by the man muttering to himself behind the bar. Having decided that a bartender talking to himself didn't pose a danger or threat, they quickly returned to their relaxed, casual conversation, then soon wandered off to their motel rooms. It was well after midnight when Doc finally turned off the lights and went to bed, only to be turned back on by Jean less than four hours later. This had become the rhythm of their days as entrepreneurs at Paleface.

## '64 Snow Would Be Welcome

The dominant weather pattern remained cold and snowless, but thanks to the early snows and cold weather, the doors remained open. In the local newspaper, Wilmington correspondent Clara E. Hazelton reported: "Variety is the spice of life. When it comes to weather, it furnishes constant conversation pieces, violent winds, snow squalls, erratic temperatures above and below that important mark, 32 degrees. Hear that wind howl. It's 28 degrees, skiing fair on Whiteface, fair also on Paleface. Snow would be welcome."

About a week later, prayers had been answered. Miss Hazelton reported as follows: "February 17 is a perfect winter day. The sun is bright, the air is a crisp 19 degrees, white snow covers the ground, the air is still and when one stops to listen one hears the sweetest bird songs from high in the trees. One enjoys the pattern of twigs against the huge blue vault of a cloudless sky. Wonderful Adirondack weather."

## '64 Ski Race at Paleface

The last Sunday in February, a great crowd of spectators from the local community turned out to watch the young racers. As was usually the case, the guests from out of town enjoyed the show as well.

The course was set up in the new expert area on the Brave trail. The boys and girls had been permitted to make practice runs, as often as they wished on Saturday.

Wayne Wright had read Walter Prager's book *Skiing* which permanently resided in the Lodge on the coffee table. Wayne had taken note of Walter Prager's advice that a skier should memorize the course, so they can visualize it. Wayne had done just that on Saturday, having made several runs at different speeds. As Mr. Prager suggested, Wayne had tried to memorize every turn, every twist and every bump.

Chuck Morgan went first, posting a nice time of 68.4 seconds. Bobby Meconi finished in 87.4 seconds. Gary Shampeny came in at 83.3 seconds. Philip Dreissigacker came in at just over a minute and a half, and his brother John came in at over two minutes, as did Mark Benoit.

Wayne watched each racer as far as he could see from where he stood, stretching and leaning to maximize his line of sight. Wayne tried to overlay every little mistake he saw the other skiers make onto the course he had memorized in his head. Last skier called, it was his turn.

Adrenaline coursed through Wayne's body. It wasn't fear. It was excitement. Drive. Wayne put on the goggles given to him a few weeks earlier by Walter Prager. A momentary distraction flashed through Wayne's head, thinking about skiing through the Italian Alps as fast as he could, dodging enemy bullets. "Focus," Wayne commanded himself, as Karl had often instructed all the boys in the ten to twelve-year-old category.

Not another thought crossed Wayne's mind until he had blown past the finish line.

At the bottom, Karl praised Wayne. "Perfect form. Not a single imperfection. Good job, son!"

"I know," said Wayne with all the honesty of a boy that age. "I skied it just like I played it in my mind."

Wayne smiled ear-to-ear during the trophy presentation after all four age groups were done, both boys and girls. Not only did Wayne win among boys ten to twelve, he also bested the boys in every other age category. Wayne's brother Richard also won a trophy in his age class, but his time was two-tenths slower than Wayne's. Beating his brother wasn't in his mind before or during the race, but it made it a little sweeter afterwards!

As if it weren't enough to have a trophy, Chuck Fitz-Gerald took a picture of Wayne standing in front of the A-Frame of the main lodge behind him. Wayne was wearing his ski jacket with the Paleface Ski patch sewn over his heart, two navy colored triangular mountains on a bright yellow field, with navy trim around the perimeter. Most importantly, Wayne's facial expression was a picture of exhilaration and triumph. His picture in the paper was "decoration" for being the fastest skier of the day. It was a picture of promise and opportunity for all the great potential yet to be fulfilled.

## '64 Grounded

The following weekend, Heidi Jost and Wayne Wright rode up the mountain together. Wayne told Heidi all about the advice he had been given, about memorizing the mountain and being able to close your eyes and see every detail.

Heidi thought, I can do that. Then she said to Wayne, "I've skied down this mountain so many times, I could do it with my eyes closed."

"I don't think that's what Mr. Prager meant," Wayne objected.

Moments later, the lift reached the station. When Heidi's skis were on the snow, she closed her eyes and demonstrated that she really could ski down the mountain with her eyes closed. Fortunately, there were no other skiers in her path. Unfortunately, Heidi's mother witnessed the conclusion of Heidi's run and instead of earning praise for her amazing feat, Heidi was grounded. No skiing. For two weeks.

## '64 Mountain Camp and Lake Scene

After a great season opener, the winter season was off and on. By early March, there wasn't enough snow left to even report conditions as fair. Skiing operations were suspended. On Tuesday, March 17th, there was some snow overnight and Paleface reopened on Wednesday.

Regardless what was happening or not happening on the ski slopes, the Monday night oil painting demonstrations remained constant. The final demonstration of the season was presented in the last week of April.

As in previous weeks, the audience was amazed to see Doc complete a painting in two hours' time, again talking about painting all the while. Doc covered the technical aspects of graduating color in the sky from horizon to zenith, lighting angles, sources of light, shadow and shading, painting masses of color and then toning them down, and stitch and sew techniques of tracing in warm colors along a water mass or a river bank.

As the season ended, the Paleface Ski Club arranged a special awards banquet and ceremony for the junior skiers. Ski Club President Waxy Gordon gave a very motivational and enlightening speech. Karl Jost talked about ski racing. Fourteen trophies were awarded to boys and girls based on their skiing performance during the season. In addition, two surprise trophies were awarded—one to Steve Haselton for most improved skier and a second to Wayne Wright for the most determined skier.

## '64 Salmon Fishing

Even with Paleface closed for the season, Doc had many things on his mind. Doc had been invited to deliver a commencement address to graduating high school seniors at Crown Point Central School on the 22nd of June. He was planning to call his speech "Tomorrow and Tomorrow." Of course, Doc wanted to deliver an inspiring future oriented send-off for the graduates.

Doc had big plans for the summer horseback riding season to be greatly expanded. He had purchased a 100 acre parcel across the street from Paleface from Cornelius Peck. A large ring was being built and a sign in front of the ring declared the moniker "Paleface Paddock." There would be almost double the number of horses that year, increasing from six to eleven, and Paleface would be boasting a network of twenty-five miles of trails.

Perhaps most present on Doc's mind was the anticipation of a long fishing trip with Carl Steinhoff and some friends from Massachusetts.

The party of six set out in mid-April for the Miramachi River in New Brunswick, Canada. They had left very early to get there, and kept a very steady pace, hardly stopping at all and finally made their destination at 4am the next day. They had planned to stop for the night along the way. Unfortunately, every motel was filled with other fishermen, also headed north.

Carl later boasted that the river was loaded with fish and that the weather was beautiful (which is saying a lot for that part of the world at that time of the year). Together Carl and Doc brought home sixty-five salmon, and that didn't count what the guys from Massachusetts took home. The largest salmon weighed twenty-one pounds. Considering the fishing was restricted to single hook fly fishing, the guys brought in quite a haul. Carl also told everyone that inspectors patrolled the river assiduously.

## '64 Diamond

During the summer, Paleface transitioned from having horses brought in, and having outside outfits run the dude ranch business to having a permanent string of horses, and hiring local guides.

There was a lot to do to get the new part of the business established. Doc's son Chuck's photographic skills were put to great use taking pictures for advertisements, press releases and tourism brochures. One particularly attractive photo shoot featured Terri Manley of Jay, riding Dunder; Patti Fitz-Gerald riding Sandy; Doc, riding Nugget; John Santor of AuSable Forks, riding Apache; Roger McLean of Jay, riding Blaze; Mark Devlin of Jay, riding Brownie; William Trumbull of Upper Jay, riding Chief; Cathy Devlin of Jay, riding Breeze; and Ray Hackett of Saranac, riding Blue Boy. Two other horses, Tony and Jigg, were left out of the picture.

The little black pony named Diamond was busy with a customer. Greg Peck had his hands full with a pushy mother who convinced him that her kid knew how to ride. The mother and child had witnessed Diamond deliberately stepping on Greg's feet. Greg warned her that this little black Shetland had a mind of its own, and therefore it would be best if Greg led the pony and rider. Despite Greg's warnings about the mean beast, the pushy mother reminded Greg that the customer was always right. The photo shoot got an early finish, as Doc galloped to the rescue of the pushy mother who was screaming at the top of her lungs as she chased Diamond up the bottom of the Glade trail. Fortunately, her kid had remained in the saddle despite Diamond's best efforts to unseat him.

After the customers had departed, Greg explained what happened to Doc. Just the way he described the scene got them both laughing. Doc suggested maybe Diamond should be sent to the glue factory, which prolonged their laughter. Doc concluded by telling Greg if this happened again, he could simply tell the customer, "Sorry, ma'am. Company policy."

The Paleface Dude Ranch was becoming a top stop on visitors' Adirondack *summer* vacation checklists.

## '64 Battle of Plattsburgh Sesquicentennial

The Battle of Plattsburgh was one of the final fights of the War of 1812, and was the last northern invasion of the United States by Great Britain. The battle was fought between the 6th of September and the 11th of September, 1814. The successful defense of Plattsburgh and Lake Champlain was followed immediately by the successful defense of Baltimore beginning the next day. Those twin victories set the stage for the negotiations at Ghent in the Netherlands. Through those victories, the United States preserved its territorial claims in the final treaty, ending the war without ceding any land to the enemy, Great Britain.

As the 150th anniversary of the battle approached, many activities were planned to commemorate the milestone. The Clinton County Artists Association planned an art exhibition as part of the festivities. Works of modern art and contemporary subjects would be on display. Paintings that could be classified as "Americana" were entered into a competition. It was announced that the judging panel of experts would include R. Ralph Maurello from the Old Mill Art School of Elizabethtown, Dr. Boylan Fitz-Gerald of Paleface Mountain, and Jack Schoof from the Art Department at the State University College in Plattsburgh.

Given Doc's love of skiing and the view from Paleface, it might not surprise anyone that he would vote in favor of a painting of Whiteface Mountain. The judges' deliberations were top secret, but one could well imagine Doc making the pitch. In any case, it was announced that the first prize winner in the Americana series in the Battle of Plattsburgh Art Exhibit was Clarence Archambault's painting of Whiteface Mountain.

## '64 Paleface Annex

In early October, Doc purchased a property from New York State Assemblyman Willis Stevens who represented Brewster, New York. The property had been operated as a Ski Lodge, having been completely redecorated in 1961. Doc renamed the property Paleface Annex. Chuck was to run it.

Jean Carol, Chuck, and their son Tim moved into the Annex just as the fall foliage was at its peak. Clara Hazelton's entry in the newspaper read as follows: "The first top week of the color season drew many cars through the beautiful Adirondacks over the weekend. The colors this year are in great variety and the reds and orange colors are a delight. There is also a chartreuse shading in many trees that did not seem to come out at all last year. Leaves are falling, people who want to see and get pictures of autumn foliage should not delay. Sunday night's vicious wind did not do much damage as expected. Gus Elliott, who retired on July 17 after thirty-four years working for the General Electric plant in Schenectady in the Steel Foundry Division of Large Generators and Motors, is now living at the family home on Springfield Road. Mr. and Mrs. Oswald of Hudson were guests of Col. And Mrs. Earl Unger over the weekend." Clara's news went from one unrelated story to another, often without changing paragraphs.

Soon the fall foliage season was over, and Paleface closed for the season.

## '64 Vacation in Mexico

With Patti off at boarding school in St. Johnsbury and Chuck and his family settled in at Paleface Annex, Doc and Jean felt like empty nesters in search of baby birds. They decided to take a long vacation in Mexico.

Their oldest son, daughter-in-law, and grandson left by car from the Adirondacks back in June for Guanajuato, Mexico. Doc and Jean arrived in Mexico by plane. They enjoyed the time away, and the time with family. For Jean, it was a very welcome break. It was nice to get in lots of relaxing time and fortunately their son's temporary teaching position provided for housing and a small pool as well.

For Doc, it was difficult to be idle and so far away from his usual activities. He couldn't work, couldn't make plans for the coming ski season or next summer's horseback riding season. He couldn't really paint or fish or hunt or ride horses. He didn't relax often, but it was during Doc's time in Mexico that Doc got the grand idea to install an indoor pool at Paleface.

Whenever Doc wasn't talking with someone, Paleface planning returned to the front of his mind almost immediately—each morning lying in bed before getting up, with eyes closed on beach chairs by the pool, and before falling asleep each night. The obsessive-compulsive planning thoughts of how to improve the business remained omnipresent.

Such was the life of an owner-entrepreneur. Doc was ever aware of the needs of the families of the staff and the opportunities that working at Paleface provided. Doc was always attuned to his guests at Paleface. He wanted their memories of Paleface to stand out. Doc wanted his guests to feel the comfort of home while at the same time be that special vacation they would never forget, and have difficulty topping. While it didn't just happen without a lot of effort, Jean and Doc's wonderful staff excelled at making it seem like their pleasure making customers feel like Paleface was built just for them.

Jean and Doc returned in early November. They were tanned and rested, and felt ready to face what they hoped would be a busy and rewarding fifth winter season for Paleface.

## '64 Planning Commission

Doc seemed never to say "no" to anything, rather preferring to take the "sure, I can do that" approach even before finding out the details. One of the things Doc had on his mind while he was in Mexico was his new position on the Planning Commission.

In November of 1964, the Essex County Supervisors formalized plans to create a fifteen person, Essex County Planning Board and unanimously voted the Planning Board a $10,000 budget. The goal was to create a first ever "master plan" for the county. The first task of the Planning Board was to conduct a study about whether creating a master plan was feasible.

Doc thought it was crazy to have a study about whether to do a plan. Perhaps a group of planners would make sense of endless planning. To him, it seemed like too much deliberation and too little action, but he didn't share his thoughts in that moment with others. Some things are better left unsaid. Then Doc though of Jean and smiled, recalling how she frequently quoted Thumper, from the Disney film *Bambi*: "If you can't say something nice, don't say nuthin' at all."

Meanwhile, the members of the new Planning Board would receive a six month indoctrination by state planners. Each of the towns in the county were to be represented on the Planning Board. Doc was named to represent the Town of Jay.

At the first meeting of the Planning Board, there was an extensive discussion about the need for a new office building in the county seat, the town of Elizabethtown. The plans also called for a "civil defense center" more commonly referred to by the public as a "bomb shelter" or even a "nuclear fallout shelter."

The rest of the meeting agenda went by the wayside as debate about whether the extra cost of having a bomb shelter in the county offices was necessary. Was there such a need, such an imminent threat that the town must have it? On the other hand, the way the plans were presented, the incremental cost of adding it didn't seem to be that much greater than the costs of the office building itself.

An hour into the conversation about a bomb shelter in Elizabethtown, and after giving thought and voice to the question of how many residents of the county could be saved if there was need for the use of such a shelter, Doc found his mind wandering to other things. One thing Doc's mind wandered to was plans to hunt grouse with friends Kingsland Ward of Cranford, New Jersey and Leon Doremus of Madison, New Jersey. Mr. Ward and Mr. Doremus came each November and would stay at Paleface for a week. It was incumbent on Doc to plan their hunting trips and escort them as well. And Doc loved doing it. As discussion about the expenses relating to a nuclear fallout shelter continued, Doc thought about the Halloween Dance the Auxiliary for the Wilmington Fire Department had held at Paleface, just a couple nights earlier. The cover charge and the ongoing collection of S&H Green Stamp books would help the Fire Department raise the funds to fill the kitchen at the Fire Department with modern appliances. Next, Doc thought about the national election being held the following day. Each candidate was making their final closing arguments. Doc thought about the civil rights legislation that had recently been passed as well as the war in Vietnam that seemed to escalate more and more each passing month. Would it be a landslide? Would the election be close? Those were the thoughts on Doc's mind. He had made up his mind which ticket to support a long time ago. (Of course, Lyndon B. Johnson and Hubert Humphrey won in a landslide, taking forty-five states and defeating Barry Goldwater.) Finally, before Doc's mind got a chance to wander further, the discussion ended and someone made a motion to adjourn. As Doc got up to leave, he wondered whether there was too much on his mind, or whether maybe that role wasn't right for him.

As it would turn out, Doc would only attend one meeting of the Essex County Planning Board, and never got the chance to be indoctrinated by the state planners.

## '64 Infectious Hepatitis

They had been home from Mexico for several weeks when Jean started to feel ill. It seemed to Jean that she had been stricken with influenza. Jean was tired, was experiencing an extremely upset stomach, and was running a fever. As Doc took Jean to the doctor's office, he had to admit he was beginning to feel poorly himself.

Their friend, Dr. Mackinnon, took one look into the whites of their eyes, and he knew. Infectious Hepatitis as it was known then. Today it would be known as Hepatitis A.

Doc asked how it could be possible. They had been home almost a month. Dr. Mackinnon informed Doc and Jean that the incubation period for Infectious Hepatitis was between two to six weeks, and worse, patients could feel ill for up to six months. Dr. Mackinnon indicated that most patients had symptoms for less than two months.

Both Doc and Jean's conditions worsened quickly.

Dr. Mackinnon suggested that Jean be treated in the hospital at Keene, and a couple of days later, Dr. Mackinnon insisted that Doc be admitted to the hospital as well.

Chuck had been getting things in order at the new Paleface Annex property, and had to let management of renovation plans at the Annex lapse. Paleface was not open for skiing, however there were many community events that needed tending during November and December.

Chuck made many trips to the hospital to check on his parents and to bring paperwork for Doc or Jean to sign in their hospital beds.

When Thanksgiving came, Chuck drove to St. Johnsbury, Vermont to bring Patti home for the holiday. Doc and Jean celebrated Thanksgiving at the hospital.

When Patti visited her Mom and Dad at the hospital that weekend, she didn't want to return to school. (To be fair, Patti never really wanted to go to school!)

Dr. Mackinnon assured Patti that Doc and Jean would be fine and that she should return to school. Jean insisted that Patti go back, and that she shouldn't worry, they were receiving the best treatment that modern medicine had to offer. On the way out, Dr. Mackinnon told Patti that while they would be fine, it was possible that they wouldn't be fully back to themselves for several months.

## '64 Rudolph the Red Nosed Reindeer

Doc and Jean shared a room at the hospital in Keene for three weeks. In addition to feeling thoroughly miserable, they were incredibly bored. They had both read everything that had been brought to them, and some things they had read two or three times. They had talked about everything they could think of to talk about. The television was immensely helpful and filled in those spots when they didn't want to read or sleep, for what else was there to do?

In Jean's mind, it seemed like the television had been on westerns non-stop. They had watched many, many westerns. Westerns dominated the prime time and late night movie schedules.

One evening, Doc was feeling particularly sick. The television had been left on CBS. It was 5pm on Sunday, December 6th when the very first broadcast of the Christmas classic, *Rudolph the Red Nosed Reindeer* came across the airwaves. Doc and Jean watched the program and were touched by the simple pleasure of watching the show. Near the end of the program, Jean said to Doc, "This program is wonderful. Children will be enjoying this, every year at Christmas for generations to come."

"Perhaps you're right," replied Doc. At 6pm when the program was over, Doc fell asleep for a while and woke up in time for *Bonanza* at 9. Unfortunately, the TV had to be changed to NBC, which required getting out of bed to turn the dial to channel 5.

## '64 Press Releases

Being trapped in the hospital gave Doc unlimited time to pen press releases. Doc's press releases generally could be counted on to keep the public well informed about the doings at Paleface. That year, the newspapers could barely keep up.

Doc wrote the news stories out by hand each day, and Chuck brought them back with him to Paleface. Jane typed them up, put them in envelopes and affixed nickel postage stamps to them and took them to the post office in town. Jane's supply of handsome red, white, and black Civil War Centennial postage stamps was disappearing fast!

Doc's first press release from his temporary office in Keene featured ticket pricing for the 1964-1965 skiing season. Then Doc wrote a long press release about the work Dana and his crew had done on the mountain while Doc and Jean were away in Mexico and continuing into their time in the hospital, noting the extensive cutting, widening, bull-dozing and grading of the upper mountain, and also the carving and sculpting of the expert Big Horn trail. Another press release announced that the new ski season would see the exciting debut of an area for sleds and toboggans, to provide a little variety for the skiers in the family, and to provide outdoor winter entertainment for non-skiing family members. Yet another press release announced the addition of Charles Draper to the staff of Paleface, to assist Dana Peck, and touted the credentials of the new and returning members of the Paleface staff.

## '64 Planning

While Doc and Jean were in the hospital, plans were finalized for the Skate 'n Ski Weekend. Sometimes it was called the Ski 'n Skate Weekend, depending on which sport was favored by whoever was mentioning it.

The president of the AuSable Jaycees announced that the event would be held on January 30 - 31, 1965. The skating races would be held in Keene at the village skating rink on Saturday. The skiing races would be held at Paleface on Sunday. Of course, Karl and Putzi Jost and members of the Paleface Ski Club would be conducting the races, and members of the Jaycees would be helping as well. It was announced that the races were open to any student of the AuSable Forks Central School or the Keene Valley Central School.

As part of the event, each school would nominate candidates for King and Queen, with balloting including all students in grades nine through twelve. Members of the local media would select from among the candidates, and a King and Queen would be named at a coronation ball at Paleface on Saturday evening. The King and Queen would each win a $50 savings bond.

Gold, Silver, and Bronze medals would be awarded in several age categories, for both the skating races and the skiing races at a ceremony immediately following the skiing races on Sunday afternoon.

Jean and Doc were still in the hospital when the Kiwanis Club held its Christmas Party at Paleface on December 19, 1964. Just days before Christmas, it was announced that the Boy Scout's 12th Annual Winter Sports Day would be held at Paleface in the middle of January.

## '64 Jailbreak

Doc's first day out of the hospital was also his first day back in the office at Paleface. His desk was clean. Jane had some checks for Doc to sign. Everything else was taken care of. The great staff at Paleface, led by Dana, Jane, and Chuck, had tended to everything.

On the way from the hospital to Paleface, Doc shared words of praise with his son, appreciation for taking care of business so well. That mood continued back at Paleface, with everyone gathered around for a brief staff meeting. Doc thanked everyone for the cards, visits, and prayers. Doc told everyone the place looked great and it felt great to have finally "busted out." Doc told everyone that Dr. Mackinnon expected to release Jean the next day, possibly the day after that. He closed by saying that Jean sent her love and looked forward to seeing everyone in a couple of days.

Though it was late December, there was no snow on the ground and according to the weather man, there was no snow in the forecast.

Half an hour later, Doc and Jane were standing just outside the slope side door looking at an overcast sky. Doc looked at the clouds and said, "Those constipated clouds need to have a movement and send us some snow!"

It was two days before Christmas Eve. The headline in the newspaper read "Awaits New Snow" and went on to describe the impact on the owner operators of the various businesses in the area that depended on snow to bring in the tourists. The situation was summed up quite succinctly with the phrase "no snow/no dough."

There was no snow Thursday, Christmas Eve.

There was no "White Christmas" on Friday.

## '64 Snow in Siberia/Dancing here Tonight

Saturday night on the triangular chalk board that stood on the floor at Paleface was a sign that said, "Snow in Siberia—Dancing Here Tonite." A picture of that sign appeared in the newspaper on December 31st. The article went on to read:

3 OWNERS CHEERFUL THROUGH $50,000 RAIN STORM—Five to eight inches of snow fell Sunday night, putting an end to the exodus of winter sports fans from Adirondack Mountain ski resorts and promising the possibility that those businessmen who gain a living from the chancy white powder may finish the season in the black. Through the Christmas weekend it appeared to be a forlorn hope, as unseasonal rain and 60 degree temperatures stripped normally white slopes down to the bare earth and drove skiers back to their homes or further north in search of better conditions. What looked like the biggest season ever turned into a nightmare, according to William Johnson of the Whiteface Mountain Authority. Sportsman's Inn in Wilmington had been sold out weeks in advance for the ten day period from Christmas through New Year's. On Sunday, December 28, Carl Steinhoff stated that not a soul was in residence there. He anticipated doing 25 percent of his winter business over that period and said that even if snow fell Sunday it was too late to help him recoup his losses and he could see no hope for a prosperous New Year. Boylan Fitz-Gerald of Paleface Lodge reported losing between $1,500 and $2,000 a day during the snowless holiday season. He fared better than either the hotels or the Whiteface Mountain facility. Due to the fact that he provides entertainment, rooms, and skiing, many of his guests remain when all are deserting the specialized facilities. Fitz-Gerald speculated that Whiteface could have been losing $6,000 to $8,000 a day. Johnson's estimate placed at $20,000 the loss for the entire weekend. We can never make it up, he said. The tension was eased somewhat Monday at Whiteface when an estimated 2,000 skiers jammed the hills to make up for time lost over the rainy period. The slopes can handle 3,000. "Closed until further notice" signs were ripped from the doors at Whiteface Lodge and the T-Bar started to operate. Ski reports there described eight inches of powder snow on a man-made base. Official spokesmen for the Authority stated that the snow making machinery

would be operated as much as possible to insure excellent slopes. Boylan Fitz-Gerald, owner of Paleface Ski Center, sits in front of a sign inside his lodge. Guests stayed at Paleface over the weekend in hopes snow would fall. Some of the disappointed visitors tried to put a cheerful face on the situation Sunday before the snow started to fall. A Ridgewood, New Jersey couple and their son, who had booked in at Paleface Lodge Thursday, admitted that they should have left their skis in New Jersey. They called Whiteface every day through the four-day period because they heard that if the temperature dropped the snow making machinery would be pressed into service. They liked the show Lake Placid put on to encourage visitors to stay; free skating and movies. In a restaurant, three young ladies from New York City poured over a map of the ski country and inquired about snow reports from the Laurentians and Vermont. At the moment, the sign in the dining room at Paleface Lodge told the whole story *Snow in Siberia—Dancing* here tonight. What a difference a day makes."

Another North Country newspaper published a picture that said it better than the words in the caption: "Through empty ski racks at Paleface Ski Center in Jay, tourists are seen walking over grass slopes where they had hoped to ski."

Clara Hazelton's report provided the final weather analysis for 1964: "The snow went down the drains and the beautiful warm days of Christmas and afterwards were green. On Sunday evening the air changed gradually colder and hoar frost covered everything giving the world a luminous look. In the night residents were awakened by machines grunting and scraping and clinking. The snow plows at work? By daylight the world was again covered with snow, about seven inches of it. The Whiteface Mountain Ski Center got out a snow report: T-Bar and one chairlift operating, skiing fair, efficient snow-making machine put out snow all night and Monday morning. Wilmington is back in business again."

## '65 Boy Scouts Winter Sports Day

The snow storm from the 27th of December kept skiers happy for about a week. Then conditions deteriorated and prayers for new snow went unanswered.

By the middle of January there was little snow left at all. To make matters worse, temperatures had plummeted. Paleface was forced to welcome the Cub Scouts, Boy Scouts, Explorers and their families with less than hospitable sub-zero temperatures and skiing conditions rated "poor." Even so, 45 Scouts earned merit badges for skiing. Regretfully, the slalom race had to be cancelled. Snowshoe races were held as scheduled.

Meanwhile, other events for the Scouts were held throughout the area. Ice skating races were held in the afternoon at the Lake Placid Municipal rink. Some Scouts enjoyed Whiteface Mountain, and other Scouts made a visit to the Mt. Van Hoevenberg Bobsled Run. The day ended with the first ever international Scout hockey game between the Rover Scouts of Montreal and the Adirondack Council Explorers (ACE). The Canadian Rovers won fourteen to two and took home the trophy. Overall, 700 Scouts participated in the various events.

Paleface made it through the 12th Annual Boy Scouts Winter Sports Day with as respectable a showing as could be hoped for under the circumstances and went right back to hoping for a hearty snow storm.

## '65 Ski 'n Skate Spectacular

The big Ski 'n Skate Spectacular had been heavily promoted for months. Everyone was talking about the event scheduled for the end of January. The races were open to all students over ten years old. The Spectacular also featured a Grand Ball on Saturday evening. Students in grades nine through twelve had been casting ballots for the King and Queen of the Ball for six weeks prior to the event. The student bodies of the AuSable Valley and Keene schools, whether skaters, skiers, or dancers, greatly anticipated the

Spectacular weekend. The skating races were planned for Saturday afternoon in Keene. The skiing races were scheduled for Sunday afternoon at Paleface.

With less than a week to go before the Ski 'n Skate Spectacular, a nasty ice storm hit the North Country. Still, optimism remained. How could snow cover be an issue at the end of January? It had to snow. It just had to. Thankfully and finally, it did, and just in time. On Saturday, just as skating races were getting underway in Keene, a light snow began to fall. All afternoon, snow fell gently.

The panel of judges that would crown the King and Queen of the Ball were enjoying dinner with Doc and Arto Monaco, the founder and creator of the Land of Makebelieve, a theme park for younger children in Upper Jay. Arto would serve as the master of ceremonies for the Grand Ball. The esteemed, independent judging panel included five judges representing local media.

Following dinner, the Judges retreated to the meeting area in the loft. The contestants were required to be available during the judges' deliberations as well and they congregated nervously in the lounge area. Mr. O'Neill, president of the Jaycees, escorted each student up the stairs to speak to the judges. In the interest of fairness, the students' presentations went in alphabetical order by last name. Somehow the students made it through their interviews.

Mr. O'Neill suggested that the judges round the contestants down to two finalists based on their applications and then pick the one who did better in the interview. The panel of judges nodded and muttered their unanimous consent. In both cases the outcome was clear, however, the judges deliberated thoroughly. No one could claim they didn't take the task very seriously. Four minutes before 9pm Mr. O'Neill wrote one name on a piece of paper, folded it in thirds and put it in an envelope labeled Queen. The King's name was placed in a second envelope. Mr. O'Neill placed both names in his sports coat pocket.

Students had been arriving all evening. Red Nadeau had been playing guitar and singing folk songs in the Lounge. A warm fire was in the fireplace behind him. The last of the dinner tables were being cleared. The Paleface Orchestra was getting set up in the corner, in front of the enormous windows on the slope side of the building. The band had worked a good number of popular current songs into the program for the ball. Normally the older audiences at Paleface appreciated songs that were a good deal less current.

At 9pm Doc was at the microphone. He extended a warm welcome to everyone present, and reviewed the details for the skiing races to be held the following afternoon. Then Doc introduced the master of ceremonies for the evening, first as a friend and hero, and then as a founder, inventor, artist, and entrepreneur whose vision had been realized. The audience clapped loudly and received Arto warmly.

Arto smiled, then squinted and surveyed the crowd. "Good evening, boys and girls. I should say men and women. I think I have seen most of you at the Land of Makebelieve. I guess that was a good number of years ago now! But you know you're never too old to use your imagination. And I guess there are sixteen of you who still want to become King or Queen! Well, I know where we can find a castle!" Of course, Arto was referring to the castle with its pastel turrets which was the central landmark at the Land of Makebelieve.

Arto told a few short stories about the work he had done at Santa's Workshop in Wilmington, at Storytown in Glens Falls, and in Florida for Walt Disney. Then Arto thanked the members of the Jaycees for sponsoring the event and for making the weekend Spectacular possible. Then, he recognized the members of the Paleface Ski Club for co-sponsoring the Coronation Ball. After that, each school principal introduced their royal candidates, and said something very nice about each one. As their names were called, each candidate came to the front of the room and stood behind the speakers to face the crowd. Each of the candidates were dressed in their best, most formal attire.

Arto told the audience that it probably wouldn't be nice to keep these poor, would-be Kings and Queens waiting any longer, however, it might be fun! With a little good natured teasing out of the way, Arto called on Miss Elaine Reilly to come forward. Miss Reilly, the art teacher at AuSable had crafted crowns suitable for Adirondack royalty. Miss Reilly was also the bearer of the bonds which she had picked up at the bank earlier in the week.

Suspense was building. Arto made a show of looking in each of his pockets for the envelopes containing the winning names. No one made a sound.

Arto held up the envelope that said Queen. "Ladies before gentlemen," Arto proclaimed as he opened the envelope and took out a sheet of paper. "It is my pleasure to announce the Queen of your ball—her majesty," and then Arto paused longer and more awkwardly than you might see on a television awards program and then finally, slowly said her name. "Marcia Thompson, and her court of seven lovely princesses."

Each of the girls hugged Marcia, who was grinning from ear to ear. Mrs. Reilly planted the one of its kind crowns on her head and attached it with bobby pins. Chuck took many pictures. Arto presented Marcia with the $50 savings bond. "On behalf of the Jaycees, it's my privilege to present you, my Queen, with this grand prize. Congratulations, young lady." Arto beamed and turned to the boys. "May I present, his royal highness, the King of your Ball—his majesty Billy Hackett and his court of seven valiant princes. King Billy, before I turn you over to Miss Reilly, I would like to present you with a savings bond on behalf of our generous Jaycees. Now I wonder, Miss Reilly, are you going to put bobby pins in the King's hair?"

The audience of 250 people laughed heartily and then Arto concluded by introducing the royal minstrels, better known as the Paleface Orchestra. After the King and Queen danced a royal waltz, the band played "The Name Game," and the kids participated in verse after verse of the latest dance craze. The song was released by Shirley Ellis late in 1964, and peaked at number three on the charts. Each of the kids tried their own name, and perfected the dance that went with it. There were so many kids at the ball that it took almost an hour to get through all of them.

The game required them to remove the first consonants from the beginning of their names and then replace them first with 'B,' then 'M,' and finally 'F.' It was a little complicated, kind of silly, yet lots of fun. Most names fit the rules nicely, but in every case it sounded like a nonsensical children's nursery rhyme.

Chuck Fitz-Gerald was working at the bar, and confided to his father that it might be wise if he didn't play that name game.

At the awards presentation the next day, twenty-four skiing medals were presented to boys and girls in each age category. Thirty skating medals were presented. Both student bodies took note of the fact that the King and the Queen, plus both the Champion ski trophies, went to students who represented the AuSable Forks school. Perhaps there was some consolation in the knowledge that the overall medal count score was dead even, twenty-seven medals for each school. Nonetheless, the stage was set for competition in the following year.

Monday morning after the Ski 'n Skate Spectacular weekend was over, Doc sat down and penned a letter to the editor of the newspapers. Later that afternoon, Jane typed the letter and mailed it to the newspaper, which was then published on Thursday February 4, 1965. Doc expressed appreciation to the members of the Jaycees and also the members of the Paleface Ski Club.

## '65 Jackie Kennedy

Well into February, Paleface was still waiting on snow. The snowfall that saved the Ski 'n Skate Spectacular had run thin. Paleface was open for business, but there wasn't enough snow on the mountain for skiing. Whiteface had most generously permitted Paleface's ski instructors to give their customers lessons at Whiteface.

On Saturday, February 20th, Karl Jost, Putzi Jost, Doc Fitz-Gerald, and Pete Pelkey were instructing their students when they noticed something a little strange. There was a large family of children, an elegantly dressed woman, and a couple of men who looked like they were prepared for battle.

As it turned out, it was the former First Lady of the United States who came to ski Whiteface with her children, Caroline and John, as well as her brother in law, the newly-elected senator from the state of New York. Senator Robert Kennedy brought his six children to Whiteface as well.

Charlie Draper, who worked with Dana at Paleface, had a sister named Caroline who was a ski instructor at Whiteface. Her husband was Mr. Serge Lussi and he operated the ski school at Whiteface.

While Jackie Kennedy, and the two heavily armed men that accompanied her, took a ski lesson with former Olympic ski coach Karl Fahrner, Charlie's sister Caroline Lussi gave lessons to Caroline and John as well as their cousins Courtney and Michael. When their lessons were done, Charlie Draper's sister Caroline got to meet Jackie Kennedy and was more than happy to report that she was every bit as beautiful and elegant as she was portrayed in the media. Additionally, Caroline Lussi reported that Mrs. Kennedy was very sweet and polite and mothering to her children and to Robert Kennedy's children.

Charlie's sister didn't get a chance to meet Robert Kennedy. While the others were skiing, Robert Kennedy had to visit Tupper Lake where the community was working overtime trying to save the Sunmount Veterans Hospital which had been slated for abandonment by the government after decades of service to veterans, particularly the veterans with tuberculosis from World War I and II.

When all was said and done, Senator Robert Kennedy couldn't save Sunmount from closure. Perhaps he had tried. Fortunately, Governor Rockefeller had been able to repurpose the hospital within a couple months of its closure as an important state hospital facility for serving patients with intellectual disabilities.

All the Whiteface Ski instructors had the pleasure of a very quick introduction to Mrs. Kennedy, and since the Paleface Ski instructors just happened to be there as well, they too had the chance to make her acquaintance. While ever so brief in the occurrence, the story made for countless hours in the re-telling, back at Paleface.

Charlie Draper got to hear it at work from the Paleface ski instructors. When Charlie got home, the phone was ringing as he came through the door. His sister told him all about it again.

Back in the office at Paleface, Doc got to feeling a little sorry for Paleface and then remembered instead to focus on expressing appreciation for being allowed to bring his crew to Whiteface. Doc pulled a piece of paper out of the desk drawer and wrote another letter to the editor to publicly express appreciation to the management at Whiteface, and their snowmaking capabilities, noting, "I am sure that most of our motel operators, inn keepers, and lodge owners in the area would agree with me in congratulating the Whiteface management for the good job to help tide us over an almost snowless winter."

## '65 Stork Shower

The first Wednesday evening in March there was a stork shower, more commonly known as a baby shower. Pearl Pierce, Paleface's legendary pastry person and breakfast chef, had a grand-daughter who was expecting. Pearl loved children, and couldn't wait for the new baby to arrive.

## '65 The Pride of Paleface

A couple days later, the pride of Paleface, Wayne Wright was at Royal Mountain in Johnstown, New York, competing in the Ahern Memorial Tournament. Wayne came in second in the slalom race and fourth place in the giant slalom. That performance qualified Wayne to be entered in the upcoming Eastern States sanctioned races featuring skiers from New Hampshire, Vermont, and New York to be held on March 20th in Middlebury, Vermont.

## '65 Boat for Sale

Meanwhile, Doc came to the sad realization that the boat he had purchased a few years earlier had not been used as much as he'd hoped. Somehow, Doc had thought he would have free time enough to explore the many beautiful lakes of the Adirondacks.

When Doc did take a day off, he always seemed to find himself fly fishing in the river instead of boating on the lakes. Doc priced it to move, and someone got a great deal on an almost new 3HP Johnson Sea Horse outboard that had logged less than twenty hours of use.

## '65 Stolen: One Caribou Head

One Sunday morning after a particularly busy Saturday night at the Happy Hunting Ground Cocktail Lounge, Doc noticed that the Caribou Head that normally resided on the wall behind the bar was missing. Doc asked everyone, and nobody had any information about it.

The next day Doc sent in an ad to the newspaper that read "Stolen: One Caribou Head (Looks something like a moose). Reward to anyone giving information leading to recovery. Contact Paleface Lodge Phone 946-2272."

The fact is Paleface had its share of pranksters, and one of those pranksters thought it would be funny to put the caribou head somewhere completely unexpected. The caribou had been temporarily located in the bathroom of suite number one, Doc and Jean's room.

Doc and Jean had spent the weekend at home. At 3pm on Monday afternoon Jean retired to the suite to relax for an hour or two before dinner. Jean opened the bathroom door and let out a blood curdling shriek. Doc had been coming down the hallway when he heard Jean's scream, then came running to help.

When Doc got to the room, and turned to enter the bathroom, then came face to nose with the caribou, he doubled over with laughter. "That was a good one." Jean was standing next to the caribou with a frown on her face. "I'll go fetch the game warden," Doc said to Jean as he went searching for someone who could help remove the beast.

Before Doc could leave, hand on her hip, Jean inquired, "Wanted. Dead or Alive. How much is my reward?" Then finally, Jean revealed a trace of a smile.

Dana moved the lost caribou back to its rightful place behind the bar before he left for home that day. Nonetheless, Jane received nearly a dozen follow up phone calls about the ad in the newspaper, mostly pranksters, perhaps those originally responsible for the caribou relocation. To this day, the mystery remains unsolved.

## '65 Representing Paleface

Everyone at Paleface was overjoyed to learn that Wayne Wright had made a great showing at the Middlebury Bowl on March 20th, coming in sixth out of seventy-five boys. Wayne's coaches, Karl and Putzi Jost, were very pleased. Wayne's mother, Jean Wright, who served skiers lunches at Paleface was enormously proud. A top ten finish at the Bowl earned Wayne the right to represent the Eastern region Nationally.

## '65 Patti Graduates High School

As winter was coming to an end in 1965, Jean was making plans to attend Patti's graduation from St. Johnsbury Academy in June. Chuck and Jean Carol also made plans to attend the ceremony. Afterwards, they would bring Patti home with them. On Tuesday, Jean planned a family celebration. Doc and Jean's oldest son Allen, his wife Carolyn, and their son, were there as well. They had recently returned from Mexico and arrived in town in time to attend Patti's graduation party. Doc and Jean would have loved to visit longer, but the following day, Doc, Jean, and Jane were scheduled to leave for the National Ski Operators Association meeting at Mount Snow in Vermont.

## '65 Christmas Trees in Boston

Chuck Fitz-Gerald was president of the Whiteface Kiwanis Club in 1965. Under Chuck's leadership, the Whiteface Kiwanis Club set their sights on Boston. Chuck appointed Ray L'Hommedieu to head the Invasion Committee.

Ray was born on Long Island, served during World War II in the Navy, and then in the Suffolk County police department, working his way up to lieutenant. In 1962, Ray retired to Wilmington, where his wife Florence was born. Ray's first retirement didn't take, so he took up a security post at The Lake Placid Club.

Chuck and Ray notwithstanding, the real inspiration behind the Invasion was a self-proclaimed "dyed-to-the-hide" Wilmingtonian named Lee Brow. Lee was born in Saranac Lake, New York in 1890. After being raised in the Town of Wilmington, Lee followed where opportunity led, to Massachusetts and New Hampshire, and finally settled in Boston. For all of Lee's adult life, he never lived in the Adirondacks, and yet the Adirondack spirit always remained within him. Each year, Lee returned to Wilmington and personally saw to it that new, fresh flags were placed at the graves of all the veterans in the cemetery. And each year Lee returned near the end of August for a vacation.

Back in Boston and at the age of seventy-five, Lee held the position of executive vice president of the State Chamber of Commerce. In addition, Lee was a long standing member of the Boston Kiwanis Club. As a guest at a Whiteface Kiwanis Club meeting, Lee suggested an idea that would forever link the people of Boston with the Town of Wilmington. The Whiteface Kiwanis Club enthusiastically and unanimously supported the proposal, and Ray L'Hommedieu's committee was authorized to implement the suggestion.

The plan called for fifty Adirondack fir trees to be planted in the Boston Commons, and in addition half a dozen white birches would be transplanted to Boston as well. Doc donated the trees. The Whiteface Kiwanis Club also authorized the placement of a commemorative plaque to be placed somewhere in the famous downtown Boston park.

The last day of April, the truckload of tiny trees got transported for transplant. The Whiteface Kiwanians making the trip with the trees included Tom Keegan of Keegan's Motel and Restaurant, and Arthur Coulson, the proprietor of the Whiteface Market, as well as Chuck and Doc. The four men made an official presentation at an inter-club meeting with the Boston Kiwanis Club. Doc presented a vision: "Just imagine, decades after all of us are gone, these trees will tower over tourists." And on the way home the next day Doc joked about their "Boston Tree Party." The Invasion was complete.

Few Wilmingtonians would ever see the plaque. However, Lee knew where to find the fifty-six trees. From then on, whenever Lee needed to feel close to his boyhood home, he would visit the Adirondack natives nestled in the big city.

## '65 Paleface Buys Whiteface

Doc couldn't wait to play a prank of his own on his unsuspecting crew. The great Caribou incident still had not been avenged. It was late June. The summer riding season was just getting under way. Doc hastily called a staff meeting one afternoon.

"It's great to have everyone back together for another great summer at Paleface. And I have some huge news to share with everyone." Doc had a newspaper in his hand. "All week long I have been dying to share this announcement. As incredible as it may sound, little old Paleface has purchased Whiteface!" Doc held up the newspaper, folded over to make the headline look as impressive as possible.

Doc's crew was stunned. Dana raised both eyebrows. Mary Wallace's jaw dropped. Bea Lincoln's eyes opened so wide you could see the whites all the way around. "Any questions?"

There was a long silence which hung in the air. Members of the crew turned and looked into each other's eyes, with elevated eyebrows, and unformed questions on lips. The silence held briefly but felt much longer. Jane had an enormous smile on her face, and couldn't help but let out the slightest laugh. The previous week, Jane had written a check for $300 to Mr. David Strong of Wilmington. Then she had typed Doc's latest press release, titled: "Paleface Buys Whiteface."

Doc continued, "That's right, the seemingly impossible has become possible!" After a long pause, Doc let the crew off the hook and shared the joke with them. "Oh, it's not what you think, in fact, the piebald gelding formerly called Baldy, owned by the David Strong family of Wilmington was purchased for the Paleface riding stable and will be renamed Whiteface. Thus "PALEFACE BUYS WHITEFACE."

Then the real meeting began. "As you know, every year we like to come back bigger and better. Over at Whiteface they have the luxury of making snow which helps them when Mother Nature can't see her way to generously providing the white gold. We have been working on plans to put in snow making at Paleface too." The crew began clapping and cheering before Doc completed his sentence.

Doc went on to explain that they would need a plentiful source of water. The property did not include a nearby lake, pond, or river. It was hoped that a grand lake could be located beneath the ground. When the lodge was originally built, sufficient water for the lodge was found at a depth of 85 feet. Doc told his staff about a man from Vermont who was introduced by Lyman Morgan from AuSable Acres, and added that he was scheduled to come to Paleface in August.

There were a few questions from the crew. One of the chambermaids asked, "Is it hard to make snow?"

Doc answered briefly that there was an art to making snow, and then deferred to Dana. Dana shared what he had heard about making snow from friends at Whiteface, and what he learned from attending skiing association meetings. Most of Dana's explanation centered around the importance of the temperatures being between ten and twenty-five degrees. "If it is too cold, then the pipes can freeze. If it is too warm the snow, if it forms at all has too high a moisture content. And then, you have to let the machine-made snow stand for six to eight hours before grooming."

The next thing Doc shared with everyone was a plan to install an indoor pool. Doc thought it would be another way to keep visitors at Paleface. As far as Doc knew, maybe only one other ski resort in the North Country had an indoor pool for its guests. "It should be a grand thing to have a pool, and will delight children of all ages," Doc concluded.

And then, as if that were not enough news, Doc announced plans to put in a game room. Not like the ping pong table in the loft, but the kind of game room with a pool table, mechanical shuffleboard style bowling, and some of those new-fangled pinball machines kids couldn't get enough of. Doc added, "I must confess that it is a lot of fun pulling that plunger and sending the ball flying around, bouncing against all the bumpers making sounds and flashing lights!"

Doc checked his watch, aware that the meeting had gone on for quite some time, and confided, "I wanted to let you know about these goings on. Normally we would be sharing all of this publicly, but I want to wait until we prove we can get the water we need. In the mean-time let everyone you know Paleface is open for the summer. We'd be glad to take them out on the trails, or just have them stop by for breakfast, lunch, or dinner!"

As always, Doc asked, "Does anyone have anything they would like to share with everybody?"

Jean reminded everyone about the Ladies' Night banquet and dance being held by the Rotary Club of AuSable forks on Saturday night. The Rotarians were being served a roast beef dinner.

## '65 Moving On

One day, Karl Jost asked Doc to take a walk with him. Outside in the fresh air, by the Rendezvous Bell, Karl told Doc that he had been offered two jobs that he was excited to accept. First, Karl would become a certifying examiner for the Canadian Skiing Association. Second, a new ski center that was being planned had convinced Karl to set up a ski school there and the developer wanted Karl to be actively involved in creating their resort from scratch. The new ski center was in Clinton County, near the Canadian border on Lyon Mountain. The developer had an extremely ambitious plan. The ski center would be an Austrian/Bavarian themed resort modeled after a small skiing village in the European Alps. The resort would be called Lowenburg, which is German for Lion Mountain.

The Lowenberg site had been carefully researched and chosen as a particularly heavy snowfall area. The business plan sounded great to Karl. Doc was very understanding. Their personal relationship made it that much harder for Karl to break the news to Doc. He was essentially going to be working for a competitor. Doc reassured Karl that his concerns were nonsense. Business was business. He had his career to manage first and foremost. Their friendship would definitely continue.

As for the Paleface Ski School, Putzi would be most welcome to stay at Paleface and become Acting Director of the Ski School. Putzi had worked very hard, was a thorough and diligent operations manager and whenever she was in charge, things ran very, very smoothly.

## '65 Drilling

It was the peak of summer, smack dab in the middle of August, when Howard Cardin of Hancock, Vermont arrived in the Paleface parking lot with his small fleet of equipment and vehicles and his entourage of junior apprentices. Doc and Jean greeted them warmly, and invited them to make themselves at home at Paleface while they were drilling. It was late in the afternoon, so all the men accomplished the first day was a long, detailed tour of Paleface, inside and outside.

Doc showed Mr. Cardin and his men where he planned to have the pool built, where he planned to have the heated shed that would house the water tanks and which trails were the top priorities.

Howard Cardin asked for a few minutes alone, and wandered as if blind, weaving around apparently without purpose. An observer might have thought perhaps Mr. Cardin had too much to drink. It might have looked like he was a shaman in a hypnotic trance being led by the "Great Spirit" to just the right spot. Finally, Mr. Cardin stopped, stood still for a minute and then with a grunt crossed his arms and simply said, "*Here*."

Mr. Cardin and his men stayed at Paleface, and enjoyed a few drinks at the bar. In the morning Doc had breakfast with Mr. Cardin and they talked about the project. Mr. Cardin warned Doc, "Don't get your hopes up too high, Mr. Fitz-Gerald. You must remember this is a mountain, we are in a mountainous area and mountains are made of giant rocks, blocks, slabs, and ledges. I guarantee you we will need to drill through a lot of this to find what we are seeking. My equipment is state of the art and cost $120,000. It can cut through solid rock at twenty feet per hour. Dirt and softer rock is much faster. Depending on what's under there it could take me all day to go 200 feet. I must remind you I can get to a maximum depth of 1,000 feet, and you will recall I had to go well over 800 feet at AuSable Acres. My site rate is $2,500 per day, and we will put in a good ten-hour day as we discussed on the telephone. Do you have a lucky rabbit's foot, or any superstitions, Mr. Fitz-Gerald?" asked Howard Cardin.

"I think a simple prayer will suffice, my friend," Doc said warmly as he bowed his head briefly and closed his eyes for fifteen seconds or so. "Very well, Mr. Cardin. Please let me know if there is anything you and your men need. We will have lunch ready for you at noon."

The first day, Mr. Cardin's equipment made great progress. At the end of the day, he had drilled 105 feet, very quickly the first hour. After that it was alternating bursts of fast and slow for another hour. Then it was clear Mr. Cardin's equipment was boring through granite, and couldn't maintain a pace of twenty feet per hour. Day two went well also. Another ninety feet, work proceeded at approximately the same pace as day one, only without the initial speed achieved at the top most level. At quitting time, they were 210 feet deep. At eight the next morning, the boring started back up again. The crew quit for lunch at noon. By noon they had reached 300 feet.

The men returned to drilling after a hearty lunch. Forty minutes later, the equipment which had been moving slowly and steadily suddenly lurched. The motor snorted and suddenly took off. Mr. Cardin said to himself, looks like we're on to something here! It didn't take him long to confirm his conclusion. Mr. Cardin said to the closest young man, "Go find Mr. Fitz-Gerald, son."

Jake took off running, and then a crazy idea grabbed hold of him. He ran to the Rendezvous Bell where the skiers met in the winter for ski class. Jake grabbed the thick knotted rope and rang that bell with all his might. The familiar sound carried throughout Paleface, and didn't stop. The crew thought it was strange to hear that sound in the summertime. And it wasn't stopping! Jane was on her way out the front door and Doc was right behind her. Only one of them was needed for the task, but both had the unstoppable momentum and insatiable curiosity.

"What the devil's going on, young man?" screamed Doc over the sound of the ringing bell.

About this time, Mr. Cardin started hoofing it toward the bell as well.

Jake stopped ringing the bell, grinning ear to ear and said, "Mr. Fitz-Gerald, Mr. Cardin needs to see you right away."

Everyone laughed mightily, and Howard Cardin said, "I told you to go get Mr. Fitz-Gerald, son. I don't know what possessed you to ring that durn bell!"

"I like this man's sense of drama, Mr. Cardin," said Doc, and everybody laughed again. Then Doc said, "You rang?"

"Yes sir, Doc," said Howard. "We have found you an underground lake. We struck it rich at a depth of 312 feet. You are a very lucky man sir! We'll be out of town by sundown, so you can rent our rooms out if you can find customers for them. I can write you out a bill if you like, but you should be glad it is only going to cost you $5,000. I would have guessed it would be twice that before we were done!"

Doc, who could be known to exhibit frivolous behavior now and then, performed an awkward move. Doc jumped in the air, knees spread wide, and touched his heels together beneath, and hollered, "Whoopty-doo!" Fictional Jed Clampett on *The Beverly Hillbillies* could not have been more excited to find the black gold beneath his soil, than Doc was to find the white gold at Paleface.

Howard Cardin returned to work, and installed the enormous

pipe that would reach deep down into the depths of Lake Paleface, far beneath the resort.

Doc returned to the dining room to find Jean. Doc found Jean organizing produce in the walk-in cooler behind the kitchen. Within the confines of the cold, dark refrigerator, Doc shared the great news with Jean and they warmly shared a chilly embrace.

Jane returned to the office and prepared a check for $5,000. That put a dent in the checkbook balance. Jane brought the check to Doc, who by then was at his desk writing a brief personal note for Mr. Cardin to go with the check. Then Doc took the check and the note, and on the way back toward the front door grabbed a painting off the wall. Doc thought it would make a nice tip. He was feeling a great sense of elation and was in a very generous mood, although that wasn't extraordinary.

Howard Cardin and his crew were almost done packing up their convoy. Doc presented Howard with the check and the note, which included an open-ended invitation to stop in and visit in the winter time for a nice long weekend. Then Doc presented Howard with the painting he had made of the converging trails.

Mr. Cardin was amazed and impressed. "Well, this is a first!" said Howard, who was happy to receive such a tip. Howard Cardin liked the painting well enough until Doc told him the story about how the painting came to feature Mrs. Kennedy and the Beatles.

Jake, who was seldom far from Howard Cardin, piped in with an enthusiastic, "FAR OUT!"

Howard Cardin and his fleet pulled out of the Paleface parking lot about 4:30 in the afternoon on their way home to Vermont."

## '65 Land of Makebelieve

It was one of those beautiful late summer days in the Adirondacks, crisp and cool in the morning, with a hint of fall not too distant on the calendar. The sky was a fresh, brilliant blue. The sunshine was abundant, with few clouds in the sky. The grass and the trees were a deep, vibrant green.

It was a rare day off for Jean. All summer, Jean had wanted to find a day to spend at the Land of Makebelieve. The opportunity presented itself perfectly one day when Doc and Jean's sons made plans to spend the day together waterskiing on Lake Placid. Jean suggested she could take Carolyn and Jean Carol and the boys to the Land of Makebelieve for the day, and went on to suggest packing the picnic basket and making a day of it.

The next morning, Jean and her daughters-in-law and her grandsons David and Tim pulled the Paleface station wagon into the Land of Makebelieve parking lot just as it was opening. Perfect timing! It was to be a truly magical day.

There were already a dozen cars in the parking lot, waiting for the attraction to open. It was a very popular part of the Adirondack experience, and a must for any family vacationing in the Adirondacks with a young family in the 1960s.

Many adults also appreciated the imaginative depiction of fairy tales brought to life, and combined into one extraordinary land where it hardly seemed strange to imagine a pastel colored castle right next to a Mississippi river boat. Just after the Fitz-Geralds arrived at the Land of Makebelieve, a bus carrying eighteen patients and residents from the Whallonsburg Home for the Aged pulled up to the entrance. Arto Monaco, the founder and proprietor himself was there to greet the elderly visitors. Arto had invited them to come spend the day, free of charge has his guests.

At the entrance to the park were two towers. The first experience of that magical land was a wooden medieval night in armor valiantly preparing to battle a scary, fire breathing dragon sculpture. Jean's grandsons couldn't wait to get through the gates, and took off running. Jean followed in hot pursuit, pushing an empty stroller. Carolyn and Jean Carol struggled to keep up under the weight of the provisions Jean had prepared for their picnic by the river, truly enough food to feed them for a week, and more variety than many restaurants.

Jean had plenty of opportunities to stop and catch her breath, as the boys darted into and out of one miniature building after another. Carolyn and Jean Carol had set the provisions at a picnic table in the shade and had rejoined Jean. Carolyn had purchased two rolls of film. Each roll had twelve pictures. The trick was to not take all the pictures quickly—you had to save film. Lots of time was spent looking into the tiny square box to try to get the perfect shot. It was expensive to process film, so it was a challenge not to waste the shots on a picture that wasn't good.

Almost every family that ever visited the Land of Makebelieve found a perfect photo opportunity at the little orange building shaped like a pumpkin, where Peter-Peter, the pumpkin eater lived. Carolyn got a nice picture of the boys there, with Tim and David peeking out through the doorway.

Carolyn also got a nice picture of Jean taking a brief break next to a giant's tricycle. In this make believe land, almost everything was child size. The giant's bike added to the sense of wonder. No human-sized child could ride such a bike, but it made for a great photo opportunity!

Jean parked the stroller near the giant's trike. The ladies followed as the boys headed off toward the brightly painted red and yellow train. They were welcomed by a very friendly, perfectly costumed conductor. Once everyone was safely in their seats the train set out for Cactus Flats, an authentic 1860s miniature replica western town.

When the boys grew tired of playing in the western town, the ladies led them on to the impressive, multi-colored, multi-towered, multi-turreted castle. It was the largest structure in the park, and it was decorated to stand out against the natural colors of the riverside setting. The castle was painted variously in cotton candy pink, lemonade yellow, and sky blue—the perfect setting for a princess. The boys didn't care, but the ladies couldn't help but be drawn to the castle. Never mind they were all too old to be princesses; Jean, Carolyn, and Jean Carol had plenty of imagination left to spare and wanted a closer look. Though the castle looked enormous on the outside, on the inside, the Fairytale Castle was perfect for kids, all the decorations placed at just the right height.

After the castle tour, the gang headed for the steam boat. Together with twenty-five other visitors, they enjoyed a brief ride down the mighty Mississippi River. Sure, the map and logic dictated it was really the AuSable River. The twenty-two-foot long Billabong Belle was unlike anything you would expect to see in the Adirondack mountains of New York state.

On the way back through the park, the little boys ran into each of the little houses again. In addition to the little pumpkin house, there was a small home for the Three Bears, and the Butcher, the Baker and the Candlestick maker; each had a little home of their own.

David and Tim enjoyed a ride on the Cactus Flats stage, which looked every bit as splendid as it did on its first voyage in the park, driven by Gene Devlin over ten years earlier, pulling into the Wells Fargo office station at 12:02pm on May 24th in 1954. The little stage was pulled by a team of miniature matching ponies.

David and Tim were too small to drive the tiny, 1920s era cars that ran along a fixed metal track to a mock service station, but each boy was able to ride as passengers with older children. At the end of the ride, the boys were given customized Land of Makebelieve driver's licenses.

Just before lunch, everyone enjoyed a spectacular parade through the park. The parade featured the stage coach, a fire engine, an assortment of ponies, a circus wagon, and a royal purple coronation coach, complete with a King and a Queen.

When the parade was over, the Fitz-Geralds headed to the picnic area. On the way there, they stopped to visit a large family of rabbits. Jean took a picture with Carolyn's camera at the rabbit house, while Jean Carol loaded her camera with another roll of film.

When the boys grew tired of watching the rabbits, Tim boarded the stroller, and promptly fell asleep on the way to the picnic area. Jean spread a thick, soft blanket over the grass, and David curled up and promptly fell asleep in the shade.

That picnic with her daughters-in-law was everything Jean imagined when she thought of the perfect picnic. The boys slept for two hours, no doubt dreaming about riverboats, castles, stage coaches, rabbits, dragons, and the Three Bears. The ladies enjoyed a leisurely lunch, featuring various sandwiches, potato salad, coleslaw, fruit salad, pickles, olives, cheddar cheese, potato chips, and chocolate cake. Jean had iced tea, Carolyn had a Tab brand diet cola, and Jean Carol sipped on a Fresca.

Tim woke up first. Jean Carol fixed Tim a plate, and Tim was finishing his lunch when David woke up as well. Once the boys were rested and fed, they were raring and ready to go again.

At the Land of Makebelieve there was a little playground. The boys wanted to ride up and down on the teeter totter. The base was painted green, the balancing board was bright red, and a grey circus elephant posed merrily at the fulcrum, with his trunk balancing on one side and his tail balancing on the other.

Of course, at one and three years of age, Tim and David were too young for the teeter totter. But with Jean Carol on one side and Carolyn Ann on the other, the ladies slowly and safely bounced the boys up and down. Jean picked up the last of the picnic and packed away the basket. Carolyn's camera was sitting on the picnic table. Jean looked in the window, the counter displayed nine pictures used from Carolyn's second roll. Jean hastily decided the picture was "worth it." It was. Jean captured a fantastic picture of her two, beautiful, young daughters-in-law with their small sons, and the beautifully landscaped lawn at the Land of Makebelieve as well.

This was the happy day that Jean recalled, and the picture in her mind, whenever she insistently and enthusiastically recommended summer guests of Paleface make sure to visit the Land of Makebelieve, just a few miles away in Upper Jay.

## '65 Flaming Leaves Antique Auto Rally

The members of the Whiteface Chamber of Commerce attended the 30th anniversary celebration of the Whiteface Mountain Highway, which had been dedicated by President Franklin D. Roosevelt on September 14, 1935. Aside from the opportunity to be present at such an historic occasion, the members of the Chamber were there to promote a new event.

Under the leadership of its new president, Colonel Earl B. Unger the Chamber came up with a new way to showcase the region. The First Annual Flaming Leaves Rally of Whiteface Mountain brought antique car enthusiasts from as far as 200 miles away.

The program began with registration at the Holiday Motel in downtown Wilmington, followed by a welcoming cocktail party at the Viking Motel Lodge. Saturday morning the motorists took chair lift rides up Whiteface Mountain, followed by a parade featuring the 125 antique autos from Wilmington to Paleface Mountain.

The automobile enthusiasts were expected to wear costumes from the period, and more specifically, the year their automobile was manufactured. The costumes were judged over lunch at Paleface.

After lunch, many of the ancient auto enthusiasts drove their vehicles up Whiteface Memorial Highway to enjoy the view from the summit. The caravan was accompanied by several area repairmen in case their services were needed. Saturday evening concluded with cocktails and dinner at Steinhoff's. Presentations of awards for the costume contest were presented at Saturday night's dinner.

The rally concluded at Whiteface Mountain Ski Center on Sunday, with judging at 11am and trophy presentation ceremony at 1pm. Gold, silver, and bronze trophies were awarded in each of eight classes. Wilmington's own Leo Cooper, town assessor, and antique car enthusiast had a great time in his 1936 Chevy Coupe. Unfortunately, Leo Cooper didn't win a trophy.

## '65 Talk Me Out of the Phone Booth

Normally during September there was plenty of room at any hotel or motel in the North Country. The Flaming Leaves Antique Car Rally accounted for a sell-out weekend. And everyone at Paleface wanted to put on a great luncheon for the event on Saturday. The kitchen was fully staffed and ready to go. Over a hundred antique autos pulled into Paleface's parking lot. The lot was close to reaching its limit.

The kitchen staff had prepared a buffet luncheon. Everyone was quickly and efficiently attended to. The tourists seemed to be enjoying their food. The staff at Paleface was hustling, yet making it look like they did that sort of thing every day.

Around noon, a more modern car, about five years old, pulled into the Paleface parking lot, and it sure looked out of place! The driver walked up the sidewalk, directly into and among the dining motorists. Jean met the young man and informed him that a private, paid luncheon event was in process. The man insisted on going to the bar. He ordered a beer and a sandwich, set his keys on the bar, and entered the payphone booth.

His call was to his girlfriend back in Pennsylvania. It was a collect call, requiring operator assistance, and Miss Barber from the AuSable Valley Telephone Company asked the man for his name several times and couldn't understand what he was saying so she called her supervisor, Mrs. Carolyn Douglas.

Finally, Mrs. Douglas was able to make out a name and dial the numbers. She reached the man's girlfriend but she refused to accept the charges. What's more, she suggested that he was drunk and despondent, and told Mrs. Douglas she should call the police.

Mrs. Douglas returned to the line and explained that his girlfriend had refused to accept the charges, and Mrs. Douglas thought he did in fact sound drunk and despondent. Things quickly went downhill from there when the man threatened to blow his guts out. Mrs. Douglas couldn't know that the man didn't have a gun in his possession.

With Miss Barber at her side, Mrs. Douglas kept the man on the phone talking while Miss Barber contacted the police. After a while, the police listened in to the conversation Mrs. Douglas was having with the man. They figured out the payphone location and the number of the payphone.

It was coming from inside Paleface. Miss Barber called the Paleface number. Jean answered the phone. Jean immediately interrupted Doc, who was visiting with folks in the dining room, and sent him into the bar.

Meanwhile, Mrs. Douglas was trying to keep the man on the phone as long as she could. She asked the man about his family. "Do you have a father?" she asked.

"No," the man answered.

"Do you have a mother?" Mrs. Douglas followed up.

"No," the man answered again.

"Do you have a brother?" Mrs. Douglas tried.

Again, he answered no.

"Do you have a sister?"

"No."

"Well, tell me about your girlfriend." Carolyn Douglas thought she might get the man talking. Instead he hung up.

Fortunately, Doc was there. The man did not open the door to the phone booth. Doc invited the man to come out and sit down and talk with him.

Then the phone in the phone booth rang. The man answered the phone.

Mrs. Douglas told the man that she was sorry, and she didn't mean to bring up such a sensitive subject. Then Mrs. Douglas went on for several minutes about how she would like to try to help, that she was a very good listener. Ironically, the man mostly did the listening and Mrs. Douglas did most of the talking.

Just about every time Carolyn Douglas asked a question that required more than a yes or no answer, he tended to hang up the telephone or tell Mrs. Douglas about the ways he might do himself in. Whenever the man hung up the phone, Miss Barber dialed Jean at Paleface as Mrs. Douglas tried to re-connect with the man.

Between Mrs. Douglas on the telephone, and Doc stationed just outside the door, the man stayed put for about a half an hour. Then finally the man was finished. He came out of the phone booth and told Doc he would need to cancel his bar order and headed for the door.

Doc followed the man to the parking lot. When he got to his

car, he realized he had forgotten his car keys. Doc said, “You left your keys at the bar, son.” The man turned to head back toward the bar and Doc said, “I have your keys now. They are in my pocket and that’s where they will stay. I can’t let you drive right now.”

The man cussed and stomped off along the side of the road as if he were going to walk from there to the town of Jay.

Doc followed at a short distance and once again asked the man if he would like to sit down and talk. Doc explained that in his many years as a minister in New Jersey, he had heard it all, and perhaps the man would find talking about his concerns would help him feel better. The tirade of foul language was about the extent of the man’s talk with Doc, and as they were walking, Doc’s questions went unanswered.

They hadn’t gotten very far in their five-minute walk toward the town of Jay when Trooper Williams from Wilmington arrived on the scene.

Doc said, “Good afternoon, sir. Are you looking for this young man here?”

Trooper Williams introduced himself to the man. He firmly informed the man that he was going to need to take him to the station in Elizabethtown. With the man in Trooper Williams’s patrol car, he spoke for a few minutes with Doc. Doc told Trooper Williams that he was unable to learn much of anything from his discussion with the man, not even his name. Doc gave Trooper Williams the keys to the man’s car. The officer put Doc in the front seat and they drove the short distance back to the Paleface parking lot. Doc stayed in the car while Trooper Williams searched the man’s car.

When Trooper Williams had completed his search, he came back to the car with some “evidence” and some paperwork from the man’s car. “Is it okay to leave this man’s car here overnight?” he asked Doc.

“Certainly,” Doc answered. Moments later, Doc was standing alone in the parking lot next to the car. Doc bowed his head and said a prayer for the unknown man, that he might find peace and his unknown burdens might be lessened.

It crossed Doc's mind that it was a good thing that he was at Paleface when this happened, considering he had just returned from a long fishing trip with his friends Carl Steinhoff, Jim Cooney, and Francis Devlin on the Michimenacus River in Quebec.

As Doc slowly walked back toward the door at Paleface, the first of the Flaming Leaves crowd was coming through the door on their way to the top of Whiteface Mountain.

"Did you know that the road to the top of Whiteface has now been in service for thirty years?" Doc said to the first bunch of people on their way to their car. Doc went on, "Yes, they just had a big commemorative celebration at the top of the mountain back in July!"

Doc remained in a sad mood, and preferred to stay outside rather than go back in. It cheered Doc up a great deal to see people off to their cars and thank them for their patronage. When most of the Flaming Leaves folks had left, Doc went back inside and told Jean that everything was going to be all right. The troubled young man would be safely tended to in Elizabethtown overnight. Jean was glad that they entertained the antique auto enthusiasts such that they were not even aware of the high drama of the day.

The young man was arraigned before Elizabethtown Justice of the Peace Stanley Pelkey. Due to public intoxication, a fine was imposed and then immediately suspended. A Trooper brought the man back to Paleface the next day. The man got in his car and drove away, presumably back to Pennsylvania, and nothing further was heard about him again.

As for Miss Barber and Mrs. Douglas, they were treated like heroes for their efforts and for preventing the man from blowing his guts out in the phone booth at the bar at Paleface in the middle of the Flaming Leaves Antique Auto Rally costume contest luncheon.

## '65 Montana Road Trip

In October, Doc and Jean made a grand road trip to Montana with their friends Mr. and Mrs. Carl Steinhoff, Mr. and Mrs. Thomas

Keegan, Dr. Goff, and Mr. James Cooney of Albany. The party spent the last week of October fishing and the first week of November hunting elk. Jean and the ladies spent a good portion of the trip shopping, and Doc had asked Jean to pick up anything that looked like it would be a great decoration that would fit within the western motif he was planning for the bar. Doc and Jean's station wagon was packed full of trinkets when they returned home.

## '65 The Miracle of Snow Making

David Torrance was happy that Doc had taken a vacation. Just as was the case when Paleface was originally built, Doc couldn't help being underfoot. David Torrance's partner Howard Trumbull was assigned the task of running interference, and trying to keep Doc occupied so the crew could keep their pace. Doc had requested a completion date of December 1st.

As Doc and Jean said goodbye and checked on the progress one last time, David couldn't help noting the irony in the fact that he was missing hunting season again. And it wasn't just him, of course. His friend Maurice Southmayd wouldn't be hunting either. He was hard at work on the plumbing challenges, and given the importance of water to the success of the project, those challenges were not to be minimized.

In the three and a half weeks that Doc and Jean were gone, most of the external work on the buildings had been completed. The two giant water storage tanks, one with a capacity of 25,000 gallons and the other with a capacity of 15,000 gallons, had arrived and been installed in their shed. The Larchmont snow making machine and compressor had arrived and had been installed. The complete system included 6,000 feet of aluminum piping, galvanized piping, couplings, accessories, nozzles, and hoses. All the technical items needed to run a snow making operation had been received, and installed. Replacement parts were organized and placed in a special workshop within the water tank shed.

Inside the pool building, the Lazy-L shaped pool had been

assembled. Mr. Southmayd had connected all the filtration and circulating systems. The Torrance and Trumbull crew had built the walls and roof around the pool after the pool had been built, and the insulation work had been completed on the building as well. By the time the Fitz-Geralds returned from Montana, Robert Gill was busy completing the final electrical work in the pool area and the Torrance and Trumbull crew was painting the building's exterior. It was painted a lovely sky blue color, identical to the color of the rest of Paleface's exterior.

The week before Thanksgiving, the inside walls were painted. Plastic trees and plastic exotic tropical plants were installed in the pool area. And a big moment of truth, filling the pool with water. Fortunately, subterranean Paleface Lake had no problem filling the pool. It was a big relief.

Once full, everyone was glad to see the pool held water. By the third day, it was clear there were no leaks! Another big relief. Then the tanks were filled from deep within the earth, replenishing at a rate of 1,000 gallons per hour. Fortunately, Howard Cardin had located a sufficient source of water beneath Paleface.

Next, the finishing work on the game room was done, and Paleface was ready to receive delivery of the machines that would delight many kids at Paleface for countless hours. And from then on, Jane had to keep big bags of rolled dimes in the safe in the office.

As the final preparations for winter came together, Doc wrote a press release that noted:

> *The management of Paleface Ski Center will not be responsible for any schizophrenic aberrations experienced by those who cannot decide whether to ski or swim. However, folks can ski in the morning and early afternoon and then relax in the pool later in the afternoon and during the evening hours, thus solving the difficult dilemma. The addition of the new indoor swimming pool and the new snow-making machine climaxes a five-year growth record at Paleface. This brings the resort to a new level*

*of distinction as one of the most unique winter country club establishments in the east. It is believed that there is only one other ski area in the east which can boast of an indoor swimming pool directly on the slope. The continuing up-dating of the facilities at both Paleface and Whiteface Ski Centers make the Jay-Wilmington area of the High Adirondacks one of the leading winter meccas of the east, as well as the Ski Capitol of New York State.*

As the family sat down to Thanksgiving dinner in 1965, Doc radiated happiness. He had realized the dream of adding snow making. The game room and the indoor pool also thoroughly pleased him. After the last two years, it was nice to enjoy a *happy* Thanksgiving. The year before, of course Doc and Jean had spent Thanksgiving at the Keene Valley Hospital. And the year before that the whole country was in mourning.

## '65 Crocheted Bikini

That fall, Doc and Jean's daughter-in-law Carolyn had taken up crochet. She made all sorts of things, from doilies to afghans.

Carolyn had heard about the new pool being built at Paleface, and decided she would crochet herself a new bikini. Carolyn's one-of-a-kind swim suit would be as unique as an indoor swimming pool in the middle of an Adirondacks winter. Maybe there weren't instructions for crocheted swim suits for a reason. It took most of the fall, and eventually her hard work paid off. It was mostly trial and error, work and re-work. Finally, she had created a swimsuit that fit her perfectly. It was a nice shade of ice blue.

There weren't a lot of people at Paleface yet. The snow making was ready for its debut, but it was too warm to make snow. Many families had taken the chance that it would get cold and snow. Almost all the rooms were sold to families who came to stay at the lodge even though there wasn't enough snow. Instead of skiing, many of those families were enjoying the pool instead of the slopes. It was Christmas Eve. The Fitz-Gerald family thought it would be nice to go swimming in the afternoon, then head home to Jay.

Patti was in the pool with her nephews. The rest of the family was sitting at a table enjoying coffee, tea and hot chocolate. Carolyn came out of the dressing room in her new swim suit. Everyone complimented the suit. Nobody had ever seen anything like it.

Seeing that she was ready for a swim, her three-year-old son pleaded with her to jump in. At 22 years of age, Carolyn was still young enough to jump in rather than take the torturous route of getting used to the water inch by inch. She stood at the deep end of the pool and jumped. Legs crossed, arms crossed, like a human cannon ball.

It happened on impact.

Strangely, no one thought of it. Least of all Carolyn. But the moment it happened, she knew it. The moment the crochet bathing suit hit water, the yarn stretched. Instantly, the swim suit was much too large. Carolyn tried to swim from the deep end to the shallow end, while keeping the enormous swim suit covering herself as best as she could.

Trying to swim while trying to keep covered caused a bit of a ruckus, the effect of which was to cause everyone at the pool to look when otherwise maybe they might have been less inclined to notice. Carolyn couldn't help it, but a case of the giggles made for an even greater spectacle.

Moments later, Carolyn was back in the changing room. She was dried and dressed in a flash, and back out of the changing room quickly. Still laughing, fully covered, and holding the offensive swim suit.

In one hand, she held the top. In the other hand, she held the bottom. Now everyone at the pool was enjoying the hilarity of the situation. Carolyn proudly showed off the crocheted creation, soaking wet and dripping. The tiny holes had grown to about an inch each. Carolyn held up the bottom by the waist band. The yarn stretched so that the crotch of the swim suit hung down to her knees.

Between uncontrollable fits of laughter, Doc debuted his new marketing slogan: "Just two feet between bikini and stretch pants!" It didn't take long for new brochures to appear with that saying, tying the new pool and the ski slopes together. Whenever Doc said the phrase out loud, the family couldn't help but think of Carolyn's unfortunate incident.

## '66 If You Can't Ski, You Can Ride Horseback

It was a good thing for the pool, because the vacationers never did get their money's worth on the slopes over the Christmas to New Year's season. To make it up to the guests, Doc had the horses brought in from the winter pasture. On New Year's Day, instead of skiing in the New Year, they would have to go riding. No charge. There was no snow, there was very little ice, but even so the ride was limited to a walk. Doc always tried to make sure the guests were safe, even while providing exciting adventures. Nine guests bundled up in their snowsuits and went for a rare winter horseback ride.

Later that afternoon, the would-be skiers were in the lodge enjoying cocktails and conversation. To the surprise of the guests, a special visitor was brought in to the bar to enjoy some liquid refreshment.

Little Chico was officially a horse but not too far from being classified as a pony. Chico entered the lounge through a special entrance. One of the cowboys somehow discovered that if you gave Chico a taste of beer, he made a very strange face, smacked his horse lips, and rolled his upper lip and lower lip in opposite directions, to the delight and mirth of observers. Chico was very good company, and made the miserable snowless après-ski activities pleasurable after all.

Clara Hazelton's column in the newspaper said it best: "One would never know that it is a mountainous country, if they visited town today. No mountains visible, dust and a bit of snow are whirled by strong, gusty winds, water is running down the gutters but it may not for long. The wind is taking on a frigid sting. The New Year's weekend was warm and mild. The Whiteface and Paleface Ski Centers were closed. The snow report from Whiteface Mt. is that until the weather is favorable for making snow or until natural snow falls, the Whiteface Mt. Ski Center is temporarily closed."

The hotel guests at least enjoyed a warm lodge, great meals, and lots of time by the fire side.

## '66 Eleven Snowless Days in January

It took eleven snowless days in January, before it was cold enough to make snow sufficient to get Paleface's lifts ready to re-open.

Finally, in mid-January, Paleface was off and running, thanks to the new Larchmont snow making equipment, and over 120,000 gallons of water. It was just in time to enable the Boy Scouts to hold their Winter Sports Day. Just like the previous year, it almost had to be cancelled, Mother Nature deciding to cooperate just in the nick of time. The previous year, Mother Nature had offered natural snow. In January 1966, at least She provided cold enough temperatures for snow making.

## '66 Fireside Chats

That winter, après-ski activities included fireside chats. Most of the talks were on topics of interest to skiers, ski racing, and local history.

Skiers were intrigued by the miracle of snow making. Doc and Dana told guests all about the system. Doc told the story of the drilling, and finding water.

Dana explained, "The water supply is not endless. What we had named Paleface Lake turned out to be more like a medium sized pond. The underground water table is good for about five hours of snow making. After we draw the water up to ground level, it takes about five hours for the underground pocket to re-fill. We have two huge storage tanks installed. If we can get them filled with water during the day time we have enough to make snow between ten to twelve hours a day, certainly not twenty-four hours a day. So, while you are fast asleep at night, we're hard at work sprinkling snow on top of the mountain."

Dana went on to explain the secrets of snow making. In addition to the consideration of optimum temperatures, another secret to snow making was the correct air to water ratio. The proper elevation of the guns was an important factor. Too high and they would shoot snow into the wind. Too low and except with the coldest temperatures, they were likely to lay down a very wet snow. Another consideration was the need to allow the new snow to have time to dry out before attempting to roll or drag it. Usually, it was best to let the snow rest overnight before grooming it early the following morning.

Everyone was interested in the snow making process. The new Larchmont snow making equipment made Dana and his crew the heroes at Paleface. The winter season was saved by the new snow making capability. By the end of the winter, Paleface boasted a skiing season of sixty-six days, not bad for a mostly snowless winter.

## '66 Jane Peck's Milestone Birthday

On February 17th, Jane turned forty years old. Her sister Laura Trumbull gave her a new outfit for her birthday, bright orange stretch ski pants and a white ski coat with brown splotchy starbursts, such as you would see in an episode of Batman with the word "POW" in it, except the centers of the starbursts were bright orange, to match the stretch pants.

That fashion, designed by Carter & Churchill of Lebanon, New Hampshire was originally featured in Ski Magazine two years earlier. It caught the eye of the style editor, Mrs. Kay Eldred who had the honors of christening Paleface during its grand opening. The outfit also caught the eye of Laura Trumbull, who had inventoried it for the past two years.

It was a fine garment that served Jane well for many, many years.

## '66 100 Members

On the 24th of February, the Ski Club met at Paleface to finish their plans for the Junior Obstacle Fun Race, which was only three days away. At the meeting, a "race committee" consisting of Gene Devlin, Howard Trumbull, Bill Sloan and Larry Sponable was appointed, and Gene Devlin was named Race Chairman.

Another meeting of the Ski Club was set for February 28th to complete planning for the Adult Obstacle Race slated for the 6th of March. The next official meeting of the Ski Club would be on March 7th.

The President of the Ski Club, Howard Trumbull, announced that a major milestone had been achieved. The Paleface Ski Club now had over 100 members! Howard thanked everyone for making the club the best it could be.

## '66 Lifties

At the start of the season, Doc had asked the "lifties" to try to establish a friendly rapport with every customer they could.

On the 31st of March, a photographer from the Plattsburgh *Press Republican* was at Paleface, working on a feature. Desmond Lawrence was working on the lift when the shot was taken that would make Des locally famous for a week or two. Des was helping Mike Chauvin and Robert Rennell from the Keeseville Central School Ski Club onto the lift.

Warren Law from South Orange, New Jersey and his wife were next in line at the lift. Des had remembered Mr. Law from the day before and said, "Good morning Mr. Law, Mrs. Law. How are you doing today?" He helped them get to their chair.

The Laws were family friends of the Fitz-Geralds from before they became ski center operators. At lunch, Mr. Law said to Doc,

"I am so impressed with the personnel at Paleface. Just this morning, your lift operator greeted us by name, and asked how we were doing."

Mrs. Law added, "Yes, Doc, you should be proud. Your employees are very friendly and so hard working. I noticed the other young man at the chairlift shoveling the snow away from under the chairs after every boarding."

Doc said, "You must be referring to Desmond Lawrence and Preston Palmer. I appreciate you telling me about them. I will make sure to let them know how happy I am with their work!"

At the end of the day as Desmond and Preston were getting ready to leave, Doc surprised them with handshakes and an envelope. Inside each envelope was ten dollars. Doc told them, "When I hear good reports from our customers about the people that work here, I can't help but feel compelled to want to share big rewards. You men deserve it, and I'm very proud of you. When you get to know our customers by name, and when you impress them with your work ethic, you make them want to come back, over and over, year after year."

Of course, that story travelled throughout the staff very quickly.

## '66 Adult Obstacle Race

At the March 7th meeting of the Ski Club, everyone was still talking about the Adult Obstacle Race held the day before. It seemed everyone had their personal favorite part of the race. There was a part of the race where skiers had to pass between slalom poles with a potato on a spoon. Traversing a teeter board on skis was a challenge, and climbing a ladder on skis disqualified many contestants. From the spectator's standpoint, watching skiers pass through a tunnel while skiing and twirling a Hoola Hoop was very entertaining.

The men's winner was Vic Pelkey with a time of fifty-eight minutes and four seconds. The women's winner was Linda Russell with a time of one hour, seventeen minutes, and twenty-four seconds. Special prizes were awarded to John Van Horn and Betty Meconi for working the hardest to get down the course. A special prize was also awarded to Peg Fountain for the best Hoola Hoop twirling.

Karl Jost brought two excellent ski movies to the Ski Club meeting, which all the members enjoyed. Next on the agenda was planning for a costumed Easter Parade on skis. Easter wasn't until the 10th of April. Would there still be snow? The Ski Club decided to plan the event anyway.

## '66 Wayne Wright – State Champion

President Trumbull waited until the end of the night for the final agenda item. He told them, "I know everyone is excited to hear all about Wayne Wright's trip to New York State's Junior Ski Championship races at Holiday Valley in Ellicottville, New York last month. Wayne couldn't be here with us tonight, but Putzi Jost can tell everyone the news."

Putzi stood and turned to face the Ski Club members. "Good evening, everybody! No more suspense. I'm delighted to share the news with you all. We have word that Wayne took first place in the Slalom race, and second place in the Giant Slalom, which was enough for Wayne to take first place in the combined point count. Our dream of having a champion skier who got his start at Paleface has been realized. As our New York State Champion, Wayne will be eligible for all sorts of other competitions, and we all look forward to hearing about the great things Wayne will do. Just next week, Wayne will compete in the New England Championship races at the Sno Bowl in Middlebury, Vermont. So, congratulate Wayne next time you see him, and wish him well!"

## '66 Final Ski Club Meeting of the Season

At the final meeting of the season, President Howard Trumbull asked this question, referring to the Fitz-Geralds' development and constant re-investment at Paleface: "What will they come up with next?"

As if by chance, the question and the promise were expanded in the Adirondack Daily Enterprise: "With their new equipment, the Fitz-Geralds have what looks like the final weather beater. Their friends in the Whiteface and Lake Placid region, however, are fairly sure they won't stop here."

## '66 A Very Special Birthday Cake

The Ski Club itself had some innovating left to do!

The first day of spring signaled the end of winter. The Ski Club focused on planning parties, golf outings, water skiing, clam bakes and summer picnics. Mrs. Irma Hildreth was appointed Social Director of the Ski Club. The main event was a big summer cook-out at David Torrance's camp on Silver Lake. Irma advised, "So put July 15th on your summer calendar. I'm sure we'll come up with some sort of competition, whether it's a water skiing competition, or a horseshoe competition, you can bet we'll do something that involves winning a trophy or ribbon."

Doc Fitz-Gerald took a few minutes to eloquently thank everyone for their friendship and for doing so much to elevate the sport of skiing. Doc concluded his remarks with a typical, "Good night and thanks for coming."

Howard Trumbull interrupted uncharacteristically. "Not so fast, Doc. It seems we have a little surprise for you!"

David Torrance and Pete Pelkey carried a large fold up table into the room. On the table was an enormous cake. More accurately, it was more like a dozen cakes laid side by side, and in places one on top of the other.

Mary Wallace and Jean Fitz-Gerald followed the cake into the room, and Mary's booming voice started the club singing "Happy Birthday." When the song was over, Mary gave Doc a big hug and a kiss on the cheek.

It was the most beautiful cake Doc had ever seen.

As an artist, Doc was accustomed to creating a poignant scene on canvass. Somehow, Mary had transformed cake into a work of art. Part sculpture, part painting, and all edible. "I have to get a picture of this amazing cake!"

While Jean went to find the camera, film and flash cubes Doc inspected all the details. The cake was a stunning replica of Paleface, including the mountains, the lifts, the trees, the lodge, and even the skiers.

Mary pointed to an individual skier. "This one is you!" The one that Mary pointed out was a tiny sculpted skier that had unfortunately collided with a tree, arms and legs spread eagle, wrapped around the trunk. "A tree hugger!" Mary concluded. The club laughed heartily at Mary's narration of her story in cake.

Before President Trumbull adjourned the meeting, ten members of the club descended on Doc, and lifted him into the air. "I don't think we've appropriately celebrated the grand opening of the new pool, and what better way to celebrate the pool and Doc's 57th Birthday than to christen the Reverend Dr. Boylan Fitz-Gerald."

Along the way, one of Paleface's regular guests, known to everyone as "The Reb," short for "Rebel," joined the processional as if he was a full, dues paying member of the Paleface Ski Club. The Reb helped carry Doc, who was making a good show of protest. Doc squirmed to make it difficult, but really didn't mind the attention or the idea of getting tossed into the pool. The Reb said, "We can make this easy or we can make it hard, but either way, you're going in!"

"Okay, okay," said Doc, "just let me get my fancy clothes off."

So, in front of friends, family, patrons, and the members of the ski club, Doc disrobed down to his long red underwear and then was carried away. Though it was pointless to resist, Doc made a good show of trying to escape.

Jean was still holding the camera from having taken pictures of the cake. Howard Trumbull asked Jean if he might borrow the camera, and caught several great pictures of Doc on his way to the pool.

No one ever made a motion to adjourn, but the final winter meeting of the Paleface Ski Club had clearly ended.

## '66 Lee Brow

In early June, the Whiteface Chamber of Commerce met at Paleface. In addition to the routine governance matters that such an august body must perform on a regular basis, the focus of the evening was on recognition.

The volunteer leader of the Chamber, Colonel Earl B. Unger had completed his two-year term as president of the Whiteface Chamber of Commerce. In recognition of his service, the Colonel was presented with a testimonial scroll which highlighted the Chamber's accomplishments under Colonel Unger's tenure as president.

The Chamber's funds were increased substantially, and the region had been well promoted, and was thus prepared for the boom that would come with the completion of the Adirondack Northway, Route 87. The new highway connected Albany, New York to Plattsburgh, New York and ultimately extended to Montreal, Quebec. Whiteface and Wilmington were ready for the spillover from the Canadian Exposition of 1967. All the gathered members of the Chamber, rewarded Colonel Unger's service with a standing ovation.

The Whiteface Chamber of Commerce also bestowed an honorary membership upon Mr. Lee Henry Brow. Colonel Unger's presentation of Lee's lifetime honorary membership highlighted four points: The previous year Lee had orchestrated the Whiteface Kiwanis Club's donation of trees to the Boston Kiwanis Club, which brought the area considerable attention; Lee, a native son of Wilmington, had risen to prominence in the Massachusetts State Chamber of Commerce, serving as it's executive vice president, at the tender age of 76 years old; each Memorial Day Lee returned to Wilmington and placed fresh new United States flags at the graves of veterans in all of the area's cemeteries; as the founding member of the Adirondack Shillelagh Club, Lee gave countless hours of his personal time to an endeavor that has done the region proud. The members of the Whiteface Chamber of Commerce rose again for another standing ovation. Colonel Unger asked Lee if he would like to say a few words. Lee never missed such an opportunity.

That evening, after Lee accepted the honorary life-time membership, and thanked the Chamber for the special recognition he had some memberships to bestow as well.

Back in 1955, as Lee was turning 65 years old, he stumbled upon a unique hobby: making canes. Lee would go into the woods of Wilmington and cut scores of saplings. Then he would return to a workbench fashioned from the trunk of his car and strip the saplings of bark and twigs. He brought them back to his Boston apartment to finish the canes.

Lee never personally profited from making canes, instead giving them away to the elderly. He also presented canes to prominent men and women that he served with in organizations like the Chamber and the Kiwanis Club. As if the gift of a handcrafted cane was not enough, the presentation was always accompanied by a membership certificate. Fortunately for all the members of the Adirondack Cane Club, there were no annual membership dues and no responsibilities tied to membership whatsoever.

Whether it was part of a plan, or not, Lee's Club became a local, then national sensation. By May 1961, the official roster of the Adirondack Cane Club included 628 members including such dignified members as New York Governor Nelson Rockefeller, President John F. Kennedy, Attorney General Robert Kennedy, and baby brother Edward M. Kennedy. Lee carried letters with him, to read aloud on such occasions, and the letter from Teddy Kennedy was an audience pleaser.

The following year, Lee succeeded in making a very special presentation of a cane and membership to former president Dwight D. Eisenhower. By 1964, former presidents Lyndon Baines Johnson, Harry S. Truman, and Herbert Hoover had also become indoctrinated into the club. Chuck Fitz-Gerald had the distinct honor of photographing the membership plaque that was presented to President Johnson.

Along the way, Lee took the advice offered by Teddy Kennedy and changed the name of the club from the Adirondack Cane Club to the Adirondack Shillelagh Club. A shillelagh [shi-LAY-lee] was defined as an Irish wooden walking stick made from blackthorn wood and often fortified with lead, giving the canes a club like property as well. The name change had the effect of making the club seem more unique. The decision was finalized one day when Lee was finishing a cane, and chuckled to think, "I'm shellacking a shillelagh!"

By the end of 1964, Lee had personally inducted 1,000 members into the Club, and in addition to five presidents, Lee had also made Evangelist Billy Graham a member of the Adirondack Shillelagh Club. Henceforth Lee would refer to the Club as being "blessed."

At that meeting of the Chamber, Lee added the following distinguished local citizens to the membership rolls of the Adirondack Shillelagh Club: Colonel Earl B. Unger for his service as president of the Whiteface Chamber of Commerce; and for their delivery of trees to Boston: Tom Keegan, Art Coulson, Chuck Fitz-Gerald, and Doc. The five new members posed for a picture with their new canes and membership certificates. Few members of the audience were jealous, since most of them had already had membership privileges bestowed upon them.

## '66 Associate Editor of Record

In early June, 1966, Stephen W. Harnett, of the *Record-Post* retired after 42 years in the business. Editor Harnett had served in both World Wars and worked briefly in Hartford Connecticut for the Royal Typewriter Company. According to legend, cited in the *Record-Post*, Mr. Harnett had "always been on the job, come fair weather or foul, sickness or car trouble. Nothing prevented him from performing his tasks." The newspaper would miss its editor and it would take some time to find a suitable replacement.

The owners of the newspaper, Mr. Fred Pelkey, and Mr. Leo A. Bailey, had come to note the formidable writing talents of Boylan Fitz-Gerald. Many of Doc's press releases and letters to the editor had crossed their desks. Doc had worked with the paper on a promotional story less than two weeks earlier.

## '66 Can the State Break the Law?

It had annoyed Doc that there were road signs in Wilmington that directed motorists to Whiteface but not Paleface. There was even a sign pointing to the Marble Mountain Ski Center, which was no longer operational. Normally, Doc didn't seem to mind competing with a state-owned business. But one day something possessed Doc to write a press release and stage a photo opportunity in the middle of Wilmington.

Doc was pictured with a three-toned station wagon with "Paleface Ski Center" in big letters on the side, parked in front of the sign and pointing to the east. The editorial questioned whether state-owned ski centers could break Adirondack forest law. Private owned enterprises weren't allowed to post billboards or have road signs that helped tourists find their way.

The feature garnered such public interest that Mr. Pelkey and Mr. Bailey took a ride to Wilmington. First, while they were in Wilmington they attended the Grand Opening of the A&W Root Beer Drive-In where they were welcomed by owners Sven and Ethel Johnson and enjoyed root beer floats delivered to them by pretty girls on roller skates. On the way back to their offices, they stopped at Paleface.

With several compliments to Doc on his writing abilities, and after hearing about his previous experience as a writer and as an editor, they offered Doc a part time, temporary job to help them do some editing and write some editorial features until they could locate a replacement for Mr. Harnett. The job didn't pay very much, but Doc thought it would be fun to do for a while, and would provide a public service to the community.

Forgetting to check in with Jean, and in Doc's usual style, Doc said, "Why not? I can do that!" And so Doc's brief association with the *Record-Post* began at once. First Doc was asked to write an article announcing his new position. The article noted Doc's college career, which included serving as news editor for "The Lafayette" weekly, art director of "The Lyre" and managing editor of "The Melange" as well as being a member of Pi Delta Epsilon, a national journalistic fraternity. The article went on to note Doc's 6 years of service as editor of the American edition of The Artist magazine, published in London, England. And finally, the article went on to note Doc's college degrees, which included an A.B. from Lafayette College, an M.A. in psychology from Columbia University, and both the B.D. and PhD degrees from Drew University.

By day, Doc managed Paleface. Little by little, Doc was becoming more active in the dude ranch operations each year. After all the rides for the day were done, and after the dinner service was completed Doc began to work his new night job. Paint brushes and canvasses were set aside for the better part of two months as Doc churned out editorials.

Doc had a unique writing style. Lots of rhetorical questions were featured. Most of his topics were philosophical. Many of his statements were emphatic. Near the end of his features, there were often lots of exclamation points. And Doc's writing appealed to mankind's better senses, full of personal responsibility messages. Doc really sought to elevate people with his words, and of course Doc's love of the Adirondacks was apparent as well.

## '66 Making the Most of Summer

Doc's first editorial in the Record Post was a feature about making the most of summer, which Doc titled "Tomorrow is Here." As Clara Hazelton would do, Doc mentioned the sorts of things that people might ordinarily miss, "Like that nest of swallows that just hatched out under the eaves. Or the horses grazing belly-deep in June grass. Or millions of forget-me-nots along the wood roads. And hundreds of trout rising in the amber pools." Contrary to Doc's positive outlook and sunny disposition, Doc contrasted the enjoyable summer activities with the less enjoyable things like heat lightning, weeds in the garden, sun burns, bee stings, poison ivy, wet hay in the barn, hay fever, and heat rash. Doc went on to highlight the more enjoyable things about summer, and talked about the summer tourist traffic, noting "The country mouse and the city mouse will become kissin' cousins for a while." Then Doc asked the readers to "Say "hello" and wave your hand and know your neighbor.

## '66 Smoke Rise Campout

Doc's duties as editor also included reviewing much of the rest of the paper as well. Looking back, perhaps it was a conflict of interest. Some of the stories featured Paleface news. For instance, in the first week of June, there was prominent mention of improvements at Paleface, announcements about the summer riding season at the Dude Ranch, and some news about a campout at the top of the mountain.

The campout story was mentioned in Clara Hazelton's Wilmington feature. Four boys, including Dan and Steve Haselton, Gregory Peck, and George Warren hiked up the mountain at Paleface and spent Sunday night in the Smoke Rise Lodge. The boys reported that it was very cold in the morning.

## '66 Hungry Trout

Miss Hazelton's article went on to report that the owners of The Blue Bowl restaurant had changed its name to The Hungry Trout. The facility had been remodeled and the owners, Mr. and Mrs. William Lowe planned to operate the restaurant throughout the year, not just during the tourist seasons. Doc liked the new name and was pleased to have it mentioned in the paper.

## '66 Firewater Teepee Debuts

The following week, Doc looked over an advertisement that Paleface had purchased. It read: "Paleface Dude Ranch Announces, The Season's Opening at our Firewater Teepee Saturday from 8pm on. Door Prizes." Doc thought about the cost of the small advertisement relative to the value of good publicity. The décor of the lounge featured old wagon wheels, branding irons, Texas longhorns, western and English saddles, riding crops, doggin' bats, Mexican sombreros and serapes, hunting and fishing trophies and mementos, horse portraits and ribbons, and a fabulous Mexican Indian rug. The decorations was meant to give Firewater Teepee a special atmosphere, and go along with the summer dude ranch business.

## '66 Dude Ranch Expands

Doc had sent in a press release shortly before being named interim editor, and it just so happens that story was schedule for front page, cover story treatment. That article's headline read: "PALEFACE DUDE RANCH EXPANDS FOR SIXTH SEASON Adds 230 Acres—New Trails—6 New Horses." The feature article went on to make many points about the operations. The 230 acres added brought the total to 1,000 acres. That allowed for a new total of thirty miles of bridle trails. The six new horses profiled included Pepsi, Koko, Ginger, Chico, Apache, and Cheyenne. Another new acquisition included a covered wagon, more specifically an army escort wagon of Spanish-American War vintage, to provide visual interest and backdrop for tourists' photo opportunities at the Paddock. The article's conclusion states that, "Facilities are ultra-modern and yet the trail system is one of the finest horseback riding opportunities east of the Rockies."

## '66 Arthur Ling Passes Away

Arthur Ling passed away on June 13, 1966.

His grand-daughter, Carolyn Ann Fitz-Gerald, lived in Rhode Island with her family. Her husband couldn't get away from his job to attend the funeral, so Carolyn made the trip home to the Adirondacks with her 4 year old son.

Doc had fond memories of meeting Arthur Ling back in 1960, and had volunteered to escort his daughter-in-law to the funeral. Jean and Patti would entertain the 4 year old. Doc admired the service offered by the Reverend Daniel Partridge, pastor of the Saranac Lake Methodist Church.

It was a relatively long ride from Saranac Lake to the Franklin Falls Cemetery, yet it was one of the most beautiful rides in the Adirondacks. A brief graveside service concluded Arthur Ling's funeral. His widow, Augusta, was not up to visiting with family and friends afterwards. She stood before the stone with her own name inscribed upon it, next to her husband's. Their birth dates were set in stone. Soon "1966" would be added next to her husband's name. Tears ran down her face.

Beneath their names was the name of their infant daughter Mabel, who had lived a short life, born and died during 1910. Also, Leona, Augusta's last baby who lived from 1926 to 1929. And finally, Arthur and Augusta's brave young son Francis who lived from 1925 to 1944.

It had been over twenty years ago, and Augusta still grieved the loss of her last baby boy. Francis had been awarded a Purple Heart and had been injured in battle in Italy in 1944 during World War II. Francis recovered quickly from those injuries and rejoined his unit on their way to invade southern France. Augusta thought about that year of waiting after learning that Francis was missing before the War Department proclaimed him killed.

Augusta stood in front of that stone for a long time, grieving the loss of her husband and her three long lost babies as well.

Augusta wasn't interested in leaving the cemetery. Following the services, everyone had expressed their condolences and returned home except for Augusta, her daughter Ada Schutz, her grand-daughter Carolyn, and Doc. Ada's husband Ernie waited in the truck parked along the road.

Doc stood at the top of the hill in the Franklin Falls cemetery as Augusta grieved. As a minister himself, he had spent a lot of time in various cemeteries. Doc couldn't remember ever seeing a more beautiful place, well set back on the top of the hill, along a seldom traveled road right where Franklin County road number 48 became Essex County road number 72, on the back side of Whiteface Mountain, almost at the point where Union Falls Pond and Franklin Falls Pond were joined by a tiny tributary in the middle of the Adirondack Forest Preserve.

Doc and Jean had already established that one day their final resting place would be in the Fairview Cemetery on a nice hillside in AuSable Forks across from a golf course. Standing on the hillside in Franklin Falls on a beautiful late spring afternoon, listening to the sounds of waterfalls in the distance, Doc was having second thoughts. Too bad Doc and Jean hadn't waited to make their final arrangements.

When Augusta finally stepped away from her husband's grave, the four mourners spent a few minutes touring the rest of the cemetery. Augusta told Ada, Carolyn, and Doc what she could remember about Arthur's ancestors buried there.

Arthur's father and mother, Baron and Flora Green Ling, were buried in Bloomingdale, but Arthur's grandfather James Ling and his grandmother Caroline Nye were buried in Franklin Falls. Carolyn asked if she had been named after her great grandmother Caroline Nye, while subconsciously rubbing her belly. Carolyn's second child was due to arrive sometime around Labor Day.

Not far from Arthur's grandfather's grave was a stone with two names on it. Arthur's grandfather James had two brothers, John Van Buren Ling (1836-1864) and Conant H Ling (1846-1865). Both were memorialized there. John had been killed in battle in New Orleans. Conant had died at Libby Prison in Richmond, Virginia. He was a prisoner of war.

Arthur's great-grandfather Abraham Ling was also buried at the cemetery in Franklin Falls. Augusta didn't recall hearing very much about him, except that he had been born in England.

Arthur Ling's other grandfather—his mother's father—was also buried in Franklin Falls. For some reason, Alanson Green was there in Franklin Falls, though Alanson's own father and wife had been buried in the town of Colton, in St. Lawrence County, just outside of Potsdam, New York. Augusta couldn't recall too much about Alanson's wife Sarah Green or his father Alba Green, except that she remembered hearing that Alba Green was a soldier in the War of 1812.

Before parting, Doc told Augusta about the day in 1960 when

he and Arthur talked for hours at Fanny's Pine Knot Restaurant. Augusta was happy to hear Doc praise her husband for being a good man, working hard to provide for his wife and children. Doc also noted that like most old trappers and Adirondack guides, Arthur Ling could tell great stories. From tall tales, to ghost stories, to funny anecdotes about wealthy camp owners' eccentric requests, Arthur could spin a yarn.

Doc had the chance to proofread and personally supervise the proper publishing of Arthur Ling's obituary in his capacity as Associate Editor.

## '66 Election Day

Doc's second editorial turned into an appeal for readers to vote on election day, as part of their civic duty. The eloquent conclusion implored, "Let us cast our votes with Plymouth Rock, with Valley Forge and Gettysburg, with Normandy Beach and Corregidor. Yes, if you've never done it before, try it now: stand up and BE somebody! And, in case you have an inferiority-complex, buck up and know that the free world needs YOU!

## '66 Are We Missing Something?

In his next piece, Doc appealed to his readers to become creative thinkers and to follow their own individual paths. The headline for that editorial was titled "Are We Missing Something?" Doc wrote about the herd mentality, and how we blindly follow each other. Rather than spend too much time consuming the creative work of others, Doc encouraged his readers to develop their inner resources. Interestingly, Doc asked, "Must we always be entertained? Are we really just armchair animals? Is life just a matter of pushing buttons and getting ourselves entertained by the efforts of other people? Have we grown *that* lazy?" Doc's prescription, "Let us stand up and be somebody, each in his own unique and rightful way... Let us not miss the one and only lifetime given to us. Let us return ever and again to the inner fountains of life-enhancement, self-realization and fulfillment. The splendor of the great society is also the multicolored radiance of the great individuals who make it most truly human."

## '66 Consider the Tortoise

Since that article didn't fill all the necessary space, perhaps it was a slow news week, Doc was asked to quickly come up with something to fill just a bit more space. So, Doc penned a little editorial encouraging people to bravely trust themselves. The title was "Consider the Tortoise," and the editorial began, "He never gets anywhere until he sticks his neck out!" It was a poetic little ditty of prose that spoke of inventing, risk taking, and failure on the way to discovering Shangri-La. Doc advanced his narrative with the saying, "Who cares to be, dares to be." The closing thoughts implored, "Enough of this senseless passion for security. To stay in your own shell is to drive a cheap bargain for a sure coffin. Why not take a chance, why not bet on yourself? Gamble a bit on *you*! Why not stick your neck out and be somebody?"

## '66 The Likes of You

Next up, Doc tried to deputize North Country residents into service as ambassadors to, and for tourists visiting the North Country. He asked the reader to think about how tourists experience the residents, not what the residents think of the tourists. "To be sure, our mountains are important, our rivers are things of beauty. BUT! Every vacation must be in large part an adventure with people. The stranger at thy gates is here. Perhaps through him you will entertain an angel unawares." Doc used himself for example, without making it clear that he was talking about himself, suggesting that a happy tourist could overstay their initial plan, keep returning to the area, and then one day end up moving to the area and perhaps, start up a business, thereby creating jobs for the reader or the reader's children. "Yes, whatever you say or do in the presence of a tourist will be a symbol of the Adirondack society. Whether it be for weal or woe, people will judge our North Country by what they find in you and me... You cannot make the stranger stay. You cannot kidnap him. But you might be able to love him into it—if you would only give it a try!"

## '66 Must We Give Up Our Dreams?

In the July 21, 1966 issue of *The Adirondack Record-Elizabethtown Post*, Doc updated his thoughts on a subject he had visited before, many, many times. Doc displayed his visionary leadership style through his writing about the importance of continually aspiring to imagine a better future.

*Headline: MUST WE GIVE UP OUR DREAMS?*

*Not so long ago I read an article which said that one of the tragedies of human life is that we all have to give up our dreams. There is, of course a profound sense in which this is true. Yet how about the poet who said "What I aspired to be, And was not, comforts me"?*

*What about those who give up dreaming too soon? And when is too soon? Well, to dream is human. It is an essential part of our humanity, inherent and integral. Never is too soon to give up our dreams. To give them up is to cease to be human. Respiration, perspiration and aspiration, each is a part of the total breath of life. As the oriole and the swallow are meant for flying, so their very nesting is aerial. So man is "a thinking need" fashioned even from pre-natal times into an "arrow of longing."*

*Give up our dreams? Why, even dreams unrealized have an important place in our lives. The very exercise of dreaming, hoping, planning keeps our minds young and our spirits eager. The blood stream moves faster when the heart is aflame!*

*A far greater tragedy than having to give up our dreams is never having any dreams at all. Dreams are like sowing seeds. Some of them never do come to fruition. Yet the very act of faithful sowing guarantees the miracle of germination.*

*It is well that we have to give up some dreams. In the retrospect of our more mature years we know full well that we spent much time dreaming the wrong dreams. WE are glad that they came to nothing. And in this sense of maturing we find that even the wrong dreams were right for us at the time. Out of their failure a new dream came to be. And often something better was born because of the sloughing-off of our stillborn dreams.*

*Sometimes we learn in the heart of hearts that a lesser dream, had it been realized, might have prevented forever a greater dream and our own fuller realization.*

*The main thing is not that we cannot have all our dreams, not the tragedy of dreams given up. The imperative is to keep on dreaming and also to keep on backing up our dreams with deeds. For it is often in the doing itself that the newer and better dream is born. Achievement often makes old dreams irrelevant. We look back upon them not with nostalgia but with the knowledge that they were necessary growing-pains, intermediary steps in the dream-deed process which is life itself.*

*Have you never had this experience? You imagine a painting. You dream it, plan it. Then you start to work. Something goes wrong – or seems to. Still you work at it. But it just will not come off. Why? Possibly because you are inept. But also, it could well be that your very dream itself has been changing all the while and you have been asleep to what has been going on within you. In any case, suddenly, a new idea comes "smiling through." No one may ever know just where it came from. But it came!*

*And now it is yours. It is you! And you go to work again. The whole thing is changed now. A new dream has replaced the old. Enthusiasm, passion, dedication, creative fire comes to a white heat and at last, if you are fortunate and able, you finish a far better painting than you knew how. Yes, again and again, you come to experience that thrill which makes you say: "I didn't know I had it in me." But if you had had your way, if you could have "forced" that first dream to take over the helm, you never would have found these "islands of the blest."*

*It is just such an experience as this which keeps a man humble and makes him realize that there is something in him, something available to him, which is far beyond the best dreams of any given moment.*

*So it is that we are glad that we have to give up many of our dreams. And in the giving-up a newer and better dream finds "lebensraum." We relinquish the dictatorship of our lives and open up our spirits to the wider, higher and greater mysteries of a life which we cannot commandeer by force of thought or will or dream.*

*Never lose faith in dreaming just because some dreams do not come true. Ask yourself questions: were they the right dreams; was I unworthy of winning them in my then state of development; was I unwilling to back them up, to bet my life on them, to give fortune a nudge; did I betray my better self and spoil my own dreams; was I too lazy, too prone to spend my hours in wishful thinking rather than in willful doing?*

*Then, after a man learns that he must give up some dreams, he has come to the cross-roads. Will he choose the path where the cynical signs say "No dreaming here"? Or will he choose the path which says "Excelsior"? As for me, I would rather climb toward the heights which are so far above me as to be forever unattainable than to lose faith in those heights themselves. The only alternative to the heights of home is "the slough of despond."*

*When you and I and millions like us lose faith in dreaming we shall be like spoiled children whose old age comes to be one long reiteration of "sour grapes."*

*There are some authors who make a real hue and cry about the fact that there are millions of people who never realize their potentiality. And this is always a tragic fact. But it is also a glorious fact. And these very authors themselves participate personally in both its tragedy and glory.*

*If people do not realize their potentiality, let us ask a few questions. Who determines the potential? Which of many potentials can we select as the true ideal for a given individual? Would you or I want to be the dictator, the arbiter, of everyman's potentiality and achievement? Again, today's potentiality may be far surpassed by tomorrow's opening vistas. Each man's possible is infinite and mysterious yet related coherently to his actual. And in the profound sense there never has been a human being who has realized his full potentiality. For which we are grateful!*

*There is something rather infernal about the spectacle of a person who has realized his full potentiality. Think of it! There is real tragedy for you. Superman all dressed up and no place to go! It would be awful to feel that you had really and finally arrived. Why go on living if you have really conquered all the worlds? And what insignificant worlds they would be if the like of you and me could conquer them! What price that kind of conquest? Suicide is the logical sequence if a man has truly and fully realized himself. Sad caricature of a man; further potentiality zero! Completely impotent, he is only the man who was.*

*But fortunately life is not like this. Man is not Sisyphus. He reaches the heights. But he always finds greater heights ahead. And he also finds that each step along the way has given him newer and greater capacity to climb.*

*Such is the wonder of human personality that there is always growing room and going room for each one of us. Titan, at an age near the century mark, knew that he was still only a schoolboy compared with what still lay possible ahead of him. No great man ever lived who did not feel that a part of the glory of the human race was the limitless potentiality, the infinite upreach of man.*

*Dreams are the foreshadowing of potentiality, the adumbrations of deeds, and the intimations of the man who is yet to be. But at the same time, we must reflect, it is this very same man here and now who is the dreamer. Today and tomorrow are wed-locked in the soul of each man. The potential and the actual, each is parent and each is child of the other.*

*Dreaming is the antenna, mysterious earnest of our fullest manhood. Dreams are patterns on the radar screens of our immortality. If only we can read them and live the aright! But, above all, whether we can read them clearly or not just now, let us keep that set turned on!*

*It is forever true, to quote a famous poet, that "a man's reach must exceed his grasp."*

## '66 Killing Time

By late July, the *Record-Post* had hired a new editor to replace Mr. Harnett, and to replace Doc, who had been filling in. Jim Goldsby had over ten years of experience with newspapers, including newspapers at the air force bases in Portsmouth, New Hampshire, and Plattsburgh, New York.

Doc continued to pen editorials while Jim Goldsby got up to speed. In his next piece, Doc took issue with the notion of killing time. The editorial was titled "Wholesale Murder!" Early into it, Doc asked, "Are we really so bored, and so unimaginative, that we have to invent ways to relieve the tedium of our existence? Do we really have to discover methods for fiddling our lives away?" Doc went on to equate such disrespect toward Father Time with suicide. Rather than all at once, in cumulative bits and pieces. He made the case that we don't just kill ourselves, we also cheat our loved ones out of "the selves we might have given them." Doc appealed to his readers to make the most of their creative potentials, essentially to build rather than destroy. Doc concluded, "Life is so short that the only way to live it is to fill it with timelessness. Wherefore let us kindle the passing hours and set them aflame with the fires of passionate significance. Kill time? No! Bring it to life!"

## '66 Shall We Clip the EXPO Crowd?

Doc's next editorial was clearly labeled with his initials. The headline asked the question "Shall We Clip the Expo Crowd?" Evidently, Doc had overheard a local businessman say, "Next year my prices will go to the moon." Instead, Doc saw the opportunity to cultivate the large number of visitors that would come through the Adirondacks on their way to Montreal for the special, World's Fair, or Exposition, or Expo for short. "Canadian Expo '67 represents a golden opportunity for us to introduce millions of new people to our beloved North Country. If we treat them fairly and honestly, we will have the opportunity to develop a whole new clientele. If we price things right next season, we will win many thousands of friends to the North Country. This will build up a following which will last for a whole generation. A tourist treated fairly now may well become a repeat customer for the next twenty years." Doc forecasted prosperity from '67 to '77 and onto '87 by taking a longer view, more strategic position on pricing goods and services, concluding, "In '67 let's make some money. But also, let's make some friends!"

## '66 Mammoth Cesspools

Doc's final editorial piece, published near the end of August, was titled: "Let's Clean Up Our Own Little Mammoth Cesspools." It offered support for a national bill passed by the U.S. Senate. Water pollution in the lakes and rivers was a severe problem, a result of decades of dumping waste into water. Doc concluded the editorial with a plea: "Each and all of us should appoint ourselves to do our personal and individual best to keep the whole North Country from becoming... mammoth cesspools!"

Doc continued to be listed as Associate Editor of the *Record-Post* through the end of September, helping occasionally after the new editor, Mr. Goldsby joined the newspaper. Then without fanfare, Doc's time as a temporary newspaperman ended, but the press releases and letters to the editor continued.

## '66 Fire on the Mountain

Bruce Hare lived on Route 86, along the highway toward Jay, at the foot of the backside of Paleface Mountain. Bruce worked for Whiteface Mountain Ski Center as an electrician.

Four nights before Halloween, Bruce stepped outside to get a breath of fresh air before going to bed. Bruce went halfway around his house and a little spot of color on the mountain caught his eye. Then it hit him.

A fire had started on the mountain! Bruce had gone from fully relaxed to highly adrenalized in a single moment. Bruce had served on the Wilmington Volunteer Fire Department for the better part of nine years, including a couple of years as fire chief. Bruce knew what he was looking at, and he knew it spelled trouble. It was a good thing he saw this fire before turning in for the night. Someone else might have missed it, or thought it was nothing. Bruce knew better. Mr. Hare wasted no time, immediately calling his wife's second cousin, Dana Peck. Dana grabbed his car keys and was out the door immediately.

While Bruce waited for Dana to arrive he called Gib Manley, the chief forest ranger, who happened to live in Jay. Moments later, Dana arrived in Bruce's driveway, and Gib arrived a minute or two later. Together the three men went to the back of the mountain, found the fire and just about had it put out when a breeze picked up. The breeze quickly became a strong wind. The fire that had almost been put out sprang to life. The men quickly realized they were going to need help. It had been a hot summer, and an extremely dry autumn, so far.

Behind them, the fire shot almost instantly from near the base of a tree to its crest. Gib didn't wait any longer to radio-in the emergency.

Bruce quickly ran back home. Dana had given Bruce Doc's home phone number. Bruce reached Doc at his home in Jay. Doc and Jean had just returned from a hunting vacation in Wyoming.

Breathlessly, Bruce exclaimed, "Doc, you better get down here right away. This is Bruce Hare, on the back side of Paleface. The mountain is on *fire*."

Doc got the message. "I'll be right down. Thanks for calling!" Quickly, Doc told Jean the news, and Jean grabbed her coat and purse. They were out the door inside of two minutes flat.

Almost immediately, men from the area began to arrive. The first responders were from Wilmington. Rod Ritchie, Earl Warren, John Follos, and Ellison Urban reported for duty. After that, the area's other volunteer fire departments began arriving.

Gib wasted no time taking command and control of all the various volunteers. Gib took a clipboard from his car and drew some lines on a blank sheet of paper. At the top, Gib titled the columns: Name, Department, In and Out. Gib made it clear that he needed to know every arrival and departure, and put Bruce in charge of it initially.

When Doc arrived, he met quickly with Gib. Doc offered, and Gib quickly accepted the proposition to make Paleface Lodge the base of operations. There was plenty of space to park the volunteers' cars. The men could be warmed, fed, and could take breaks at the lodge.

"And what's more, Ranger Manley," Doc offered, "if you need it, there's water in the pool you can use and we have 25,000 gallons of water stored for making snow that you can use."

Gib thanked Doc, and told him he hoped it would not come to that. Gib said he would keep it in mind. Gib thought about what would happen if the fire made it around the mountain and threatened structures. He would need every drop of water he could find.

## '66 Backpack Pumps

Most of the equipment brought by the firemen from their local fire departments turned out to be useless. There was no way to get their equipment to the scene of the fire.

One piece of equipment that was exceedingly useful for fighting the fire on Paleface Mountain was the Indian brand fire pump, model number 90, marketed, manufactured and distributed for about seventy years by D.B. Smith & Co on Main Street in Utica, New York. Every fireman was equipped with an Indian backpack.

The pumps were constructed from galvanized aluminum, a lightweight material as metals go. The tanks were slightly rectangular, almost square, and held five gallons of water. Baffles inside the tanks helped to cut-down on the problem of water splashing too freely within the tanks. A gasket on the cap and a small hole in the cap prevented the tank from becoming pressurized during use so that it wouldn't cave in. Straps turned the tanks into backpacks and a hose affixed to a hand operated, slide action pump ejected water from the tank, either in a direct stream or in a spray.

## '66 Jeeps

A couple firemen who lived nearby and who had jeeps or other four-wheel drive vehicles dashed home to get them.

It was kind of like a relay race, as a steady stream of jeeps drove up the mountain with full backpacks and back down with empty ones. Gib came to refer to them as Four Wheeled Mountain Goats. Fast as the men moved, and sure-footed as the goats were on the mountain, it just didn't seem like they could get ahead of the rapidly moving fire.

Frankly, Gib was worried. Extremely worried.

A couple of hours into the epic battle, Gib and Doc were talking briefly. It was about eleven o'clock in the evening. Gib was giving Doc another update on the situation. As they talked, both men had their gazes fixed on the top of Paleface Mountain.

A few feet away, Rod Ritchie, one of the Wilmington firemen, was at the truck filling his Indian backpack. Rod turned around again to face the mountain, to wait for the next Jeep to bring him back up.

And it seemed to happen in an instant.

The wind had kicked up and the fire used that moment to propel itself toward the summit. As it approached the summit, it seemed to spread around, rather than up the final peak. Gib later explained that there is not much dirt or groundcover near the top of the mountain, so not much to burn there.

Rod exclaimed, "Jeez! It looks like a volcano. The fire is headed toward the ski slopes!"

Gib thought it resembled a hurricane. A strong fire could create its own wind gusts, and that wind on its own could spread the fire. It was as if a little bit of a breeze was amplified by the raging fire, which made it spread further and faster.

A Jeep came and whisked Rod Ritchie back up the mountain. Rod thought about the fire, the ski slopes, and the lodge. For a moment, Rod also thought about his half-grown Christmas trees over on the Hardy Road, not too far away from Paleface Mountain.

As the Mountain Goats returned, Gib re-directed everyone toward the top.

Doc watched as Paleface appeared to bellow out lava. Paleface seemed twice as tall a mountain on that night. The bright orange and red flames contrasted brilliantly against the bluish black night sky, and the gray smoke made the horrible scene even more ominous in appearance. The scene permanently impressed itself on the canvass of Doc's mind.

The Paleface parking lot was packed with people from the community that had come out to see the fire in the night. The teenaged sons of the Wilmington firemen took a ride down to check out the fire and didn't return home for hours. They watched from the parking lot, in hopes someone would ask for their assistance.

An hour later, the wind had died down. The Mountain Goats, volunteers, and Indian backpacks were winning the day. As it turned out, the fire near the summit was mostly dried grass, which burned fast and then burned out.

At one o'clock in the morning, the front face of the mountain looked safe for the time being. The fire had been pushed back over the other side of the mountain.

## '66 Operation Food

As soon as Jean got inside the lodge, she began fixing coffee, turned on the lights, turned up the heat, preheated the oven, and put a big pot of water on the stove to cook.

The coffee disappeared almost as fast as Jean could make it. Likewise, biscuits were in high demand. Usually, Jean would have been fast asleep by eleven o'clock at night. Like the fireman battling the blaze, Jean was powered by adrenaline.

Jean single-handedly kept Operation Food running all night.

An army of women descended on "Operation Food" the next day. Ladies from every church in the area brought baked goods, prepared sandwiches, and dropped off covered dishes, as did the wives and girlfriends of the fire-fighters. At all times, there was something hot, something sweet, plenty of bread, and lots of coffee.

Jean's friend Mary Wallace arrived at 9am. Within fifteen minutes, Mary had taken over, and ordered Jean to get some rest. Jean went to lie down and fell asleep right away, jumping up at two o'clock in the afternoon. She hadn't meant to be away that long!

When Jean returned to the dining room, she was greatly relieved to see that everything looked to be in fine shape. Mary was in charge, happily presiding over rows of food. If Jean didn't know better, she would have thought that she was at a church social rather than a forest fire.

## '66 Breaking Even

None of the men got any rest Thursday night.

Jeeps and backpacks continued their circuitous route. After the initial gusts, and the wind that blew the flames to the summit, the wind subsided substantially. The firemen kept up with the fire during the overnight hours.

Gib was like a wartime general in a battle. Every couple of hours, Gib took a quick tour by Jeep. Otherwise, Gib communicated with men in the field using his radio.

At dawn, Gib reported to Doc, "We are just about breaking even."

## '66 Employment Record

About four o'clock Friday morning, Esther Manley arrived on scene. Her job was to supervise the recording of the payroll. Gib turned over the clipboard to his wife. All comings and goings were to be signed-in at Esther's table.

Early Friday morning, firemen from Saranac Lake, Bloomingdale, St. Armand, Tupper Lake, and Black Brook arrived on the scene. Toward mid-morning, thirty-seven students from the forestry program at Paul Smith's College arrived. The first fifteen students were taken out at once, and the others were given some instruction.

That weekend set a record for employment at Paleface. At the peak on Friday, 280 men reported to work on the mountain. Some volunteers worked tirelessly day and night, and others came to help for just a couple of hours.

## '66 Bulldozers Cut Fire Breaks

At daybreak, three bulldozers went to work. Glenn Ryan from the Conservation Department arrived with a bulldozer he had towed over from Saranac Inn. Another dozer came from the Haselton Lumber Company up the road in Wilmington. The third came from the nearby real estate development called AuSable Acres. Yet another bulldozer had been expected to arrive from Whiteface Mountain.

After a couple of hours, the bulldozers had pushed dirt between one half and two-thirds of the way around Paleface Mountain at an elevation of about half way between the base and the summit. The plan was for the fire break to dead-end the flames, preventing the spread of fire across it. The jeeps and four-wheel drive vehicles used the breaks as a super highway to move around the mountain quickly.

## '66 Converted Torpedo Plane

By the middle of the morning, a World War II era Torpedo Bomber Martin (TBM) plane arrived on the scene.

The plane had been manufactured by the Glenn L. Martin Company of Santa Ana, California (in business between 1912 and 1961). Most likely the plane on duty that morning had been manufactured at the Omaha, Nebraska plant in the early 1940s.

The TBM had been converted, removing the armaments. Two large, 320-gallon capacity tanks had been retrofitted into the plane. The tanks were filled with a mixture of water and chemicals, and yet the TBM could still fly 120 miles per hour.

Earlier that summer, the same plane had assisted firemen with forest fires at Long Pond Mountain and Sawtooth Mountain. The plane was piloted by Jerry Tyrrell and departed from the airport in

Saranac Lake, or Lake Clear airport as the locals preferred to refer to it.

Between the two trips, the plane was filled from the Village of Saranac Lake's white fire truck, and the fire truck had been refilled from a stream on the Lake Clear Road. Fully loaded, the plane made it from Saranac Lake to Paleface in half an hour.

The TBM was used primarily to get to those areas that the firefighters had difficulty reaching by foot. On Paleface Mountain, there were a couple of ledge areas that the plane could reach that the men couldn't navigate. Mostly, the plane was used to cool areas that would be too hot for the firemen to enter otherwise.

After the plane had swooped through, it was safe to let the forestry students onto the mountain.

## '66 Jumping the Break

Late morning, Gib got a call on the walkie-talkie. One of his men was reporting that the blaze had jumped the break on the eastern slope.

Gib jumped on the next Jeep. Of course, he didn't have long to wait. When it took off with a refill, Gib was on the way up to check out the situation. He diverted dozens of the men to fight the blaze that jumped the break.

It took about ninety minutes. That fire was no match for three dozen Indian backpacks, and just as many firemen. Unfortunately, of course that gave the other fires on the mountain a chance to get going again.

Late afternoon was slowly giving way to evening. Everyone was busy. Thankfully, the wind remained at bay. There were still many spots where smoldering leaves, twigs and roots could be found. Gib thought, "Just because you can't see it, doesn't mean it isn't there!"

Just after lunch, one of the men claimed that the fire was under control. But someone had missed the fire that jumped the berm. Gib asked the men to withhold their judgment. It may be under control in one area, and still be out of control in another.

## '66 I Won't Rest Until There's a Foot of Snow Covering the Ground

Gib generally wasn't eager to update reporters and the public. There was work to do! Even so, at the end of the day Gib looked for Doc. Gib thought it would be wise to make sure Doc had current information.

Gib sighed and wiped his brow, "I'd like to say I'm confident the fire is well beyond its zenith. Today we brought in everyone we could bring, and fought the fire aggressively. The problem is when it is dry like this, a little ember can burn slowly at the ground or just under the surface. The glow can travel through roots, and can cross on logs underneath foliage. I won't rest until there's a foot of snow covering the ground. It can't come fast enough for me! Then I will be willing to claim victory. It is the age-old story of man versus his environment. To be sure, even when we think there is no more fire, we must continue with vigilant patrols. Tonight, however, I think we can start out with less men than we had last night. We'll bring back more guys if we need them."

Doc thanked Gib for his time, his hard work, and complimented his leadership.

## '66 Case Closed

The Jeep trips up and down the mountain had slowed down tremendously. All the volunteers traipsing around the woods still carried full Indian backpacks. It had been hours since any volunteers had reported suspicious patches of ground.

Gib had become comfortable enough with his command that he had spent the afternoon meeting with reporters from the local television and radio stations. Gib took every opportunity to report the suspicion that the fire had been caused by careless hunters' cigarettes. There wasn't any other explanation that made sense to Gib.

When the media left, Doc asked Gib about some of the other ways the fire could have started. "Doesn't matter," Gib responded. "We have the perfect opportunity to use the press to increase awareness for fire safety. There's no way we're going to miss this opportunity. Of course, I don't really have any way of knowing or proving it. But if it helps prevent future forest fires, this one is officially case closed!"

"I understand," Doc replied. "Say no more."

## '66 Grouse Hunters

At that moment, Doc and Jean's friends and frequent guests of Paleface arrived for their annual grouse hunting expedition. Doc had forgotten all about them! Doc introduced Leon Doremus of Madison, New Jersey and Robert Connelly of South Orange, New Jersey.

Gib said, "Good afternoon, gentleman. I'll keep you up to date, Doc." With that, Gib was off to his next task.

"Change of plans, men," said Doc. "We're going to have to put you up at home instead of at the lodge!" Doc's friends understood. Doc told them which rooms they should take their things to. Leon and Robert rode over to the house and unpacked the car before returning to Paleface.

## '66 Tease

Doc didn't know it, but his friends had a surprise in store for him. It had been all they could do to keep it bottled up. When they arrived in the midst of disaster, they had to save their fun surprise for a more appropriate time.

Fortunately, when Leon and Robert returned to Paleface after settling in at Overlook, early Saturday evening the fire-fighting was winding down, and in the hands of the trained professionals. It was between seasons, so except for Operation Food there was no dinner service in the restaurant.

Doc was relaxed and available. Doc was in a very good mood, feeling at that point that the business was safe and would go on to prosper in the coming seasons. There was time to visit. The three friends settled down for Irish coffee.

Doc planned a detailed itinerary for the hunters weeks before, planning each day, and arranging permission to hunt on various properties. Doc had intended to go with his friends, as he did each year. Instead, Doc told Leon and Robert they were on their own. Doc felt he needed to remain at Paleface.

Doc started to give his friends their plans for the next three days, but Leon Doremus stopped him. “First we have a surprise for you!”

Doc was taken aback. The last thing he expected was to receive a present.

Leon went on, “Do you recall last November when we spent an evening debating whether an old dog could be taught new tricks?”

“Yes, I do,” answered Doc hesitantly, and with some trepidation.

Leon reminded him, “You took the position that if you went about it correctly, you could teach an old dog. I took the position that once an old dog is used to laying around and doing nothing all the time, there was no way to get him to do otherwise. Robert argued an in between position, stating that it depended on that dog’s temperament and demeanor. Perhaps the right trainer could help that lazy old dog become the cracker jack bird dog that he always wanted to be.”

Robert jumped in and added, “Leon has some experience with just this sort of bird dog gone wrong.”

“That’s right,” said Leon, flashing his customary grin, “which brings us to our surprise. Cover your eyes, and I’ll be right back.”

Leon was gone for a few minutes, leaving Robert and Doc alone.

Leon went to the car and helped his Brittany spaniel named Tease to the ground. Leon had an enormous red florist’s bow ready for that moment. With the bow perched at the nape of Tease’s neck, the gift was as wrapped as it was going to be.

Four years earlier, he had brought him home as a puppy. The dog was very smart. He was also loving and gentle. It should have been easy to train that dog, because he was extremely motivated by food. When it came to meals or potential snacks, he had the demeanor of a pug rather than a Brittany spaniel. Mr. Doremus and his wife did their best to try to help the dog stay fit and trim. Their daughter couldn't help but share snacks with him.

The dog went everywhere with Mr. Doremus, and in fact, he spent his days at Leon's florist shop in Madison, New Jersey. Leon wasn't particularly attached to the dog, but carted him around more out of obligation than out of affection.

Ever since the previous year's bird hunting trip, Mr. Connelly and Mr. Doremus had been conspiring to give that dog to Mr. Fitz-Gerald.

Imagine Doc's surprise when he uncovered his eyes. How could Doc refuse the gift of "man's best friend" so thoughtfully wrapped and so affectionately given? Doc sure was a sucker for a challenge.

"I see how this is!" he exclaimed. "I accept your generous gift, but under one condition. If I can turn this dog into a passable bird dog by this time next year, you can bring him home with you. If I fail, this dog shall remain here as a constant reminder that you were right, and I was wrong!"

It had taken just that much time for Tease to make himself at home at Paleface, asleep on the floor, his chin on Doc's foot. Tease was home.

## '66 If Only It Would Snow

Sunday afternoon, only eight men remained to patrol the woods. Increasingly, Gib was having to admit the fire was no longer an emergency. Gib was still worried. If only it would snow or rain!

## '66 It Takes a Lot of Heroes at Times Like These

Mary Wallace was back at the Lodge managing Operation Food. A grateful Russell Mulvey told Mary, "The food here made for positively luxurious fire-fighting conditions. We are used to having a loaf of bread and a package of bologna and putting sandwiches together with our own fire-blackened hands."

Mary told Russell, "It is very kind of you to be so complimentary.

Mrs. Fitz-Gerald has worked tirelessly, almost continually, since Thursday night."

Jean interrupted Mary. "Thank you for the compliment, Mary, but it's nothing compared to the work of the firemen, many of whom haven't rested at all, and the volunteers and the students, and Ranger Manley, and Mrs. Manley." They turned to look at Esther at her sign-in table. She was asleep at that moment, sitting on her chair, head on her table, pencil in her hand. "It takes a lot of heroes at times like these and nobody anywhere can beat the local heroes we have right here in the North Country." As she finished her thought, Jean became choked up with gratitude.

## '66 A Cowboy and a Fireman

The last two men on the job were the "fire boss" and his colleague, Ranger Russell Mulvey, a resident of Wilmington who held a similar job as Gib, but who had to travel great distances in his conservation efforts as regional forester for the district including Warren, Washington, and Saratoga counties, to the south.

Russell and Gib toured Paleface by jeep three times together that day. The first time through the woods, Gib talked about the fire two years earlier on neighboring Hamlin Mountain, Paleface's little brother across the street. Gib recalled another dry summer, and getting a call from Charles Haselton one afternoon. A couple dozen residents from Jay were gathered up immediately. Gib recalled that it was a stubborn little fire that had burned about three quarters of an acre. Fortunately, the crew put the Hamlin fire out after a couple hours. Nonetheless, Gib checked on the fire every day for two weeks, and concluded, "I shudder to think what would have happened if that fire got out of control. It was the middle of summer. Not much rain, and certainly no snow to look forward to."

On their last trip through the woods together, Gib confided to Russell, "You know I am always the last one to proclaim any fire over. With my own eyes, I can see no remaining apparent risk here. And yet, this fire, this mountain, and this season... they have me spooked. I can't turn my back on this until I know for certain it is safe. What would you do?"

Russell reassured Gib. "You are right to be cautious. On the other hand, it was probably safe to walk away yesterday. Tomorrow I will have to catch up on my work elsewhere. And if I were you, I would probably make a tour once a day until you get your soaking rain or snow storm."

Russell Mulvey went on to compliment his fellow Ranger. "I admired your serious, tireless, organized leadership over the course of the last couple of days." Russell concluded his praise by adding, "Ranger Manley, you're my hero," in a mock recently rescued damsel in distress voice.

The two Rangers shared a well-earned laugh.

Back in his living room in Jay, late Monday afternoon, Gib completed his reports so he could close the official files on the fire at Paleface Mountain. Then he took out his large, dark brown, leather-bound diary and wrote his own reflections looking back at the four day battle.

There was a knock on Gib's front door. Doc had stopped by to thank him, once again and a bit more officially, with a gift.

Most of Doc's landscapes were combinations of blue and green, bright and beautiful, happy and uplifting. That afternoon, Doc had sent his friends on a grouse hunting adventure without him, and remained behind to paint a scene he named "Fire on the Mountain" as a gift for Gib.

Gib thanked Doc for the painting. The two men looked at it together in silence for about a minute before Gib told Doc that looking at it felt exactly like standing there late Friday night. As sometimes is the case, a tragic disaster can appear on canvass as a thing of beauty.

Their art appreciation was interrupted by another knock on the door. It was Gib's grandchildren in Halloween costumes. One was a cowboy. Another was a fireman. Doc looked at Gib briefly, wondering if he noticed the irony.

Doc excused himself and left Gib to visit with his family.

## '66 Letter of Gratitude

A couple of weeks later, after talking with Jean, Doc penned another letter to the editor. He officially expressed their appreciation before the whole community. There were lots of people to thank, and Doc's warm letter was warm and conveyed the depth of Jean and Doc's gratitude.

## '66 Promotion for Putzi

Paleface kicked off the new season with a series of announcements.

First and foremost was news that Putzi Jost was officially named Director of the Paleface Ski School. Putzi held both the Canadian Ski Instructors Alliance and United States Eastern Ski Association's certifications and was a member of the Professional Ski Instructors of America. After five years as Assistant Director and one year as Acting Director, Putzi was more than ready to lead that most important part of the Paleface operation. In addition to Putzi's years at Paleface, she spent two years as an instructor at the Harvey Clifford Ski School at Mt. Snow in Vermont. Putzi had also worked as an instructor at the Real Charette Ski School at Grey Rocks in the Laurentians.

Soon after Putzi was named Director came an announcement that Cecil Victor Pelkey, known to everyone as Pete, had been named Assistant Director. Pete had five years of service with Paleface, and before that was a member of the ski patrol at Whiteface.

Next, Paleface announced that two recent high school graduates, Marla Hildreth and Tommy Thomas, had been added to the Paleface Ski School staff. Marla and Tommy had skied for years as part of the after-school ski program sponsored by the Rotary Club, led by Waxy Gordon and attorney Dan Manning, Jr. It was also announced that Howard and Laura Trumbull and Theresa Devlin would be returning for the 1966-67 winter season.

Doc was pleased and proud to see the after-school ski program had produced new ski instructors and was happy that Putzi Jost had decided to add Marla and Tommy to her ski school.

## '66 Making Snow

Dana started the new winter ski season by adding a new employee to a crew of four local boys from Wilmington.

Preston Palmer was seventeen years old and recently moved to the neighboring town of Upper Jay. Preston had lost his parents at a young age. The responsibility for raising Preston fell to his mother's oldest brother, Preston's uncle and best friend Harold Greene. Preston and Harold moved to Upper Jay following Harold's retirement from the General Electric Company in Schenectady.

It had been Harold's dream to retire to the country. Harold wanted to live in a small cabin or cottage, in the woods, near a stream and far from any city. Harold's plan was to spend his time fishing and riding snowmobiles. The only problem was that neither Harold nor Preston had ever done either before moving to the Adirondacks.

After talking with Preston for a few minutes, Dana decided that he really liked the young man. He seemed very nice, eager to please, and ready to learn. First and foremost, Preston was polite and respectful. Dana thought, "I can work with this kid."

It didn't take long for Preston and Dana to form a strong bond. Whenever Dana asked Preston to do something, Preston almost ran to get it done. Whenever Preston saw Dana working on something, he jumped to try to help Dana.

Perhaps the only drawback Dana noticed was that he needed to be very specific and literal when he asked Preston to do something. And Dana needed to make sure not to skip any seemingly small detail. Preston would do just exactly what Dana asked. Preston didn't have those skills that folks in the country are assumed to possess naturally, and Preston didn't ask questions. The response to pretty much everything was a cheerful, "Yes, sir." And Preston would be off and running between the "yes" and the "sir."

Dana and the other men on the mountain found Preston was well worth the training time. He was happy to do all the tasks customarily assigned to the new guy, with no complaints. He was strong and hard-working and always seemed to be whistling along with his work, almost dancing along to songs playing in his head.

Dana's brother, who also worked at Paleface, took to calling Preston by the nickname "Presto" and mostly, it seemed to stick. The more they called him Presto, the faster he seemed to go.

Preston had completed the eleventh grade in Schenectady and decided after moving with his uncle that he would work instead of going to school. They had moved to town almost four months earlier, and it had taken that much time for Preston to find work in the off season of a North Country autumn.

The coming winter would be Paleface's second winter of snowmaking. After the first season, Doc had invested in a 600 cubic-foot compressor which would provide sufficient pressure to cover two full trails rather than just one trail. Now Paleface would be sure to have enough snow on the all-important Paleface Glade trail where the team of Paleface ski instructors schooled their students.

Dana was happy to have the new compressor and was looking forward to seeing the compressor help the Larchmont brand snow making equipment realize its full potential.

## '66 Season Open

The lodge was busy during its season opening weekend. There was always something going on at Paleface. Paleface looked beautiful and festive, fully decorated for the Christmas season. Patti and Jean had decorated the dining room and lounge with boughs of balsam, and the beautiful bountiful piney smell filled the space.

The first skiers of the season were bustling in and out of the lodge.

At the same time, the volunteers from the Whiteface Kiwanis Club were busy packing fruit cakes to send to all the servicemen from the area. After a couple of hours, all the fruit cakes were packed in boxes, the boxes were sealed and addressed.

After a brief break, the members of the Club held their annual meeting. The nominating committee had presented a slate of officers for the members' consideration. As always, the members affirmed the slate and Jack Dreissigacker, a vice president at Santa's Workshop was named president of the Whiteface Kiwanis Club, replacing John Manning.

Another brief break allowed for the arrival of Kiwanians from the eleven clubs representing the Adirondack Division. Paleface was hosting the gala annual Christmas party for the combined clubs. The cocktail party was followed by dinner and then dancing to the house orchestra. Well-dressed philanthropists from across the Adirondacks danced their way into a Christmas spirit until well past midnight. And with that, Paleface was open for the winter season.

## '66 How the Grinch Stole Christmas

Mary Wallace joined her friend Jean for babysitting duty at Paleface on the night of December 18th. The two friends had planned to spend the evening together until it became clear that nobody was going to show up for work in the nursery that night.

No matter, Mary and Jean enjoyed spending time with children, and there was a brand new children's Christmas special scheduled on TV for that evening. First, they read Dr. Seuss's 1957 book, *How the Grinch Stole Christmas*. Then they watched the debut airing of the cartoon.

"That was a little scary," said Mary when it was over.

"I tend to prefer *Rudolph the Red Nosed Reindeer*," said Jean.

Three of the children were still awake at the end of the program. They agreed it was the best thing they had ever seen on television.

## '66 White Christmas

As if Paleface didn't have enough to be grateful for, with a solid early season kicked off over a week before Christmas, and with temperatures cool enough to make snow throughout the second half of December, Mother Nature delivered a big, beautiful whopper of a snowstorm that began late in the afternoon on Christmas

Eve and continued in to Christmas day. The blizzard brought seventeen inches of wonderful white winter gold.

## '67 Mr. and Mrs. Tommy Thomas, Jr.

Nine days into the new year, Thomas Matthew Thomas, Junior of AuSable Forks married Linda Russell of Keene. Tommy and Linda became yet another married Paleface couple. Tommy was a ski instructor and Linda was assistant to the Head Patrolman. Somehow, Paleface would get by while the Tommy Thomases enjoyed their honeymoon at Stratton Mountain in Vermont.

## '67 Shadows

Doc had taken notice of Preston. There was a lot to appreciate about him. In the month since Preston had started work at Paleface, they had enjoyed several conversations.

Preston was eagerly saving money, and was extremely motivated to pick up as much work as he possibly could. It had occurred to him that if he got to Paleface a couple hours early each night, he might be asked to start early. The strategy seemed to be effective, as Preston had a fifty percent success rate with it.

That meant sometimes, Preston would be hanging around waiting for his 11pm to 7am shift to begin. Most times, Preston would be sitting somewhere reading a book. Often, he could be found writing in a notebook.

Doc was intrigued by Preston. He was very studious, busily reading and writing. And yet, Doc learned that he had not completed high school. Preston was extremely motivated and hardworking when he was at work. Yet he seemed to be the most easygoing person one could hope to find. He was very friendly, comfortable talking with people and as polite a person as one could expect to meet. But he didn't seem to have any close bonds with people his own age. That didn't make sense to Doc, who had always had lots of friends his own age, at every stage of his life.

One Sunday night, Preston arrived two hours early for work. Sunday evenings weren't generally very busy. Preston was seated in a corner of the lounge, making sure not to take up space that a guest might want to occupy. He was writing in a notebook. As usual, he was lost in the fictional world of his own creation.

Doc wandered over to talk with Preston. "Good evening, Preston," said Doc.

Startled, Preston jumped, and dropped his pen and his notebook. "Yes, sir. Doc Fitz-Gerald. How are you tonight?" He rose to his feet.

"Just fine, Preston. Please, sit down. I brought you a mug of hot chocolate, on the house. May I join you for a few minutes?" Doc sat down nearby, not waiting for an answer to his question. "Sometimes I see you busily writing in a notebook. What are you working on?"

Strangely, no one had ever asked Preston that. "It's just nothing," Preston replied. "I guess I just kind of like to write down stories that I think up. They just kind of come to me, and I just kind of write them down. Then if it sounds good, I try to re-write them and make them better. Mostly, they're just silly little stories."

Ever curious, Doc asked, "May I read one?"

Preston passed Doc his notebook. It didn't occur to him to say no. Doc owned Paleface. Doc was the "big boss." And the more times Preston met Doc, the better he liked talking with him.

"Where should I begin?" asked Doc.

"Here, let me show you," Preston said, taking the notebook back for a minute. "The last story I finished starts here." Preston sat quietly while Doc read the story. It was hard to sit there patiently, while someone, the big boss no less, read his story.

Preston closed his eyes, and Doc slowly read aloud.

*Shadows, by Preston Palmer III*

*On and on he ran. Dark shadows of looming trees bent over the tired runner. Many night creatures hovered about him, everywhere he looked. Thick stringy-barked grape vines that were coiled about the bases of the trees were seen as thousand-tongued serpents. Time passed and the forest darkened.*

*After a while, his head was throbbing with the noises of the drums. The trees and the monsters, too, seemed to shake at every blast. His eyes filled with tears and his vision was blurred. In the trees he saw his pursuers, tall, hunched over, demanding, and demeaning. The sounds of the drums grew louder, for he was running slower. The deep hypnotic thumps became so closely spaced, that it seemed to him as if the trees were screaming at him, louder and louder. He kept going.*

*His clothes had been worn out from his long hard journey. Even though they were very ragged, fragments of them still clung to his body, plastered to it by the steaming sweat, or even attached to it by clotted blood. His feet, too, were bloody, but they had not gotten the chance to harden, for the wounds were constantly being reopened. Fragments of his moccasins were left along the trail with the drops of blood that were staining the ground. From his fall, sweat-stained mud was streaked across his body.*

*The noise had nearly caught him. He stumbled on, and cried out in sobs, coughing and wheezing from the exertion. Inside him burned a twinge of pain, which increased with every step. Before him, he saw it. The forest was slowly giving way. The last of these trees passed him by like bats in the night. Unaware, he flung himself out, into the sky and over the cliff. He was falling. The speed he was moving at was incredible, and it felt so good, too, for he didn't have to do anything. Over and over he turned. The air that rushed past him, felt cool against his over-heated body. He relaxed.*

*Finally, he hit it, but with a smack that entered him through every pore in his body. The cool bubbling water now gurgled around him. It cleansed him. It cooled him. It strengthened him. The morning sun, and warmth opened his senses to the chirping of the birds, the babbling of the fall, and the beauty of a perfectly clear day. The river had washed away the mud, blood, ragged clothes, and all his memories. A golden winged gull flew off toward the sun.*

When Doc finished the story, he handed the book back to Preston. "That's very good, son. I liked that story a lot. I think you have a gift. Is there room for improvement? Certainly! I would definitely encourage you to keep writing your stories!"

Doc thought Preston seemed like a happy-go-lucky, friendly kind of kid. His story was brooding, dark, serious, tragic even. Interesting. "Sometimes I think a writer feels the need to fill in the whole story," Doc said aloud, "leaving nothing to the imagination of the reader. Your story almost paints a picture. While I was reading I really enjoyed filling in the rest."

Preston said, "I think I saw a movie where a tribe of Indians held a captive. For their amusement, the captive was given a small chance of escape. I wanted to write about what it could have felt like for the captive who was attempting to escape."

"I think I saw that movie too," Doc laughed. "And that's exactly what I pictured when I read your story. I noticed you drew a long twisty vine around three sides of the page too. I found that was a nice touch. It really helped add to the mood your words created."

Doc and Preston talked for about an hour. Doc asked lots of questions, and Preston answered them all. Doc concluded that Preston was very smart in many ways. He also noted that Preston was naïve. There were many things that Preston didn't seem to know much about, and while Doc appreciated Preston's determination to maximize the hours in his paycheck, Doc got a sense that Preston didn't have any future ambitions.

It was almost time for Preston to begin work for the evening. Doc felt compelled to share some parting thoughts with him. "I think a man your age should be working toward something big. You should be trying to realize a higher purpose. I understand you are saving money to buy a car, and a snowmobile and to help your uncle. At the same time, you have talents and skills, unique qualities, a potential that needs to be fulfilled. I want you to name it. And then I want to talk to you about what to do next! Have a great night out on the mountain, Preston!"

Preston was startled. Doc had come on a little strong near the end. Preston said, "Yes, sir," and added a quick, "Thank you, Mr. Fitz-Gerald."

Doc reflected on his conversation with Preston, and resolved to find a way to help him. At the very least, he was certain of the need to help that boy get a high school diploma, for starters. Preston was the sort of young man that people wanted to help, whether he needed or wanted it.

## '67 UFO's

The new winter season was off to a fantastic start. The early snow in December never melted, and temperatures remained cold enough that Paleface was able to make lots and lots of snow. By the middle of January, the winter season was well underway.

It was Sunday, January 22nd. Preston Palmer was working the overnight shift, from 10pm to 6am, making snow. By about fifteen minutes after ten, Preston was up on the top of the glade trail. Something in the sky caught his eye.

It took Preston a moment to deduce that he was seeing a UFO. It shot across the sky, like a comet except that it kind of zigged and zagged. Preston dropped the snow gun he was pointing toward a patch of trail that desperately needed more snow. The snow gun landed on his foot. He didn't feel a thing, as his jaw dropped. Finally, Preston watched the object disappear behind Hamlin Mountain, just across the road from Paleface.

He raced down Paleface mountain as fast as he could, and must have looked quite a sight. Part running, part hopping, and almost rolling through the snow down the mountain, completely forgetting his snowshoes.

Preston Palmer wasn't quite eighteen years old, and though he would not have cared to admit it, he was afraid of the dark. There was the tiniest sliver of a crescent moon, so there wasn't much natural light. Most nights, Preston half expected old Slewfoot to appear from the darkness and maul him. That night, Preston was quite sure a rocket ship full of fuzzy green aliens had unloaded its occupants who were at that moment climbing down from their spacecraft and making themselves at home on the other side of Hamlin Mountain.

Preston found Dana Peck in the tank room. Dana could tell something was troubling his assistant. Dana put down his tools and said, "Hold on son, calm down. Everything will be all right. Now what's wrong?"

Preston told Dana about seeing the UFO and how he thought it had landed less than a mile away. Contrary to Dana's best advice, Preston had become more animated since Dana's soothing attempt to help calm him down.

"Should we evacuate Paleface?" Preston asked. "Clearly, immediate action should be taken to save the guests! What about the police? Or maybe the fire department?"

Dana wondered what in the world the police would think if he let Preston call in a report that Paleface was being invaded by aliens. It took Dana's maximum restraint to summon his composure and show compassion for Preston's paranoia.

"I tell you what, son," Dana said slowly. "You go inside, take your walkie-talkie with you. I'll go up and finish putting the guns in place. I'll bring along my walkie-talkie. If I see anything, I'll let you know and you can alert everybody."

Preston nodded vigorously while Dana was talking, and when he was finished, Preston said, "Be careful, Mr. Peck," in the way one would say it if they were sure a multitude of perils waited around every corner. Preston turned and ran for the front door of the lodge, not looking back until he was there.

Dana waved to Preston, and wondered whether Preston had just set a world's record for the hundred-yard dash. Dana shook his head in wondrous disbelief, chuckled to himself, and gathered his things to head up the mountain and finish preparing for a night of snow making.

## '67 Sightings

Preston explained to Doc that Dana had sent him and his walkie-talkie into the lounge. While Preston was telling, and retelling the story of his UFO sighting in the Firewater Teepee to an audience of five, three young boys in AuSable Forks were trying to figure out who *they* should tell about what they saw.

Randy, Wayne, and Steve were killing time in the parking lot near the bank. Each boy told the other what they saw as if they weren't all there witnessing it together. They agreed it looked a bit like a comet. They agreed it had a vapor trail like a jet would leave, which might be hard to see in a dark sky on a moonless night. They agreed it looked like a basketball on the front end, and stretched into a cone on the back end.

The next day, Randy told the librarian, Mrs. Maicus, about the UFO. He had been thinking about it most of the night and added that it wasn't like a shooting star that faded out quickly. Mrs. Maicus confided to Randy that she had seen it also. She and her husband Paul, president of the School Board and owner of the Rex Theater in Keeseville, were on their way from AuSable to Jay that night. Paul Maicus pulled the car over and Mr. and Mrs. Maicus watched the UFO go behind a cloud, then reappear on the other side of the cloud. The object never faded, but eventually disappeared behind the mountains.

When Mr. and Mrs. Maicus retold the story, Mrs. Maicus reminded people that Paul had flown more than fifty missions during World War II. She told them, "With all of his training, and all of the things he saw, I can tell you Mr. Maicus never saw anything like it.

Although Mrs. Maicus and Randy were equally certain what

they saw was not a comet, they researched the subject in the library's collection. The conclusion was that no comets would be visible to the human eye in January.

Meanwhile, George Yando of AuSable Forks was in his driveway, getting ready to drive to work at the J. & J. Rogers Co for his 11pm shift. Mr. Yando noticed that the object was "about twice as big as a star" and further described it as "a bright ball of white fire with a long trail behind it."

Howard Snow, an appropriately named ski instructor and member of Gore Mountain's ski patrol, reported that it was in the sky long enough for him to run inside and bring someone else outside to witness it. Howard Snow concluded, "It might have been a comet, because of the tail but it certainly didn't act like any comet I ever heard of."

Usually Dana could count on his crew to tend to the snow making at night. Under normal circumstances, unless there was a breakdown, Dana could sleep a normal night's sleep and work the day shift at Paleface. On that particular night, there was no way Dana could leave Preston Palmer alone on the mountain. Dana didn't let Preston remain in the lodge more than an hour before sending the signal on the walkie-talkie that all was clear. Dana worried that if he didn't get Preston back out on the mountain right away, he might not come back again the next night. The two men worked together all night.

Early the next evening, at Dana's insistence, Preston and Dana snowshoed all over Hamlin Mountain. Dana knew that if Preston didn't see it for himself, Preston would be certain that the forces of an alien invasion were gathering on the back side of the mountain.

Even with the personal inspection, Preston Palmer kept an eye out all winter. If he had to be honest, it wouldn't have surprised him in the slightest to see the aliens. At least it helped ease his fear of a midnight bear attack. Preston was saving his money to buy a snowmobile, otherwise he might have quit that job at Paleface!

## '67 King of the Ball

At the Third Annual Ski and Skate held on January 21st, Dana and Jane's son Greg was named King of the ball. Greg had come close to being named king two years earlier. It might not even have crossed his mind that he was being crowned in a resort that was sitting right on top of where he once lived. Who better to serve as king than someone with such close ties to the kingdom?

## '67 A Young Man's Imagination

A couple of weeks later, on a Saturday in the middle of February, there was a violent blizzard. Visibility was nearly zero and the roads were very slippery. There were numerous car accidents in the area.

Billy Ward was driving Ward Lumber Company's 1966 Plymouth across the stone bridge in Wilmington and scraped the left side of the car against the bridge. Mrs. Bernard Roberts was headed toward Jay and Ira Winch was driving the town's snowplow in the other direction toward Wilmington. Mrs. Roberts was blinded by a whiteout and collided with Mr. Winch's plow. Fortunately, Mrs. Roberts wasn't badly hurt. Jane Peck was headed home toward Wilmington after a quick stop at Paleface. Mr. Lukosevicius from Verdun, Quebec was coming up the hill, and due to the whiteout, he stopped his 1967 Ford in the middle of the road. Mr. Bartholemew Gaffney from Isalin, New Jersey stopped right behind him. Jane's car slid on the turn, colliding with Mr. Lukosevicius pushing his car into Mr. Gaffney's car. Fortunately, none of the drivers were injured in those accidents.

Although the natural snow kept Dana and his staff plenty busy with grooming, making as much new manufactured snow as possible remained a priority as well. They just never knew when they might need it.

Preston Palmer couldn't help but think about whether the severe weather could have been caused by the UFO. Of course, control of the weather would be a skill the aliens would possess.

Maybe they also liked to cause auto accidents for their amusement. Perhaps they used the white-outs from the storm as cover to prepare for their world-wide attacks which would of course utilize Paleface as their base of operations.

Preston had recently learned not to repeat those kinds of thoughts. Nobody wanted to hear about the UFO's and the aliens on Hamlin Mountain anymore. But working alone all night on a dark snowy mountain does wonders for a young man's imagination.

## '67 Chamber Changes

During the winter of 1967, The Whiteface Chamber of Commerce had failed to find a volunteer to serve as chamber president. Doc Fitz-Gerald continued as acting president in that interim period. It was a busy time for the chamber.

The chamber members were engaged in coordinating a vote by petition. Each participating business collected signatures indicating whether their customers preferred to honor the country's first president by celebrating his birthday as part of a long weekend, or whether to continue to celebrate in traditional fashion on his actual birthday.

It was no surprise that the results of the local voting were about four to one in favor of the long weekend, and who wouldn't want to extend a two-day weekend whenever possible? The local businessmen in the tourist trade figured people from the cities would travel farther if the holiday were attached to a weekend. It took a few years, but eventually President Washington's birthday was turned into a long holiday weekend, first in New York and then subsequently the national holiday that became known as Presidents' Day was established in 1971.

A more contentious topic was whether the town of Wilmington should be encouraged to consider changing its name to Whiteface. The Whiteface Chamber of Commerce couldn't resolve that discussion topic in one meeting, and Doc Fitz-Gerald appointed a subcommittee to discuss the issue further.

The name of the town had been changed before, so there was some precedent. At its founding, the town was named Danville. Unfortunately, there was another town in the State of New York with that name, and to avoid confusion, the town changed its name to Wilmington two years later, in 1822. Ultimately, there was insufficient appetite for changing the name of the town to match the name of the state-owned ski center.

Doc also appointed a nominating committee to work on pressing some new volunteer board members into service, and to recruit a new president from among the ranks of members.

The chamber board also discussed the highly contentious issue of merging the AuSable and Keeseville High Schools. Doc argued in favor, thinking of the taxpayer money that could be saved by having one instead of two schools. The most vocal voices in the room spoke of school spirit and community spirit, and one man made the argument that "few things are made better merely by making them larger." That statement stopped the debate momentarily while everyone in the room considered the wisdom of those words.

Doc didn't change his mind, but it was clear that there was no consensus on that topic. Furthermore, Doc possibly held a minority position on it. Unlike most of the community, Doc hadn't grown up in town, attending one or the other of the two rival schools. The issue wasn't up to the chamber anyway. In the end the chamber did not take a position. It did not endorse either point of view. Boylan Fitz-Gerald continued to argue in favor of the merger personally, just not as a volunteer leader of the chamber. Ultimately, the two schools did merge.

## '67 A Job Offer

As the winter ski season began to wind down, Doc got to thinking about his daughter Patti more and more. Finally, he put his thoughts together, and made the case for Patti to return to the North Country.

*Thursday*

*Hi Patti:*

*Everything's at a standstill here this morning. Very high winds, so we can't run the chair lift. Snow squalls, however, so maybe we're in for something.*

*Just got a nice letter from Ray Kaufman accepting the job of Corral Boss for next summer. His wife Pat has shown horses on the Sunshine Circuit in Florida since she was eleven years old, western pleasure, equitation, stock, etc. They should make us quite a team. He is bringing a friend to help him, name's Terry. Ray says he's nice, neat and clean and responsible. So, all in all it looks like we're in for a nice summer. As I told you, I want to buy 4 or 5 Pinto geldings if I can find them. They should help us really look "western". With the big Canadian Exposition opening in Montreal in the spring, we should have a great year.*

*We've been having a good winter and are quite a bit ahead of last year. I've enjoyed full time teaching, it's a lot healthier than bar tending and more fun seeing people progress. This week we have 45 ski-weekers. My class started at the stem Christie level and now we've moved up to sloppy parallel with a two-hour session yesterday on hop Christies. I've found a new way to get them into the hops without psyching them out, you know that problem.*

*Speaking of which, I've been doing quite a bit of thinking about our general problems here and about your set-up there in Utica. It seems to me that if you're making $50 a week take home pay, you have to deduct almost $10 a week for room rent. That's down to $40, then it must cost you at least $20 for food and incidentals, which brings you down to $20 a week net. I personally* *think you're worth a lot more than that both to yourself and to people.*

*You have some terrific gifts of personality and a real liking for people, and these things shouldn't be allowed to go to waste.*

*As far as your training is concerned it is true you had that course in Utica that gives you something specific to fall back on in case of real need. However, when it comes to other matters, you've had a lifetime of training with people and with wholesome fun situations. Your latest training had to do with accuracy and responsibility in business details and that's useful anywhere any time.*

*Now! As I said before we are in a very crucial spot in our business here. We should be moving out of the red and into the black for the first time this year. As we really make the big push into the Dude Ranch business I'm going to need real help. I'm delighted to have that western trio here. The Canadian Expo will give us a long season, from May 15 to October 15. I need people on the staff who will be responsible and good with the public.*

*Mom and I have talked it over and would like you to think of the possibility of helping us go Gung Ho into this program this summer. I would like to see you with us in a position where you'd be meeting the public and helping with the general fun spirit of a swingin' resort. We need you Patti and what your bubbly personality can do for us.*

*It's hard to spell it out, but you know what Putzi means to our winter program. Ninety percent of the success or failure of our kind of business has to do with the personality and character of our key personnel. The fact that we have so many repeat customers shows that they like the people who work here.*

*Now, as we go into a new phase, we'll be drawing a younger group together, and, again, what you can do for us is terribly important.*

*We need help at the level of counter girl, hostess, someone at the front desk to sell rooms, check in house guests, make up their bills and check them out, etc., etc. Later on as things get swinging we'll need help with social directing, fun and games, organizing parties, picnics, square dances. There's no limit to the future. And, you should have a larger part in the growth of Paleface!*

*As far as the economics of it are concerned, here are a few things to think about: When you work for us, there are quite a few "fringe" benefits which you are now in a position to appreciate. 1) You don't have to report every dollar you receive from a parent!!! 2) Room and board don't even have to be considered. They're here as part of the general set-up and don't have to be reported as "income". 3) Transportation is always available somewhere around the ranch. 4) Even though the top spots are now in the hands of western-trained wranglers, there is still going to be need for help with the horses and horse shows. 5) As I mentioned above, to be able to do what you enjoy doing, to work with people you like, to help folks enjoy life, all these things are really worthwhile.*

*Mother and I both appreciate your spirit of independence and your pride in making your own way. We know you can do it, you don't have to "prove" something to us.*

*However, you know by now that you can be well worth your "pay" to us as a regular key employee in our expanding business. It's easy to hire chambermaids and dishwashers, etc. But it's hard to find key people such as you should be.*

*So far as "salary" is concerned I prefer to think of it that way more than "hourly wages" we could talk about that later. You know and we know that you'd be making a lot more "net" with us than you would where you are, not to mention some of the "fringe benefits" I discussed above.*

*Well, think about all these things, and if another full season here, helping good old Paleface makes sense, then plan to jump in the saddle come May 15th! You belong here and we miss you.*

*We'll have a good talk about it next time you come home. Incidentally, the enclosed check may help you get the diddy-bop-bug [a $450, 1954 Rambler] on the road again. You'll be wanting to get it in shape to trade in before long.*

*Give our love to your side-kick when and if you see her.*

*Love, Dad*

*We really miss you and would love to have you around for a while before you try your wings out west, we don't mean you can't ever leave but maybe Ray would have ideas on that line. We won't be able to use Jean Carol much with the new baby coming and anyway it's you and your umph we miss.*

*Bought you a new parka, I think you'll love it, it's long! It's dark blue. If you are coming home soon, maybe you should leave me your car and take mine again for the rest of the winter. Shall I mail the parka?*

*Lots of love, Mom*

## '67 A Letter to Mother

Half a week later, Doc wrote a late-night letter to his wife, for Jean to find in the morning.

*March 28, 1967*

*Hi Snooks!*

*Howdaya like our new writing paper? Not too bad, eh? Dude Ranch paper and all!!*

*Now that we're closed for the season, we get a chance to do the things we want to do, like writing to our girl-kid.*

*Anyhow! I guess I told you how I bought a new Pinto named Navajo. Real cutie, mate, or I should say twin of Cheyenne. Just comin' four, bridle tooth half on. Real gentle. Douggie Peck loves him. A real kid's horse.*

*Tonight, I got a phone call from Glendive, Montana, about 11:00 p.m. from Ray Kaufman (photo enclosed in case you forgot how he looks). I told him that his wife Pat and my Pat could take parties out end of May in case his best wrangler Terry couldn't get here until June 1st.*

*Yeah man! I think we'll have a great year! Ray is really hot to trot and I think he and Pat and Terry will help us a whale of a lot. In fact, the more I think of it the better our team looks for this year!! You too kid!!*

*We've got a couple new brochures on the way, which should help.*

*Incidentally the Peck boys are having a lot of fun riding the new Pinto, Navajo, and Trigger and your cutie, Chico. All of our horses have wintered well except old Brownie and Whiteface who seem a bit thin. Soooo! We'll fatten them up on the June grass and not use them until July. That should help.*

*Oh! I gotta tell ya, our ole pal Ralph Calkins died last week. He sure was a lotta man for 75 years. We'll miss him at the horse shows. Remember how he shod Dunder for the Dannemora show and said, "go out and win that ribbon Son!" And we sure did! They don't come too plentiful like that Ralph. A real guy. He'd put many a young kid, boy-kid I mean, to shame when it comes to muscle and handling horses! I'm sure glad I knew him!*

*Incidentally, this past winter even though it died three weeks too soon was our best winter to date. In fact, the year just over is our best year to date. I really feel good about it all! This year was $18,000 better than any year we've ever had. We grossed $130,000. Hooray for Paleface!! And we have only just begun to fight! Just watch our new team, next year!*

*Paleface has stood the test, and is now starting to go into the black!!!!!!!!!!*

*All of which shows that you've got to be a good fisherman, patient and all that. You have to keep on trying!! Soooo! In about three weeks our gang will be going to New Brunswick for salmon. Steinhoff, and Behrle Todd and Doc Mackinnon and Bob Connolly and this year, Chuck will be going too!*

*Then, the Mackinnons and Mom and Patti will have to go to Wolfe Island for a try at those Canadian bass!! I mean summer-time.*

*Oooooh! I forgot to told you! We just made a coupla bucks!*

*We sold that juniper pasture where we used to keep the sick or tired horses – the side hill between Mother Pecks and Willard Haselton's. Bought it for $1,300 and sold it for $4000, not bad, eh? Sometimes lightning strikes in our favor! Soooo! From now on things are lookin' up, up, UP!*

*Here's to we, us and Company*

*Love, Popeye!*

## '67 Fishing Expedition

Each spring, fishermen come from around the world to fish the mighty West Branch of the AuSable River.

Each spring, Doc liked to travel with friends on a fishing expedition. Jean thought there were plenty of good fish to be had nearby. Of course, Jean understood it was also an opportunity for the men to get away with friends.

Between seasonal operations, nothing much happened in April and November. There was no point being open, and Paleface was usually closed during those months. Doc and Jean used those opportunities to travel. Often while Doc went on adventures, Jean visited family or old friends in New Jersey.

The late April fishing expedition in 1967 included Doc Fitz-Gerald, his son Chuck, Fran Devlin, Curtis Fountain, Robert Connelly of Underwood Street in Newark, New Jersey, and Carl Steinhoff. The men fished the Miramichi River in Nova Scotia. As always, two large station wagons carried the men, their gear, and their provisions to the distant location.

## '67 The Mystery Spot

After Paleface closed for the season, Preston Palmer got a job working for Chuck Kurutz, who was quickly building a roadside attraction he called The Mystery Spot. The attraction was practically right across the street from Paleface, at the base of Hamlin Mountain.

Mr. Kurutz had a plan all drawn out. It was basically a three-year development plan. Most of the building for the first phase was done in May and June of 1967. A crew put the buildings together according to Mr. Kurutz's specifications and instructions.

Preston Palmer was Mr. Kurutz's assistant. Whatever errand needed doing was assigned to Preston, and when there were no such errands, Preston helped with painting and landscaping projects. Mr. Kurutz liked Preston's outgoing personality. When the attraction was open, Preston would make a perfect tour guide.

On the 19th of May, Mr. Kurutz was having lunch with the building crew. Preston took a break from painting to eat a ham sandwich. Mr. Kurutz passed around a newspaper for everyone to see. There was a big circle drawn around the brief news story that said: "The Mystery Spot, Wilmington's newest attraction, is being built on the left side of Route 86 going east at the foot of the hill near Paleface Mountain Inn."

When the newspaper came around to Preston, another little story in the paper caught his eye. According to that story, a public relations officer from the Plattsburgh Air Force Base had concluded that "no further information was available locally" about the UFO sightings seen by countless North Country residents in January and that "the matter had been referred to the Pentagon for analysis." Preston scoffed. He thought that was the last anyone would ever hear about it. Preston didn't normally exhibit such cynical tendencies.

Preston's final thought on the matter was a conclusion that "there's something mystical about this Hamlin Mountain. I wonder if those aliens have burrowed their way underground somewhere." Preston had reconciled to working nights during the winter on Paleface's Basset Mountain. Good thing his summer job at The Mystery Spot was a daytime job.

Next, Mr. Kurutz shared with everyone the news that he and

his wife Pam would be expecting a child near the end of the year. It was an exciting time, with a new business in development and a baby on the way.

The grand opening for The Mystery Spot was on Saturday, June 17th. The Mystery Spot was a "fun house" attraction. Visitors were led through a series of connected houses in which optical illusions were designed to confound, and leave guests wondering, "How is that possible?"

Some of the mini houses featured trick mirrors that re-shaped people's physical appearances. One made guests shorter and wider, another made guests seem taller and extremely thin. Yet another made guests look like they were zig zag shaped, like a lightning bolt. Other houses made it seem like guests were walking through them sideways rather than walking through normally. For those visitors prone to motion sickness, The Mystery Spot could be most upsetting. Most guests were amazed by the miraculous things they saw, or thought they saw. For instance, in one building, there was a water feature which seemed to exhibit water running *uphill*.

As spring gave way to summer, Mr. Kurutz created much excitement locally, making presentations to the boards of the Chambers of Commerce, churches, and civic groups.

In May, Mr. Kurutz attended a meeting of the Whiteface Kiwanis. He told them about the "topsy turvy" fun house world he was creating, and his plans for an enormous dinosaur themed fun park that would surround it in the future. Beyond that, Mr. Kurutz imagined rides, giant slides, miniature golf, and all sorts of amusements.

Everyone was so enthralled with Mr. Kurutz's vision, they decided to visit The Mystery Spot as part of their July monthly meeting. In July, the Kiwanis Club met at Tirolerland. Joe Wallace of Upper Jay gave a lecture on road building, and then the Kiwanians made a road trip to The Mystery Spot where Mr. Kurutz gave eighteen members of the club a personally guided tour through the fun houses.

## '67 Jean has a Heart Attack

At Paleface, it was time to gear up for another busy summer season.

The Expo, or The Exposition in Montreal was expected to bring many new tourists through the Adirondacks on their way from New York City, New Jersey, and other locations to the south, and for that matter, across the country and throughout the world.

The local Chambers of Commerce had worked hard and in united fashion to place enticing advertisements in front of potential visitors. For over a year, Doc had been one of the leading voices for seizing the opportunity to welcome Expo visitors to the Adirondacks, perhaps on their way to Expo, or on their way home.

The phone had been ringing, and between Doc and Jane, most of the calendar on the wall had been filled in solid from about a week before the Fourth of July through Labor Day. Even September's reservations looked good.

Patti, who was almost twenty years old, planned to remain in Utica over the summer. Patti had taken a part-time job, and was taking classes at Cazenovia College. If she had to be honest, she would have preferred to work at Paleface year-round, skiing, riding horses, and entertaining tourists instead of going to college.

Doc had recruited a couple Montana cowboys to give Paleface's Dude Ranch a western flair and to amplify the western theme. That would be the busiest summer ever for the cowboys and horses.

Doc had expansive plans, which he announced in his longest press release ever. The press release was so long that the newspaper had to reduce it by half, cutting out some of Doc's more colorful descriptions of each new horse.

As usual, Doc put the latest press release in Jane's hands, and Jane set out for the post office.

Jean had been going over the menu, looking at whether to make changes to any of the meal offerings for the summer, and double checking the cost to make each meal.

As the morning continued, Jean felt more and more out of sorts. And then it occurred to Jean that she might have a couple of the signs that she might be having a heart attack. Fortunately, Doc had come to the dining room after Jane left for the post office. It didn't take him long to decide to call the Wilmington Rescue Squad.

The ambulance rushed over from Wilmington to Paleface and took Doc and Jean to the Keene Valley Hospital. Doctor Mackinnon told Doc it was a good thing they had come right away.

Jean remained in the hospital for the rest of May and all of June. It took Doc about two days to realize that he was going to need help.

Jean would have been furious to know that Doc had told their daughter Patti that she was seriously ill in the hospital. Jean felt it was wrong to burden young people with their parents' concerns, plus Jean had hoped that Patti would take an interest in her college studies.

Doc set out in the Paleface station wagon early one morning for Utica instead of driving to the hospital to visit his wife. He didn't stop until he reached his destination.

Doc arrived in Utica just as Patti had completed her last exam.

Doc said to Patti, "I haven't got a right to ask, and I really shouldn't suggest you come home and help. If you say no, that's fine, it will be alright. We'll certainly figure things out. But on the other hand, I feel like I want to beg you to come home as a personal favor to me. Aside from the fact that I miss you, I need your help with your mother and I need your help at Paleface this summer."

And it wasn't just Patti. Patti's childhood friend, Linda Cooke, shared an apartment with Patti. Between them, they didn't have a full-time job. They were barely making the rent each month.

It didn't take any arm twisting. It was very easy to convince Patti to move home. Cookie figured she could make it on her own. If she had to, she could find a way. Without particularly trying to be persuasive, Doc offered Cookie a full-time job as a chambermaid for the summer, and topped the job offer off with the promise of lots of extra overtime money for baby sitting and waitressing in the evenings. The girls were packed within two hours.

A couple of phone calls later, both girls had quit their jobs and dropped their summer classes. Cookie was very close to completing a two-year degree. Patti had a good deal further to go than Cookie did. Patti was barely matriculated anyhow, having come up with a temporary major until a more permanent future plan could be formed. There was no time to think about college classes at that point. Patti was anxious about her mother's health, and in a hurry to get home to see her. She was a little afraid of seeing her mother ill, but part of her soul soared to think of leaving the big little city of Utica behind and returning to her beloved mountain home in the Adirondacks.

After an hour on the road, with the station wagon dragging a small rented trailer full of the girls' possessions, the travelers briefly began to forget their worries and troubles. They talked most of the way from Utica to Albany.

With a brief pause in the conversation, Doc turned on the radio. The volume was quiet at first, then Doc and the girls turned the volume louder and louder, as one hit song followed another.

Doc was amused and thoroughly entertained as Cookie and Patti sang "These Boots Are Made for Walkin'," a big hit from the year before, along with Nancy Sinatra. They almost got into singing along too much. Doc was laughing out loud by the time the song ended.

By the time Doc pulled into the parking lot at the Keene Valley Hospital, he had been brought up to date on the modern music of the day. The girls had to admit they enjoyed the road trip. Though Jean scowled at Doc from her hospital bed, she was beside herself with happiness to see Patti there, and she summoned all of her energy to look as "well" as possible during Patti's visit. She didn't yet realize that Patti was home for good. It was late in the evening, and visiting hours were almost over. Though she wouldn't have let on, Jean was tired but full of gladness at having had the company.

As was often the case through the years, the extraordinary staff of people that worked at Paleface rose to the occasion and did all the things necessary to keep the business functioning. The Dude Ranch operations were in good hands with the cowboys. Jane and

Dana took care of the things that needed taking care of in the office and around the lodge. Patti and Doc alternated days at the hospital and days at Paleface.

## '67 Preston Meets Cookie

Memorial Day was busier than previous Memorial Day weekends. It would turn out to be good preparation for even busier weeks to come. Few guests remained by Monday evening, however.

After a busy weekend, Cookie made quick work of making up the rooms. Patti and Cookie had plans to spend the afternoon together. Patti had the day off, and started her day with an early visit to see her mother in the hospital.

It was just about five minutes before noon. Cookie was passing by the lodge's entrance, distracted by a bag she was carrying, not paying close enough attention to where she was going, and walked right into Preston Palmer.

Their eyes met. Words came slowly to each. "Excuse me," Cookie said.

"Pardon me, Miss," Preston replied.

Without taking time to think or analyze, it was as if Preston and Cookie had spent scores of past lifetimes together. Was it a chance, accidental encounter? Or were these two people destined to walk into each other at that time on that day?

Cookie gestured with her arm to indicate the direction of the dining room. "I'm sorry. I wasn't looking where I was going. I was on my way to change. You must be here for lunch."

Preston replied, without thought or plan. Preston liked girls well enough but had never chased or caught one. "Yes, I was going to have lunch in the lounge. I've just finished work for the day. Would you like to join me? After you change that is. If you don't have plans."

Cookie told Preston she was planning to have lunch with her friend who was due to come along any minute, but then added, "Perhaps you could join *us* for lunch. I'll just be a couple minutes."

With that, Cookie started to walk away. "You don't mind waiting," Cookie added, turning her head back to look at Preston and blinking a couple of times. She smiled and added, "Do you?" Then she laughed, feeling like she had just imitated some famous movie star.

While she was getting ready, it occurred to her that Preston looked like a very young Elvis Presley—a very *blond* Elvis Presley. The fact that Cookie immediately associated him with a famous person bode well for Preston.

By the time Patti arrived, Cookie was just finishing getting dressed.

Patti didn't mind the extra company at lunch. The three young adults got along marvelously. Of course, Patti and Cookie had been friends for many years. Patti had met Preston briefly at some point since he had worked at Paleface over the winter, even if it was the late night shift.

Preston told the girls his life story, in his typical unassuming, self-effacing manner. Likewise, Cookie told Preston about growing up in the town of Jay, and going away to college in Utica. Being raised by his uncle, Preston hadn't spent much time around girls or women. Cookie dominated the conversation. Patti's friendly manner and sense of humor made Preston completely at ease. Though it hadn't crossed their conscious thoughts, deep down all three of them knew that Preston and Cookie were destined for one another.

After lunch, Patti suggested they go for a ride to look at the new baby reindeer at the Santa's Workshop reindeer farm between Jay and AuSable Forks. In the past couple of days, two new reindeer had been born, bringing the total number of new fawns up to four. The roadside reindeer ranch was perfect graze for the herd, and a great promotion for the attraction, far better than any billboard.

There was a spot at the side of the road big enough for five cars. When Patti pulled her car in, there were two other cars already there. One belonged to Jack Dreissigacker, who was the vice president of Santa's Workshop. The other was a cherry red 1957 Ford

Thunderbird convertible, with a red and white interior and Kansas license plates.

Preston and Cookie got out and watched the baby reindeer, running around and playing like a litter of baby kittens. Patti searched her car, and finally found her camera. She took lots of pictures of Cookie and Preston with the reindeer in the background. When they weren't looking, she also took a picture of the two men talking by the fence.

As she backed up to get a wide shot of the herd and her friends, Patti overheard some of the conversation.

Jack said, "Please tell me more about your experiences as Santa in Wichita, Mr. Scholtz."

The man with the red car, red pants and long, natural white beard said, "Please, call me LeRoy. Or better yet, call me Roy. Or better still, call me Santa!"

Patti thought, "Way to *ace* your job interview!"

Patti smiled and exchanged brief pleasantries with the men, when she realized she had gotten close enough to the men that she had distracted them from their conversation.

Patti tried to find a place at the fence where she could give Cookie and Preston some space to themselves. At the same time, she was trying to avoid intruding on Mr. Dreissigacker and Mr. Scholtz. Patti was able to remain just within earshot, and heard Mr. Scholtz say, "My greatest joy is when a child rushes up to me and, with stars in his eyes, and bursts out, 'Santa Claus, I found you! And I love you so much!' There is so much happiness in this recurring scene that to be part of it gives me great satisfaction. And to be able to dispense a little happiness in this world is all I am asking for."

With the reindeer visit over, Patti drove Preston back to The Mystery Spot where his uncle's car was parked. Then Patti and Cookie drove to Plattsburgh. They didn't have specific plans, but immediately after dropping off Preston, Cookie told Patti that she was going to the drive-in movies with Preston on Friday night. Cookie wanted to buy some new clothes.

Cookie always had magazines at her fingertips. She pulled a

magazine from her bag and flipped to some pictures of Doris Day from the movie *Caprice*.

In one picture, Doris was wearing a black and white coat with a houndstooth pattern. In another, she was wearing a bright yellow skirt with knee high white boots and enormous yellow sunglasses. The article referred to the style of clothing from the movie as "mod."

Cookie was supposed to be saving her money for her final college classes in the fall, not spending all her money on new clothes. To do both, she was going to have to work a lot of overtime during the summer!

It struck Patti as funny that she hadn't felt like a third wheel while the three of them were at lunch, in the car, or while they were visiting the reindeer. But now that it was just she and Cookie, between the shopping and the fact that all Cookie could talk about was Preston, she definitely felt like a third wheel.

Patti knew Cookie very well. This wasn't just a date or just a boyfriend. It was the kind of sixth sense that didn't require psychic powers. It would have been clear to anyone. Those two belonged together, just as Mr. Scholtz was made to be Santa Claus.

## '67 Preston and Cookie's Big Date

Patti and Cookie had succeeded at finding Cookie a mod new outfit, almost identical to the ones in the pictures, for her date with Preston.

Preston had to work until four on Friday afternoon. Then he raced home. He showered, changed into his Sunday best slacks and a sweater, and pulled into Cookie's driveway at five-thirty.

Cookie didn't keep Preston waiting, or make him wait in the living room with her parents. Instead, she flung open the front door and walked slowly down the front steps of her house in a mock movie star gait down the walkway to the driveway, hamming it up as much as possible. Cookie and Preston laughed at the ridiculousness of the mannerisms, although both Cookie and Preston thought

Cookie looked very pretty in the Doris Day knock-off outfit.

They didn't have the time or the budget for a fancy dinner, and the main attraction that night was the movies. Preston took Cookie to the Carrol's Restaurant in the Skyway Plaza, the first significant development in Plattsburgh, just beyond where Denny Miller's fifty mile hike had concluded.

Carrols was a popular chain of drive-in hamburger restaurants. The building was fairly small, and square shaped. The square parts were a dark orange color with vertical white pinstripes all around. The front face of the building featured square glass panels. At the right and left side of the building were large, angular boomerang shaped structures which added interest and affect to the appearance of the structure, and in front of the building a larger aquamarine colored boomerang served as the back drop for the Carrol's logo.

The restaurant's brand featured the Carrols name spelled out in cursive script. The letter C looked a little like a bottle opener, and the loop at the top of the letter "L" was shaped like a heart.

Above the cursive name in giant size was "15" followed by the cents symbol on an orange background. At the bottom of the sign was the word, HAMBURGERS in giant-sized printed capital letters on an orange parallelogram.

The bright aquamarine added contrast to the dark orange of the building, just as the orange tops of the garbage cans added contrast to the bright white bases of the trash receptacles. Carrols was known for this color combination, the name in cursive, the fifteen cent hamburger, and most especially, the club burger.

Preston and Cookie finished their dinner at Carrols in plenty of time to arrive by dusk at the Stardust Drive-in Movie Theater in Plattsburgh. Preston hung the big gray speaker over the car window, and cranked the window up, almost to the top.

It was a little chilly that early June evening. Preston had a warm blanket in the back seat of the car. With his arm over Cookie's shoulder and the blanket covering both of them, Preston and Cookie settled in for the show.

A short cartoon presentation aired first.

Cookie had been looking forward to seeing that movie since seeing it featured in her magazine. It wasn't a very successful movie and the critics hated it, but Cookie and Preston found it very entertaining.

The critics and the moviegoing public found it hard to imagine Doris Day as a James Bond 007 style spy. Preston had to admit he had a hard time keeping track of who was double crossing whom at any given time. The concept of a secret formula for waterproof hairspray was quite intriguing. It was amazing seeing one of the characters come out of the swimming pool with her wet hair turning instantly dry as she got out of the pool.

If Cookie could have purchased all the clothes Doris Day wore in the movie, she would have done so, right then and there.

Preston had the good sense to tell Cookie that she looked better in the big yellow sunglasses, tall white boots, yellow miniskirt, and houndstooth jacket than Doris Day looked in hers, and Preston sincerely meant it. Cookie showed her appreciation for Preston's compliment with a kiss, quickly followed by a second, then hundreds after that.

They continued the marathon kiss through the third feature, Ray Charles' movie *Blues for Lovers* which was a re-release of his 1964 film. It didn't do much better the second time around, but Preston and Cookie enjoyed the background music.

The double feature finished at about eleven thirty. Preston put the speaker back on the pole, the blanket back in the backseat, and turned on the car radio. It took almost half an hour to get all the cars out of the field and back on the road. Cookie went into conversation mode, and talked happily about a variety of subjects.

They were almost home at about one in the morning. Rather than going home and getting a few hours of sleep before work in the morning, Preston asked Cookie if she wanted to park for a while. Cookie smiled and said, "Uh huh." Preston easily found an old abandoned logging road. There were lots of old abandoned logging roads in the North Country.

About an hour later, they were wrapped up together in a blanket in the back seat. Neither Cookie nor Preston had ever been happier. Preston told Cookie that if they were Indians they would now be married, and they laughed. Preston had been a big reader his whole life, however all of the books he read were about Indians, cowboys, and the wild west. That was one subject about which he was an expert.

It was almost four in the morning when Preston dropped Cookie off in her driveway. "When will I see you again?" he asked.

Cookie said, "How about tomorrow, the next day, and the day after that?" They both smiled, shared a quick parting kiss, then Preston sped away.

Preston's uncle was awake already when Preston got home. As was always the case, Preston told Harold all about his evening. Harold himself had never found someone special, and couldn't help but be pleased that his young nephew had. Harold made coffee and a big breakfast, then Preston headed back down the driveway in Harold's car for a busy Saturday showing tourists the amazing miracles and wonderful optical illusions at The Mystery Spot.

From that point on, Preston and Cookie were inseparable. They cruised from one town to the next and back, racking up miles and burning gas. On a typical evening, they would drive from Wilmington to Lake Placid, then back to Wilmington then to Upper Jay, then to Jay, then to Paleface, then to AuSable Forks, off to Fern Lake or Silver Lake then back to Jay then back to Upper Jay, all the fun of a road trip, without going anywhere or spending very much money.

Whether the words meant anything to them or not, they sang all the songs as they came on the radio. The one song that represented Preston and Cookie together became their song and it was the huge hit by The Turtles from earlier that year: "Happy Together." Preston and Cookie thought of each other, and that time in their lives together, whenever they heard that song.

## '67 We've Got Our Work Cut Out for Us Today

Paleface was running behind on staffing up for the busy summer season. During June, the summer staff should have been locked in. Doc's recruiting trip to Utica brought Patti home and completed staffing in the barn. Cookie completed the maid staffing. Unfortunately, the restaurant was far from ready.

By early June, Jean would have lined up the summer crew. A basic schedule would have been created. And by Wednesday morning, the official schedule for the coming week would be posted on the wall in the office by the little mailboxes.

With all that was going on, Doc kept forgetting to post the schedule each Wednesday morning. It was the fourth weekend in June. The Fourth of July was little more than a week away.

By the time Doc realized there was nobody working Saturday morning, it was too late. Doc called everyone who he could think of. Carrie McDonald and Pearl Pierce, who normally worked Monday through Friday, said they would be there. Everyone else had plans.

Doc left Patti a little note in her mailbox, like he often did. For the most part, Doc treated Patti the same as he would any other employee. Doc wanted the employees to perceive that they were treated fairly and that the boss's daughter didn't get special treatment. Aside from the father-daughter notes, Doc did a pretty good job demonstrating impartiality. This little mailbox note asked Patti if she could come in early Saturday morning and work breakfast in the lodge.

After all, it was only the 24th of June, so aside from the guests in the hotel, Doc didn't expect that it would be too busy Saturday morning. Frankly, more effort had been put into getting staffed up for a wedding reception at Paleface Saturday afternoon and evening than for breakfast in the morning.

When Saturday morning rolled around, Pearl Pierce was there. Carrie McDonald was sick—perhaps it was the 24-hour stomach bug—and had called Paleface just as Patti and Pearl were arriving at five that morning.

Another young lady that Doc had hired to work weekends

during the summer had failed to arrive at seven. Pearl said to Patti, "We've got our work cut out for us today, Patti." They shared a look of realization; it was going to be a long, long morning. Fortunately for Patti and Pearl, everyone didn't decide to have breakfast at once. Unfortunately for Patti and Pearl, there were no vacancies in the motel the night before. Every room was occupied. Most of the rooms were occupied by full families. Then almost all of them decided to have breakfast at Paleface!

Patti and Pearl had kept up just fine with the early risers. By 6am, four breakfasts had been served, and Pearl had everything set up for the rest of the morning. By 7am, another eight people had been fed. By 8am, sixteen more had been served. So far so good. At 8am, the dishwasher failed to materialize. Patti and Pearl realized they were completely on their own! Patti was delivering an order to Pearl and noticing the dishwasher wasn't there. Pearl said to Patti, "Don't look now!" and pointed over Patti's shoulder. Patti looked. Four families of four arrived at once. "Here we go!" Patti exclaimed. As Patti was taking those orders, another three families arrived. Patti raced back and forth to the kitchen with orders, made coffee, and delivered orange juice. Hectic, yes and Patti might not have wanted to admit it at the time, but it was fun in a way too. It was definitely a challenge. By nine o'clock, Pearl had prepared another thirty-four breakfasts.

Cookie and Jane arrived at 9am. Instead of getting to work cleaning rooms, Cookie helped clear the tables and washed some dishes. Between selling tickets for rides and selling sundries at the front desk, Jane helped by making sure the coffee pots were full, and helping Patti top off everyone's coffee. Jane hadn't really been scheduled to work that morning. Usually Jane didn't work on Saturdays, and that Saturday in particular there was a wedding in her family. Her niece was going to be married early that afternoon, to be followed by a reception at Paleface.

Before Jane left, Patti asked Jane if she could wake up Doc who had spent the night in room number one as he usually did while Paleface was open. Jane stopped in the ladies' room before waking

Doc, and couldn't help but notice Cookie was vomiting. Cookie made a feeble attempt to blame it on the dishwashing.

Jane, of course, knew better. Jane said, "It's okay dear, I understand. You'll need someone to talk with. Please feel free to confide in me."

Cookie was feeling a little better. She thanked Jane for her understanding and concern, and recognizing Jane had a busy afternoon suggested talking on Monday morning.

Fortunately, the late crowd of breakfast diners were in a lazy mood, which made them more patient, perhaps. Pearl was a professional. Patti had boundless energy. Most guests didn't even realize that Paleface's morning breakfast crew was functioning in disaster mode.

After Doc's quick wake up call, a couple splashes of cold water across his face and a quick shave, Doc took over at the front desk. Before she left to go home and get her family ready for the wedding, Jane made a couple more pots of coffee, emptied Pearl's trash cans, whipped up a big batch of pancake batter and gave Cookie a hug. Cookie raced through the dishes as quickly as possible between making up bedrooms. When Doc didn't have customers at the front desk, he engaged customers in conversation to distract them from the fact they didn't have their breakfasts yet.

By ten o'clock, Pearl had prepared another twenty-eight breakfasts.

Pearl and Patti had made it. It was all over except the stragglers now!

At eleven o'clock, breakfast was over. Pearl asked Patti, "What's the final breakfast count?"

Patti said, "It will take me a couple minutes to figure that out!"

## '67 96 Breakfasts

And Pearl had plenty to do anyway, putting breakfast away, getting things ready for the lunch crew and helping Cookie with dishes. Eventually, Patti returned to the kitchen with the answer. "Okay,

Pearl, would you believe it? This morning you made ninety-six full breakfasts, all by yourself! I don't know what we would do without you." Patti gave Pearl a kiss on the cheek and a big hug. "I'm so proud of you."

Pearl told Patti she did an excellent job as well.

Pearl was very proud of her work that day, as well she should have been. And though she hadn't told anyone yet, Pearl had begun to think about her retirement, considering she would be turning seventy-five years old at the end of the summer. It was a stand-out day in Pearl's life, so much so that the details were included in Pearl's obituary when she passed away decades later at the age of 106.

## '67 A Wedding Reception

Jane had been a little worried as she was getting ready, and she worried a little more while she was at church, waiting for the bride to walk down the aisle. Would Doc and the crew at Paleface be able to get through the day? Would they be able to handle the wedding reception later in the afternoon? And what about Cookie, poor thing. At that point, Jane thought, there was nothing to do except pray it would all work out.

The sight of the bride in her beautiful dress, and the smell of the pretty white cascading Stephanotis bouquet she was carrying, brought Jane back into the moment. Jane's nieces, the bride's sisters, looked beautiful in their floor-length yellow bridesmaid's gowns.

How special to have her brother perform the ceremony for their sister's daughter. Jane was glad the wedding was at their church in Wilmington. She thought it was perhaps the most beautiful wedding ceremony she had ever witnessed there.

With the anxiety over breakfast, it was fortunate that the lunch and dinner crews were well staffed.

Still, the kitchen remained very busy. Paleface had developed a great reputation for lunch. Burgers and fries, fried chicken, and BLT's were very popular. Most people who came to ride horseback tended to stay for a meal if their ride was anywhere near meal time. And even when it wasn't meal time, the "dudes" would often have a drink and perhaps a snack.

With the lunch crew in charge of the restaurant, Patti accompanied Cookie during her chambermaid duties for a while so they could talk. Cookie had rescued the breakfast disaster by helping with the dishes, and now she was behind on cleaning the rooms.

While they were making up the last room, Cookie told Patti about her predicament. They sat down and talked for an hour. Surprisingly, Cookie was in very good spirits. One trait Cookie and Preston shared, and that was acceptance of whatever situation they found themselves in. Cookie shrugged, then sighed, "Que Sera, Sera..." Patti and Cookie started laughing until tears squeezed out of the corners of their eyes.

"Does anyone know about this yet?" Patti asked Cookie as their laughing fit waned.

"Well," said Cookie, "I don't officially know myself. I haven't seen the Doctor yet. I haven't told Preston anything. Of course I haven't told anyone else either. Except for you and me, and Jane who happened into the ladies' room as I was having the sickness, nobody else knows."

Patti told Cookie, "I know you'll find your way through all of this, and you'll be a great momma. You'll see, it will be okay. I already can't wait to hold your baby!" Patti and Cookie shared a comforting embrace and then Patti was off to the barn.

All the rides for the afternoon were sold out. It was time for Patti to do her "regular" job.

Doc thought, "This is great! It's not even the Fourth of July yet! Business is booming! Paleface is flourishing!" Not everything was great, however. Jean was still in the hospital. Doc made a quick trip to Keene to visit Jean early in the afternoon. Doc didn't tell Jean about the ninety-six breakfasts. If he did, Jean would probably have tried to defy Doctor's orders and get back to Paleface immediately!

The lodge hosted a beautiful reception for Jane's niece and her new husband. Perhaps the only glitch was the punch. Some of the children giggled that the groom's grandmother had accidentally gotten into the wrong sauce! She had evidently thought she was drinking Hawaiian Punch. Lucky for her, someone had noticed and advised her she might want to drink from the other punch bowl.

It was rough at Paleface without Jean. Of course, if Jean had been there, things would have gone much more smoothly. Doc and Patti knew it wasn't a very smooth day, and Jane knew it was a challenging day for the family. However, the guests were well tended. Nobody felt slighted. The wedding reception went pretty much according to plans.

Jean was recovering slowly, but Doctor Mackinnon was optimistic about Jean's progress. Dr. Mackinnon thought Jean might need a couple more days in the hospital, and then Jean would need rest at home. She should not return to work for a couple of weeks, and then she must not push herself too hard.

Before Doc turned in for the night, he thought about staffing, and determined he was going to have to do a better job of getting Paleface ready for the summer. If Doc hadn't previously fully appreciated Jean's contribution at Paleface, he certainly developed a full measure of respect for Jean's leadership and work ethic during her absence in June, 1967.

## '67 Montana Cowboys

If Doc had to admit it, he was much more interested in what was happening across the street. As if Doc didn't have enough to contend with as spring was giving way to summer, Doc was undertaking to double the dude ranch operations. There were several aspects to Doc's aggressive growth strategy. Tuesday morning, after the Memorial Day holiday weekend was over, Doc put pencil to paper. It was time for another one of Doc's press releases. Doc noted the expansion of the dude ranch operations, the arrival of western cowboys Ray Kaufman and Terry Dohrmann, from Intake and Glendive Montana, as well as the local staff, which included Marla Hildreth, Roger McLean, and Patti Fitz-Gerald. Doc noted that Paleface had joined the Eastern Dude Ranch Association, which he thought gave the operation a higher degree of credibility. Then Doc mentioned two of the horses, Tomahawk and Cherokee, which added character to the press release.

Doc sent the press release with a photograph of Ray Kaufman, in a red bandana shirt and a white cowboy hat. Perhaps there wasn't much else going on in the world or in the area during the first week of June, or perhaps it was the strength of the story. Doc's press release was featured on the front page of the *Record-Post* that week, complete with Ray's picture.

To each side of the huge headlines, two small boxes highlighted the article, perhaps to inform readers who wouldn't read the paragraphs.

A month earlier, Doc had written an open letter to operators of other hotels, motels, and attractions. The *Adirondack Record-Elizabethtown Post* published that letter as if the letter had been written to the editors. The letter said:

*Dear North Country Host:*

*Once again, as summer approaches, Paleface Dude Ranch will be making a unique contribution to our whole community. We are the only approved Dude Ranch within a radius of 75 miles with horseback riding open to the general public!*

*This year our riding program will feature three Montana experts.*

*Head wrangler Ray Kaufman is well-known as the men's rodeo champ of the Lake George area. For the past two years he has been the Assistant Wrangler of the famous Roaring Brook Dude Ranch. His wife Pat, is ladies' rodeo and barrel racing champ and has shown on the Sunshine Circuit of Florida since she was twelve years old. They will be assisted by Terry Dohrmann, another keen young rodeo rider from Montana. And, our own Marla Hildreth of AuSable Forks will again be helping in the instruction ring with beginners and with English equitation.*

*Although our major emphasis will be western, we shall continue to have our good English horses and tack for those who prefer.*

*We have thirty miles of woodland bridle trails, well maintained and located off the highways. At least half of our horses are ribbon-winners. Please remember, our horses are not rented. We own them all and can vouch for them!*

*Contrary to the practice of most Dude Ranches our horses will not be restricted to our own house guests. Frankly, with only sixteen motel units, we would not have enough guests of our own to keep four pros and twenty some horses busy. For this reason, we are happy to share our fine horseback riding opportunities with our fellow motel operators in the area.*

*Last, but not least, our horse-back riding rates will be the same as last year, only $3.00 per hour. The services of one of the above-mentioned trail guides are included in the price.*

*We shall deliver a supply of our horseback riding literature to you early in May. Our opening date will be the May 12th week-end.*

*May we all have a wonderful summer as we do our best to enhance THE ADIRONDACK EXPERIENCE of our guests! The*

*Montreal Expo hasn't got ALL the aces in the North Country!*

*Cordially yours,*
*Doc Fitz-Gerald, Pres.*
*Paleface Dude Ranch*
*The only one between Lake George and Greenland*

## '67 Yankee Code of Thrift

Monday morning, Jane took an hour away from her office duties and helped Cookie make up a couple rooms. It gave them a chance to talk a little more.

"How in the world are we going to make ends meet?" Cookie asked.

Jane gave Cookie advice about how to carefully manage expenses. "When Dana and I were just getting started, there was a saying 'eat it up, wear it out, make it do, or do without.' It was called The Yankee Code of Thrift and was attributed to President Calvin Coolidge. You and Preston will find your way, but you'll have to ask yourselves all the time: 'Do we need this? Do we really need that? Are we absolutely sure we can't live without it?' Anyway, you and Preston are hardworking, and you have lots of great people around you who love you. You will find a way to make it work. I believe in you!"

Cookie and Jane talked a while longer. Jane's advice was perfectly timed, and just what Cookie needed to hear. Before Jane returned to her own work, she implored, "Please let me know if there's anything I can do to help."

## '67 New Brochures

Doc had waited for the new brochures like a kid waits for Christmas. Doc couldn't wait to see how they turned out and Doc couldn't wait to take the new brochures out into the world.

Patti had been home from Cazenovia College on spring break, and it was an uncommonly warm, dazzlingly beautiful sunny day back in April when the family took the beautiful pictures that were going to be featured in the promotional materials. And it wasn't just the brochures and flyers. Postcards were very popular with the guests. Doc was always looking for an opportunity to add new post cards to the post card tree that spun on the front desk where guests checked in and checked out.

The printer had indicated that it would probably take between ten and fourteen weeks to get the job done. Doc was disappointed to hear it. He was hoping to be able to get the new brochures out before the Fourth of July weekend. Doc told the printer, "I understand. If you can fit it in any earlier, I would be eternally grateful."

The brochures arrived on Friday, June 30th. Doc was ecstatic. The order had been delivered exactly ten weeks to the day. The printer had told Doc they would do their best. Doc tipped the delivery man handsomely and thanked him profusely. Then Doc called the printer and expressed his gratitude. The printer told Doc that they had pushed his order ahead of the others because he was so nice, polite, patient, and understanding.

When Doc hung up the phone he said to himself, "Doesn't that just beat all. It just goes to show that it pays to be a good guy, even in business."

Jane said, "And I'll bet they really appreciated your phone call, Doc."

Doc hadn't realized that he had spoken out loud. "Come take a look, Jane."

Everything was perfect.

One postcard featured the beautiful A-Frames that made up the Paleface complex. The three tall triangles with their powder blue shingles, pale blue trim and enormous windows with a bright blue sky behind them and bright, lush green new spring grass in the foreground. "Oh!" Jane exclaimed. "How wonderful."

Doc tried to look at the picture with his trained artist's eye. And Doc had to admit, he was thoroughly impressed as well. Doc couldn't help but think of the Great Pyramids in Egypt when he looked at the postcard, although the construction had been inspired by a ski resort in Colorado, not the Great Pyramids.

Next, they opened a box of postcards featuring Jean, Doc, and Patti on the iconic Pinto horses, again with Paleface in the background. Jean, Doc, and Patti had worn the matching red paisley western print shirts, white cowboy hats, and blue jeans that made such a winning combination when they competed in the family class at area horse shows. Most striking was the vibrant sorrel and white color of the three Pintos. Jean on her favorite, the gentle, loving Cheyenne. Doc was on one of his favorites, Dunder. Dunder was "the elder statesman" of the Paleface string, an accomplished trophy and ribbon winner, fast in the gymkhana events, and equally expert in the equitation and pleasure classes. Patti was on Apache, a newer addition to the string. Doc thought Apache's small face, blond mane and blond eyelashes made him particularly striking to look at. Doc felt Apache had spirit and therefore enormous development potential in the gymkhana events.

Jane exclaimed, "How special!" Jane's expressions of exclamation were always full of warmth and amazement, and were so endearing that those exclamations drew people to feel like Jane's lifelong friends.

Doc said, "Thank you, Jane. This picture fills my heart with joy and wonder, I must admit. Maybe I can get an 8 X 10 and frame it." Mentally, Doc put that on his list of things to do someday.

The next box of postcards featured Doc's handsome painting of Paleface's mountain, with its network of ski trails in white. Whiteface stands in the background, off in the distance. In the painting, Whiteface almost seems smaller and less inviting. The white webs of trails on the bright amber colored mountain make Paleface seem very welcoming.

Patti on the Pinto Dunder, and Roger on the tall, pretty Palomino named Ginger came out of the next box. The horses and riders were the prime features in the photo, however a small mountain in the background, and a little bit of sky at the left and right of the picture gave a strong sense of summer though it was really only April when the picture was taken. The Palomino was perfectly posed, and it was as if a wind machine had been carefully placed to blow Ginger's mane to perfect affect.

The next postcard featured the indoor pool. The photo angle highlighted the Lazy-L shape of the pool, the shiny red paneling around the pool and the pale blue color of the five-step slide that dropped swimmers into the deep end. The post card included seven people, one couple in the pool, another couple on the green and white checkered beach chairs and another couple at the back end of the pool under a yellow umbrella, placing an order with the waitress who wore the Paleface cocktail waitress uniform: white blouse, red knee-length skirt with white trim at the bottom.

Next, Doc opened the bigger boxes. The first box he opened contained the brochures for the Dude Ranch. In addition to the images from the post cards there was a picture of four riders in front of the enormous metal sign that stood in front of Paleface, the shape of which mirrored the three A-Frame outline of the Paleface buildings against the sky. Another picture showed the new cowboy Terry Dohrmann riding the lightning fast Tomahawk around a barrel.

On the front of the brochure was a picture featuring every single one of the twenty-five horses in the Paleface string, with a rider. Doc chuckled, recalling how difficult it was to get twenty-five people together to take the picture given that Paleface wasn't open yet. The front also featured the picture of Doc's painting of Paleface and Whiteface.

The back panel featured all the details. It was a lot of words packed into a fairly small space, but Doc thought it looked great and represented Paleface and the North Country very well. It was divided into three sections.

The first section heading said *"The Family Fun Place"* and continued: *"A two-season FAMILY RESORT in the high northern Adirondacks. Close to Whiteface Mountain and Lake Placid. Only 5 hours from New York City. 1 ½ hours from Montreal. Modern A-Frame Lodge, family size rooms, all meals, full bar, cocktail lounge, indoor heated swimming pool, outdoor sun-deck, game rooms. Children and pets always welcome! Always something for the whole family!"*

The second section started with "*IN SUMMER IT'S Paleface Family Ranch*" and went on to add the by-line "*THE BEST WEST IN THE EAST.*" Underneath those headings, Doc advertised "*Horseback rides on a tract of 8000 acres. 30 miles of woodland roads, off highway, 20 dependable prize-winning horses for all riding abilities. Our cowgirls and cowboys are experienced trail guides. Also – nearby attractions include Santa's Workshop, Land of Makebelieve, Whiteface Mountain Chair Lift and Memorial Highway, Mystery Spot, AuSable Acres, High Falls Gorge, AuSable Chasm and Lake Placid Boat Rides. Fine trout fishing and golf courses nearby.*"

The third section led with "*IN WINTER IT'S Paleface Ski Center*" and the second headline added to that was "*THE BIGGEST LITTLE ONE.*" The skiing highlights were mentioned as follows "*Skiing for all abilities. Double Chair Lift, T-Bar, 15 Trails Snow Maker, Night Skiing, Complete Ski Shop. Our families play together and stay together. Our Ski School of 8 professionals, many of them certified, has a long-standing reputation for quality teaching at all levels. And it is only 200 feet from your Bedroom to the Chair Lift!*" The section ends with "*FAMILY FUN SKIING AT ITS BEST.*"

Another box had the one-page riding flyer, featuring a picture of Doc Fitz-Gerald riding Dunder in one of his winning pole bending gymkhana races. The picture was a great close-up, capturing horse and rider working together, preparing to bend and twist, turning around the pole as closely as possible without touching, tipping or knocking down the pole. The mild-mannered Dunder almost looked fierce, like a painting of an Indian war pony carrying a brave into a particularly fierce battle.

The last box had four reams of eight and a half by eleven inch rate sheets. Doc liked the handsome red lettering on the creamy, cloudy light yellow background. At the top of the rate sheet was the phrase: "*THE HIGH ADIRONDACK'S FINEST RESORT WHERE YOU ARE THE V.I.P.*"

Doc and Jane each read through the rate sheet carefully, making sure that everything was spelled correctly, and all the prices were right. The daily room rates were $12 to $16 per couple. The modified American Plan featured the room and two meals for $12 to $14 per adult. The weekly ski package pricing was $89 for adults and $69 for children, and included five 2-hour lessons, five-day lift tickets, five nights lodging, five breakfasts, and five dinners, provided at least two people occupied a room. For 50 cents to a $1.50 extra, lobster tails and steaks could be added to meals.

The weekly ranch package was also $89 for adults and $69 for children, and included ten hours of horseback riding (two hours per day) plus chair lift rides to the top of the mountain, use of the swimming pool, game room, ping pong table, sun deck, shuffle board, swings, and playground.

Even in the late 1960s, those rates would have seemed very modest.

Doc was pleased with the work the printers had done. He couldn't wait to show his son Chuck how everything came out. Chuck did all the photography, and Doc was very proud of Chuck's work on this project.

Doc loaded up the station wagon with the brochures. In addition, he took a couple of each post card with him. Before he made the rounds, delivering brochures to all the area businesses that would display them, he stopped by the house to see Jean. She was out of the hospital and resting at home, following the doctors' orders and taking it easy.

## '67 Ticonderoga Show

A couple of weeks earlier, Doc had asked Dana if he could build a display shelf behind the front desk to show off the trophies won by the Paleface horses and riders. Doc also asked Dana if he could find a way to display the ribbons, and maybe some of the other horse related items.

Dana had been collecting bits and pieces of wood left over from other projects around Paleface, and had crafted the shelving.

On Dana's day off, while Doc was still sleeping, Dana installed the shelving behind the front desk, right at eye-level for guests checking in. Above the shelving, Dana had a series of pegs connected by a spider-web like network of string. And on the outer periphery, Dana nailed several used horse shoes, a dogging bat, and an old pair of worn out spurs to the wall.

Dana asked Jane if she could find a ribbon. Jane didn't have to look too hard. There were plenty of ribbons on display behind the bar in the lounge. Dana and Jane hung several ribbons from the strings using the wires on the back of the ribbons. "I think they can take it from here!" Dana said, standing back. Dana and Jane admired Dana's handiwork for a minute or two more before heading home.

Doc was surprised to see the display when he woke up later that morning. As soon as he saw it, he raced across the street. Patti was out leading a trail ride. Doc knocked about the barn impatiently, inspecting each horse like Santa inspecting his reindeer.

When Patti got back with her twelve beginning riders, Doc helped the riders dismount, and helped bring each horse back to the barn. With the guests on their way back across the street, Doc asked Patti, "Where are the trophies and ribbons from the Ticonderoga show?"

"I have them all right here," she said, taking a box out from under the desk in the little barn office. She had carefully written in neat handwriting on the back of each ribbon so that she would know which show, which event, which rider, and which horse that ribbon pertained to. On the bottom of the trophies, she had written the same information on beige masking tape.

"Great," said Doc. Then he picked up the box and headed back across the street. The Paleface horses and riders had their best showing ever, back on the 11th of June in Ticonderoga. There were eighteen events listed. The Paleface horses and riders had won twenty-six ribbons. And the new head wrangler from Montana, Ray Kaufman won a tall trophy as the Reserve Champion, racking up points in several different events.

The Paleface crew included Doc, Ray Kaufman, and long-time Paleface cowboys Roger McLean, and Mark Devlin. In addition to the Reserve Champion Trophy, the Paleface crew brought home first place trophies in several other categories.

In the Old Shoe Race, Mark Devlin finished first, and Roger McLean finished fourth. In that timed event riders simultaneously raced to a pile of boots, including their boots plus the other riders' boots. When the riders found their own boots, they had to lead their horses back to the start/finish line, carrying their own boots. The contestants groaned as they watched kids shovel dirt from the ring into their boots at the other end of the ring.

In the Musical Chairs race, Doc finished first and Mark came in third. Instead of chairs, a series of "stalls" were outlined using ground posts. When the music stopped, the last rider to get their horse into a "stall" was eliminated. And then the ground posts were removed, so that there was always one less stall than contestant, until there was one and only one winner.

In the Rescue Race, Ray and Roger took the trophy for first place and Mark and Doc teamed up to take third place. In the rescue race, one rider galloped to a barrel at the other end of the ring, picked up a second rider and galloped back to the start/finish line with both riders on a single horse.

In the Pony Express Race, Ray came in second, riding Dunny and Dunder. The pony express race was a timed event run on a pre-determined pattern. A second horse was placed at a particular point in the pattern. The rider raced the first horse through the pattern to the second horse, dismounted, untied the second horse, tied the first horse, mounted the second horse then returned to the start/finish line in the fastest time possible.

In the Tack Race, Roger came in first, and Mark came in fourth. The tack race was another timed event. The rider raced bareback, which is to say without a saddle, from the start line through a pre-determined course pattern. At a point along the way were the saddle and blanket. The rider dismounted, saddle up their horse and raced back to the start/finish line.

In the Key Hole Race, Ray came in first. Doc came in fourth. In that obstacle race a horse sprinted into the ring, entered an area marked out with chalk, stopped and turned, on a dime and raced back out without disturbing the markers.

In the Pole Bending Race, Ray came in first, Mark came in second, and Doc came in third. Pole bending was an obstacle course consisting of six posts set in a straight line. Riders quickly rode to the last post then weaved their way through the course and back to the end, then sprinted back to the start/finish line.

In the Barrel Race, Ray came in fourth place. In the barrel race, riders raced a clover leaf pattern around three barrels as quickly as possible. The Barrel Race was probably the most famous gymkhana event in the country.

In the Western Equitation Class Ray came in fourth place. In equitation, the judges evaluated the skills of the rider, not the performance of the horse. In the Western Pleasure Class Ray came in third place. In pleasure classes, the judges considered the manners, disposition, temperament and training of the horse. If Ray and his horse Dunny had been more known in the area at that time, perhaps he might have placed higher in those classes.

The prize for traveling the greatest distance to the show was a sack of grain. That honor also went to the gang from Paleface, and that prize was the only award the horses themselves could appreciate.

After Doc set up the trophies on the shelf, Doc hung the ribbons on the strings. It was amazing to think that the trophies and ribbons from just one event filled all the available space. At the bottom of the box there was a newspaper clipping. It was from the Ticonderoga Sentinel, and was dated June 15th, 1967.

There were details about the winners in each category. There was also a feature story that said, “Sunday we went to the horse show which is to be an annual event of the Ticonderoga Riding Club. We went early in order to be there to admire all the horses as they were unloaded. There were some beautiful ones. The horses brought from Paleface Dude Ranch at Jay showed that the ones responsible for them were aware of their health and comfort. Each horse wore a blanket and each horse had his legs well wrapped and padded against injury in the truck."

The article was attributed to Eleanor Murray, a spectator and local correspondent for the Ticonderoga Sentinel. Also, in her regular feature column "Facts and Notion" Eleanor went on to report: "From around the area more thoughts about 'horsey people.' Horsey people are a clique and talk horses and the background of horses entirely but spectators also enjoy the horse shows."

Doc chuckled at Eleanor Murray's thoughts about horsey people, but was very touched by her comments on Paleface's commitment to the safety of the horses. Doc taped the newspaper to the wall. Doc thought it would go along great with the trophies and ribbons, and guests might appreciate knowing about the care Paleface's ranch hands took to make sure the horses were well cared for.

A couple of days later, Doc noticed someone had removed the newspaper from the wall and placed it inside of a frame. And next to that a second frame held an 8 X 10 color photo of Jean, Doc, and Patti. Doc didn't need to hire a private investigator to figure out who to thank. Next time Doc saw Jane, he thanked her most profusely.

When Jean returned to Paleface, just after the Fourth of July holiday, she teared up at the sight of the beautiful picture in the big frame. She was touched by the warm welcome from her friends, and co-workers. It was hard to be away knowing that everyone was busy at Paleface, and all the more so because of her absence. To top it all off, Jean was grateful to have recovered to the point where she could return to making her normal contribution to the family business. The crew had gotten along without her, but were mighty glad to have her back.

## '67 Give the Little Woman a Night Out at Paleface

At the beginning of that summer season, a new ad was being run locally that implored, in large letters: "*Yes! GIVE THE LITTLE*

*WOMAN A NIGHT OUT at Paleface."* The advertisement went on to note that Paleface was *"The Dining Room and Cocktail Lounge with the Western Look!"*

## '67 Preston Marries Cookie

By the 4th of July, which fell on Tuesday that year, Cookie had confirmed her pregnancy with her doctor.

Pregnancy or not, 4th of July or not, Cookie had rooms to tend to at Paleface. Preston was busy at The Mystery Spot. They had made plans for the evening, but would miss the parade and Fireman's Field day. Cookie was looking forward to seeing Preston, but was understandably apprehensive about seeing him that evening.

After work, Preston stopped at home for dinner, and then headed back out in his uncle's car. It was a good thing Preston's uncle hardly ever wanted to go anywhere! Preston picked Cookie up at her house, and as usual they drove from town to town just to pass the time. As dusk approached, they returned to Jay. Just up the hill from the covered bridge and the river rapids, Preston parked the car in the cemetery, facing the direction of town.

It was a beautiful evening, as it almost always was around the 4th of July. Preston and Cookie got out of the car. Standing in front of the car, leaning against the hood and fender, Preston and Cookie waited for the fireworks, and Preston drew Cookie closer.

There was a whole row of cars in the still undeveloped section of the cemetery. A whole row of cars was parked there. It was a great spot to watch the annual fireworks display, except for the mosquitos which really couldn't be avoided anywhere.

Cookie decided that was the time, and that was the place. Cookie told Preston that she was pregnant, and that they were going to become parents early the next year.

Cookie had to admit that Preston's reaction surprised her. Without thought or hesitation, Preston let out a yell, the sort of holler you might expect from someone who was just told that they had won the lottery.

"You're *happy* about this?" Cookie said incredulously when Preston settled down a little bit. Cookie couldn't believe it. Maybe Jane was right. Everything would be okay. "What about our not being married, Preston?" Cookie asked.

"We should do that," said Preston breathlessly. "A baby's going to want Mommy and Daddy to get married, isn't it! Besides, I told you already, the way I see it, we already are married."

"I guess the baby agrees with you, Preston," joked Cookie. "But what about the government, the church, my parents, and your uncle?" And what about me, thought Cookie.

"Well, let's get married right away then," said Preston.

"Like, when?" Cookie pressed.

"I don't know. How does it work? Right now? Like, yesterday! How about tomorrow?" Obviously, Preston didn't care when, and Preston didn't have any anxiety about making a lifelong commitment to Cookie and their baby.

"Let me check my calendar," said Cookie. "You know, I'll need at least a day to plan such a big deal as a wedding!" They laughed and hugged. Then Preston impetuously took off running at top speed down the length of cars, no less than twice, periodically jumping in the air and spreading his arms and legs, all the while hooting and hollering, "WE'RE GETTING MARRIED!" over and over again.

When Preston regained some of his composure, Cookie was waiting back in front of Preston's uncle's car. Shaking her head from side to side, Cookie thought, "What in the world have I gotten myself into?" Cookie thought for a minute about the fact that Preston was two years younger than she was. Then Cookie thought, "Even if Preston was ten years older than me, it probably wouldn't change anything!"

Cookie said, "You know, Preston, this is a pretty small town. I haven't told my Mom and Dad about this yet. Now you've gone and announced it to the whole town!"

The look on Preston's face changed instantly. "We should tell them. They're gonna need to know!"

Cookie thought to herself, "You don't suppose?!"

Another thing Preston and Cookie shared was the propensity to face something like that head on and quickly. No use letting it eat away at them. Rather than stay and enjoy the fireworks, Cookie and Preston left the cemetery and headed for Cookie's house. Cookie's parents were sitting on their screen porch in matching armchairs, waiting for the fireworks to start. Their porch was perfectly situated to see the fireworks without having to leave the house.

Cookie's parents couldn't help but like Preston in spite of the situation. Truth be told, they were as happy as Cookie and Preston. They had only met Preston once, and that meeting had been brief. That night they fell in love with Preston too. Preston and Cookie stayed on the porch with Cookie's parents through the fireworks. Then they got back in the car to go find Patti.

After they left, Cookie's father joked, "I didn't even need to get my shot gun." Cookie's mother found the comment strangely amusing, and oddly endearing.

It was a very strange wedding. Patti took the day off and she and Cookie spent a whole day planning it.

They decorated the Smoke Rise lookout just as they had decorated Paleface for a dance a couple years earlier. The only difference was a change in color scheme, and the addition of some groovy modern touches, far out colors, beads, and soforth. It might have looked like a rainbow exploded inside the A-Frame building at the top of Paleface Mountain. Cookie thought it looked beautiful.

Patti had arranged for the groom and bride to ride the matching Palomino horses, Ginger and Señior, up the mountain.

There was one old-fashioned English style sidesaddle in Paleface's possession, a throwback to earlier times. That saddle was only used in costume classes at horse shows or at the parade on the 4th of July.

Everyone else rode up to the chalet on the chairlift.

It was a modest affair anyway. Cookie's parents were there, and Preston's Uncle Harold, of course. Doc, as a former minister, was called to officiate, and Jean served as a witness. Dana was surprised when Preston dropped by the day before to ask him to serve as his best man. He was surprised to learn he had made such an impression on him. Jane was there too, and Doc's son Chuck was there taking pictures. Patti had cashed in a favor to get Chuck to take the job on a volunteer basis!

Preston and Cookie got married in the clothes they wore on their first date, little more than a month earlier. Cookie rode up Paleface mountain riding a Palomino horse, sidesaddle, wearing knee-high, shiny white boots, a yellow mini skirt, a black and white patterned jacket, and big, round, yellow plastic-rimmed sun glasses. To top it all off, Cookie had spent the afternoon at Alma's getting her hair piled up high on top of her head in a stunning bouffant that wouldn't have moved if a tornado or hurricane had struck Paleface that afternoon.

Preston was wearing gray slacks, a three-color argyle sweater, and penny loafers. Preston's clothes were definitely on the tight side, and his pant legs were a little short. Those clothes only two years prior had been almost too large to wear. He had reached his full height and maturity. New clothes hadn't been a priority. Preston had more important things to save up for, namely a brand new snowmobile. Cookie liked Preston in the tight-fitting clothes anyway.

Jean and Jane looked at each other. The look they shared seemed to say something like, "Get a load of this." Not in a judgmental way, really. What a sight those two looked. It was as if Doris Day was marrying Wally Cleaver from the television show *Leave it to Beaver*, if only Wally Cleaver was wearing a wig of thick, straight blond hair.

The wedding was as unique as the couple God had brought together.

## '67 Ticonderoga Gymkhana

Paleface cowboys and horses made a remarkable showing in Ticonderoga at a horse show back in June. The spoils of victory were on display right at the front desk of Paleface. As the summer of 1967 waned, Ticonderoga was the site for another major event of interest to horsey people in the North Country.

The cowboys from Paleface included Doc, Patti, Roger, and Paleface's brand new head wrangler Terry Dohrmann. During the summer, Ray Kaufman and his wife Pat jumped the fence for greener pastures, resulting in a promotion for Terry. In addition to being in charge of operations, all of the responsibility for embodiment of the western theme fell to Terry as well. Just like in the movies, sometimes an actor wanted to be the director as well.

In fact, Terry looked and acted like the real Montana, rodeo cowboy that he was, and that was just what Doc was looking for. By the end of Terry's first summer at Paleface, the rest of the cowboys and cowgirls looked a lot more western too. Doc couldn't have been more pleased, unless perhaps Terry had been a little more like Roy Rogers and a little less like Clint Eastwood.

The competition at Ticonderoga was fierce. It wasn't just a horse show. It was a tri-county event, and it attracted riders from towns far and wide. The Paleface crew did well. Not as well as the previous trip to Ticonderoga, judging by the number of trophies and ribbons. Doc enjoyed the challenge of competition; a hard-fought victory was far sweeter than a battle easily won.

The first victory was in the pairs class. Patti and Terry took first place in the synchronized horseback riding event on Tomahawk and Koko.

In the Western pleasure class, Doc took a third place on his favorite little Pinto Chippewa, and Patti took fourth on Chico. A little later, Roger rode a newer horse named Cherokee, to a third place finish in the Barrel Race and a fourth place finish in the Key Hole Race.

The Paleface cowboys had practiced and trained for several weeks to improve their performance in the Flag Races at gymkhana events, and finished very strong. Only none of the riders were able to turn in a trophy winning performance. Roger took second place, Terry took third and Doc placed fourth. They would have to train harder still to win that event in the future!

With bluster and bravado, Terry had been promising all day to win a trophy in the Pole Bending class. He came very close, losing by what the announcer described as a heart breaking one eighth of a second. Still, it was another ribbon for the team and added to the record of Paleface's horse named Tomahawk who was catching up to Dunder according to the records Patti kept. Tomahawk was fast, and seemed to be getting faster at every show.

So, except for the trophy in the pairs class, the only trophy Paleface brought home that day was the second most important of the day. Not the Grand Championship hardware, but the Reserve Championship accolade. Roger McLean was the winning cowboy from Paleface that day. Although he hadn't cleared first place in any event, the number of second, third and fourth place finishes that Roger had racked up earned him the second most points overall.

## '67 Tourist Dies of a Heart Attack

Paleface was very particular about providing safe riding experiences for its guests. At the same time, horses could be extraordinarily unpredictable. Even very well trained, gentle horses could panic and things could go horribly wrong.

All of the Paleface wranglers gave specific, detailed instructions at the beginning of each trail ride, and frequently during the course of a ride, the wranglers would check that each guest was following the rules. In particular, guests were advised to keep their feet in the stirrups at all times, their hands on the reins and be ready to grab the saddle horn if something should happen. Mostly accidents happened to riders who weren't focused on what they were doing.

One day in the middle of July, one of Paleface's most seasoned cowboys was leading a string of riders toward the dirt paths in the AuSable Acres development. Roger was guiding eight beginning riders that morning. They had set out at 11am, and planned to return by noon.

The eight riders included three couples, a single young woman from Ottawa, and a young girl from New Jersey. One of the couples on the ride was Mr. and Mrs. Connelly, dear old friends of Doc and Jean's from South Orange, New Jersey. The Connelly children were on the intermediate ride. The other two couples were young newlyweds, conveniently a couple of young ladies who were best friends married a couple young men who were best friends. They saved money by getting married on the same day, and sharing a station wagon on their honeymoon. They were guests of the Town and Country Motel in Wilmington. At the front desk, it was suggested they might enjoy going for a trail ride at Paleface. The brochure in the lobby convinced them to make reservations.

It was a beautiful warm pleasant morning. Roger had gone over the safety instructions before everyone set off down the trail. The riders were vigilantly following all of the rules. Usually about ten or fifteen minutes down the trail, everyone settled into the rhythm of the ride.

The riders may have settled in that day, but some of the horses had not settled in at all.

Horses were very hierarchical. Like chickens, they always needed to establish where each other were in the pecking order. Like dogs there was always a leader, an "alpha dog." Usually all of this was worked out, between the horses when they were in pasture, perhaps over the winter, or in the evening when they were set to graze.

Because Susan was so young, and because she was a beginner, Roger had Susan's horse on a lead rope. In that situation, the horse in the following position got very close to the horse in the leading position.

On that particular July morning, the horse being ridden by Susan had an unresolved issue with the horse Roger was riding. Susan's horse took a notion to bite Roger's horse's butt, just to the left of his tail. Roger's horse reacted instinctively, kicked, turned, and bucked, throwing Roger to the ground. Roger was knocked unconscious by contact with the ground. The horses in the string went in all different directions.

Fortunately, all of the guests were able to get their horses under control. Even Susan, who had listened closely to the instructions and who had decided that she would hold on to the saddle horn throughout the ride, managed to stay in the saddle. Roger's horse ran back toward the barn, about a half a mile away. Mr. Connelly confidently hurried back to the barn to get help. Mrs. Connelly dismounted to try and help Roger.

Back at the barn, Mark Devlin was tending to chores between rides. Patti was out with a string of intermediate riders. Marla Hildreth was out leading a string of experts, happily galloping down an old logging trail at the moment Roger was thrown to the ground.

It took a moment for the appearance of Roger's horse to register with Mark Devlin.

It didn't take any time at all for it to register with Susan's Dad, a guest of Paleface visiting from Union City, New Jersey. Against his better judgement, he had legally consented to turn his daughter Susan over to strangers and permit her to ride a 2,000 pound beast.

As Mark Devlin was trying to invite Susan's dad to remain calm, Mr. Connelly rode quickly up the trail toward the barn. "Excuse me, sir, our wrangler was thrown from his horse and he is hurt."

Mark asked Mr. Connelly about the other riders. Mr. Connelly told Mark everyone was fine, but to hurry and call the emergency rescue squad.

Susan's dad had waited long enough. It wouldn't be over reacting to say that he was in a complete panic. Mark needed to get help quickly. "Begging your pardon, sir, I'll be with you in a minute or two," and with that, Mark Devlin turned his back on Susan's dad. Fortunately, the new barn had a phone, and Mark reached Mr. Winch on the first ring. Meanwhile, Susan's dad took off running down the trail. It had been a long time since he had run anywhere. It was fair to say that he was not in good physical condition. Even though Mr. Connelly had said all the other riders were fine, Susan's dad couldn't stop until he saw for himself that his daughter was okay.

Mark Devlin had forgotten about Susan's dad, and hadn't even noticed his disappearance. Mark was trying to think of how he could get the rescue squad up the trail, and had set out for the main lodge when he ran into Greg Peck, Dana and Jane's son. Greg was working on grounds maintenance, mowing lawns, tending gardens, and putting up hay for the horses to enjoy during the winter.

Greg ran for the Jeep, and Mark ran back to the barn. Moments later, Mr. Ira Winch from the Wilmington Rescue Squad arrived in an ambulance.

Mark Devlin, Ira Winch, and Robert Connelly jumped into the Jeep. Greg drove the Jeep up onto the horse trail as quickly as he could go. The Jeep arrived in the clearing about a minute behind Susan's dad who had run faster than he had run anywhere in the past twenty years. Unfortunately, he collapsed upon arrival in the clearing. His frightened daughter started screaming and sobbing on the top of her horse.

Ira glanced quickly at the cowboy who had been thrown. Apparently, he had come to while waiting for help to arrive. Mr. Winch couldn't fully assess Roger's condition in that moment, but clearly Susan's dad was more in need of assistance than Mr. McLean.

Mrs. Connelly told Roger to sit down on the ground, and not to move. Then Mrs. Connelly went to console the young girl, helping her from the back of her horse. Mr. Winch rolled Susan's dad onto his back, and ripped open the front of his shirt. He had quit breathing. Ira tipped his head back, and administered mouth-to-mouth resuscitation. Then Ira pushed down on his chest. Ira began working on Susan's dad, alternating between massaging the heart with chest compressions and trying to breathe air back into his lungs.

Mrs. Connelly had concluded that Susan's dad had died and that there was no way to save him. She picked Susan up and headed down the trail on foot.

Susan was far too old for a lullaby, but Mrs. Connelly didn't have suitable words of consolation. Susan cried so hard, and so intently that she happily let herself fall asleep in Mrs. Connelly's arms before they made it back to the barn.

For fifteen minutes, Ira worked on Susan's dad without the slightest indication that he was helping. The sight of his daughter stayed in Ira's mind while Ira tried in vain to bring him back.

After another five minutes, Mark Devlin took over. Ten minutes later, Ira tried again. Eventually the men had to admit defeat. It had been more than an hour since the Jeep pulled up to the clearing.

Greg Peck, Mark Devlin and Ira Winch propped Susan's dad up in the back of the Jeep. Greg helped Roger into the Jeep as well. Then Ira Winch drove the Jeep up the trail back to the barn.

Mark Devlin mounted Mrs. Connelly's horse and led the two pairs of newlyweds back to the barn, and Greg Peck tailed the way back to the barn on Susan's horse. It was a slow, sad trip back. Greg had to admit that it was a little disturbing to have seen a dead body that had just been a living person.

Back at the barn, Ira made a quick call for a second ambulance. The first ambulance took Susan's dad to Lake Placid. His wife quickly packed their things, and she and their daughter followed the ambulance in their car to Lake Placid. Ira Winch was so exhausted from trying to save Susan's dad that he himself required treatment at the Lake Placid Hospital.

The second ambulance took Roger to the Keene Valley Hospital, where he remained overnight. Roger was a bit disoriented, and couldn't recall a single event from that day, but the Doctor was sure that Roger would be okay.

By Monday morning, Roger was back to himself and back to work.

The news was devastating. It was hard to believe a man of only 44 years of age had died of a heart attack. A daughter couldn't hope for a more devoted father than one who would react such as Susan's dad did when he believed his young daughter was in danger.

No one from Susan's family was there to hear it, but Doc felt the need to say a few words. Most of the staff at Paleface gathered around as Doc said a prayer. The other riders had received a refund to replace the money they had spent. Solemn, heartfelt prayers of condolence were all that Doc could think to offer Susan's family.

## '67 Bees on the Trail

That same season, Patti Fitz-Gerald had a misfortunate incident on the trails also.

For the most part everything was routine. It was a varied group of riders. Men, women, some kids, some adults, mostly beginners, a few riders had some limited experience riding horses. Everyone was very nice, and followed instructions, and listened carefully as Patti cheerfully explained the house rules. With one exception.

There was one man who was particularly disruptive. As Patti explained the rules, he mocked Patti. Perhaps he thought he was being funny. Patti had concluded that he was just a miserable son of a gun. Without missing a word of her presentation, Patti rode her horse over so that she was immediately beside the man.

Patti thought that had done the trick. Until about five minutes later. They were on the first section of the beginner's trail, and Patti turned back to check on the riders in the string. And there he was, feet out of stirrups, hamming it up at the back of the line. Patti felt sorry for Koko, the name of the horse that had been assigned to that customer.

Patti stopped the ride, rearranging the riders so that the miserable man was immediately behind her. She looked at her watch, and thought about how slowly that hour ride was going.

Confidentially, Patti told the man that he needed to keep his feet in the stirrups at all times. Patti tried to blame the insurance company for that rule. That had worked well on other occasions.

This customer didn't take feedback or direction very well.

"I don't guess I need some young, amateur little *girl* bossing me around and telling me what to do. I'm a grown man, and I paid good money for this ride. These miserable old beasts are trained to quietly plod along, dumbly playing follow the leader all day. If you want to keep your job, I guess you'll have to learn to treat your customers better, and let them have a little fun."

Every word the man said stung. Patti could feel tears of anger building behind her eyes. She clenched her jaw, determined not to let tears be her response to this idiot's diatribe.

"For your information, I am a trained professional. I have been riding horses for over ten years. I have ridden in horse shows all around the North Country. What's more, I am personally responsible for the safety of all of our guests. Now, if you please, we have other riders among us here today who paid good money and would like to get back on the trail."

By the time Patti finished her speech, she was feeling quite pleased with herself. She hadn't let the tears of anger loose. She had calmly and professionally addressed the situation, and what's more, when she came to the end, the rest of the riders clapped. Mr. Grouchy-pants hung his head.

Patti turned and started her horse back down the trail. The rest of the horses followed. The next half hour or so was pretty uneventful. They were three quarters of the way around the loop. Almost home, she thought. Then she turned back, yet again to check on the riders.

Patti couldn't believe it, even though she had seen it with her own eyes. The man made an ugly face, stuck his tongue out, and removed his feet from the stirrups. Then he slouched his bulk from one side to the other.

Right then and there, Patti resolved that when they got back to the barn she was going to give him his money back, all $3, and tell him never to show his ugly face around there again. And if he didn't like the way he was treated, he should go in and ask for the owner.

Just as Patti was congratulating herself on the righteousness of her thoughts, Mr. Bully's horse was thrown off the straight and narrow path by the erratic behavior of his rider. This caused poor Koko to step on a ground nest of bees. Once the bees had begun to exit the hole, mass continuous swarms of bees commenced to stinging anything that moved. That meant every horse, and ever rider. In a matter of seconds, horses were hopping all around trying to get away from the bees. Bucking and hopping, twisting, then stopping, then starting again. Patti later described it as looking like "Mexican jumping beans."

One by one, all but the last horse in the string of riders got thrown off. Patti jumped in and took over the situation. Patti instructed the riders to run, or walk as fast as possible down the trail a safe distance, until no bees were present.

Then Patti gathered horses. One by one, Patti reunited each

rider with their horse and helped them get mounted back up. Each time Patti went back, she got stung again, many times over.

As it happened, the last horse Patti caught was the chauvinist's horse. Of course, he had been thrown to the ground. For some reason, he hadn't gotten back up. He kind of sat there, moaning and groaning. Patti ignored him; she just thought he was being selfish and miserable, but then she discovered that, in addition to being selfish and miserable, he'd broken his leg.

Even so, he was able to make it to his feet. One of the other guests helped Patti get the large man back on his horse. Fortunately, there wasn't too far to go before they made it back to the barn.

As they were approaching the barn, Patti waved her arms furiously. Roger McLean saw Patti, and came running. Patti quickly told Roger what had happened and asked if he could give their guest a ride to the hospital.

Then Patti turned to the guest and said, "Mister, the next time some *young, amateur little girl* bosses you around may I suggest you do what *she* tells you, *sir*! Broken leg! Serves you right!" Patti turned away, leaving her former customer in Roger's hands.

The other guests were very gracious and sympathetic. Patti got many compliments for standing up to the miserable son of a gun. They told Patti they appreciated how well she took care of them, remaining calm and getting them safely back to the barn. And Patti had never been tipped more handsomely.

And then, Patti began to swell up. If she hadn't had the allergy to bees previously, she definitely developed one that day. One of the other cowboys called the office and got Doc to come over. Doc quickly whisked Patti off to the Doctor where they were informed they had made it just in time. From then on, Patti had to carry an emergency bee sting kit with her everywhere she went. Patti couldn't help but think of the day she socked it to a bully twice her size whenever she saw that bee kit.

On the way home from the doctor's office, Patti confessed to Doc and told him exactly what had happened on the trail, and how she couldn't help but say what she did.

Doc told Patti, “I’m proud of you. Maybe I have never been more proud of you than I am right now. It does serve him right. If he comes back to complain, I can assure you I won’t be as professional as you were!”

Then Patti said, “Do you think I should have cussed? I didn’t cuss. Should I have done it?”

Both of them laughed. It was a silly thing to say. Maybe it was the bee poison, maybe it was the medicine. What made Doc laugh was the sight of his daughter saying something so ridiculous with her face and body all swollen and puffed up. They laughed so hard it was almost hard for Doc to keep the car on the road.

## ’67 Girl-Kid

Doc picked up a pen and wrote a note to his daughter later that evening. Leaving the bees behind, Doc had another horse matter on his mind.

*Dear Patti:*

*Just a little good-nite note to ya. I’ve been thinkin’ things over a bit.*

*Bravo on that big ribbon for you and Mandy! Even if it hadn’t rained, your combo would have scored!*

*But I didn’t like what I saw in our ring here the other day. I didn’t like that head tossing and tail switching. Something was wrong. It’s up to you to work it out. Gentle her, play her cool. Keep her mouth soft. Figure out where she’s at her best and don’t push beyond her temperament. There are very few “all-around” horses. She’s so marvelous when you pleasure her, trail her (what a performance, one in a thousand!)*

*But remember, she's young! That barrel racing article I told you about, remember, a National Champ says she wants a barrel horse to be ten to fourteen years old. Not five!*

*So, cool her, and figure out her mouth. I believe two things are important just now, for quite a while, the right bit and a light hand.*

*The hell with the flashy roll backs and slide stops, they'll come later if need be, much later. And as far as gym stuff is concerned, settle her first. You can ride other gym horses. (Parenthetically, I don't think Terry has gotten the best out of Tom yet, much as I love Terry.)*

*You'll notice that Chip is best in the cool. He's still young. In pleasure, trail, and command, he's good. But no conformation. Dunder is a one event horse – unless you count pairs. A wonderful old boy, but severely limited now.*

*So, figure that Mandy. I'd say cool her for quite a while. But most of all, figure out her mouth. I think that's the secret to head tossing and tail switching.*

*The advice I gave you in the article, makes a lot of sense. I'm glad to see you use her as a lead horse, give her some fun and variety. Don't spend too many hours pushing her, perfectionist style, driving her, nagging her, making her bored with the ring and that ever-lasting fence.*

*Use her like a fun horse, girl kid, enjoy her and let her enjoy herself. Trail her, use her for lead horse, fun her and yourself, stay loose. Don't try to grab all the ribbons in all the classes. That's the way you both could go, or get ulcers. Don't be too serious, or too demanding. Don't push either one of you so hard that it ceases to be fun.*

*You've got a jewel there. Keep her that way, where she and you can both say, together, I gotta be me. Not somebody else, but just me. And even more than that, perhaps, "we've gotta be US." Gradually, you'll adjust to each other. You're at your best as a team.*

*After all, ribbons are secondary, they are only symbolic of something more important. Mainly like, are you both having fun together? That's the important question. If the answer to that is "yes," then other things fall in place.*

*Yes, I want you both to win many ribbons over the years, but, more than that, I want you both to love and enjoy life. There are enough people who are just too damned serious! And all too few Patti's.*

*So just be yourself and let Mandy be Mandy at her best, and you've got a great little horse going for you.*

*I'm proud of the way you're handling her. Keep it up. Always remember, fun her plenty, and fun yourself. That way neither one of you will (turn) sour or, to put it positively, both of you will always stay sweet, the way the both of you always should be.*

*Stay feminine! Muscles make men take only second place in horsemanship. I know, sometimes you want to be a tomboy. But, few men can out-finesse an honest gal when it comes to handling horses. No 150 to 200-pound man can out-muscle a 1,000-pound horse, but an intelligent 120-pound girl can finesse that same 1,000-pound horse into doing her bid.*

*The world is geared for male superiority. Soldiers, astronauts, presidents, priests, lawyers, cops are men, BUT, you girl-kids know what the score is, Finesse and not muscularity!! I'm with YOU, and Mandy,*

*Love Dad (at 5am or anytime)*

## '67 Dana and Jane Take Their Son to College

The busiest summer in Paleface history was headed for an end. As the days of August flew by, the change of season was around the corner. The Peck family was facing enormous change as well. They packed up the car with their oldest son's belongings, and the whole family took Greg to college. Dana and Jane were proud as parents could be, and were struck by the impact. Jane reflected that it was bittersweet when children left home to follow their dreams and discover their futures.

## '67 Paleface Horse Show

The Annual Kiwanis Horse Show at Paleface was held late in 1967. Due to the distraction caused that summer by all the extra business as a result of the Exposition in Montreal, the annual event was re-located on the calendar to the 10th of September. It was not nearly as well attended as in prior summers, but the annual tradition was maintained nonetheless.

The Grand Champion award went to Tomahawk, ridden by Terry Dohrmann of Glendive, Montana. And the Reserve Champion award went to Chippewa, ridden by Doc. It might have made a better story if Paleface cowboys and horses hadn't dominated the show. To be fair, many ribbons were awarded to riders not affiliated with Paleface.

## '67 Rescue at Ledgerock

One afternoon in early October, several of the local heroes from the Wilmington Rescue Squad stopped by Paleface for a late lunch.

Doc was having a late breakfast at the next table, and couldn't help but get drawn in to the story the men were telling Bea Lincoln, their waitress.

Rod Ritchie explained, "It happened at Grossmann's Ledgerock Motel at around ten o'clock. Two small boys were playing outside by the pool, seven-year-old Robbie Androvetti and four-year-old David Garbe. They were throwing rocks in the pool when Robbie accidentally fell in to the deep end. David ran into the motel to get his Dad, Mr. William Garbe from Rochester, New York. Mr. Garbe jumped out of his pants and shoes, dove into the pool and recovered young Robbie from the bottom of the pool, ten feet below. We were told that Mr. Garbe had difficulty getting Robbie out over the edge in the cold water. Fortunately, Mrs. Garbe came along in time to help. They got Robbie out, and then Mr. Garbe got out of the pool. Meanwhile, Mrs. Grossmann had called us. Mr. Grossmann put our training to good use. First, he tried to resuscitate the boy, then he turned Robbie over, working water out of his lungs. And then he returned to mouth-to-mouth resuscitation. When we got there, we took over. The boy's body was blue. We were both sure the boy was lost. We got the boy, Robbie on the oxygen and the resuscitator and we revived him. His Mom and Dad rode with us to Placid Memorial Hospital. Just imagine, every parent's worst nightmare. One minute, everything's fine. The next minute, your child is facing a life threatening emergency!"

Ellison Urban told Bea and Doc, "It was a beautiful rescue. Everybody and everything clicked."

Rod agreed. "Our equipment did its job and it looks like this story has a happy rather than tragic ending!"

Doc praised, "Bravo, men! Every time I see you or hear about your brave, heroic acts I am reminded of how lucky the local citizenry is to have you men tending to the public welfare and all of our various emergencies. You are the best! Absolutely the best."

Rod and Ellison thanked Doc for saying so. Then Rod said, "You have no idea how much satisfaction it gives the men of the Rescue Squad to succeed in a mission such as this one."

## '67 Tease Gets to Stay

There was no shortage of excuses, but when the first Saturday in November rolled around, Doc had to admit that Tease was not a bird dog. He was, however, a phenomenal host. In October, Doc had finally had some time to work with Tease. His best trick was to sit and stay where placed for long periods of time.

Doc found a large stool, just the right size for a dog to sit on and be seen by guests coming in the front door. Then Doc worked tirelessly to coax Tease to bark twice when someone came in. Once Tease got the idea that he would be fed when he performed this trick, Tease performed it consistently, with 100 percent reliability.

So, finally, that late afternoon in early November, when Mr. Doremus came through the front door and came face to face with his old dog, Tease greeted him with a pair of barks, and then a yawn. Doc jumped up quickly from his chair in the office, gave Tease his pay and hugged his old friend.

Leon Doremus said to Doc, "That dog don't hunt, am I wrong?"

Doc shrugged. "No, but Tease has found his calling!"

"No matter," Mr. Doremus replied, "I want you to come meet my new seven-month old puppy named Toldyaso!" Doc had to shake his head in mild amusement, with a touch of amazement wrapped into the gesture. Then in mock shame, Doc hung his head briefly.

"I will admit defeat. And I couldn't let you have Tease back even if you wanted him. You see, he has fallen hopelessly in love with us. And he plays a very important role here at Paleface. In addition to greeting guests as they arrive, Tease takes care of all the little bits of fat and gristle that diners chop off their steaks."

"And while I have failed at my task, I haven't been proven wrong exactly. You can teach an old dog new tricks. Let me show you."

Doc called Tease over, and Tease demonstrated an amazing ability to perform indoor, fireside tricks. Tease easily went through the basics, then some extraordinary tricks. Doc had Tease performing like a circus pony for about ten minutes before he let the dog take a well-deserved nap.

Doc's parting thought on the matter was that the old dog could learn new tricks, however the tricks had to befit the character of the dog. After all, you couldn't make a silk purse out of a sow's ear. The gentlemen philosophers then debated for an hour and a half about the wisdom or lack thereof in that old saying.

Toldyaso turned out to be an excellent hunting dog. Mr. Doremus loved the dog that reminded him of vacationing at Paleface in the Adirondacks.

Tease continued his role as fireside mascot, garbage can, and Adirondack host.

## '67 New Snowmobiling Club

Paleface was bustling with activity during the off-season of 1967. The front doors were locked, but behind closed doors many new innovations were being readied.

Dana and his trail crew had been working all fall, getting ready for a new winter season. In addition to putting up snow fences, grooming the trails and inspecting the chair lift and T-Bar, the crew did extensive work on several trails.

The "Brave" trail was made to be twice as wide as before, and the terrain was sculpted to make for exciting moguls, jumps, and airplane turns. Even after being widened, the Brave trail was a spectacularly scenic tour through the woods, twisting and turning down and through the evergreens. With the trail widened, instructors could bring beginner and intermediate skiers to the long trail to practice their slow turning and stem Christies.

Three other trails were made significantly wider as well, the Tenderfoot and Papoose trails, as well as the Walter Prager trail. The Walter Prager trail was named after the famed 1931 World Champion skier.

Inside the lodge, the under-utilized area between the lounge and the pool was completely re-decorated and re-purposed into a junior game room. About the only thing that remained in that area was the pool table. Several new pinball machines and a pitch-and-bat pinball baseball game served to provide an additional form of entertainment for kids of all ages. No doubt, parents and grandparents would return home from vacation with empty change purses.

Christmas parties were scheduled for every Friday and Saturday night, and in some cases, Paleface was booked for overlapping Christmas parties, using the dining room for one party, the lounge for another and the balcony area for a third on at least two different occasions. The Christmas season ran so long that the six Christmas trees had to be replaced and re-decorated twice, a lot of work, but worth the effort. Paleface looked stunning at Christmas. Particularly when there was a blanket of sparkling white snow outside the giant picture windows.

All summer, Doc had been planning to bring snowmobile enthusiasts to Paleface. During the previous winter, the sport had quickly grown popular with the local population.

The Paleface Ski Mobile Club organized during the early summer months of 1967. A couple prominent local citizens were invited as founding members of the club. Word spread quickly, and by the end of the summer, friends of friends were attending meetings.

Just as the Ski Club and the Junior Ski Club had turned Paleface's best customers into an advisory committee, and volunteer boosters, the new Snow Mobile Club ensured the successful launch of Paleface's new endeavor. The December meeting drew a crowd of sixty people. The founding members of the Paleface Ski Mobile Club formalized its governance structure by electing a president, a vice president, and a secretary-treasurer. Then the founding members debated which were best: Moto-Skis, Ski-Doos, Polaris, or Evinrudes.

The agenda for the December meeting also included remarks from Doc, who emphasized that the Ski Mobile Club was to be a family organization. Not just men, but also women and children would be welcome to enjoy snowmobiling. Doc encouraged the members to commit to the principles of good sportsmanship and safety.

After a lengthy discussion, everyone agreed on a safety plan wherein snowmobilers would file a flight plan to include an estimated return time. A patrol would then ride to the rescue if a rider failed to return on time.

Another priority of the Club was to be courteous neighbors. The previous winter many area residents complained of excessive noise, particularly at night. The sport was growing quickly in the community, especially within the past year or two. The Club committed to "strict prohibitions on use of private roads, such as log roads, etc. without the consent of the owner."

Doc's local relationships also helped establish a network of lands through which snowmobilers could ride continuously, connecting all the local towns. Just as Doc had connected Paleface, the AuSable Acres real estate development and the Agnes Ward Tree Farm for riding trails, Doc's local friends consented to allowing members of the Club to travel on their properties.

The horses had to give up a portion of their eighty-acre winter pasture to allow for the creation of a snowmobile arena where riders could race around in circles, and over jumps and around obstacles. The arena also included an inviting fire-pit. Snowmobilers enjoyed parking their sleds almost as much as riding them. The arena provided a nice spot for rallies.

The new Club also made plans for its next meeting on January 26th of the coming new year at seven thirty in the evening. Mr. Cal Lawrence, the vice president formally filed a resolution to "blast off to the Smoke Rise Lookout for a social hour following the business meeting." The resolution passed unanimously.

Also over the summer of 1967 a slope between the mountain and the snow-mobile arena was developed for tobogganers. Between the lodge, the lounge, skiing, snowmobiling and sledding, Paleface had something for everyone during their winter vacations.

Although Doc hated to do it, Paleface implemented its first-ever price increase. Adult day ticket prices were raised from $4 to $5, in 2017 dollars, that would be about $36. Children's tickets remained at $2.50 and Season Lift Tickets remained at $50 for adults and $25 for children.

Finally, in mid-December news spread through the local community that Chuck Morgan and Wayne Wright had been chosen to represent the State of New York in the United States Eastern States Amateur Ski Association (USESASA) pronounced USE-sas-uh. Chuck and Wayne were two of ten boys that would represent the state. Just before Christmas, the two boys would attend a training camp at Franconia, New Hampshire.

## '67 Snow Guns

With the help of "Dame Nature" as Doc liked to put it, Paleface's snow making crew was able to get a head-start, taking full advantage of an early cold snap. The Larchmont snow making machinery was entering its third winter with a blast. Dana's snow making crew got right to work laying down a deep base on the Chair Lift and Paleface Glade trails. Still, Doc was hoping for a good amount of natural snow as well, to add "frosting on the cake."

## '67 Dance Clubs

The members of the Paleface Ski Club and the members of the newly formed Paleface Ski Mobile Club had their Christmas party on Saturday December 9th.

The beautifully decorated lodge, and the snow guns running full blast created a festive note and helped put all the Club members in the Christmas spirit. Of course, it didn't hurt to remind members that the skiing and riding season had arrived as well.

Just outside Paleface's front door, a beautifully decorated Christmas tree was all trimmed out with shiny ornaments, and a fair amount of natural snow looked perfectly placed, alongside the fancy decorations.

## '68 Outstanding Service Award

For months, the Whiteface Chamber of Commerce had been planning its annual meeting and dinner dance. The planning subcommittee included Carroll Yard, Jack Dreissigacker, and Ed Cozette.

Bill Johnson, the secretary of the Chamber of Commerce was placed in charge of tickets and reservations.

The main event of the evening was the Chamber's award for Man of the Year. This award was being made for only the fourth time in the Chamber's history. Previous honorees included John Zachay, Abe Kilburn, and Donald Peterson.

In 1968, the Chamber added town Supervisor, Mr. George Haselton to its list of honorees. The inscription on the plaque read, "In recognition and appreciation of unselfish service to the town of Wilmington."

Next, the Chamber honored Doc with an Outstanding Service Award.

It was a special night with friends, business contacts and colleagues. Doc and his family appreciated the recognition and the honor. Both Jean and Doc appreciated that the Chamber chose to hold their annual dinner at Bertha and Carl Steinhoff's Sportsman's Inn. If they had to admit it, it was nice to get away from Paleface for an evening, and let their friends do the hosting honors!

Of course, Doc made a few remarks, gratefully accepting the recognition of his peers. Doc went on for several minutes about his love for the Adirondacks, his respect for the fine men and women of the North Country and the patience and tolerance of his family, particularly Jean. "When it comes to unselfish service to others, I don't know of anyone who sets a finer example than my wife." Doc got caught up in the emotional content of his remarks, and concluded perhaps a little prematurely, compared to other occasions on which Doc was called to make remarks before an audience.

The men and women at the dinner appreciated Doc's brevity, because there were several guests present that evening. The presidents of the Lake Placid, Saranac Lake, and Plattsburgh Chambers were all in attendance, and each made brief remarks. George Haselton, Man of the Year honoree had a few things to say as well. The big speech of the night was delivered by the editor of Saranac *Lake's Adirondack Daily Enterprise*, Mr. James Loeb.

Editor Loeb had lots of interesting stories to share with the audience. Aside from his experience as editor of the only *daily* newspaper within the Adirondack State Park, James Loeb had also served as ambassador to Peru in South America and New Guinea in the South Pacific. The audience enjoyed hearing James' interesting stories and witty remarks.

Next on the program were remarks from Republican State Senator Ron Stafford and Democratic Assemblyman Louis Wolfe.

The evening ended with the screening of an 8 millimeter color movie produced by the Eastman Kodak company featuring the Adirondacks. The audience enjoyed and applauded whenever they recognized local landmarks within the film.

## '68 Famous Figure Skaters

On the last Saturday evening in January, the Paleface Ski Mobile Club held its planned meeting on the balcony at Paleface.

Meanwhile, in the lounge Doc, Putzi, and Pete Pelkey hosted famous figure skating royalty.

The 1967 U.S. National Pair Champions, and three-time World Bronze medalists, Cindy Kauffman and her brother Ron Kauffman of the Seattle Skating Club relaxed by the fire after a day of skiing at Paleface. Former Canadian National Junior Champion Toller Cranston was also visiting Paleface.

Doc's son Chuck was on hand to photograph Paleface's famous visitors. After Chuck took pictures of the famous skaters, Chuck and his friend Charlie Draper, one of Dana's snow makers, set to work to put in motion another one of their pranks. Charlie Draper had that particular night off, but was at Paleface anyhow.

At the request of one of Chuck's portrait customers, Chuck had rented a gorilla suit for a photo shoot. The customer was a wealthy, frequent Lake Placid visitor with an eccentric sense of humor. Chuck had read an account of a motorist who had claimed to see a giant gorilla like creature late one night between Tupper Lake and Saranac Lake. All week long, Charlie had been talking about that sighting at

Paleface, especially whenever the gullible young Preston Palmer was nearby.

Doc had been left with instructions to call Preston Palmer on the walkie-talkie at precisely eight o'clock. Preston and his young wife Cookie were expecting their first baby any day.

At the appointed time, Doc radioed Preston. "You better get down here to the lodge on the double," Doc said loudly into the walkie-talkie.

"Yes sir!" Preston responded a couple moments later. With all the excitement of an expectant father, Preston hurried down the dark trail.

Behind a tree, Chuck was perched on the shoulders of his friend Charlie. Chuck wore the top part of the rented gorilla suit, Charlie wore the bottom part of the suit, and Charlie wore a small bearskin rug over his shoulders, covering the space between where the top and bottom part of the gorilla suit didn't meet.

Chuck and Charlie had another accomplice, who shall remain unnamed. After Chuck and Charlie had suited up in their costume, the accomplice helped cover them in snow from the snow jet near the bottom of the trail. Then the accomplice helped them to their hiding place behind the tree.

At just the right moment, the accomplice put Chuck and Charlie directly in the path of poor Preston Palmer.

Good thing for Chuck and Charlie, Preston was an unarmed man!

Preston screamed at the sight of the snow-covered Yeti, and took off running so fast he tripped over a small snow bank. Then he rolled, quickly and desperately, trying to get away from the beast, which he was sure was in hot pursuit. Preston didn't hear Chuck and Charlie's laughter.

Preston scrambled to his feet again and ran for Paleface's front door.

Safely inside, Preston wasted no time finding Doc and the famous figure skaters at the fireplace. Preston's wife Cookie had returned to his consciousness the moment he made it safely inside.

At the same time, Doc need to know there was a dangerous beast outside Paleface's front door.

Preston was in the middle of telling Doc about the Abominable Snowman, and Doc put his hand on Preston's shoulder. "Excuse me, Preston. Is that the beast you were talking about?"

Chuck and Charlie's accomplice had helped them waddle through the front door of Paleface. Preston delivered another full-throated scream at the sight of the snow saturated Sasquatch, every bit as frightening under the bright indoor lighting as it was in the outdoor darkness.

Fortunately, the guests of honor had been properly prepared for this most entertaining prank. Their laughter was Preston's first clue that he had been duped. Again.

Doc went over and shook the Abominable's hand. That was Preston's second clue.

Then Doc and the accomplice helped Chuck off Charlie's shoulders. Preston sat down in an empty chair, shaking his head incredulously.

With the gorilla suit and the bearskin rug slowly steaming by the fireplace, and the jokers laughing about their prank Preston finally found his voice and said to Doc, in an injured tone, "And you were in on this, sir?"

The sir part, especially, made Doc feel bad. Honestly, Doc had to confess to Preston that yes, he was in on the prank. As Doc was explaining to Preston that the elaborate hoax was an indication of how much everyone liked him and enjoyed his company, Jean came around the corner with news from the office. Preston's wife and in-laws had sped off to the Keene Valley hospital.

Doc left the famous figure skaters in the company of Putzi, Pete, Charlie, and Chuck and took Preston to the hospital in Paleface's station wagon. Doc would have let him take the wagon of course, but between the impending fatherhood and the Yeti sighting, Preston wasn't in any condition to drive.

When the Paleface Snow Mobile Club convened, all the riders set out for the Smoke Rise Lookout. The Paleface Staff had laid out a fine feast at the Lookout. Chuck and Charlie took the skaters, Cindy and Ron Kauffman and Toller Cranston to the Lookout to enjoy the party as well.

After the social hour on the mountain top, Chuck and Charlie took the skaters for a long snowmobile ride and stopped for a rest in the snowmobile arena. It was a beautiful, midwinter's evening. The moon shone brightly, just two-days shy of official full-moon status.

The next day, the figure skaters would return to their long days of full-time training and relentless pursuit of gold medal superstardom. It was a nice break, and change of pace to be able to enjoy other winter sports for a change.

At ten minutes to midnight, Preston Melvin Palmer IV was born. The news was promptly delivered to Preston, his uncle, Doc, and Cookie's father in the waiting room. Doc vigorously shook Preston's hand, then slapped him on the shoulder. Then Doc left the happy family to enjoy their time together.

Of course, Preston would never forget the day his son was born anyhow. The re-telling of the story of the day Preston's son "Four" was born would always include the Abominable Snowman tale as well.

## '68 Mt. Marcy

It was the middle of May.

It had been a very busy season for Mr. Archibald Robinson, president of the Hudson River Bank in Edgewater, New Jersey. Between board meetings, visits with customers, approving loans and searching out high net worth individuals throughout Bergen County, Archibald visualized himself standing in the West Branch of the AuSable River. It was the same every spring.

Archie and Doc Fitz-Gerald attended grade school together, years earlier. Archie's father Thankful Robinson had been friends with Doc's father, the senior Aaron Boylan Fitz-Gerald. Also, their fathers were Freemasons.

Like many of Paleface's customers, Archie and Rosemary were multi-season guests. Each year there was a winter skiing vacation. Each year there was a summer vacation, and each year there was a spring fishing vacation.

To celebrate Archie's milestone birthday, Archie and Rosemary decided to spend a full two weeks in the Adirondacks. Archie planned to spend every day in the river.

Meanwhile, Rosemary had a big bag full of a dozen books and as many magazines to occupy her time. She left a trail of used books wherever she went, as a public service to others who might be interested in reading them also. In each book, Rosemary included a postcard which she used as a book mark, and on each postcard, she left a brief note for future readers. To this day, antique book dealers are probably finding those notes she left behind long ago.

The first day of their vacation, Archie and Rosemary got up early and left as the sun was rising. Three and a half hours later they were waiting for the doors to open at the Orvis shop in Manchester, Vermont. Archie needed to invest in a new pair of waders.

Another two and a half hours in the car and they arrived at Paleface. Without unpacking a thing, Archie dropped his things in room number seven. Moments later, Archie was back at the front desk. Doc and Archie sped off in the Paleface station wagon to visit Fran Betters' Adirondack Sport Shop.

Archie couldn't wait to get into the river, but more than that he couldn't wait to visit with the experts that could always be found telling stories and sharing jokes at Fran's shop. To top it all off, a little bit of expert advice and a couple of Fran's world famous AuSable Wulff flies, and Archie would be ready first thing in the morning.

Though Archie hardly needed one, he always insisted on hiring a guide. Archie found a couple of candidates at Fran's. Fran advised, "None of these guys are licensed professionals, but any of them would be able to help you find the smart fish." After a brief negotiation, Archie hired Desmond Lawrence. Des worked lifts at Paleface during the winter.

Archie was paying good money, and would of course tip heavily if he was successful. And so, Des was hired to work every day for the next two weeks except Tuesdays. Archie and Doc had planned to hike in the High Peaks of Keene Valley each Tuesday while Archie was on vacation. Fran recommended a guide, smiling ear to ear, and wrote a phone number and the name Joe York on a piece of paper. Archie gave the paper to Doc, so that Doc could hire the guide. Fran told Archie and Doc that their guide was an Adirondack 46-er and had led many groups up the tallest peaks. When Doc dialed the number, a sweet young lady answered and she told Doc that their guide would meet them at Fran's on Tuesday morning at 7am promptly.

Rosemary Robinson was in the lounge reading the first of her brand-new books, *Chariots of the Gods*, by Erich von Däniken, who hypothesized that extraterrestrials had a hand in creating ancient monuments such as the Pyramids of Giza and Stonehenge. Over dinner, Rosemary repeated many of von Däniken's theories.

Archie rebutted by singing the chorus of "Everybody's Going to the Moon," a popular song by Jonathan King. Case dismissed.

Rosemary thought that it was easy to be skeptical until you read the book yourself. Rosemary decided against vocalizing a defense on behalf of the author.

Early the next morning, Archie met Desmond Lawrence at the muster point, Fran Betters' shop in Wilmington. From there Des escorted Archie to all the best spots. For the next two days, Archie had great luck, using Fran's flies and placing them exactly where Des told him. Desmond didn't fish himself. He was far too busy scouting the river for the best rocks and pools. Archie threw most of the fish he caught back, but kept a couple of the largest, and gave some to Des.

By the middle of the afternoon on Monday, Archie was done for the day. They returned to Fran's shop, and shared the news of their day—what worked and what didn't. You could think of it as "Fran Central Station," an information clearing house. Combining the news of each fisherman's experience, Fran would be in a position to advise anglers in the days to come.

While Archie and Des drank coffee, Fran tied fly after fly and told extraordinary stories. One of Fran's favorite stories was the one where he caught a decent sized fish just as it was being consumed by a much, much larger one.

The next morning, Archie and Doc returned again to Fran Betters' shop. Archie and Doc waited at the iconic sign at Fran's shop that featured a pretty young blond angler, in a bikini, cowboy hat and cowboy boots, who had managed to hook the back of her bikini bottoms with her fishhook.

Jo York drove up in a beat up, rusted out pickup truck, and screeched into the parking lot way too fast, slamming on the breaks and throwing gravel almost to where Doc and Archie waited for their guide. She jumped out of the truck, landing firmly on both feet. She stood barely five feet tall, wore hiking boots, short shorts, a white ribbed tank top shirt under a red plaid shirt. When her feet hit the ground she tied the bottom of the plaid shirt into a knot at her belly. Then she tossed her long blond hair around her head before putting it up into hat. Then she took a large pack from the back of the truck that looked too big for a girl Jo's size to carry. She lifted the pack so easily, it looked to Doc and Archie like Jo's pack were completely empty. Then she greeted Archie, offering her hand, "Morning y'all, I'm Jo."

It took a moment for the men to realize what was happening. It had never dawned on them that this young girl, perhaps 20 years old, could be their guide, Jo York. Doc asked, "Are you the young lady I spoke with on the phone?"

Jo confirmed, "Yes, I told you your guide would meet you at 7am promptly. I'm guessing you are surprised that the guide turned out to be me." She giggled, and put her big pack in the back of Doc's station wagon. As they drove away from Fran's shop, it occurred to Archie that Jo looked just like the girl on the sign.

They exchanged pleasantries on the way to the trailhead. Jo was very warm, friendly, talkative, and so likeable that Doc and Archie weren't the slightest bit inclined to inform Jo that her guide services would not be required. Perhaps they were a little apprehensive about following Jo's guidance, if they had to admit it.

For years, Doc had meant to hike Mount Marcy. It had been put off far too long. Five years earlier, Adirondack 46-er Jim Bailey spoke of the beauty of Mount Marcy and the tiny Lake Tear of the Clouds. Ever since, Doc had been meaning to make the climb.

The trailhead at the Adirondak Loj was a few miles outside of Lake Placid. The turnoff lay between the Ski Jump Complex and the Mount Van Hoevenberg Bobsled course. The Loj was remote, and the trails from the Loj all the more so.

It was a good thing the men got an early start, just as they would if they had gone fishing instead. Archie and Doc scoffed when Jo led them in leg stretching exercises. Jo persisted nonetheless. The final preparations included a heavy application of bug spray for each of the hikers. Jo took a moment to apply some bright pink lipstick, and then lifted her heavy pack. “Off we go!” Jo urged. They headed down the trail. First Doc, then Archie, and then Jo.

It wasn’t long before Doc was way out in front, and Archie wasn’t too far behind. Jo, kept a slow and steady pace. Jo warned them to pace themselves. The old men thought at first, that Jo was going to hold them back and prevent them from reaching their destination. Doc offered to switch packs with Jo. She sweetly declined.

The first couple of miles went fairly easy, with slight inclines and declines as well. They reached Marcy Dam in good time.

Beyond Marcy Dam, the trail got dramatically steeper. Instead of keeping a pace of three miles per hour, the group was hardly able to keep a pace of one mile per hour. The old men began to appreciate the enormity of the task they had set out to accomplish.

Jo advised her elders to take tiny steps, set a visible goal, and walk to that. Then take a couple deep breaths and set the next goal. Perhaps a big rock or a funny looking tree, anything that looked different made for a good milestone. “Take as long as you like, take a break whenever you need it. We have all day.”

Earlier in the day, Doc and Archie might have thought Jo couldn’t possibly carry her pack to the top of the highest mountain in New York. As the day went on, Jo barely seemed to tire as the old men plodded on. As was the case with many men from their generation, neither Archie nor Doc uttered so much as one syllable of complaint.

A couple of hours later, they finally reached Lake Tear of the Clouds. Fortunately, it was a beautiful, clear day—not at all warm out, but not cold either, though about twenty degrees cooler than at the base.

Jo showed Archie where to stand, so that he could make the claim that he stood with one foot on either side of the mighty Hudson River, which left Lake Tear as a tiny trickle. Jo wondered how long it might take for a drop of water to float all the way from the source to the mouth of the river near Archie's home in Edgewater, New Jersey. Just as the thought entered Archie's mind, a drop of sweat rolled off the tip of his nose and made a tiny splash in the river.

Doc wished for his easel and palette, and about five hours of time to make an artist's rendering of the beautiful little jewel of a lake. Doc said, "this is as heavenly a spot as I have seen anywhere on earth!" Doc took lots of pictures with a Kodak camera. That would have to spur his memory, and his imagination would have to take care of the rest. It was a short break at the tiny lake.

There was much hiking yet to do. And the main prize, the summit of Mount Marcy still lay ahead. Jo pointed to a little, almost invisible path that led to the summit of Gray Mountain. Then Jo invited Archie and Doc to return to the prominent, marked trail that led toward the summit of Mount Marcy.

Not too far from the little lake, they hiked their way to the other side of the tree line. The hearty trees that fought for their survival at elevations above 4000 feet above sea level often appeared tortured, twisted and tiny. Between the lack of soil, the extreme winds and the short growing seasons trees don't get very big near the top of the tallest mountains.

Of course, Doc and Archie were accustomed to seeing trees at the tree-line from their years of skiing at Whiteface. Walking through the stunted forest was a bit different from riding over it on a chairlift or swiftly sailing through it on a ski trail. The delicious, heavy fir scent of the balsams and the rotten, pungent aroma of the trail mud conflicted for olfactory attention below the tree line.

Above the tree line, it was hard not to stop and gawk at the spectacular sight of the views below. However, the summit still was quite a distance ahead. Jo encouraged the men to keep moving. Not swiftly, but steadily. Jo always preferred to enjoy the views on the way back down, but focus on the quest on the way up. You never could tell when a nice day would turn ugly all of a sudden. It would be a pity to have to turn back short of their goal after getting so far up the mountain.

Fortunately, there were no issues with the weather that fine, cool spring day. It was early in the season, and they had the top of the mountain to themselves. In every direction was a magnificent view. From the top of the tallest mountain on that clear afternoon, Doc could see Whiteface and Lake Placid. In another direction, Doc could see Lake Champlain off in the distance. The other High Peaks looked magnificent, seemingly very close and far away at the same time, depending on whether the person looking at them had to hike to them or float off toward them in their imaginations.

Jo pointed out the mountains in the McIntyre range, which was on their travel plan for the following Tuesday. "Imagine yourself on the top of that mountain right there, looking up here and thinking 'yeah, I did that!'"

They ate their packed sandwiches and drank water from their canteens. Fortunately for Doc and Archie, Jo had carried an enormous burden of extra water in her large pack. Doc and Archie had traveled lightly.

Though they would have liked to stay on the top of the world a lot longer, the wind chill had turned their warm sweaty bodies to cold sweaty bodies in a hurry. It was time to return back down the path.

All the way up, Jo let Archie and Doc lead. On the way down, Jo took the lead. Inexperienced hikers often find their legs go rubbery on the way down, and often don't know that it can be more dangerous hiking down than up. Jo felt it was important to keep a slow and steady, careful pace. Jo's companions were in very good physical condition, but they were also almost 60 years old, and smokers.

The next morning, neither Doc nor Archie could walk very comfortably. When Archie's guide, Desmond Lawrence showed up at Fran's, Archie asked if perhaps there was a way they could fish from a dock instead of standing in the fast moving current of the West Branch of the AuSable River in waders all day.

Des laughed all the way home. Archie was happy to wait in a classic Adirondack chair in front of Fran's shop until Des returned with his canoe. They spent the day fishing in Lake Placid instead. Archie appreciated getting off his feet for the day, though he greatly preferred fly fishing in the river to fishing in the lakes and ponds.

The following Tuesday went much the same. The trail up Algonquin was significantly shorter. Doc and Archie's legs had fully recovered, no worse from the experience a week earlier, in fact the previous week's conditioning made the Algonquin trip easier. Even so, both Doc and Archie had to use Jo's little trick of making lots of baby step goals to make it up the steepest inclines.

As Doc was leaving the tree line on Algonquin Mountain, it occurred to him that Algonquin had a different personality from Mount Marcy. It was the same kind of terrain, similar elevations, but there was something that just felt different. On Algonquin, there was a greater sense of an ancient spiritual connection. Almost eerie, and perhaps a little scary at first, but then strangely comforting and welcoming, so Doc gave in to the notion.

When they got to the top they just stood there, and rested a little, taking in the view. Doc felt a little like he was flying through time and space as he looked from Algonquin Mountain to the slides on Colden Mountain and to Mount Marcy beyond it. Doc allowed his gaze to very slowly take in the panorama, soon settling on that most familiar sight, Whiteface Mountain. Doc's heart warmed to the happy thought of deep appreciation for being able to live in the shadow of Whiteface, rather than at the other end of the Hudson River, like his friend Archie.

Jo dug into her enormous backpack and pulled out three square

Tupperware containers. Each container held a piece of chocolate cake. One container had a tiny inscription: *Happy Birthday, Archie* in light blue letters on the top. Jo stuck a tiny birthday candle in the piece of cake and lit it with a butane lighter. The wind at the top of Algonquin Mountain beat Archie to the flame. The men laughed, Jo shrugged her shoulders. Flaming candle or not, Doc began to sing into the wind, "Happy Birthday to you...."

Jo reached into her pack again and pulled out a small package and handed it to Archie. Archie unwrapped the package and found an intricate, gold antique pocket watch and chain with a scene of a man standing on the top of a mountain. Archie opened the watch and on the inside, was an engraving that read, "Happy 60th Archie, Love Rosemary."

Rosemary and Jean had conspired to burden Jo with Archie's birthday celebration at the top of Algonquin Mountain. Rosemary had found the old watch in Lake Placid during their winter vacation back in December. Doc's wife Jean took care of the cake duty and called Jo to arrange a surprise delivery.

Doc laughed, "I have something for you as well, my friend, but we'll have to get back down to earth first!"

After the men finished their lunch, and birthday celebration Jo said, "All right, so we have three choices! One, we can return down Algonquin Mountain, and call it a day. Two, we can make a side trip up Wright Mountain on the way back. Three, we can continue over the other side of Algonquin here to Iroquois Mountain. I guess a fourth choice would be to do Iroquois and Wright, but I'm guessing that's not in the cards for today!"

Doc told Jo, "I can keep going. After last week, I took a couple Bayer aspirins this morning, knowing what was coming!"

Archie laughed, "So did I! Since chances are, we'll never pass by here again, I'd say let's continue on."

Jo affirmed, "Good choice. I think you'll find the walk from Algonquin to Iroquois is the best walk in the Adirondacks! But I have to tell you, there is no official trail, and you will get wet from the dew of the branches of the trees in the col, which is to say the valleys between the mountains. I also have to tell you there are two lesser mountains between Algonquin, and Iroquois, namely Pyramid and Boundary. So, there will be plenty of work to do, going up and down."

Jo went on to explain the belief that the peak of Boundary Mountain was the border between Iroquois lands and Algonquin lands. Until just a couple of years ago, Algonquin Mountain had been known as McIntyre Mountain, named after an iron magnate from the 1800s.

On the way to Iroquois, Doc experienced the feeling Jo had described. It was an exhilarating feeling. Doc thought life above 4000 feet was splendid. Compared to the trek up Algonquin, the hike to Iroquois from Algonquin was a cake walk.

Of course, the extra miles took their toll and made for a long climb back down Algonquin. Back at the car, Archie joked, "Thank you partners! There's no way I'll ever *top* this birthday!"

## '68 Prehistoric Gardens

Early in the spring, Preston was back at work at The Mystery Spot in advance of the summer season. There was much to do to get ready for a busy second season.

Craftsmen and artisans were hard at work building enormous life-size replicas of long extinct dinosaurs and gardens to look absolutely prehistoric, which was not so easy to do in an alpine climate.

Mr. Charles Kurutz, the owner-operator of The Mystery Spot had hired Chuck Fitz-Gerald to take pictures for postcards, and for the newspaper. One sunny spring morning, about a week before the season opening, Chuck Fitz-Gerald arrived to take pictures. Clara Hazelton, the Wilmington correspondent was on hand as well, conducting an interview for the newspaper. Chuck saw Preston Palmer in the flower bed, busily planting flowers for the summer season. Chuck couldn't help telling Clara and Mr. Kurutz about the day Preston's son Four was born.

While Chuck went to work photographing dinosaur statues, Clara sat on a bench and wrote:

*Wilmington is the scene of another look, aside from mod, bikinis, fishing toggery, mini-skirts and all. The new look is paradoxically, pre-historic. Charles Kurutz, who ran Mystery Spot last year with success has added a prehistoric garden, complete with mammoth, dinosaur and twenty-one other ancient animals we can't spell or pronounce. He even has a group of prehistoric men and a Volcano.*

*All very educational and immensely entertaining, along with the many illusions he has planned. One really gets a jolt when riding along one sees a huge, long necked, long tailed creature beside Route 86. And as one glances up one sees the mammoth on the hill standing in the natural forest. Walks are laid out for the curious to follow to see monsters and pre-historic men. And don't forget your camera, says Mr. Kurutz.*

## '68 Correspondents' Dinner

Margaret Madden had been meaning to get around to calling her acquaintance Clara Hazelton for a couple of years. Something always seemed to come up, and she just never got around to it.

After reading the *Adirondack Daily Enterprise* one Thursday afternoon in early June, Margaret picked up the phone and called.

"Clara," Margaret started, "I've been wanting to call you for ages and see if we could get together. I hate to admit, the news of Robert Kennedy's death finally made me pick up the phone and call you. Anyway, I thought it might be wonderful to talk about our work for the newspaper, perhaps over lunch or dinner."

Clara replied, "I would love to get together. I was thinking of going to Santa's Workshop on Monday the 17th. They're having an Open House to celebrate the start of their 20th season. You could join me and then we could have a late lunch at Paleface if that sounds good."

With their plans formalized and finalized, the two ladies went back to talking about the big news that was on everyone's mind that day. How awful for the Kennedy family, as well as for the country, of course. Margaret said, "I still cry every time I think about Martin Luther King, and it's been two months already since he was killed."

Clara said, "These are very troubled times we're living in, that's for sure." Just then, a customer came into Clara's shop and she excused herself. "I've got a customer to tend to. I look forward to seeing you a week from Monday, Margaret."

The two ladies enjoyed their visit to Santa's Workshop. They rode the Candy Cane Express, a small steam train that made a loop above and through the village. The Christmas Carousel took them round and round. The ladies sat in a bright red sleigh rather than riding side-saddle on the reindeer. Reindeer took the place of the more traditional horses on that carousel. They enjoyed a brief conversation with the talking Christmas Tree, aptly named Tannenbaum. Clara and Margaret went through the reindeer barn, and got to feed live reindeer. Each stall had the name of one of the famous reindeer on it, and Dasher decided to take a bite from the hem of Clara's skirt.

In the center of the park, they sat on small wooden benches and enjoyed a Christmas pageant. At the end of the pageant, the owner of Santa's Workshop, Robert Reiss made a few remarks:

> *We want to thank you all for coming out to Santa's Workshop today. It is a pleasure to welcome you here as we kick off our 20th season. As you know, Santa's Workshop is America's oldest theme park. Since we opened our tourist attraction, we have entertained over ten million visitors. On behalf of the management and the employees at Santa's Workshop, thank you for your continued support. Tell your friends and family all about us, and send any tourists you might encounter our way!*

John Zachay, a manager at Santa's Workshop, followed Mr. Reiss briefly. "I would like to introduce a new artisan to you all today. May I present Mr. John Cudequest, a Bavarian glassblower who is taking up residence here at Santa's Workshop?" Mr. Cudequest smiled and took a bow.

After the show, Margaret and Clara checked out the frozen ice pole, the "North Pole" as it were. "What a fun place this is!" exclaimed Margaret. "I had no idea. I have heard all the children talk about it, but just never got around to coming myself!" The ladies couldn't resist buying a magic wand with a glitter colored star on the end, and a personalized Santa hat while they were in the village.

Shortly after 1pm, the ladies headed out for a late lunch. They arrived in separate cars at Paleface on schedule. They had the dining room to themselves, and Margaret and Clara sat across from each other at a table near the window. They were still wearing their personalized Santa hats, and carrying their personalized magic wands.

Jean Fitz-Gerald greeted them, chatted briefly and took their lunch order. Margaret waved her magic wand at Jean and all three ladies giggled. Jean told Margaret and Clara, "You would be surprised maybe, but that happens here *all the time!* And yet it still tickles my funny bone."

Pearl Pierce, who had worked from breakfast through lunch, was getting ready to leave for the day when she saw Clara and Margaret in the dining room. Pearl stopped over to say hello before leaving. Clara said to Margaret, "Did you know that Pearl Pierce was a correspondent for the *Record-Post* for many, many years."

"I don't know about many, many years," chuckled Pearl, "but I loved working for the paper, collecting the local stories and mailing them in each week. And then seeing the news all typed up on Thursday afternoon."

"If you're not rushing off to somewhere important, would you like to join us, dear?" asked Margaret.

Clara said, "Well how about this! We can call this the first annual meeting of the North Country Correspondents Association."

"It's funny you should say that, Clara. I have been carrying around this article for over a month." Margaret pulled a folded up piece of newsprint out of her enormous pocket book.

While they waited for Jean to bring them their lunch, Margaret Madden read a transcript of President Johnson's speech to the

White House Correspondents Association, verbatim. The President appeared at their annual dinner on May 11th.

Margaret's best imitation of President Johnson's Texan drawl left much to be desired, but she stuck to it steadfastly as she mentioned Vice President Hubert Humphry, the outgoing president of the Correspondents' Association, the incoming association president, and the ladies and gentlemen in the audience. Then Margaret as LBJ told a funny story about not being recognized, emphasizing the feeling of invisibility that comes with declaring yourself a lame duck by declining to run for reelection. President Johnson joked about having to wear a pass, and Margaret drawled on, "One day, as I was walking over to my *nap*," Margaret paused for a long time, "a guard stopped me in the hall and looked at me very carefully and said, 'Excuse me, buddy, but do you work here?' So, I am so glad you all remembered me tonight. You do remember me, don't you, *Hubert*?" In a different voice, Margaret delivered the Vice President's line, "And how."

Margaret continued on, through LBJ's comedic jabs at the media, partisan politicians, and as her favorite part of the speech came closer, Margaret's voice got louder and louder. At top volume, Margaret read, "Well, this may be my valedictory address to the press. So tonight I can be even more frank with you than I have customarily been in the past, if that is humanly possible." Margaret captured just the right level of sarcasm with the tone of her voice. Continuing with appropriate cadence, Margaret said, "As some of you may have heard, I have had my troubles with the press. But that's not at all unusual. There has always been some friction between the press and us in the *academic community*. Why this friction? We *intellectuals* agree that it is not so much a matter of substance, we just plain don't like your style, much too earthy. As you know, the relationship between presidents and the press has always been a very intriguing one, kind of a sort of a lover's quarrel." Margaret paused slightly after delivering each sentence fragment, and imagined the members of the press laughing at the thought of LBJ claiming to represent the academic community of intellectuals, though he had some reasonable basis to do so. As Margaret went on, President Johnson compared himself and his relationship with the press to previous president Thomas Jefferson's press relations. In the speech Margaret went on to tease the press for failing to believe that LBJ really, seriously was not a candidate for reelection, supposing perhaps it was a brilliant ruse to galvanize support for the electorate to insist upon drafting him. Then came the joke, "And I am told that my March 31 decision not to run surprised some people. But if you think that was a surprise, you just wait till you hear Lady Bird's announcement!"

The president's speech was interrupted when Jean dropped by and placed lunch on the table. During the brief pause, Margaret wished wistfully that the joke was instead a fact, wouldn't it be marvelous to have a lady be president? Then Margaret continued with her dramatic reading. Clara gestured to the empty chair at her left, across from Pearl and Jean sat down and listened to the rest of Margaret Madden's presidential address. Margaret hadn't missed a beat, and continued in character, more serious and more patriotic than previously. Margaret drawled through deep, weighty thoughts about struggling for peace, solutions to the problems of poverty and race, and the pace at which history turned. After a mostly dark address, LBJ concluded his speech with soaring, optimistic, uplifting rhetoric.

Margaret folded up the article and put it back in her purse. Margaret's eyes misted over a little. President Johnson's words had worked as he might have imagined. He had certainly impressed Margaret Madden. "Perhaps President Johnson will change his mind and run again," Margaret added with a sniffle.

Pearl said, "Those are some beautiful words. And I almost forgot, somewhere along the way that you weren't really the president!"

The ladies shared a good laugh.

In all seriousness, however, Margaret Madden was on the ballot in November. In addition to working as a book-keeper and sales clerk in Hurley and Madden's country store AND in addition to serving as the *Record Post*'s correspondent for the Town of Jay, Margaret Madden was also the duly elected Town Clerk.

Margaret had been curious to ask Clara about her writing. "Your articles are just wonderful, Clara. The editor always tells me to just keep it to the facts. How do you get your beautiful descriptive prose past them?"

"I don't know," Clara answered, "I just send it in and they publish it."

Jean told Clara she couldn't wait to read her column every week. Jean and Clara shared a love for watching birds, and for garden flowers. Sometimes Jean got too busy to stop and appreciate the gardens and the birds, and Clara's column always reminded her to stop and appreciate the moment.

"What are you working on for this week's column, Clara?" asked Margaret.

Clara had her stenographer's notebook with her. In fact, Clara always had her notebook with her. "I'd be happy to read what I've got so far," said Clara. She made eye contact with Jean. She noticed the ladies were listening intently.

"Summer is coming on apace. Things are growing fast. The rains came in abundance on Saturday but did not penetrate very deeply into the ground. The soil is very dry, yet growth is rapid. Gardens are gay with petunia plants, columbine, iris and other flowers. We met a new one to us on Sunday in Vermont. Baptisia, a very interesting four-foot perennial. Birds which were calling in the late afternoon were Red-Eyed Vireo, Blackburnian Warbler, Wood Thrush, Robins and many others. The water level is high in most streams, in Lake Champlain and ponds."

Clara licked her finger and flipped the page in her notebook. "I also have a little story on the ditches and culverts being placed on Springfield Road. I have a paragraph about a young soldier in Vietnam named Fred Betters. And I have a story about Mrs. Ada Schultz who took a bad fall down her cellar stairs. The rescue squad took her to the hospital in Lake Placid and then she was flown to the hospital in Burlington. There was a very deep cut in the back of her head."

Jean said, concerned, "Ada is our daughter-in-law's mother. I hadn't heard anything about this." She excused herself and went to make a phone call.

Clara went on to talk about the Northland Rock and Mineral Club's field trip. Only the day before Clara and the Club went to Richford, Vermont, then on to Sherbrooke in Canada. At each stop the Club members hiked to likely locations where they collected rock specimens for their collections. At a river near Sherbrooke they found a huge collection of Pyrite, also known as Fool's Gold. When the club crossed the border back into New York, the back of their cars looked like they were dragging on the road, they were so weighed down with rocks.

For many years, Clara had been a rock hunter and was past president of the Northland Rock and Mineral Club. She kept the public as up to date on the rocks in the region as she did the weather, gardens, and birds.

"What do you have in the news this week, Margaret?" inquired Clara.

"I have a sad story about the death of Paul Harrison in Vietnam. Major Harrison was A.H. Thompson's grand-nephew. Mr. Thompson lives in AuSable Acres. That family has had fifteen members of the family serve, in World War I, World War II, Korea, and now Vietnam, and this is the first member of their family that has been lost in war."

The ladies talked for some time about the war in Vietnam. Many from the community had served or were serving at that time. Pearl thought of her friend and co-worker Dorothy McLean and about her son Roger McLean, Jr, who was on leave from his job as a wrangler at Paleface and who was actively serving in Vietnam.

During a lull in the conversation, Pearl offered a prayer for the family of Major Harrison, for Roger McLean and his Mom and Dad, and for all the folks who served our country in Vietnam. Margaret and Clara added an "amen" when Pearl finished.

Margaret Madden went on to add, "There is some good news in the paper this week! I can report that Carl Steinhoff and Doc Fitz-Gerald returned from St. Edward Lake in Quebec with lots of trout.

And I can report that Patti Fitz-Gerald has won a blue ribbon and a first place trophy riding Tomahawk, just yesterday at the Keeseville Riding and Driving Club Horse Show. Meanwhile, Doc won a first place ribbon in the costume class riding one of the beautiful Paint horses, Chippewa."

The ladies had so much fun getting together that afternoon in June, they got out their calendars and decided to do it again in September.

The summer rolled by fast, as it always seemed to do in the North Country. Margaret Madden arrived at Paleface a few minutes before 11am, and ran into Jane Peck. "How was your summer, Jane?" Margaret inquired.

Jane told Margaret about her husband Dana's thirtieth class reunion, and the dinner celebration they had at Paleface. "It was wonderful to see so many people come out. Lena Torrance did a wonderful job organizing the reunion. Of course, both Lena and her husband David were graduates of the class of '38. The roast beef dinner was delicious. It's hard to believe in a couple of years all these people will be fifty years old!" Jane concluded, shaking her head from side to side in disbelief.

"How are the boys?" asked Margaret.

"Well, we are so proud of all of them, of course. This summer our son Greg toured with a group from college. They covered 7,000 miles, ten states, seventy-six services, and fifty-two churches. Greg sings bass, you know, and I could just listen to him sing all day. Greg will be a sophomore this year. It's hard to believe the boys are growing up so fast, Margaret." Jane would have gone on to talk about Doug and Dana-D, but Clara and Pearl arrived. "I'll let you get to your lunch, Margaret. It was so nice talking with you."

As they sat down, Pearl Pierce observed, "It's funny how much change we have seen in the world during our lifetimes, and yet people are such creatures of habit. Here we sit in exactly the same seats we sat in last time we got together!"

Clara suggested, "Let's all move! Lest we be too predictable."

The ladies got up and each moved one seat to the right. When they were all comfortably seated again, Clara said, "Now what did I have last time we were here!" Everyone laughed, but in fact Clara did have exactly the same lunch—a bacon, lettuce, and tomato sandwich with a big glass of iced tea.

The ladies caught up on the national news. Election Day was fast approaching. Would Richard Nixon finally be elected President? Would the Vice President, Hubert Humphrey win? "It won't be long before the nation decides!" concluded Margaret.

Clara added, "And good luck to you, Margaret. We will root for your re-election!" Clara always referred to herself as we, whether in her column or in conversation. It had become second nature. Pearl nodded agreement, though she wasn't in the habit of voting for Democrats. And Margaret was very definitely a Democrat.

The ladies talked about the death of Charley McDonald the previous week. Clara asked, "How is Carrie holding up, Pearl?" Charley's wife Carrie worked at Paleface with Pearl.

Pearl said, "I think Carrie is doing as well as she can under the circumstances. Jean told her to take off as much time as she needed, but Carrie insists that it is good for her to get out of the house. The funeral was yesterday, and do you know what? Carrie is back at work today!"

Pearl went on, "You know, while Charley was alive, every day Carrie would leave Paleface promptly at noon, right in the middle of the big lunch hour to go home and make Charley his lunch, and then race right back to Paleface," Pearl laughed wistfully, as if she were recalling events from long ago, rather than just the week before.

Margaret noted, "It must be hard on everyone else at Paleface to have Carrie up and leave in the middle of the lunch hour."

Pearl generously allowed, "You would think so, but we are all used to it. Carrie gets everything ready for lunch, and helps us catch up quickly when she gets back. I guess we understood that if we wanted Carrie to work with us, this was just how it had to be. And Carrie is a very hard worker."

Clara added, "And you would think by 1968, men would have evolved to the point where they could make a ham sandwich on their own!" The ladies laughed. Neither Clara Hazelton nor Margaret Madden ever married.

"Well, I have to tell you ladies. I celebrated my 75th birthday on the 4th of September and Mr. Pierce and I celebrated fifty-six years of marriage together on that same day. You would think men have evolved to look at all the modern stuff around us. But if you spend five decades with a man, you will find they don't evolve at all! Quite the contrary...."

After a bit more laughter at the expense of men everywhere, Margaret complimented Clara about her column in the paper. "I don't think your writing has ever been better. Maybe you should write a book instead of a weekly newspaper column." Margaret added, "And I enjoyed your piece on the clean-up at the Wilmington Flume. I hate to see a bunch of garbage on the side of the road. But it's all too common these days, I'm afraid. What is wrong with people? Why do they think it is okay to just toss their trash out of the windows of their cars?"

Clara's feature heralded the young people from the local businesses who volunteered one evening to clean up the road side. Over forty employees from Santa's Workshop, Whiteface Mountain, The Mystery Spot, Paleface, and the members of the Whiteface Chamber of Commerce got together to clean up. To make the work seem like fun, prizes were offered to the volunteer who picked-up the most junk, to the volunteer who found the most unusual item, and to the volunteer that found the oldest looking item. The most common item found was the tear-off part from Polaroid film. There was plenty of other trash, including bottles, rags, papers, and cans. There was enough to fill a small truck to its limits. Bill Johnson found a Model T fender, qualifying as the winner of the oldest looking item. John McKenna from Lake Placid, who worked at Santa's Workshop found a suit of red flannel underwear, such as one might expect Santa Claus himself to wear under his red and white suit. With that find, John was the undisputed winner of the most unusual item.

Thanks to all the volunteers, the scenic waterfalls collectively known as the Wilmington Flume, was restored to its proper, photogenic condition. To celebrate, the members of the Board of Directors of the Chamber of Commerce roasted hot dogs for the volunteers, in the fully restored, picture postcard pretty setting.

Doc stopped by to visit with the ladies for a few minutes. He had been awake for almost two hours and hadn't had a conversation with anyone yet. Margaret asked Doc if he had any news for her column.

Doc talked about the big plans he had for the end of the season, an employee appreciation dinner at the Smoke Rise Lookout. "As soon as the leaves fall from the trees, we'll be up that chairlift with all the steaks, corn, and fixings we can carry." Doc and Jean did all the cooking for the end of season party, just a small personalized token of appreciation for their hardworking summer staff.

Doc elaborated, "And this year, we have extra cause for celebration. The wranglers of Paleface can now boast 400 ribbons to their credit. What an accomplishment! We have a great string of horses and the best wranglers you could hope to find." From the way Doc was talking, one might not have known that a good percentage of those ribbons and trophies were won by Doc himself.

## '68 Return on Investment

After turning a decent profit in 1967, Doc had hoped that Jean would begin to see Paleface as having been a good investment. 1968 was shaping up to be a decent year as well. The fact that they had generated an $18,000 profit in 1967 would have corresponded to something like $130,000 fifty years later. However, considering the substantial investments made between 1960 and 1966, the profit generated in 1967 was extraordinarily inconsequential.

Yes, Jean was happy that Paleface wasn't losing money. But

Jean was concerned, especially after having had a major heart attack, that Paleface would be better off in the possession of someone else. Another point Jean made was that selling Paleface during a time of increasing profits made sense. You never knew what was coming down the road.

The notion was hard for Doc to accept. In his brain, Doc understood the points Jean made. In his heart, he hoped that he could yet demonstrate that Paleface had upside potential. Meanwhile, Doc consented, it wouldn't hurt to quietly market the potential sale of Paleface to qualified investors.

Doc made a few half-hearted inquiries and had a brief conversation with his attorney and his accountant. Yes, being able to demonstrate two years of increasing profits was nice. If four or five years could be strung together, that would really bring a handsome sale potential.

## '68 Doc and Jean's 35th Wedding Anniversary

Late in the evening, a couple days before their anniversary, long after Jean had turned in for the night, Doc wrote his wife the following letter:

*2:30am*

*Hey sweetie:*

*I'm really trying to communicate wid ya. And I know I'm not so good at it. BUT, let's saddle up a coupla good little trail horses and get lost for a coupla hours. We owe it to us. You name it. Sunday, Monday, only let's do it, now that the leaves are turning you set the pace!*

*Please ride my sweetie, little Chip, the best little hoss I've ever known, tho I still love ole Dunder! This is the best place to live in our Halcyon years. Chip and Dunder are real solid pals. Where you can have a real woodsy day. Or, if you want Trigger or Pepsi, that's ok with me. You name it, but let's just let "Heavenly lost-ness overwhelm" us, to quote good old Robert Frost.*

*Come on, let's go! And I seem to remember Lowell saying, "Let's give our soul a loose!"*

*Tomorrow or Sunday, you name it.*

*Here's to the sweetest little wife a guy could ever want, and this is our time of the year.*

*And I don't care if its 5 am or 11 pm, only the latter would spoil the flaming leaves part of the fun.*

*Just say "yes." Put on your jeans and your boots the dog mutilated (am sorry about that!) and it's a date.*

*Love Popeye*

Doc and Jean celebrated their 35th wedding anniversary with a long afternoon trail ride. Later that evening Doc wrote Jean another letter:

*Sept 20 '68*

*Hello Sweetie Pie:*

*I just feel like writing you a letter. Guess that sometimes I'm not so hot on communications either!*

*When a guy has these 4 things going for him, he's more than lucky: #1, a wonderful, loyal, patient wife who knows how to put up with his stubborn folly; #2 a sweet little girl kid whom he loves just one sixteenth of an inch from the good Lord himself; #3, two boy kids who have a lot going for them (and we all make mistakes!); and #4 two little spotted woods pals, the horse and the dog of me old age, yes, he's got his share of the world's best!*

*Please ride my little Chippy sometime. You'll love him. He's alive, but he's sensitive (like Tease) he wants to please you. You must do some riding the next two or three weeks. The color is picking up every day. So, let's go diddy-bopping, you and I. Like we did 35 years ago in the Maple Leaf glory of the Laurentians. That 3-hour ride today was a lot o' living.*

*A new world has come into being in 35 years, and yet, so help me, it's still our kind of a world! Let's you and I make the most of it. You don't darn well know how much I'm looking forward to this trip of ours, to Jackson Hole and 2 Bar 7 and Taos. We are both of us hill-billies and this will be our honeymoon and our holiday. God knows we've worked hard and we need it! Let's not let anything keep it from being the best holiday we've ever had. Here's to your beloved Rockies, and mine! Hope they still have cowboy and cowgirl out there at 2 Bar 7!*

*Don't forget to bring warm clothes and gloves. Wool sox too! Let's be ready to live it to the full.*

*We've had our ups and downs but we've had an interesting and, I like to believe, a somewhat useful life. Right now, I feel a wee bit selfish. People are wonderful, but you and I are a lit bit special. You often speak of friends, and how few they really are. Thank God, we've got us. Speaking for me, your hubbie, that's everything I want. You and me, just like 35 years ago!*

*Good nite darling. I love's ya. Even though I sometimes make a durn poor job of showing it!*

*Fitzey.*

*P.S. Just checked in the Swansons, from Short Hills, Room 12 and 14 at 2:15 am.*

## '68 Landslide Business

The North Country was blessed with a major early winter snowstorm and the slopes were already crowded for the weekend of December 14th and 15th. Doc thought that finally, Paleface had turned the corner to success. They were just about to begin to realize a fine return on their investments.

## '69 Wright to Alaska

In late March of 1969, Wayne Wright competed in the National Junior Championships held at Mount Alyeska, Alaska. It was an extraordinarily distance to travel, and expensive as well.

Of course, Paleface was proud to boast that Wayne learned to ski at Paleface, and his first coaches Karl and Putzi Jost were proud of his accomplishments. The community at large had come to root for Wayne. Wayne had just returned from Alaska, and he and his parents were special guests of the Whiteface Mountain Kiwanis Club. Wayne had been asked to keep the results a secret until revealing them at the club meeting that night.

The Kiwanis Club held their meeting at Tirolerland, in Jay, New York and Jack Dreissigacker led the meeting. As Jack conducted the club's business, and spoke of all the many recent achievements of the members of the club, everyone was waiting impatiently to hear about Wayne's trip to Alaska.

Finally, Jack turned to face the guest of honor. "I don't have to tell you how proud we all are of you, Wayne. Congratulations on all your success, and we can't wait until the day you represent us all in the Olympics! Please tell us how you fared in Alaska."

Wayne stood and told everyone about his trip to Alaska, making them wait to hear how he placed in the competition. Wayne told everyone about the big snow storm that hit while they were there—ten inches of wet snow, and howling winds at forty knots. Wayne told everyone about the ski jumping competition, and the downhill races. Wayne told everyone about how Alyeska has the only chairlift in the entire state of Alaska. Wayne told everyone about the broken bones suffered by a boy named Andy from Colorado and a girl named Gigi from Montana, plus all the other injuries from the competition.

Finally, Wayne came around to tell the audience about the slalom event. "The slalom was my best event," Wayne told the audience, "and my total time was 105.90 seconds, the sum total of two great runs."

And then Wayne told them about his competitors, one by one, and the total times posted by each, referring to a piece of paper Wayne held in his hand. He saved the top finishers for last.

Finally, Wayne revealed that Perry Thompson of Mammoth Lakes, California had a faster time, with a time of 105.62. All together the crowd let out a gasp. Everyone was sure Wayne was going to tell them that he had won.

And then Wayne reported that Steve Lathrop from Plymouth, New Hampshire had a time of 101.68. Again, the crowd showed their supportive disappointment.

And then Wayne revealed the conclusion—that he had come in third. The room let out a sigh of relief. Wayne reported that he had bested sixty-seven other young men. Then he dug a bronze medal out of his pocket and passed it around the room for everyone to look at.

Everyone stood up and clapped. Karl Jost hooted and Putzi Jost hollered. Heidi Jost jumped up and down. Wayne's mother, Jean Wright yelled the loudest, and she had already known how the story ended!

Finally, Wayne mentioned that he had come in fourth place overall. Never mind that the crowd assembled at Tirolerland that night was thrilled with Wayne's success in Alaska.

Jack Dreissigacker then told the assembled crowd about the cost of the trip Wayne had made to Alaska. Jack further demonstrated his leadership by placing twenty dollars in a big beer stein and passed it around the room. Fortunately, the large showing at the Kiwanis Club meeting that night and the compelling storytelling on Wayne's part, helped raise $580 to go against the cost of Wayne Wright's trip to Alyeska, Alaska.

## '69 Dana and Jane's 25th Wedding Anniversary

On the 4th of June, Dana and Jane Peck celebrated the 25th anniversary of their June 3rd wedding in 1944 in the Fellowship Room at the Nazarene Church. It was a joint celebration with Mr. and Mrs. Rodney Ritchie, who were also celebrating their silver anniversary.

Both couples received nice gifts, including a silver tea and coffee service for each. Dana and Jane were happy to be among friends and relatives. It was hard to believe twenty-five years had gone by already!

As the party was winding down, Mrs. Ritchie asked Jane if she had pictures from her trip with the family to Washington DC. As it happened, Jane had just gotten the film developed and had the pictures in her pocket book. The pictures the Pecks had taken at Arlington National Cemetery came out particularly well.

## '69 Moon Landing

Personally, I was much more interested in the wild west, cowboys and Indians, horses, and my idol, Aunt Patti. She drove a blue Camaro, ate Snickers bars, smoked Marlboros, and rode horses. Lots of other kids at the time were captivated by space, and dreams of becoming astronauts and joining the space race. Even for tiny cowboys it was impossible to avoid getting caught up in the magic of space during the summer of 1969.

I remember being at home in Rhode Island, just Mom and us kids. Dad was out of town on a job-hunting trip. I didn't yet fully appreciate that job-hunting tips meant we would be moving somewhere before long. Change was in the air. Things were different.

The babies couldn't tell, of course, and I couldn't understand why our happy, sweet, fun-loving Mom seemed to stare blankly off into the corner for long periods of time. Sometimes I would find her with tears in her eyes, which struck fear into my heart. What could be so bad as to make a Mommy cry? It must be really horrible. Mom would just scoop me up, hug the stuffing out of me, tell me I was wonderful and not to worry about adults' problems.

Mom's sadness wasn't like my childish concerns. At seven years old, you can cry your eyes out over nothing and an hour later, completely forget whatever it was that made you sad. Though it felt like years, it was probably only months. And yet it was beginning to feel like Mom would always be very sad; that's just the way it was going to be.

On Sunday, July 20th, 1969 Mom suddenly seemed like her old self again.

We had one television, and it was on all day. It had been on almost continuously since we watched a rocket blast three astronauts off into space on Wednesday morning. Mom was fascinated by space, and couldn't stand to be away from the television for fear she might miss an update. There were only three channels on television then, and none of them played news all day.

It seemed like every fifteen minutes, she would scoot me away from what I was doing to watch with her. A rapid-fire succession of "ooh-ooh-ooh" was the signal. "We're witnessing history unfolding, right before our eyes," Mom said. "Hubba, hubba, hubba! Something's about to happen!" When Mom became excited about something, it was hard not to get sucked into it yourself.

My younger sister Barbara, and younger brother Jeffrey were toddlers at the time. We spent the whole day camped out with Mom in the bedroom. Mom sat on the bed with her legs crossed Indian style. The floor was littered with toys, and there were toys all around Mom on the bed. The television was unusually loud, to drown out the not so quiet sound of three kids playing, which could be hard to accomplish. Every once in a while, Mom would jump off the bed, race to the television, and turn the dial on the set to make it even louder, or to see if maybe there was better coverage happening on one of the other two channels.

Just before two in the afternoon, it was announced that the landing craft had separated from the command module. The landing craft began circling the moon. Mom tried to explain that the landing craft was going to go around the moon once or twice then it was going to try to land on the moon. And Mom tried to explain that they wouldn't be able to show us the landing craft on television when it was on the other side of the moon.

"Mommy, what happens on the dark side of the moon?" I asked.

Mom gave a fantastic, imaginative answer with lots of details that modern science had yet to prove or disprove. I could tell by the voice she used that she was making stuff up. Mom had just read *Chariots of the Gods*, the book Rosemary Robinson had left behind at Paleface. Mom's imagination took the author's theories much farther and incorporated fantastic, vivid details.

At about 3:40 in the afternoon, Mom turned the volume down on the television and rocked the babies to sleep. While they were falling asleep, I asked lots of questions. With a seven-year-old brother, babies had to learn to fall asleep while people talked.

Mom answered in soothing, sleep-inducing tones. By about ten minutes to four, the landing craft had completed its orbit of the moon, emerging from the dark side, and was preparing to land on the surface.

With one sleeping toddler on each side and me on her lap, Mom answered questions about all the confusing spaceship names. "Saturn Five is the name of the rocket; Columbia is the name of the space ship. Eagle is the name of the tiny ship that is about to land on the moon. Apollo is the name of the mission. Apollo 11 to be more specific because other astronauts have made ten space missions before this one."

That should have cleared it up, but I wanted to call it just one thing. Forget Apollo, Saturn, and Columbia. I just called it the Eagle.

"Mommy, if you could go to the moon, would you?" I asked.

"Yes, of course!" she exclaimed. "What an adventure that would be!"

"Mommy, do they have lady astronauts?"

She sighed dreamily. "No, not yet, but I bet someday there will be."

"Mommy, wouldn't you be scared to go out into space?"

"Maybe a little, but probably more excited than scared."

"I think space is scary," I told her. "Did you know that someday the sun will burn out and we'll all die!"

"Where did you hear that?"

"At school. And in this book." I picked up a book that had a picture of all the planets on the cover. The one that Mom had been trying to get me to read.

"Don't spend your time worrying about that, that's millions of years in the future. By then we will discover a way to blast ourselves off into space and build new homes on other planets." Mom was very reassuring and very persuasive.

I still had my doubts.

"Space is so full of black nothingness. What if all that nothingness sucked you in and swallowed you up?" Though I hated to admit it, I was quite afraid of the dark.

And vampires! A few months earlier I was taken to see a vampire movie although I was only seven. Just the thought that a person, who was really a vampire, and could turn from a bat back into a person, and bite you on the neck, and make you into a vampire, was a horrifying thought.

For weeks, every night at dark, I carried on and on at bed time. It wasn't until Mom made me a cross out of aluminum foil and gave me a whole fistful of garlic cloves that our family had peace and quiet at bed time.

"Mommy, since vampires only like the dark, do you think the dark side of the moon is full of vampire bats?" I asked, afraid of the answer.

"No, I'm sure vampires and bats are not allowed on the moon!" Mom answered emphatically and convincingly. She sold that conclusion, putting a stake through the heart of thoughts about vampires.

Fortunately, it was the middle of the afternoon in the summer, and vampires only come out at night, so I went back to worrying about the nothingness of space.

"What if the Eagle crashes and the astronauts die, Mommy? What then?"

Mom said, "Well, we've never done this before. I guess that could happen. Maybe thousands of the world's smartest scientists have been working on this project since President Kennedy told them we need to go to the moon. I'll bet they have thought of everything, and will know just what to do in order to boldly go where no man has gone before." That last part Mom had copied from the television show *Star Trek*, of course.

"How far is it to the moon, Mommy?"

"I think they said it was two hundred and nineteen thousand miles."

"How many miles is it to Paleface, Mommy?"

"I think it is about 325 miles to Paleface." She thought for a moment, and then began muttering math. "Seven times three equals twenty-one, so 700 trips times 300 miles would be 210,000 miles, which is almost 219,000 miles, more or less." After calculating an approximation, Mom said, resolutely, "So going to the moon would be like going to Paleface almost 700 times! Keep in mind that rocket ships go much faster than Chubby does."

Chubby was the name of our car. It was an old Checker taxi cab that had been retired from service as a taxi and wound up becoming our family car. Instead of yellow and black it had been painted solid black all over. In the back seat, there were two fold up chairs, with small round seats. Kids could ride on those chairs, and rock back and forth on them. Just like those metal animals on giant springs at the playground which you could rock back and forth. Behind the back seat was a shelf that was big enough for a seven-year-old boy to climb up onto. On a long trip to Paleface I would often lie on that shelf by the back window and fall asleep. I couldn't remember ever wearing seat belts as a kid, and often the driver would entertain us all by swerving or punching the breaks, sending us three kids flying around like future generations of kids in a bouncy house.

"When are we going to Paleface, Mommy? I want to see Nana and Grampa and Aunt Patti and ride the horses. It is summer now. We should be at Paleface!"

Mom gently hushed my questions and whispered in my ear, asking me to turn up the television a little louder, but not so loud that the babies would wake up. In those days, before every television came with a remote control, children were very useful channel changers.

It was about quarter after four in the afternoon. They were getting closer to landing on the moon. We had been watching the countdown clock and a simulation of a spaceship and the moon. Walter Cronkite and the famous astronaut Wally Schirra were preparing us to witness the historic event.

We didn't say a word as the clock counted off the final ten minutes. You could hear beeping sounds and voice transmissions from the astronauts and ground control. CBS alternated between footage of the moon, and what they called a simulated model. The seconds clicked by in what seemed like slow motion.

As it was being confirmed that the module had landed, the camera showed Wally Schirra appearing to wipe a tear from his eye. Walter Cronkite removed his glasses, saying "geez" and "oh boy" and pinching his nose with his thumb and index finger. Mr. Cronkite was clearly overwhelmed by the enormity and the importance of what he was witnessing. This never happened. Mr. Cronkite was generally calm, cool, and collected in any given situation.

Walter said to Wally, "Wally, say something... I'm speechless."

Wally said, "I'm just trying to hold on to my breath."

I looked at Mom, and tears were streaming down her face. She had her hands clasped together over her heart and her chin rested lightly on top of her knuckles. She smiled at me and pulled me close on her lap. She was crying and laughing at the same time. Overjoyed! It made me feel good to see Mommy so happy.

Mr. Cronkite went on to say, "You know we've been wondering what this guy Armstrong or Aldrin would say... just to hear them do it, we're left absolutely dry mouthed and speechless." Moments later, Walter added, "And there they sit on the *moon*."

The astronauts and ground control could be heard: "Roger we have it... he has landed, tranquility base, Eagle is in Tranquility, over... we have unofficial time for that touch down of 102 hours 45 minutes 42 seconds and we will update that...."

Walter Cronkite added, "Time which will be in the history books forever."

That was corrected moments later by another voice, marking the official time as being a couple minutes later. In any case, it was about quarter after four in the afternoon as we were watching. The Eagle had landed in the waterless "Sea of Tranquility."

## '69 Fifth Annual Kiwanis Horse Show at Paleface

Meanwhile, at Paleface the fifth annual Kiwanis sponsored horse show was in full gear. Rain or shine, with or without a moon landing! The members of the Kiwanis Club depended on the annual fundraiser to provide for all the needy causes they supported each year—causes like buying a plane ticket to send young Mr. Wright to the Junior National Skiing Championship in Alyeska, Alaska! Causes like planting trees in Boston.

Thanks to radio station WKDR, Plattsburgh, the participants, spectators, and sponsors of the biggest horse show ever staged at Paleface were able to hear live continuous coverage of the lunar landing. Between updates from space, an announcer on a podium called the day's program in the ring.

The competition was extremely fierce. More riders than ever participated in the eighteen events. The judges were challenged to name the best horsemen and horses on that particular day.

Several riders during the pole bending competition and the barrel race found themselves removed from their saddles, making their own moon landings in the dusty ring.

At the end of the afternoon, the ribbon and trophy ceremony had to wait.

Imagine standing outside on a platform or around a large fenced off ring on a big field on a warm summer afternoon with hundreds of other people, watching dozens of cowboys, cowgirls, and horses and silently listening to a radio broadcast coming out of giant speakers mounted on wooden poles. The greatest applause of the afternoon came at the conclusion of the broadcast from the ABC network. "The most historic moment in space exploration is a success!"

Doc Fitz-Gerald announced over the loudspeaker, "Ladies and gentlemen, cowboys and cowgirls, we have landed a man on the moon. How about that! Many years from now, when someone says to you, do you remember where you were on the day you learned that man had landed on the moon, you can think about this horse show on this beautiful summer afternoon, the view of Whiteface Mountain in the distance and the excitement of our annual horse show! And our champions can remember that they *also* achieved greatness on this day." The champions were presented their trophies, Doc thanked everyone for coming and the audience dispersed.

## '69 Moon Walk

Back at our house I returned to my toys. The previous summer I had been given a burlap bag full of plastic western toys, with fencing, a covered wagon, horses and gear. Combined with my Lincoln Logs and Erector set, I could create my own dude ranch and horse shows.

My brother and sister woke from their naps. With an ear out for the television, household life returned to normal for a while. The babies had a bath, we all had dinner, and everyone played on the floor for a couple hours before bed at around eight.

After I had been asleep for a couple hours, I was jostled awake. "Why is mommy waking me up in the middle of the night?" I thought. It wasn't very often adults woke children in the middle of the night on purpose.

"David! Wake up! It's about to happen. The astronauts are going to walk on the moon!" It took a little bit of effort, but Mom managed to wake me up enough to stay awake for a while at least. Mom had a drink and a snack and some toys handy to keep me busy while we waited. Mom was animated and excited.

The sight of the earth from outer space was amazing. The picture looked shadowy and the astronauts looked like ghosts. I understood that most of television was stories, or entertainment, but I understood *that* night's television program was real, live, and happening at that very moment, somewhere out in space. 109 hours and 24 minutes after the flight began.

I watched Neil Armstrong come down the ladder, and heard Mr. Cronkite say, "There he is, foot coming down the steps." It was really hard to make out that an astronaut was walking down a big step ladder.

I heard Neil Armstrong say, "I'm at the foot of the ladder" and say the most famous space words of all: "That's one small step for man, one giant leap for mankind."

Strangely, Walter Cronkite and Wally Schirra couldn't hear the second part of the phrase. Someone had to tell them in the television studio what Neil Armstrong had said.

Neil Armstrong talked about the moon dirt on his moon boots. Mom read the words from the screen out loud. "Live voice of astronaut Armstrong from surface of moon." At this point, they were no longer showing us a simulated model.

A little bit after that, the television image reversed so that the black spaces were white and the white spaces black. Walter Cronkite talked about the negative polarity, and hoped that NASA would figure out how to return the transmission to normal. It was a little spooky to watch. Fortunately, it didn't take long to return to normal.

I don't think I stayed awake too long. Mom watched, riveted, hanging on to every word uttered by the astronauts or the anchormen. Before long, as Neil Armstrong was gathering moon rocks, I fell back to sleep. Mom woke me up again when Buzz Aldrin came down the steps. And Mr. Cronkite said, "Now we have two Americans on the moon."

Buzz said, "Beautiful view."

Neil said, "Isn't that something."

Buzz said, "Magnificent desolation."

Walter Cronkite added, "Like walking on a trampoline."

"Why do you keep waking me up, Mommy?" I asked.

"Someday you'll be happy I woke you up. This could be the most important day in the history of the world and I bet you'll never forget it!" Mom smiled warmly, which made me feel like this was a special moment, just between the two of us. I tried as hard as I could to stay awake.

Mom woke me up again to see the astronauts place the American Flag on the moon, and again when the astronauts got a phone call from President Nixon. I had fallen asleep for good when Walter Cronkite summed up the night with the following words:

> *The first tourists on the moon. From their description, it sounds like some place we might want to go after all. Aldrin called it magnificent desolation. Armstrong, stark beauty all its own. Well for thousands of years now, it's been man's dream to walk on the moon. Right now, after seeing it happen, knowing that it happened, it still seemed like a dream and it is, it's a dream come true.*

Half a minute past midnight, CBS' broadcast from the moon had ended.

Somewhere on the moon the astronauts placed a plaque, to inform future generations: "Here men from planet Earth first set foot on the moon. July 1969 A.D. We came in peace for all mankind."

## '69 Nylorac

Before the sadness, Mom went through great creative entrepreneurial enterprises. Taking care of a home, two toddlers, and a young school age son kept her busy most of the day. Each day there was less than an hour all to herself. It was usually dedicated to such businesses.

One year it was batik. The previous year it was driftwood furniture. During our annual summer vacation to the Adirondacks, several days were spent combing the area's lakes for the most perfectly deformed pieces of drift wood that just happened to be aged to perfection. Late August was the perfect time. With water levels low, the natural creations were exposed or within reach. We filled Chubby the Checker and we filled the Paleface Station Wagon with driftwood. Then we rented a one-way U-Haul trailer and dragged them home to Rhode Island. Some of the driftwood creations were turned into lamps and decorative furniture. Most of the driftwood became lawn art, garden sculptures and made their way into garage sales throughout the following decade.

In the summer of 1969 it was *Nylorac* art, which read backwards was Mom's name: Carolyn. Perfectly shaped, and sized to fit in the palm of an adult hand, smooth and oval shaped river rocks collected from the AuSable River between Upper Jay and Keene, New York, Nyloracs were a precursor to the pet rock craze that would follow a few years later. Except that a Nylorac was actually a beautiful work of art. Each one had a unique hand painted design, kind of a paisley inspired modern art doodle with lots of twists and turns that might bring dragons' tails and sea monsters' backs to mind. After each Nylorac was painted, it got a couple coats of some kind of finish, like polyurethane, only I'm not sure exactly what kind of chemical concoction it was. Whatever it was, those doodles will never be lost in time, and are bound to outlast the petroglyphs and hieroglyphs left behind by our ancient ancestors.

After the Moon Landing, the sadness returned. Mom worked on the Nylorac art, not with the jubilation that carried her through the first big basket of rocks. It seemed to take forever to complete the second big basket.

Shortly after the moon landing, we began to plan for a long trip to the Adirondacks during the second half of August. I counted the days. I couldn't wait to see our family. Most of all, I couldn't wait to be at Paleface—at the barn and on the trails. Seven-year-old boys were not very patient!

## '69 Road Trip

We rolled into town on Wednesday, August 13th.

After 328 miles in a car with three young children, everyone was relieved to have arrived, especially and including those three young children. The last half hour was probably the hardest.

From North Hudson to Keene Valley and Keene, we knew we were deep in the heart of the Adirondacks. We knew we were almost there. We were among the high peaks, and we couldn't wait for Chubby to roll up the driveway.

Mom was an expert in diversionary tactics, and a right fine singer as well. On the dark highway between the tallest mountains, Mom sang about how there was a mountain, and then there was no mountain, finally followed by the declaration that there was. Mom was particularly good at singing songs with repetitive lyrics, which was very helpful in getting young children to sing along. That Donovan song from two years earlier was the perfect choice. From Buddhist saying to hit folk song, it was perfect for the Adirondacks in the late 1960s. Mom sang the chorus over and over again, and now and then included the song's intriguing verses as well.

After that, Mom broke into one of her very favorite songs, "Freight Train." At home she often played Peter, Paul, and Mary's 1963 recording of the song from the album *Into the Wind*. One time, after singing that song, Mom told us about her grandmother, Stella Elliott, whose own grandmother lived to be 106 years old. She was born in in Trois-Rivieres Quebec, in 1817. When she moved to New York her name changed from Marguerite Rouette to Margaret Wheel LaBombard.

Anyway, I remember hearing Mom sing that song on every long road trip we ever took, and certainly on every trip home to the Adirondacks. Usually, she would sing a modified version of the first line of the chorus twice, and then add her own lyrics afterwards, shielding us from the dark subject matter that followed, so what we heard was: "Freight train, freight train, going so fast; Freight train, freight train, going so fast," over and over again.

## '69 Woodstock

After a day of reconnecting with family, Dad set out on another job-hunting trip. Nana eagerly agreed to entertain the grandchildren for the weekend. Mom headed off with some artist friends and her baskets of Nyloracs. She was supposed to be selling them as collector's items at a road side flea market, to help make ends meet. Instead Mom and her friends made a round trip to Woodstock and the Nyloracs never left the trunk of her friends' car. We didn't hear about Mom's trip to the most infamous music festival in the history of the world until many years later.

It was the peak of the summer season at Paleface. With Mom and Dad on their road trips, we were delighted to go along with Nana to work. The free babysitting service at Paleface entertained the babies during the peak breakfast and lunch service hours, and Nana played with and read to them when the restaurant wasn't busy.

Paleface's expert cooks and servers really didn't need much supervision, of course! Nana and the babies spent most of the weekend in room number one. Our Grandfather had to find somewhere else to enjoy his late afternoon mini-naps.

## '69 Picnic with Aunt Patti

Whenever I wasn't with Aunt Patti or at the barn across the street, I was constantly pestering, pleading and plotting to get there. I was at a difficult age, not old enough to come and go as I pleased, and not so easily put off either. Somehow, we all made it through the busy weekend.

Aunt Patti had Monday off, her first day off in the better part of two weeks. After sleeping in until mid-morning, as young people were wont to do on their days off, Aunt Patti showed up at Overlook, where we had spent Sunday night.

Nana fed us all a hearty breakfast and packed picnic foods into a basket and into saddle bags. We were so excited to see Aunt Patti, and so glad she was there, we were literally running around the kitchen, randomly bumping into things and screaming way too loud for Nana and Aunt Patti to talk about anything.

Aunt Patti scooped me up and took me into the living room. She asked me in a confidential whisper, "How would you like to spend the day with me today? Just you and me?"

"You know it!" I shouted.

"I have a special surprise for you today," Aunt Patti continued. "But first, do you think you can help quiet down the babies while Nana and I get ready? We need maybe ten or fifteen minutes."

I had butterflies in my stomach, and I was too excited to want to play with the babies, but I understood the faster they were made happy, playing on the floor, the sooner we'd be able to go.

It wasn't long before Aunt Patti and I were headed out the door. I hugged and kissed Nana, and darned if the babies didn't want to be hugged and kissed too. I flew out the door, my feet barely touching the ground on the way to Aunt Patti's car. Aunt Patti was right behind me.

A kid my age never got to sit in the front seat, let alone ride in a fancy modern sports car. Aunt Patti opened the door to the car, and on the front seat were two big boxes with wrapping paper on them.

I turned to look at Aunt Patti, and she had a giant, prodding smile that seemed to suggest those two presents were for me. It's not Christmas, I thought. "It's not my birthday," I said out loud. I was so happy, I gave Aunt Patti a huge hug. It didn't even matter what was in the boxes. I felt so lucky.

I didn't happen to notice Nana looking out the window next to the front door. Aunt Patti and Nana exchanged satisfied grins through the window. Aunt Patti got all the credit, even though she told me it was Nana who got and wrapped the gifts.

Aunt Patti put the picnic packed saddle bags in the car and handed me the first box. I ripped through the wrapping paper in seconds flat. Inside was a shoe box. I took the cover off and inside was a pair of buckskin colored boots with a design stitched over the toes. I put them on right away. They were a little bit large, good enough to last the season and the next, perhaps! Nana had picked out the widest ones she could get her hands on, and then had them stretched even wider from the inside. Even when my feet were small, they were very wide.

The next box was unwrapped just as fast as the first. Inside was a white straw cowboy hat. A red and white Paleface patch was glued on the front and center of the hat. I think I wore that hat every day. All summer. Every summer, for several years.

I felt like a full-grown cowboy.

"What do you say we go riding?" Aunt Patti asked.

"Can we?" I exclaimed. It didn't occur to me to ask where we were going or what we were going to do. If Aunt Patti was going, and willing to take me, then I was up for anything. Moments later Aunt Patti was behind the wheel, and we were ready. Aunt Patti waved to Nana in the window, and so did I. Aunt Patti had her summer shadow. Whatever she did, I copied.

On the way to Paleface, we stopped at Mac's store just off the town square. Aunt Patti bought a one-dollar slab of cheddar cheese off the wheel under the big glass dome. Ada McDonald wrapped the cheese in paper, ripped from a giant roll and tied a string that she pulled from a pulley above her head around the package. Aunt Patti also bought a pack of Marlboro's, a box of candy cigarettes, two Peppermint Patty candies, a Pepsi, and a Mountain Dew.

I showed off my new boots and hat, and Helen McDonald gave them her approval. Ada McDonald came over to look at them more closely, and told me she thought I was the most handsome cowboy she ever saw. She pinched my cheek and told me I was getting so big that it wouldn't be long before I was taller than she was. She was probably right; Ada wasn't a very tall woman.

Aunt Patti put the Peppermint Patty candies and the chunk of cheese in the saddle bags, started the Camaro, and turned the radio on. On the way to the barn at Paleface we "smoked" our cigarettes and drank our sodas. We sang along with the radio, first to the song "More Today Than Yesterday" by Spiral Staircase and then "Bad Moon Rising" by Credence Clearwater Revival.

We pulled up in front of the barn. Aunt Patti parked on the grass rather than in the parking lot. We were just steps away from the horses. As it turned out, that was a good thing—walking in my new boots took a little getting used to.

There were three cowboys on that day—Terry Dohrmann, Dick Mihill, and Dave Reiner. I wanted to show them all that I was a cowboy now too.

After a short visit with the cowboys, I was ready to visit with all the horses. I didn't want to hear about how I needed to drag my new boots through horse poop before I could be a real cowboy.

We started on the right side of the long pole barn. There were six stalls, then a small tack room with a desk in it. Then there were six more stalls. Instead of a wall at the back of the barn, there was a large swinging gate that led to a pasture.

The left side of the pole barn was similarly situated. First there were six stalls, then a small corridor across from the small office on the opposite side. There was a three-step stairway at the end of the little corridor that led to a long, elevated hallway which allowed a kid such as myself great access to the horses from the front. We called this the hall of noses.

Aunt Patti took me into each stall, told me the name of each horse and answered every question I could think to ask. By the time we had made it all the way around, Aunt Patti could tell I liked the Paint horses best. Perhaps she could have predicted that!

After the tour, Aunt Patti asked me which horses we should ride that day. That question meant we had to go around a second time. I was happy to be making such an important decision.

For Aunt Patti, I picked Cheyenne. Aunt Patti told me that was a great choice, and that Cheyenne was Nana's favorite horse.

For myself I picked Dunder. I wanted to pick Navajo, by far the most handsome horse, in my opinion, but I had been told that because I was only seven years old, I wasn't old enough to ride him yet.

Aunt Patti left me in the hall of noses while she got our horses brushed, bridled and saddled. It took a little longer than expected because Terry and Dick had riders heading out at 11:30. I visited with the horses along the hall of noses, and then I explored the big attached barn.

I opened one door. It led to a huge room filled to the brim with freshly cut rectangular bales of hay. Another day I would have to come back and explore that part of the barn.

I opened the second door. That room was very long and narrow, and the roof wasn't very high even for a short kid like me. The tack room was enormous, and had as many saddles in it as there were horses in the barn, except some of the saddles were missing from their posts. Those saddles were sitting on horses, and ready for the next ride. Since it was a Monday, about half of the horses were left rider-ready for the day. Dick was heading out with four beginners and Terry was headed out with three experts.

I opened the third door. It was a fairly small room, with a big grain bin to the right side as you walked in, and another door to the left. I opened the grain bin, and grabbed a little handful. Dave Reiner walked into the grain room just as I was smelling the grain.

Dave playfully pushed my head into the grain in my hand. It's a little known fact that cowboys of all ages tend to be pranksters.

Dave asked, "Why don't you try a bite?"

It smelled pretty good, so I thought, "Why not?" I took a little nibble. Not bad. Kind of plain. "It might be good with milk and sugar," I said. I tried another little nibble. Maybe some cinnamon would improve it!

Dave Reiner laughed and hooted and hollered so much and generally made such a big deal about me eating the grain that it actually made me want to eat more of it. It became my thing. It made me feel unique among the cowboys, and it made me feel like I was a part of the inside jokes, though I was plainly the butt of that joke.

Dave went out the door across from the grain bin, and I went back into the pole barn. Aunt Patti had the horses ready. She told me to follow Dave out the grain room door, and we would meet out by the front gate.

For many summers, Aunt Patti had put me on the backs of various horses and led me around. The previous summer I rode around the ring on Blueboy. Blueboy was a tall, mostly white, dapple-gray horse with a silver mane. He was the oldest horse in the string, and despite his height, Blueboy was the wrangler's first choice for beginning riders, even the smallest of children.

That was the first summer I was getting to ride on my own, while Aunt Patti rode a horse of her own. We started out on a long lead rope. Dave Reiner opened the pasture gate, and Aunt Patti led us out the gate, down the foot path that connected Paleface Lodge and the Dude Ranch and we crossed Route 86. Patti led us down a slight hill into the parking lot. We crossed it diagonally and went up a trail that led into the woods.

Now that we were away from the road, the parking lot, people and the cars Aunt Patti jumped off Cheyenne and asked me if I wanted her to take the lead rope off. Of course, I said, "You bet!"

Dunder was a seasoned professional dude hauler. He knew to follow the lead horse. Although he was the most decorated show horse, and the second most decorated gymkhana horse Dunder knew the expert rider from the amateur, and Dunder knew the show ring from the trail.

Dunder was fun to ride on the trail because he seemed to be interested in everything. He walked with his head held high, and often turned it left or right. You could see Dunder's eyes when he turned his head. He was attentive to every move a rider made and his surroundings as well. It made you want to turn to see what had caught Dunder's eyes. Many of the trail horses walked with their heads held lower, kind of sleepwalking through their work day, trudging along at a slow plodding pace. Dunder and Cheyenne had good quick walking gates. It seemed they were as happy to be on the trail as we were.

I asked question after question, and chattered nonstop the whole way. Aunt Patti led us up one ski trail and down another. To me it felt like we had gone miles and miles. In fact, we really hadn't gone that far, just zigging and zagging our way across the mountain—up the Paleface Trail to the Tenderfoot Glade, almost all the way up to the Smoke Rise Lookout, then back down the Walter Prager Trail, cutting across the access trail to ride down the Brave Trail for a while before heading back up again on the Cross Trail, then the Teepee Trail to the Big Rock Mid Station before riding back down the Peace Pipe Trail, taking a diversion along the Long Trek Trail, which offered the best views of Whiteface Mountain.

After a while, we came to a patch of wild blueberry bushes near the edge of the forest where the woods gave way to the wide, cultivated Lower Big Horn ski trail, just a little below the point where the Long Trek Trail merged into the Lower Big Horn ski trail. It was a little past blue berry season really, but there were still enough blueberries to sweeten the pallet before lunch time. While we ate blueberries, Dunder and Cheyenne snacked on grass.

A short while later, we were back on the horses. We followed the Big Horn trail almost back to the base, before leaving the ski trail near the far end of the parking lot and around the base of the mountain. Aunt Patti got off and opened a gate for us. About a hundred yards further the path led to a perfect, sweet spot right at the foot of Paleface Mountain.

There was a big rectangular rock. The shape of that rock was perfect for a picnic. With Paleface just behind us, and a wide open clearing in front of us we had another splendid view of Whiteface Mountain. That part of the valley had become known as Paleface Flats, though some people called it Haselton Flats.

Aunt Patti tied the horses to a tree, which was almost unnecessary considering we had two of the gentlest, friendliest horses with us. They would far rather be with us than to run away from us. There was little chance Dunder or Cheyenne would bolt.

We enjoyed the picnic Nana had packed for us. We ate a little bit of everything there was. There was so much food, there wasn't a chance we could eat it all. It was fun being able to sit on the picnic table you were eating off of—the rock was that big!

Aunt Patti told me that it was her favorite spot at Paleface. "Every direction you look you see something different. And the view in every direction is beautiful. And from here you can't see anybody else. It's just you and me and the great outdoors." Aunt Patti smiled. "It feels like Paleface Mountain was put here just to admire Whiteface, don't you think? Here we are, in the shadow of a giant!" Aunt Patti's right arm gestured toward the magnificent mountain.

"Aren't we lucky, Aunt Patti?" I said, attempting to wink back at Aunt Patti, first with one eye and then the other. "Someday I would like to own this piece of land right here. Do you think I could, Aunt Patti?"

"Maybe if you work hard, and save all your money!"

Soon we were full, and I was ready to get back on the horses. We left everything on the rock and rode out further into the clearing.

"Can we run, Aunt Patti?" I pleaded.

"Sure. Let's give it a try!"

We were in the pasture where the horses spent most of the winter. There was plenty of room for us to ride side by side. Aunt Patti told me what to expect, what would happen, and to hold on tightly to the saddle horn. We were riding close enough that when Aunt Patti made the "click, click" sound and squeezed her legs to signal Cheyenne, Dunder responded as well and both horses trotted. To make that click, click sound, I had been taught to close my lips tightly on one side, and open my mouth wide for a big smile on the other, then I put my tongue along my teeth on the open side, near the roof of my mouth, and made a click by creating a vacuum between my tongue and the roof of my mouth.

I giggled and then I laughed out loud. I yelled into the wind, "This is the best day of my whole life!"

Aunt Patti hollered, "Hold on tighter, tighter, tighter!" Another click, click sound and both horses fell into the rhythmic loping gate that riders most enjoy. A bit faster than a trot, not as fast as a full on gallop, but fast enough to make me feel like I was a feather bouncing along on a brisk breeze. And fast enough that my brand new hat flew off.

I panicked, and shouted. Aunt Patti looked over, smiling. Then she noticed right away my hat was gone. Patti gently slowed Cheyenne's gate to a trot and then a walk, and Dunder followed in turn. "Don't worry, David," Aunt Patti reassured. "We'll get that hat back, it's just a little way back!"

Of course, if Aunt Patti said so, I knew it was true. Now that we were back to walking, I couldn't stop smiling, ear-to-ear. Dunder had loped and I stayed on. It was an awesome fun feeling, and yet deliciously dangerous too. I wanted to do it again. In fact, riding running horses non-stop all summer long, every summer, would suit me fine.

After we found my hat, we walked the horses back to picnic rock. As we packed the picnic goods back into the saddle bags I said, "Aunt Patti, I have a secret to tell you. I love you more than anybody body else in the whole wide world. *Don't tell anybody.* It will just be our secret!"

Aunt Patti said, "That's funny, I was just about to tell you I love you more than anybody else in the whole wide *universe*."

We agreed that we wouldn't tell anyone about our secret, and then we wouldn't tell anybody what it was. Of course, I loved my Mommy more than anybody else in the whole wide world too. What little Momma's boy doesn't? But the fact remained, I could just never get enough of Aunt Patti!

The saddlebags were loaded onto the backs of the horses and we headed back the way we came. Not far up the path, Aunt Patti turned on to a different path and led us up the Papoose Trail. That trail led all the way up to what I thought was the top of the mountain. Finally, we arrived at the Smoke Rise lookout, the warming station that allowed skiers to warm up a little bit on cold days before skiing down the mountain.

We tied the horses to the railing and went inside. Aunt Patti pulled out a deck of cards and we played a few rounds of Go Fish.

I always won. Aunt Patti was an expert reverse cheater! I was just about to win the second game when Aunt Patti noticed the horses seemed agitated.

"What's happening, Aunt Patti," I said quickly, worried. "Is it werewolves?"

"I don't think so."

By the time we got to the door, the horses were nearing a state of panic. "Stay here until I come back," she said, quickly and seriously. "You can watch through these windows."

Just then, a huge bear ran behind the horses and off into the woods. It made so much noise crashing into the branches of the trees, it sounded like the trees were falling over. Both horses had run off down the hill back toward Paleface. Aunt Patti had tied them very loosely, not expecting anything like that to happen.

I was frozen in awe. The bear had passed close enough I saw his huge fingers. His giant claws. All summer long I had worried about werewolves. Maybe I should worry instead about bears, I thought.

Aunt Patti made it better by exalting, "Wasn't that wonderful? Some people never get to see a bear. We got a close up view! What an animal!"

"What's that smell?" I asked. We walked out the door to the Smoke Rise Look Out.

"You can smell him?" asked Aunt Patti. "Kids can smell better than adults. And horses can smell bears too! That's how they knew he was coming."

"How are we going to get the horses back?"

"We might have to walk," she said. "But let me give something a try." She let out a whistle, like some men did when a pretty woman walked by. Dunder was just within range and remembered his training. Aunt Patti kept whistling and Dunder turned toward the whistle. Cheyenne followed Dunder.

Aunt Patti laughed, "Looks like we won't have to walk down the mountain."

I was amazed. "I thought that only happened on television!" I exclaimed. Of course, I had seen many re-runs of *The Lone Ranger*!

"You're right, David. it's not every horse that can do that. Dunder has many special talents." I was in awe of Dunder, and so proud to have picked him that day.

On the way down, Aunt Patti told me that the bear was famous at Paleface. Everyone called him Slewfoot. You could tell it was him by the way he ran. Aunt Patti talked of him fondly all the way down the mountain. The more she talked, the more my fear of bears evaporated. By the time we made it down the mountain, I was so un-afraid of Slewfoot the bear that it might as well have been a teddy bear we saw that afternoon.

Old Slewfoot ambled down the mountain that afternoon, and must have been headed somewhere important when he took a notion to cross the street. As luck would have it, Anna Otto who lived in a small cabin had just crossed the road to her mailbox when Slewfoot broke out of the heavy woods near her cabin.

Anna told the story like this. "Was I scared of that big old bear? Heck, no! He doesn't want me. I'm much too skinny."

Anna Otto stood her ground, just like an old-time pioneer woman. Anna weighed all of 100 pounds, and Old Slewfoot was 400 pounds of muscle, flesh, fur, and claws.

Anna stood in the middle of Route 86 with her mail in one hand, her other hand on her hip staring down the bear. The bear stood between Anna and her cabin. And then all at once the bear thunder-limped across the highway.

About three yards was all that separated Anna and Old Slewfoot. And Anna boasted that she didn't so much as bat an eye-lash. Anna Otto's account of her bear encounter was so compelling it became a local legend, and it was carried by newspapers as far away as Pennsylvania.

The rest of our ride down the mountain was un-eventful, but quite enjoyable. If it were up to me, I would have ridden non-stop across the country and back with Aunt Patti that day. Before it was over, I wanted to go again. "We'll go again real soon," Aunt Patti reassured.

When we got back to the barn, I gave Dave Reiner the update, all in one breath, as fast as I could. Old Slewfoot had returned from teddy bear status to towering menace again.

When I finished the story, my mind wandered off. I was busy fantasizing that I had rancher parents instead of hippie parents. Earlier in the summer I had read Mary O'Hara's trilogy of books that started with *My Friend Flicka*, continued with *Thunderhead* and concluded with *Green Grass of Wyoming*. Reading those books made me feel envious of Ken, the main human character of the books.

When my mind returned to the present world, Dave Reiner was saying something about giving me a ride in the honey wagon. He must have said something important, and I must have neglected to respond to it. I said, "I'll take a ride in the honey wagon if you can go really, really fast!"

Dave Reiner laughed, and then said, "Maybe tomorrow. It's been a long day."

Aunt Patti returned from putting the horses in the barn just in time to hear me say to Dave, "Yes, maybe tomorrow. I'm free tomorrow, you know!"

The next day it rained. It wasn't a heavy rain. All day long it seemed like it would stop at any time, but it never did. If the cowboys had known that it was going to rain all day, they would have closed up and left. Instead they played cards in the office.

I curled up in the manger at the front of Dunder's stall and read a book from cover to cover. The book was called *The Trumpet of the Swan* by E.B. White. The main character in the book, Louis the Swan was from Montana, just like Terry Dohrmann and Dave Reiner.

Over the course of the next couple of days, I got to spend the afternoons at the barn. If Aunt Patti was leading a beginner's ride, I got to go along as well. Most afternoons I got the chance to go on the 1pm ride and the 3:30 ride.

When I wasn't on the trail, I was left to entertain myself along the hall of noses. Most of the horses didn't mind me climbing into their hay manger. Perhaps it was because I brought small handfuls of grain from the grain bin, which I was happy to share with the horses. Perhaps it was because the cowboys went to the trouble of making sure the friendly horses were parked in stalls along the hall of noses, and the kickers, biters, stompers, and squashers were parked in stalls along the opposite side of the barn.

## '69 Paleface Potpourri

One afternoon, after I got tired of reading, I thought about how Paleface smelled different from anywhere else I knew of.

I was curled up in my makeshift sofa at the front end of Dunder's stall, a furnishing that only a 7 year old child would think of as comfortable. Dunder seemed to like the company, sometimes nibbling around me for small scraps of hay. Other times, he nuzzled me, perhaps to see if I might like to brush him, or rub between his ears. I liked to gently pet the unbelievably soft tip of his nose, which felt like a satin pillowcase. Dunder seemed to like it when I would breath heavily into his enormous nostrils. I had read in a book that was how Indians created unbreakable bonds with their horses. I spent lots of time with Dunder in his stall. I was a great conversationalist, and he was an equally good listener.

Another hour left behind, too busy for me to tag along with the wranglers and dudes. So I asked Dunder how I could describe the smell of a horse to someone who had never smelled a horse. He didn't make any suggestions, so I thought out loud. I really missed the smell of Paleface when I was back home.

Nana left petite balsam pillows here and there, and replaced them periodically whenever they seemed to weaken. Not just in the guest rooms, but on the coffee tables, end tables, and any old un-occupied nook, knothole, or cranny. I thought about the story of Johnny Appleseed, and also the story of Hansel and Gretel. Nana's breadcrumbs and apple seeds were balsam pillows. What if I could make one of those little pillows, but make it smell like Paleface? What would I put in it? A horse for sure.

Then I thought about how I could lasso the smell of horse. I thought it was a happy smell, easy to recognize, yet hard to describe. I buried my face into Dunder's neck, and breathed deeply. One of the cowboys had told me that each horse had its own distinct smell, and that horses were products of their environments. So that meant that horses smelled like lots of different things. I tried to think of all the smells that reminded me of horses. I thought of dry hay stored in the lofts of barns on sweltering hot, early August afternoons. I thought of green hay, the first of several cuttings from a warm day, late in the month of May. I thought of the ground, the very dirt itself, picked up from a good roll on the packed soil. I thought of the grain, sweetened with a touch of molasses. I thought of the stuffing at Thanksgiving, the combination of roasted chestnuts and sage. I thought about scraping the sweat off the horses' necks when they returned from a long ride on the advanced trails. Then I thought about adding a little bit of horse poop to my imaginary pillow. I giggled to think about putting sweat and poop in a pillow. Dunder didn't mind my outburst of laughter, and wasn't fazed by it at all. I wondered if everybody thought horse poop smelled nice, or whether it was just me and Dunder who felt that way.

Next, I thought about the kitchen and dining room at Paleface. It was different depending on what time of day it was. In the morning, the sweet citrus scent of fresh squeezed orange juice, real—not imitation maple syrup, the strong salty savory smell of bacon and eggs frying on melted Crisco, and percolating coffee. Mixed in with the smells of breakfast, the sweet and doughy smells of pies and pastries baking away for use later in the day. The smell of fresh baked bread wafting out from the kitchen was enough to make you want to grab a stick of butter and have a feast. In the afternoon, the smell of the fryer boiling potatoes into crispy, crunchy, golden French fries and burgers on the grill that hours before cooked bacon, eggs, and pancakes replaced the breakfast smells. In the evening the smell of thick steaks sizzling over charcoal that had been ignited by a heavy saturation of lighter fluid to start, plus the combination of wine and mushrooms, and the combination of wine, whiskey, and coffee that often was part of the dinner meals at Paleface. The bar near the jukebox had its foul, boozy scent, forgiven and overlooked since it invoked the feeling of being at Paleface.

Some smells hung around Paleface in all the seasons, and at all times of the day. Unmistakably, Paleface smelled like leather. It's hard to imagine that smell traveled from the barn all the way across the street, so it probably wasn't just the hides the horses were still wearing, or their saddles and tack. There was a small saddle on a saw horse that stood just between the dining room and the cocktail lounge. Kids like me posed for pictures on an unseen horse, fully saddled, with an authentic Hudson Bay striped blanket underneath, and the A-Framed wooden girders made an attractive backdrop. One saddle probably wasn't enough to make the strong leather smell. The smell of leather couldn't possibly come from the false Naugahyde and pleather coverings of the chairs in the lounge. Perhaps the mounted deer, elk, and caribou heads on the walls together with the chemicals used to preserve them made an aromatic contribution. It could have been Grampa's leather chair in the office, seldom seen by kids or customers. One way or another, Paleface definitely smelled like leather.

Another perennial, prominent Paleface collection of smells were the woodsy ones: Balsam, cedar, pine, even wet moss, and decomposing leaves lying on the forest floor. Some of that smell came naturally from the woods outside of Paleface, of course. The natural scent was fortified with a heavy dose of bleach and pine scented cleaners plus air fresheners, applied liberally every day in effort to mask the ever-present smell of cigarette smoke. In those days people smoked indoors, and not just in the bar or in the evening.

In addition to the smells that could be found every day, some smells were more seasonal. In the winter, the smell of melted paraffin which was the key ingredient in most brands of ski wax, and even the almost imperceptible smell of snow added to the stew of smells. An expert snow maker could tell you that machine made snow smelled different from its exact chemical equal, the snow that came from the sky. And the snow smelled different at 30 degrees below zero than it did at 30 degrees above zero.

Finally, there was often a floral palette of perfumes at Paleface as well. In the spring time, Jean brought lily of the valley and purple lilacs from home, and daffodils as well. In the summer, roses could often be found in vases on each table. Sometimes wildflowers, including daisies, black-eyed Susan's and purple cone-flowers were on the table. Sometimes, Jean would pick up some gardenia from the florist particularly when a more formal event was planned.

The smell at Smoke Rise Lookout came from parties and cookouts. Just like a backyard barbecue, corn on the cob, hot dogs, hamburgers, and steaks sizzling on the grill. Beyond the lounge was the game room, where you could smell the chalk for the pool table's cue sticks, and the smell of chlorine from the swimming pool beyond the game room.

On sunny spring days, skiers relaxing on the deck would apply Coppertone lotion to avoid sunburns, and that had a nice strong beachy smell. So, I thought I should add a little Coppertone to my pillow.

I chuckled to myself to think of putting balsam needles, horse poop, maple syrup, and suntan lotion in a pillow. Maybe, I thought, if it were all boiled up it could be made into a perfume or a candle. The more I thought about it, it wasn't really like the smells were all stirred together, but rather each smell was kind of stacked in very thin layers, just blowing around in the breeze, combining almost randomly like songs played from the jukebox full of records from a variety of genres. Then I thought, maybe someday somebody would invent that, a jukebox for smells.

I got so tired thinking about the smell of Paleface, I dozed off briefly. I woke up a little later and the only sound I could hear was the sound of horses munching hay. I noticed that when that was the only sound being made, it sounded incredibly loud. I wondered whether the sound of munching hay was the same as the sound of munching grain. Who knows how long I would have thought about the sounds of Paleface, except for the fact that it hit me all of a sudden that I was starving, and the thought of Nana's German chocolate cake moved to the front and center of my mind.

## '69 Comfortable in the Saddle

By the time a week had gone by, I was as comfortable in the saddle on the back of Dunder as I was walking across the floor. I had mastered staying in the saddle, even during a bumpy trot. I had gotten good at using the reins to direct my horse in whichever direction I wanted him to go. I had learned not to let my horse eat grass while we were riding.

I had also learned a little trick. Aunt Patti, as the professional wrangler, always rode in the front. Half the time it seemed her body was twisted around so she was almost riding backwards, making sure all the riders in the chain were accounted for and their horses were behaving themselves. Sometimes I could hold my horse back long enough to put a little distance between me and Aunt Patti. Then I could kick my horse and make him run a little bit to catch up.

One afternoon I tried my little trick as the horses were entering the small roundup pasture just outside the pole barn. I picked the wrong time to do that! The head wrangler, Terry Dohrmann saw me. Foreman Dohrmann really gave me the business. Terry Dohrmann said it was not safe to run the horses on the way into the barn. They were already in a hurry to get to their water and hay. If the horses got trained to run to the barn they'd be ruined, and wouldn't be able to work at Paleface anymore because it wouldn't be safe for the guests to have a horse take off for the barn like that.

Terry made a lot of sense. I never did that again.

But the next afternoon, business was a little slow. When there were no guests, the cowboys did chores. The chore for that afternoon was haircuts for horses. It was a lot of work every day to brush and clean the horses. Because the guests would all want pictures of themselves on the horses, the horses had to be looking their best at all times.

So rather than comb the horses' manes all the time, most of the horses got haircuts. Usually a little bit was left at the bottom of the mane, by the saddle horn. From there the clippers trimmed the horses' manes all the way up to the forelock, between the horses' ears.

The horses went for their haircuts in pairs. They got their haircuts on the back side of the lodge, which is to say the side that didn't face Whiteface Mountain.

Next up was Tomahawk (also known as Tommy and Tom interchangeably) and Pepsi, two of the fastest horses in the Paleface string. On the way to their haircuts Terry rode Tommy and Dave Reiner rode Pepsi. Dave Reiner had it in his mind that Pepsi had a lot of potential as a gymkhana horse, in fact, Dave Reiner claimed, "Pepsi might be faster than Tom."

Of course, cowboys could be very competitive, and also very loyal and Terry was both. Tomahawk was the top Gymkhana horse for several years running. Terry wasn't about to let his friend Dave Reiner, or Pepsi for that matter, beat Tomahawk in a race.

After both horses had gotten their haircuts, and after they had walked the horses through the parking lot and across the highway, the race was on. It was a very short distance all in all, but that matter needed to be settled at once.

Pepsi kept up well, no doubt about it. For a brief flash even, Pepsi was in the lead. But neither Terry nor Tommy were having any of it. As Terry and Tommy passed through the gate, Terry leaned forward further and kicked Tommy harder and Tommy bolted. As the entrance to the barn approached, Tommy turned to the left a little sooner than Terry expected. Terry flew off. Tomahawk won the race, without his rider.

Terry broke his arm against the wall of the pole barn.

It wasn't good, that's for sure. Dave Reiner had to take Terry to the Doctor to get the broken arm set in a cast. To make matters worse, there's lots of work Terry wouldn't be able to do with a broken arm, which meant double chores for his friend Dave. It hadn't occurred to either Terry or Dave until they got back and saw Aunt Patti laughing at them that there was a honey wagon load of irony in the situation.

Aunt Patti reminded the boss that it wasn't prudent to run the horses to the barn. I wasn't there to see it, but I had to admire Terry Dohrmann the next day when he told me all about it and said he should yell at himself. Then Terry let me write my name on his cast.

It seemed like we had just arrived but two weeks were on the verge of ending very quickly. My parents had long since returned from their respective road trips. In a short couple of weeks, I had gone from a lead rope led kid rider to a fully confident, independent junior wrangler. Whenever I thought about returning home I got sad, so I put off thinking about it. That didn't stop it from coming though, and the last night of vacation was upon us.

## '69 Engagements

We got to go for a swim at the Paleface pool, exactly twenty minutes after eating dinner. I enjoyed my usual chicken in a basket, my favorite kids choice on the Paleface dinner menu.

At the pool, Aunt Patti told me she wanted me to meet somebody special.

Vince Smith met us at about 8pm and changed into an old pair of swimming trunks. I thought he seemed nice enough, until I learned that Aunt Patti wasn't going to marry me when I grew up, she was going to marry Vince someday. Someday soon. I was asked not to tell anyone. It was a secret. And I was part of it. I was the only one who knew. Nana didn't know. Grampa didn't know. Just us.

About a half an hour later Aunt Patti's friend Maureen White joined us at the pool. The cowboy from Montana, Dave Reiner was with her. Then I found out that Maureen and Dave Reiner were going to get married also.

Shortly after Maureen and Dave arrived, Nana relieved Aunt Patti and the rest of the young adults from entertaining me and my brother and sister. We went back to Jay with Nana. Patti, Vince, Maureen, and Dave Reiner finished their swim and spent the evening square dancing at Paleface. Our parents also remained at Paleface for the evening.

The next day we returned to Rhode Island. I wore my new hat and boots the whole way home.

Maureen and Dave were married on September 13th and Patti and Vince eloped the following Saturday, September 20th.

## '69 Tenth Anniversary

Doc and Jean liked the young man who married their daughter. Patti and Vince seemed very happy and had settled in a small apartment in AuSable Forks, the next town over. With the children now undeniably grown and gone from the house, Doc was in a reflective mood. Taking stock, he took out a piece of paper and penned a new press release.

Though the article jumped the gun by a year, and a couple months as well, Doc felt warm and satisfied putting the words to paper.

*Press release:*

*Nine years ago the lumberjacks were felling trees and burning brush. Bulldozing, dynamiting, seeding and trail grooming was in high gear. The construction crew of Torrance and Trumbull was making like crazy with the giant A-Frame beams for the Lodge.*

*Well, time has flown by. We, at Paleface, feel proud of these nine years. A lot has been accomplished.*

*Somehow, someway, each one of you who reads this review is a part of the on-going, creative and re-creative life of Paleface. YOU have helped us to bring something special, something personal and friendly. Something unique, real and permanent to the North Country.*

*How the Paleface family has grown! Many people and things have been added since this time nine years ago, since that day when Kay and Bill Eldred broke the bottle of champagne on that first chair lift tower.*

*A FEW ITEMS AT RANDOM:*

*A new indoor swimming pool, complete with insulated building, dressing rooms and heating units was added.*

*Eight new AAA quality motel units were built.*

*A snow-making machine insulated water building housing a 23,500-gallon water tank, 300 foot well and special pumps, was installed and set in operation*

*Night skiing under flood lights became a regular feature. We have added more new lights this year.*

*A large patio with sun-deck and glass walls was added.*

*The Big Horn Upper Mountain with its T-Bar and Expert Trails gave Paleface a range of terrain for all abilities.*

*Parking lots have been tripled. Trail grooming and widening continues each year.*

*An additional 320-acre Dude Ranch came into being with some twenty horses and tack, stables, tack-rooms and pastures. Our five cowboys and cowgirls have won well over 400 ribbons and trophies over the years and Paleface Dude Ranch can boast some of the best gymkhana horses and riders in the North Country. Paleface Dude Ranch is "The Best West in the East."*

*A network of thirty miles of bridle trails, doubling in the winter as snowmobile trails has been established, with the generous cooperation of good neighbors like AuSable Acres, Ward Lumber Company, Haselton Lumber Company, Albert Peck and the late Mrs. John Peck, Gux Maxon and others.*

*Paleface has been honored with approved membership in three fine organizations: The American Automobile Association, the Eastern Ski Area Operators Association and the Eastern Dude Ranches Association.*

*A Paleface Ski Club of ninety members sponsors junior racing.*

*A Paleface Ski-Mobile Club of sixty families adds its own festive fun all through the winters.*

*Our winter house guest roster now includes over 600 families, friends and patrons from all over the North Country, Eastern U.S. and Canada.*

*The Paleface Ski School program, launched by Karl Jost and more recently enlarged by Putzi Jost, has grown fantastically over the years. It now includes some 400 pupils from Keene and Keene Valley Schools, Jay and Upper Jay Schools, the AuSable Forks Rotary Club School program, the Keeseville School, the Willsboro-Essex Kiwanis Club School program, Plattsburgh University faculty and student groups, Miner Institute, Plattsburgh Air Force Base, Camp Poke-O-Moonshine and other groups.*

*Because of our excellent teaching staff, and because of our confidence building terrain and trails, Paleface has helped in the development of hundreds of accomplished skiers, including top-flight racers and certified ski pros.*

*Over the years, Paleface has been fortunate to have had the loyal service of a friendly and dedicated staff averaging between fifty and sixty North Country people many of whom have been with us since the beginning.*

*Yes, in the North Country, our closest neighbor, Whiteface is deservedly "the Big One." But just as surely Paleface has become "The Biggest Little One." In winter, Paleface is the North Country's favorite "Winter Country Club", a great little mountain with truly recreational skiing. Paleface is "The Family Fun Place", where "Everybody Knows Everybody!"*

*So, on the eve of our tenth anniversary, Paleface invites you to celebrate with us! Here's to a wonderful tenth winter for all of us – and to Family Fun Skiing at its Best!*

*As always, yours,*
*Aunt Jean and Uncle Doc Fitz-Gerald*
*Paleface Ski Center*
*Route 86*
*Jay, N.Y.*

## '70 Doc Has a Heart Attack

Just after the holidays, and ringing in a new decade Doc had a heart attack.

Everyone was surprised since Doc always seemed so robust, energetic, vital, and healthy. Of course, everyone who knew Doc thought he had a big heart, however the doctor's diagnosis of an enlarged heart didn't sound like it was intended to be a compliment.

After the better part of a month away, Doc was released from the Saranac General Hospital on the 10th day of February. It was the heart of the winter ski season. Doc returned to Paleface without even stopping at home.

The doctors had ordered a strict new diet. It was recommended that Doc quit smoking, and limit alcohol to one per day. Another recommendation was that he assume a normal sleeping schedule rather than staying up half the night and sleeping through the morning hours. Finally, the doctors insisted Doc limit his work schedule to a couple of hours per day. For the next month, the doctors recommended that he not work at all, and he should rest a lot and take short leisurely walks a couple times a day.

While Doc was in the hospital, the Assistant Director of Paleface's ski school Pete Pelkey was lured from Paleface to Whiteface. Pete had a friendly and fun manner that disarmed the fears of beginning skiers so that they could learn to ski. Pete was one of the most popular instructors, and one of the busiest. Putzi Jost, the director of the ski school, needed a new Assistant Director.

Putzi took stock. Her ski school staff had many, many instructors but when it came down to it there weren't that many who worked full time. Most had other part time jobs, full time jobs, or were students. She could pick the instructor with the longest tenure. She could pick the instructor who was the best skier.

One busy afternoon after the lifts had closed, the instructors were at the bar interacting with the day's skiing public. Après-ski at the bar was part of the job, forming a lasting relationship in hopes of stimulating repeat customers.

Putzi was observing Patti Smith, formerly Patti Fitz-Gerald. Though she hadn't thought about it seriously before, it dawned on Putzi that nobody was better at connecting with the skiing public, except for Pete Pelkey... and nobody was more dedicated, willing to drop everything to show up on a moment's notice and work every minute available, except for Putzi herself, than Patti.

Putzi was accustomed to blazing trails. Who should follow in her footsteps? What if Paleface had not only a woman Director of the Ski School, but also Assistant Director? Momentarily alone at the bar with her drink, Putzi asked for a second drink, lit a smoke, and thought about it some more. Would it be too weird to promote the bosses' daughter to be her second in charge? Would the other instructors resent it? Putzi thought for a couple minutes more, her steely resolve thickened. She had made the decision.

But the decision had to be approved by her boss, or at least not vetoed. Although it was a strange way to organize a reporting structure, Putzi's boss, the owner of Paleface, Doc Fitz-Gerald was also a ski instructor, so Putzi was also Doc's boss!

Doc was in the hospital and didn't need to be bothered with any kind of intrigue. By the time Doc returned to Paleface, Putzi had made the decision, implemented it, and Patti had three weeks under her belt as Assistant Director of the Paleface Ski School, and Patti still found time to visit Doc in the hospital every day.

When Doc learned about it on his return, he told Putzi he was proud that she made a great decision, and didn't wait for him to do it. Doc told Patti he was proud of her promotion. When the boss's daughter gets a promotion in a family owned business, perhaps people tend to grumble or criticize. The fact was, Patti worked as hard, if not harder and with more determination, than anyone else and Doc required her to prove herself more than other Paleface employees, not less.

In fact, several times Patti had been passed over for promotion at the barn. Doc had remained committed to the idea of having a cowboy as the head wrangler at Paleface, not a cowgirl. Having been inspired by Putzi's decision, and getting swept away in the moment, and with his heart condition weighing somewhat on his mind, Doc promoted Patti to head wrangler for the dude ranch, completely without warning, planning, or discussion.

Nobody cared more about the horses, or the riding public. Just as Patti had been the most reliable ski instructor, Patti was also at the barn every day it was open, even on the occasional summer day off it seemed. Though Patti was short, she was strong for her size. From a physical standpoint, Patti did all the work the cowboys did, and then some. And the other cowboys respected Patti, not because she was the bosses' daughter but because of work ethic and skill with horses.

Patti's new job couldn't start for several months, however. It was the middle of February! That gave Patti a few months to think about and plan for how the dude ranch might be different in the coming summer.

Most of Patti's thinking about dude ranch operations happened when she found herself alone on the chairlift. It didn't take more than a day after being named head wrangler to decide she wanted to make some personnel changes. In fact, no less than five changes! As she thought about it, she came to realize that some of the guys were just hanging around all day eating, and taking up space, not doing their fair share. It was time for them to move along. Of course, Patti was thinking about some of the horses in the string, not her fellow wranglers and co-workers. First on Patti's list was Comanche.

Comanche had the requisite Paleface Pinto markings, sorrel and white. He was stout, maintaining his peak spring weight even through the winters. The problem was, he was mean. Comanche was the horse most likely to bite the wranglers when he was being saddled or brushed. Comanche was the horse most likely to kick someone if they walked too close behind his stall. And short as he was, Comanche was the horse most likely to escape. On more than one occasion, Comanche had figured out how to escape his stall and nudge open the grain bin. Comanche was round enough without the extra rations. To top it all off, Comanche wasn't very good at riding single file. Many times, Comanche tried to bite the butt of the horse in front of him, and kick the face of the horse behind him on the trail. No doubt about it, Comanche was first on Patti's hit list.

Also, Whiskey Joe had to go. Whiskey Joe was a dark brown horse, bordering on black with a very dark mane. Old Whiskey Joe was actually a wrangler favorite. Though he was older than most of the other horses, approaching twenty years he was very, very fast in short distances. In the earliest years, Whiskey Joe was able to compete in gymkhana events. In recent years, however Paleface acquired horses that were even faster. For the last couple of years Whiskey Joe had difficulty making it through a beginner's hour long trail ride, and didn't have it in him to go out on the trail more than once a day. Sadly, it was time to retire old Whiskey Joe.

Finally, Patti had decided Paleface should sell Whiteface. As could be the case, sometimes those high-profile mergers just don't work out the way they were expected to! Whiteface was a big, strong Paint horse with a big head. Whiteface didn't bear the markings of the typical Paleface Paint horse. Rather than the sorrel and white coloring, Whiteface was black, brown and white. There had been high hopes for Whiteface as a gymkhana horse, but he didn't seem to be able to develop the necessary agility. It was as if Whiteface was a standard size horse trapped in a large horse's body. Whether it was knocking over the poles when running the pole bending race or knocking over barrels when barrel racing, Whiteface just couldn't get comfortable in his skin. In fact, the most honest assessment of his gymkhana skills would be to say he was clumsy. Even if he couldn't make it as a gymkhana horse, there remained lots of opportunity on the trails, hauling the dudes up and down the trails. Unfortunately, the previous year, Whiteface had thrown a couple dudes off his back, no telling what possessed him to do so. Whiteface also had the habit of trying to lean on the wranglers when they came into his stall, as if to try and squeeze them against the wall. As one of the biggest horses in the string, getting flattened by Whiteface was most uncomfortable and very unnerving. Perhaps the biggest problem with Whiteface, ironically was that he didn't winter well.

If they could find some great replacements, there were a few other horses Patti had her eye on replacing. They may not have known it, but they were "on notice" during the summer of 1970. Like any great operations manager, Patti tracked in great detail the job performance of every member of the team.

The horses carried riders over 5,000 hours a summer, with most of those hours happening during July and August. Patti could tell from her log, on any given day exactly how many hours each horse had worked that summer. And Patti could tell how long it had been since any horse had a day off. Patti kept charts and graphs on each horse before computers made such depictions easy. The head wranglers from Montana had been happy to leave that record keeping up to Patti.

As the winter rolled on, Patti thought more and more about the dude ranch operations. What to change? What to improve? How could it be even better? Would the cowboys treat her differently now that she was in charge? Would the cowboys still threaten to give her a ride in the honey wagon—also known as wheelbarrow full of horse poop—as they often threatened to do? Would she treat the cowboys differently now that she was in charge?

Patti had to keep reminding herself it was still winter. There would be time to worry about the barn when the lifts closed.

## '70 Staff Meeting

By the time it was announced at the monthly staff meeting on the 6th of March, of course everyone knew that Patti had been named Assistant Director. Putzi noted with pride that Paleface not only had a woman Director of its Ski School, but a woman Assistant Director as well, not to mention a woman head wrangler.

After Patti's promotion was confirmed and affirmed, Doc said, "I'd like to share with you a note that we received last week from one of our regular guests, Mr. Emil Romagnoli, a Brazilian born printer from the Bronx. Actually, Mr. Romagnoli's note comes to us in the form of a poem, which also serves as a compliment to all of you that work hard here at Paleface to make our guest's stays something they'll always remember. Mr. Romagnoli titles this poem Paleface Inn."

*Where the northern breeze*
*cools the summer air*
*And the clouds float slowly by*
*Where mountains in the distance*
*Lend enchantment to the sky*
*Where the sunset casts its colors*
*at the close of the day*

*Where trails wind through the forest*
*and nature's creatures play*
*Where the White Birches mingle*
*with the Hemlock and the Fir*
*Where the river's mood changes*
*as winter's spell begins to stir*
*Where the aura lights prevail*
*as it spreads its cosmic ray*
*There Paleface sits, in nature's splendor*
*At the Inn I love to stay*

Doc took his time reading the poem, adding dramatic flair to his favorite words and phrases. More than a couple members of the Paleface staff were touched by the poem. Doc got a little choked up. Jean wiped a tear from the corner of her eye. Putzi smiled proudly.

Doc updated everyone on his medical condition. He was feeling much stronger after being back for several weeks, and doctor's orders were agreeing with him. He was following most of the orders, most of the time. While Doc portrayed confidence that he was making a full recovery, worry was evident on Jean's brow.

Jean announced changes to the breakfast menu. It would now include grapefruit and cottage cheese for those who wanted to set a good example. Doc joked about going back to sleeping until noon if that's what breakfast was going to be like.

It looked like a good winter season was poised to continue well into spring. Good for skiers, not so good for deer.

Dana and Albert Peck took turns telling the story of how the men from Paleface got to a deer in the meadows just as several feral dogs were closing in. Even domestic dogs seemed to take to chasing deer sometimes, most particularly in late winter. The snow was deep, the does were pregnant, hungry, and vulnerable. The doe that was saved by the men of Paleface was very fortunate. She fell in with the horses and ate some of their hay.

That season, there were reports of dogs killing deer in Willsboro, and Westport, and the Essex County Board of Supervisors ordered the agriculture commissioner to impose a quarantine, meaning people were forced to keep their dogs inside or on leash for twenty-four hours.

Of course, troubled deer and aggressive dogs weren't the only good sign of a hearty winter season. Jean told everyone that records were broken the past weekend. In addition to record crowds on the slopes, there were fifty riders arriving from the North Country Snowmobile Club and from the Black Mountain Snowmobile Club, all of which made for an extremely busy dinner service.

The staff discussed plans for the annual winter fun days planned for March 7-8, plus the dance and the crowning of the King and Queen as in years past. Plans were also reviewed for the Miss Paleface, 1970 contest event coming up quickly on the calendar. Doc told the staff he was hopeful the event would be popular and become an annual tradition. Doc also told everyone that David Yando had won the poster contest held in Miss Elaine Reilly's art class and that David Yando had won a $5 prize. Frank Sprague and Monica Lanzoni also won prizes for their submissions. Doc concluded, "All the posters you see around town feature David's artwork."

Jane told everyone, "Once again this year, the members of the Beta Tau fraternity from Clarkson College in Potsdam will be staying at the lodge April 25th and April 26th for their annual spring weekend. Between the students, their friends, and their faculty chaperones, we should expect about eighty people. Another event you'll want to make sure you have on your calendar," Jane continued, "is the AuSable Valley High School's Junior Prom which will be held Saturday May 16th."

Doc asked whether anyone had news they'd like to share, as was the tradition at the monthly staff meetings.

Pearl Pierce beamed with pride. Though she had mentioned it many times in the previous two weeks, Pearl had become a Great Grandma and couldn't stop talking about the baby who weighed seven pounds nine ounces. Pearl was proud of her granddaughter and her husband. While she was at it, Pearl also talked proudly about her grandson and was looking forward to his graduation from

Murray State College in Kentucky.

Jane told everyone that Dana and Jane's son Douglas had been chosen from among seventeen applicants to attend an international meeting of the Nazarene Young People's Society Institute in Colorado in July.

Dana told everyone, "My baby sister Natalie is getting married tomorrow."

Next Jane mentioned that their son Greg had been named to play the lead in the musical *The Sound of Music* which was being presented by the senior class at the Eastern Nazarene College. "We are looking forward to going to Wollaston, Massachusetts to see his performance and then visiting with my brother Deane and his family in Melrose, Massachusetts," Jane added. Of course everyone was aware of the 1965 movie starring Julie Andrews and Christopher Plummer. Greg had a big job to do, memorizing all those lines and learning all those songs.

With all the news fully shared, the meeting ended and everyone returned to their work. It was sure to be a busy weekend. It was one week into March, and there wasn't much evidence that spring was around the corner. There was lots of snow, lots of ice, and the temperature remained very cold.

One day in the newspaper, correspondent Clara Hazelton of Wilmington put it like this:

*Our snow keeps being renewed, one three inch fall and almost every day or night an inch or so. Ice conditions are bad. We have to drive the car to get to the post office or church. Both just across the street. The lawn is a ten-foot strip of solid smooth ice. Crows are being heard and that means the maple sugaring time is here. As leaders the birds are as hungry as ever and so interesting to watch. Any piece of paper or cardboard left loose out of doors has started its journey toward Lake Champlain. March is living up to its tradition of being a windy month. Trees and shrubs in sheltered sunny locations show unmistakable changes of color. The gold color of the poplars is the most noticeable.*

*Bird songs are more joyous and frequent and humans are anticipating an end to snow and ice. 'Think Snow' is definitely a discarded repudiated saying.*

Of course, anyone who worked at Paleface would never repudiate the saying, "Think snow!"

## '70 Writer's Club I

Clara Hazelton, the long-time correspondent for the local newspaper, had been talking about starting a writer's club for many years. Her gift shop and her newspaper duties kept her quite busy, but one day, she decided not to put it off any longer.

Clara was also a member of the Northland Rock and Mineral Club. Without her, that club might well have folded. Clara's boundless passion for the subject kept the club going, and her leadership brought in dozens of people that otherwise might never have known they had an interest in geology. Perhaps she could spark an interest in writing within the local community. News of the new club spread by word of mouth and also through Clara's weekly column.

Fifteen people showed up for the organizational meeting of the new club on the 15th of March, some out of curiosity, but most of them were serious about writing. A couple showed up by accident.

The accidental writers included Jean Fitz-Gerald and her friend Mary Wallace, who was at Paleface to judge the Miss Paleface Pageant that had generated a lot of local interest. Mary had accidentally shown up two hours early, and was visiting with her friend Jean over a cup of tea. Before they realized it, they had become surrounded by people arriving to attend the meeting of the club, and Clara opened the introductory meeting before Mary and Jean had a chance to excuse themselves.

Jean thought about her diary. It occurred to her that she had not been particularly diligent or frequent in making new diary entries.

Mary Wallace was already the co-author of one cook book. It had been in the back of Mary's mind to present the history of the town of Jay in the form of another cook book.

Preston Palmer had taken a couple writing classes at North Country Community College, and over the past couple of years he had finished a series of short stories. Working two jobs to support his family took most of Preston's time, and taking time to write his stories seemed selfish and self-indulgent, but most days Preston found at least half an hour to write. Since Preston Palmer's UFO encounter, and since reading science fiction books left at Paleface by Rosemary Robinson, Preston had expanded his writing from stories about Indians to science fiction as well. Now that he had a small son, Preston also took to writing for children. Like Mary Wallace and Jean Fitz-Gerald, Preston Palmer had been sitting at a table and got swept up into the club's organizational meeting.

Clara presented a page of club rules, a calendar of proposed meetings and pressed the attendees to join the club as charter members. It was agreed that the club would meet on the third Monday of each month from six to nine in the evening. "The next scheduled meeting is tomorrow," she concluded.

Clara asked Jean if they could meet at Paleface the next day. Jean nodded, and said, "Yes, we would be glad to have everyone back tomorrow!"

With no further business to be conducted, President Clara Hazelton adjourned the founding meeting of the North Country Writer's Club.

## '70 Miss Paleface, Jean Nye

While the Writer's Club met, the staff of Paleface had been busy decorating the bar and lounge area, transforming it to look like a television beauty pageant. The Indian blankets, longhorns, and the heads of the caribou, moose, elk, and deer had been covered by white sheets. Flowers, balloons, banners, crepe paper, and glitter formed the basic backdrop for the contest of the day.

About a hundred members of the local community came out to witness the pageant, most being friends and family members of the young ladies who were entered in the contest. Hotel guests and skiers who normally enjoyed après-ski in the lounge found themselves treated to a talent show.

Of course, instead of modeling swimsuits and evening gowns, the young ladies modeled parkas and fine warm fashions from the ski shop.

The centerpiece of the Miss Paleface 1970 Pageant was the talent show program. Most of the talent presentations were dances, including ballet dancing and tap dancing. There was a magic show and two baton twirling presentations. Several young ladies sang songs. One girl sang "Sweet Caroline" by Neil Diamond, and another sang Jackie DeShannon's hit song from the year before, "Put a Little Love in Your Heart."

Each girl received praise and jubilant feedback from judge Mary Wallace, widely known as Aunt Mary. Every girl got one of Aunt Mary's warm, fully engulfing hugs and one of Aunt Mary's joyful, affectionate, affirming smiles.

It was very hard for Aunt Mary and her fellow judge Frank Scsigulinsky to pick winners among the talented young ladies. In the end, they chose 16 year old Jean Nye of Upper Jay. Of course, she was very pretty, but it wouldn't have been possible to win the title of Miss Paleface 1970 without a very impressive showing in the talent competition. The runner up, 13 year old Carol Trumbull sang "Scarborough Fair," and played the guitar.

Jean Nye easily differentiated her talent performance from the much more traditional displays by demonstrating the first aid skills she had learned at a course she was taking in Plattsburgh. Lee Torrance played the role of victim, turning in a convincing performance himself. Inside of five minutes, Jean had applied a leg splint to Lee Torrance's fictional broken leg.

Miss Paleface 1970 received several nice prizes. In addition to a beautiful trophy, Jean Nye received a $25 gift certificate from the Ski Hut at Paleface, and a season lift ticket for the 1971 ski season. All in all, about a hundred people attended the Miss Paleface Pageant.

## '70 Writer's Club – II

Doc and Patti were preoccupied with delivering Patti's mare, Smugglers Amanda to stud, with hopes that a new member of the family would come along the following spring. Jean was far more focused on her thoughts about the Writer's Club meeting that evening. All day long, it was never far from her thoughts.

Most of the founding club members made it to the second meeting, and a few brought friends. The fledgling club was off to a fast start.

Over the course of the next three hours, Clara challenged the writers to several writing exercises.

First, Clara Hazelton asked everyone to write for thirty minutes about a friend. Everyone quietly wrote until Clara interrupted. "In the next minute or two, please finish your thoughts and then begin a second writing exercise. For your second exercise, I would like you to write about something you love to do."

For a moment, Mary Wallace touched her chin with the pink eraser at the top of her pencil and looked sideways into the corner where the ceiling met the wall, and then she was off and writing.

Mary wrote about her love for baking, and in her half hour recited some of her favorite recipes. Mary wrote about discovering legendary singer Kate Smith's recipe for Popovers in a cook book called Placid Eating by local author Climena M. Wikoff, founder of the Mirror Lake Inn in Lake Placid. Mary had a signed copy of the book that she purchased about ten years earlier. Kate Smith's recipe listed the ingredients and described how to combine them, what temperature to bake them at, and finally instructed: "After fifteen minutes open the oven door and slam it hard, then bake for fifteen minutes more."

Though Mary had the recipe memorized, whenever dinner plans called for popovers, she couldn't stop herself from opening the cook book and re-reading that part about slamming the oven door. It was as if Mary wanted to make sure it still said that! It always made her smile or laugh to think of it.

When Mary looked up, her half hour was only half over, so she wrote about her friend Bea Lincoln's recipe for oatmeal raisin cookies. It seemed that every North Country cook was known for at least one favorite dish, and Bea's cookies ranked up there with Mary's cakes and Pearl's pies.

As Mary finished writing, she chuckled to herself, or so she thought. It seemed everyone looked up at Mary, who was smiling.

"Oh my," said Mary, "it seems I forgot to have dinner tonight, and all I've been doing for the past half hour is writing about deserts!"

Everyone laughed. Clara asked if anyone would like to share something from their first or second writing exercise.

With a sly smile that belied her usual anything-but-sly nature, Jean raised her hand and read aloud:

> *Cakes... many are the cakes that Mary does bake, and many more she will... for hers is a talent she loves to share. She gives—and others take! What happiness Mary spreads in this community! Long before some little one comes along, his advent is heralded with a cake—cradle and all. How the mother–to–be can enjoy this cake, making her realize for sure a new life will join hers. Even before this, she remembers the gorgeous white creation of many tiers, topped by a bride and groom, surrounded by roses and bells for this joyous event—a true beginning. The Wedding! And later on the birthdays come and go—each one celebrated by the cake. It may be a clown, or a doll, or what about Raggedy Ann? For little boys there are cowboys, trains, and guitars. Later on, these same children are suddenly facing graduation! And there is a cake of course! And before you know it, the cycle starts all over... but now a silver or gold decked cake has joined the parade for Mom & Dad. These cakes are landmarks in a life! They are a trail of memories. Each one punctuates an event. God bless Mary.*

As her friend finished, a tear rolled down Mary's right cheek. The body language was unmistakable. Mary tucked her chin to her chest, tipped her head, and blinked both eyes. Mary deeply appreciated her friend's recognition. Jean had explained why Mary's hobby meant so much to both women.

Jean smiled. "It seems I forgot to have dinner also." And at that moment, Jean's stomach rumbled loudly enough that others heard.

As if he were introduced, Doc Fitz-Gerald entered the room pushing a small snack cart.

Clara Hazelton took the opportunity to suggest everyone take a fifteen minute break. "And when you're done, please write for half an hour about how you would like to be remembered by future generations."

Jean wrote the following passage:

*For years I never knew whether twilight was the ending of the day or the beginning of the night and then, suddenly, one day I understood that this did not matter at all for time is but a circle and so there can be no beginning and no ending. And this is how I came to know that birth and death are one and it is neither the coming or the going that is of consequence. What is of consequence is the beauty that one gathers in this interlude called life. And so I have slowly come to understand that beauty has a thousand different faces. Stark branches against a wintry sky, a snow drop welcoming the spring, the delicate tracery of a spider web, the rich fragrance of the damp woods, the timpani of distant thunder, and yes, do not forget the dusty pink and molten golds of the sunset, the music of the raindrops upon the leaves, the sleepy call of a robin in the gathering dusk and the glittering stars that fill the darkness with the symbols of time and space unending. Beauty holds a thousand different faces toward the searching heart. We who have lived some of our years here at 'Overlook,' in the shadow of Jay Mountain, have so much to be thankful for. Always the big sky, the wind whispering or wild, the evergreens with their message of hope and beauty, the flashing wings and sweet songs of many birds, the space to have animals all about us to teach us that as they are dependent on us, so we too, are dependent on others and on a source above us, greater and wiser and kinder than we. So let us learn from our heritage of great people in our past, great beauty–to love more and criticize less–to help each other more. All the world is our neighbor and all the world needs love as never before."*

Oliver Winch, who was in town visiting friends and relatives, wrote the following:

*Teaching is a very pleasant way of life, and if I had my life to live over again I would be a teacher above all else. Recording what it was like in the Town of Wilmington in earlier times helps people understand what life was like before we had all the modern conveniences of life today. For instance, one little story that I think should be captured for future generations:*

*While I was in Keene, I came to know Mrs. Martin, granddaughter of Horace Mann. She was a wealthy summer visitor and the patron saint of Keene Center as well as a sponsor of the school of philosophy on East Hill. She gave a library filled with excellent books to the Town and employed me at her expense to act as librarian. Thus, I had two paying jobs at once. Besides, I gardened quite extensively. The three years there were happy and profitable.*

*Mrs. Martin owned a donkey that she called Bob. She was often seen riding in a gig drawn by Bob. One time, she was entertaining Maxim Gorki, the Russian novelist. He expressed a desire to drive the outfit on a trip to Keene Valley. The expedition disappeared. Eventually, search parties found them; Bob was climbing the steep sides of a mountain looking for tasty bits still attached to the cart with Gorki clinging desperately to the emblems of authority that did not exist, feet up - head down.*

*When Mrs. Martin returned to the city, she left Bob to board with me. He was supposed to work for his board but he never acknowledged any such agreement. I soon found that, if I were in a hurry, it was quicker to walk. If I were not in a hurry (which was seldom the case) I might go along with Bob, the driver to the contrary, notwithstanding.*

*At that time, there were no automobiles in Keene to frighten the horses - but Bob did. Especially did the horses of the stagecoach resent this monstrosity. When they essayed to pass the stable where Bob resided on the route up by the Cascade mountain, a loud "H E E. H A W" threw them into a panic. They turned and bolted back down the road to Elizabethtown. The driver struggled with them and dragged them by the stable, all the while cussing "that devilish jackass."*

*However, in a way, he could put on a pretty good show. On Saturdays, the boys would come to ride the donkey. It made a good show: I stood by convulsed with laughter as boy after boy tumbled off his back. One boy turned a reproachful look at me and said, "Why don't you ride him?"*

*Then came the chorus, "Yes, you ride him! Ride him! Ride him, cowboy!*

*So I felt honor bound to ride him. I mounted and, I found myself on a whirlwind! He did everything in the Dictionary but I held on–there was nothing else that I could do. There remained a cedar thicket, and he took it, emerging, without a rider and I remained hanging in the branches.*

*However, I didn't mind–I was one of the boys again.*

*On the whole, Bob proved to be a nuisance and a farmer was persuaded to board him until Mrs. Martin returned.*

The Writer's Club adjourned promptly at nine, as Miss Clara was a stickler for deadlines. One by one, the club members said "good-night" and headed for home.

Doc came in to help pick up after the meeting, and Jean helped as well. It only took a moment for Doc to find himself engaged in conversation with Oliver Winch. They got to talking about Oliver's history book, and Oliver started to tell Doc about his writing exercise that evening.

Doc inquired, "Would you permit me to read your writing, sir? I once fancied myself a writer also!"

Oliver watched as Doc read the story. Doc had a most expressive face, and Oliver could see his comic tale played out on Doc's face as he read. "What a wonderful yarn!" Doc exclaimed. "I wouldn't change a thing."

Then Doc scratched his chin and raised one eyebrow and said, "Unless maybe we re-name Bob. What if the old donkey was named Aristophanes instead, after the Athenian comic play writer. The story might be all the more engaging than if the donkey was named Bob."

Oliver smiled, and flipped pages in his notebook until he came to the page he was looking for. Then he handed Doc a page that said:

> *Tall story telling was an art among the most accomplished story tellers of the Adirondacks. The purpose was to tell the biggest lie and, at the same time, not to deceive the listener. A falsehood that tended to injure another was taboo. Exaggerations to excel other exaggerations and cause merriment, without deceit, were works of art. If the simple and gullible should "fall" for the story, he would be put wise by the resultant laughter. He could only redeem himself by telling another and a bigger one.*

"Exactly," said Doc. "Is it more important that you capture the name of the jackass accurately or is it more important to keep your reader flipping pages? When I am painting a picture, I have the power to move mountains, trees, barns, and streams. I don't have to be limited by the actual reality I see before me."

And so, Bob became Aristophanes.

## '70 Carrie McDonald

As Paleface opened its doors for the 1970 summer season, the staff came together to recognize the loss of Carrie McDonald. Carrie had a large family and would be missed by her daughter, her sisters, her four grandchildren, three great-grandchildren, and by her nephew, who she raised like a son. Carrie was also Dana Peck's aunt.

Jean was very sad to lose her friend Carrie, who had worked beside her in the kitchen for many years. A reliable, dependable employee was one thing, but after a couple of years Jean became very attached to the people she worked with. Jean was technically the owner-operator but she also felt a close kinship with her staff.

Jean thought back to when Carrie lost her husband, Charlie, almost two years earlier. Dana led the Paleface staff in prayer, just as Dana had done at the funeral home earlier in the week. There wasn't a dry eye at Paleface when Dana finished. Carrie was only sixty-seven years old.

Everyone shuffled off from the staff meeting. Jane went to the office, and turned on the piped in music. The haunting sound of Patsy Cline filled Paleface, as it often did. Jean froze in her tracks, as the empty silence was replaced by the warm rich sound. Jean got goose bumps. It had always been Carrie's favorite song.

## '70 The Annex

We arrived in the Adirondacks at the end of June.

The school year had finally come to an end. I had heard we were going to spend the entire summer in the Adirondacks and I couldn't wait to get there. I didn't know anything about Grampa's heart attack. I was eight years old, and I just felt lucky to be heading for the mountains.

Being a teacher left my father the freedom to do different things each summer. To help out at home, Mom and Dad spent the summer of 1970 managing the Paleface Annex property. It was an enormous house. We had a couple rooms to ourselves, a living area and a couple of bedrooms. Some rooms we shared with guests, like the kitchen and bathrooms. It was a one year deal for us. A more permanent host would be hired to run the Annex the following year.

I liked being there. However, I spent most of my time at the Annex waiting. Waiting for someone to take me to Paleface. Waiting for Aunt Patti to come. Waiting to go on some sort of Adirondack adventure. We also fell into a rhythm of Wednesdays with Nana.

## '70 Dandelion Wine

Mom's new endeavor that summer was Dandelion Wine.

The idea of turning a plentiful weed into a delicious adult treat *and* a possible business simultaneously appealed to Mom's entrepreneurial spirit and her hippie sensibilities.

To me, it seemed like the craziest idea. Ever. And I had to help. The babies were getting bigger and always seemed to be running in different directions. Mom spent more time chasing children than picking dandelions.

Paleface had a baseball machine in the game room that I loved playing, but not as much as riding horses, of course. The baseball machine ate dimes. I got good enough at the machine that I could make a dime last as long as fifteen or twenty minutes sometimes.

It turned out that the going rate for picking a quart sized bowl of dandelion heads was exactly one dime. So the idea was, if I picked the dandelions, I could fill my pockets with dimes for later. It crossed my mind that there never seemed to be a shortage of people at Paleface willing to lend me a dime. Especially Nana.

I resigned myself to picking dandelions anyway. It was our first day at Paleface since late last summer. Instead of being at the barn or on the trails, I was popping the heads off of sunny little weeds. Nana was busy in the distance replacing the pansies in her gardens with petunias and marigolds. Further off in the distance, Doug Peck was riding the lawn mower, a turquoise Pennsylvania Panzer riding mower around the chairlifts.

Finally, Barbara and Jeffrey had dozed off on a blanket on the lawn. I had picked two dimes worth of dandelions already and was on my third. It was much more fun to pick them with Mom than it was to pick them by myself. Working together, we filled the bowl five more times. As plentiful as dandelions were in the Adirondacks in late June, we were beginning to run out of dandelions to pick on the lawn at Paleface.

Fortunately, nap time was over. Plus, Doug Peck was ready to mow the lawn where we had been picking. Eight bowls of dandelions. Eight dimes for future use in the game room. A bigger priority remained trying to figure out how to get myself back to the barn. Then it hit me. I could shovel stalls for dimes. They'd have to let me go to the barn if I did something useful there.

It was a good plan, but it would have to wait. Mom was in a hurry to get back to the Annex and get the dandelion blossoms washed and into pots of boiling water.

Back at the Annex, Mom combined slices of lemons and oranges with sugar, yeast, boiling water and dandelion blossoms. Then it was left to ferment. I guess it looked like orange juice. Mom said we needed to wait for about two weeks before the dandelion wine would be ready. Every day we would need to watch and see if we could see bubbles. If we saw bubbles in there, we would know it was working.

It was hard not to get interested in something Mom was interested in. Though I had no use for wine, Mom turned it into kind of a fun science experiment. Now that the work was done, I was ready to get back to figuring out how to get from the Annex to Paleface. I tried to figure out whether it was close enough for me to walk from the Flume to Paleface.

Fortunately, the next morning Aunt Patti picked me up and brought me to work with her. My parents had instructed me that if I wanted to go with Aunt Patti again I needed to give her lots of time to do her job, taking care of the guests and the horses. I should keep myself quiet and I should pitch in and help with things without having to be asked, and more important than anything else, I needed to stay away from the back ends of the horses.

The busy summer season was just getting under way. The 4th of July was two days away. The lodge was filled with guests. It would be a busy day at the barn. Some days, guests would schedule a "sunrise" ride. Aunt Patti picked me up at 5am. We were at the barn at quarter after five. There were eight riders scheduled for the sun rise ride. Five beginners and three experts. Aunt Patti quickly brushed the horses, saddling and bridling half of them. Stan Smith, who was also on early duty that day, took care of the other horses.

Aunt Patti and I set out with the beginners. I hadn't been riding since we left at the end of the previous summer. It was great to be back in the saddle again. I tried to remember not to bother Aunt Patti too much. Aunt Patti was pleased that I had not forgotten anything since the previous summer.

We got back from the sunrise special at 8am. The horses were put in the stall. The other wranglers had arrived at work while we were on the trail and they were taking care of the morning chores. The horses that worked the sunrise special had their breakfast waiting for them.

Aunt Patti, Stan Smith and I went across the street to the lodge where Nana, Pearl, and Dot had breakfast going. Aunt Patti stopped by the front desk to check in with Jane. It looked like we had a full day of reservations. There were a couple openings left for the 9:30-10:30 beginners ride, and also a couple openings for the 11am-12pm intermediate ride. The afternoon rides, from 1pm-2pm and 3:30-4:30 were sold out.

Over breakfast I talked Aunt Patti into letting me try the intermediate ride. So far, I had only been on the beginner's rides. Of course, only if there were still horses available. It looked like I was destined to sit the afternoon out.

There was a long string of beginners at 9:30. Aunt Patti asked me if I would ride at the end of the string. She needed to talk to the guests more while she was working, and I needed to be polite and talk nicely to the guests as well. Aunt Patti explained that if guests were happy with their rides then they would give the wranglers tips. Extra money. Kind of like the dandelion dimes.

The second to last rider in the string was a young lady named Cathy. She was from Montreal, Canada. Fortunately for me, she spoke English clearly, and didn't mind talking with a child while she rode her horse. Cathy was riding Cheyenne. I had memorized every detail about every horse, and I was happy to tell Cathy everything about her horse, and how lucky she was to ride that particular horse, which happened to be my Nana's favorite.

At the end of the ride, Aunt Patti asked each guest if they would like to have a picture taken on their cameras with their horse. I noticed that every guest gave Aunt Patti some money on their way out. The last guest off her horse was Cathy. She asked Aunt Patti if she could get a picture with me and her horse. Then Cathy gave me a dollar on her way out. My first tip! I was shocked. I smiled at Aunt Patti. "This is a lot better than the eight dimes I got picking dandelions!"

Aunt Patti told me I did a very good job riding at the back of the string and looking out for the safety of all the riders between us. Aunt Patti was great at reading the riders, and knew exactly who to put on the second to last horse most of the time.

On the intermediate ride at 11am, Aunt Patti put me right behind her instead of at the end of the string. The beginner ride was mostly walking, plus a little bit of slow trotting. On the intermediate ride the horses would do a lot more running. Three or four times in the course of the one hour ride the horses would lope.

I told Aunt Patti that I wanted to be able to run without holding on to the saddle horn like the other wranglers did. Aunt Patti told me I should probably wait until next summer. Only the experienced wranglers could do that; there was no shame in holding on tight!

I loved the intermediate ride. I talked non-stop at lunch about going fast, and asked all kinds of questions, as usual. I was on cloud nine! I didn't mind the fact my day was over. All the horses were needed for guests that afternoon.

One of the cowboys walked me back to Paleface. I took my dollar tip and spent fifty cents at the jukebox playing "Hitchin' a Ride" by Vanity Fare and "Red Rubber Ball" by The Cyrkle, which fortunately was still in the jukebox after having been there for a couple of years. The other 50 cents I spent on the baseball machine, hitting home run after home run. I never regretted spending a single dime on that baseball machine, or on the jukebox for that matter.

After all the guests were served their lunches, Nana and I got in the station wagon and headed toward the Annex.

## '70 Skyslide

We had no sooner gotten into the station wagon and gone around the corner, when Nana pulled the car into The Mystery Spot. Since the prior summer, the attraction had added a giant yellow slide. We went in, and Nana told me that I could ride the slide a couple of times and then she'd take me back to the Annex.

The Skyslide, newly installed at The Mystery Spot, was enormous, and seemed as tall as a mountain climbing up those steps. The ride was thrilling. There were three drops, and the burlap sacks really slid fast down the giant yellow plastic mountain.

I could have gone down that slide a hundred times, but I probably couldn't have climbed up the stairs too many times that afternoon. Nana had said that I could slide a couple of times. Yet she said yes to the third ride, the fourth ride, and the fifth ride. I didn't even ask for a sixth ride!

It had been a perfect day.

## '70 4th of July

Growing up, I always loved the 4th of July, especially when we were in Jay. It had started many years before as a typical small town celebration. Then each tradition was perfected over a hundred years or more. It was the premier community event in Jay. It wasn't just the kids in town, it was the adults too. For example,

Pearl Pierce who was 77 years old in 1970, baked 200 pies for the event, with assistance provided by Heidi Jost.

Mrs. Viola McLean who was a patient in a nursing home in Elizabethtown was brought home to Jay to celebrate the 4th of July. Viola was Paleface wrangler, Roger McLean, Jr.'s grandmother. She sat in a car, parked near the park for several hours visiting with old friends and people passing by. Most folks inquired about Roger, and asked Viola if she knew when he would be coming home from Vietnam. Roger was on leave from his wrangler duties to serve his country.

Most adults knew the importance of the 4th of July in Jay was to serve as a fundraiser for the Volunteer Fire Department, but the budget for the fireworks was so generous, the firemen probably didn't raise as much money as people thought.

The parade was the best in the area. Many of the towns in the county participated in the parade in Jay rather than stage their own. Many participants were very serious about competing for the top honors in the judging of the parade.

Mom took us kids to the parade, and we got to watch Aunt Patti, dressed as an Indian, riding her horse Sandy through the covered bridge. We made so much noise cheering her on, it was a wonder her horse didn't pitch her off. Aunt Patti was riding without a saddle, which could be risky. If a horse got spooked, it could buck and throw off its rider.

After the parade, the firemen ran the concession booths. Back then it was in the village green rather than in the meadow by the fire station.

In 1970, there were some challenges. First of all, the brand new fire engine didn't arrive in time to be showcased in the parade. Then there was road construction to contend with. Then in the afternoon, it rained for a couple of hours. Most people left, but when the weather cleared they came back, so all in all, the day was a huge success. The firemen raised just as much cash as they had the year before, and all of the town's beloved traditions continued, rain or shine.

After Aunt Patti took Sandy back to his stall, she came and got me and took me around the village green. There was a band playing in the pavilion at the center of the green. Couples were dancing around the pavilion. The concession stands and games of chance were positioned around the perimeter of the village green. Aunt Patti gave me money and let me play each game, though there was little chance I would win anything.

Aunt Patti gave me money for B-I-N-G-O, which kept me busy for a while as she talked to some of her friends and acquaintances. I lost the first game, like most everybody else. Shockingly, I won the second game—the competition was fierce! I got my choice of the prizes that were left. I chose wisely—A brightly colored lime green stuffed dog with magenta ears that surely looked like it could glow in the dark. This dog was just a little smaller than I was. Aunt Patti had to carry my winnings back to her car and then the three of us rode back to Overlook.

On the way back I asked Aunt Patti about the bicentennial. "Won't it be something, when our country turns *200 years old*?"

Aunt Patti said that was six years away, but it would be here before I knew it. I wasn't so sure. Six years sounded like an awfully long time.

## '70 Harry and the Aliens

Preston and Cookie's son was sick, so Cookie called in regrets that she would be unable to work one evening in the middle of July. Cookie was scheduled to work the babysitting service. So, after working during the breakfast shift and the lunch shift Jean ended up providing the free babysitting service also, as was often the case.

In addition to the guests' children, Jean had three of her own grandchildren with her that evening. The younger children scribbled in coloring books and played with stuffed animals. The older children made symmetrical Spirograph drawings and played Kerplunk, pulling long wooden sticks out of a clear plastic cylinder, and trying to avoid dropping the most marbles to the bottom of the cylinder.

When the kids had mostly grown tired of playing with the toys available, Jean settled down to read the kids a story. Jean picked up the first book, and held up the book so the children could see the cover. The book was handmade by Preston Palmer, who wrote the story for his little boy.

Jean read the title: *Harry & The Aliens*. She pointed to a drawing of an animal whose four feet, tail, and half of its hairy body appeared on the cover of the book. The head and top half of the body were outside of the picture. Also on the cover were two stick figure aliens, one with pony tails, and both with astronaut's helmets and antennae.

Jean opened the book and read to the children:

*Once upon a time, there was a very, VERY, hairy wildebeest named... you guessed it! Harry.*

*One night, Harry was enjoying a grassy snack by the light of the moon. When all of a sudden a UFO landed and a bunch of ALIENS got out. HARRY'S EYES BUGGED OUT OF HIS HEAD!*

*The biggest alien said give us all your gold BEAST. Harry didn't like to be called BEAST. He just walked away. Which of course made the aliens very ANGRY.*

*Soon Harry forgot all about the aliens, found a rock for a pillow and went to sleep. When Harry woke up the next morning Harry realized that he was trapped." Jean held up the book so the kids could see a drawing of Harry the wildebeest in a square cage.*

*AGAIN the aliens said "GIVE US ALL YOUR GOLD, BEAST." Harry kicked the biggest alien between his antennae and broke its helmet. And it evaporated.*

*The other aliens picked all the goldenrod they could find and brought it to Harry. Harry was so happy he ate all the goldenrod. And pooped gold nuggets all night long.*

As you might imagine, all the children laughed at this part.

I said, "Nana, read that page again!" And again, all the kids laughed when Jean said, "And pooped gold nuggets all night long." When the kids settled down, Jean told the kids, "Do you know what? I am allergic to goldenrod. When the goldenrod blooms each summer, I get all stuffed up like I have a cold, and my eyes get swollen and I cry a lot. But at least I don't poop gold nuggets!" This time, the kids howled with laughter. That was the last thing I ever expected to hear Nana say.

Getting back to the story, Jean continued:

*The aliens couldn't have been happier. They loaded up all the poop and zoomed off into space again.*

*The moral of the story is... if aliens land on our planet, and if you are lucky, the aliens will bring you food and clean up your messes OR... always do what they tell you because they ARE going to get what they WANT.*

The children loved the story, and begged to have it read again. Nana mumbled, "What kind of person thinks of a story like this?" Then Nana read it again.

## '70 Summer Jobs

It was a sunny, hot summer day, and there were only two days left until the 6th Annual Kiwanis Horse Show at Paleface.

On top of getting the grounds ready to look their best, it was time to cut, bale, load, and store the hay for the following winter. Dana assembled a crew, mostly brothers, uncles, and cousins to put up the hay. Dana's son Doug drove the truck, and Dana himself arranged the bales that were thrown up onto the truck by the rest of the men who followed along behind. It was very hard, dusty work and when it was done, everyone enjoyed a nice cool dip in the river.

Dana's youngest son Dana-D had taken over the lawn mowing task from his brother Doug. It was a rite of passage, and Dana-D felt he had truly arrived when he was entrusted with such an important task. Dana-D did a meticulous job mowing the lawn.

The longer he spent mowing, the longer he could put off dead-heading the marigolds and petunias in Jean's long strip gardens at Paleface. Dana-D had been in charge of that task for a couple of years, and was looking forward to moving on to other chores instead.

Unfortunately, no one else had come along to take up that task. Even so, Jean could often be found helping with the task herself. She often thought about her mother Maggie's love for gardening. While Jean's father John J. Allen was occupied with running a successful business and then in public service as the mayor of Ottawa, Maggie enjoyed hours in her flower gardens, and hosting parties in the evenings. Jean's gardens at Paleface connected her to happy childhood memories.

In the decades since, petunias were perfected to the point where they no longer required dead-heading. Marigolds, on the other hand, were not.

Shoveling horse manure was another great summer job for young men looking to make a few bucks. In addition to cleaning up fresh messes in the barn, it always seemed there was a pile of the stuff that needed to be relocated from one place to another.

The day before the horse show was a Saturday. The haying was finally finished. It should have been a busy day, with lots of customers in saddles on horses on the trails. For some reason, it was a little slow. To capture the attention of passing motorists, Doug and Dana-D saddled up two of the showiest horses in the barn, Sioux Scout and Navajo. The boys loved riding Navajo, a spunky little sorrel and white Pinto. Sioux Scout was okay, maybe a little on the lazy side, but a tall and striking black and white Paint horse.

After an hour of showing off in the ring, the horses were booked for most of the rest of the day. Doug and Dana-D had to give up their mounts to seat the dudes, and the boys were demoted back to landscaping tasks.

## '70 Square Dancing

Just as the ski instructors were expected to participate in the après-ski activities at Paleface, Doc had come to expect the cowboys and cowgirls that worked in the barn to come to the Saturday Western Square Dancing held each Saturday night, dressed authentically and playing a hosting role, and to help perpetuate one of Doc's marketing slogans. Paleface really was "The Best West in the East."

The real talent was California Ray Columbe, a tall, handsome, ex-marine who "called" the dances, every Saturday night in July and August. Many in the community came out every Saturday, and got quite good at square dancing in the process. The loyal local dancers became known as Ray's "Funtastic Fan Club." The fact that there was no admission charge and no cover charge helped assure a big local crowd.

Sometimes the Paleface cowboys would celebrate too much on Saturday night, but with the big show the following day, Doc encouraged most of the cowboys to head home early that particular Saturday night.

## '70 Horse Show at Paleface

No doubt about it, as a kid I wanted nothing more than to be a cowboy: full-time, year-round, 100 percent. Whenever I wasn't at Paleface, I wished I was.

Everyone was talking about the upcoming horse show. It was going to be at Paleface. I was surprised to learn that this wasn't the first time, in fact this would be the 6th Annual Kiwanis Horse Show. Somehow, I had managed to be in the wrong place every time for the past five previous years. I was thrilled and excited to get the chance to go; I couldn't wait.

Then, two days before the big show, I learned my parents had different plans. Couldn't they have had different plans for us almost any other day that summer? I'm certain I pitched a fit, stomped my boots on the floor, pouted, and attempted to use what limited powers of persuasion I possessed. Nothing seemed to work.

I'm sure there wasn't any doubt I would make everyone around me miserable until I got my way, or until the show had passed. As any kid that age knew, you never wanted to give up. At the last minute, something could fall into place and all of a sudden, a possibility could emerge.

Then Aunt Patti came to the rescue yet again. She used the right words, at the right moment, and in the right manner. "Why don't you let David come with me? He can be a big help to me."

I was stunned. It looked like those words were gaining traction. It occurred to me not to say one word to try to help plead my case. It was all up to Aunt Patti to seal the deal. I held my breath. I didn't move a muscle. I didn't so much as blink.

"Nah, he won't be any trouble."

"Nah, he won't be in the way."

"I'm sure he will be on his best behavior."

Aunt Patti successfully navigated the minefield of questions. I would have to broaden my horizons another time. It would seem that my parents would have to visit Montreal without me!

Maybe the 6th Annual Whiteface Mountain Kiwanis Horse Show at Paleface on Sunday, July 19th was all the more enjoyable because of the fact that I almost didn't get to go!

Finally, the magic date arrived. My parents packed up Chubby the Checker, and the babies and set off for Parc Safari and a couple of days in Montreal, beyond. Parc Safari was a great place to go and normally I would have jumped at the chance.

I understood my job was to be good, polite, quiet, and do exactly as I was told. If the slightest thing went wrong, I knew I could be moved across the street to the lodge and placed in the care of the expert babysitters at Paleface. There was no chance I was going to allow that to happen.

Nana, Grampa, Aunt Patti and I had a nice, early lunch together at the restaurant in the lodge, finishing up around quarter to twelve. Then Nana went to work with the kitchen crew to get ready for a busy day feeding hungry customers.

I went with Aunt Patti and Grampa across the street where the Paleface cowboys were working on the final preparations for the day's event. Grampa seemed satisfied that everything was in place. One after another, horse trailers pulled up and dropped off their contents.

Aunt Patti went to the Paleface barn to help the cowboys. I stayed at Grampa's side.

Grampa knew everyone, and greeted them by name, and inquired after their family members. It was all the same, whether the arrival was a fellow member of the Whiteface Chamber of Commerce, a fellow member of the Kiwanis Club, a contestant in the show, a spectator, or one of the wranglers, Grampa treated everyone with equal respect and genuine affection. Paleface held lots of events throughout the year. For my Grampa, this was his favorite, truly the social event of the year.

Not to diminish the esteem Grampa held for the humans, Grampa was just as glad to have the horses visiting Paleface. I tagged along as he visited with each new arrival. He had something nice to say to each horse's human companion, complimenting something about their horse or their preparation for the show. It wasn't just dogs—Grampa had a way with horses too. Even the ones that had a bit of a reputation for being wild seemed to soften to his touch.

Shortly before the show was set to begin, the judges, Mr. Favor Smith of Lake Placid, and Mr. Larry Spaulding of Malone, arrived along with the ringmaster, Mr. Bob Cane Jr. After them, Dr. Robert Lopez arrived in a small pick-up truck with a little girl about my age.

We stood for the National Anthem which was broadcast over the loud speaker, then the Ringmaster, Mr. Cane led everyone as they recited the pledge of allegiance. Then Bing Crosby & the Andrews Sisters' version of the song "Don't Fence Me In" was played, and most of the spectators and competitors sang along. I had never heard that song before.

Then the first of the seventeen events got underway. I stood quietly by Grampa's side as he watched the show and visited with Dr. Lopez, from Westport New York. Dr. Lopez took care of all the Paleface horses, so Grampa was perhaps Dr. Lopez's best customer.

Dr. Lopez's daughter Lori had joined him that day. After we watched the costume class on horseback, which occurred to me was like Halloween in the middle of summer, came some of the least interesting events. Grampa and Dr. Lopez talked all through these events, neither taking their eyes off the horses in the ring, both feeling responsible for the safety of the horses and riders. Eventually, Lori and I got to talking about subjects more interesting to kids that what Grampa and Dr. Lopez were discussing.

Lori asked me what I wanted to be when I grew up. Of course, I told her that I wanted to be a cowboy. Maybe I would compete in horse shows. Maybe I would compete in rodeos. Maybe I would take dudes on trail rides, like my Aunt Patti. Maybe I would work on a ranch out west. But, something like that, for sure. Lori was a good listener. When I finished, she told me she was going to be a horse doctor, just like her Dad.

Then Lori told me about all her brothers and sisters. I couldn't count how many names she listed, but it was a very long list. As Lori finished telling me about her family, the spotted horse class began. I liked that event, no boring brown horses, just Pintos, Appaloosas, and Dapples. I asked Lori which horse she liked best.

Lori didn't hesitate. It was like she had been asking herself the exact same question. She said, "I like that one," and she pointed to Chippewa. "One day I'm going to buy that horse," she said.

I replied, "But he lives here!"

Lori repeated, "Yes, one day I'm going to buy that horse and I'm going to name him 'Truly Scrumptious' just like that lady in the movie *Chitty, Chitty, Bang, Bang* with the magical flying car."

I said, "But his name is Chippewa. We call him Chip for short. Besides, he's a boy, not a lady. You can't give him a girl's name!"

Lori said, "Why not? Of course I can. I can call him whatever I want when I buy him. Besides, a horse doesn't know his own name anyway!"

I concluded the debate with, "Well, I guess we'll just have to ask Aunt Patti about that!" I was glad Lori didn't want to buy Dunder or Navajo!

After a while, the show transitioned into the gymkhana events. It was exhilarating watching the galloping horses speed through their events, one by one. Aunt Patti was always a star in the barrel racing. After Aunt Patti finished, she came over to take Grampa's place with me.

Dr. Lopez introduced Aunt Patti to his daughter Lori. Aunt Patti said some nice things to Lori, then asked Dr. Lopez how many children he had. Dr. Lopez told Aunt Patti that he had fourteen children!

Aunt Patti said, "I don't know how you do it, spending as much time as you do on the road!"

Dr. Lopez joked, "I must have found some time at home, given I wound up with fourteen children."

A little embarrassed, Aunt Patti laughed and said, "I meant I don't know how you find time to spend *with* the children."

Dr. Lopez responded a little more seriously, "I try to take one of them with me everywhere I go, so I get a little one-on-one time with each of them."

Lori smiled. She said she was glad that her turn was an afternoon horse show rather than one of the more ordinary rounds of house calls.

Then Grampa went to get Dunder for his run at the pole bending class. Since his heart attack back at the beginning of the year, Grampa hadn't ridden very much, but nothing would stop him from competing that beautiful July afternoon.

Another very determined pole bender that afternoon was Paleface cowboy Stan Smith. Stan had been trying to convince Aunt Patti that she and Doc had overlooked the talent of the horse named Pepsi.

Pepsi was a nice looking, cola colored, dark brown horse,

practically the color of Pepsi Cola. A few years back, Pepsi had shown some signs that he had what it took to be a good gymkhana horse. Stan had been working with Pepsi for the past couple of weeks, and Stan had talked Patti into chancing the entry fee on him.

Pepsi jumped out of the gate quickly, and made a fast run to the end pole. He wound his way back to the first pole, and turned nicely for the return. He was on his way to a great finish, perhaps a first place ride. When Pepsi got back to the end pole, and rounded it snugly against the poll, something went wrong. His feet slid, went out from under him, and dropped poor Stan between the last two poles.

Pepsi skidded on his side, and came to a stop almost twenty feet away.

Dr. Lopez seemed to jump the fence in a single bound, his feet moving before his brain fully recognized it was time to go to work. Dr. Lopez hit the ground on the other side of the fence, without making a good landing. Nonetheless, Dr. Lopez jumped up from the ground and ran to check on Stan. Stan was fine.

Pepsi was laying on his side, right where his slide had come to an end. He was looking around, a little confused, as if to say, "What the heck just happened? This isn't how this works!"

Dr. Lopez checked Pepsi's legs. Fortunately for Pepsi, his legs were fine. In fact, there was nothing wrong with Pepsi, he just needed a little encouragement regaining his feet. As Pepsi stood back up, Ringmaster Bob Cane's voice came out over the loudspeaker: "How about a round of applause for Pepsi, and his rider Stan Smith. It looks like horse and rider are both going to be fine. Right, Doctor?"

Dr. Lopez shook his head up and down, in an animated a fashion, like a rodeo clown would do. Competitors and spectators alike applauded Pepsi's final gymkhana event.

After Stan had returned Pepsi to the barn, he came out to tell Aunt Patti she was right and he was wrong.

Aunt Patti told Stan he was right about one thing—Pepsi sure could move, but weaving the poles was another matter! Then Patti smiled and told Stan, "There's no use crying over spilled Soda Pop!"

At the end of the show, there was a presentation of the ribbons and trophies. The horse show took most of the afternoon, but to me it seemed to go by way too fast. It was so exciting, one competitive drama following quickly after the other. Great people, fast horses, beautiful weather—it was every bit as much fun as I thought it would be.

As the last of the horse trailers were loaded up, I was alone with Aunt Patti and Grampa. Aunt Patti reported that Paleface's total ribbon count had reached 489 ribbons that day.

It sounded like the adults were between subjects, and there was just enough silence for a kid to interrupt politely. I said, "Do you think I could be in a horse show? Even just the costume class, maybe? I could ride old Blueboy if you don't think I'm ready to ride one of the other horses."

Grampa looked at Aunt Patti and smiled, then turned to me and said, "We'll see, we'll just have to see. Meanwhile, it wouldn't hurt to practice all you can. I've seen you riding lately. You should stick with Dunder and forget about old Blueboy. Leave Blueboy to the dudes and the kids."

"Yes *sir*!" I stood as straight and tall as I could, like a toy soldier, and I smiled from ear to ear. Best to leave it at that for the moment.

## '70 Writer's Club III

Mr. Oliver Winch, who grew up locally and taught school at Glens Falls, was back in town. Mr. Winch usually visited friends and family during the summer. Oliver Winch had worked on his book for several years, and finally had completed *The History of Wilmington*.

Oliver did the printing and binding of the book himself—about 100 copies made completely by hand—at the ripe old age of ninety-seven years. For the front cover, Oliver Winch rubber-cemented a beautiful picture post card of Wilmington displaying its fall foliage.

Everyone in attendance received a signed copy. It was a special gift for the members of the fledgling club.

Adeline Frances Jaques was another Wilmington native, who also became a teacher and moved away. Like Mr. Winch, Miss Jaques also returned each August. Adeline Jaques accompanied her friend Gus Elliott at the August meeting of the Writer's Club. Flipping through Mr. Winch's book, Adeline got the idea of writing her own account of Wilmington's past. Adeline wrote two little stories during the meeting. One was an account of her service in the Navy and her very brief service in the 1944 movie *Waves*, starring Bing Crosby.

Adeline Jaques kept a folder full of old newspaper clippings, various features that interested her for one reason or another. Adeline's second writing exercise was a rebuttal to a clipping from the *Adirondack Daily Enterprise* feature dated November 13, 1956 that basically stated what a horrible thing Whiteface Mountain did, and the need to keep Mt. McIntyre, which is what they used to call Algonquin Mountain, and Mt. Marcy from the same fate.

Jean brought her daughter-in-law Carolyn Fitz-Gerald to the Writer's Club meeting as a guest. Carolyn wrote the following:

*My Journey*
*Each being is just a glowing vibration*
*And is part of the crust of the planet*
*Because each person is needed*
*To make the planet glow.*
*Each vibration has its own circle*
*On which it stands and glows.*
*This gives the planet a red glow*
*Which pleases the Universal Being*
*And gives Mars its glory*
*In the eyes of God.*
*Each vibration is needed*
*And there are rules for each vibration.*
*Each vibration must learn to glow*
*In its own circle*
*And no vibration is allowed to glow any brighter*
*Than another vibration*
*Because then certain parts of the surface*

*Would be uneven and cause problems*
*That could endanger the whole surface.*
*Whenever a vibration breaks the rules*
*And gets out of hand*
*They are exiled to another planet*
*Until the lesson is learned*
*And when the vibrations return to their own circle*
*They know how to be*
*And they are more grateful*
*And they know how to be a part of the surface*
*And they don't get out of line*
*But are happy with where they are*
*And with their own glowing.*
*Time is not the same on Mars as it is on earth*
*It takes ten Earth years to equal one Mars year.*
*I know that this idea of being from mars is silly*
*But it is something that makes good sense to me*
*Though it may not to anyone else.*
*So I am here.*
*Since I am here,*
*I'll have to deal with it as best I can*
*I have to become a good human*
*Or I can't go back.*
*When I reach the end of this existence,*
*I will become a much better vibration,*
*And I will look out from my circle*
*Toward the earth*
*Which is like a sparkling diamond*
*In the sky of Mars,*
*And remember what I was*
*And I will always be able to see my children*
*Who will be here.*

Over the summer, Fran Betters had joined the Writer's Club. For a couple of years, Fran had it in the back of his mind to write a book about fishing. Fran figured that maybe joining the new club would help him get started. The idea was still fairly vague in his mind, but he had a title that he thought would be catchy: *Fish Are Smarter in the Adirondacks*. Maybe it would be collection of short stories, perhaps it might include some poetry and tall tales.

Fran thought that his title was deliciously ironic. He wrote down everything he knew and believed regarding the difference between the indigenous trout and the trout that had been brought over from Germany. No doubt about it, the brown trout were the smarter, and more challenging variety and, so—in Fran's estimation—catching a big brown trout was a more-worthy accomplishment than landing a large rainbow trout. Yes, fish were smarter in the Adirondacks, but it was those German transplants more than the native brook trout whose brilliance Fran so admired.

After all the writers completed their evening practice, Clara asked if anyone would like to read what they wrote, maybe a small passage, or even just a conversation about their subject matter.

After everyone said a little bit about what they had worked on that evening, Clara shook her head and chuckled. "I thought tonight's assignment was to write about what you did this summer. Sounds like you all felt like writing about other things instead!"

## '70 Back from Vietnam

The first week of August, Paleface cowboy Roger McLean, Jr. returned from Vietnam. Roger's parents both worked at Paleface and were glad to have him back after three years in the army and nineteen months in Vietnam. Roger returned just in time to help get ready for the big show of the season, The Essex County Fair, later that month.

## '70 Horse Show at Essex County Fair

Ever since the horse show at Paleface the month before, I had hoped to be in a horse show myself. Grampa said, "We'll see, we'll just have to see." And then he told me to practice. I knew the summer was quickly passing by. So, every chance I got, I asked for help getting me to the barn and into the saddle and into the ring. Mostly, of course, I asked Aunt Patti. I wasn't the only one. When the Paleface cowboys weren't leading dudes along the trails, they would often run Paleface's best horses around the barrels in the ring or weave them through the poles.

Riding a horse around in circles wasn't my favorite way to spend time with a horse, but I was determined. Grampa gave me some great advice. For instance, "Don't kick your horse when they tell you to trot, send him a signal." Grampa instructed me to use the clicking sound with my tongue, with lips closed on one side but not the other. "At the same time, squeeze your legs as hard as you can. Usually you don't need to kick a good horse. If you do need to kick him, pay attention to where the judges are sitting, then kick give him a good little kick with the heel of your boot on the opposite side so the judges won't see it."

Fortunately, the horse didn't need training, just the young rider. Dunder was a proven professional, and it didn't matter to him if he was racing for an expert rider, responding to commands in the spotted horse class, or hauling dudes. Dunder knew how to handle all his tasks and seemed to appreciate each for what it was. Many horses were specialists. For instance, old Blueboy was good for the dudes, and most gentle and loving for people experiencing horses for the first time, but Blueboy wasn't showy and wasn't a racer.

There was less than a week left before the fair. I kept asking the cowboys, "How many more days until the fair?" Still, I hadn't gotten the nod. Had Grampa forgotten? I knew he was busy over in the office and had to run all of Paleface. I knew he couldn't just worry only about the horses and the dude ranch and the horse show at the fair.

Though he hadn't told me, Grampa had registered me and paid an entry fee for a couple of classes, just in case I had managed to follow through and practice. It was late Monday night and Doc left this note for Patti:

*Patti:*

*Just because I'm so lousy at "communications"–here's to advise you that I've written notes to alert both Allen and Mother that we should plan on making Friday a family day at the Essex County Fair, knowing by now David can enter Dunder in Open Pleasure, Spotted Horse and Family Class. I'll ask for Wallace to tend bar so that both Allen and Carolyn can go to the County Fair. We'll plan to take a good goodie-box and make a day of it. O.K.? Tell Vince. P.S. We have to practice family class with the Paints!*

Tuesday afternoon, Roger McLean was in the ring with a new horse named Sundance, renamed after coming to Paleface, and based on the phenomenally successful cowboy movie *Butch Cassidy and the Sundance Kid.* Roger was trying to determine the highest and best use for him and determine his demeanor. As it turned out Sundance was a gentle horse, good for beginners. He was a lovely, almost golden brown color, not quite as golden as the horse named Nugget.

While I was practicing with Dunder in the ring, all of a sudden Aunt Patti joined me in the ring. She was riding Apache, which I thought was a little unusual, but I was sure glad to see her. A couple of minutes later, Grampa led his favorite little Pinto Chippewa into the ring.

"So here is the deal, son," Grampa said, "we're going to practice for the family class and if it goes good, the three of us will see if maybe we can win a ribbon. The idea of the family class is that we need to try and keep all three horses as close together, side by side throughout the entire event. As we walk, side by side. As we trot, side by side. As we lope, same thing—side by side. If we can do that, we have a good chance of winning a ribbon! And remember what I told you about kicking your horse? Since you'll be in the middle, between me and Chip, and Aunt Patti and Apache, you can kick old Dunder all you want. But Dunder has done the family class before, he should be fine. He knows what to do. Two years ago, Nana, Aunt Patti and I took a blue ribbon in the family class on these Pintos."

It seemed to me like we should have practiced more. We practiced for about a half an hour on Tuesday, a little longer on Wednesday, and again for half an hour on Thursday afternoon. On Thursday afternoon, Grampa said, "I think that's going to be great. You've done your homework. Now just focus on having fun. We've got a horse show to go to tomorrow!"

In the weeks between the Paleface show and the Essex County Fair, the Paleface cowboys had increased their ribbon count from 489 to 498. Even without the practicing, it should be possible to pass the 500 ribbon count. We probably made much more of it than was warranted; somehow it had become an epic milestone accomplishment, and it was looking like it was all coming down to the wire at the 122nd Annual Essex County Fair, held each year in Westport, along Lake Champlain.

Aunt Patti picked up the first blue ribbon in the costume class. Mounted on Dunder, riding bareback, with her very, very long hair, a doe skin dress, some beads and a feather in her hair, Aunt Patti's portrayal of an Indian maiden was very convincing. Ribbon number 499.

The Family Class was our next event. It isn't as easy as one might think to find horses and riders that can match up and ride together in a horse show. There were only six teams competing that day, and they were awarding four ribbons, so our chances were good.

All of the other teams were pairs. A team of three was more difficult, so if we did a good job riding like when we practiced, we stood to do really well.

As we were getting ready, Aunt Patti changed in the horse trailer from an Indian maiden into blue jeans and a green, brown and white shirt. Grampa gave me a smaller version of that same shirt, and put one on himself. Mine was a little big, but not too bad. We finished our preparations just in time to enter the ring when announced.

I don't know how well I rode, but I do know I concentrated on following all the instructions I could remember, and I also know I smiled throughout. I was as pleased as I could be to be riding with my Grampa and my Aunt Patti in the horse show.

Once or twice, I couldn't help but notice my Mom and Nana at the fence, snapping pictures.

Sometimes, things just worked in your favor. It seemed our three horses were in the mood to cooperate with each other. Dunder and Chip were steady and reliable, but sometimes Apache could be a handful. Fortunately, we walked, trotted, and loped in unison. Aunt Patti and Grampa were able to speed their horses to match the pace Dunder set beneath me. I had been practicing my tongue clicks, and Dunder had responded perfectly. At one point late in the event, Apache got a little bit ahead of the other two horses, but fortunately for us, that was on the opposite side of the ring from where the judges were sitting.

At the end of our class, all of the teams lined up in the middle of the ring, facing the judges, and the bleachers. Then the announcements began.

I snuck a sideways glance to the left, and then I looked quickly to the right. All I saw was plain old boring black and brown horses. I closed my eyes and pictured how flashy and alive we must look on our fancy spotted horses.

They called fourth place. It wasn't us. The fourth place team rode up to the get their ribbon, and exited the ring. Then the same thing with the third place team, also not us. And then the second place team was announced, a pair of jet black horses that looked like they were identical twins, and two young ladies that looked very much like sisters rode forward to get their ribbon.

And there we were, three teams left. One of the teams would get first place, the other two teams would leave without a ribbon.

I felt yet another rush of adrenaline. There were butterflies in my stomach and my heart beat faster. It felt like it was going to jump up into my throat. I tried to tell myself that I would behave very dignified if we lost. I imagined telling the winners how happy I was for them.

Then came the announcement. They were saying our names. Grampa and Aunt Patti began to ride forward to get our ribbon. I just sat there. Fortunately, Dunder knew to follow even if I forgot to make the sound.

When we left the ring and got off the horses, I hugged Aunt Patti tightly, and I clung to her, not wanting to let go. I couldn't remember ever having been so happy.

We earned that milestone 500th ribbon, together, as a family!

But there was no time to bask in our glorious moment. There were more classes to come, and more competing to prepare for. In fact, I had to turn around and go right back in! And so did Grampa. We were both entered in the spotted horse class, which came next on the program.

Decades later, when I looked back, I wondered whether maybe he entered that class so he could be nearby in case I needed him to come to the rescue. I was only 8 years old, after all.

In that class, there were eight participants. It crossed my mind that I was going to need to do everything right if I was going to get a ribbon. Fortunately, again old Dunder preformed magnificently. There was one time when the ringmaster called a command to lope when we had only been walking. I had never gone from a walk directly to a lope. Fortunately, we got there pretty quickly. Another command I hadn't practiced was to reverse directions at a lope. The spotted horse class was a lot harder than I thought it would be.

There was one point during the event when I thought I saw Grampa ahead of me kicking Chip, and in front of the judges no less. I couldn't believe it.

When the spotted horse class was over, and we were lined up waiting for the announcements, I remember thinking I should pinch myself. "I'm just glad to be here, I don't even need another ribbon." My head was still in the clouds from our first place finish in the family class.

The first name was called. "In fourth place, Doctor Boylan FitzGerald, representing Paleface, and riding Chippewa." I was happy to see Grampa get a ribbon, I almost forgot where I was.

The second name was called. "In third place, David Fitz-Gerald, representing Paleface, and riding Dunder." My jaw dropped. I was getting a ribbon in the spotted horse class? I kicked Dunder forward without even thinking, but the judging was over! It didn't matter. I picked up my ribbon and slowly rode out of the ring.

As I was riding out of the ring, it occurred to me that I had beaten my Grampa! I was stunned.

It didn't occur to me until much later that my Grampa may have "thrown" the event on purpose. I was relieved afterwards to find out that Grampa wasn't sore about me beating him.

By the time the show was over, the Paleface riders had scored three first place ribbons, 2 seconds, 3 thirds and 2 fourths. If I had to be honest, though it wasn't humble to say so, I was very proud of myself. But I was even more proud of old Dunder. Not only did he carry me to first place in the family class, he had also carried Aunt Patti to first place in the costume class, and then Stanley Smith rode Dunder to a first place finish in the Pole Bending Class. Dunder also finished fourth in the Barrel Race.

I could never imagine loving a horse more than I loved Dunder.

## '70 Torrance's Maple Candy

It was always sad to be leaving the Adirondacks, but the start of the new school year was fast approaching. After the tearful goodbyes, we settled into the old Checker Cab for a long ride home. The smell of the stinky fermenting dandelion wine filled the car. Eventually, I was distracted from thoughts about the horrible smell by thoughts about all the future horse shows I would compete in, and how happy I was to have gotten the chance to ride for Paleface at the Essex County Fair.

After a couple hours of driving, Mom opened the Coleman cooler and pulled out a tube of tuna sandwiches, which had been packed back into the wrapper the bread came in. After we each ate a sandwich, Mom passed out maple candies that she had picked up at Frank Torrance's house. Frank drove a school bus, worked at the Land of Makebelieve, was a member of the volunteer fire department in Upper Jay and Frank and his wife Rose made the best maple candy in the North Country.

After lunch, Mom began to sing verse after verse of her own musical creation, "Proud to be a Pig Farmer's Daughter" which replaced the famous lyrics from Loretta Lynn's brand new, monster hit song from that summer. As the verses went on, Mom's voice got quiet and quieter, the pace of the song got slow and slower, and all three of us kids fell fast asleep. By the time we woke up, we were within an hour's drive of being home.

Summer was officially over.

## '70 Coy Dog

Back in the North Country, a couple of days after Labor Day, Helen Pierce picked up Pearl Pierce at Paleface. They planned to make an afternoon trip to Lake Placid. They had no sooner pulled out of the parking lot, when a strange creature crossed their path.

It looked like a giant, wild dog. It had tan fur, with long patches of gray fur, and giant fangs. It would have looked really scary if it weren't for the lazy, loping, unimpressed manner in which it ran from the direction of the corrals near the Paleface barn, across the highway and down into the meadow where the Paleface horses spent most of the winter, just across from The Mystery Spot.

Helen and Pearl stopped by to report to Clara Hazelton that they had seen a werewolf crossing the road near Paleface. Sometimes Clara had to work hard to come up with interesting stories for her column. She knew the story would fascinate her readers.

About two weeks later, James Warren who was the manager, and a co-owner of The Mystery Spot got the strange beast in his sights and brought it down. It had been lurking around the prehistoric gardens, under the giant yellow slide and darting in and out from between the legs of the giant dinosaur figures. The Mystery Spot wasn't quite closed for the season, and Mr. Warren didn't want to risk the safety of their visitors.

Mr. Warren brought the carcass to the conservation office in Ray Brook and was paid a $10 bounty for ridding the world of the frightful beast. The animal was identified as a coy dog, which was a cross between a dog and a coyote. Nobody had ever heard of coy dogs in the North Country in 1970, but that's what the experts said it was. The conservation officer returned the dead body to Mr. Warren, and Mr. Warren dropped off the remains at the dump in Jay.

Nana sent us a long letter telling us all about the situation. All of us kids were frightened by Uncle Vince's stories about the wild fanged North Country werewolf. Nana thought we would be less fearful knowing that it had met its demise. The world was now a safer place. A month removed from the North Country, we had forgotten to worry about werewolves anyway.

## '70 Survival

Doc had a special gift in mind for his daughter Patti on her birthday. It came with a letter that read as follows:

*Dear Patti,*

*Just feel like talking a bit.*

*This book, Survival is a great experience. The adventure is thrilling in itself. But far more important than that, the book is a great storehouse of woods-man-ship.*

*I know that you have a great bit of common sense, and that is perhaps the greatest gift of all. And I also know that Vince in particular has had a lot of woodland experience.*

*But we can never have too much "savvy" when it comes to nature.*

*Tennyson, who love d nature for her beauty and fragrance and peace, also reminded the readers of his poems that nature could be "red in tooth and claw." She can be both a wonderful friend and also a terrible foe.*

*So read this book well. It contains a tremendous storehouse of knowledge.*

*I hope you'll understand some of the reasons why I'm going to say what I have to say. I've spent hundreds, or thousands of hours in the out-of-doors. When I was between the ages of 27 & 29 I was scoutmaster in Califon, NJ. You can bet we weren't arm-chair scouts.*

*Those two years, with eighteen boys in charge, taught me an awful lot about the woods and woods-man-ship. Those were two wonderful years!*

*Someday, Patti, with your wonderful way with children, let me encourage you to work with Girl Scouts. Here's one teaching job where the only diploma you'll need is your heart. In order to teach them, you'll learn an awful lot yourself: compass, fire, rain shelter, first aid, a thousand things about "survival" as well as enjoyments of nature and people who need friends.*

*In my book, too, the best answer to all the fuss and fury about dope and LSD or whatever, is the positive approach and the girls can love the outdoors and be at home there. They'll never be so bored that they have to resort to artificial "kicks."*

*Here are a couple things that come to my mind: Always carry a compact survival kit–each of you–in case you become separated in the woods. Always travel together, within calling distance. You can break a leg or drown awful quick, we all need each other, no matter how strong we are. Some of these stories prove this. Learn to make an emergency crutch out in the woods. Try putting together a travois, Indian style, especially you, Patti. Vince is a heavy guy. With a travois, you could haul him a long way. Especially with a tumpline. Here's hoping he never breaks a leg to test you!*

*Learn how to make a fire in the woods on a rainy day without one match. Learn how to send out a simple S.O.S, by light and by sound.*

*Know your compass like a watch and how to use it, and believe in it. Sometimes rain and snow and fog obliterates land markers.*

*Learn to respect water, for the depth of it and the power of it, and also, at times, for the filth of it. Several years ago, a brain surgeon drowned while fishing alone in the Saranac. Rather expensive trout!*

*You may think I'm being a cautious ole fuddy-duddy. Well, the older a guy gets, the more he loves life, and the more he loves nature, and the more he wants his loved ones to have this, the happiest, fullest, and longest heritage of all. Here's to many wonderful years in this marvelous North Country.*

*Bye now. See you soon. Love, Dad*

## '71 Bar Lee

It was very cold for late March, and Patti worried every day that the new foal would freeze to death the instant it was born. Patti and Vince took turns checking on Mandy several times each night. Doc assured Patti that everything would be all right. Nonetheless,

Patti had warned Dr. Lopez to be prepared for an emergency phone call at any time. It was a long drive from Westport to Jay, and he needed to be ready, just in case.

Patti had been around horses more than half her life, but this was the first time one of the Paleface horses had been bred. Patti was proud of her mare, Mandy. As horse and rider, they were a great team, both seemingly equally happy to spend time with each other. Patti thought that she and Mandy were natural partners, simpatico. The sire had been carefully selected to produce just the most desirable offspring. After a half year search, Doc and Patti had selected the stallion Aledo Bar Ben.

Finally, the foal arrived without incident. Even so, Dr. Lopez was called to check up on the new mother and her filly. The foal was a pretty baby girl, with a very strong resemblance to her mother. Patti and Vince spent hour after hour with the horses. After experiencing the miracle of birth, neither of them could get enough of the beauty of new life.

The new filly would need a name to fit her. Patti giggled when she thought of it. Aledo Bar Lee, or Barley for short. It reminded her of her niece Barbara, and the song Patti always sang to her: "Barley soup is good to eat, but not as good as barley meat," and then of course Aunt Patti would pretend to bite off one of her niece's limbs.

Patti and Vince were filled with joy, not unlike the joy they would later experience as parents of human babies.

## '71 Local Heroes

Winter was coming to a close, and it was a busy day for local hero Ed O'Connor. Ed was looking forward to the opening of fishing season and thinking about the evening meeting of the Wilmington Fish, Game, and Sport Club at Paleface. Mr. O'Connor was a co-owner of the Town and Country Motel in Wilmington, and the long-serving president of the WFG&S Club.

Ed was just about to write down a note for the evening's meeting when something caught his attention. Out the window, he noticed sparks coming from the power line, raced out his doorway, fired up his snowmobile and raced to his neighbor's trailer, which was parked at the North Pole Campsites. The trailer was on fire and flames were coming out of the windows.

Major Virginia Cundiff, a World War II and twenty year veteran army nurse, and her old dog Ajax had just come out of the trailer. Other than her pet companion, a small box and an armful of clothing was all that Miss Cundiff could scoop up on the way out the door.

Ed O'Connor rushed to disconnect the power and fuel connections to the trailer. The manager of the campsites, Mr. Donald Hodson arrived at that moment and quickly hooked up his truck to Virginia Cundiff's car and quickly dragged it a long distance from the trailer.

Mr. Hodson and his wife drove Virginia to Placid Memorial Hospital. She was suffering from severe burns on her face and hands. Virginia explained to the doctors that she had just lit her camping lantern when it exploded. She said she shouldn't have lit the lantern inside the trailer, but she did it anyway. The fire jumped to the curtains immediately. Virginia said she vaguely remembered jumping out the trailer door as fast as she could. And then perhaps two seconds later she remembered her dog was in the trailer. With the fire quickly spreading it was hard to get the dog through the flames and out the door.

Whether the first degree burns on her face came from the combustion or from the flames on the way out the door the second time, Virginia Cundiff had suffered some awful, dreadful burns in that fire.

Ajax had stayed with Ed O'Connor as the Hodsons drove away with Miss Cundiff.

The Wilmington Volunteer Fire Department quickly arrived on the scene and extinguished the fire in the blazing trailer. By the time the fire was put out, all the neighbors had arrived on the scene.

All the firefighters praised Ed O'Connor and Donald Hodson's heroic actions. All the neighbors clapped. Mr. O'Connor humbly nodded his head, almost imperceptibly. Mr. Winch added, "What was already a tragedy could have turned catastrophic."

Dana Peck was one of the neighbors that had arrived on the scene. Dana took Ajax home with him, and when Virginia Cundiff was released from the hospital, she stayed with the Peck family also until she was feeling better and could find a place to stay on her own.

## '71 WFG&S Club

Ed O'Connor returned home after the fire, took a shower, brushed his hair, combed his long beard, and finished his notes just in time to get to the show. Three Dog Night's song "Joy to the World" was playing on Ed's little transistor radio as he finished getting ready to head out the door. With a kiss for his wife Louise, Ed was on his way.

The same snowmobile that carried Ed to Virginia's trailer fire now carried him to Paleface. The warm, late March sun was quickly melting all the snow but enough remained to make one last ride of the season. Maybe it was night or dusk when he left home. Ed felt great on his machine, sliding across the snow, happily singing to himself about the joy experienced by you and me and all "the fishies in the deep blue sea."

Jim Wright was setting up all the food for the meeting and then the double feature film presentation. Paleface provided the coffee and donuts. It was a potluck dinner, and the club members each brought a dish. About sixty people showed up for the meeting. If the rest of the club knew that Della Straight's famous, mouth-watering donuts were being served, they probably all would have shown up too.

The club members ranged in age from 8 to 90. There were plenty of father-son as well as grandfather-father-son members. There weren't too many girls and ladies in the Wilmington Fish, Game & Sports Club, but in the last year that membership category had begun to grow nicely as well.

If Ed O'Connor were the sort to brag about his leadership as president of the club, he could boast having started in 1970 with fourteen members, increasing membership to 216 members by August 1970, up to 410 members in the middle of 1971, and 532 members by December 1971.

The main focus of the meeting that evening was planning for a fishing derby. The season would open in a matter of days and they needed to work very quickly. The derby should have been planned months ago, but as President O'Connor exclaimed, "There's no time like the present."

It was suggested that a trophy for the biggest catch be awarded in each of the following categories: adult, teens, and children. Another trophy would be awarded for the big three, that is the combined length of the three longest fish taken. Members were responsible for measuring their own catches and reporting the results on the honor system. There were no parliamentary procedures when it came to the WFG&S Club, but everyone voted in favor of the impromptu fishing derby.

Another suggestion was to have an awards ceremony and fish fry. Someone proposed Thursday evening, April 15th. "File your taxes, drop off your fish at Paleface, then get ready for a feast," Ed O'Connor concluded. It was decided that on Thursday, April 15th there would be an awards ceremony and fish fry. Everyone could drop off frozen fish at Paleface, and the Paleface chefs would serve them up at 7pm.

Boylan Fitz-Gerald, a member in good standing, told the members that he had prior obligations. A previously planned fishing trip with friends in Canada would prevent him from being able to join them for the fish fry. "Nonetheless," Boylan advocated, "by all means you should proceed with your plans. It sounds like a splendid idea."

Another topic of discussion for the club that evening was the recommendation for a club patch. Members had discussed the concept of a depiction of a rod and a rifle, a duck and a fish, and the official club colors brown, green, and orange. The final design was approved and the club authorized an order for a thousand patches to be distributed to members at future club meetings.

The members of the WFG&S Club then enjoyed their evening program. The first film was titled *Beaver Dam* and the second film was called *Great Adventures*.

The evening out ended late, and the youngest members were yawning mightily as they bundled up and headed out the door. It was late March, but it still got quite cold in the North Country on an early spring evening.

## '71 Tax Accountants

The last thing on Doc's schedule before heading out with his friends on their annual hunting and or fishing excursion was a meeting with his accountant. Though it could be extended, Doc and Jean liked to have their taxes prepared on time.

Donald Feldstein from Gloversville, New York arrived at Paleface mid-morning on Friday the 9th of April, right on schedule. Doc and Jean met with Don in the corner of the dining room. There were very few guests at Paleface. Skiing had lasted longer than usual, making it almost until the end of March. The few guests in residence were mostly fishermen. And fishermen weren't ever having breakfast at 10am—lunch, perhaps.

Doc was expecting a quick meeting, signing the tax returns, and a nice little visit with Mr. Feldstein.

Poor Mr. Feldstein had been dreading that trip for days.

Don Feldstein enjoyed doing the figuring, putting the numbers on the forms, and making sure all the rules were followed. The two things Don hated to do were tell a client that they owed the government a huge sum of money, and tell a client they owed the government nothing, for that meant they weren't making any money.

Don Feldstein had worked on the chart himself. With a ruler and some graph paper he had carefully charted the amount of cash Paleface had lost each year since it had opened. Each year except one, that was. Don kept colored pencils to use in such situations, and each of the bars on the chart was colored in a different hue. It would have been a handsome sight if it weren't such an ugly picture.

As Don explained the chart to Doc and Jean, with all the accompanying apologetic words and phrases designed to make the bitter pill easier to swallow, Don pointed out, "Look, the last two years, two of your best years here, we failed to put more money in the checkbook than went out. True, we almost made it to positive, but look how far down some of these other years go." Don thought it made it seem nicer to say "we."

"The bottom line is," Don concluded somewhat insistently, "that if things continue as they're going now, Paleface has *at best* five years left to live. After that, you're out of cash. Out of investments. Busted. I hate to put this so bluntly. You are wonderful people, and one of my favorite clients. I think you need to give some thought to the future."

Doc and Jean received the bad news from the "Dollar Doctor" as well as could be expected. Doc's face turned red, from a cross between embarrassment and anger. Even so, Doc remained cordial and polite. He had expected Don to note the improvement in the books compared to other years. Jean looked back and forth between Doc and Don, and felt equal measure of sympathy for both.

The returns were signed and Doc took them to the office and asked Jane to mail them. While Doc was away from the table, Jean thanked Don for addressing the situation. "This conversation needed to happen, and I appreciate having you looking out for us."

When Doc returned to the table, he told Don that he and Jean would think about it, talk about it, and let him know if they had any questions. They exchanged pleasantries, and Mr. Feldstein was on the road back to Gloversville.

After Don Feldstein left, Doc said to Jean, "Next year, let's not have Don come to see us right before I head out of town!"

Don thought on the way home, "I wonder if I'll be fired!" Unfortunately for accountants, a good dose of honesty was often harshly rewarded.

Within an hour of Don's departure, Doc gathered all his fishing gear and packed the station wagon. It was a gloomy afternoon. Hours later, Jim Cooney arrived from Albany and shortly after that, Fred Arnold arrived from Gloversville. Together they rode over to Steinhoff's Sportsmen's Inn. Robert Arms from Jay and Dr. John Mackinnon from AuSable Forks were already there.

The men enjoyed a long leisurely dinner together. Everyone looked over the Rand McNally Road Atlas pages. There were three ways to get there. For some reason, nobody had thought of the first and shortest route, driving north to Montreal, to Quebec City, and around the tip of Maine.

After studying the atlas and checking each other's figures, it was hard to argue that one of the two proposed routes was significantly better than the other. In any case, everyone agreed—at a minimum, it would be a ten and a half-hour drive. More like twelve hours if they made a lot of stops.

The friends parted early. A six o'clock start the next morning would put them at their destination by dinner time. Jim and Fred rode back to Paleface with Doc.

Doc enjoyed the relaxed comfort of having dinner, making plans and sharing laughs with his close friends at Steinhoff's, and Doc was looking forward to getting away and doing a lot of fishing with them. Doc hadn't thought about the checkbook or Mr. Feldstein for a couple of hours. Unfortunately, it all came back as soon as Doc's head hit the pillow. It was hard to fall asleep with Mr. Feldman's ugly chart imprinted on the inside of Doc's eyelids.

Jean was up at four thirty, just as she was every morning. That season, breakfasts were served early. Jean woke Doc at 5:30am, and phoned Jim and Fred from the front desk. Carl Steinhoff arrived at five minutes to six.

Winifred Arms dropped off her husband Robert at Paleface at six o'clock exactly. With a quick hug and a kiss, Robert said, "I love you."

Winifred said, "Love you too, have a great time." Winifred got back in the car, lit a cigar, and drove away.

The men enjoyed a quick, yet hearty breakfast—the usual eggs, bacon, toast, orange juice, and coffee. Jean had a big lunch sack packed for each of the men. Each lunch sack had two sandwiches, an apple, small paper bags of peanuts, and four of those famous home-made donuts. None of the men would go hungry on their road trip.

Jean gave Doc Mackinnon's lunch sack to Carl Steinhoff.

Moments later, the men were gone. Jean signed deeply, cleared the dishes from the table, and nestled into her comfy chair with a book.

## '71 New Brunswick

The two station wagons pulled up in front of Dr. John Mackinnon's house in AuSable Forks. Some of John's gear was laying on the grass next to the driveway. As the wagon pulled up, Dr. Mackinnon came out the door, followed by his wife and four daughters. They had all gotten up early to see him off.

For young children, having Dad away for two weeks seemed like an eternity. From oldest to youngest, John Mackinnon hugged his wife and each of his daughters, told them he loved them, and wiped the tears off the cheek of his youngest.

Ten hours later, the six friends arrived at Lake Edward in the town of Denmark, province of New Brunswick, Canada.

The men had a wonderful time together, as they did every year. During the day, they caught more salmon than they could handle—almost. During the evening, they enjoyed hearty debates and collegiate, philosophical conversations. They also enjoyed recalling and retelling hunting and fishing stories from their past, even though they all knew those stories by heart.

The days went by quickly, yet the men were happy two weeks later to contemplate returning home to their families and their normal lives. The last night at camp they did some brainstorming. "Where should we go next fall?" asked Doc. Doc had a philosophy that the key to happiness was to always plan the next vacation before finishing a vacation. That way there was always something grand to look forward to.

Perhaps they stayed up a little too late, but everyone was excited with the plan for the following fall. The men decided they would like to go west the following year. It was almost midnight before everyone went to bed.

The next morning everyone had a simple breakfast, packed up the cars, cleaned the cabin, and headed south for Maine.

About two hours later, Carl Steinhoff was feeling a little tired. He pulled the lead car into a roadside parking area. The parking area had a phenomenal view of Mount Kathadin, a huge mountain with a long ridge. Rather than having a conical shape, Mount Kathadin looked like three or four mountains joined together as one.

Doc took some pictures with a Kodak instamatic camera, some just of the Mountain, and some of the gang of six with Kathadin in the background. Doc thought that one day, he might want to paint that mountain.

Everyone finished stretching their legs and got back into the cars.

In the back seat of the lead station wagon, Carl pulled a blanket up over his head and closed his eyes.

## '71 Tragedy

Meanwhile, down the road, a truck driver was headed north on highway 95. Some have said he was in too much of a hurry, some have said he was too tired to stay awake, and yet others concluded that he was drunk. Whatever the case, the results quickly turned tragic.

The truck had crossed into a southbound lane after sideswiping two vehicles.

In the front seat of the lead station wagon, Dr. John Mackinnon and Robert Arms saw it coming. There were vehicles in the northbound lane. The truck was coming at them in their lane.

There was barely time for it to register that it was happening.

There didn't seem to be any safe path for the station wagon to go. The truck was coming at them. There was no time to stop the station wagon. The wagon couldn't go anywhere else but off the edge of the road. A horrible choice to ever have to make. The station wagon flipped over on the way down the hillside. Unfortunately, the driver of the truck made the same choice a fraction of a second after the station wagon began its fall.

The truck landed upside down on top of the upside down station wagon. The authorities later concluded that Carl Steinhoff, Doc Mackinnon, and Robert Arms had been killed instantly.

The men in the second station wagon were a short distance behind, and were on the scene just moments later. Jim, Fred, and Doc jumped out as fast as they could. Doc told Fred to go for help. Doc and Jim jumped and slid down the hill.

No time to grieve. Doc and Jim hoped it was a rescue operation, but panic was starting to set in.

There was no way they could get to the car. They could see it, and it was plainly squashed, having completely collapsed. There were no sounds coming from the vehicle. Doc and Jim couldn't find any evidence of their friends within the wreckage. It was flattened.

Doc and Jim helped the driver of the truck descend from the cab of his upside down truck. They made it back to the road above the drop off just as Fred made it back with a police officer following him. There was nothing that could be done.

It took the whole afternoon for the rescue team to lift the truck off the car, then to bring the car up to the road level. The police escorted the friends to town, insisting they leave the work at the scene of the accident to the professionals.

Not even a former Methodist minister could find the words to make the phone calls he had to make. It had to be done. Each passing minute made it harder to contemplate. Instead, the policeman from Medway, Maine insisted that they call their counterparts in New York and have a policeman inform Bertha Steinhoff, Katherine Mackinnon and Winifred Arms.

Doc called Jean, who was home at Overlook. Doc wasn't able to talk for long.

Next, the men arranged for the bodies to be flown to Saranac Lake, New York.

The authorities insisted that the men stay in Medway overnight. They were so grief-stricken and drained there was no way they could have driven through the night.

Doc managed to sleep somehow that night, perhaps by sheer will. Awake was the last thing Doc wanted to be.

Next morning the grieving began anew.

Overnight the policemen had typed up their reports, which the men signed. It was understood that they might be called back to testify. There was a plan to charge the driver, and if he pleaded not guilty they would need to come back and bear witness.

Back home, the entire community mourned and grieved the loss of its prominent citizens and pillars of their community. Things would never be the same. One of Doc's friends tried to console Doc by saying, "Every fatal auto accident is a tragedy and they happen all too frequently. Every time you get into a car, you are placing yourself in the path of danger. Yet, for the survivors, life marches on."

The young Mackinnon girls would have to be raised without their father. The hospital and the patients that depended on the young doctor would have to settle for someone else. Mrs. Steinhoff would eventually have to decide what to do with the business, and the patrons would miss the best part about the place they loved almost as much as its proprietor. Mrs. Arms would eventually have to decide whether to remain in the retirement home she and her husband had built in Jay or return to her native Massachusetts.

After Doc's friends were buried, Doc spent most of his time alone. For weeks. Doc hardly left the house, ate infrequently and spent most of his time in his study.

One day, about a month after the accident, the phone rang. Doc would be needed in Maine. The other men would need to appear as well. Jim and Fred made the trip to Maine on their own.

Jean insisted on driving Doc to Maine. All those weeks later, Doc still hadn't been able to talk to Jean about the tragedy. Mostly the round trip to the court in Maine was quiet as well. Jean had encouraged Doc to talk about it. Specifically, Jean had asked Doc to consider talking with one of the local ministers. Doc wasn't ready. His faith was shaken. The most consistent thought Doc had been able to communicate was, "It should have been me. I almost switched places with Dr. Mackinnon at that parking area."

It shouldn't have been anybody.

Although he pleaded innocent, the truck driver was convicted of causing the deaths of Carl Steinhoff, Dr. John Mackinnon, and Robert Arms. The driver was fined $750. The case was closed.

As best they could, the living had to carry on.

## '71 Prize Trout

The West Branch of the AuSable River was serving up increasingly larger fish with each passing year. Fran Betters had attributed the increase in the size of the fish in the river to the restrictions, one per fisherman! In the Wilmington Notch, there were reports of fine fish being taken near the Monument.

The Monument was a large rock with an engraved tablet embedded in the rock. The tablet had an engraving of two beavers, an evergreen tree and a pine branch with two pine cones. At the top of the tablet, were the years 1885 to 1935. The words on the tablet, all in capital letters, were as follows: "This tablet commemorates the 50th anniversary of conservation in New York State on May 15, 1885, Governor David B. Hill signed the law establishing the forest preserve. The surrounding mountains streams and woodlands have been acquired for the free use of all the people of the state and are maintained as wild forest land for the enjoyment of future generations. Erected 1935 by Conservation Department State of New York."

The Monument sat by a parking spot, big enough for several vehicles. Mostly the parked cars at the roadside stop belong to fishermen.

The biggest fish of the season was caught by Paleface ski-lift operator Desmond Lawrence at the Wilmington Dam. The prize trout was 26 ½ inches long and weighed 6 pounds, 14 ½ ounces. It was such a beautiful brown trout that Ed O'Connor rallied the members of the Wilmington Fish, Game & Sports Club to vote to pay to have the fish mounted and engrave a plate with Desmond Lawrence's name on it. The members of the Club appreciated the diversion of the prize trout. Even so, the tragic news hung over the members of the Club as they mourned the loss of local legend Carl Steinhoff and his friends.

## '71 Garden Tour

Business was good at Paleface during the summer of 1971.

Customers stayed at the lodge, the dude ranch did a brisk business across the street. The restaurant was always busy, the dances continued to draw crowds and Paleface remained popular for local events and meetings of civic organizations. But the business never seemed to have much to show after subtracting all the disbursements from the receipts.

Doc remained friendly with everyone in his life, but the tragedy and the checkbook problems made Doc feel hopeless and apathetic for the first time in his life. Those weren't the kind of things someone could just snap out of in a week or two.

One nice summer afternoon, Jean insisted that Doc join her for the Keene Valley Garden Club's tour of neighborhood houses and Gardens. The tour included the Reidemeister's, the Buresh's and the Bohling's houses. The tour also included Mrs. Robert Arms' house.

Doc had known Winnifred Lefferts for a long time, even before she married Robert Arms, a Traveler's Insurance agent. Like Doc, Winnifred had been, and still was, a prominent artist, having illustrated many book covers in the 1920s through the 1940s. Jean thought it would be good for Doc to see Winnifred, and perhaps it might be good for Winnifred also.

Doc and Jean stayed at Winnifred Arms' house for about an hour after the Garden Tours had ended. It did turn out to be helpful for both. Winnifred Lefferts Arms didn't remain in Jay for long, and Jean was glad she had convinced Doc to visit with her when they had the chance.

Doc's demeanor improved somewhat after that, at least outwardly.

## '71 Wolfe Island – Lake Ontario

Just after Labor Day, Tom and Ruth Keegan, Doc and Jean Fitz-Gerald, and Bertha Steinhoff set out for a fishing trip to Wolfe Island.

Wolfe Island was the largest in The Thousand Islands region, located where the St. Lawrence River met Lake Ontario, at the northeastern quadrant of the lake. From Wilmington, it was about a four-hour drive, followed by a long ride on a ferry.

It was nice to spend some quiet time together with friends, and yet it was very hard not to notice the missing presence of lost loved ones. The five friends enjoyed long boat rides and fishing. In the evenings, it was nice to go to restaurants and be served meals. Doc couldn't help but order salads with Thousand Island dressing, which was said to have originated in the region sometime around the 1900 to 1905 timeframe. After dinner they played cards, retold happy stories and reminisced. One day, Doc and Jean took a side trip to Maynard Ontario, not too far from Ogdensburg, New York. Doc's great-grandfather, William Young and great-grandmother Amanda Waldron Young were buried there.

Doc and Jean had already chosen their own eternal resting places, the Evergreen cemetery in AuSable Forks. It had been hard for Doc to admit he didn't want to be buried in the family plot with his ancestors just outside of Newark, New Jersey in the town of Linden.

After visiting the graveyard, Doc and Jean toured the Battle of the Windmill National Historic Site in the neighboring town of Prescott, Ontario before returning to Wolfe Island.

The Battle of the Windmill occurred in 1838 when a small group of would-be revolutionaries attempted to lead an American style revolution in Canada, to achieve independence from Great Britain. The uprising was a miserable failure however the small band of insurgents held out at the windmill long enough that it was necessary for artillery bombardment from gunboats and steamers to dislodge them and force their surrender.

Jean had an interest in history, and enjoyed reading every roadside sign and historical marker she could find.

Mrs. Steinhoff and the Keegans kept busy with a shopping trip to Kingston, Ontario while the Fitz-Geralds were away on their side trip.

## '71 Wilmington Sesquicentennial

Saturday, September 18th was a busy day in Wilmington, New York. The weekend long celebration of the Town's sesquicentennial kicked off at nine o'clock in the morning. An Antique Show was displayed at the Town Hall.

A parade commenced from the Beach Road at 1 o'clock in the afternoon. The parade proceeded along Route 86 past the judges' station in the parking lot of the Holiday Motel, and on past the Town Hall to the Park.

The four judges had their work cut out for them, picking winners in several categories. Lee Brow was one of the judges.

Awards were presented in the Park at the conclusion of the parade, followed by a couple of speeches. The Queen and King of the event were recognized. The Best Band Award went to AuSable Forks. The Best Marching Unit Award went to the Golden Eagle Drum and Bugle Corps of Port Henry. The Best Float was the King and Queen's float. The Best Fire Department Award went to the Lake Placid Fire Department. Each of the awards came with a $100 prize.

The Most Humorous Float Award went to the Wilmington Fire Department, which featured a still. Clara Hazelton's articles in the newspaper reminded everyone in town of Wilmington's 150 years of history, including its first industry: the production of Rye Whiskey.

A couple of other awards were presented. Mary Goetschius won a $25 award for her Old Time Peddler costume, complete with pots and pans that clinked and clanked as she walked. Peggy Mihill won $12.50 for the best horse in the parade, and Karen Benson won $12.50 for the best decorated bicycle in the parade. A lot of the antique autos rode along in the parade, giving the appearance of a really old time procession. The awards for the cars would be given in a separate program the next day.

Finally, many dignitaries and local politicians appeared in the parade. Nobody gave the politicians any awards. Dana began his long political career that fall, marching in the parade with a sign that said “Pick Peck.” Dana was running un-opposed, so chances looked good that he would get the nod from the voters to serve as assessor.

Then the judges were recognized for their volunteer service. The Town Supervisor, BJ Cook did a great job of keeping remarks to a bare minimum. The keynote speaker, on the other hand, did not!

81-year-old Lee Brow proudly stood at a podium in the park and delivered a long, relaxed keynote address as if he had all the time in the world and nothing else to do.

He started by speaking about the glories of the Adirondack region. Lee expressed profound appreciation for the beauty of the AuSable Valley and called the area between Mount Marcy and Whiteface Mountain, God’s Rock Garden. Lee’s eloquent words flowed from his tongue like the AuSable River, fast in some places and slow in others.

Lee went on to tell the audience that to completely appreciate the beauty of the area, one should have to experience being away, and to make frequent periodical visits. Such was Lee’s experience, having been born into one of Wilmington’s first families, and having been raised in Wilmington. As an adult, Lee moved away, but returned to Wilmington for vacations twice each summer. He went on to tell the audience about the founding history of the town and his ancestors.

The speaker had a great time comparing the modern conveniences with the experience of living in Wilmington 150 years earlier. Lee talked about the advent of the automobile and the wonderful roads, the "magnificent series of motels and eating places. Great areas of enticing entertainment have been developed." Wherever Lee lived or traveled, he spoke of all the Adirondack mountains had to offer, from the winter sporting activities to hunting and fishing. Lee confided that he liked to think of the great AuSable Valleys as being "the house by the side of the road" in the poem immortalized by Sam Walter Foss, which implored people to be kind to tourists and travelers passing by their homes and through their towns. Lee challenged residents to be conscious of their roles as local ambassadors so that visitors would be encouraged to "stop awhile and enjoy what we who were born here treat at times altogether too lightly."

Lee spoke lovingly about his inspiring grandfather, the late Landon "Jack" Wilkins. Lee mentioned Jack's service during the Civil War, shared memories of Jack's home spun philosophies. From then on Lee spoke of Jack as Gramps. He told a story about how Gramps had instructed that should Lee ever become lost in the woods, he should simply look for a brook and follow the brook home. Lee told the crowd that recently he was resting under a tree on Marble Mountain, next to Whiteface, "drinking in the wondrous vista of the valley below" and recalled Gramps' advice and became inspired to write a poem of his own, inspired by his grandfather and by Robert Frost. Lee read his poem to the crowd, the advice on how not to become lost was conveyed simply, and the affection between grandfather and grandson was apparent.

After intentionally speaking for as long as he possibly could, Lee said "I hope that I have not trespassed too long upon your time. When one stirs up his thoughts and memories of the Adirondacks, he runs the risk of over extension."

Lee concluded as he began, trumpeting the "wondrous glories of God's Rock Garden." Then he prayed, asking that God bless Wilmington for another 150 years.

The crowd awarded Lee Brow with vigorous applause, and then disbursed.

Dozens of citizens stood in line to shake Lee's hand and congratulate him on delivering such a fine speech. Doc Fitz-Gerald had admired Lee's presentation from the back of the crowd, and stood last in line.

"Would you like to sit down and talk for a while, Mr. Brow?" asked Doc. Doc and Lee sat on a bench under a tall tree. They talked briefly about public service, public speaking, and their shared love for the Adirondacks. Then they talked for a while about poetry. Doc didn't often come across people with a knowledge of poems. From his memory, Doc very slowly recited another Sam Walter Foss poem, called *The Calf-Path.* He had memorized it as a student, and often featured in his sermons. It documented the case of an ancient herd path that through the ages evolved to become a super highway, and followed the same course, just because it had always been there. It was a good reminder how easy it was to just blindly follow long-established traditions.

Doc paused for a long moment of reflection. Lee Brow did not disturb it. Doc concluded with the observation that poet Foss appealed to him because the poet saw the average man as extraordinary. Lee Brow nodded in agreement.

Lee reflected, "I guess that's why I enjoy serving as justice of the peace. Last year I married 700 average men to 700 average women. The best part is that I got to spend part of the best day of each of their lives with them. And I got to share a little bit of advice with them as well."

Doc inquired, "If you don't mind me asking, were you ever married?"

"No, of course. I don't mind at all. It's been years since anyone asked me that question. I was married in 1921, and we had a daughter. It didn't end well, I'm sorry to say and I hate to have to admit the fault was all mine. So, the advice I give comes from lessons learned the hard way."

Next the men talked for a few minutes about the Adirondack

Shillelagh Club. Lee told Doc that there were now over 1,200 members in the club. Doc told Lee, "I admire all that you have accomplished, the example that you set, and the vigor with which you have approached your *golden* years. When I am your age, I hope to be just as interesting a fellow!" Doc concluded.

Doc and Lee took a leisurely stroll through the flea market tables in the park, and were first in line when the Wilmington Fire Department served barbecue at 4:30 in the afternoon. Next in line were Leo Cooper and Gus Elliott. Leo and Gus were talking about the festivities planned for the next day, which really all related to the Antique Auto Rally. The planners had thought to tack the anniversary celebrations on to the annual classic car convention.

## '72 Debut of Crazy Horse

Going into the winter season, the members of the ski club and the ski instructors were looking forward to the debut of Crazy Horse. A new ski trail, which promised to be of interest to expert skiers, had been in development all summer.

Doc thought about the Indian after whom the trail was named, the last great hope of the Sioux Nation almost a hundred years earlier. Doc also thought about the mountain in South Dakota near Mount Rushmore where sculptor Korczak Ziolkowski had been toiling away since 1948 creating a megalithic memorial monument.

It felt a little like the good old days as Doc advertised Paleface's new ski trail coming into the new ski season.

## '72 Hot Winter

The winter of 1972 was a hot winter—what would be the first of two such hot winters. There was a little bit of snow early, and so Christmas had been okay, but not long after that there wasn't enough snow to ski on. No snow from the sky. Too hot to make snow. Paleface had no choice but to shut down skiing operations, laying off seventy workers, smack dab in the middle of January. Two weeks into the new year, and Paleface's year to date net income was *minus* $40,000.

The rest of the winter wasn't much better. It was very difficult to eke out a season. Doc and Jean worked twice as hard, trying to do all the work themselves, with just a skeleton crew. The restaurant, hotel, and bar remained open. There were not enough customers to cover the cost of employees *and* the costs to operate the facilities, such as property taxes, insurance, heat, lights, and power. Even so, Doc and Jean felt bad about having to have the employees on furlough, knowing they all had bills to pay as well. Each day Doc fretted over the cash report. And every day Doc thought about the accountant, and dreaded his next visit.

## '72 Rosemary Robinson

Rosemary Robinson had been coming with her husband to the North Country two or three times a year for over a decade. Mr. Robinson's passions included skiing, hunting, and fishing. Fortunately, Mrs. Robinson had no difficulty keeping herself entertained in his absence.

Rosemary continued to make an effort to learn how to ski. Several years earlier, when Pete Pelkey left Paleface for Whiteface, Rosemary followed. Ol' Pete might have preferred Mrs. Robinson *not* tell everyone what a wonderful ski instructor Pete was, since she would always add that she had been taking his beginner classes for over a decade. A good ski instructor was supposed to graduate his pupils to intermediate and then advanced levels of skiing fairly rapidly.

Rosemary Robinson was very expert at relaxing in the ski lodge all afternoon. Fortunately for Paleface, Mrs. Robinson insisted that they stay at Paleface, even though they didn't ski at Paleface anymore.

Laura and Trum, who ran the Ski Hut at Paleface, greatly appreciated Mrs. Robinson's visits to Paleface. Rosemary loved to show off her ski fashions when she returned home to New Jersey. Each year when Laura put out the new merchandise, she could almost predict what Rosemary Robinson would buy. Or maybe Laura made it easy on Rosemary by always dressing the Manikin in the latest, best, highest priced, highest margin outfit of the season.

Unbeknownst to Mrs. Robinson, Laura had taken to calling the manikin Rosemary. Laura and Trum were always careful to avoid conversing with Rosemary the manikin when Rosemary the customer was a guest at Paleface.

Rosemary Robinson was also a collector. Given Rosemary's expensive tastes in fashions, Mr. Robinson appreciated that Mrs. Robinson's collection specialty was postcards.

The Robinsons came to Paleface three to four times a year, enjoying all the seasonal changes of the Adirondacks. This vacation was a fishing vacation. Mr. Robinson got up before dawn and drove off in the car in search of trout.

Jean was having breakfast with Carolyn and her kids at the lodge when Mrs. Robinson came out to dine. There were no other guests at the lodge. Carolyn had seemed to hit it off with Rosemary, and Jean suggested to Carolyn that she take Rosemary on a Lake Placid shopping trip. Jean was more than happy to spend the day with her grandchildren. Mr. Robinson was somewhere on the banks of the West Branch of the AuSable River. Jean could relate.

In the middle of the afternoon, Carolyn and Rosemary returned with bags full of boxes. Carolyn proudly said to Jean, "It seems Mrs. Robinson has completed her Christmas shopping, Mother!"

As it turned out, Carolyn had done some shopping of her own. Three of the boxes held brand new dresses Carolyn had purchased, plus some clothes for her children. Plaid, bell bottom pants for everyone, in a wide range of vibrant colors. Plus a new poncho made of mismatched patches for her daughter Barbara.

That afternoon, Carolyn and Rosemary put on a fashion show for Doc and Jean at Paleface, changing from one outfit to the next. Doc and Jean showered each outfit with compliments and praise.

"You are every bit the high priestess of polyester!" Doc exclaimed to a laughing Carolyn as she modeled a lovely pink, brown, and white paisley polyester dress.

"You are number-one in Naugahyde," Doc told Carolyn when she returned in a brown pleather skirt and burnt orange, mohair sweater.

The compliments Mrs. Robinson received from Doc went a little more like this: *How gallant, what a lovely hat, that is such a pretty dress*, and *you look exquisite, Mrs. Robinson!*

Carolyn, Jean, and the kids left Paleface for Jay. Doc, Jane, and Mrs. Robinson remained at Paleface.

After school, Dana and Jane's sons arrived at Paleface. Doc had work for the boys, who were always saving for something.

Mrs. Robinson spent the afternoon sipping hot chocolate, and filling out postcards, just as she did during her winter vacations. Rosemary had an enormous address book, filled with hundreds of her closest friends back home.

Rosemary had sheets of postage stamps and stacks of new postcards that she had purchased in Lake Placid during her shopping spree.

On one card, she wrote: "Wish you were here. Heavy rain last night. Nicer today. Spent the day in Lake Placid."

On another card, she wrote, "Look at this! A chimp in a go-cart! Only in the Adirondacks." Never mind that Rosemary only went to the gift shop at the famed, Land of 1000 Animals, and only long enough to buy a couple dollars-worth of postcards. One would think she had toured the entire iconic Adirondack attraction!

Ironically, the job Doc had for the boys was to send postcards to every guest that ever stayed at Paleface. All afternoon, the boys wrote, "Join us for our best summer yet! Love, Aunt Jean and Uncle Doc." The boys were told that the successful summer season that year would depend on their best penmanship. The message was easy enough, but the addresses took a little more effort and concentration to copy correctly. The boys made fun of the names of the towns they had never heard of before. Places like Hoboken, New Jersey; Penobscot, Maine; and Contoocook, New Hampshire.

Shortly after five o'clock, Jane brought Rosemary another hot chocolate, and then checked the boys' work. Doc gave each boy $5 for their troubles. Then the Peck family headed home for a busy evening of homework in preparation for school the next day.

Dana-D. had a book report due the next day. He had read Drums Along the Mohawk by Walter Edmonds, all about the hardship endured by fictional Gill and his wife Lana during the revolutionary war. Dana-D. just had to put 200 words to paper by first thing the next morning.

Doc fed the jukebox, and played: "I'd Like to Teach The World to Sing (In Perfect Harmony)" by The New Seekers and "Family Affair" by Sly and the Family Stone. Then Doc sat down with Rosemary Robinson. Rosemary set aside her address book and blank cards, and said, "Let me show you what I picked up in town today!"

Slowly, one by one, Rosemary showed Doc the old post cards she had picked up at the antique shop in Lake Placid. They marveled at the picture post cards from the past.

Doc's favorites were the two cards featuring little Lake Tear of the Clouds, in the shadow of the behemoth Mount Marcy, also known as Tahawus or Cloud Splitter. The older was a black and white picture taken by Seneca Ray Stoddard. The more recent card was a hand colored picture printed on linen. Doc and Rosemary joked about the time a few years earlier when Doc and Rosemary's husband Archie hiked up Mount Marcy and stopped at Lake Tear of the Clouds before making the final long, hard ascent to the summit.

There were several old cards from the early days of the Whiteface Memorial Highway, showing the twists and turns up the mountain, hairpin turns, the castle at the top, the tunnel to the elevator that brought visitors up the final couple hundred feet.

Many of the old cards featured spectacular views of Whiteface Mountain from the other side, which is to say from the Lake Placid side. Until that afternoon, Mrs. Robinson hadn't realized that Lake Placid was physically located on the shores of Mirror Lake. The actual lake named Lake Placid was just beyond. "The view from the Town of Lake Placid to Whiteface, with the Lake and its islands in between is nothing short of spectacular!" exclaimed Rosemary.

"You should go out on the steamer, the Doris II," Doc replied, "you'll get a great view and have a marvelous time." There were several old cards among Rosemary's purchases that featured the Doris, and Rosemary had to agree they made a compelling case for jumping aboard.

Rosemary had also managed to find some postcards featuring some of the stately, iconic old hotels in Lake Placid and in Wilmington, including the Lake Placid Club, The Stevens House, The Whiteface Inn, and The Wilmington Inn.

One old postcard tickled Doc's funny bone. It was a drawing of the old covered bridge in the Town of Jay, with a farmer and a whip driving a happy beast of burden onto the bridge.

A dreamer at heart, Doc was often drawn much more to thoughts of the future than to thoughts of the past. It was hard to think of postcards written during his own lifetime as antiques, or collectibles. The world had changed a lot in the past sixty years! Though he might not have wanted to admit it, the years were flying by faster and faster.

Finally, Mr. Robinson returned from his day in the river with an enormous speckled beauty. Mrs. Robinson gloated, "I think I did as well as you did." And handed her husband a picture postcard of a creel and a fine collection of the Adirondacks' finest food source.

Doc took Mr. Robinson's catch to the kitchen, cleaned it, cooked it, and brought a fine feast of trout to the table. Mr. Robinson insisted that Doc join them for dinner, and the three of them enjoyed a nice meal.

Mr. Robinson remarked, "It is lots of fun to be here in the winter or the summer with people all over the place, but I have to say having the place all to ourselves and being served by the owner, the very proprietor himself is very special."

"We like to think of you as cherished friends," Doc replied.

Doc cleared the table, then cleaned up in the kitchen, leaving the Robinsons to themselves for a while.

## '72 God Bless America

It was early in the afternoon, late in the 1972 summer season. Just as the last guests were finishing lunch a very famous visitor stopped into Paleface.

A man entered through the front door, and asked the first person he met whether he could speak with the owner or the manager. Jean introduced herself as the owner's wife and asked how she might be of service.

Behind his hand, the man very quietly told Jean that he had in the car a very famous woman who needed to use the rest room. As Jean was suggesting she could use a vacant room to freshen up, she saw the very famous woman getting out of the vehicle parked out front. It seemed she could not wait for her driver to return with permission.

Jean would have recognized her anywhere.

For years, Jean had followed her on radio, television and enjoyed her recordings. Jean was not one to idolize celebrities although she had admired this cultural icon who had remained in the public spotlight for decades.

Moments later, "America's Songbird" Kate Smith walked through the front door of Paleface. Her driver, who also served as her manager had tried to keep a low profile. Kate Smith sauntered in, and immediately began singing along with the piped in music, her pace increasing as she went along. Jean got an extraordinary opportunity to hear Kate Smith join Mavis and the Staple Singers on their minor hit song "Respect Yourself."

Locally, it was common knowledge that Kate Smith had a vacation home in Lake Placid. Fewer people knew that she had a dear friend that lived in Keeseville, New York, and from time to time Kate Smith would make the trip from Lake Placid through Wilmington, Jay, and AuSable Forks on the way to Keeseville.

Kate Smith was best known for singing "God Bless America," which she debuted on Armistice Day in 1938. As a recording artist, Kate Smith's greatest popularity occurred in the 1940s and Kate Smith was a major radio star during the 1930s and 1940s. Her career extended far into the television era as well.

Her manager introduced Jean Fitz-Gerald and Jean escorted Miss Smith to room number one. Once there, Jean said, "Please make yourself at home, dear. Take all the time you need. I'll be at the front desk if you need anything."

Miss Smith's driver waited near the entrance.

Jane came out of the office, which was just behind the front desk. Jane was holding the outgoing mail and the bank deposit bag. Jean stopped her and whispered a quick update in her ear. Jane set down the mail and the bag on the desk and scurried off to ask the driver if she could get him something to eat or drink.

A couple minutes later, Kate Smith emerged from Jean and Doc's chambers. Jean was waiting for her at the desk, and Jane had just returned from getting Miss Smith's driver an iced tea. Jean introduced Kate Smith to Jane Peck.

Jane said, "It's an honor to meet you, Miss Smith. You sing like an angel. It's a pleasure to meet you. Have a lovely afternoon." Jane shook hands with Kate Smith and then, picking up the mail and the bank bag, Jane excused herself.

Jean asked, "Can we get you some lunch or something to drink?"

"You know, that sounds wonderful," said Kate, "but only if you will join me."

Jean showed Miss Smith to the best table at Paleface, and with her right hand suggested Kate Smith take the window seat with the best view of Whiteface. The table was kind of in the corner, just beneath Paleface's mascot, Fuzzy Wuzzy and with Miss Smith's back to the dining room, she was less likely to be recognized or fussed over by other guests and staff.

Once it was clear that Kate Smith planned to stay at Paleface for a while, Kate Smith's driver sat at a table near the front of the dining room, about five tables away from Kate and Jean. Jean suggested bacon, lettuce and tomato sandwiches for lunch, and told Kate she would be back in moments.

The rest of the lunch crew had cleared out for the day. Jean Wright was cleaning up, and getting things prepared for the dinner crew when Jean Fitz-Gerald came in with the order: two BLT's with French fries, two Tab's, and two chocolate puddings. "And would you mind bringing them to my table in the dining room?" Jean asked. "It would seem I am entertaining the legendary Kate Smith of radio and television this afternoon."

Jean Fitz-Gerald returned to Kate Smith's table, and settled into the chair to Miss Smith's left. Neither woman noticed that it seemed to take forever for lunch to arrive. Jean Wright, who was normally very efficient, was consumed with trying to make every single detail perfect.

Mrs. Wright had never paid such close attention to a bacon, lettuce, and tomato sandwich in her life. With the bacon cooking, Jean Wright put the French fries in the deep fryer and went in search of produce. Jean Wright rejected several perfect leaves of lettuce before finally settling on two pristine leaves and then tried to pick out the perfect tomato.

Finally, Jean Wright had gathered everything on a round waiter's tray. It looked to Mrs. Wright like everything was perfect and ready to go, and of course, it was. Jean Wright's hands were shaking as she picked up the tray and headed for the front of the dining room.

As lunch arrived, Jean Fitz-Gerald took advantage of the pause in the conversation to introduce Miss Kate Smith to Jean Wright. Kate Smith said, "It's nice to meet you, Jean."

Jean Wright said, "Pleasure to meet you, ma'am, I hope you enjoy your lunch." With a slight bow Mrs. Wright disappeared. Back in the kitchen, Jean Wright let out a huge sigh of relief, just glad not to have spilled anything, not to have dropped anything, and not to have tripped over her own feet, even though she wasn't in the habit of doing any of those things.

Mrs. Wright felt star struck. Every two minutes, she peered out of the window from the kitchen to the dining room at the back of Kate Smith's head.

About ten minutes after delivering lunch, Mrs. Wright forced herself to return to the dining room to ask if everything was alright and whether she could bring anything else. Jean Fitz-Gerald and Kate Smith had both finished their Tab's.

After Mrs. Wright delivered more soda she stopped to check on Miss Smith's driver who was grateful for the offer of a newspaper and a magazine. Waiting for famous people could be very boring.

After the brief, initial shock of seeing Kate Smith get out of a car and walk through the front door of Paleface, Jean Fitz-Gerald felt like she was talking with an old friend, a kindred spirit. Conversation between the two women came so easy, Jean Fitz-Gerald half forgot that she was talking to an international superstar.

And Kate Smith talked to Jean about ordinary things, like the summer weather, the birds in the feeders, the flowers in the garden and repair work needed around their homes. The two women also talked about more consequential things, from religion to politics to health care.

Both women were diabetic. A very long conversation about living with diabetes began as Miss Smith and Mrs. Fitz-Gerald enjoyed their chocolate puddings. Jean Fitz-Gerald listened very sympathetically as Kate Smith talked about trying to manage her weight and keep a positive attitude while living in the public eye. Comedians and gossip columnists loved to ridicule celebrities of size, particularly the ladies.

For the most part, Miss Smith avoided talking about performing or the trappings of fame. Jean Fitz-Gerald did mention to Kate Smith that she was a fan of her music, and mentioned how much she had enjoyed seeing Kate Smith, Dean Martin, and Lucille Ball perform a vaudeville medley on Dean Martin's television show five or six years earlier.

Kate Smith told Jean that it was a lot of fun, and a little hard to sing with a straight face as Lucille Ball was doing her bits in the background. Other than that brief exchange, Jean might as well have been talking with an old friend from Church.

During their afternoon together, Jean confessed to Kate Smith that she was feeling like she had reached the point where it was time to slow down. It had been in the middle or the back of her mind for a couple of years, and since the tragic car accident the year before it was clear that Jean and Doc needed to confront the fact that it was time to enter a new phase in their lives. Or maybe it was just clear to Jean.

It wasn't so much that Kate Smith gave specific advice, as it was lending her ear and asking questions. As Jean Fitz-Gerald answered Kate Smith's questions, she was clearly answering her own questions as well, questions she had been avoiding asking herself. Miss

Smith helped Jean realize that Jean had devoted herself to helping her husband realize his dream. And though it shouldn't have to be, Jean would have to lead what was to come. It was time to find new owners for Paleface.

Kate Smith's own career had similarly declined to such a point that she was much less in demand. She told Jean about how nice it was to live at a slower pace, and then joked about the strange twists and tangles of life.

As circumstance would have it, both Jean Fitz-Gerald and Kate Smith were hockey fans. Kate Smith told Jean the story about how the Philadelphia Flyers had begun featuring "God Bless America" late in 1969 during important home games periodically. And on those occasions, there was a perception that the team was more successful. Kate Smith laughed, "It's kind of fun being a good luck charm!"

Kate Smith and Jean Fitz-Gerald wiled away the entire afternoon. Kate seemed to be in no hurry to rush off and visit her dear friend in Keeseville, and Jean certainly wasn't about to excuse herself from such a thoroughly enjoyable afternoon.

After the last gang of trail riders had purchased their tickets at the front desk and made their way across the street to the dude ranch, Kate Smith visited Jean and Doc's private room again. Then Miss Smith borrowed the phone in the office to call her friend, who seemed to understand that something had come up and that Kate Smith would visit at another time.

By late afternoon, Kate Smith and Jean Fitz-Gerald kissed each other's cheeks and Kate and her manager put the car on the road back toward Lake Placid.

## '72 Anniversary Note - 1972

*Darling,*

*Here's to the best little wife a guy ever could want. You're all the woman I could ever dream about or ask for. I haven't always made it easy for you, maybe that's male pride. Maybe it's Irish.*

*I dunno! But I sure love you and want you to know it. Just be patient you little loveable Sunfish.*

*I'm trying to unload this joint, the best way I know how. Without a distress sale and without too much loss for our 3 kids. Maybe you sometimes feel like calling Paleface "Fitz-Gerald's Folly." Sometimes I do too!!! But I know who it is that has really stuck by the old fool.*

*The trouble is, for one thing, I'm a hill-billy at heart. I hate the city and never want to go back. They can buy Paleface—but they'll never buy any horse you or Patti want.*

*Yes! Right now it's tough. Galloping socialism has given us problems. But, I still believe in us. You and me especially! You've been a real team-mate. May it go on a long, long while! Not the problems. I hope they'll be over in a year or so. But the feeling of one-ness, of loyalty, of a lot of the same way of loving life, close to the essential things, the real things that count.*

*- Popeye*

## '73 Baby Courtney

We got the news by telephone, the news we'd been waiting to hear. Aunt Patti and Uncle Vince had a baby and they named her Courtney! It was so exciting, I remember running wild around the house, repeating the news over and over again.

For fun and profit, our Mom was breeding Betta fish, otherwise known as Siamese Fighting Fish. It was a difficult thing to accomplish, but we had about a hundred tiny baby fish, each growing slowly in its own glass. Beyond breeding Betta fish, Mom had the idea to open a tropical fish store, and we had gone so far as to visit the supply stores and hatcheries, one of which was near Buffalo,

New York. Anyway, my brother, sister and I had to share the news, at the top of our lungs, with each and every single baby Betta, that we had a new cousin.

Aunt Patti's dream of being a cowboy *and* a mommy had finally come true.

And baby Courtney was the most beautiful baby I had ever seen in my life.

## '73 El Nino

Nobody had ever heard of El Nino in 1972, however its impact on the tourism industry in the North Country during the two year period from 1972 to 1973 was devastating.

When Ed Stransenback, the reporter from the Plattsburgh *Press-Republican* called Paleface on March 19th, Doc Fitz-Gerald glumly reported: "It's been too warm this winter. Had temperatures been lower we would be okay. But with this warm weather, we have had no chance to make snow."

Doc gloomily continued, "Prior to our March 4th closing, we had only four days of skiing in the past month and a half. We've only had forty-three ski days overall this winter."

When Doc read the newspaper article that included the Paleface Ski Report, he found the following analysis: "...most weathermen contacted were not sure why the winters in the East are getting milder and those in the West worse. Both last winter and the present one have shown this characteristic. However, Jerome Namias, research meteorologist with the Scripps Institution of Oceanography in LaJolla, California has recorded an interesting bit of information. The former chief long-range forecaster for the U.S. Weather Service said the changed weather pattern is due to a changing of ocean temperatures. When the East was cold, it was cold in the Central Pacific, But Namias has noted that for the last two years the central Pacific has become warmer and the Eastern Pacific has been colder, changing the wind patterns that carry the weather. The East is now getting the warmer air that used to flow over the West and vice versa." Namias stated that he wasn't sure what caused the shift in ocean temperatures. He mentioned that water is sluggish and a return to former temperatures could take years. Whatever the problem, Eastern winter recreation centers could not suffer the financial loss of too many more years like that winter.

Doc didn't know to blame the Little Boy in Spanish, but sure had a few choice words for Mother Nature in English. Words that a former member of the clergy would not have been proud to utter.

## '73 Year-End Numbers

With winter's early demise, there was plenty of time to close the prior year's books. A final analysis of the gross receipts, compared to all previous years showed a sad decline. Doc looked at the columns of numbers. How exhilarating it had been when Paleface first topped $100,000 in 1963, Doc thought.

A fraction of a second later, Doc snorted with disdain at the thought of declining numbers in the following two years, 1964 and 1965.

Then 1966 was much better, almost back to 1963 levels. When revenues hit $141,000 in 1967 Paleface generated a handsome, respectable profit. 1968 revenues declined again before returning to higher levels in 1969, 1970, and 1971. Doc thought about how impressed he had been with Gross Receipts in 1967, the year the Montreal Exposition dropped hordes of tourists on Paleface's doorstep. Even with great repeat visits, revenues failed to exceed the rising costs of doing business as the years progressed.

The devastation caused by 1972's snowless winter felt like a kick in the gut.

Looking at historical figures in their future equivalents could be more revealing. In contemporary dollars, 1967 was certainly the pinnacle of Paleface's success, the modern equivalent of a $1,000,000 dollar a year business.

## '73 Summer Floated by Like a Warm Breeze

At Paleface, the summer of 1973 just kind of floated by like a warm breeze. Mostly we weren't there to enjoy it but with every fiber of my being I wished I was there. As soon as school let out at the end of spring, I always believed we belonged at Paleface.

Unfortunately, Dad taught summer school that year so our family vacations in the Adirondacks were very brief. In addition to teaching classes to students who didn't pass during the regular school year, Dad also taught a typing class for extra money.

For some reason, I went to work with Dad that summer and I remember being in the back of the class, with an old typewriter in front of me—the kind where each key individually plunged down through a ribbon onto paper when you pounded on the round key.

I became a very proficient typist that summer. To this day, my fingers easily land in the home position, out of habit.

## '73 Rock Party

Fortunately, we got to spend some of August in the Adirondacks.

For two weeks, Nana and Grampa rented us a camp on Fern Lake. It was the last camp on the lake. Beyond that point there was a trail through the woods to a sandy beach on the north side of the lake. Mostly people visited Sand Beach by boat, but the trail was well utilized also.

The camp had a sign that said Fitzie's Trail's End. It would seem the owners of the camp had gone to great length to make us feel welcome, with our last name being Fitz-Gerald and all. Actually, the owners' name was Fitzsimmons, so the name of the camp made complete sense.

We had a new puppy that summer. He was the runt of the litter, and the sweetest dog the world has ever known. He was a mutt through and through, white and tan, sort of like a Pinto pony except the tan coloring was so light it almost looked white. The veterinarian identified the puppy as part terrier, part beagle, part pug, and who knows what else! Each of those breeds had its faults. Fortunately for us, our puppy got all the great traits from his doggie ancestors and none of their faults. Except for shedding after he reached maturity. He did tend to leave tiny white hairs everywhere. Mom gave the puppy the gift of a name. The first day we had him he was so small, and had very little hair on his body. He had lots of little black spots on his belly. He was weaned too soon and we had to give him little bottles of milk. He looked just like a tiny piglet. Mom named him after Winnie the Pooh's loyal sidekick. Anyway, we were lucky to be able to have our little dog with us at the rented camp.

Along the road to Fern lake there were lots of wild blueberries growing in the woods. Fortunately, we arrived early enough in August to catch the end of the blueberry season. We were warned to keep a look out for bears, who are known to love the berries almost as much as kids! We made a contest out of berry picking, to see who could finish with the most berries in the bucket. I couldn't help but eat most of the berries I picked. The berries that survived made their way into one of Nana's pies.

Aunt Patti had recently become great friends with Sue (Meconi) Pulitzer. Patti had known Sue for many years. Before Patti went to boarding school in St. Johnsbury, she attended school in AuSable. Sue was secretary of the Class of '64. Patti was treasurer of the band. That was about the extent of their overlap as kids.

When Patti married Uncle Vince, and Sue Meconi married Spike Pulitzer, Patti and Sue were brought back together and discovered that they had greatly compatible personalities. They might have discovered it years earlier, except Sue wasn't interested in skiing or horseback riding, and Patti didn't seem to have time for much else! Sue had every opportunity to take an interest in skiing. Her mother Betty and her brothers Billy and Bobby were all great skiers, and spent lots of time skiing at Paleface. Billy and Bobby were very active in the Junior Racing Program, and Betty was an officer of the Paleface Ski Club for many years.

The Meconis had a beautiful camp just a stone's throw away from Fitzies Trails End. Sue wanted to plan a memorable event while we were visiting. Given that we took to calling her Aunt Sue during that week, despite the lack of genealogically recognizable connections, she certainly succeeded at making it special.

Aunt Sue was very creative, and with Aunt Patti's help they planned a Rock Party. Aunt Sue collected a bunch of rocks, each one very recognizably different from the other. On a piece of paper, Aunt Sue made a list of each rock's features. Then Aunt Sue baked a delicious cake, and dropped the rocks (which she had cleaned very thoroughly, to be sure) into the batter at various spots so that no two rocks would end up in the same slice.

Then to the list of rocks and their features, Aunt Sue added silly little challenges. Most of the challenges were very silly, and not hard to take at all.

In addition to the cake, Aunt Sue planned a cookout, leaving the grilling to Uncle Spike. Aunt Sue had prepared several side dishes, and Aunt Patti brought several with her. Nana came as well, and contributed a couple of her favorite picnic items.

Uncle Vince bought torches. To make the torches, Uncle Vince collected about a dozen swamp water cattails. The cattails were soaked in kerosene for a full day. The torches were on display in their bucket, waiting for the right moment.

And finally, there was a small campfire in a built-up stone pit. At the ready were graham crackers, Hershey bars, marshmallows, and sticks for toasting the marshmallows.

Aunt Patti had been talking up the Rock Party all week, but revealing almost no details. By the time the evening of the Rock Party came around, everyone was very excited. It started in the middle of the afternoon, with a trip around the lake on the Meconi's boat and a stop at the sandy beach for a long swim. When we got back to Meconi's camp, we were hungry enough for a great feast. And Spike was an expert master of the grill.

After dinner was over, we took a walk down the road to make room for dessert. When we got back a short while later, Aunt Sue had cleared away all the remains from the cookout, and in the middle of the long table that had been set out in the yard was a beautiful Chocolate Cake under a big glass cover. Next to the cake were plates, napkins, and forks, and a strangely shaped spatula that was perfectly shaped for serving a single slice of cake.

As Aunt Sue cut the cake, she very slowly and seriously warned us that there were rocks in the cake. She might as well have said there were rocks in her head. It didn't make sense. We looked at each other, and wondered what in the world she was talking about. Aunt Sue warned us that we should take little bites of the cake with our forks, and make sure we didn't eat any rocks.

There was also a pile of hand towels on the end of the table, and next to the table was a big bucket of water. Aunt Sue said that those of us who were lucky enough to get a rock should wash them in the bucket and then she would tell us what each rock meant.

While we ate our cake, and searched for rocks, Uncle Vince lit the torches. It was getting kind of late, not dark yet but headed in that direction. Uncle Vince had brought a couple buckets of sand and the lit torches were placed into the buckets all around the yard.

I was not lucky enough to get a rock. I had to volunteer for a second slice of cake to get a rock! My rock choice dictated that I run around the camp three times, clucking like a chicken, flapping my arms and stretching my neck. Aunt Sue had a large pheasant feather ready to go for whoever drew this rock. I was more than happy to stick the pheasant feather down the back of my pants and run around the camp as a chicken. It must have been a sight to see the way everyone roared with laughter.

One of the challenges was to reach your hand into a bag full of eyeballs and pull out a walnut from the bag. My little brother Jeff who was seven drew that rock. When Aunt Patti told him what his task was, she tried to minimize the part about the eyeballs in the bag, but Jeff heard it, and Jeff had questions. Jeff's eyes were wide as saucers. But like a champ, he reached his hand into the bag of eyeballs and quickly found the walnut and got his hand out of that gooey mess as quick as he could.

Jeff was greatly relieved when he found out that the bag of eyeballs was really a bag full of grapes Aunt Sue had set into a mold full of yellow Jell-O and then dumped into a plastic bag inside of a sandwich bag. The Walnut was placed in the bag just before the Jell-O was dumped in, so that it would theoretically be at the bottom of the bag.

One of the challenges was to eat a live goldfish. My little sister Barbara, who was 6 years old, drew that rock. There was no way Barbara wanted to swallow a goldfish. We kept giving her the chance to do her task, and kept skipping her until there were no other tasks to perform.

The second to last task was Aunt Patti's. Her challenge was to sit in a chair and get a bucket of slime dumped slowly over her head. Aunt Sue needed Uncle Vince's help for this one. The bucket was full, and very heavy! Aunt Sue prepared the bucket of slime by melting a pound of gum drops until they were only half melted. She dumped the molten gum drops into the bucket of water and added an entire container of green food coloring. Aunt Sue felt bad for Aunt Patti, with Aunt Patti's thick, beautiful, waist length, brown hair, Aunt Sue knew those half-melted gum drops were going to be just awful for her. Aunt Patti sat in an aluminum lawn chair with green woven strips of fabric and closed her eyes. Before the first drop of bright green sloppy slime landed on her head she began to giggle, and as Uncle Vince very slowly poured the bucket of slime over Aunt Patti's head, we all began to giggle until we were doubled over with laughter at the thought and the sight of Aunt Patti's plight.

When the bucket of slime was empty, Aunt Patti stood up from the chair and curtsied. Then she bowed. And then she ran for the dock and jumped in the lake. Nana was holding baby Courtney, who had long ago fallen fast asleep and missed all the fun! Who knows what a 6 month old baby would think of seeing her father dump a bucket of bright green goo on her mother's head. Perhaps it would be just the kind of thing that made a baby laugh too.

Then we came back around to Barbara. Barbara had allowed herself to get lost in the fun of watching Aunt Patti do her challenge. Now it was back to the front of her mind that she was still supposed to swallow a live goldfish. While blindfolded.

Finally, Aunt Patti convinced Barbara that it would be okay. It was only a small goldfish, and Aunt Patti told Barbara that she herself had swallowed hundreds of them. She told Barbara they tasted kind of like cobbler. Barbara was fully brought to tears. She knew everyone else had completed their Rock Party challenges. She was determined to do hers too. And yet she just couldn't bring herself to eat a live goldfish, straight out of a pet store baggie. No one else in the world could have convinced Barbara to do it, but eventually Aunt Patti did. Barbara tipped her head back and opened her mouth. Aunt Patti dropped the goldfish in.

Barbara jumped up out of the chair, blindfolded, gagging, and trying to keep the goldfish in her mouth. It didn't take long before that goldfish came flying out of Barbara's mouth, flew through the air and landed in Uncle Spike's shirt pocket. Aunt Patti helped Barbara take the blindfold off. The torture had ended. She may not have swallowed the goldfish, but she had given the task a valiant effort. Aunt Sue let Barbara off the hook. "I have to give you a lot of credit. There's no way I would have done that. I say you accomplished your task!" At that moment, Barbara felt like Aunt Sue was a super hero—Wonder Woman came to mind.

Then Aunt Sue said, "Where is that goldfish? Maybe we can save it and Barbara can put it in a glass bowl and take it home with her!"

Spike said, "It landed in my shirt pocket! I hope it doesn't leave a stain! Let's see, oh I think I feel it flopping around." Uncle Spike reached into his pocket and pulled out a small slice of slippery canned peach.

Everyone laughed when it was revealed that Aunt Sue had pranked Barbara with a simple peach slice.

After the Rock Party Challenges, we paraded around Meconi's camp with the torches as the sun set. It was the kind of evening that made for memories to last a lifetime.

## '73 AuSable Chasm

When the rental period at Fitzie's Trails End came to an end, we moved into Overlook, Nana and Grampa's house in Jay for our final week. We had been underfoot for a couple of days, and Nana suggested Dad take us to AuSable Chasm. Nana was always glad to see us. I always felt so happy around her. She had a great appreciation for natural beauty, and she wanted us to become impressed with it too.

I revolted. I didn't want to go.

I wanted to spend the day at the barn with Aunt Patti and the cowboys. Or I wanted to spend the day in Jay with Aunt Patti and baby Courtney. I was all for Barbara and Jeffrey going to AuSable Chasm.

I had never been to see this natural wonder, so it was decided I must make the trip to the Chasm as well. Nana went with us, but since there was a lot of walking involved, she planned to read a book and take a nap in the station wagon while we toured the Chasm. The fact that Nana recommended it ultimately won me over.

On the way there, Nana told us a story about the French family that visited Paleface the week before. They weren't from France, it was just that their last name was French.

It was busy when they arrived at AuSable Chasm. For some reason, there was nobody there selling tickets. And the rope with its hook clasp on the end that served as a gate leading to the walking portion of the tour was also unmanned. They walked through, without giving it any apparent thought.

At the end of the walking portion there was a boat ride through another portion of the chasm. To get on board the boat, and the bus that would come later, they were supposed to have tickets.

They told the ticket taker that Grandma had taken sick all of a sudden and headed back to the car, with the tickets in her purse. Not wanting to drag three children back up the path and up all the stairs and steps, they asked if the ticket requirement could be waived.

Then Nana told about how they came back to Paleface, bragging about how they had saved the money and gotten away with a great "deal." Mr. French, the father in the family, rationalized that the AuSable Chasm had to pay an "idiot tax" just like at the grocery store when the clerk neglected to notice a case of Utica Club beer on the shelf beneath the food basket.

I had never seen Nana so furious in my life, retelling that story from the week before. I did recall that she scolded me one time when I asked her for a chocolate pudding at Paleface, and when she returned with it I was long gone. Nana was right—if I wanted some pudding and she was getting it for me, I should wait to receive it so she wouldn't have to hunt throughout Paleface to find me to deliver pudding to me, especially when she was busy serving customers. I probably wasn't even that hungry, it just is one of the great things about being a kid. Sometimes adults wanted to spoil you, and it felt good to be spoiled. I didn't care much for the spoiled pudding that day!

Business owners have a hard enough time keeping businesses afloat on three months a year's worth of business without people stealing from them. And that was just exactly what Nana thought of it.

So, when we went in and paid our admission, Nana came in with us. She told the cashier about the family of freeloaders from the previous week, and then she insisted the cashier ring up a family of five. And Nana paid that bill.

Nana had a very strong sense of right and wrong. And while she hadn't meant to make a lesson for us, her ethics lesson has served me well. I thought about it all the way down the steps into the Chasm as the water furiously roared through the channels. I thought about it on the boat ride through the gentler part of the river. And I thought about it on the bus ride back to the main parking lot.

## '73 Westerns and the News

During that summer trip, Grampa spent some time in Jay instead of spending all his time there at the Paleface office. Though I always wanted to be at Paleface instead, it was nice to be at home with everyone all together at Overlook.

Uncle Vince told great stories about werewolves and trees coming to life and moving around the property while we slept at night. And it was fun to curl up in Grampa's chair and watch westerns, though he always seemed to nod off and miss the good parts.

When the news was on we weren't allowed to talk. At all. Except during the commercials. They were still talking about Watergate. It seemed they had been talking about Watergate all year.

As if Watergate wasn't bad enough there was a lot of adult talk about unrest in the middle-east. What if war broke out there? What would happen to the price of the gas we put in our cars?

We didn't know it yet, but the Arab-Israeli War and the energy crisis was only one month away as the summer of 1973 ended. During that energy crisis, the price of oil went from $12 per barrel to $75 per barrel. No doubt that would have an impact on the ability of families to gas up the station wagon and head out on vacations, summer or winter.

Secretly I wished we wouldn't be able to find any gas to drive home, and would be stuck in the Adirondacks forever. I also wondered how in the world Grampa could stay awake for the boring old news and fall asleep during the exciting shows, like *Bonanza!*

## '73 Succession

Finally, a buyer had been found. Nana and Grampa had known it was potentially in the works when we visited them the month before, but they never mentioned it. Best be sure before telling the family!

In the beginning, Paleface had been created in less than a year. Each year for ten years Paleface came back better than it was the year before—new and improved, exciting and full of promise.

The last few years were a different story.

Since the tragic loss of the dearest of friends, Doc had lost the entrepreneurial drive to innovate. Doc lived with the grief on a constant basis; it was an overwhelming and pervasive sense of loss. Doc felt that instead of his friends, it should have been he that was killed in that car crash in Maine.

Both Doc and Jean were having ongoing health issues. Jean wanted to retire. Doc didn't want to leave Paleface, yet the challenge of continuing to build and innovate had completely and devastatingly waned. Instead of dreaming and imagining forth new innovations, Doc and Jean lived each day as it came.

It had been a couple of years since Paleface had invested money in anything new or inspiring. The newspapers had been running the same advertisements for several years, nothing new, perhaps just a reminder to the community: "We're still here." The press releases had stopped. No new and unique marketing campaigns or slogans. Doc seldom painted. Doc rarely rode or skied any more.

Most days, Doc moped around the office, asking Jane questions and providing help where help wasn't needed. Doc watched the daily balance in the checkbook. Every time he looked at the running balance, the image of a leaky faucet crossed his mind, that dreadfully vivid image ingrained in his mind since that meeting with the tax accountant a couple years earlier.

Doc knew he was getting old, faster than he thought he would. If only there was someone to leave Paleface to. For the ten thousandth time, it would seem Doc went down the list in his mind.

Oldest son—no interest, Paleface was clearly not for him.

Second son—lived too far away, and no chance he would return home.

Third child, daughter Patti—Patti loved Paleface more than anyone. Patti had proven she could manage the barn and was active in the leadership of the ski program. If only Patti had a couple more years of business school, maybe! Plus, Patti was a new mother, and wanted to maximize the time she spent with her new daughter Courtney.

Nieces, nephews, cousins? Doc's older half-sister Estelle had disappeared in her twenties. Kidnapped, ran away, nobody ever knew what became of her. Jean was an only child, and for all intents and purposes, so was Doc. Doc's extended family remained in New Jersey. Jean's extended family remained in Ontario.

Grandchildren? There were six of them now, unfortunately the oldest one was only 11 years old. Doc knew he and Jean could not keep the business afloat long enough for one of them to demonstrate the interest, skill, and ability.

What about giving it away? Doc couldn't think of a way to do it. If there was only a way to give Paleface to the people that had helped make it great. Could the employees become the owners? One person could run it, Doc thought. Putzi!

Jean insisted that Paleface must be sold for whatever it could bring. They needed money to sustain them, whatever years they had left. And Jean wanted to be able to leave the kids something, whatever they could.

One way or another, Doc might just have given it away. But Doc had come to the sad realization that perhaps the gift would become a curse. Even the most brilliant manager would be hard pressed to turn the business into a money maker.

At the end of the previous season, Doc and Jean went to Lake Placid for a quiet dinner together at the Steak and Stinger restaurant. "How can we sell Paleface to someone knowing the business model just doesn't work?" Doc said to Jean, as they sipped on lemonade and waited for dinner.

Jean said, "Whoever buys it will have to have their own plan. We have to answer every question honestly. Maybe if they can buy the business cheap enough they can figure out a way to make money at it. Whoever they are, they can't come along soon enough. I just want to go home," she concluded weakly. When Jean said she wanted to go home, she was talking about Overlook, their beautiful year-round vacation home in Jay.

Finally, at the end of the summer of 1973, a couple named George and Marjorie Winters came along. They fell in love with the building and the view. They reviewed the accountant prepared financial statements for the past three years, and Doc and Jean explained that they were selling the business because of their health and because none of the kids were in a position to take over the business.

On September 6, 1973 George and Marjorie Winters formed

a corporation for the purpose of operating a ski center and dude ranch, though they weren't yet 100 percent sure about continuing the dude ranch.

George felt certain he could make Paleface a prosperous business.

Jean prayed that the Winters would do well at Paleface.

Patti and Doc joked that it must be destiny! With the name Winters, perhaps Paleface would no longer suffer hot, snowless winters like it had during the past two years.

After waiting a year for the business to sell, Doc and Jean were not inclined to negotiate aggressively when the Winters' offer came. And it was far less than ideal.

The Winters purchased the business for a very small up-front cash payment. Doc and Jean financed most of the sale price. The Winters had half a year to complete a purchase of the real estate. Doc and Jean rented them the land and buildings for a nominal price during that half year period. That would give them time to convince a bank to extend them a mortgage, certainly! Or perhaps they would find an investor.

Labor Day had come and gone. The last of the summer tourists had returned to their lives back home. School was back in session. Business slowed down to a crawl as it usually did in September.

Doc and Jean's lawyer, Dan Manning of AuSable Forks was in touch on a daily basis with an update on negotiations with the attorney representing George and Marjorie. What about this? What about that? It seemed that every day an unimaginable consequence appeared in the imagination of one lawyer or the other.

## '73 Happy Double Anniversary

One evening in late September, a couple days after the new tennis playing sensation, Billie Jean King defeated Bobby Riggs, in a match hyped as the "Battle of the Sexes," Doc and Jean celebrated their 40th wedding anniversary. Coincidentally, it was also Patti and Vince's 4th anniversary.

Patti had arranged for a surprise party at the Smoke Rise Lookout, up the chairlift from the Paleface lodge below. After Patti spent about a month making secret arrangements, Vince inadvertently spilled the beans. Sometimes anticipating a special evening with friends and family is sweeter than having the dramatic element of surprise. About a week before the party, Doc told Patti that he knew about the party she was planning, and that the distraction was a very, very welcome intrusion. Doc was looking forward to setting aside thoughts of lawyers and business affairs for the evening. Patti wasn't too cross with Vince for spoiling the surprise.

It was a small gathering, by Paleface standards anyway. Patti had invited relatives and close friends.

Doc wore a light tan pair of slacks, a camel colored sports coat, and a western print shirt with a bolo tie and a bright red carnation pinned to his lapel. Jean wore a bright blue, knee length dress with a powder blue colored blouse and a matching scarf at her neck, and a red rose bud corsage with baby's breath and white ribbon. Patti wore a smart looking navy blue pantsuit with blue and white striped piping. Vince wore a heavy plaid sports coat and a burgundy colored, button down shirt.

The menu included beef stroganoff, garlic bread, an enormous garden salad, tuna stuffed tomatoes, musk melon stuffed with green Jell-O, and for dessert, lime chiffon pies.

Baby Courtney had just fallen asleep in her travel bassinet, and dessert was just about to be served. Patti took advantage of the opportunity to stand up and say a few words about the fine example her parents set, and about their strength getting through difficult times together, as well as the way they put others' wishes, wants, thoughts, and desires ahead of their own.

Also, Patti spoke about the family's love of Paleface, and tellingly Patti spoke in the past tense: "Paleface was the tangible physical realization of a dream, the dream of its founder." She spoke warmly of the business, like it was a member of the family, with a personality and a humanity all its own.

Patti closed her eyes so that she could finish thinking. "The rich legacy of Paleface is that the happy memories, which maybe seemed like dandelion fluff in the moment, can't help but leave a lasting, positive imprint on the souls of the people who lived, worked, and vacationed here. Long after they've forgotten other memories, people will remember the place that only my father and mother could have created." Patti opened her eyes, having gotten all her thoughts out, and she smiled. Her eyelids had been holding back tears, tears of sadness mixed with tears of joy.

Mary Wallace handed Patti a slice of pie, and said, "That was beautiful, dear, so lovely." Patti and Mary talked breezily about the weather between forks full of lime chiffon, then Patti checked on her beautiful, angelic, sleeping baby.

Together, and separately, the guests of honor received many nice gifts, including: a Dynamic brand 6-Transistor radio, made in Japan; a pair of camel colored, moccasin styled Clark's Wallabee brand shoes for Doc; a Rival brand Crock-Pot; a Jim Beam whiskey decanter, commemorating the 14th Annual Desert Classic golf tournament, featuring a caricature of Bob Hope with a golf ball on a tee perched on the tip of his ski jump shaped nose; a matching pair of 1-quart sized, red Tartan plaid Thermos brand coffee containers, one with a beige colored top that served also as a coffee cup, and the other with a red cup; a new picnic basket, with lots of compartments, filled with red speckled stoneware dishes, linens, and silverware; and some Aqua Velva, Ice Blue brand aftershave lotion for Doc. Patti gave Jean a beautiful polka dotted blouse, with white dots on blue, not unlike the blouse that the popular, talking Mrs. Beasley doll wore, however the blue background was navy rather than sky blue, and coincidentally the blouse looked almost identical to the one Kate Smith wore when she stopped by Paleface the previous summer.

It was a happy evening with friends and family. After dinner and gifts, Doc added a few warm thoughts, speaking for himself and for Jean. Doc told the story about how he had fallen in love with a beautiful young lady while sailing around the world. She was on a voyage to distract her mind from a relationship with a former beau. He was on a trip around the world, a graduation gift. Having fully expressed his love and gratitude in words, Doc and Jean joined hands, then shared a brief kiss. Friends and family clapped and cheered.

After the party, as friends and family were leaving, Doc thought the wonderful evening was a happy celebration, and yet also seemed something like a going away party. Like setting out on a trip around the world, things would never be the same afterwards.

## '73 Date Set

Monday morning, the 1st of October, word came that all the details were in place. The purchase agreement had been reviewed by the buyers, the sellers, and their lawyers. The closing was set for Thursday, October 4th at 11am.

## '73 Ramblin' Man

Business was fairly brisk the last couple of days. Mostly older couples stopped in for a for a hearty meal and a good night sleep. The beautiful fall colors attracted them like a magnet to the North Country. Occasionally the guests would enjoy a highball or two. But mostly Doc had the bar to himself in the evening.

Doc occupied his time thinking about all the special people that had gathered at Paleface over the years. Doc puttered around the bar, feeding his own money into the jukebox.

The man from the vending company had just brought in some new records. One new song sounded like nothing Doc could remember hearing before. "Ramblin' Man" by the Allman Brothers seemed to capture his current mood, and make him long for days long past. It made Doc think about his many careers, his trip around the world, and it also made Doc think about plans for travel after the sale of Paleface.

It was a comforting consolation.

## '73 On Top of the World

The last full day Doc and Jean owned Paleface, Doc waited for the weather to improve. On and off it rained, and finally in the afternoon it cleared.

The Carpenter's had a new song. Doc hummed the words to himself as he hiked up the trail: happy, optimistic lyrics combined with a sort of melancholy melody. Of course, the most famous words from the song spoke of "lookin' down on creation" from "the top of the world."

When Doc reached the top of the mountain, tears were streaming down his face. He was grieving over the loss of a precious friend. For an inanimate object, Paleface the mountain had a beautiful old soul. He had never felt a stronger spiritual connection to a single geographical location in his life, though Doc had travelled the world extensively.

Doc spent several hours enjoying the view of Whiteface on a pretty, partly cloudy, mild fall afternoon. How many times had Doc enjoyed that view? How many times had Doc painted Whiteface Mountain from Paleface, in different seasons or from different angles? How many times had Doc skied down one, while enjoying the view of the other?

Doc was fully aware it was the last trip he would ever make up his lovely little mountain.

## '73 The Closing

At the closing, Doc and Jean wished the Winters the best of luck and much happiness. The lawyers had completed gathering signatures on all the documents. There was nothing left to do.

Jane had called people to come and see Doc and Jean off, even those that had retired or taken other jobs over the years. Jane told everyone to arrive at five minutes after eleven, not a moment sooner.

Most couldn't make it, having returned to their off-season activities. The gang congregated in the area between the kitchen, the dining area, and the lodge area, where the long hall led to the double doors, and the parking lot beyond.

It warmed Doc and Jean's hearts to see their friends.

Ray Charles' hauntingly beautiful and poignantly sad song "Take These Chains from My Heart" was playing quietly in the background. Treasured old friends said goodbye. Things would never be the same again.

The lyrics amplified the emotion. The music harkened back to earlier times. Orchestral. Big Band. Piano.

Doc, never at a loss for words, found only a few to share with the gathered crowd that day. "Thank you for being here with us on our journey. We could not have done it without you. We are so proud to have known you all, and worked with you. On a personal note, you have made my dream come true, and you'll never know how much it means to me."

Doc made no attempt to hide his emotions. The words in the last sentence were accompanied by tears streaming down Doc's face, and two or three sniffles. Near the end, Doc's voice broke but he powered through and finished.

Jean tried to blink her eyes free of tears as well. She added, "Yes. You have meant the world to us. Working with you has been such a blessing. From the bottom of our hearts, we love you all very, very much."

Jean and Doc hugged everyone. Not the short hugs for greetings but the long sort of hugs that generally accompany a parting, or a deep and permanent change. Then Jean and Doc hugged each other.

They shared a brief kiss.

Jean said to Doc, "I'm so proud of you." Then Jean turned to face their friends, gestured toward Doc and said uncharacteristically, in her best Jane Russell voice, "our hero!"

Doc smiled and took Jean's hand in his.

Hand in hand they walked slowly down the long hall and out the front door.

*The End*

## Bibliography

Adirondack Daily Enterprise. (Various). Saranac Lake, New York: James Loeb, Jr.

Betters, F. (1982). *Fishing The Adirondacks.* Wilmington, NY: Adirondack Sporting Goods.

Betters, F. (1983). *Fish Are Smarter In The Adirondacks.* Burlington, VT: The George Little Press.

Beyea, W. E. (2008). *The Captain of the Juniper.* Bloomington, IN: iUniverse.

Davis, J. K. (2014). *Lost Ski Areas of the Northern Adirondacks.* Charleston, SC: The History Press.

De Sormo, M. C. (1969). *Noah John Rondeau Adirondack Hermit.* Utica, NY: North Country Books.

Drew University. (June 7-11, 1961). *Journal and Year Book, Newark Annual Conference, The Methodist Church, One Hundred Fourth Session.* Madison, New Jersey.

Drew University. (May 31-June 3, 1981). *Northern New Jersey, Annual Conference – The United Methodist Church – One Hundred Twenty-fourth Session.* Madison, New Jersey.

Edmonds, W. D. (1936). *Drums Along The Mohawk.* Boston: Little, Brown, and Company.

Fitz-Gerald, B. (1955, Jan). The Romance of Painting I: The Approach. *The Artist,* 77.

Fitz-Gerald, B. (1955, Feb). The Romance of Painting II: Composition. *The Artist,* 102.

Fitz-Gerald, B. (1955, Mar). The Romance of Painting III: The Romance of Dynamic Composition. *The Artist*, 141.

Fitz-Gerald, B. (1959, February). Must We Give Up Our Dreams. *The Artist*, 120.

Fitz-Gerald, D. (1979). *Literary Magazine.* Rochester, NY: The Harley School.

Fitz-Gerald, J. A. (1998, December). Boylan Fitz-Gerald, Profile of Adirondack artist, angler and entrepreneur: one man's many lives. *Adirondack Life*, pp. 48-67.

Hayes, R. K. (1995). *Kate Smith A Biography, with a Discography, Filmography and List of Stage Appearances.* Jefferson, NC: McFarland & Co, Inc.

Jaques, A. F. (1980). *Echoes from Whiteface Mountain, A Brief History of Wilmington, New York.* Wilmington, NY: Adeline F. Jaques.

Kanze, E. (2014). *Adirondack Life and Wildlife in the Wild, Wild East.* Albany, NY: State University of New York Press.

Lake Placid News. (Various). Lake Placid, New York.

McLeod, N.Z. (Director). (1948). *The Paleface* [Film].

Ortloff, G. C. (1985). *A Lady In The Lake.* Lake Placid, NY: With Pipe And Book.

Peck, D. D. (2005). *The E.M. Cooper Memorial Library: A Brief History, 1918 to 2001.*

Plattsburgh Press-Republican. (Various). Plattsburgh, New York.

Prager, W. (1951). *Skiing* (éd· 2nd)· New York: A·S· Barnes and Company, New York·

Ski [World's Largest Ski Publication]. (Various). Hanover, New Hampshire: William T. Eldred.

Smith, A. «. (1962). *I Will Look Unto the Hills.* Keeseville, NY: The Essex County Republican Co. Inc.

Sulavik, S. B. (2005). *ADIRONDACK: Of Indians and Mountains, 1535-1838.* Fleischmanns, NY: Purple Mountain Press.

Tashlin, F. (Director). (1967). *Caprice* [Film]

The North Countryman. (Various). Rouses Point, New York.

The Record-Post [The Adirondack Record-Elizabethtown Post]. (Various). AuSable Forks, New York: Fred P. Pelkey, Leo A. Bailey, Stephen W. Harnett, Boylan Fitz-Gerald, Jim Goldsby.

Weeks, N. (s.d.). *Lucky Star.* Chicago, Illinois: Adams Press.

Wikoff, C. M. (1959). *Placid Eating* (éd. 2nd).

Wilmington Historical Society. (2013). *Wilmington and the Whiteface Region (Images of America).* Charleston, South Carolina: Arcadia Publishing.

Winch, O. W. (1974). *Wilmington of the Adirondacks - a brief history.*

CPSIA information can be obtained
at www.ICGtesting.com
Printed in the USA
BVHW041017041222
653419BV00015B/71

9 781432 770754